DREAMSONGS

VOLUME II

DREAMSONGS

VOLUME II

George R. R. Martin

BANTAM BOOKS

DREAMSONGS: VOLUME II
A Bantam Spectra Book / December 2007

Originally published in one volume as *GRRM: A RRetrospective*
by Subterranean Press in 2003

Published by
Bantam Dell
A Division of Random House, Inc.
New York, New York

Illustrations by Michael Wm. Kaluta
Book design by Susan Turner

Bantam Books, the rooster colophon, Spectra, and the portrayal of a boxed "s" are trademarks of Random House, Inc.

Library of Congress Cataloging-in-Publication Data
Martin, George R. R.
Dreamsongs / George R. R. Martin.
p. cm.
ISBN: 978-0-553-80545-1 (Volume I)
ISBN: 978-0-553-80658-8 (Volume II)
Originally published in one volume as: *GRRM*. Michigan: Subterranean Press, 2003.
2007017681

Printed in the United States of America
Published simultaneously in Canada

www.bantamdell.com

BVG   10 9 8 7 6 5 4 3 2 1

Contents

George R. R. Martin:
A Retrospective Fiction Checklist
by Leslie Kay Swigart

for Phipps, of course,
there is a road, no simple highway,
between the dawn and the dark of night.
I'm glad you're here to walk it with me.

DREAMSONGS

VOLUME II

SIX

A Taste of Tuf

MY CAREER IS LITTERED WITH THE CORPSES OF DEAD SERIES.

I launched my star ring series with "The Second Kind of Loneliness" and "Nor the Many-Colored Fires of a Star Ring," then lost interest and never did a third story.

"A Peripheral Affair" was meant to be followed by the further adventures of the starship *Mjolnir* and the *Good Ship Lollipop*. None ever appeared, for the simple reason that none was ever written.

My corpse handler series went all the way to three: "Nobody Leaves New Pittsburg" began it, "Override" followed, and "Meathouse Man" brought it to... well, a finish, if not an end. A fourth story exists as a four-page fragment, and there are ideas in my files for a dozen more. I once intended to write them all, publish them in the magazines, then collect them all together in a book I'd call *Songs the Dead Men Sing*. But that fourth story never got finished, and the others never got started. When I did finally use the title *Songs the Dead Men Sing* for a collection (from Dark Harvest, in 1983), "Meathouse Man" was the only corpse story to make the cut.

I fared somewhat better with the Windhaven series, perhaps because Lisa Tuttle and I were collaborating on that one, so I had someone to give me a swift kick whenever my creative juices dried up (Lisa also added some swell creative juices of her own). We started out trying to write a short story, which turned into the novella "The Storms of Windhaven" (a Hugo and Nebula loser) at the prompting of *Analog* editor Ben Bova. "One-Wing" and "The Fall" followed, two more novellas. Then Lisa and I put the three of them together, added a prologue and epilogue, and published *Windhaven*, a classic example of the "fix-up" novel; a novel made by cobbling together a series of previously published short stories or novellas.

Windhaven wasn't supposed to be the end of Windhaven, however. Lisa and I meant to continue the tale through two more books and two more generations, showing how the changes Maris started in "The Storms of Windhaven" continued to transform her world. The second book was to be entitled *Painted Wings*. The protagonist would be the little girl we'd introduced in "The Fall," all grown up.

We never wrote it. We *talked* about writing it for years, but the timing never worked out. When I was free, Lisa was in the throes of a novel. When she was free, I was out in Hollywood, or doing *Wild Cards,* or a novel of my own. We were a thousand miles apart even when we were closest; then I went west (to Santa Fe and Los Angeles) and she went east (to England and Scotland), and we saw each other less and less often. Also, as we grew older, our voices and styles and ways of looking at the world became more and more distinct, which would have made collaborating far more challenging. Literary collaboration is a game for young writers, I think…or for old, cynical ones trying to cash in on their names. So our *Painted Wings* never took flight.

My other series all proved to be even shorter, as I've mentioned here and there throughout these commentaries. There was the Steel Angel series (one story). The Sharra series (one story). The Gray Alys series (one story). The Wo & Shade series (one story). The Skin Trade series (one story). It's enough to make one suspect a terminal case of *creatus interruptus*.

Ah, but then comes Tuf.

Haviland Tuf, ecological engineer, master of the *Ark,* and the protagonist of *Tuf Voyaging,* which is either a collection of short stories or a fix-up novel, depending on whether you're a critic or a publisher. 'Twas Tuf who broke my series bugaboo for good and all, and opened up the gates for *Wild Cards* and *A Song of Ice and Fire*.

As a reader, I had my own favorite series characters. In fantasy, I was drawn to Moorcock's Elric and Howard's Solomon Kane, and I loved Fritz Leiber's dashing rogues, Fafhrd and the Gray Mouser. In SF, I was fond of Retief, of Dominic Flandry, of Lije Bailey and R. Daneel Olivaw. But my favorites had to be Jack Vance's galactic effectuator Magnus Ridolph and Poul Anderson's fat, scheming merchant prince of the spaceways, Nicholas van Rijn.

As a writer, I still had dreams of establishing a popular, long-running series of my own. I had an idea that I was certain could sustain one as well. It was 1975, and "ecology" was a word on everyone's lips. It seemed to me that a series about some sort of biogenetic engineer, who moves from world to world solving (or in some cases, creating) ecological problems, would offer no end of story possibilities. The subject matter would allow me to explore all sorts of juicy issues...and best of all, no one else had done anything remotely like it, so far as I knew.

But who was this fellow? It seemed to me I had a terrific concept, but to sustain a series I needed a terrific *character* as well, someone the readers would enjoy following story after story. With that in mind, I went back and looked at some of the characters that I loved as a reader. Nicholas van Rijn. Conan. Sherlock Holmes. Mowgli. Travis McGee. Horatio Hornblower. Elric of Melnibone. Batman. Northwest Smith. Flashman. Fafhrd and the Mouser. Retief. Susan Calvin. Magnus Ridolph. A diverse bunch, certainly. I wanted to see if they shared any traits in common.

They did.

Two things leapt out at me. One, they all had great names, names that fit them perfectly. Memorable names. *Singular* names. You were not likely to meet two Horatio Hornblowers. Melnibone's phone book would not list four Elrics. Northwest Smith was not required to use his middle initials to distinguish himself from all the other Northwest Smiths.

Secondly, every one of them was larger than life. No average joes in this bunch. No danger of any of them vanishing into the wallpaper. Many of them are supreme in their own spheres, be that naval warfare (Hornblower), deduction (Holmes), hand-to-hand combat (Conan), or cowardice and lechery (Flashman). Most of them are severely idiosyncratic, to say the least. There is surely a place in fiction for small, commonplace, realistic characters, subtly rendered...but not as the star of an ongoing series.

Okay, I thought to myself, *I can do that.*

Thus was born Haviland Tuf, merchant, cat lover, vegetarian, big and bald, drinking mushroom wine and playing god, a fussy man and formal, who has long since veered past idiosyncrasy into out-and-out eccentricity. There's some of Holmes and Ridolph in him, a pinch of Nicholas van Rijn, a little Hercule Poirot and a lot of Alfred Hitchcock...but not much me at all. Of all my protagonists, Tuf is the least like myself (although I did own a cat named Dax, though he was not telepathic).

The name? Well, "Haviland" was a surname I noticed on the wall charts at a chess tournament I was directing. I'm not at all certain where the "Tuf" came from. When I put the two of them together, though, that was *him,* and never a doubt.

Back in the '70s, I was still trying to place my stories in as wide a variety of markets as possible. I wanted to prove that I could sell to *anybody*, not just the same few editors. Also, I figured that every time I had a story in a new market I would reach new readers, who might then go on to look for my stuff else-where.

Working on that theory, I sold the first Haviland Tuf story to a British hardcover anthology called *Andromeda*, edited by Peter Weston. Perhaps "A Beast for Norn" did indeed win me legions of new British readers, I couldn't say; unfortunately, very few of my old American readers ever found the story until St. Martin's printed an American edition of *Andromeda* three years later. By that time, I had already published the second Tuf story, "Call Him Moses." I'd sold that one to Ben Bova. Thereafter Tuf became a familiar figure in the pages of *Analog*. Ben and his successor Stanley Schmidt got first look at each new Tuf story, and bought them all.

Not that there were a great many. Tuf was fun, but he was by no means the only fish in my frypan. In the late '70s I was still teaching at Clarke College, so my writing time was limited, and I had other stories I wanted to tell. And when I moved to Santa Fe at the end of 1979, to try and make a go of it as a full-time writer, my attention shifted to novels. *Fevre Dream* occupied most of my writing time in 1981, *The Armageddon Rag* in 1982, *Black and White and Red All Over* in 1984. (We won't talk about 1983, my Lost Year.) The Tuf series might well have petered out at three or four stories, but for Betsy Mitchell.

Betsy had been the assistant editor at *Analog* under Stan Schmidt, but in 1984 she left the magazine to become an editor at Baen Books. Not long af-ter joining Baen she phoned to ask if I had ever considered doing a collection of Haviland Tuf's adventures. I had, of course...but that was for "eventually," some future time when I had accumulated enough Tuf stories to make a book.

In 1984 I had maybe half a book at best. Still, Betsy's offer was not one I could refuse. My career was in serious trouble just then. The readers had ig-nored *The Armageddon Rag* in droves, and as a result no editor would touch *Black and White and Red All Over*. This was a chance to get back into the game. I could write some more Tuf tales, sell first serial rights to Stan Schmidt at *Analog*, put them all together for Betsy, and make enough money to pay my mortgage for a little while longer.

So I wrote "The Plague Star," the tale of how Tuf came to be the master of the *Ark*, followed by the S'uthlam triptych, which gave the book a spine. Baen published *Tuf Voyaging* in February, 1986, as a novel. My fifth novel, some say...though I've always counted *Tuf Voyaging* as a short story collection. (In my own mind, *Black and White and Red All Over* will forever be my fifth novel, broken and unfinished though it is.)

No sampling of my checkered career could possibly be complete without a taste of Tuf, so I've included two stories here. The rest can be found in *Tuf Voyaging,* for those who want more.

"A Beast for Norn" was the earliest Tuf story, written in 1975 and published in 1976. When it came time for me to assemble *Tuf Voyaging* for Betsy in 1985, a decade had passed, and Haviland Tuf had changed somewhat, coming more into focus, as it were. The Tuf of "A Beast for Norn" no longer quite fit, so I decided to revise and expand the story, to bring the proto-Tuf more in line with the character as he'd evolved in the later stories. It is the revised version of "A Beast for Norn" that appears in *Tuf Voyaging.* For this retrospective, however, I thought it might be interesting to go back to my first take on Tuf. So what follows is the *original* version of "A Beast for Norn," as it appeared in *Andromeda* in 1976.

"Guardians" is of somewhat later vintage, having first been published in *Analog* in October, 1981. It was the most popular entry in the series with the readers, winning the *Locus* poll as Best Novelette of the year, and garnering a Hugo nomination. It finished second in the final balloting, losing the award to Roger Zelazny's superb "Unicorn Variations." (Roger was a dear friend of mine, and I had suggested the idea for "Unicorn Variations" to him jokingly one day, as we drove to Albuquerque for a writers' lunch. Roger acknowledged that with a tip o' the hat by naming his protagonist Martin... and then went right out and took my Hugo.)

At one time there was supposed to be a second Tuf book. *Tuf Voyaging* did well enough so that Betsy Mitchell suggested a sequel; either another book of collected stories or perhaps a genuine full-length novel. I was willing. I had ideas for another dozen Tuf stories in my files. So contracts were duly drawn up and signed, and the book was even announced in *Locus.* Our working title was *Twice as Tuf,* although if I had gone the novel route I would probably have changed that to *Tuf Landing.*

It never happened. Hollywood intervened, and I found myself out in L.A., making as much money in two weeks as the *Twice as Tuf* contract would have paid me for a year's work. I needed money badly at that time, in the wake of *Armageddon Rag*'s disastrous sales and the failure of *Black and White and Red All Over* to sell.

When the deadline came and went without a book, I suggested to Betsy that I might bring in a collaborator, who could write the stories from my outlines. I take contracts seriously, and wanted to fulfill mine with Baen if at all possible...but taking on a partner really wasn't a very good idea. Betsy Mitchell did not think so either, and she talked me out of it. For that I remain grateful. She was right; Tuf stories written by someone else would not have been the same. I would have been cheating Baen Books, my readers, and myself. I ended up settling the *Twice as Tuf* contract by granting Baen Books the right to reprint some of my older books, so everyone ended up reasonably happy except the Tuf fans.

There are still a number of those about, actually. Every year for a decade or more, a few letters have come trickling in, urging me to stop writing *Wild Cards,* or those TV shows, or that series of big fat fantasy novels, so I can write some more Haviland Tuf stories instead.

To which I can only say, "Maybe one of these days, when you least expect it..."

A Beast for Norn

HAVILAND TUF WAS RELAXING IN AN ALEHOUSE ON TAMBER WHEN the thin man found him. He sat by himself in the darkest corner of the dimly lit tavern, his elbows resting on the table and the top of his bald head almost brushing the low wooden beam above. Four empty mugs sat before him, their insides streaked by rings of foam, while a fifth, half-full, was cradled in huge calloused hands.

If Tuf was aware of the curious glances the other patrons gave him from time to time, he showed no sign of it; he quaffed his ale methodically, and his face—bone-white and completely hairless, as was the rest of him—was without expression. He was a man of heroic dimensions, Haviland Tuf, a giant with an equally gigantic paunch, and he made a singular solitary figure drinking alone in his booth.

Although he was not *quite* alone, in truth; his black tomcat Dax lay asleep on the table before him, a ball of dark fur, and Tuf would occasionally set down his mug of ale and idly stroke his quiet companion. Dax would not stir from his comfortable position among the empty mugs. The cat was fully as large, compared to other cats, as Haviland Tuf was compared to other men.

When the thin man came walking up to Tuf's booth, Tuf said nothing at all. He merely looked up, and blinked, and waited for the other to begin.

"You are Haviland Tuf, the animal-seller," the thin man said. He was indeed painfully thin. His garments, all black leather and grey fur, hung loose on him, bagging here and there. Yet he was plainly a man of some means, since he wore a thin brass coronet around his brow, under a mop of black hair, and his fingers were all adorned with rings.

Tuf stroked Dax, and—looking down at the cat—began to speak. "Did you hear that, Dax?" he said. He spoke very slowly, his voice a deep bass with only a hint of inflection. "I am Haviland Tuf, the animal-seller. Or so I am taken to be." Then he looked up at the thin man who stood there impatiently. "Sir," he said. "I am indeed Haviland Tuf. And I do indeed trade in animals. Yet perhaps I do not consider myself an animal-seller. Perhaps I consider myself an ecological engineer."

The thin man waved his hand in an irritated gesture, and slid uninvited into the booth opposite Tuf. "I understand that you own a seed-ship of the ancient Ecological Corps, but that does not make you an ecological engineer, Tuf. They are all dead, and have been for centuries. But if you would prefer to be called an ecological engineer, then well and good. I require your services. I want to buy a monster from you, a great fierce beast."

"Ah," said Tuf, speaking to the cat again. "He wants to buy a monster, this stranger who seats himself at my table."

"My name is Herold Norn, if that is what's bothering you," the thin man said. "I am the Senior Beast-Master of my House, one of the Twelve Great Houses of Lyronica."

"Lyronica," Tuf stated. "I have heard of Lyronica. The next world out from here towards the Fringe, is it not? Esteemed for its gaming pits?"

Norn smiled. "Yesyes," he said.

Haviland Tuf scratched Dax behind the ear, a peculiar rhythmic scratch, and the tomcat slowly uncurled, yawning, and glanced up at the thin man. A wave of reassurance came flooding into Tuf; the visitor was well-intentioned and truthful, it seemed. According to Dax. All cats have a touch of psi. Dax had more than a touch; the genetic wizards of the vanished Ecological Corps had seen to that. He was Tuf's mindreader.

"The affair becomes clearer," Tuf said. "Perhaps you would care to elaborate, Herold Norn?"

Norn nodded. "Certainly, certainly. What do you know of Lyronica, Tuf? Particularly of the gaming pits?"

Tuf's heavy and stark white face remained emotionless. "Some small things. Perhaps not enough, if I am to deal with you. Tell me what you will, and Dax and I will consider the matter."

Herold Norn rubbed thin hands together, and nodded again. "Dax?" he said. "Oh, of course. Your cat. A handsome animal, although personally I have never been fond of beasts who cannot fight. Real beauty lies in killing-strength, I always say."

"A peculiar attitude," Tuf commented.

"Nono," said Norn, "not at all. I hope that your work here has not infected you with Tamberkin squeamishness."

Tuf drained his mug in silence, then signaled for two more. The barkeep brought them promptly.

"Thank you, thank you," Norn said, when the mug was set golden and foaming in front of him.

"Proceed."

"Yes. Well, the Twelve Great Houses of Lyronica compete in the gaming pits, you know. It began—oh, centuries ago. Before that, the Houses warred. This way is much better. Family honor is upheld, fortunes are made, and no one is injured. You see, each House controls great tracts, scattered widely over the planet, and since the land is very thinly settled, animal life teems. The lords of the Great Houses, many years ago during a time of peace, started to have animal-fights. It was a pleasant diversion, rooted deep in history—you are aware, maybe, of the ancient custom of cock-fighting and the Old Earth folk called Romans who would set all manner of strange beasts against each other in their great arena?"

Norn paused and drank some ale, waiting for an answer, but Tuf merely stroked a quietly alert Dax and said nothing.

"No matter," the thin Lyronican finally said, wiping foam from his mouth with the back of his hand. "That was the beginning of the sport, you see. Each House had its own particular land, its own particular animals. The House of Varcour, for example, sprawls in the hot, swampy south, and they are fond of sending huge lizard-lions to the gaming pits. Feridian, a mountainous realm, has bred and championed its fortunes with a species of rock-ape which we call, naturally, *feridians*. My own house, Norn, stands on the grassy plains of the large northern continent. We have sent a hundred different beasts into combat in the pits, but we are most famed for our ironfangs."

"Ironfangs," Tuf said.

Norn gave a sly smile. "Yes," he said proudly. "As Senior Beast-Master, I have trained thousands. Oh, but they are lovely animals! Tall as you are, with fur of the most marvelous blue-black color, fierce and relentless."

"Canine?"

"But *such* canines," Norn said.

"Yet you require from me a monster."

Norn drank more of his ale. "In truth, in truth. Folks from a dozen near worlds voyage to Lyronica, to watch the beasts fight in the gaming pits and gamble on the outcome. Particularly they flock to the Bronze Arena that has stood for six hundred years in the City of All Houses. That's where the greatest fights are fought. The wealth of our Houses and our world has come to depend on this. Without it, rich Lyronica would be as poor as the farmers of Tamber."

"Yes," said Tuf.

"But you understand, this wealth, it goes to the Houses according to their honor, according to their victories. The House of Arneth has grown greatest and most powerful because of the many deadly beasts in their varied lands; the others rank according to their scores in the Bronze Arena. The income from each match—all the monies paid by those who watch and bet—goes to the victor."

Haviland Tuf scratched Dax behind the ear again. "The House of Norn ranks last and least among the Twelve Great Houses of Lyronica," he said, and the twinge that Dax relayed to him told him he was correct.

"You know," Norn said.

"Sir. It was obvious. But is it ethical to buy an offworld monster, under the rules of your Bronze Arena?"

"There are precedents. Some seventy-odd standard years ago, a gambler came from Old Earth itself, with a creature called a timber wolf that he had trained. The House of Colin backed him, in a fit of madness. His poor beast was matched against a Norn ironfang, and proved far from equal to its task. There are other cases as well.

"In recent years, unfortunately, our ironfangs have not bred well. The wild species has all but died out on the plains, and the few who re-main become swift and elusive, difficult for our housemen to capture. In the breeding kennels, the strain seems to have softened, despite my efforts and those of the Beast-Masters before me. Norn has won few victories of late, and I will not remain Senior for long unless something is done. We grow poor. When I heard that a seedship had come to Tamber, then, I determined to seek you out. I will begin a new era of glory for Norn, with your help."

Haviland Tuf sat very still. "I comprehend. Yet I am not in the habit of selling monsters. *The Ark* is an ancient seedship, designed by the Earth Imperials thousands of years ago, to decimate the Hrangans through ecowar. I can unleash a thousand diseases, and in the cell-banks I have cloning material for beasts from more worlds than you can count. You misunderstand the nature of ecowar, however. The deadliest enemies are not large predators, but tiny insects that lay waste to a world's crops, or hoppers that breed and breed and crowd out all other life."

Herold Norn looked crestfallen. "You have nothing, then?"

Tuf stroked Dax. "Little. A million types of insects, a hundred thousand kinds of small birds, full as many fish. But monsters, monsters—only a few—a thousand perhaps. They were used from time to time, for psychological reasons as often as not."

"A thousand monsters!" Norn was excited again. "That is more than enough selection! Surely, among that thousand, we can find a beast for Norn!"

"Perhaps," Tuf said. "Do you think so, Dax?" he said to his cat. "Do you? So!" He looked at Norn again. "This matter does interest me, Herold Norn. And my work here is done, as I have given the Tamberkin a bird that will check their rootworm plague, and the bird does well. So Dax and I will take *The Ark* to Lyronica, and see your gaming pits, and we will decide what is to be done with them."

Norn smiled. "Excellent," he said. "Then I will buy this round of ale." And Dax told Haviland Tuf in silence that the thin man was flush with the feel of victory.

THE BRONZE ARENA STOOD SQUARE IN THE CENTER OF THE CITY OF All Houses, at the point where sectors dominated by the Twelve Great Houses met like slices in a vast pie. Each section of the rambling stone city was walled off, each flew a flag with its distinctive colors, each had its own ambience and style; but all met in the Bronze Arena.

The Arena was not bronze after all, but mostly black stone and polished wood. It bulked upwards, taller than all but a few of the city's
scattered towers and minarets, and topped by a shining bronze dome
that gleamed with the orange rays of the sunset. Gargoyles peered from
the various narrow windows, carved of stone and hammered from
bronze and wrought iron. The great doors in the black stone walls
were fashioned of metal as well, and there were twelve of them, each
facing a different sector of the City of All Houses. The colors and the
etching on each gateway were distinctive to its House.

Lyronica's sun was a fist of red flame smearing the western horizon
when Herold Norn led Haviland Tuf to the games. The housemen had
just fired gas torches, metal obelisks that stood like dark teeth in a ring
about the Bronze Arena, and the hulking ancient building was surrounded by flickering pillars of blue-and-orange flame. In a crowd of
gamblers and gamesters, Tuf followed Herold Norn from the half-
deserted streets of the Nornic slums down a path of crushed rock, passing between twelve bronze ironfangs who snarled and spit in timeless
poses on either side of the street, and then through the wide Norn Gate
whose doors were intricate ebony and brass. The uniformed guards,
clad in the same black leather and grey fur as Herold Norn himself, recognized the Beast-Master and admitted them; others stopped to pay
with coins of gold and iron.

The Arena was the greatest gaming pit of all; it *was* a pit, the sandy
combat-floor sunk deep below ground level, with stone walls four meters high surrounding it. Then the seats began, just atop the walls, circling and circling in ascending tiers until they reached the doors.
Enough seating for thirty thousand, although those towards the back
had a poor view at best, and other seats were blocked off by iron pillars.
Betting stalls were scattered throughout the building, windows in the
outer walls.

Herold Norn took Tuf to the best seats in the Arena, in the front of
the Norn section, with only a stone parapet separating them from the
four-meter drop to the combat sands. The seats here were not rickety
wood-and-iron, like those in the rear, but thrones of leather, huge
enough to accommodate even Tuf's vast bulk without difficulty, and
opulently comfortable. "Every seat is bound in the skin of a beast that
has died nobly below," Herold Norn told Tuf, as they seated them-

selves. Beneath them, a work crew of men in one-piece blue coveralls was dragging the carcass of some gaunt feathered animal towards one of the entryways. "A fighting-bird of the House of Wrai Hill," Norn explained. "The Wrai Beast-Master sent it up against a Varcour lizard-lion. Not the most felicitous choice."

Haviland Tuf said nothing. He sat stiff and erect, dressed in a grey vinyl greatcoat that fell to his ankles, with flaring shoulder-boards and a visored green-and-brown cap emblazoned with the golden theta of the Ecological Engineers. His large, rough hands interlocked atop his bulging stomach while Herold Norn kept up a steady stream of conversation.

Then the Arena announcer spoke, and the thunder of his magnified voice boomed all around them. "Fifth match," he said. "From the House of Norn, a male ironfang, aged two years, weight 2.6 quintals, trained by Junior Beast-Master Kers Norn. New to the Bronze Arena." Immediately below them, metal grated harshly on metal, and a nightmare creature came bounding into the pit. The ironfang was a shaggy giant, with sunken red eyes and a double row of curving teeth that dripped slaver; a wolf grown all out of proportion and crossed with a saber-toothed tiger, its legs as thick as young trees, its speed and killing grace only partially disguised by the blue-black fur that hid the play of muscles. The ironfang snarled and the Arena echoed to the noise; scattered cheering began all around them.

Herold Norn smiled. "Kers is a cousin, and one of our most promising juniors. He tells me this beast will do us proud. Yes, yes. I like its looks, don't you?"

"Being new to Lyronica and your Bronze Arena, I have no standard of comparison," Tuf said in a flat voice.

The announcer began again. "From the House of Arneth-in-the-Gilded-Wood, a strangling-ape, aged six years, weight 3.1 quintals, trained by Senior Beast-Master Danel Leigh Arneth. Three times a veteran of the Bronze Arena, three times surviving."

Across the combat pit, another of the entryways—the one wrought in gold and crimson—slid open, and the second beast lumbered out on two squat legs and looked around. The strangling-ape was short but immensely broad, with a triangular torso and a bullet-shaped head, eyes sunk deep under a heavy ridge of bone. Its arms, double-jointed and muscular, dragged in the Arena sand. From head to toe the beast was hairless, but for patches of dark red fur under its arms its skin was a dirty white. And it smelled. Across the Arena, Haviland Tuf still caught the musky odor.

"It sweats," Norn explained. "Danel Leigh has driven it to killing frenzy before sending it forth. His beast has the edge in experience, you understand, and the strangling-ape is a savage creature as well. Unlike its cousin, the mountain feridian, it is naturally a carnivore and needs little training. But Kers' ironfang is younger. The match should be of interest." The Norn Beast-Master leaned forward while Tuf sat calm and still.

The ape turned, growling deep in its throat, and already the iron-fang was streaking towards it, snarling, a blue-black blur that scattered Arena sand as it ran. The strangling-ape waited for it, spreading its huge gangling arms, and Tuf had a blurred impression of the great Norn killer leaving the ground in one tremendous bound. Then the two animals were locked together, rolling over and over in a tangle of ferocity, and the Arena became a symphony of screams. "The throat," Norn was shouting. "Tear out its throat! Tear out its throat!"

Then, as sudden as they had met, the two beasts parted. The iron-fang spun away and began to move in slow circles, and Tuf saw that one of its forelegs was bent and broken, so that it limped on the three remaining. Yet still it circled. The strangling-ape gave it no opening, but turned constantly to face it as it prowled. Long gashes drooled blood on the ape's wide chest, where the ironfang's sabers had slashed, but the beast of Arneth seemed little weakened. Herold Norn had begun to mutter softly at Tuf's side.

Impatient with the lull, the watchers in the Bronze Arena began a rhythmic chant, a low wordless noise that swelled louder and louder as new voices heard and joined. Tuf saw at once that the sound affected the animals below. Now they began to snarl and hiss, calling battle cries in savage voices, and the strangling-ape moved from one leg to the other, back and forth, in a macabre dance, while slaver ran in dripping rivers from the gaping jaws of the ironfang. The chant grew and grew—Herold Norn joined in, his thin body swaying slightly as he moaned—and Tuf recognized the bloody killing-chant for what it was. The beasts below went into a frenzy. Suddenly the ironfang was charging again, and the ape's long arms reached to meet it in its wild lunge. The impact of the leap threw the strangler backwards, but Tuf saw that the ironfang's teeth had closed on air while the ape wrapped its hands around the blue-black throat. The ironfang thrashed wildly, but briefly, as they rolled in the sand. Then came a sharp, horribly loud snap, and the wolf-creature was nothing but a rag of fur, its head lolling grotesquely to one side.

The watchers ceased their moaning chant, and began to applaud and whistle. Afterwards, the gold and crimson door slid open once again and the strangling-ape returned to where it had come. Four men in Norn House black and grey came out to carry off the corpse.

Herold Norn was sullen. "Another loss. I will speak to Kers. His beast did not find the throat."

Haviland Tuf stood up. "I have seen your Bronze Arena."

"Are you going?" Norn asked anxiously. "Surely not so soon! There are five more matches. In the next, a giant feridian fights a water-scorpion from Amar Island!"

"I need see no more. It is feeding time for Dax, so I must return to *The Ark.*"

Norn scrambled to his feet, and put an anxious hand to Tuf's shoulder to restrain him. "Will you sell us a monster, then?"

Tuf shook off the Beast-Master's grip. "Sir. I do not like to be touched. Restrain yourself." When Norn's hand had fallen, Tuf looked down into his eyes. "I must consult my records, my computers. *The Ark* is in orbit. Shuttle up the day after next. A problem exists, and I shall address myself to its correction." Then, without further word, Haviland Tuf turned and walked from the Bronze Arena, back to the spaceport of the City of All Houses, where his shuttlecraft sat waiting.

———

HEROLD NORN HAD OBVIOUSLY NOT BEEN PREPARED FOR *THE ARK.* After his black-and-grey shuttle had docked and Tuf had cycled him through, the Beast-Master made no effort to disguise his reaction. "I should have known," he kept repeating. "The size of this ship, the *size.* But of course I should have known."

Haviland Tuf stood unmoved, cradling Dax in one arm and stroking the cat slowly. "Old Earth built larger ships than modern worlds," he said impassively. "*The Ark*, as a seedship, had to be large. It once had two hundred crewmen. Now it has one."

"You are the *only* crewman?" Norn said.

Dax suddenly warned Tuf to be alert. The Beast-Master had begun to think hostile thoughts. "Yes," Tuf said. "The only crewman. But there is Dax, of course. And defenses programmed in, lest control be wrested from me."

Norn's plans suddenly withered, according to Dax. "I see," he said. Then, eagerly, "Well, what have you come up with?"

"Come," said Tuf, turning.

He led Norn out of the reception floor down a small corridor that led into a larger. There they boarded a three-wheeled vehicle and drove through a long tunnel lined by glass vats of all sizes and shapes, filled with gently bubbling liquid. One bank of vats was divided into units as small as a man's fingernail; on the other extreme, there was a single unit large enough to contain the interior of the Bronze Arena. It was empty, but in some of the medium-sized tanks, dark shapes hung in translucent bags, and stirred fitfully. Tuf, with Dax curled in his lap, stared straight ahead as he drove, while Norn looked wonderingly from side to side.

They departed the tunnel at last, and entered a small room that was all computer consoles. Four large chairs sat in the four corners of the square chamber, with control panels on their arms; a circular plate of blue metal was built into the floor amidst them. Haviland Tuf dropped Dax into one of the chairs before seating himself in a second. Norn looked around, then took the chair diagonally opposite Tuf.

"I must inform you of several things," Tuf began.

"Yesyes," said Norn.

"Monsters are expensive," Tuf said. "I will require one hundred thousand standards."

"*What!* That's an outrage! We would need a hundred victories in the Bronze Arena to amass that sum. I told you, Norn is a poor House."

"So. Perhaps then a richer House would meet the required price. The Ecological Engineering Corps has been defunct for centuries, sir. No ship of theirs remains in working order, save *The Ark* alone. Their science is largely forgotten. Techniques of cloning and genetic engineering such as they practiced exist now only on Prometheus and Old Earth itself, where such secrets are closely guarded. And the

Prometheans no longer have the stasis field, thus their clones grow to natural maturity." Tuf looked across to where Dax sat in a chair before the gently winking lights of the computer consoles. "And yet, Dax, Herold Norn feels my price to be excessive."

"Fifty thousand standards," Norn said. "We can barely meet that price."

Haviland Tuf said nothing.

"Eighty thousand standards, then! I can go no higher. The House of Norn will be bankrupt! They will tear down our bronze ironfangs, and seal the Norn Gate!"

Haviland Tuf said nothing.

"Curse you! A hundred thousand, yesyes. But only if your monster meets our requirements."

"You will pay the full sum on delivery."

"Impossible!"

Tuf was silent again.

"Oh, very well."

"As to the monster itself, I have studied your requirements closely, and have consulted my computers. Here upon *The Ark*, in my frozen cell-banks, thousands upon thousands of predators exist, including many now extinct on their original homeworlds. Yet few, I would think, would satisfy the demands of the Bronze Arena. And of those that might, many are unsuitable for other reasons. For example, I have considered the selection to be limited to beasts that might with luck be bred on the lands of the House of Norn. A creature who could not replicate himself would be a poor investment. No matter how invincible he might be, in time the animal would age and die, and Norn victories would be at an end."

"An excellent point," Herold Norn said. "We have, from time to time, attempted to raise lizard-lions and feridians and other beasts of the Twelve Houses, with ill success. The climate, the vegetation..." He made a disgusted gesture.

"Precisely. Therefore, I have eliminated silicon-based life forms, which would surely die on your carbon-based world. Also, animals of planets whose atmosphere varies too greatly from Lyronica's. Also, beasts of dissimilar climes. You will comprehend the various and sundry difficulties incumbent in my search."

"Yesyes, but get to the point. What have you found? What is this hundred thousand standard monster?"

"I offer you a selection," Tuf said. "From among some thirty animals. Attend!"

He touched a glowing button on the arm of his chair, and suddenly a beast was squatting on the blue-metal plate between them. Two meters tall with rubbery pink-grey skin and thin white hair, the creature had a low forehead and a swinish snout, plus a set of nasty curving horns and dagger-like claws on its hands.

"I will not trouble you with species names, since I observe that informality was the rule of the Bronze Arena," Haviland Tuf said. "This is the so-called stalking-swine of Heydey, native to both forests and plain. Chiefly a carrion-eater, but it has been known to relish fresh meat, and it fights viciously when attacked. Said to be quite intelligent, yet impossible to domesticate. The stalking-swine is an excellent breeder. The colonists from Gulliver eventually abandoned their Heydey settlement because of this animal. That was some two hundred years past."

Herold Norn scratched his scalp between dark hair and brass coronet. "No. It is too thin, too light. Look at the neck! Think what a feridian would do to it." He shook his head violently. "Besides, it is ugly. And I resent the offer of a scavenger, no matter how ill-tempered. The House of Norn breeds proud fighters, beasts who kill their own game!"

"So," said Tuf. He touched the button, and the stalking-swine vanished. In its place, bulking large enough to touch the plates above and fade into them, was a massive ball of armored grey flesh as featureless as battle plate.

"This creature's homeworld has never been named, nor settled. A team from Old Poseidon once explored it, however, and cell samples were taken. Zoo specimens existed briefly, but did not thrive. The beast was nicknamed the rolleram. Adults weigh approximately six metric tons. On the plains of their homeworld, the rollerams achieve speed in excess of fifty kilometers per standard hour, crushing prey beneath them. The beast is all mouth. Thusly, as any portion of its skin can be made to exude digestive enzymes, it simply rests atop its meal until the meat has been absorbed."

Herold Norn, himself half-immersed in the looming holograph, sounded impressed. "Ah, yes. Better, much better. An awesome creature. Perhaps...but no." His tone changed suddenly. "Nono, this will never do. A creature weighing six tons and rolling that fast might smash its way out of the Bronze Arena, and kill hundreds of our patrons. Besides, who would pay hard coin to watch this *thing* crush a lizard-lion or a strangler? No. No sport. Your rolleram is *too* monstrous, Tuf."

Tuf, unmoved, hit the button once again. The vast grey bulk gave way to a sleek, snarling cat, fully as large as an ironfang, with slitted yellow eyes and powerful muscles bunched beneath a coat of dark blue fur. The fur was striped, here and there; long thin lines of bright silver running lengthwise down the creature's flanks.

"Ahhhhhhhh," Norn said. "A beauty, in truth, in truth."

"The cobalt panther of Celia's World," Tuf said, "often called the cobalcat. One of the largest and deadliest of the great cats, or their analogs. The beast is a truly superlative hunter, its senses miracles of biological engineering. It can see into the infrared for night prowling, and the ears—note the size and the spread, Beast-Master—the ears are extremely sensitive. Being of felinoid stock, the cobalcat has psionic ability, but in its case this ability is far more developed than the usual. Fear, hunger, and bloodlust all act as triggers; then the cobalcat becomes a mindreader."

Norn looked up, startled. "What?"

"Psionics, sir. I said psionics. The cobalcat is very deadly, simply because it knows what moves an antagonist will make before those moves are made. It anticipates. Do you comprehend?"

"Yes." Norn's voice was excited. Haviland Tuf looked over at Dax, and the big tomcat—who'd been not the least disturbed by the parade of scentless phantoms flashing on and off—confirmed the thin man's enthusiasm as genuine. "Perfect, perfect! Why, I'll venture to say that we can even train these beasts as we'd train ironfangs, eh? Eh? And *mindreaders*! Perfect. Even the colors are right, dark blue, you know, and our ironfangs were blue-black, so the cats will be most Nornic, yesyes!"

Tuf touched his chair arm, and the cobalcat vanished. "So then, no need to proceed further. Delivery will be in three weeks standard, if that pleases you. For the agreed-upon sum, I will provide three pair, two sets of younglings who should be released as breeding stock, and one mated set full-grown, who might be immediately sent into the Bronze Arena."

"So soon," Norn began. "Fine, but..."

"I use the stasis field, sir. Reversed it produces chronic distortion, a time acceleration if you will. Standard procedure. Promethean techniques would require that you wait until the clones aged to maturity naturally, which sometimes is considered inconvenient. It would perhaps be prudent to add that, although I provide Norn House with six animals, only three actual individuals are represented. *The Ark* carries a triple cobalcat cell. I will clone each specimen twice, male and female, and hope for a viable genetic mix when they crossbreed on Lyronica."

Dax filled Tuf's head with a curious flood of triumph and confusion and impatience. Herold Norn, then, had understood nothing of what Tuf had said, or at any rate that was one interpretation. "Fine, whatever you say," Norn said. "I will send the ships for the animals promptly, with proper cages. Then we will pay you."

Dax radiated deceit, distrust, alarm.

"Sir. You will pay the full fee before any beasts are handed over."

"But you said on delivery."

"Admitted. Yet I am given to impulsive whims, and impulse now tells me to collect first, rather than simultaneously."

"Oh, very well," Norn said. "Though your demands are arbitrary and excessive. With these cobalcats, we shall soon recoup our fee." He started to rise.

Haviland Tuf raised a single finger. "One moment. You have not seen fit to inform me overmuch of the ecology of Lyronica, nor the particular realms of Norn House. Perhaps prey exists. I must caution you, however, that your cobalcats will not breed unless hunting is good. They need suitable game species."

"Yesyes, of course."

"Let me add this, then. For an additional five thousand standards, I might clone you a breeding stock of Celian hoppers, delightful furred herbivores renowned on a dozen worlds for their succulent flesh."

Herold Norn frowned. "Bah. You ought to give them to us without charge. You have extorted enough money, trader, and..."

Tuf rose, and gave a ponderous shrug. "The man berates me, Dax," he said to his cat. "What am I to do? I seek only an honest living." He looked at Norn. "Another of my impulses comes to me. I feel, some-how, that you will not relent, not even were I to offer you an excellent discount. Therefore I shall yield. The hoppers are yours without charge."

"Good. Excellent." Norn turned towards the door. "We shall take them at the same time as the cobalcats, and release them about the es-tates."

Haviland Tuf and Dax followed him from the chamber, and they rode in silence back to Norn's ship.

THE FEE WAS SENT UP BY THE HOUSE OF NORN THE DAY BEFORE delivery was due. The following afternoon, a dozen men in black and grey ascended to *The Ark*, and carried six tranquilized cobalcats from Haviland Tuf's nutrient vats to the waiting cages in their ships. Tuf bid them a passive farewell, and heard no more from Herold Norn. But he kept *The Ark* in orbit about Lyronica.

Less than three of Lyronica's shortened days passed before Tuf ob-served that his clients had slated a cobalcat for a bout in the Bronze Arena. On the appointed evening, he disguised himself as best a man like he could disguise himself—with a false beard and a shoulder-length wig of red hair, plus a gaudy puff-sleeved suit of canary yellow com-plete with a furred turban—and shuttled down to the City of All Houses with the hope of escaping attention. When the match was called (it was the third on the schedule), Tuf was sitting in the back of the Arena, a rough stone wall against his shoulders and a narrow wooden seat attempting to support his weight. He had paid a few irons for admission, but had scrupulously bypassed the betting booths.

"Third match," the announcer cried, even as workers pulled off the scattered meaty chunks of the loser in the second match. "From the House of Varcour, a female lizard-lion, aged nine months, weight 1.4 quintals, trained by Junior Beast-Master Ammari y Varcour Otheni. Once a veteran of the Bronze Arena, once surviving." Those cus-tomers close to Tuf began to cheer and wave their hands wildly—he had chosen to enter by the Varcour Gate this time, walking down a green concrete road and through the gaping maw of a monstrous golden lizard—and, far away and below, a green-and-gold enameled door slid up. Tuf had worn binoculars. He lifted them to his eyes, and saw the lizard-lion scrabble forward; two meters of scaled green reptile with a whip-like tail thrice its own length and the long snout of an Old Earth alligator. Its jaws opened and closed soundlessly, displaying an array of impressive teeth.

"From the House of Norn, imported from offworld for your amusement, a female cobalcat. Aged—aged three weeks." The announcer paused. "Aged three years," he said at last, "weight 2.3 quintals, trained by Senior Beast-Master Herold Norn. New to the Bronze Arena." The metallic dome overhead rang to the cacophonous cheering of the Norn sector; Herold Norn had packed the Bronze Arena with his housemen and tourists betting the grey-and-black standard.

The cobalcat came from the darkness slowly, with cautious fluid grace, and its great golden eyes swept the arena. It was every bit the beast that Tuf had promised; a bundle of deadly muscle and frozen motion, all blue with but a single silvery streak. Its growl could scarcely be heard, so far was Tuf from the action, but he saw its mouth gape through his glasses.

The lizard-lion saw it too, and came waddling forward, its short scaled legs kicking in the sand while the long impossible tail arched above it like the sting of some reptilian scorpion. Then, when the cobalcat turned its liquid eyes on the enemy, the lizard-lion brought the tail forward and down. Hard. With a bone-breaking crack the whip made contact, but the cobalcat had smoothly slipped to one side, and nothing shattered but air and sand.

The cat circled, yawning. The lizard-lion, implacable, turned and raised its tail again, opened its jaws, lunged forward. The cobalcat avoided both teeth and whip. Again the tail cracked, and again, the cat was too quick. Someone in the audience began to moan the killing chant, others picked it up; Tuf turned his binoculars, and saw swaying in the Norn seats. The lizard-lion gnashed its long jaws in a frenzy, smashed its whip across the nearest entry door, and began to thrash.

The cobalcat, sensing an opening, moved behind its enemy with a graceful leap, pinned the struggling lizard with one great blue paw, and clawed the soft greenish flanks and belly to ribbons. After a time and a few futile snaps of its whip that only distracted the cat, the lizard-lion lay still.

The Norns were cheering very loudly. Haviland Tuf—huge and full-bearded and gaudily dressed—rose and left.

———

Weeks passed; *The Ark* remained in orbit around Lyronica. Haviland Tuf listened to results from the Bronze Arena on his ship's comm, and noted that the Norn cobalcats were winning match after match after match. Herold Norn still lost a contest on occasion—usually when he used an ironfang to fill up his Arena obligations—but those defeats were easily outweighed by his victories.

Tuf sat with Dax curled in his lap, drank tankards of brown ale from *The Ark* brewery, and waited.

About a month after the debut of the cobalcats, a ship rose to meet him; a slim, needle-bowed shuttlecraft of green and gold. It docked, after comm contact, and Tuf met the visitors in the reception room with Dax in his arms. The cat read them as friendly enough, so he activated no defenses.

There were four, all dressed in metallic armor of scaled gold metal and green enamel. Three stood stiffly at attention. The fourth, a florid and corpulent man who wore a golden helmet with a bright green plume to conceal his baldness, stepped forward and offered a meaty hand.

"Your intent is appreciated," Tuf told him, keeping both of his own hands firmly on Dax, "but I do not care to touch. I do require your name and business, sir."

"Morho y Varcour Otheni," the leader began.

Tuf raised one palm. "So. And you are the Senior Beast-Master of the House of Varcour, come to buy a monster. Enough. I knew it all the while, I must confess. I merely wished—on impulse, as it were—to determine if you would tell the truth."

The fat Beast-Master's mouth puckered in an "o."

"Your housemen should remain here," Tuf said, turning. "Follow me."

Haviland Tuf let Morho y Varcour Otheni utter scarcely a word until they were alone in the computer room, sitting diagonally opposite. "You heard of me from the Norns," Tuf said then. "Is that not correct?"

Morho smiled toothily. "Indeed we did. A Norn houseman was

persuaded to reveal the source of their cobalcats. To our delight, your *Ark* was still in orbit. You seem to have found Lyronica diverting?"

"Problems exist. I hope to help. Your problem, for example. Varcour is, in all probability, now the last and least of the Twelve Great Houses. Your lizard-lions fail to awe me, and I understand your realms are chiefly swampland. Choice of combatants being therefore limited. Have I divined the essence of your complaint?"

"Hmpf. Yes, indeed. You do anticipate me, sir. But you do it well. We were holding our own well enough until you interfered; then, well, we have not taken a match from Norn since, and they were previously our chiefest victims. A few paltry wins over Wrai Hill and Amar Island, a lucky score against Feridian, a pair of death-draws with Arneth and Sin Doon—that has been our lot this past month. Pfui. We cannot survive. They will make me a Brood-Tender and ship me back to the estates unless I act."

Tuf quieted Morho with an upraised hand. "No need to speak further. Your distress is noted. In the time since I have helped Herold Norn, I have been fortunate enough to be gifted with a great deal of leisure. Accordingly, as an exercise of the mind, I have been able to devote myself to the problems of the Great Houses, each in its turn. We need not waste time. I can solve your present difficulties. There will be cost, however."

Morho grinned. "I come prepared. I heard about your price. It's high, there is no arguing, but we are prepared to pay, if you can..."

"Sir," Tuf said. "I am a man of charity. Norn was a poor House, Herold almost a beggar. In mercy, I gave him a low price. The domains of Varcour are richer, its standards brighter, its victories more wildly sung. For you, I must charge three hundred thousand standards, to make up for the losses I suffered in dealing with Norn."

Morho made a shocked blubbering sound, and his scales gave metallic clinks as he shifted in his seat. "Too much, too much," he protested. "I implore you. Truly, we are more glorious than Norn, but not so great as you suppose. To pay this price of yours, we must need starve. Lizard-lions would run over our battlements. Our towns would sink on their stilts, until the swamp mud covered them over and the children drowned."

Tuf was looking at Dax. "Quite so," he said, when his glance went back to Morho. "You touch me deeply. Two hundred thousand standards."

Morho y Varcour Otheni began to protest and implore again, but this time Tuf merely sat silently, arms on their armrests, until the Beast-Master, red-faced and sweating, finally ran down and agreed to pay his price.

Tuf punched his control arm. The image of a great lizard materialized between him and Morho; it stood three meters tall, covered in grey-green plate scales and standing on two thick clawed legs. Its head, atop a short neck, was disproportionately large, with jaws great enough to take off a man's head and shoulders in a single chomp. But the creature's most remarkable features were its forelegs; short thick ropes of muscle ornamented by meter-long spurs of discolored bone.

"The *tris neryei* of Cable's Landing," Tuf said, "or so it was named by the Fyndii, whose colonists preceded men on that world by a millennium. The term translates, literally, as 'living knife.' Also called the bladed tyrant, a name of human origin referring to the beast's resemblance to the tyrannosaur, or tyrant lizard, a long-extinct reptile of Old Earth. A superficial resemblance only, to be sure. The *tris neryei* is a far more efficient carnivore than the tyrannosaur ever was, due to its terrible forelegs, swords of bone that it uses with a frightful instinctive ferocity."

Morho was leaning forward until his seat creaked beneath him, and Dax filled Tuf's head with hot enthusiasm. "Excellent!" the Beast-Master said, "though the names are a bit long-winded. We shall call them tyrannoswords, eh?"

"Call them what you will, it matters not to me. The animals have many obvious advantages for the House of Varcour," Tuf said. "Should you take them, I will throw in—without any additional charge—a breeding stock of Cathadayn tree-slugs. You will find that. . . ."

———

WHEN HE COULD, TUF FOLLOWED THE NEWS FROM THE BRONZE Arena, although he never again ventured forth to the soil of Lyronica. The cobalcats continued to sweep all before them in the latest featured encounter; one of the Norn beasts had destroyed a prime Arneth strangling-ape and an Amar Island fleshfrog during a special triple match.

But Varcour fortunes were also on the upswing; the newly introduced tyrannoswords had proved a Bronze Arena sensation, with their booming cries and their heavy tread, and the relentless death of their bone-swords. In three matches so far, a huge feridian, a water-scorpion, and a Gnethin spidercat had all proved impossibly unequal to the Varcour lizards. Morho y Varcour Otheni was reportedly ecstatic. Next week, tyrannosword would face cobalcat in a struggle for supremacy, and a packed arena was being predicted. Herold Norn called up once, shortly after the tyrannoswords had scored their first victory. "Tuf," he said sternly, "you were not to sell to the other Houses."

Haviland Tuf sat calmly, regarding Norn's twisted frown, petting Dax. "No such matter was ever included in the discussion. Your own monsters perform as expected. Do you complain because another now shares your good fortune?"

"Yes. No. That is—well, never mind. I suppose I can't stop you. If the other Houses get animals that can beat our cats, however, you will be expected to provide us with something that can beat whatever you sell them. You understand?"

"Sir. Of course." He looked down at Dax. "Herold Norn now questions my comprehension." Then up again. "I will always sell, if you have the price."

Norn scowled on the comm screen. "Yesyes. Well, by then our victories should have mounted high enough to afford whatever outlandish price you intend to charge."

"I trust that all goes well otherwise?" Tuf said.

"Well, yes and no. In the Arena, yesyes, definitely. But otherwise, well, that was what I called about. The four young cats don't seem interested in breeding, for some reason. And our Brood-tender keeps complaining that they are getting thin. He doesn't think they're healthy. Now, I can't say personally, as I'm here in the City and the animals are back on the plains around Norn House. But some worry does exist. The cats run free, of course, but we have tracers on them, so we can..."

Tuf raised a hand. "It is no doubt not mating season for the cobalcats. Did you not consider this?"

"Ah. No, no, don't suppose so. That makes sense. Just a question of time then, I suppose. The other question I wanted to go over concerned these hoppers of yours. We set them loose, you know, and they have demonstrated no difficulty whatever in breeding. The ancestral Norn grasslands have been chewed bare. It is very annoying. They hop about everywhere. What are we to do?"

"Breed the cobalcats," Tuf suggested. "They are excellent predators, and will check the hopper plague."

Herold Norn looked puzzled, and mildly distressed. "Yesyes," he said.

He started to say something else, but Tuf rose. "I fear I must end our conversation," he said. "A shuttleship has entered into docking orbit with *The Ark*. Perhaps you would recognize it. It is blue-steel, with large triangular grey wings."

"The House of Wrai Hill!" Norn said.

"Fascinating," said Tuf. "Good day."

BEAST-MASTER DENIS LON WRAI PAID THREE HUNDRED THOUsand standards for his monster, an immensely powerful red-furred ursoid from the hills of Vagabond. Haviland Tuf sealed the transaction with a brace of scampersloth eggs.

The week following, four men in orange silk and flame red capes visited *The Ark*. They returned to the House of Feridian four hundred fifty thousand standards poorer, with a contract for the delivery of six great poison-elk, plus a gift herd of Hrangan grass pigs.

The Beast-Master of Sin Boon received a giant serpent; the emissary from Amar Island was pleased by his godzilla. A committee of a dozen Dant seniors in milk white robes and silver buckles delighted in the slavering garghoul that Haviland Tuf offered them, with a trifling gift. And so, one by one, each of the Twelve Great Houses of Lyronica sought him out, each received its monster, each paid the ever-increasing price.

By that time, both of Norn's fighting cobalcats were dead, the first sliced easily in two by the bone-sword of a Varcour tyrannosword, the second crushed between the massive clawed paws of a Wrai Hill ursoid (though in the latter case, the ursoid too had died)—if the great cats had escaped their fate, they nonetheless had proved unable to avoid it. Herold Norn had been calling *The Ark* daily, but Tuf had instructed his computer to refuse the calls.

Finally, with eleven Houses as past customers, Haviland Tuf sat across the computer room from Danel Leigh Arneth, Senior Beast-Master of Arneth-in-the-Gilded-Wood, once the greatest and proudest of the Twelve Great Houses of Lyronica, now the last and least. Arneth was an immensely tall man, standing even with Tuf himself, but he had none of Tuf's fat; his skin was hard ebony, all muscle, his face a hawk-nosed axe, his hair short and iron grey. The Beast-Master came to the conference in cloth-of-gold, with crimson belt and boots and a tiny crimson beret aslant upon his head. He carried a trainer's pain-prod like a walking stick.

Dax read immense hostility in the man, and treachery, and a barely suppressed rage. Accordingly, Haviland Tuf carried a small laser strapped to his stomach just beneath his greatcoat.

"The strength of Arneth-in-the-Gilded-Wood has always been in variety," Danel Leigh Arneth said early on. "When the other Houses of Lyronica threw all their fortunes on the backs of a single beast, our fathers and grandfathers worked with dozens. Against any animal of theirs, we had an optimal choice, a strategy. That has been our greatness and our pride. But we can have no strategy against these demon-beasts of yours, trader. No matter which of our hundred fighters we send onto the sand, it comes back dead. We are forced to deal with you."

"Not so," said Haviland Tuf. "I force no one. Still, look at my stock. Perhaps fortune will see fit to give you back your strategic options." He touched the buttons on his chair, and a parade of monsters came and went before the eyes of the Arneth Beast-Master; creatures furred and scaled and feathered and covered by armor plate, beasts of hill and forest and lake and plain, predators and scavengers and deadly herbivores of sizes great and small. And Danel Leigh Arneth, his lips pressed tightly together, finally ordered four each of the dozen largest and deadliest species, at a cost of some two million standards.

The conclusion of the transaction—complete, as with all the other Houses, with a gift of some small harmless animal—did nothing to soothe Arneth's foul temper. "Tuf," he said when the dealing was over, "you are a clever and devious man, but you do not fool me."

Haviland Tuf said nothing.

"You have made yourself immensely wealthy, and you have cheated all who bought from you and thought to profit. The Norns, for example—their cobalcats are worthless.

"They were a poor House; your price brought them to the edge of bankruptcy, just as you have done to all of us. They thought to recoup through victories. Bah! There will be no Norn victories now! Each House that you have sold to gained the edge on those who purchased previously. Thus Arneth, the last to purchase, remains the greatest House of all. Our monsters will wreak devastation. The sands of the Bronze Arena will darken with the blood of the lesser beasts."

Tuf's hands locked on the bulge of his stomach. His face was placid.

"You have changed nothing! The Great Houses remain, Arneth the greatest and Norn the least. All you have done is bleed us, like the profiteer you are, until every lord must struggle and scrape to get by. The Houses now wait for victory, pray for victory, depend on victory, but all the victories will be Arneth's. We alone have not been cheated, because I thought to buy last and thus best."

"So," said Haviland Tuf. "You are then a wise and sagacious Beast-Master, if this indeed is the case. Yet I deny that I have cheated anyone."

"Don't play with words!" Arneth roared. "Henceforth you will deal no longer with the Great Houses. Norn has no money to buy from you again, but if they did, you would not sell to them. *Do you understand?* We will not go round and round forever."

"Of course," Tuf said. He looked at Dax. "Now Danel Leigh Arneth imputes my understanding. I am always misunderstood." His calm gaze returned to the angry Beast-Master in red-and-gold. "Your point, sir, is well-taken. Perhaps it is time for me to leave Lyronica. In any event, I shall not deal with Norn again, nor with any of the Great Houses. This is a foolish impulse—by thus acting I foreswear great profits—but I am a gentle man much given to following my whim. Obedient to the esteemed Danel Leigh Arneth, I bow to your demand."

Dax reported wordlessly that Arneth was pleased and pacified; he had cowed Tuf, and won the day for his House. His rivals would get no new champions. Once again, the Bronze Arena would be predictable. He left satisfied.

Three weeks later, a fleet of twelve glittering gold-flecked shuttles and a dozen work squads of men in gold-and-crimson armor arrived to remove the purchases of Danel Leigh Arneth. Haviland Tuf, stroking a limp, lazy Dax, saw them off, then returned down the long corridors of *The Ark* to his control room, to take a call from Herold Norn.

The thin Beast-Master looked positively skeletal. "Tuf!" he exclaimed. "Everything is going wrong. You must help."

"Wrong? I solved your problem."

Norn pressed his features together in a grimace, and scratched beneath his brass coronet. "Nono, listen. The cobalcats are all dead, or sick. Four of them dead in the Bronze Arena—we knew the second pair were too young, you understand, but when the first couple lost, there was nothing else to do. It was that or go back to ironfangs.

"Now we have only two left. They don't eat much—catch a few hoppers, but nothing else. And we can't train them, either. A trainer comes into the pen with a pain-prod, and the damn cats know what he intends. They're always a move ahead, you understand? In the Arena, they won't respond to the killing chant at all. It's *terrible*. The worst thing is they don't even breed. We need *more* of them. What are we supposed to enter in the gaming pits?"

"It is not cobalcat breeding season," Tuf said.

"Yesyes. When *is* their breeding season?"

"A fascinating question. A pity you did not ask sooner. As I understand the matter, the female cobalt panther goes into heat each spring, when the snowtufts blossom on Celia's World. Some type of biological trigger is involved."

"I—Tuf. You *planned* this. Lyronica has no snowthings, whatever. Now I suppose you intend charging us a fortune for these flowers."

"Sir. Of course not. Were the option mine, I would gladly give them to you. Your plight wounds me. I am concerned. However, as it happens, I have given my word to Danel Leigh Arneth to deal no more with the Great Houses of Lyronica." He shrugged hopelessly.

"We won victories with your cats," Norn said, with an edge of desperation in his voice. "Our treasury has been growing—we have something like forty thousand standards now. It is yours. Sell us these flowers. Or better, a new animal. Bigger. Fiercer. I saw the Dant garghouls. Sell us something like that. We have nothing to enter in the Bronze Arena!"

"No? What of your ironfangs? The pride of Norn, I was told."

Herold Norn waved impatiently. "Problems, you understand, we have been having problems. These hoppers of yours, they eat anything, everything. They've gotten out of control. Millions of them, all over, eating all the grass, and all the crops. The things they've done to farmland—the cobalcats love them, yes, but we don't have enough cobalcats. And the wild ironfangs won't touch the hoppers. They don't like the taste, I suppose. I don't know, not really. But, you understand, all the other grass-eaters left, driven out by these hoppers of yours, and the ironfangs went with them. Where, I don't know that either. Gone, though. Into the unclaimed lands, beyond the realms of Norn. There are some villages out there, a few farmers, but they hate the Great Houses. Tamberkin, all of them, don't even have dog fights. They'll probably try to *tame* the ironfangs, if they see them."

"So," said Tuf. "But then you have your kennels, do you not?"

"Not any more," Norn said. He sounded very harried. "I ordered them shut. The ironfangs were losing every match, especially after you began to sell to the other Houses. It seemed a foolish waste to maintain dead weight. Besides, the expense—we needed every standard. You bled us dry. We had Arena fees to pay, and of course we had to wager, and lately we've had to buy some food from Taraber just to feed all our housemen and trainers. I mean, you would never *believe* the things the hoppers have done to our crops."

"Sir," said Tuf. "You insult me. I am an ecologist. I know a great deal of hoppers and their ways. Am I to understand that you shut your ironfang kennels?"

"Yesyes. We turned the useless things loose, and now they're gone with the rest. What are we going to do? The hoppers are overrunning the plains, the cats won't mate, and our money will run out soon if we must continue to import food and pay Arena fees without any hope of victory."

Tuf folded his hands together. "You do indeed face a series of delicate problems. And I am the very man to help you to their solution. Unfortunately, I have pledged my bond to Danel Leigh Arneth."

"Is it hopeless, then? Tuf, I am a man begging, I, a Senior Beast-Master of Norn. Soon we will drop from the games entirely. We will have no funds for Arena fees or betting, no animals to enter. We are cursed by ill fortune. No Great House has ever failed to provide its allotment of fighters, not even Feridian during its Twelve Year Drought. We will be shamed. The House of Norn will sully its proud history by sending dogs and cats onto the sand, to be shredded ignominiously by the huge monsters that you have sold the other Houses."

"Sir," Tuf said, "if you will permit me an impertinent remark, and one perhaps without foundation—if you will permit this to me—well, then, I will tell you my opinion. I have a hunch—mmm, *hunch*, yes, that is the proper word, and a curious word it is too—a hunch, as I was saying, that the monsters you fear may be in short supply in the weeks and months to come. For example, the adolescent ursoids of Vagabond may very shortly go into hibernation. They are less than a year old, you understand. I hope the lords of Wrai Hill are not unduly disconcerted by this, yet I fear that they may be. Vagabond, as I'm sure you are aware, has an extremely irregular orbit about its primary, so that its Long Winters last approximately twenty standard years. The ursoids are attuned to this cycle. Soon their body processes will slow to almost nothing—some have mistaken a sleeping ursoid for a dead one, you know—and I don't think they will be easily awakened. Perhaps, as the trainers of Wrai Hill are men of high good character and keen intellect, they might find a way. But I would be strongly inclined to further suspect that most of their energies and their funds will be devoted to feeding their populace, in the light of the voracious appetites of scampersloths. In quite a like manner, the men of the House of Varcour will be forced to deal with an explosion of Cathadayn tree-slugs. The tree-slugs are particularly fascinating creatures. At one point in their life cycle, they become veritable sponges, and double in size. A large enough grouping is fully capable of drying up even an extensive swampland." Tuf paused, and his thick fingers beat in drumming rhythms across his stomach. "I ramble unconsciously, sir. Do you grasp my point, though? My thrust?"

Herold Norn looked like a dead man. "You are mad. You have destroyed us. Our economy, our ecology . . . but *why*? We paid you fairly.

The Houses, the Houses . . . no beasts, no funds. How can the games go on? *No one* will send fighters to the Bronze Arena!"

Haviland Tuf raised his hands in shock. "Really?" he said.

Then he turned off the communicator and rose. Smiling a tiny, tight-lipped smile, he began to talk to Dax.

GUARDIANS

———————— ❖ ————————

HAVILAND TUF THOUGHT THE SIX WORLDS BIO-AGRICULTURAL
Exhibition a great disappointment.

He had spent a long, wearying day on Brazelourn, trooping
through the cavernous exhibition halls, pausing now and then to give a
cursory inspection to a new grain hybrid or a genetically improved insect. Although the *Ark's* cell library held cloning material for literally
millions of plant and animal species from an uncounted number of
worlds, Haviland Tuf was nonetheless always alert for any opportunity
to expand his stock-in-trade.

But few of the displays on Brazelourn seemed especially promising,
and as the hours passed Tuf grew bored and uncomfortable in the
jostling, indifferent crowds. People swarmed everywhere—Vagabonder
tunnel-farmers in deep maroon furs, plumed and perfumed Areeni land-
lords, somber nightsiders and brightly garbed evernoons from New
Janus, and a plethora of the native Brazeleen. All of them made excessive
noise and favored Tuf with curious stares as he passed among them.
Some even brushed up against him, bringing a frown to his long face.

Ultimately, seeking escape from the throngs, Tuf decided he was
hungry. He pressed his way through the fairgoers with dignified distaste, and emerged from the vaulting five-story Ptolan Exhibit Hall.
Outside, hundreds of vendors had set up booths between the great
buildings. The man selling pop-onion pies seemed least busy of those

nearby, and Tuf determined that a pop–onion pie was the very thing he craved.

"Sir," he said to the vendor, "I would have a pie."

The pieman was round and pink and wore a greasy apron. He opened his hotbox, reached in with a gloved hand, and extracted a hot pie. When he pushed it across the counter at Tuf, he stared. "Oh," he said, "you're a big one."

"Indeed, sir," said Haviland Tuf. He picked up the pie and bit into it impassively.

"You're an offworlder," the pieman observed. "Not from no place nearby, neither."

Tuf finished his pie in three neat bites, and cleaned his greasy fingers on a napkin. "You belabor the obvious, sir," he said. He held up a long, calloused finger. "Another," he said.

Rebuffed, the vendor fetched out another pie without further observations, letting Tuf eat in relative peace. As he savored the flaky crust and tartness within, Tuf studied the milling fairgoers, the rows of vendors' booths, and the five great halls that loomed over the landscape. When he had done eating, he turned back to the pieman, his face as blank as ever. "Sir. If you will, a question."

"What's that?" the other said gruffly.

"I see five exhibition halls," said Haviland Tuf. "I have visited each in turn." He pointed. "Brazelourn, Vale Areen, New Janus, Vagabond, and here Ptola." Tuf folded his hands together neatly atop his bulging stomach. "Five, sir. Five halls, five worlds. No doubt, being a stranger as I am, I am unfamiliar with some subtle point of local usage, yet I am perplexed. In those regions where I have heretofore traveled, a gathering calling itself the Six Worlds Bio-Agricultural Exhibition might be expected to include exhibits from six worlds. Plainly that is not the case here. Perhaps you might enlighten me as to why?"

"No one came from Namor."

"Indeed," said Haviland Tuf.

"On account of the troubles," the vendor added.

"All is made clear," said Tuf. "Or, if not all, at least a portion. Perhaps you would care to serve me another pie, and explain to me the nature of these troubles. I am nothing if not curious, sir. It is my great vice, I fear."

The pieman slipped on his glove again and opened the hotbox. "You know what they say. Curiosity makes you hungry."

"Indeed," said Tuf. "I must admit I have never heard them say that before."

The man frowned. "No, I got it wrong. Hunger makes you curious, that's what it is. Don't matter. My pies will fill you up."

"Ah," said Tuf. He took up the pie. "Please proceed."

So the pie-seller told him, at great rambling length, about the troubles on the world Namor. "So you can see," he finally concluded, "why they didn't come, with all this going on. Not much to exhibit."

"Of course," said Haviland Tuf, dabbing his lips. "Sea monsters can be most vexing."

NAMOR WAS A DARK GREEN WORLD, MOONLESS AND SOLITARY, banded by wispy golden clouds. The *Ark* shuddered out of drive and settled ponderously into orbit around it. In the long, narrow communications room, Haviland Tuf moved from seat to seat, studying the planet on a dozen of the room's hundred viewscreens. Three small gray kittens kept him company, bounding across the consoles, pausing only to slap at each other. Tuf paid them no mind.

A water world, Namor had only one landmass decently large enough to be seen from orbit, and that none too large. But magnification revealed thousands of islands scattered in long, crescent-shaped archipelagoes across the deep green seas, earthen jewels strewn throughout the oceans. Other screens showed the lights of dozens of cities and towns on the nightside, and pulsing dots of energy outlay where settlements sat in sunlight.

Tuf looked at it all, and then seated himself, flicked on another console, and began to play a war game with the computer. A kitten bounded up into his lap and went to sleep. He was careful not to disturb it. Some time later, a second kitten vaulted up and pounced on it, and they began to tussle. Tuf brushed them to the floor.

It took longer than even Tuf had anticipated, but finally the challenge came, as he had known it would. *"Ship in orbit,"* came the demand, *"ship in orbit, this is Namor Control. State your name and* business. State your name and business, please. Interceptors have been dispatched. State your name and business."

The transmission was coming from the chief landmass. The *Ark* tapped into it. At the same time, it found the ship that was moving toward them—there was only one—and flashed it on another screen.

"I am the *Ark*," Haviland Tuf told Namor Control.

Namor Control was a round-faced woman with close-cropped brown hair, sitting at a console and wearing a deep green uniform with golden piping. She frowned, her eyes flicking to the side, no doubt to a superior or another console. *"Ark,"* she said, "state your homeworld. State your homeworld and your business, please."

The other ship had opened communications with the planet, the computer indicated. Two more viewscreens lit up. One showed a slender young woman with a large, crooked nose on a ship's bridge, the other an elderly man before a console. They both wore green uniforms, and they were conversing animatedly in code. It took the computer less than a minute to break it, so Tuf could listen in. "... damned if I know what it is," the woman on the ship was saying. "There's never been a ship that big. My God, just look at it. Are you getting all this? Has it answered?"

"Ark," the round-faced woman was still saying, "state your homeworld and your business, please. This is Namor Control."

Haviland Tuf cut into the other conversation, to talk to all three of them simultaneously. "This is the *Ark*," he said. "I have no homeworld, sirs. My intentions are purely peaceful—trade and consultation. I learned of your tragic difficulties, and moved by your plight, I have come to offer you my services."

The woman on the ship looked startled. "What are *you*..." she started. The man was equally nonplussed, but he said nothing, only gaped open-mouthed at Tuf's blank white visage.

"This is Namor Control, *Ark*," said the round-faced woman. "We are closed to trade. Repeat, we are closed to trade. We are under martial law here."

By then the slender woman on the ship had composed herself. *"Ark,* this is Guardian Kefira Qay, commanding NGS *Sunrazor.* We are armed, *Ark*. Explain yourself. You are a thousand times larger than any trader I have ever seen, *Ark*. Explain yourself or be fired upon."

"Indeed," said Haviland Tuf. "Threats will avail you little, Guardian. I am most sorely vexed. I have come all this long way from Brazelourn to offer you my aid and solace, and you meet me with threats and hostility." A kitten leapt up into his lap. Tuf scooped it up with a huge white hand, and deposited it on the console in front of him, where the viewer would pick it up. He gazed down at it sorrowfully. "There is no trust left in humanity," he said to the kitten.

"Hold your fire, *Sunrazor,*" said the elderly man. "*Ark,* if your intentions are truly peaceful, explain yourself. What are you? We are hard-pressed here, *Ark,* and Namor is a small, undeveloped world. We have never seen your like before. Explain yourself."

Haviland Tuf stroked the kitten. "Always I must truckle to suspicion," he told it. "They are fortunate that I am so kind-hearted, or else I would simply depart and leave them to their fate." He looked up, straight into the viewer. "Sir," he said. "I am the *Ark.* I am Haviland Tuf, captain and master here, crew entire. You are troubled by great monsters from the depths of your seas, I have been told. Very well. I shall rid you of them."

"*Ark,* this is *Sunrazor.* How do you propose doing that?"

"The *Ark* is a seedship of the Ecological Engineering Corps," said Haviland Tuf with stiff formality. "I am an ecological engineer and a specialist in biological warfare."

"Impossible," said the old man. "The EEC was wiped out a thousand years ago, along with the Federal Empire. None of their seedships remain."

"How distressing," said Haviland Tuf. "Here I sit in an illusion. No doubt, now that you have told me my ship does not exist, I shall sink right through it and plunge into your atmosphere, where I shall burn up as I fall."

"Guardian," said Kefira Qay from the *Sunrazor,* "these seedships may indeed no longer exist, but I am fast closing on something that my scopes tell me is almost thirty kilometers long. It does not appear to be an illusion."

"I am not yet falling," admitted Haviland Tuf.

"Can you truly help us?" asked the round-faced woman at Namor Control.

"Why must I always be doubted?" Tuf asked the small gray kitten.

"Lord Guardian, we must give him the chance to prove what he says," insisted Namor Control.

Tuf looked up. "Threatened, insulted, and doubted as I have been, nonetheless my empathy for your situation bids me to persist. Perhaps I might suggest that *Sunrazor* dock with me, so to speak. Guardian Qay may come aboard and join me for an evening meal, while we converse. Surely your suspicions cannot extend to mere conversation, that most civilized of human pastimes."

The three Guardians conferred hurriedly with each other and with a person or persons offscreen, while Haviland Tuf sat back and toyed with the kitten. "I shall name you Suspicion," he said to it, "to commemorate my reception here. Your siblings shall be Doubt, Hostility, Ingratitude, and Foolishness."

"We accept your proposal, Haviland Tuf," said Guardian Kefira Qay from the bridge of the *Sunrazor*. "Prepare to be boarded."

"Indeed," said Tuf. "Do you like mushrooms?"

The shuttle deck of the *Ark* was as large as the landing field of a major starport, and seemed almost a junkyard for derelict spacecraft. The *Ark*'s own shuttles stood trim in their launch berths, five identical black ships with rakish lines and stubby triangular wings angling back, designed for atmospheric flight and still in good repair. Other craft were less impressive. A teardrop-shaped trading vessel from Avalon squatted wearily on three extended landing legs, next to a driveshift courier scored by battle, and a Karaleo lionboat whose ornate trim was largely gone. Elsewhere stood vessels of stranger, more alien design.

Above, the great dome cracked into a hundred pie-wedge segments, and drew back to reveal a small yellow sun surrounded by stars, and a dull green manta-shaped ship of about the same size as one of Tuf's shuttles. The *Sunrazor* settled, and the dome closed behind it. When the stars had been blotted out again, atmosphere came swirling back in to the deck, and Haviland Tuf arrived soon after.

Kefira Qay emerged from her ship with her lips set sternly beneath her big, crooked nose, but no amount of control could quite conceal the awe in her eyes. Two armed men in golden coveralls trimmed with green followed her.

Haviland Tuf drove up to them in an open three-wheeled cart. "I am afraid that my dinner invitation was only for one, Guardian Qay," he said when he saw her escort. "I regret any misunderstanding, yet I must insist."

"Very well," she said. She turned to her guard. "Wait with the others. You have your orders." When she got in next to Tuf she told him, "The *Sunrazor* will tear your ship apart if I am not returned safely within two standard hours."

Haviland Tuf blinked at her. "Dreadful," he said. "Everywhere my warmth and hospitality is met with mistrust and violence." He set the vehicle into motion.

They drove in silence through a maze of interconnected rooms and corridors, and finally entered a huge shadowy shaft that seemed to extend the full length of the ship in both directions. Transparent vats of a hundred different sizes covered walls and ceiling as far as the eye could see, most empty and dusty, a few filled with colored liquids in which half-seen shapes stirred feebly. There was no sound but a wet, viscous dripping somewhere off behind them. Kefira Qay studied everything and said nothing. They went at least three kilometers down the great shaft, until Tuf veered off into a blank wall that dilated before them. Shortly thereafter they parked and dismounted.

A sumptuous meal had been laid out in the small, spartan dining chamber to which Tuf escorted the Guardian Kefira Qay. They began with iced soup, sweet and piquant and black as coal, followed by neograss salads with a gingery topping. The main course was a breaded mushroom top full as large as the plate on which it was served, surrounded by a dozen different sorts of vegetables in individual sauces. The Guardian ate with great relish.

"It would appear you find my humble fare to your taste," observed Haviland Tuf.

"I haven't had a good meal in longer than I care to admit," replied Kefira Qay. "On Namor, we have always depended on the sea for our sustenance. Normally it is bountiful, but since our troubles began..." She lifted a forkful of dark, misshapen vegetables in a yellow-brown sauce. "What am I eating? It's delightful."

"Rhiannese sinners' root, in a mustard sauce," Haviland Tuf said.

Qay swallowed and set down her fork. "But Rhiannon is so far, how do you..." She stopped.

"Of course," Tuf said, steepling his fingers beneath his chin as he watched her face. "All this provender derives from the *Ark,* though originally it might be traced back to a dozen different worlds. Would you like more spiced milk?"

"No," she muttered. She gazed at the empty plates. "You weren't lying, then. You are what you claim, and this is a seedship of the . . . what did you call them?"

"The Ecological Engineering Corps, of the long-defunct Federal Empire. Their ships were few in number, and all but one destroyed by the vicissitudes of war. The *Ark* alone survived, derelict for a millennium. The details need not concern you. Suffice it to say that I found it, and made it functional."

"You *found* it?"

"I believe I just said as much, in those very same words. Kindly pay attention. I am not partial to repeating myself. Before finding the *Ark,* I made a humble living from trade. My former ship is still on the landing deck. Perhaps you chanced to see it."

"Then you're really just a trader."

"Please!" said Tuf with indignation. "I am an ecological engineer. The *Ark* can remake whole planets, Guardian. True, I am but one man, alone, when once this ship was crewed by two hundred, and I do lack the extensive formal training such as was given centuries ago to those who wore the golden theta, the sigil of the Ecological Engineers. Yet, in my own small way, I contrive to muddle through. If Namor would care to avail itself of my services, I have no doubt that I can help you."

"Why?" the slender Guardian asked warily. "Why are you so anxious to help us?"

Haviland Tuf spread his big white hands helplessly. "I know, I might appear a fool. I cannot help myself. I am a humanitarian by nature, much moved by hardship and suffering. I could no more abandon your people, beset as they are, than I could harm one of my cats. The Ecological Engineers were made of sterner stuff, I fear, but I am helpless to change my sentimental nature. So here I sit before you, prepared to do my best."

"You want nothing?"

"I shall labor without recompense," said Tuf. "Of course, I will have operating expenses. I must charge a small fee to offset them. Say, three million standards. Do you think that fair?"

"Fair," she said sarcastically. "Fairly high, I'd say. There have been others like you, Tuf—arms merchants and soldiers of fortune who have come to grow rich off our misery."

"Guardian," said Tuf, reproachfully, "you do me grievous wrong. I take little for myself. The *Ark* is so large, so costly. Perhaps two million standards would suffice? I cannot believe you would grudge me this pittance. Is your world worth less?"

Kefira Qay sighed, a tired look etched on her narrow face. "No," she admitted. "Not if you can do all you promise. Of course, we are not a rich world. I will have to consult my superiors. This is not my decision alone." She stood up abruptly. "Your communications facilities?"

"Through the door and left down the blue corridor. The fifth door on the right." Tuf rose with ponderous dignity, and began cleaning up as she left.

When the Guardian returned he had opened a decanter of liquor, vividly scarlet, and was stroking a black-and-white cat who had made herself at home on the table. "You're hired, Tuf," said Kefira Qay, seating herself. "Two million standards. *After* you win this war."

"Agreed," said Tuf. "Let us discuss your situation over glasses of this delightful beverage."

"Alcoholic?"

"Mildly narcotic."

"A Guardian uses no stimulants or depressants. We are a fighting guild. Substances like that pollute the body and slow the reflexes. A Guardian must be vigilant. We guard and protect."

"Laudable," said Haviland Tuf. He filled his own glass.

"*Sunrazor* is wasted here. It has been recalled by Namor Control. We need its combat capabilities below."

"I shall expedite its departure, then. And yourself?"

"I have been detached," she said, wrinkling up her face. "We are standing by with data on the situation below. I am to help brief you, and act as your liaison officer."

THE WATER WAS CALM, A TRANQUIL GREEN MIRROR FROM HORIZON to horizon.

It was a hot day. Bright yellow sunlight poured down through a thin bank of gilded clouds. The ship rested still on the water, its metallic sides flashing silver-blue, its open deck a small island of activity in an ocean of peace. Men and women small as insects worked the dredges and nets, bare-chested in the heat. A great claw full of mud and weeds emerged from the water, dripping, and was sluiced down an open hatchway. Elsewhere bins of huge milky jellyfish baked in the sun.

Suddenly there was agitation. For no apparent reason, people began to run. Others stopped what they were doing and looked around, confused. Still others worked on, oblivious. The great metal claw, open and empty now, swung back out over the water and submerged again, even as another one rose on the far side of the ship. More people were running. Two men collided and went down.

Then the first tentacle came curling up from beneath the ship.

It rose and rose. It was longer than the dredging claws. Where it emerged from the dark green sea, it looked as thick as a big man's torso. It tapered to the size of an arm. The tentacle was white, a soft slimy sort of white. All along its underside were vivid pink circles big as dinner plates, circles that writhed and pulsed as the tentacle curled over and about the huge farming ship. The end of the tentacle split into a rat's nest of smaller tentacles, dark and restless as snakes.

Up and up it went, and then over and down, pinioning the ship. Something moved on the other side, something pale stirring beneath all that green, and the second tentacle emerged. Then a third, and a fourth. One wrestled with a dredging claw. Another had the remains of a net draped all about it, like a veil, which didn't seem to hinder it. Now all the people were running—all but those the tentacles had found. One of them had curled itself around a woman with an axe. She hacked at it wildly, thrashing in the pale embrace, until her back arched and suddenly she fell still. The tentacle dropped her, white fluid pulsing feebly from the gashes she had left, and seized someone else.

Twenty tentacles had attached themselves when the ship abruptly listed to starboard. Survivors slid across the deck and into the sea. The ship tilted more and more. Something was pushing it over, pulling it down. Water sloshed across the side, and into the open hatchways. Then the ship began to break up.

Haviland Tuf stopped the projection, and held the image on the large viewscreen: the green sea and golden sun, the shattered vessel, the pale embracing tentacles. "This was the first attack?" he asked.

"Yes and no," replied Kefira Qay. "Prior to this, one other harvester and two passenger hydrofoils had vanished mysteriously. We were investigating, but we did not know the cause. In this case, a news crew happened to be on the site, making a recording for an educational broadcast. They got more than they bargained for."

"Indeed," said Tuf.

"They were airborne, in a skimmer. The broadcast that night almost caused a panic. But it was not until the next ship went down that things began to get truly serious. That was when the Guardians began to realize the full extent of the problem."

Haviland Tuf stared up at the viewscreen, his heavy face impassive, expressionless, his hands resting on the console. A black-and-white kitten began to bat at his fingers. "Away, Foolishness," he said, depositing the kitten gently on the floor.

"Enlarge a section of one of the tentacles," suggested the Guardian beside him.

Silently, Tuf did as she bid him. A second screen lit up, showing a grainy close-up of a great pale rope of tissue arching over the deck.

"Take a good look at one of the suckers," said Qay. "The pink areas, there, you see?"

"The third one from the end is dark within. And it appears to have teeth."

"Yes," said Kefira Qay. "All of them do. The outer lips of those suckers are a kind of hard, fleshy flange. Slapped down, they spread and create a vacuum seal of sorts, virtually impossible to tear loose. But each of them is a mouth, too. Within the flange is a soft pink flap that falls back, and then the teeth come sliding out—a triple row of them, serrated, and sharper than you'd think. Now move down to the tendrils at the end, if you would."

Tuf touched the console, and put another magnification up on a third screen, bringing the twisting snakes into easy view.

"Eyes," said Kefira Qay. "At the end of every one of those tendrils. Twenty eyes. The tentacles don't need to grope around blindly. They can *see* what they are doing."

"Fascinating," said Haviland Tuf. "What lies beneath the water? The source of these terrible arms?"

"There are cross-sections and photographs of dead specimens later on, as well as some computer simulations. Most of the specimens we took were quite badly mangled. The main body of the thing is sort of an inverted cup, like a half-inflated bladder, surrounded by a great ring of bone and muscle that anchors these tentacles. The bladder fills and empties with water to enable the creature to rise to the surface, or descend far below—the submarine principle. By itself it doesn't weigh much, although it is amazingly strong. What it does, it empties its bladder to rise to the surface, grabs hold, and then begins to fill again. The capacity of the bladder is astounding, and as you can see, the creature is *huge.* If need be, it can even force water up those tentacles and out of its mouths, in order to flood the vessel and speed things along. So those tentacles are arms, mouths, eyes, and living hoses all at once."

"And you say that your people had no knowledge of such creatures until this attack?"

"Right. A cousin of this thing, the Namorian man-of-war, was well-known in the early days of colonization. It was sort of a cross between a jellyfish and an octopus, with twenty arms. Many native species are built along the same lines—a central bladder, or body, or shell, or what have you, with twenty legs or tendrils or tentacles in a ring around it. The men-of-war were carnivores, much like this monster, although they had a ring of eyes on the central body instead of at the end of the tentacles. The arms couldn't function as hoses, either. And they were much smaller—about the size of a human. They bobbed about on the surface above the continental shelves, particularly above mud-pot beds, where fish were thick. Fish were their usual prey, although a few unwary swimmers met a bloody awful death in their embrace."

"Might I ask what became of them?" said Tuf.

"They were a nuisance. Their hunting grounds were the same areas we needed—shallows rich with fish and seagrass and waterfruit, over mud-pot beds and scrabbler runs full of chameleon-clams and bobbing freddies. Before we could harvest or farm safely, we had to pretty much clean out the men-of-war. We did. Oh, there are still a few around, but they are rare now."

"I see," said Haviland Tuf. "And this most formidable creature, this living submarine and ship-eater that plagues you so dreadfully, does it have a name?"

"The Namorian dreadnaught," said Kefira Qay. "When it first appeared, we theorized it was an inhabitant of the great deeps that had somehow wandered to the surface. Namor has been inhabited for barely a hundred standard years, after all. We have scarcely begun to explore the deeper regions of the seas, and we have little knowledge of the things that might live down there. But as more and more ships were attacked and sunk, it became obvious that we had an army of dreadnaughts to contend with."

"A navy," corrected Haviland Tuf.

Kefira Qay scowled. "Whatever. A *lot* of them, not one lost specimen. At that point the theory was that some unimaginable catastrophe had taken place deep under the ocean, driving forth this entire species."

"You give no credit to this theory," Tuf said.

"No one does. It's been disproved. The dreadnaughts wouldn't be able to withstand the pressures at those depths. So now we don't know where they came from." She made a face. "Only that they are here."

"Indeed," said Haviland Tuf. "No doubt you fought back."

"Certainly. A game but losing fight. Namor is a young planet, with neither the population nor the resources for the sort of struggle we have been plunged into. Three million Namorians are scattered across our seas, on more than seventeen thousand small islands. Another million huddle on New Atlantis, our single small continent. Most of our people are fisherfolk and sea-farmers. When this all began, the Guardians numbered barely fifty thousand. Our guild is descended from the crews of the ships who brought the colonists from Old Poseidon and Aquarius here to Namor. We have always protected them, but before the coming of the dreadnaughts our task was simple. Our world was peaceful, with little real conflict. There was some ethnic rivalry between Poseidonites and Aquarians, but it was good-natured. The Guardians provided planetary defense, with *Sunrazor* and two similar craft, but most of our work was in fire and flood control, disaster relief, police work, that sort of thing. We had about a hundred armed hydrofoil patrol boats, and we used them for escort duty for a while, and inflicted some casualties, but they were really no match for the dreadnaughts. It soon became clear that there were more dread-naughts than patrol boats, anyway."

"Nor do patrol boats reproduce, as I must assume these dread-naughts do," Tuf said. Foolishness and Doubt were tussling in his lap.

"Exactly. Still, we tried. We dropped depth charges on them when we detected them below the sea, we torpedoed them when they came to the surface. We killed hundreds. But there were hundreds more, and every boat we lost was irreplaceable. Namor has no technological base to speak of. In better days, we imported what we needed from Brazelourn and Vale Areen. Our people believed in a simple life. The planet couldn't support industry anyway. It is poor in heavy metals and has almost no fossil fuel."

"How many Guardian patrol boats remain to you?" asked Haviland Tuf.

"Perhaps thirty. We dare not use them anymore. Within a year of the first attack, the dreadnaughts were in complete command of our sea lanes. All of the great harvesters were lost, hundreds of sea-farms had been abandoned or destroyed, half of the small fisherfolk were dead, and the other half huddled fearfully in port. Nothing human dared move on the seas of Namor."

"Your islands were isolated from one another?"

"Not quite," Kefira Qay replied. "The Guardians had twenty armed skimmers, and there were another hundred-odd skimmers and aircars in private hands. We commandeered them, armed them. We also had our airships. Skimmers and aircars are difficult and expensive to maintain here. Parts are hard to come by, and we have few trained techs, so most of the air traffic before the troubles was carried by airships—solar-powered, helium-filled, large. There was quite a sizable fleet, as many as a thousand. The airships took over the provisioning of some of the small islands, where starvation was a very real threat. Other airships, as well as the Guardian skimmers, carried on the fight. We dumped chemicals, poisons, explosives, and such from the safety of the air and destroyed thousands of dreadnaughts, although the cost was frightful. They clustered thickest about our best fishing grounds and mud-pot beds, so we were forced to blow up and poison the very areas we needed most. Still, we had no choice. For a time, we thought we were winning the fight. A few fishing boats even put out and returned safely, with a Guardian skimmer flying escort."

"Obviously, this was not the ultimate result of the conflict," said Haviland Tuf, "or we would not be sitting here talking." Doubt batted Foolishness soundly across the head, and the smaller kitten fell off Tuf's knee to the floor. Tuf bent and scooped him up. "Here," he said, handing him to Kefira Qay, "hold him, if you please. Their small war is distracting me from your larger one."

"I—why, of course." The Guardian took the small black-and-white kitten in hand gingerly. He fit snugly into her palm. "What is it?" she asked.

"A cat," said Tuf. "He will jump out of your hand if you continue to hold him as if he were a diseased fruit. Kindly put him in your lap. I assure you he is harmless."

Kefira Qay, appearing very uncertain, shook the kitten out of her hand onto her knees. Foolishness yowled, almost tumbling to the floor again before sinking his small claws into the fabric of her uniform. *"Ow,"* said Kefira Qay. "It has talons."

"Claws," corrected Tuf. "Tiny and harmless."

"They aren't poisoned, are they?"

"I think not," said Tuf. "Stroke him, front to back. It will make him less agitated."

Kefira Qay touched the kitten's head uncertainly.

"Please," said Tuf. "I said *stroke,* not pat."

The Guardian began to pet the kitten. Instantly, Foolishness began to purr. She stopped and looked up in horror. "It's trembling," she said, "and making a noise."

"Such a response is considered favorable," Tuf assured her. "I beg you to continue your ministrations, and your briefing. If you will."

"Of course," said Qay. She resumed petting Foolishness, who settled down comfortably on her knee. "If you would go on to the next tape," she prompted.

Tuf wiped the stricken ship and the dreadnaught off the main screen. Another scene took their place—a winter's day, windy and chill by the look of it. The water below was dark and choppy, flecked with white foam as the wind pushed against it. A dreadnaught was afloat the unruly sea, its huge white tentacles extended all around it, giving it the look of some vast swollen flower bobbing on the waves. It reached up as they passed overhead, two arms with their writhing snakes lifting feebly from the water, but they were too far above to be in danger. They appeared to be in the gondola of some long silver airship, looking down through a glass-bottomed viewport, and as Tuf watched, the vantage point shifted and he saw that they were part of a convoy of three immense airships, cruising with stately indifference above the war-torn waters.

"The *Spirit of Aquarius,* the *Lyle D.,* and the *Skyshadow,*" said Kefira Qay, "on a relief mission to a small island grouping in the north where famine had been raging. They were going to evacuate the survivors and take them back to New Atlantis." Her voice was grim. "This record was made by a news crew on the *Skyshadow,* the only airship to survive. Watch."

On and on the airships sailed, invincible and serene. Then, just ahead of the silver-blue *Spirit of Aquarius,* there was motion in the water, something stirring beneath that dark green veil. Something big, but not a dreadnaught. It was dark, not pale. The water grew black and blacker in a great swelling patch, then bulged upward. A great ebony dome heaved into view and grew, like an island emerging from the depths, black and leathery and immense, and surrounded by twenty long black tentacles. Larger and higher it swelled, second by second, until it burst from the sea entirely. Its tentacles hung below it, dripping water, as it rose. Then they began to lift and spread. The thing was fully as large as the airship moving toward it. When they met, it was as if two vast leviathans of the sky had come together to mate. The black immensity settled atop the long silver-blue dirigible, its arms curling about in a deadly embrace. They watched the airship's outer skin tear asunder, and the helium cells rip and crumple. The *Spirit of Aquarius* twisted and buckled like a living thing, and shriveled in the black embrace of its lover. When it was over, the dark creature dropped the remains into the sea.

Tuf froze the image, staring with solemn regard at the small figures leaping from the doomed gondola.

"Another one got the *Lyle D.* on the way home," said Kefira Qay. "The *Skyshadow* survived to tell the story, but it never returned from its next mission. More than a hundred airships and twelve skimmers were lost in the first week the fire-balloons emerged."

"Fire-balloons?" queried Haviland Tuf. He stroked Doubt, who was sitting on his console. "I saw no fire."

"The name was coined the first time we destroyed one of the accursed things. A Guardian skimmer put a round of explosive shot into it, and it went up like a bomb, then sank, burning into the sea. They are extremely inflammable. One laser burst, and they go up spectacularly."

"Hydrogen," said Haviland Tuf.

"Exactly," the Guardian confirmed. "We've never taken one whole, but we've puzzled them out from bits and pieces. The creatures can generate an electric current internally. They take on water, and perform a sort of biological electrolysis. The oxygen is vented into the water or the air, and helps push the things around. Air jets, so to speak. The hydrogen fills the balloon sacs and gives them lift. When they want to retreat to the water, they open a flap on top—see, up there—and all the gas escapes, so the fire-balloon drops back into the sea. The outer skin is leathery, very tough. They're slow, but clever. At times they hide in cloud banks and snatch unwary skimmers flying below. And we soon discovered, to our dismay, that they breed just as fast as the dreadnaughts."

"Most intriguing," said Haviland Tuf. "So, I might venture to suggest, with the emergence of these fire-balloons, you lost the sky as well as the sea."

"More or less," admitted Kefira Qay. "Our airships were simply too slow to risk. We tried to keep things going by sending them out in convoys, escorted by Guardian skimmers and aircars, but even that failed. The morning of the Fire Dawn...I was there, commanding a nine-gun skimmer...it was terrible..."

"Continue," said Tuf.

"The Fire Dawn," she muttered bleakly. "We were...we had thirty airships, *thirty,* a great convoy, protected by a dozen armed skimmers. A long trip, from New Atlantis to the Broken Hand, a major island grouping. Near dawn on the second day, just as the east was turning red, the sea beneath us began to...seethe. Like a pot of soup that has begun to boil. It was *them,* venting oxygen and water, rising. Thousands of them, Tuf, thousands. The waters churned madly, and they rose, all those vast black shadows coming up at us, as far as the eye could see in all directions. We attacked with lasers, with explosive shells, with everything we had. It was like the sky itself was ablaze. All those things were bulging with hydrogen, and the air was rich and giddy with the oxygen they had vented. The Fire Dawn, we call it. It was terrible. Screaming everywhere, balloons burning, our airships crushed and falling around us, bodies afire. There were dreadnaughts waiting below, too. I saw them snatching swimmers who had fallen from the airships, those pale tentacles coiling around them and yanking them under. Four skimmers escaped from that battle. Four. Every airship was lost, with all hands."

"A grim tale," said Tuf.

Kefira Qay had a haunted look in her eyes. She was petting Foolishness with a blind rhythm, her lips pressed tightly together, her eyes fixed on the screen, where the first fire-balloon floated above the tumbling corpse of the *Spirit of Aquarius.* "Since then," she said at last, "life has been a continuing nightmare. We have lost our seas. On three-fourths of Namor, hunger and even starvation hold sway. Only New Atlantis still has surplus food, since only there is land-farming practiced extensively. The Guardians have continued to fight. The *Sunrazor* and our two other spacecraft have been pressed into service—bombing runs, dumping poison, evacuating some of the smaller islands. With air-cars and fast skimmers, we have maintained a loose web of contact with the outer islands. And we have radio, of course. But we are barely hanging on. Within the last year, more than twenty islands have fallen silent. We sent patrols out to investigate in a half-dozen of those cases. Those that returned all reported the same things. Bodies everywhere, rotting in the sun. Buildings crushed and ruined. Scrabblers and crawling maggies feasting on the corpses. And on one island they found something else, something even more frightful. The island was Seastar. Almost forty thousand people lived there, and it was a major spaceport as well, before trade was cut off. It was a terrible shock when Seastar suddenly stopped broadcasting. Go to the next exhibit, Tuf. Go on."

Tuf pressed a series of lights on the console.

A dead thing was lying on a beach, rotting on indigo sands.

It was a still picture, this one, not a tape. Haviland Tuf and Guardian Kefira Qay had a long time to study the dead thing where it sprawled, rich and rotten. Around and about it was a litter of human corpses, lending it scale by their proximity. The dead thing was shaped like an inverted bowl, and it was as big as a house. Its leathery flesh, cracked and oozing pustulence now, was a mottled gray-green. Spread on the sand around it, like spokes from a central wheel, were the thing's appendages—ten twisted green tentacles, puckered with pinkish-white mouths and, alternately, ten limbs that looked stiff and hard and black, and were obviously jointed.

"*Legs,*" said Kefira Qay bitterly. "It was a walker, Tuf, before they killed it. We have only found that one specimen, but it was enough. We know why our islands fall silent now. They come from out of the sea, Tuf. Things like that. Larger, smaller, walking on ten legs like spiders and grabbing and eating with the other ten, the tentacles. The carapace is thick and tough. A single explosive shell or laser burst won't kill one of these the way it would a fire-balloon. So now you understand. First the sea, then the air, and now it has begun on the land as well. The *land.* They burst from the water in thousands, striding up onto the sand like some terrible tide. Two islands were overrun last week alone. They mean to wipe us from this planet. No doubt a few of us will survive on New Atlantis, in the high inland mountains, but it will be a cruel life and a short one. Until Namor throws something new at us, some new thing out of a nightmare." Her voice had a wild edge of hysteria.

Haviland Tuf turned off his console, and the telescreens all went black. "Calm yourself, Guardian," he said, turning to face her. "Your fears are understandable but unnecessary. I appreciate your plight more fully now. A tragic one indeed, yet not hopeless."

"You still think you can help?" she said. "Alone? You and this ship? Oh, I'm not discouraging you, by any means. We'll grasp at any straw. But..."

"But you do not believe," Tuf said. A small sigh escaped his lips. "Doubt," he said to the gray kitten, hoisting him up in a huge white hand, "you are indeed well named." He shifted his gaze back to Kefira Qay. "I am a forgiving man, and you have been through many cruel hardships, so I shall take no notice of the casual way you belittle me and my abilities. Now, if you might excuse me, I have work to do. Your people have sent up a great many more detailed reports on these creatures, and on Namorian ecology in general. It is vital that I peruse these, in order to understand and analyze the situation. Thank you for your briefing."

Kefira Qay frowned, lifted Foolishness from her knee and set him on the ground, and stood up. "Very well," she said. "How soon will you be ready?"

"I cannot ascertain that with any degree of accuracy," Tuf replied, "until I have had a chance to run some simulations. Perhaps a day and we shall begin. Perhaps a month. Perhaps longer."

"If you take too long, you'll find it difficult to collect your two million," she snapped. "We'll all be dead."

"Indeed," said Tuf. "I shall strive to avoid that scenario. Now, if you would let me work. We shall converse again at dinner. I shall serve vegetable stew in the fashion of Arion, with plates of Thorite fire mushrooms to whet our appetites."

Qay sighed loudly. "Mushrooms again?" she complained. "We had stir-fried mushrooms and peppers for lunch, and crisped mushrooms in bitter cream for breakfast."

"I am fond of mushrooms," said Haviland Tuf.

"I am weary of mushrooms," said Kefira Qay. Foolishness rubbed up against her leg, and she frowned down at him. "Might I suggest some meat? Or seafood?" She looked wistful. "It has been years since I've had a mud-pot. I dream of it sometimes. Crack it open and pour butter inside, and spoon out the soft meat... you can't imagine how fine it was. Or sabrefin. Ah, I'd kill for a sabrefin on a bed of seagrass!"

Haviland Tuf looked stern. "We do not eat animals here," he said. He set to work, ignoring her, and Kefira Qay took her leave. Foolishness went bounding after her. "Appropriate," muttered Tuf, "indeed."

FOUR DAYS AND MANY MUSHROOMS LATER, KEFIRA QAY BEGAN TO pressure Haviland Tuf for results. "What are you *doing*?" she demanded over dinner. "When are you going to act? Every day you seclude yourself and every day conditions on Namor worsen. I spoke to Lord Guardian Harvan an hour ago, while you were off with your computers. Little Aquarius and the Dancing Sisters have been lost while you and I are up here dithering, Tuf."

"Dithering?" said Haviland Tuf. "Guardian, I do not dither. I have never dithered, nor do I intend to begin dithering now. I work. There is a great mass of information to digest."

Kefira Qay snorted. "A great mass of mushrooms to digest, you mean," she said. She stood up, tipping Foolishness from her lap. The kitten and she had become boon companions of late. "Twelve thousand people lived on Little Aquarius," she said, "and almost as many on the Dancing Sisters. Think of that while you're digesting, Tuf." She spun and stalked out of the room.

"Indeed," said Haviland Tuf. He returned his attention to his sweet-flower pie.

A week passed before they clashed again. "Well?" the Guardian demanded one day in the corridor, stepping in front of Tuf as he lumbered with great dignity down to his work room.

"Well," he repeated. "Good day, Guardian Qay."

"It is not a good day," she said querulously. "Namor Control tells me the Sunrise Islands are gone. Overrun. And a dozen skimmers lost defending them, along with all the ships drawn up in those harbors. What do you say to that?"

"Most tragic," replied Tuf. "Regrettable."

"When are you going to be ready?"

He gave a great shrug. "I cannot say. This is no simple task you have set me. A most complex problem. Complex. Yes, indeed, that is the very word. Perhaps I might even say mystifying. I assure you that Namor's sad plight has fully engaged my sympathies, however, and this problem has similarly engaged my intellect."

"That's all it is to you, Tuf, isn't it? A problem?"

Haviland Tuf frowned slightly, and folded his hands before him, resting them atop his bulging stomach. "A problem indeed," he said.

"No. It is not just a problem. This is no game we are playing. Real people are dying down there. Dying because the Guardians are not equal to their trust, and because you do nothing. *Nothing.*"

"Calm yourself. You have my assurance that I am laboring ceaselessly on your behalf. You must consider that my task is not so simple as yours. It is all very well and good to drop bombs on a dreadnaught, or fire shells into a fire-balloon and watch it burn. Yet these simple, quaint methods have availed you little, Guardian. Ecological engineering is a far more demanding business. I study the reports of your leaders, your marine biologists, your historians. I reflect and analyze. I devise various approaches, and run simulations on the *Ark's* great computers. Sooner or later I shall find your answer."

"Sooner," said Kefira Qay, in a hard voice. "Namor wants results, and I agree. The Council of Guardians is impatient. Sooner, Tuf. Not later. I warn you." She stepped aside, and let him pass.

Kefira Qay spent the next week and a half avoiding Tuf as much as possible. She skipped dinner and scowled when she saw him in the corridors. Each day she repaired to the communications room, where she had long discussions with her superiors below, and kept up on all the latest news. It was bad. All the news was bad.

Finally, things came to a head. Pale-faced and furious, she stalked into the darkened chamber Tuf called his "war room," where she found him sitting before a bank of computer screens, watching red and blue lines chase each other across a grid. *"Tuf!"* she roared. He turned off the screen and swung to face her, batting away Ingratitude. Shrouded by shadows, he regarded her impassively. "The Council of Guardians has given me an order," she said.

"How fortunate for you," Tuf replied. "I know you have been growing restless of late from inactivity."

"The Council wants immediate action, Tuf. *Immediate.* Today. Do you understand?"

Tuf steepled his hands beneath his chin, almost in an attitude of prayer. "Must I tolerate not only hostility and impatience, but slurs on my intelligence as well? I understand all that needs understanding about your Guardians, I assure you. It is only the peculiar and perverse ecology of Namor that I do not understand. Until I have acquired that understanding, I cannot act."

"You *will* act," said Kefira Qay. Suddenly a laser pistol was in her hand, aimed at Tuf's broad paunch. "You will act now."

Haviland Tuf reacted not at all. "Violence," he said, in a voice of mild reproach. "Perhaps, before you burn a hole in me and thereby doom yourself and your world, you might give me the opportunity to explain?"

"Go on," she said. "I'll listen. For a little while."

"Excellent," said Haviland Tuf. "Guardian, something very odd is happening on Namor."

"You've noticed," she said drily. The laser did not move.

"Indeed. You are being destroyed by an infestation of creatures that we must, for want of a better term, collectively dub sea monsters. Three species have appeared, in less than half a dozen standard years. Each of these species is apparently new, or at least unknown. This strikes me as unlikely in the extreme. Your people have been on Namor for one hundred years, yet not until recently have you had any knowledge of these things you call dreadnaughts, fire-balloons, and walkers. It is almost as if some dark analogue of my *Ark* were waging biowar upon you, yet obviously that is not the case. New or old, these sea monsters are native to Namor, a product of local evolution. Their close relatives fill your seas—the mud-pots, the bobbing freddies, the jellydancers and men-of-war. So. Where does that leave us?"

"I don't know," said Kefira Qay.

"Nor do I," Tuf said. "Consider further. These sea monsters breed in vast numbers. The sea teems with them, they fill the air, they over-run populous islands. They kill. Yet they do not kill each other, nor do they seem to have any other natural enemies. The cruel checks of a nor-mal ecosystem do not apply. I have studied the reports of your scientists with great interest. Much about these sea monsters is fascinating, but perhaps most intriguing is the fact that you know nothing about them except in their full adult form. Vast dreadnaughts prowl the seas and sink ships, monstrous fire-balloons swirl across your skies. Where, might I ask, are the little dreadnaughts, the baby balloons? Where indeed."

"Deep under the sea."

"Perhaps, Guardian, perhaps. You cannot say for certain, nor can I. These monsters are most formidable creatures, yet I have seen equally formidable predators on other worlds. They do not number in hun-dreds or thousands. Why? Ah, because the young, or the eggs, or the hatchlings, they are less formidable than the parents, and most die long before reaching their terrible maturity. This does not appear to happen on Namor. It does not appear to happen at all. What can it all mean? What indeed." Tuf shrugged. "I cannot say, but I work on, I think, I endeavor to solve the riddle of your overabundant sea."

Kefira Qay grimaced. "And meanwhile, we die. We die, and you don't care."

"I protest!" Tuf began.

"Silence!" she said, waving the laser. "I'll talk now, you've given your speech. Today we lost contact with the Broken Hand. Forty-three islands, Tuf. I'm afraid to even think how many people. All gone now, in a single day. A few garbled radio transmissions, hysteria, and silence. And you sit and talk about riddles. No more. You *will* take action now. I insist. Or threaten, if you prefer. Later, we will solve the whys and hows of these things. For the moment, we will kill them, without pausing for questions."

"Once," said Haviland Tuf, "there was a world idyllic but for a single flaw—an insect the size of a dust mote. It was a harmless creature, but it was everywhere: It fed on the microscopic spores of a floating fungus. The folk of this world hated the tiny insect, which sometimes flew about in clouds so thick they obscured the sun. When citizens went outdoors, the insects would land on them by the thousands, covering their bodies with a living shroud. So a would-be ecological engineer proposed to solve their problem. From a distant world, he introduced another insect, larger, to prey on the living dust motes. The scheme worked admirably. The new insects multiplied and multiplied, having no natural enemies in this ecosystem, until they had entirely wiped out the native species. It was a great triumph. Unfortunately, there were unforeseen side effects. The invader, having destroyed one form of life, moved on to other, more beneficial sorts. Many native insects became extinct. The local analogue of bird life, deprived of its customary prey and unable to digest the alien bug, also suffered grievously. Plants were not pollinated as before. Whole forests and jungles changed and withered. And the spores of the fungus that had been the food of the original nuisance were left unchecked. The fungus grew everywhere—on buildings, on food crops, even on living animals. In short, the ecosystem was wrenched entirely askew. Today, should you visit, you would find a planet dead but for a terrible fungus. Such are the fruits of hasty action, with insufficient study. There are grave risks should one move without understanding."

"And certain destruction if one fails to move at all," Kefira Qay said stubbornly. "No, Tuf. You tell frightening tales, but we are a desperate people. The Guardians accept whatever risks there may be. I have my orders. Unless you do as I bid, I will use this." She nodded at her laser.

Haviland Tuf folded his arms. "If you use that," he said, "you will be very foolish. No doubt you could learn to operate the *Ark*. In time. The task would take years, which by your own admission you do not have. I shall work on in your behalf, and forgive you your crude bluster and your threats, but I shall move only when I deem myself ready. I am an ecological engineer. I have my personal and professional integrity. And I must point out that, without my services, you are utterly without hope. Utterly. So, since you know this and I know this, let us dispense with further drama. You will not use that laser."

For a moment, Kefira Qay's face looked stricken. "You . . ." she said in confusion; the laser wavered just a bit. Then her look hardened once again. "You're wrong, Tuf," she said. "I *will* use it."

Haviland Tuf said nothing.

"Not on you," she said. "On your cats. I will kill one of them every day, until you take action." Her wrist moved slightly, so the laser was trained not on Tuf, but on the small form of Ingratitude, who was prowling hither and yon about the room, poking at shadows. "I will start with this one," the Guardian said. "On the count of three."

Tuf's face was utterly without emotion. He stared.

"One," said Kefira Qay.

Tuf sat immobile.

"Two," she said.

Tuf frowned, and there were wrinkles in his chalk-white brow.

"Three," Qay blurted.

"No," Tuf said quickly. "Do not fire. I shall do as you insist. I can begin cloning within the hour."

The Guardian holstered her laser.

So HAVILAND TUF WENT RELUCTANTLY TO WAR.

On the first day he sat in his war room before his great console, tight-lipped and quiet, turning dials and pressing glowing buttons and phantom holographic keys. Elsewhere on the *Ark,* murky liquids of many shades and colors spilled and gurgled into the empty vats along the shadowy main shaft, while specimens from the great cell library were shifted and sprayed and manipulated by tiny waldoes as sensitive as the hands of a master surgeon. Tuf saw none of it. He remained at his post, starting one clone after another.

On the second day he did the same.

On the third day he rose and strolled slowly down the kilometers-long shaft where his creations had begun to grow, indistinct forms that stirred feebly or not at all in the tanks of translucent liquid. Some tanks were fully as large as the *Ark*'s shuttle deck, others as small as a fingernail. Haviland Tuf paused by each one, studied the dials and meters and glowing spyscopes with quiet intensity, and sometimes made small adjustments. By the end of the day he had progressed only half the length of the long, echoing row.

On the fourth day he completed his rounds.

On the fifth day he threw in the chronowarp. "Time is its slave," he told Kefira Qay when she asked him. "It can hold it slow, or bid it hurry. We shall make it run, so the warriors I breed can reach maturity more quickly than in nature."

On the sixth day he busied himself on the shuttle deck, modifying two of his shuttles to carry the creatures he was fashioning, adding tanks great and small and filling them with water.

On the morning of the seventh day he joined Kefira Qay for breakfast and said, "Guardian, we are ready to begin."

She was surprised. "So soon?"

"Not all of my beasts have reached full maturity, but that is as it should be. Some are monstrous large, and must be transshipped before they have attained adult growth. The cloning shall continue, of course. We must establish our creatures in sufficient numbers so they will remain viable. Nonetheless, we are now at the stage where it is possible to begin seeding the seas of Namor."

"What is your strategy?" asked Kefira Qay.

Haviland Tuf pushed aside his plate and pursed his lips. "Such strategy as I have is crude and premature, Guardian, and based on insufficient knowledge. I take no responsibility for its success or failure. Your cruel threats have impelled me to unseemly haste."

"Nonetheless," she snapped. "What are you doing?"

Tuf folded his hands atop his stomach. "Biological weaponry, like other sorts of armament, comes in many forms and sizes. The best way to slay a human enemy is a single laser burst planted square in the center of the forehead. In biological terms, the analogue might be a suitable natural enemy or predator, or a species-specific pestilence. Lacking time, I have had no opportunity to devise such an economical solution.

"Other approaches are less satisfactory. I might introduce a disease that would cleanse your world of dreadnaughts, fire-balloons, and walkers, for example. Several likely candidates exist. Yet your sea monsters are close relatives of many other kinds of marine life, and those cousins and uncles would also suffer. My projections indicate that fully three-quarters of Namor's oceangoing life would be vulnerable to such an attack. Alternatively, I have at my disposal fast-breeding fungi and microscopic animals who would literally fill your seas and crowd out all other life. That choice too is unsatisfactory. Ultimately it would make Namor incapable of sustaining human life. To pursue my analogy of a moment ago, these methods are the biological equivalent of killing a single human enemy by exploding a low-yield thermonuclear device in the city in which he happens to reside. So I have ruled them out.

"Instead, I have opted for what might be termed a scattershot strategy, introducing many new species into your Namorian ecology in the hopes that some of them will prove effective natural enemies capable of winnowing the ranks of your sea monsters. Some of my warriors are great deadly beasts, formidable enough to prey even on your terrible dreadnaughts. Others are small and fleet, semi-social pack hunters who breed quickly. Still others are tiny things. I have hope that they will find and feed on your nightmare creatures in their younger, less potent stages, and thereby thin them out. So you see, I pursue many strategies. I toss down the entire deck rather than playing a single card. Given your bitter ultimatum, it is the only way to proceed." Tuf nodded at her. "I trust you will be satisfied, Guardian Qay."

She frowned and said nothing.

"If you are finished with that delightful sweet-mushroom porridge," Tuf said, "we might begin. I would not have you think that I was dragging my feet. You are a trained pilot, of course?"

"Yes," she snapped.

"Excellent!" Tuf exclaimed. "I shall instruct you in the peculiar idiosyncrasies of my shuttle craft, then. By this hour, they are already fully stocked for our first run. We shall make long low runs across your seas, and discharge our cargoes into your troubled waters. I shall fly the *Basilisk* above your northern hemisphere. You shall take the *Manticore* to the south. If this plan is acceptable, let us go over the routes I have planned for us." He rose with great dignity.

FOR THE NEXT TWENTY DAYS, HAVILAND TUF AND KEFIRA QAY crisscrossed the dangerous skies of Namor in a painstaking grid pattern, seeding the seas. The Guardian flew her runs with élan. It felt good to be in action again, and she was filled with hope as well. The dreadnaughts and fire-balloons and walkers would have their own nightmares to contend with now—nightmares from half a hundred scattered worlds.

From Old Poseidon came vampire eels and nessies and floating tangles of web-weed, transparent and razor-sharp and deadly.

From Aquarius Tuf cloned black raveners, the swifter scarlet raveners, poisonous puff-puppies, and fragrant, carnivorous lady's bane.

From Jamison's World the vats summoned sand-dragons and dreerhants and a dozen kinds of brightly colored water snakes, large and small.

From Old Earth itself the cell library provided great white sharks, barracuda, giant squid, and clever semi-sentient orcas.

They seeded Namor with the monstrous gray kraken of Lissador and the smaller blue kraken of Ance, with waterjelly colonies from Noborn, Daronnian spinnerwhips, and bloodlace out of Cathaday, with swimmers as large as the fortress-fish of Dam Tullian, the mockwhale of Gulliver, and the ghrin'da of Hruun-2, or as small as the blisterfins of Avalon, the parasitical caesni from Ananda, and the deadly nest-building, egg-laying Deirdran waterwasps. To hunt the drifting fire-balloons they brought forth countless fliers: lashtail mantas, bright red razorwings, flocks of scorn, semi-aquatic howlers, and a terrible pale blue thing—half plant and half animal and all but weightless—that drifted with the wind and lurked inside clouds like a living, hungry spiderweb. Tuf called it the-weed-that-weeps-and-whispers, and advised Kefira Qay not to fly through clouds.

Plants and animals and things that were both and neither, predators and parasites, creatures dark as night or bright and gorgeous or entirely colorless, things strange and beautiful beyond words or too hideous even for thought, from worlds whose names burned bright in human history and from others seldom heard of. And more, and more. Day after day the *Basilisk* and the *Manticore* flashed above the seas of Namor, too swift and deadly for the fire-balloons that drifted up to attack them, dropping their living weapons with impunity.

After each day's run they would repair to the *Ark,* where Haviland Tuf and one or more of his cats would seek solitude, while Kefira Qay habitually took Foolishness with her to the communications room so she could listen to the reports.

"Guardian Smitt reports the sighting of strange creatures in the Orange Strait. No sign of dreadnaughts."

"A dreadnaught has been seen off Batthern, locked in terrible combat with some huge tentacled thing twice its size. A gray kraken, you say? Very well. We shall have to learn these names, Guardian Qay."

"Mullidor Strand reports that a family of lashtail mantas has taken up residence on the offshore rocks. Guardian Horn says they slice through fire-balloons like living knives—that the balloons flail and deflate and fall helplessly. Wonderful!"

"Today we heard from Indigo Beach, Guardian Qay. A strange story. Three walkers came rushing out of the water, but it was no attack. They were crazed, staggering about as if in great pain, and ropes of some pale scummy substance dangled from every joint and gap. What is it?"

"A dead dreadnaught washed up on New Atlantis today. Another corpse was sighted by the *Sunrazor* on its western patrol, rotting atop the water. Various strange fishes were picking it to pieces."

"*Starsword* swung out to Fire Heights yesterday, and sighted less than a half-dozen fire-balloons. The Council of Guardians is thinking of resuming short airship flights to the Mud-Pot Pearls, on a trial basis. What do you think, Guardian Qay? Would you advise that we risk it, or is it premature?"

Each day the reports flooded in, and each day Kefira Qay smiled more broadly as she made her runs in the *Manticore*. But Haviland Tuf remained silent and impassive.

Thirty-four days into the war, Lord Guardian Lysan told her, "Well, another dead dreadnaught was found today. It must have put up quite a battle. Our scientists have been analyzing the contents of its stomachs, and it appears to have fed exclusively on orcas and blue kraken." Kefira Qay frowned slightly, then shrugged it off.

"A gray kraken washed up on Boreen today," Lord Guardian Moen told her a few days later. "The residents are complaining of the stink. It has gigantic round bite-marks, they report. Obviously a dreadnaught, but even larger than the usual kind." Guardian Qay shifted uncomfortably.

"All the sharks seem to have vanished from the Amber Sea. The biologists can't account for it. What do you think? Ask Tuf about it, will you?" She listened, and felt a faint trickle of alarm.

"Here's a strange one for you two. Something has been sighted moving back and forth across the Coherine Deep. We've had reports from both *Sunrazor* and *Skyknife,* and various confirmations from skimmer patrols. A huge thing, they say, a veritable living island, sweeping up everything in its path. Is that one of yours? If it is, you may have miscalculated. They say it is eating barracuda and blisterfins and larder's needles by the thousands." Kefira Qay scowled.

"Fire-balloons sighted again off Mullidor Strand—hundreds of them. I can hardly give credence to these reports, but they say the lashtail mantas just carom off them now. Do you..."

"Men-of-war again, can you believe it? We thought they were all nearly gone. So many of them, and they are gobbling up Tuf's smaller fish like nobody's business. You have to..."

"Dreadnaughts spraying water to knock howlers from the sky..."

"Something new, Kefira, a *flyer,* or a glider rather, swarms of them launch from the tops of these fire-balloons. They've gotten three skimmers already, and the mantas are no match for them..."

"...all over, I tell you, that thing that hides in the clouds...the balloons just rip them loose, the acid doesn't bother them anymore, they fling them down..."

"...more dead waterwasps, hundreds of them, thousands, where are they all..."

"...walkers again. Castle Dawn has fallen silent, must be overrun. We can't understand it. The island was ringed by bloodlace and waterjelly colonies. It ought to have been safe, unless..."

"...no word from Indigo Beach in a week..."

"...thirty, forty fire-balloons seen just off Cabben. The council fears..."

"...nothing from Lobbadoon..."

"...dead fortress-fish, half as big as the island itself..."

"...dreadnaughts came right into the harbor..."

"...walkers..."

"...Guardian Qay, the *Starsword* is lost, gone down over the Polar Sea. The last transmission was garbled, but we think..."

Kefira Qay pushed herself up, trembling, and turned to rush out of the communications room, where all the screens were babbling news of death, destruction, defeat. Haviland Tuf was standing behind her, his pale white face impassive, Ingratitude sitting calmly on his broad left shoulder.

"What is happening?" the Guardian demanded.

"I should think that would be obvious, Guardian, to any person of normal intelligence. We are losing. Perhaps we have lost already."

Kefira Qay fought to keep from shrieking. "Aren't you going to *do* anything? Fight back? This is all your fault, Tuf. You aren't an ecological engineer—you're a trader who doesn't know what he's doing. That's why this is..."

Haviland Tuf raised up a hand for silence. "Please," he said. "You have already caused me considerable vexation. Insult me no further. I am a gentle man, of kindly and benevolent disposition, but even one such as myself can be provoked to anger. You press close to that point now. Guardian, I take no responsibility for this unfortunate course of events. This hasty biowar we have waged was none of my idea. Your uncivilized ultimatum forced me to unwise action in order to placate you. Fortunately, while you have spent your nights gloating over transient and illusory victories, I have continued with my work. I have mapped out your world on my computers and watched the course of your war shudder and flow across it in all its manifold stages. I've duplicated your biosphere in one of my great tanks and seeded it with samples of Namorian life cloned from dead specimens—a bit of tentacle here, a piece of carapace there. I have observed and analyzed and at last I have come to conclusions. Tentative, to be sure, although this late sequence of events on Namor tends to confirm my hypothesis. So defame me no further, Guardian. After a refreshing night's sleep I shall descend to Namor and attempt to end this war of yours."

Kefira Qay stared at him, hardly daring to believe, her dread turning to hope once again. "You have the answer, then?"

"Indeed. Did I not just say as much?"

"What is it?" she demanded. "Some new creatures? That's it—you've cloned something else, haven't you? Some plague? Some monster?"

Haviland Tuf held up his hand. "Patience. First I must be certain. You have mocked me and derided me with such unflagging vigor that I hesitate to open myself to further ridicule by confiding my plans to you. I shall prove them valid first. Now, let us discuss tomorrow. You shall fly no war run with the *Manticore*. Instead, I would have you take it to New Atlantis and convene a full meeting of the Council of Guardians. Fetch those who require fetching from outlying islands, please."

"And you?" Kefira Qay asked.

"I shall meet with the council when it is time. Prior to that, I shall take my plans and my creature to Namor on a mission of our own. We shall descend in the *Phoenix,* I believe. Yes. I do think the *Phoenix* most appropriate, to commemorate your world rising from its ashes. Markedly wet ashes, but ashes nonetheless."

Kefira Qay met Haviland Tuf on the shuttle deck just prior to their scheduled departure. *Manticore* and *Phoenix* stood ready in their launch berths amidst the scatter of derelict spacecraft. Haviland Tuf was punching numbers into a mini-computer strapped to the inside of his wrist. He wore a long gray vinyl greatcoat with copious pockets and flaring shoulderboards. A green and brown duck-billed cap decorated with the golden theta of the Ecological Engineers perched rakishly atop his bald head.

"I have notified Namor Control and Guardian Headquarters," Qay said. "The council is assembling. I will provide transportation for a half-dozen Lords Guardian from outlying districts, so all of them will be on hand. How about you, Tuf? Are you ready? Is your mystery creature on board?"

"Soon," said Haviland Tuf, blinking at her.

But Kefira Qay was not looking at his face. Her gaze had gone lower. "Tuf," she said, "there is something in your pocket. Moving." Incredulous, she watched the ripple creep along beneath the vinyl.

"Ah," said Tuf. "Indeed." And then the head emerged from his pocket, and peered around curiously. It belonged to a kitten, a tiny jet-black kitten with lambent yellow eyes.

"A cat," muttered Kefira Qay sourly.

"Your perception is uncanny," said Haviland Tuf. He lifted the kitten out gently, and held it cupped in one great white hand while scratching behind its ear with a finger from the other. "This is Dax," he said solemnly. Dax was scarcely half the size of the older kittens who frisked about the *Ark*. He looked like nothing but a ball of black fur, curiously limp and indolent.

"Wonderful," the Guardian replied. "Dax, eh? Where did this one come from? No, don't answer that. I can guess. Tuf, don't we have more important things to do than play with cats?"

"I think not," said Haviland Tuf. "You do not appreciate cats sufficiently, Guardian. They are the most civilized of creatures. No world can be considered truly cultured without cats. Are you aware that all cats, from time immemorial, have had a touch of psi? Do you know that some ancient societies of Old Earth worshipped cats as gods? It is true."

"Please," said Kefira Qay irritably. "We don't have time for a discourse on cats. Are you going to bring that poor little thing down to Namor with you?"

Tuf blinked. "Indeed. This poor little thing, as you so contemptuously call him, is the salvation of Namor. Respect might be in order."

She stared at him as if he had gone mad. "What? That? Him? I mean, Dax? Are you serious? What are you talking about? You're joking, aren't you? This is some kind of insane jest. You've got some thing loaded aboard the *Phoenix,* some huge leviathan that will cleanse the sea of those dreadnaughts—something, anything, I don't know. But you can't mean . . . you can't . . . not that."

"Him," said Haviland Tuf. "Guardian, it is so wearisome to have to state the obvious, not once but again and again. I have given you raveners and krakens and lashtail mantas, at your insistence. They have not been efficacious. Accordingly, I have done much hard thinking, and I have cloned Dax."

"A kitten," she said. "You're going to use a *kitten* against the dreadnaughts and the fire-balloons and the walkers. One. Small. *Kitten.*"

"Indeed," said Haviland Tuf. He frowned down at her, slid Dax back into the roomy confines of his great pocket, and turned smartly toward the waiting *Phoenix*.

KEFIRA QAY WAS GROWING VERY NERVOUS. IN THE COUNCIL CHAMbers high atop Breakwater Tower on New Atlantis, the twenty-five Lords Guardian who commanded the defense of all Namor were restive. All of them had been waiting for hours. Some had been there all day. The long conference table was littered with personal communicators and computer printouts and empty water glasses. Two meals had already been served and cleared away. By the wide curving window that dominated the far wall, portly Lord Guardian Alis was talking in low urgent tones to Lord Guardian Lysan, thin and stern, and both of them were giving meaningful glances to Kefira Qay from time to time. Behind them the sun was going down, and the great bay was turning a lovely shade of scarlet. It was such a beautiful scene that one scarcely noticed the small bright dots that were Guardian skimmers, flying patrol.

Dusk was almost upon them, the council members were grumbling and stirring impatiently in their big cushioned chairs, and Haviland Tuf had still failed to make an appearance. "When did he say he would be here?" asked Lord Guardian Khem, for the fifth time.

"He wasn't very precise, Lord Guardian," Kefira Qay replied uneasily, for the fifth time.

Khem frowned and cleared his throat.

Then one of the communicators began to beep, and Lord Guardian Lysan strode over briskly and snatched it up. "Yes?" he said. "I see. Quite good. Escort him in." He set down the communicator and rapped its edge on the table for order. The others shuffled to their seats, or broke off their conversations, or straightened. The council chamber grew silent. "That was the patrol. Tuf's shuttle has been sighted. He is on his way, I am pleased to report." Lysan glanced at Kefira Qay. "At last."

The Guardian felt even more uneasy then. It was bad enough that Tuf had kept them waiting, but she was dreading the moment when he came lumbering in, Dax peering out of his pocket. Qay had been unable to find the words to tell her superiors that Tuf proposed to save

Namor with a small black kitten. She fidgeted in her seat and plucked at her large, crooked nose. This was going to be bad, she feared.

It was worse than anything she could have dreamed.

All of the Lords Guardian were waiting, stiff and silent and attentive, when the doors opened and Haviland Tuf walked in, escorted by four armed guards in golden coveralls. He was a mess. His boots made a squishing sound as he walked, and his greatcoat was smeared with mud. Dax was visible in his left pocket all right, paws hooked over its edge and large eyes intent. But the Lords Guardian weren't looking at the kitten. Beneath his other arm, Haviland Tuf was carrying a muddy rock the size of a big man's head. A thick coating of green-brown slime covered it, and it was dripping water onto the plush carpet.

Without so much as a word, Tuf went directly to the conference table and set the rock down in the center of it. That was when Kefira Qay saw the fringe of tentacles, pale and fine as threads, and realized that it wasn't a rock after all. "A mud-pot," she said aloud in surprise. No wonder she hadn't recognized it. She had seen many a mud-pot in her time, but not until after they had been washed and boiled and the tendrils trimmed away. Normally they were served with a hammer and chisel to crack the bony carapace, and a dish of melted butter and spices on the side.

The Lords Guardian looked on in astonishment, and then all twenty-five began talking at once, and the council chamber became a blur of overlapping voices.

"...it *is* a mud-pot, I don't understand..."

"What is the meaning of this?"

"He makes us wait all day and then comes to council as filthy as a mudgrubber. The dignity of the council is..."

"...haven't eaten a mud-pot in, oh, two, three..."

"...can't be the man who is supposed to save..."

"...insane, why, just look at..."

"...what is that thing in his pocket? Look at it! My God, it *moved*! It's alive, I tell you, I saw it..."

"*Silence!*" Lysan's voice was like a knife cutting through the hubbub. The room quieted as, one by one, the Lords Guardian turned toward him. "We have come together at your beck and call," Lysan said acidly to Tuf. "We expected you to bring us an answer. Instead you appear to have brought us dinner."

Someone snickered.

Haviland Tuf frowned down at his muddy hands, and wiped them primly on his greatcoat. Taking Dax from his pocket, Tuf deposited the lethargic black kitten on the table. Dax yawned and stretched, and ambled toward the nearest of the Lords Guardian, who stared in horror and hurriedly inched her chair back a bit. Shrugging out of his wet, muddy greatcoat, Tuf looked about for a place to put it, and finally hung it from the laser rifle of one of his escorts. Only then did he turn back to the Lords Guardian. "Esteemed Lords Guardian," he said, "this is not dinner you see before you. In that very attitude lies the root of all your problems. This is the ambassador of the race that shares Namor with you, whose name, regrettably, is far beyond my small capabilities. His people will take it quite badly if you eat him."

EVENTUALLY SOMEONE BROUGHT LYSAN A GAVEL, AND HE RAPPED it long and loud enough to attract everyone's attention, and the furor slowly ebbed away. Haviland Tuf had stood impassively through all of it, his face without expression, his arms folded against his chest. Only when silence was restored did he say, "Perhaps I should explain."

"You are mad," Lord Guardian Harvan said, looking from Tuf to the mud-pot and back again. "Utterly mad."

Haviland Tuf scooped up Dax from the table, cradled him in one arm, and began to pet him. "Even in our moment of victory, we are mocked and insulted," he said to the kitten.

"Tuf," said Lysan from the head of the long table, "what you suggest is impossible. We have explored Namor quite sufficiently in the century we have been here so as to be certain that no sentient races dwell upon it. There are no cities, no roads, no signs of any prior civilization or technology, no ruins or artifacts—*nothing*, neither above nor below the sea."

"Moreover," said another councillor, a beefy woman with a red face, "the mud-pots cannot possibly be sentient. Agreed, they have brains the size of a human brain. But that is about all they have. They have no eyes, ears, noses, almost no sensory equipment whatever except for touch. They have only those feeble tendrils as manipulative organs, scarcely strong enough to lift a pebble. And in fact, the tendrils are only used to anchor them to their spot on the seabed. They are hermaphroditic and downright primitive, mobile only in the first month of life, before the shell hardens and grows heavy. Once they root on the bottom and cover themselves with mud, they never move again. They stay there for hundreds of years."

"Thousands," said Haviland Tuf. "They are remarkably long-lived creatures. All that you say is undoubtedly correct. Nonetheless, your conclusions are in error. You have allowed yourself to be blinded by belligerence and fear. If you had removed yourself from the situation and paused long enough to think about it in depth, as I did, no doubt it would become obvious even to the military mind that your plight was no natural catastrophe. Only the machinations of some enemy intelligence could sufficiently explain the tragic course of events on Namor."

"You don't expect us to believe—" someone began.

"Sir," said Haviland Tuf, "I expect you to listen. If you will refrain from interrupting me, I will explain all. Then you may choose to believe or not, as suits your peculiar fancy. I shall take my fee and depart." Tuf looked at Dax. "Idiots, Dax. Everywhere we are beset by idiots." Turning his attention back to the Lords Guardian, he continued, "As I have stated, intelligence was clearly at work here. The difficulty was in finding that intelligence. I perused the work of your Namorian biologists, living and dead, read much about your flora and fauna, re-created many of the native lifeforms aboard the *Ark*. No likely candidate for sentience was immediately forthcoming. The traditional hallmarks of intelligent life include a large brain, sophisticated biological sensors, mobility, and some sort of manipulative organ, such as an opposable thumb. Nowhere on Namor could I find a creature with all of these attributes. My hypothesis, however, was still correct. Therefore I must needs move on to unlikely candidates, as there were no likely ones.

"To this end I studied the history of your plight, and at once some things suggested themselves. You believed that your sea monsters emerged from the dark oceanic depths, but where did they first appear? In the offshore shallows—the areas where you practiced fishing and sea-farming. What did all these areas have in common? Certainly an abundance of life, that must be admitted. Yet not the same life. The fish that habituated the waters off New Atlantis did not frequent those of the Broken Hand. Yet I found two interesting exceptions, two species found virtually everywhere—the mud-pots, lying immobile in their great soft beds through the long slow centuries and, originally, the things you called Namorian men-of-war. The ancient native race has another term for those. They call them guardians.

"Once I had come this far, it was only a matter of working out the details and confirming my suspicions. I might have arrived at my conclusion much earlier, but for the rude interruptions of liaison officer Qay, who continually shattered my concentration and finally, most cruelly, forced me to waste much time sending forth gray krakens and razorwings and sundry other such creatures. In the future I shall spare myself such liaisons.

"Yet, in a way, the experiment was useful, since it confirmed my theory as to the true situation on Namor. Accordingly I pressed on. Geographic studies showed that all of the monsters were thickest near mud-pot beds. The heaviest fighting had been in those selfsame areas, my Lords Guardian. Clearly, these mud-pots you find so eminently edible were your mysterious foes. Yet how could that be? These creatures had large brains, to be sure, but lacked all the other traits we have come to associate with sentience, as we know it. And that was the very heart of it! Clearly they were sentient as we do not know it. What sort of intelligent being could live deep under the sea, immobile, blind, deaf, bereft of all input? I pondered that question. The answer, sirs, is obvious. Such an intelligence must interact with the world in ways we cannot, must have its own modes of sensing and communicating. Such an intelligence must be telepathic. Indeed. The more I considered it, the more obvious it became.

"Thereupon it was only a matter of testing my conclusions. To that end, I brought forth Dax. All cats have some small psionic ability, Lords Guardian. Yet long centuries ago, in the days of the Great War, the soldiers of the Federal Empire struggled against enemies with terrible psi powers; Hrangan Minds and *githyanki* soulsucks. To combat such formidable foes, the genetic engineers worked with felines, and vastly heightened and sharpened their psionic abilities, so they could esp in unison with mere humans. Dax is such a special animal."

"You mean that thing is reading our minds?" Lysan said sharply.

"Insofar as you have minds to read," said Haviland Tuf, "yes. But more importantly, through Dax, I was able to reach that ancient people you have so ignominiously dubbed mud-pots. For they, you see, are entirely telepathic.

"For millennia beyond counting they have dwelled in tranquility and peace beneath the seas of this world. They are a slow, thoughtful, philosophic race, and they lived side by side in the billions, each linked with all the others, each an individual and each a part of the great racial whole. In a sense they were deathless, for all shared the experiences of each, and the death of one was as nothing. Experiences were few in the unchanging sea, however. For the most part their long lives are given over to abstract thought, to philosophy, to strange green dreams that neither you nor I can truly comprehend. They are silent musicians, one might say. Together they have woven great symphonies of dreams, and those songs go on and on.

"Before humanity came to Namor, they had had no real enemies for millions of years. Yet that had not always been the case. In the primordial beginnings of this wet world, the oceans teemed with creatures who relished the taste of the dreamers as much as you do. Even then, the race understood genetics, understood evolution. With their vast web of interwoven minds, they were able to manipulate the very stuff of life itself, more skillfully than any genetic engineers. And so they evolved their guardians, formidable predators with a biological imperative to protect those you call mud-pots. These were your men-of-war. From that time to this they guarded the beds, while the dreamers went back to their symphony of thought.

"Then you came, from Aquarius and Old Poseidon. Indeed you did. Lost in the reverie, the dreamers hardly noticed for many years, while you farmed and fished and discovered the taste of mud-pots. You must consider the shock you gave them, Lords Guardian. Each time you plunged one of them into boiling water, all of them shared the sensations. To the dreamers, it seemed as though some terrible new predator had evolved upon the landmass, a place of little interest to them. They had no inkling that you might be sentient, since they could no more conceive of a nontelepathic sentience than you could conceive of one blind, deaf, immobile, and edible. To them, things that moved and manipulated and ate flesh were animals, and could be nothing else.

"The rest you know, or can surmise. The dreamers are a slow people lost in their vast songs, and they were slow to respond. First they simply ignored you, in the belief that the ecosystem itself would shortly check your ravages. This did not appear to happen. To them it seemed you had no natural enemies. You bred and expanded constantly, and many thousands of minds fell silent. Finally they returned to the ancient, almost-forgotten ways of their dim past, and woke to protect themselves. They sped up the reproduction of their guardians until the seas above their beds teemed with their protectors, but the creatures that had once sufficed admirably against other enemies proved to be no match for you. Finally they were driven to new measures. Their minds broke off the great symphony and ranged out, and they sensed and understood. At last they began to fashion new guardians, guardians formidable enough to protect them against this great new nemesis. Thus it went. When I arrived upon the *Ark,* and Kefira Qay forced me to unleash many new threats to their peaceful dominion, the dreamers were initially taken aback. But the struggle had sharpened them and they responded more quickly now, and in only a very short time they were dreaming newer guardians still, and sending them forth to battle to oppose the creatures I had loosed upon them. Even as I speak to you in this most imposing tower of yours, many a terrible new lifeform is stirring beneath the waves, and soon will emerge to trouble your sleep in years to come—unless, of course, you come to a peace. That is entirely your decision. I am only a humble ecological engineer. I would not dream of dictating such matters to the likes of you. Yet I do suggest it, in the strongest possible terms. So here is the ambassador plucked from the sea—at great personal discomfort to myself, I might add. The dreamers are now in much turmoil, for when they felt Dax among them and through him touched me, their world increased a millionfold. They learned of the stars today, and learned moreover that they are not alone in this cosmos. I believe they will be reasonable, as they have no use for the land, nor any taste for fish. Here is Dax as well, and myself. Perhaps we might commence to talk?"

But when Haviland Tuf fell silent at last, no one spoke for quite a long time. The Lords Guardian were all ashen and numb. One by one they looked away from Tuf's impassive features, to the muddy shell on the table.

Finally Kefira Qay found her voice. "What do they *want*?" she asked nervously.

"Chiefly," said Haviland Tuf, "they want you to stop eating them. This strikes me as an eminently sensible proposal. What is your reply?"

———

"Two million standards is insufficient," Haviland Tuf said some time later, sitting in the communications room of the *Ark*. Dax rested calmly in his lap, having little of the frenetic energy of the other kittens. Elsewhere in the room Suspicion and Hostility were chasing each other hither and yon.

Up on the telescreen, Kefira Qay's features broke into a suspicious scowl. "What do you mean? This was the price we agreed upon, Tuf. If you are trying to cheat us..."

"Cheat?" Tuf sighed. "Did you hear her, Dax? After all we have done, such grim accusations are still flung at us willy-nilly. Yes. Willy-nilly indeed. An odd phrase, when one stops to mull on it." He looked back at the telescreen. "Guardian Qay, I am fully aware of the agreed-on price. For two million standards, I solved your difficulties. I analyzed and pondered and provided the insight and the translator you so sorely needed. I have even left you with twenty-five telepathic cats, each linked to one of your Lords Guardian, to facilitate further communications after my departure. That too is included within the terms of our initial agreement, since it was necessary to the solution of your problem. And, being at heart more a philanthropist than a businessman, and deeply sentimental as well, I have even allowed you to retain Foolishness, who took a liking to you for some reason that I am entirely unable to fathom. For that, too, there is no charge."

"Then why are you demanding an additional three million standards?" demanded Kefira Qay.

"For unnecessary work which I was cruelly compelled to do," Tuf replied. "Would you care for an itemized accounting?"

"Yes, I would," she said.

"Very well. For sharks. For barracuda. For giant squid. For orcas. For gray kraken. For blue kraken. For bloodlace. For water jellies. Twenty thousand standards per item. For fortress-fish, fifty thousand standards. For the-weed-that-weeps-and-whispers, eight..." He went on for a long, long time.

When he was done, Kefira Qay set her lips sternly. "I will submit your bill to the Council of Guardians," she said. "But I will tell you straight out that your demands are unfair and exorbitant, and our balance of trade is not sufficient to allow for such an outflow of hard standards. You can wait in orbit for a hundred years, Tuf, but you won't get any five million standards."

Haviland Tuf raised his hands in surrender. "Ah," he said. "So, because of my trusting nature, I must take a loss. I will not be paid, then?"

"Two million standards," said the Guardian. "As we agreed."

"I suppose I might accept this cruel and unethical decision, and take it as one of life's hard lessons. Very well then. So be it." He stroked Dax. "It has been said that those who do not learn from history are doomed to repeat it. I can only blame myself for this wretched turn of events. Why, it was only a few scant months past that I chanced to view a historical drama on this very sort of situation. It was about a seedship such as my own that rid one small world of an annoying pest, only to have the ungrateful planetary government refuse payment. Had I been wiser, that would have taught me to demand my payment in advance." He sighed. "But I was not wise, and now I must suffer." Tuf stroked Dax again, and paused. "Perhaps your Council of Guardians might be interested in viewing this particular tape, purely for recreational purposes. It is holographic, fully dramatized, and well-acted, and moreover, it gives a fascinating insight into the workings and capabilities of a ship such as this one. Highly educational. The title is *Seedship of Hamelin*."

———

They paid him, of course.

SEVEN

THE SIREN SONG OF HOLLYWOOD

When I was in seventh grade *The Twilight Zone* was my favorite television show. I never dreamed that one day I'd be writing it.

Now, let us make it clear that we're talking about two different shows here. I must look one hell of a lot older than I think, because sometimes when I mention that I worked on *The Twilight Zone,* I get the response, "Oh, I loved that show. What was it like to work with Rod Sterling?" (The clueless inevitably drop a "t" into Rod Serling's name.)

I loved that show too, but sad to say I never worked with Rod Sterling, or even Rod Serling. I did, however, work with Phil DeGuere, Jim Crocker, Alan Brennert, Rockne S. O'Bannon, and Michael Cassutt, as well as a host of terrific actors and directors, on the short-lived and much-lamented *Twilight Zone* revival of 1985–87. Call it *TZ-2.* (There have been two more incarnations since, *TZ-3* and *TZ-4,* but we prefer not to talk about them in polite company.)

It was *The Armageddon Rag* that sent me off to *The Twilight Zone.* Published by Poseidon Press in 1983, the *Rag* was supposed to be the breakout novel that would transform me into a bestselling author. I was proud of the book, and my agent and my editor were high on it as well. Poseidon paid me a whopping big advance for the rights, and I went right out and bought a larger house.

The *Rag* received some wonderful reviews. It was nominated for the World Fantasy Award, losing out to John M. Ford's superb *The Dragon Waiting.* And it died the death. It had all the hallmarks of a big bestseller save one. No one bought it. Far from building on the success of *Fevre Dream,* it sold badly in hardcover and miserably in paperback. The full extent of the disaster was not brought home to me until 1985, when Kirby tried to sell my unfinished fifth novel, *Black and White and Red All Over,* and found that neither Poseidon nor any other publisher was willing to make an offer.

Yet even as *The Armageddon Rag* slammed one door shut behind me, it was opening another. Dismal though its sales had been, the *Rag* did have its ardent fans. One was Phil DeGuere, the creator and executive producer of the hit television series *Simon & Simon.* DeGuere was a huge fan of rock music, especially the Grateful Dead. When our mutual agent Marvin Moss showed him my book, Phil saw a feature film in it, and optioned the movie rights. He intended to write and direct the film himself, and to shoot the huge concert sequences at Grateful Dead shows.

I'd sold other film options previously. My usual involvement was limited to signing the contract and cashing the check. Phil DeGuere was different. The ink was hardly dry on the deal before he flew me out to L.A. and put me up at a hotel for several days, so we could talk about the book and how best to adapt it. Phil went on to write several drafts of the screenplay, but was never able to get a studio to bite for the financing. No movie was made. During the course of this, however, he and I got to know each other a bit... enough so that, when he decided to revive *The Twilight Zone* for CBS in 1985, Phil phoned to ask me if I would like to try a script.

Surprisingly, I did not immediately leap at the chance. I had been weaned on television, sure, but I'd never written for it, had never *wanted* to write for it, knew nothing about scriptwriting, had never even seen a screenplay or a teleplay. Besides, all you ever heard about writing for Hollywood was the horror stories. I'd read Harlan Ellison's *Glass Teat,* after all. I'd even read *The Other Glass Teat.* I knew how crazy it was out there.

On the other hand, I liked Phil and respected him, and he had Alan Brennert on his staff, another writer whose work I had admired. DeGuere had brought Harlan Ellison aboard as well, as a writer and consultant. Maybe this new *Twilight Zone* would be different. And if truth be told, I needed the money. At the time I was madly writing Haviland Tuf stories to fill out *Tuf Voyaging* and keep my mortgage paid, but *Black and White and Red All Over* still had not sold, and my career as a novelist lay in ruins. I was still hesitating when Phil cinched the deal by promising my lady Parris backstage passes to all the Grateful Dead shows we cared to see. You couldn't say no to *that.*

He mailed me the show's bible and a stack of sample scripts, and I sent him a stack of tearsheets and xerox copies of stories I thought might make good *Twilight Zone* episodes. Since I had never done a teleplay before, I wanted to make things easier for myself by doing an adaptation rather than an original story. That way, I could concentrate on mastering the form, rather than having to come up with the plot and characters and dialogue as well. Adaptations did not pay as well as originals, but I was more concerned with not making an utter fool of myself than I was with making money.

DeGuere liked a number of the stories I sent them, and half a dozen would end up becoming episodes of *TZ-2*, some adapted by me, some by other hands. For my first outing, however, the tale that was chosen was "Nackles," a Christmas horror fable by a writer named Curt Clark. I'd found it in an obscure Terry Carr anthology.

"Nackles" was the sort of idea that makes you slap your head and cry, "Why didn't *I* think of that?" Every god must have his devil. Nackles was the Anti-Santa. On Christmas Eve, while Santa Claus is flying around the world in his sled, sliding down chimneys to leave presents for good boys and girls, Nackles is moving through pitch-dark tunnels beneath the earth in a railroad car pulled by a team of blind white goats, and crawling up through the furnace grate to stuff bad boys and girls in his big black sack.

I was delighted by Phil's choice. "Nackles" seemed to me to be a perfect *Twilight Zone*, given a faithful adaptation. I also took a little pleasure imagining the thrill the sale would give Curt Clark, this obscure, forgotten little writer, who I pictured teaching English composition at some community college in Nowhere, North Dakota or Godforsaken, Georgia.

It turned out that "Curt Clark" was a pseudonym for Donald E. Westlake, the bestselling author of the wonderful Dortmunder series and a hundred other mysteries and crime novels, half of which had been turned into feature films. It also turned out, once rights had been secured and I had signed my contract, that the guys at *Twilight Zone* did not want a faithful adaptation of Westlake's story. They liked the notion of the Anti-Santa, but not the rest of it: the abusive former football star who invents Nackles to terrorize his children, his wife and kids, the brother-in-law who narrates the story. All of that had to go, I was told. Before I could start my script, I would need to come up with a whole new story for Nackles and present it in a treatment.

(So much for adaptations being easier.)

I came up with half a dozen ways to handle "Nackles." The first one or two I wrote up as formal treatments, the later ones I pitched to Harlan over the phone. He didn't like any of them. After a month of this, I hit a wall. I had no more fresh ideas for "Nackles," and remained convinced that the best way to handle the material was the way Westlake handled it in his story. Harlan was growing as frustrated as I was, and I got the impression that Phil DeGuere was ready to pull the plug.

At that point Harlan came up with an idea. Another episode had also been giving trouble, an original called "The Once and Future King," about an Elvis impersonator who travels back in time and finds himself face-to-face with

Elvis. A freelancer named Bryce Maritano had done several drafts of the script, but DeGuere and his team still felt it needed work. I was no stranger to rock 'n' roll, as *The Armageddon Rag* bore witness. Harlan suggested a switch. He would take over "Nackles" himself, and I would move to the Maritano script. Phil thought that was worth a try, and the swap was made . . . with fateful consequences for all concerned.

The subsequent tale of "Nackles" is as horrifying as Nackles himself. Harlan Ellison's approach to the story met with more approval than mine had, and his script was duly written and given the green light. Ed Asner was cast in the lead role, and Harlan himself was set to direct. He had added a new twist to the Westlake story, however, one that drew the ire of the network censors. In the midst of preproduction, "Nackles" was brought to a screeching halt by Standards and Practices. For those who are curious, all the grisly details of what followed can be found in Harlan's collection *Slippage* (Houghton Mifflin, 1998), along with Westlake's original story and Harlan's teleplay. Despite good faith efforts by Phil and Harlan to address the network's concerns, the CBS censors proved unrelenting. "Nackles" was scrapped, and Harlan left the show.

Meanwhile, I was still at home in Santa Fe, a thousand miles away from the storms, reading up about the King. Elvis had shouldered Nackles aside. I wrote my treatment of "The Once and Future King," and when that was approved, I launched into the script. It was the first teleplay I had ever attempted, so it took me longer than it should have. I shot it off to *The Twilight Zone* with considerable trepidation. If Phil did not like what I'd done, I figured, my first teleplay would also be my last.

He did like it. Not well enough to shoot my first draft, mind you (I soon learned that in Hollywood no one ever likes a script *that* much) . . . but well enough to offer me a staff job after "Nackles" blew up and Harlan's departure left the *Zone* shorthanded. Suddenly I was off to a land of both shadow and substance, of things and ideas, somewhere between the pit of man's fears and the summit of his knowledge: Studio City, California.

I joined the series near the end of its first season, as a lowly Staff Writer (you know the position is lowly if the title includes the word "writer"). My first contract was for six weeks, and even that seemed optimistic. After a strong start, the ratings for *TZ-2* had slumped off steadily, and no one knew whether CBS would renew the series for a second season. I began my stint by doing several more drafts of "The Once and Future King," then moved on to new scripts, adaptations of Roger Zelazny's "The Last Defender of Camelot" and Phyllis

Eisenstein's "Lost and Found." Six weeks of talking story with DeGuere, Crocker, Brennert, and O'Bannon, reading scripts, giving and taking notes, sitting in on pitch meetings, and watching the show being filmed taught me more than I could have learned in six years back in Santa Fe. None of my own scripts went before the cameras until the very end, when "The Last Defender of Camelot" was finally sent into production.

Casting, budgets, preproduction meetings, working with a director; all of it was new to me. My script was too long and too expensive. That would prove to be a hallmark of my career in film and television. *All* my scripts would be too long and too expensive. I tried to keep Roger Zelazny informed of all the changes we had to make, so he would not be too taken aback when he saw his story on the air. At one point, our line producer Harvey Frand came to me with a worried look on his face. "You can have horses," he told me, "or you can have Stonehenge. But you can't have horses *and* Stonehenge." That was a hard call, so I put the question to Roger. "Stonehenge," he said at once, and Stonehenge it was.

They built it on the sound stage behind my office, with wood and plaster and painted canvas. If there had been horses on the stage, Stonehenge would have trembled like a leaf every time one pounded by, but without horses, the fake rocks worked fine. Not so the stuntwork, alas. The director wanted to see Sir Lancelot's face during the climactic swordfight, which entailed removing the visor from Richard Kiley's helm...and that of his stunt double as well. All went well until someone zigged instead of zagging during the swordplay, and the stunt man's nose was cut off. "Not the whole nose," Harvey Frand explained to me, "just the end bit."

"The Last Defender of Camelot" was broadcast on April 11, 1986, as part of *TZ-2*'s first season closer. After we wrapped I went home to Santa Fe, not knowing if there would be a second season. For all I knew, my brief stint in television was done.

But when the networks announced their fall schedules in May, it turned out that CBS had renewed *The Twilight Zone* after all. I was promoted from Staff Writer to Story Editor, and headed back to Studio City. Several new writers and producers joined us for that abbreviated second season, most notably Michael Cassutt, who took my place at the bottom of the food chain as the lowly Staff Writer. Cassutt had the office next to mine. Short, cynical, talented, funny, and wise in all the ways of Hollyweird, he showed me how to get a better office (come to work early and move in), and joined me in trying to teach Phil DeGuere's cockatoo to say, "Stupid idea," which we thought would enliven pitch meetings no end.

The second season of *TZ-2* got off to a great start for me. Both of my leftover season one scripts, "Lost and Found" and "The Once and Future King," were put into production; the latter became our second-season opener. As Story Editor, I did more duties, more rewrites, and had a bigger role in pitch meetings. I wrote two new teleplays as well. "The Toys of Caliban" was another adaptation, this time of a story by Terry Matz. "The Road Less Traveled," which you'll find presented here, was my first (and last) original for the *Zone*. The idea was one that I'd come up with a few years earlier for an anthology about the War in Vietnam, but had never gotten around to writing.

On an anthology show like *The Twilight Zone,* the stories are the stars. We had no leads with fat weekly salaries, no recurring characters to service, no continuing storylines. As a result we could sometimes attract feature actors and directors who would never have consented to appear on an ordinary episodic drama. I got very lucky with "The Road Less Traveled." My script was sent to Wes Craven. He liked it, and agreed to direct.

We speak of television programs running an hour (most dramas) or a half-hour (all sitcoms), but of course the shows themselves are nowhere near that long, since commercials eat up a large amount of that time. In the mid '80s, an "hour-long" drama was roughly forty-six minutes long, a "half-hour" sitcom about twenty-three minutes.

Of course, when you shoot a script, it is very rare that you will get exactly as much film as you need. Most rough cuts run long, by anywhere from a few seconds to a few minutes. No problem. The show's editors, working with the director and the producers, simply take the tape into the editing room and trim, until they have forty-six or twenty-three minutes of footage, as required.

Rod Serling's original *Twilight Zone* was a half-hour program for most of its run. It is those episodes that most fans recall. The show actually expanded to a "full hour" for one season, but those hours are seldom seen in syndication, since they will not fit into the same time slots as the rest of the series run. Whether an hour or a half-hour, however, Serling's *Twilight Zone* featured only one story per episode.

TZ-2 was an hour-long show, but it used the format of another Serling series, *The Night Gallery,* rather than that of the original *Zone*. Each hour was made up of two or three unconnected tales of varying length. It was seldom as neat as dividing one forty-six-minute hour into two twenty-three-minute half-hours. One week, the show might have a thirty-minute episode teamed with one that ran sixteen minutes; the next week, a twenty-one-minute segment with a twenty-five; the week after an eighteen, a fifteen, and a thirteen. It did not matter how long the individual segments ran, so long as they added up to forty-six minutes after editing.

"The Road Less Traveled" was too long (and too expensive). But it was felt to be a strong script, and had a very strong director in Wes Craven, who shot some terrific film. When Wes turned in his director's cut, it was longer than all but a few of our previous segments, but it was also a powerful little film. The decision was made to make only minor trims to Wes Craven's cut. If the hour ran long, time could always be taken out of the other segment to get us down to the necessary forty-six minutes.

The show as finally assembled paired a thirty-six minute cut of "The Road Less Traveled" with a ten-minute version of . . . well, to tell the truth, I no longer recall which second-season episode I had drawn as my running mate. The show was edited, color-timed, scored. Effects were added, along with the opening and closing narrations. Around the office, Mike Cassutt and my other friends were congratulating me. There was talk of Emmy Awards for Wes Craven and Cliff DeYoung. The show was delivered to the network, locked and finished and ready for broadcast.

Then CBS took *The Twilight Zone* off the air.

It should not have come as a shock. Our ratings had been weak at the end of the first season, and had only gotten weaker during the second. Even so, the network was not canceling the show. Not quite. Instead they were taking us off the air for "retooling."

Gloom descended on the MTM lot as we sat around our offices waiting for the other shoe to drop. Soon enough it did. We were going back on the air, in a new time slot . . . as a *half-hour* show. The original *Twilight Zone* had enjoyed its greatest success as a half-hour, CBS reasoned; perhaps we could do the same. And by the way, no more of this two or three stories per show stuff. From now on each episode would be a single story, twenty-three minutes in length. As for those episodes already in the can, they would have to be re-edited to fit the new half-hour format.

"The Road Less Traveled" was broadcast on December 18, 1986, but it was not the show that I had been so proud of. A truncated, mutilated remnant aired instead. Thirteen minutes had been excised, more than a third of the episode's original length. The pacing was shot to hell, and much of the character development was gone.

If any of you chanced to catch "The Road Less Traveled" in syndication, it was the butchered version you saw. The original thirty-six-minute cut was never aired, and so far as I know only two copies of it still exist on tape. Wes Craven has one, I understand. I have the other. I would show it to you if I could, but I can't. All I can do is let you read my script.

For what it's worth, I can't really quarrel with the network's decision. *The Twilight Zone* was dying; CBS had to try something. The half-hour format was worth a shot. In hindsight, the series might have been better off if it had been a half-hour show right from the start. So I cannot fault the suits for making the change. I only wish they had waited a week, until *after* "The Road Less Traveled" had been aired.

Sad to say, ratings showed no notable improvement, and CBS finally pulled the plug halfway through the second season. A short time later, a third incarnation of *The Twilight Zone* arose from our ashes, and produced thirty cheap new half-hour shows which were bundled with our episodes to make a syndication package. *TZ-3* inherited our unproduced scripts and filmed a few of them (most notably Alan Brennert's fine adaptation of "The Cold Equations"), but otherwise had no connection to its predecessor. Or to me.

The Twilight Zone was a unique show, the perfect series for someone like me. My first thought when it went off the air was that I was done with Hollywood. Hollywood was not done with me, however. The corpse of *TZ-2* had scarcely cooled before I found myself writing a treatment for *Max Headroom*. A few months after that one of my *TZ* scripts got into the hands of Ron Koslow, the creator and Executive Producer of a new urban fantasy series called *Beauty and the Beast* that would be making its premiere in the fall of 1987. I was not convinced I wanted to do another show, but when my agents sent me a tape of Koslow's *Beauty and the Beast* pilot, the quality of the writing, acting, and cinematography blew me away.

I joined the staff of *Beauty and the Beast* in June of 1987, and spent three years with the series, rising from Executive Story Consultant to Supervising Producer. It was a very different sort of show than *The Twilight Zone* had been, but once again I found myself working with some terrific actors, writers, and directors. The show was twice nominated for an Emmy Award as Best Dramatic Series. I wrote and produced thirteen episodes, did uncredited rewrites on a score of others, and had a finger in everything from casting and budgeting to post-production, learning a great deal in the process. By the time *Beauty and the Beast* died its premature death, I had the experience and the credits to dream about creating and running a show of my own.

Fast forward to the summer of 1991. I was back at home in Santa Fe (though I worked in Hollywood for ten years, I never actually moved to Los Angeles, and would flee back to New Mexico and Parris the moment my current project wrapped). Since the end of *Beauty and the Beast*, I had written the pilot for a medical show and the screenplay for a low-budget science fiction movie (it wasn't so low-budget after I got done with it). Neither had gone anywhere, and no new assignment was in the offing, so I started work on a new novel. *Avalon* was science fiction, a return to my old future history. The writing seemed to be going well, until one day a chapter came to me about a young boy who goes to see a man beheaded. It was not a part of *Avalon*, I knew. I knew I had to write it too, so I put the other book aside and began what would ultimately become *A Game of Thrones*.

When I was a hundred pages into the fantasy, however, my lovely and energetic Hollywood agent Jodi Levine called to report that she'd gotten pitch meetings for me at NBC, ABC, and Fox. (CBS, the network that had aired both *The Twilight Zone* and *Beauty and the Beast*, was the only network that did not want to hear my ideas. Go figure.) I had been telling Jodi that my werewolf novella "The Skin Trade" would make a swell franchise for a series, and asking her to get me in to pitch it. Now she had. So I put *A Game of Thrones* in the same drawer with *Avalon* and flew out to L.A. to try and sell the networks on a buddy series about a hot young female private eye and an asthmatic hypochondriac werewolf.

It's always best to have more than one string to your bow when fiddling for networks, so I noodled with some other notions on the plane. Somewhere over Phoenix, the opening line of "The Lonely Songs of Laren Dorr" came back to me. *There is a girl who goes between the worlds . . .*

By the time I got off the plane, that line had mutated into a concept for an alternate-world series I called *Doors* (it was later changed to *Doorways*, to avoid confusion with Jim Morrison's band and Oliver Stone's film). It was *Doors* that ABC, NBC, and Fox all responded to, not "The Skin Trade." I flew home thinking that Fox was the most likely of the three to bite, but ABC was faster on the trigger. A few days later, I had a pilot.

Doorways became my life for the next two years. I took the project to Columbia Pictures Television, where my old *Twilight Zone* colleague Jim Crocker joined me as Executive Producer. The rest of 1991 I spent writing and rewriting the pilot. I did several story treatments and beat outlines before going to script. The toughest question I faced was deciding what sort of alternate world Tom and Cat should visit in the pilot. After long consultations with Jim

Crocker and the execs at Columbia and ABC, I went with "winter world," a stark post-holocaust Earth locked in the throes of a nuclear winter. My first draft, as usual, was too long and too expensive, but Crocker seemed pleased with it, as was Columbia.

ABC was pleased as well... with the first half of the script. Unfortunately, the network guys had changed their minds about what should happen when Tom and Cat go through the first door. Winter world was too grim, they now decided. If we went to series, we could go there for an episode, certainly, but for the pilot ABC felt we needed a less depressing scenario.

It meant tearing up the entire second half of my script and doing it all over, but I gnashed my teeth, put in some late nights and long weekends, and got it done. In place of winter world, I sent Tom and Cat to a timeline where all the petroleum on Earth had been eaten some years earlier by a bioengineered virus designed to clean up oil spills. Needless to say, this caused a rather major... ah, *burp*... but civilization recovered after a fashion, and the resulting world was far less grim than winter world had been.

In January 1992, ABC gave us a production order for a ninety-minute pilot. To offset some of the projected budget deficits (my script was too long and too expensive), Columbia also decided to produce a two-hour version for European television. Academy Award winner Peter Werner was hired to direct, and preproduction began. Casting was a hell and a half, and actually caused us to delay the shoot (with fateful consequences further down the road), but we finally found our regulars. George Newbern was perfect as Tom, Rob Knepper made a splendid Thane, and Kurtwood Smith was so good in his dual role as Trager that we would have brought him back many times had we gone to series. For Cat, we had to go across the ocean to Paris, where we discovered a brilliant and beautiful young Breton stage actress named Anne LeGuernec. I remain convinced that if *Doorways* had gone to series, Anne would have become a huge star. There was no one like her on American television, then or now. We found some great people for our guest roles too, adding Hoyt Axton as Jake and Tisha Putman as Cissy. Finally we were go to roll.

When we screened the rough cut for ABC that summer, we got an enthusiastic reception and an order for six back-up scripts, so we would be ready to go into production as a mid-season replacement in 1993. I wrote one of the six scripts myself, hired some terrific writers to do the other five, and spent the remainder of 1992 and the first few months of 1993 doing rewrites, going over pattern budgets, and getting ready to go to series.

It never happened. ABC passed. The *why* of that remains a matter of conjecture, though I have my theories. Bad timing might have been a part of it. By the time we finally found our Tom and Cat, we had missed the development window for the '92 fall season. We seemed to be a lock for the fall of '93, but there was a shakeup at ABC before that decision day rolled around, and both of the execs who had supervised the pilot ended up leaving the network. We might also have made a mistake when we agreed to scrap winter world, which would have given the second half of the show a visual and visceral impact that no-oil world could not match. The test audiences and focus groups would have gotten a much different idea of the dramatic potential of the series from a world in more desperate straits.

Or maybe it was something else entirely. No one will ever know for certain. After ABC pulled the plug, Columbia screened the pilot for NBC, CBS, and Fox, but it is a rare thing for one network to pick up a project developed for another. Heinlein said it best: if you let them piss in the soup, they like the flavor better.

Doorways died. I mourned a while, and went on.

You don't forget, though. Ten years have passed, but it still makes me sad to think what might have been. It gives me great pleasure to include the script in this retrospective. No writer wants to see his children buried in an unmarked grave.

I debated a long time over which version of the script to use here. The later drafts are more polished, but in the end I decided to use the first draft, the one with winter world. The two-hour European cut of *Doorways* has been released on videotape everywhere but in the U.S.A., and large crowds saw the rough cut of the ninety-minute version at the test screenings we did for MagiCon, the 1992 worldcon in Orlando, Florida. But no one has ever visited winter world till now. And what could be more appropriate for an alternate-worlds story than to present an alternate version of the script?

Doorways will always be the great "what if" of my career. I wrote other pilots—*Black Cluster, The Survivors, Starport*—but *Doorways* was the only one to get beyond the script stage, the only one to be filmed, the only one to come within a whisker of winning a spot on a network's primetime schedule. If it had, who knows? It might have run for two episodes, or for ten years. I might still be writing and producing the show today, or I might have been fired two months into the series. The only certainty is that I would be much, much richer than I am at present.

On the other hand, I would never have finished *A Game of Thrones,* or written the other volumes of *A Song of Ice and Fire.* So maybe it all turned out for the best after all.

THE TWILIGHT ZONE: "THE ROAD LESS TRAVELED"

FADE IN

INT.—LIVING ROOM—NIGHT

JEFF MCDOWELL and his wife DENISE, an attractive couple in their late thirties, are cuddled together on their couch, watching TV. She's sleepy but contented; he's rapt on the screen. The light of the TV plays over their faces. The furnishings are eclectic, not expensive or terribly chic, but comfortable. There's a fireplace, with bookshelves to either side stuffed with magazines and plenty of well-read dog-eared paperbacks.

O.S. we HEAR dialogue from the original version of *The Thing*: the exchange "What if it can read minds?" "Then it'll be real mad when it gets to me." Jeff smiles. Behind them, we SEE their five-year-old daughter, MEGAN, enter the room.

                          MEGAN
          Daddy, I'm scared.

As Megan comes over to the couch, Denise sits up. The girl climbs up into Jeff's lap.

JEFF

Hey, it's only a space carrot.

Vegetables are nothing to be scared of.

(beat, smile)

What are you doing down here anyway?

Aren't you supposed to be in bed?

MEGAN

There's a man in my room.

Denise and Jeff exchange looks. Jeff hits the pause button.

DENISE

Honey, you were just having a bad dream.

MEGAN

(stubborn)

I was *not*! I saw him, Mommy.

JEFF

(to Denise)

My turn, I guess.

Jeff picks up his daughter, carries her toward the stairs.

JEFF

(cheerful, reassuring)

Well, we'll just have to see who's scaring my girl, huh?

(aside, to Denise)

If he reads minds, he'll be real mad when he gets to me.

CUT TO

INT.—MEGAN'S BEDROOM

as Jeff opens the door. A typical untidy five-year-old's room. Dolls, toys, a small bed. A huge stuffed animal, fallen on its side, fills one corner. The only light is a small nightlight in the shape of some cartoon character. Megan points.

MEGAN

He was over there. He was watching me, Daddy.

JEFF'S POINT OF VIEW

as he looks. Under the window is a shape that does indeed look like a man sitting in a chair, staring at them.

BACK TO THE SCENE

Jeff turns on the overhead light, and suddenly the man in the chair is nothing but a pile of clothes.

JEFF

See. It's nothing, Megan.

MEGAN

It was a man, Daddy. He scared me.

Jeff musses his daughter's hair.

JEFF

Just a bad dream, Megan. My big girl isn't scared of a little nightmare, is she?

He carries her to bed, tucks her in. Megan looks uncertain about the whole thing; she sure doesn't want to be left alone.

JEFF

Can you keep a secret?

Megan nods solemnly.

                              JEFF

(conspiratorially)
       When I was a kid, I had lots of bad dreams. And monsters.

                             MEGAN

(wide-eyed)
       Monsters?

                              JEFF

       In the closet, under the bed, everywhere. Then my dad told
       me the secret. After that I wasn't scared anymore.
(whispers in her ear)
       Monsters can't get you if you hide under the blankets!

                             MEGAN

       They can't?

                              JEFF

(solemn, definite)
       Those are the rules. Even monsters have to obey the rules.

Megan pulls up her blankets and ducks underneath, giggling.

                              JEFF

       That's my girl.
(lifts blankets, tickles her)
       But blankets can't hide you from daddies.

They tussle playfully for a moment. Then Jeff kisses her, tucks her
back in.

                              JEFF

       Now go to sleep, you hear?

Megan nods, ducks under the blanket. Jeff smiles, goes to the door, and
pauses to look back before turning out the light.

JEFF'S POINT OF VIEW

Of the room, the bed, Megan's small form huddled under the blankets, the scattered toys. He flicks the switch.

SMASH CUT TO

INT.—HUT IN VIETNAM—NIGHT

Everything is the same; everything is grotesquely different. The walls and roof are thatched, the floor is dirt. The arrangement of objects is a distorted echo of Megan's room. Outside the window a nearby fire illuminates the scene (instead of a streetlamp). In a dark corner, where the stuffed animal lay in Megan's room, a body slumps instead. Every toy, block, and object from Megan's room has a counterpart placed identically; pots and pans, a rag doll, a gun, etc. The bed is a pile of straw, and the blanket is ragged, but there's still a child's body beneath. Only now there's a dark stain spreading on the cloth. We HEAR Jeff's shocked gasp. The Vietnam shot should be held very briefly, almost a subliminal. Then Jeff turns the light back on and we

SMASH CUT TO

MEGAN'S ROOM

As before. Everything is normal.

CLOSE ON JEFF

Disoriented, confused, he stares for a beat, shakes his head.

BACK TO THE SCENE

Jeff turns off the light again. This time nothing happens. He closes the door softly, and we FOLLOW him downstairs.

LIVING ROOM

Denise is glancing over some legal briefs, oversized glasses on the end of her nose. She glances up at Jeff, and notices something in his expression that makes her put away the papers.

DENISE
What's wrong? You look like death warmed over.

JEFF
(still shaken)
It's nothing...I thought...ah, it's absurd. Like daughter like father, I guess.
(forced laugh)
The "man" was a chair full of clothes.

DENISE
She's got your imagination.

JEFF
I *wondered* who took it.

DENISE
She's okay, though?

Jeff seats himself, picks up the remote control, turns the movie back on just in time for the "Keep watching the skies" speech.

JEFF
Sure.

CUT TO

MEGAN'S ROOM

The girl is huddled under the blankets in the soft glow of her nightlight. We HEAR her soft, steady breathing. The camera MOVES IN slowly, with the faint SOUND of a wheelchair moving across a hardwood floor.

CLOSE ON MEGAN

As a shadow falls across her. She does not stir, not even when a man's hand moves in from off camera, grasps the corner of her blanket, and pulls it back with ominous slowness.

FADE OUT

FADE BACK IN

INT.—CLASSROOM—THE NEXT DAY

A college lecture hall. Twenty-odd students are watching and taking notes while Jeff paces in front of the class, tossing a stub of chalk idly as he lectures. On the blackboard is written NY JOURNAL—HEARST and NY WORLD—PULITZER.

> JEFF
> —when Remington complained that he couldn't find a war, Hearst supposedly cabled him back and said, "You provide the pictures. I'll provide the war." Now, that anecdote is probably apocryphal, but the role the yellow press played in whipping up war fervor was beyond dispute.

A sullen dark-haired student with the look of a jock interrupts the lecture before Jeff can proceed.

> JOCK
> At least they were on our side.

Jeff stops, looks at him, sits on the edge of his desk.

> JEFF
> You have a point to make, Mueller?

> JOCK
> (points at board)
> These guys, at least they were behind our boys. The real yellow journalists were the ones who ran down everything we did in Nam.

JEFF

(drily)

Not every war can be as box office as Hearst's little shoot-em-up, I guess.

JOCK

Yeah, well, at least we won that one. We could have won in Nam too.

JEFF

I wouldn't go that far, Mueller. You need to spend more time with your text and less with Rambo.

The class breaks into laughter, but the jock looks angry. Before Jeff can resume his lecture, the class bell RINGS. The students begin to rise, gather up their books, etc.

JEFF

Remember, chapter twelve of Emery is due by next week.

He puts down the chalk and begins to clear his papers into a briefcase as the students file out. The jock lingers until he and Jeff are alone. He steps up to the desk. Physically he is bigger than Jeff, who closes the briefcase and looks up at him.

JOCK

So where were you during Nam, Mister McDowell?

The two men lock eyes for a long, solid beat. It is Jeff who breaks and looks away first, his eyes averted as he replies.

JEFF

(brusquely)

I was in school. Not that it's any of your business.

He brushes past, walking a little faster than necessary, while the jock watches him go.

CUT TO

EXT.—DAY CARE PARKING LOT—DAY

Denise and Megan emerge from a Day Care Center, and cross the parking lot to her Volvo. Denise, on her way home from work, is dressed in a chic tailored suit, carrying a briefcase. As she unlocks the car, we HEAR the sound of a wheelchair.

ANGLE OVER VET'S SHOULDER AT DENISE

In f.g., we see a man's shoulder and the back of his head. Denise backs out of the parking spot, turns toward the camera.

ANGLE ON CAR

As it passes we get a quick glimpse of a legless man in a wheelchair (THE VET) turning to follow it with his eyes. He is long-haired, bearded, his trousers pinned up at mid-thigh, wearing a shapeless olive drab jacket without badges. We should not see his face clearly.

CLOSE ON MEGAN

staring out the car window, she SEES the Vet, follows him with her eyes until they turn a corner.

TIME CUT TO

EXT.—MCDOWELL HOUSE—EVENING

Denise pulls up and parks the Volvo in the driveway, behind Jeff's modest Datsun. The house is a two-story suburban tract home; pleasant, respectable, in a decent neighborhood, but nothing too large or expensive. A comfortable middle-class sort of house.

CUT TO

INT.—KITCHEN

Denise & Megan enter, to find Jeff tossing a salad. A small TV set sits on the counter, and Jeff watches the news from the corner of his eye. The newscaster is reading a story about El Salvador. An open bottle of wine and half-empty glass are close at hand. Jeff turns when they enter.

> JEFF
> Roast beef, baked potatoes, tossed salad, and wine.
> (kisses Megan)
> Except for you. You get milk.
> (to Denise)
> So how does that sound?

> DENISE
> Like paradise regained.
> (to Megan)
> Go wash up, honey.

Megan rushes off upstairs.

> DENISE
> So what's wrong?

> JEFF
> Wrong? What makes you think something's wrong?

Denise gives him a rueful smile, picks up the wine bottle, sloshes it thoughtfully.

> DENISE
> Clues, Sherlock. The last time you served wine was the day your car got banged up in the school lot. What is it this time?

Jeff looks as though he's going to deny it, then stops, shrugs. She knows him too well.

> JEFF
> This morning in class, a student asked me where I was during Vietnam.

(beat, grimace)

    I told him I was in school.

DENISE

You were. I remember it distinctly. I was there with you, re-member?

JEFF

I left out the part about the school being in Canada.

DENISE

It's none of his business anyway.

JEFF

That's what I said. I just feel . . .

(beat, hesitant)

    I don't know. Guilty. Like I did something wrong. Dumb, huh?

He opens the oven, pokes at the roast with a long fork.

JEFF

Well, it didn't moo. I think it's done.

CUT TO

INT.—DINING ROOM

Denise is filling bowls of salad as Jeff carries the roast out on a platter. Megan has not yet reappeared. Denise goes to the stairs to call.

DENISE

Megan! Come on down, Hon, dinner's ready.

A beat, then a DOOR CLOSES upstairs and Megan comes down. Denise takes her by the hand, frowns.

> DENISE
>
> Megan, you didn't wash up.

> MEGAN
>
> The man was upstairs, Mommy. He talked to me.

> DENISE
>
> (put upon)
>
> Honestly. Come on, let's get you scrubbed up for dinner.

We TRACK with them as they go up the stairs and into the bathroom. Kneeling, Denise takes a facecloth and begins to wash a dirty spot off of Megan's face.

> DENISE
>
> Honey, it's okay to play pretend, but you shouldn't try to blame someone else when you forget to do something.

> MEGAN
>
> It's not pretend, Mommy.

> DENISE
>
> There, that's a little better.

She puts down the washcloth, looks at Megan's reflection in the mirror, smiles. We move in TIGHT on the mirror as Denise's eyes rise. Behind them, the open bathroom door is reflected, and outside in the hallway, sitting in his wheelchair, is the Vet. Denise spins around, and off her shocked reaction we

CUT TO

DINING ROOM

Jeff grabs a baked potato, winces as it burns his fingers, tosses it onto a plate, and then reacts as we HEAR Denise scream O.S. He's up like a shot, running for the stairs.

ANGLE ON JEFF

on the staircase, as he almost runs into Denise coming down.

> JEFF
>
> What's wrong?

> DENISE
>
> (frantic)
>
> Where is he? Did he come past you?

> JEFF
>
> (confused)
>
> What? Come past me? Who?

> DENISE
>
> The man in the wheelchair.
>
> (impatient, off Jeff's confusion)
>
> He was there, in the mirror...I mean, he was in the hall, but I saw him in the mirror, and then...he *must* have come by you!

> JEFF
>
> (baffled)
>
> A man in a *wheelchair*?

He takes Denise by the shoulders, tries to calm her down.

> JEFF
>
> (continued)
>
> I think I would have noticed a man in a wheelchair, honey. Besides, how the hell could anyone get a chair down these stairs?

Denise gapes at the narrow steps, realizes that Jeff is right. But she knows she saw the Vet; she's totally lost.

DENISE

He was there, I tell you. If he didn't come down—
(whirls, scared he's still up there)
Megan appears at the top of the stairs, calm, unafraid.

MEGAN

He's gone, Mommy.

Denise wraps her in a tight hug.

MEGAN

Don't be scared, Mommy. He's a nice man.

ANGLE ON JEFF

as he watches wife and daughter embrace.

JEFF

There is *no way* anyone could have gotten out of this house.
What the hell is going on here?
(starts up stairs)
Whatever it is, I'm going to find out.

JEFF'S POINT OF VIEW

As he moves upstairs, down the carpeted hall, slamming open doors,
peering into the rooms, finding nothing. Bathroom, linen closet,
Megan's room, the master bedroom and bath; all empty.

ANGLE ON JEFF

Standing in his bedroom, looking angry, disgusted. He starts back out
into the hall, takes a few steps... and stops dead outside the bathroom.
He drops to one knee, reaches out.

CLOSE ON CARPET

As Jeff traces the clear, unmistakable track of a wheelchair tire in the thick shag carpet.

JEFF

What the . . .

SMASH CUT TO

CLOSE ON MUDDY GROUND

Matching shot, the motion of Jeff's fingers CONTINUOUS from the last shot, but now the carpet is mud, the tracks are footprints, and Jeff's sleeve is an army uniform.

EXT.—JUNGLE TRAIL—DAY—JEFF'S POINT OF VIEW

Jeff looks up from the footprints. It's a jungle trail in Vietnam, narrow, overgrown, thick foliage all around. A black grunt stands a few feet away: a kid, no more than nineteen, his uniform dirty, a crude bandage wrapped around a head wound and soaked with blood. He's holding an M-16.

GRUNT

Hey, man, what's wrong?

JEFF

As he staggers to his feet. It's Vietnam, he's in cammies, an M-16 slung over his shoulder. He can't believe any of it. He gapes—at himself, the trees, the gun, at everything.

GRUNT

(disgusted, scared)
Don't freak on me, Spaceman. I need you, man.

Jeff backs away from him, shaking his head.

JEFF

No. No way. This can't be—

He backs hard into a tree, stumbles. He's lost. When the grunt approaches, Jeff shrinks away from him.

JEFF

Stay away from me!

GRUNT

(confused)

What the hell's wrong? It's me, man!

He grabs Jeff by the shoulders, shakes him as Jeff struggles.

GRUNT

Cut it out, man. It's me! Hey, Spaceman, it's only me.

CLOSE ON JEFF

as the grunt shakes him.

GRUNT (O.S.)

It's me, man. It's me, it's me, it's me, it's me . . .

Off Jeff's SCREAM, we
SMASH CUT TO

INT.—HALLWAY

Where Denise has a hysterical Jeff by the shoulders, shaking him, shouting at him.

DENISE

. . . it's me, Jeff. It's only me! It's *me*!

Jeff suddenly realizes that he's back, wrenches free, staggers back away from her, panting.

                              JEFF
          I...I...where...my God, what *happened* to me?

                             DENISE
          I heard you yelling. When I came up, you were on the floor. It
          was like you were terrified of me.

                              JEFF
          It wasn't *you*!
(beat, confused)
          I mean...I don't...Denise, I was...here, and then suddenly I
          wasn't...I was in *Nam*!
(beat, continues off Denise's worried look)
          I know. It doesn't make sense. None of it makes sense.

                             DENISE
(timidly)
          Maybe...I don't know...maybe you had some kind of...
          flashback or something?

                              JEFF
          How the hell can you flash back to a place you've never been?

                             DENISE
          Jeff, I'm scared.

Jeff takes her in his arms.

                              JEFF
          You're not the only one.

DISSOLVE TO

INT.—BEDROOM—LATE THAT NIGHT

Dinner's been reheated and eaten, Megan's been put to bed, but Jeff is
still shaken. Denise, in pajamas, sits up in bed, pillows propped up

against the headboard bookcase. Jeff, still dressed, stands by the window, looking out, his back to her.

JEFF

(dully)

I have to go away.

DENISE

Go *away*? You're talking crazy, Jeff.

JEFF

(turns to face her)

Crazy? Tell me what's crazy! A man in a wheelchair who leaves tracks in my carpet and vanishes into thin air, that's crazy. One moment I'm in Megan's room and the next I'm in some hut in Nam, *that's* crazy. But it's happening, all of it's happening.

(beat, then earnestly)

Denise, don't you see? It's happening on account of me. I don't know what's going on, but I'm the cause of it.

DENISE

You haven't done anything—

JEFF

(interrupts)

No? I can think of something I did. I was drafted, Denise. I chose Canada instead. And now...

(beat, confused)

...now it's catching up with me, somehow. Maybe Nam was my *fate*, maybe I was supposed to die there. Maybe this legless ghost is the guy who went instead of me, or someone who died because I wasn't there.

He turns away again, stares back out the window.

> DENISE

That's your guilt talking, not you. And for what? You said no to a dirty little undeclared war. You helped to *stop* the war, damn it. You know that.

> JEFF

All I know is that I've got to leave. If I go, maybe you and Megan will be safe.

Denise gets up from bed, walks over to the window, puts her arms around Jeff, hugs him. He does not turn.

> DENISE

Jeff, *please*. Whatever is happening, we can face it together.

CLOSE ON JEFF

Worried, but softening. He doesn't want to go, not really.

> JEFF

Maybe you're right.

He turns toward her, to kiss her.

SMASH CUT TO

INT.—BROTHEL—NIGHT

Jeff completes the turn to find himself standing in the bedroom of a brothel in Saigon, a young Vietnamese prostitute standing there with her arms around him, waiting for his kiss. The light flooding through the window is red, garish. Jeff CRIES OUT and thrusts the prostitute away roughly. She stumbles and falls.

> JEFF

No, *no*! Not again.

He backpedals, and runs from the room wildly as the woman gets back to her feet.

CUT TO

EXT.—MCDOWELL HOUSE—NIGHT

As Jeff's Datsun revs up, backs out of the driveway, and screams off down the street, Denise comes running out of the house, a bathrobe flapping around her legs, shouting for him to stop.

> DENISE
>
> Jeff! *Jeff! Wait!*

The car screeches around a corner and Denise stands there, shaking, slumped in despair.

TIME CUT TO

INT.—DENISE'S OFFICE—THE NEXT DAY

A busy Legal Aid office. Denise is a staff attorney, with a private glass-walled cubicle. She's working on some briefs, although it's clear from her face that she's depressed, unhappy, worried. When her com line BUZZES, Denise lifts the phone.

> DENISE
>
> Yes, Susan.

> SUSAN
> (O.S.)
>
> Your husband's on five.

> DENISE
>
> Thanks.
> (pushes phone button, eager)
> Jeff? Where have you been? I've been so worried.

We HEAR Jeff's voice over the phone. It has a hoarse, raspy tone; he sounds strained, uncertain.

> JEFF (O.S.)
>
> Denise? Is it you?

> DENISE
>
> Of course it's me. Where are you? Are you all right? You sound strange.

> JEFF (O.S.)
>
> Strange?

(beat)

> I . . . I'm fine, Denny. How are you?

> DENISE
>
> Denny? You haven't called me Denny since high school. Jeff, what's the matter?

> JEFF
>
> I just . . . need to see you, Denny. Just for a little while. I'm at home, Denny. I need to see you.

> DENISE
>
> I'll be right there.

She HEARS the click as the phone is hung up. She rises, hurriedly stuffs her briefcase, heads through the door into the outer office, where she pauses by the receptionist's desk.

> DENISE
>
> Susan, I'm going home for the afternoon. Ask Fred to cover for me.

> SUSAN
>
> Sure. I hope nothing's wrong.

Denise nods grimly, and exits.

CUT TO

INT.—DENISE'S CAR

She has a worried look on her face as she drives home.

CUT TO

LEGAL AID OFFICE

The outer office. Susan has just hung up the phone as Jeff comes through the outer door, haggard and unshaven, wearing the same clothes we saw him in the night before. Susan's obviously surprised to see him.

> JEFF
>
> (weary, abashed)
>> Hi, Susan. Denise in?

> SUSAN
>
> She went home about five minutes ago. Right after you called.

> JEFF
>
> Right after... *I* called? I never called.

> SUSAN
>
> Of course you did. I put you through myself not ten minutes ago. I ought to know your voice by now.

> JEFF
>
> (stares, with dawning apprehension and fear)
>> My God!

He turns and runs from the office.

CUT TO

EXT.—MCDOWELL HOUSE—DAY

as Denise's car pulls up. She walks to the kitchen door.

INT.—KITCHEN

as Denise enters.

> DENISE
>
> (calls loudly)
> > Jeff? I'm home.

There's no answer. Denise frowns. We TRACK with her as she walks through the kitchen and into the living room.

> DENISE
>
> Jeff? Are you there?

Silence for a long beat, and then, from upstairs, comes Jeff's voice . . . except that it's not quite his voice, it's a little harsher somehow, with a bitter edge to it, a rasp. And it's weak, a bit faint, as if talking was an effort.

> VET
>
> Denny? I . . . I'm here, Denny.

Denise moves upstairs, down the hall.

> DENISE
>
> Jeff?

> VET
>
> Here. Back here.

The voice is coming from the bedroom. Denise enters. The drapes are pulled tight, the room is very dark.

DENISE

Honey?

Silence. She crosses the room, pulls back the drapes, and as daylight floods the bedroom, the door SLAMS, Denise whirls.

DENISE'S POINT OF VIEW—WHAT SHE SEES

The Vet, legless, in fatigues, sits in his wheelchair, blocking the only exit from the room. We HOLD on him for a long beat, and for the first time we see that he is Jeff McDowell. A gaunt, hollow-cheeked Jeff McDowell, his scraggly beard doing little to disguise obvious ill-health. His speech patterns are rougher, cruder; this Jeff has been educated by Vietnam and VA hospitals, not colleges and universities. His eyes are deeply sunken; he looks at her like a starving man staring at a feast.

BACK TO THE SCENE

Denise is terrified for a beat, and then she recognizes him.

DENISE

(scared whisper)
    Jeff?

The Vet smiles a tremulous, tentative smile. He looks almost as scared as she does.

VET

They call me Spaceman. I got the name in Nam, on account of the movies I liked.
(beat)
You're looking good, Denny. Even better than you did back . . . back when we were together.

She backs away, shaking her head.

DENISE

This isn't happening...Jeff...what am I *saying*, you're not Jeff, you can't be Jeff.

The Vet rolls toward her.

CUT TO

EXT.—FREEWAY—DAY

Jeff's car is barreling through freeway traffic, cutting in and out, hurrying home. He comes down an exit ramp, speeds along a residential street.

INT.—JEFF'S CAR

Behind the wheel, he looks grim and intent, a little frightened.

CUT TO

THE BEDROOM

The Vet rolls forward as Denise backs away from him.

VET

You want to see my dogtags? I'm Jeff McDowell, just as much as *he* is. You want to test me? Go on, I know all the answers. We met in high school, working on the school paper. Your parents are named Pete and Barbara. The first time we went all the way was on your couch, the night they went out for an anniversary dinner and I came over to watch *War of the Worlds* on your color TV. You've got a birthmark on the inside of your thigh, about an inch—

DENISE

(interrupting)

My God...you *are* Jeff. What...What...

VET

(looks down at missing legs)

What happened? Is that the question? Vietnam happened, Denny. Vietnam and the draft lottery and a mine.

DENISE

You didn't go to Vietnam. You went to Canada. *We* went to Canada, together, we got married up there. You taught up there until the amnesty.

VET

(bitter laugh)

I'm still waiting for my amnesty.

DENISE

How...how did you get here? Where did you come from? And *why*? What do you want from us?

VET

I just want...

Before he can finish, they HEAR the sound of squealing brakes from outside.

CUT TO

EXT.—MCDOWELL HOUSE—DAY

Jeff's Datsun screeches up into the driveway, behind Denise's Volvo. He opens the door, rushes inside.

INT.—LIVING ROOM

as Jeff bursts in through the kitchen door.

JEFF

(wild, yells)

Denise! Where are you? *DENISE!*

He looks around the room, snatches up a fireplace poker.

CUT TO

BEDROOM

where Denise hears him yelling.

                    DENISE
(shouts)
          JEFF! Here, I'm up here.

                         VET
          Denny, please. I don't have—

                         DENISE
(louder)
          JEFF!

We HEAR Jeff's footsteps pounding up the stairs and a moment later the door bursts open as he enters, brandishing the poker. The Vet wheels his chair around and backs off.

                         JEFF
          Stay away from her! Leave her alone—

Jeff stops dead, as the full realization hits him. He stares.

                         JEFF
(softly)
          You're . . . me.

                         VET
(soft, weary)
          Bingo.

                         JEFF
          This isn't happening, this is some kind of—

                          VET
(interrupts)
        Dream? Yeah. But are you dreaming me or am I dreaming
        you?
(beat)
        I don't give a damn either way. I think we're both real. I think
        that back around 1971 we came to this fork in the road, and
        you went one way, and I went the other, and we got to . . .
        different places.

Jeff slowly lowers the fireplace poker. He's pale, scared.

                          JEFF
        Then . . . those flashbacks I've been having . . . those are . . .

                          VET
(hard smile)
        Mine, brother. Part of the baggage. I guess they just come with
        me. And you and me, we're the same person, right? I could feel
        it happening . . . leaking. But I couldn't stop it. We just got too
        close.

                        DENISE
        Jeff—

Both of them turn to look at her.

                        DENISE
(continues, with difficulty)
        I mean . . . *Spaceman* . . . in your . . . road . . . what happened to . . .

                          VET
        To us, Denny? You and me?

Denise nods.

                              VET
You died in a motorcycle crash while I was in Nam. The guy
you were riding with didn't believe in helmets.

Denise looks sick, turns away. The Vet stares off into space, remembering something, and when he continues his voice is dead, hollow, full of
pain.

        All the time I was over there, I knew I'd be coming back, I
        knew I'd find you again and make it right between us...and
        then your mother wrote me that letter.
(beat, with great difficulty)
        I was short, man. I was so short. I shoulda known better, but I
        wasn't thinking right, wasn't paying attention. You got to pay
        attention. I felt it when I stepped on it. It makes this sound, this
        little click.
(looks at them)
        That kind of mine...it don't go off when you step on it, you
        know. It's when you take your weight off. The rest of the guys
        just looked at me. I told them to get the hell away, and they
        backed off one by one, but they all kept looking at me, staring
        at the dead man who was standing there shouting at them.
        Even when they were all out of range, I couldn't move. But
        they were watching me, all of them watching me, and finally I
        couldn't take it no more. I jumped.
(bitter laugh)
        We never could jump very far, huh, Jeffy?

CLOSE ON JEFF

For a beat, the silence is profound.

                              JEFF
        You saved them. You saved their lives.

BACK TO THE SCENE

VET

Yeah. They gave me a medal.

JEFF

You saved them.

(turns away)

And I didn't. That's it, isn't it? I wasn't there.

He *flings* the poker away violently, and it smashes off a wall. Jeff turns back, angry.

JEFF

All right, then. Guilty, I'm guilty. I took...the other road. But whatever...retribution is due, it's mine. Denise and Megan have nothing to do with it. Whatever you have to do, leave them out of it.

ANGLE ON DENISE

as she listens to Jeff with fear, horror.

DENISE

No!

(looks to Vet)

I went with him to Canada. We decided together. I'm part of him, and everything that happens to him.

ANGLE ON THE VET

After a long beat, he smiles gently.

VET

I know. That's why I loved you, Denny.

(to Jeff)

You don't understand, man. You think I'd hurt *them*?
(laughs)
And they say us vets are crazy.

BACK TO THE SCENE

JEFF

Then ... *why*? Why are you here?

VET

Good question.
(grim smile)
I'm dyin', man.

DENISE

My God ...

VET

The doctors never tell you, but I feel it coming. And it's okay ... I lost everything important a long time ago ... my legs, my girl, my future. Even Jeff. And Spaceman, he didn't have nothing but some real nasty memories.
(beat)
I was in the VA ... waiting to get it over with ... and I kept thinking about Denny, you know? Wondering how it would of come out if I'd done it different. I guess I just ... *wondered* myself here, huh?
(laughs)
I always liked ghosts, but I never thought I'd be one.

The Vet turns his wheelchair to face Jeff.

VET
(continues)
I just wanted ... to see them.
(beat, smile)
You did okay, McDowell.

Jeff shakes his head, obviously eaten up by guilt. He's sound and whole, but he's the guy in the chair too, and his face is corroded by self-doubt.

                              JEFF
          You did okay. I wasn't there—

Unable to face his crippled counterpart, Jeff turns away.

                              VET
(softly)
          I wasn't there either. Not for Denise. Not for Megan.

The Vet rolls himself over to a dresser, and picks up a framed photograph of Megan, stares at it.

                              VET
(continues)
          If you can hold your little girl in your arms and think for even
          a second that you did anything wrong, then you're the dumb-
          est human being ever walked the face of the earth. Believe me,
          Jeff. You didn't miss nothing.

ANGLE ON JEFF

As he turns back, reacting to what the Vet has said, to the obvious truth of it. He's choked up. Denise goes to him, wordlessly. They embrace.

                              VET
          I think . . . maybe it's time I went.
Denise turns to him.

                            DENISE
          You don't have to. I mean, you can stay.

                              VET

(sadly)

    No. I can't. At least now I've got a few things to remember, huh?

Jeff reacts sharply; he's had a thought.

                              JEFF

    The flashbacks—

(beat)

    You and me, we're the same person. It has to work both ways.

(beat, decisively)

    I've got memories too. Maybe if we touched, or—

He steps forward, but the Vet rolls backward, away from him.

                              VET

    No! You don't know what you're talking about.

                              JEFF

(softly, with compassion)

    I'm talking about the day Denise and I got married. Our honeymoon. The day Megan was born.

                              VET

(bitterly)

    It ain't one way, Jeff. Think of what you'll get in return. You'll remember them dyin' around you. The hospitals, the years in the chair.

(beat)

    You'll remember standing there while they backed away from you, watching you, all of them watching you. You won't sleep so good, and sometimes you'll wake up screaming.

Jeff hesitates, looks to Denise. She nods. He kisses her, steps toward the Vet.

JEFF

I'm not afraid of a few nightmares.
(wry smile)
I can always hide under the blankets, right?

He holds out his hand. The Vet stares up at him, then, very slowly, reaches out and takes Jeff's hand in both of his. Jeff winces sharply, as if in pain. The Vet closes his eyes. Tears begin to run down his cheek.
CLOSE ON DENISE

as she watches.

ANGLE PAST DENISE ON SCENE

The two Jeff McDowells seem to glow with a strange blue-green light, as ghostly afterimages flicker about each of them. Her Jeff, standing, seems for a moment to be wearing a uniform, and then a long straggly beard. The Vet appears to be dressed in a 60s-style tux, then in civilian clothes; his trouser legs FILL OUT as LEGS shimmer into view, spectral and glowing, but legs nonetheless. He opens his eyes, stares in wonder, then RISES from the chair.

VET

I guess maybe we're both heroes, huh?

The Vet, now standing, EMBRACES Jeff, the strange light playing all about them. Then the two bodies seem to MELT into each other, to MERGE and become one. The light grows so intense that Denise shies away, covers her eyes.

When the glow fades, the wheelchair and the Vet are gone, and only the original Jeff McDowell remains. Denise runs to him, and they embrace, holding each other very tight and hard. We HOLD the shot as the NARRATOR'S voice comes up.

NARRATOR

We make our choices, and afterwards wonder what that other road was like. Jeff McDowell found out, and paid the toll. A lesson in courage and cartography, from the mapmakers of the Twilight Zone.

THE END

Doorways

FADE IN

EXT.—FREEWAY—NIGHT—AERIAL

Traffic is fast and heavy. Suddenly we hear a CRACK, as loud as a clap of thunder, as sharp as a sonic boom.

SMASH CUT TO
TIGHT ON CAT

A girl stands trapped in the center of the freeway, as speeding traffic surges around her. Call her CAT. She's twenty. Her figure is lean, boyish, wiry-tough. Her hair is short, raggedly shorn. There is something wild about her, something quick and feral and not-quite-tamed. Her pants are leather, old, cracked, badly worn. She wears a loose black uniform shirt several sizes too big for her, unbuttoned, over a tight silver-gray undershirt. Her feet are bare. She looks lost, confused...

INTERCUT—CAT'S POV

HEADLIGHTS are coming at her from all directions, it seems, cars are missing her by inches.

RESUME CAT

She tries to dart toward the shoulder, misjudges the speed of traffic. A car almost hits her, its horn BLARING. Cat jumps back.

A second car SWERVES to avoid her. Brakes SQUEAL. More HORNS sound. Cat spins, searching for a way out. She takes a step in the other direction, jumps back as two cars SLAM TOGETHER. Metal CRUNCHES with impact. More HORNS. Off in the distance, we HEAR police SIRENS too.

CLOSE ON CAT

She covers her ears against the noise, draws herself in protectively, closes her eyes amidst the chaos . . .

Suddenly she is AWASH IN BLINDING LIGHT, and we hear the deep, terrifying sound of a big truck's AIR HORN. Her eyes snap open.

REVERSE ANGLE

A huge SEMI is bearing down on her.

RESUME CAT

She freezes, like a deer pinned by the truck's lights. Then the fear is replaced by defiance. From under her shirt, she pulls a WEAPON; sleek and strange, like no gun we have ever seen. Cat swings it up quickly, aims with both hands, and FIRES. The only sound is a soft PHUT of compressed air as the weapon spits out a needle.

ANGLE ON THE SEMI

One moment it is roaring forward at sixty miles an hour, its horn screaming, its headlights blinding. Then it EXPLODES. The cab blows apart, sending chunks of glass and metal flying in all directions. The huge truck careens wildly out of control, veers off to one side, and CRASHES. A second EXPLOSION rocks the truck as its gas tank blows, sending up a towering ball of flame.

CAT

is turning to make a break for the shoulder when a spinning piece of debris from the explosion comes flying at her. She ducks, but not fast enough. She catches a glancing blow on the forehead. The impact sends her sprawling.

PUSH IN TIGHT

Cat lies on the road, unconscious, bleeding from a cut over one eye. The weapon has slipped from her grasp, and the sleeve of her shirt has ridden up to reveal an ornate bracelet clasped around her right forearm. It's a strange piece, a Gigeresque tangle of silvery metal inset with three parallel slashes of dark plastic, that coils around her arm like a nest of snakes.

OFF that image, we

FADE OUT

END OF TEASER

ACT I

FADE IN

EXT.—HOSPITAL—NIGHT

SIRENS scream through the night as an ambulance races down the freeway, closely followed by two POLICE CRUISERS with lights flashing.

CUT TO

INT.—EMERGENCY ROOM—NIGHT

An eight-year-old BOY sits on an examination table, surrounded by his MOTHER, a young doctor (TOM), and a heavyset nurse (MADGE).

TOM

Not like that. Look at that mess. No, you have to keep your hand steady. It's a delicate operation. Mistakes can be fatal. Here, watch.

REVERSE ANGLE

Tom holds up his hand, palm down. He is twenty-seven, dark-haired, rumpled, confident. The nameplate on his greens reads LAKE. He has a quarter between two fingers. He "walks" it across his hand, flips it up in the air, catches it, opens his hand. He pulls it out from behind the boy's ear.

TOM

What did I tell you. Magic is easy. Diagnosis is hard.

He grins at the young patient, who LAUGHS with delight. The nurse and the mother smile fondly. In b.g., we HEAR the sound of SIRENS. Tom hears it too.

TOM

(to boy)
　　　And for my next trick, I make you disappear.
(to mother)
　　　He'll be fine.

INT.—HOSPITAL—NIGHT

Two PARAMEDICS rush a gurney down a corridor to the Emergency Room. A pair of cops (CHAMBERS and SANCHEZ) follow close behind.

TRACKING WITH THE GURNEY

Tom falls in beside the gurney.

TOM

What do we have?

PARAMEDIC

Head injury, facial lacerations, maybe some internal. Her vitals are real strong, but she's non-responsive.

A gauze bandage covers Cat's cut; it's PINK with blood.

SANCHEZ

She was playing tag out on the freeway. Blew the crap out of a semi with some weird gun.

INT.—EMERGENCY ROOM—CONTINUOUS

They push through a set of double doors into the ER.

TOM

We'll take it from here. Madge, notify X-Ray I'm sending someone up. Tell them I'll need a full set of cranials.

The nurse scrawls a signature for the paramedics. They EXIT as Tom begins his examination of Cat. He feels gently around her neck, searching for breaks. Lifts the gauze pad to examine her head injury. When he pushes up her sleeve to take her pulse, he reveals her strange bracelet. He touches it.

TIGHT ON CAT

Her eyes snap open and Cat MOVES. She grabs Tom by the crotch and SQUEEZES. Tom GASPS in shock and pain.

RESUME

Cat rolls off as Tom collapses, on her feet with all the speed of her namesake. Chambers jumps her. Cat tries to punch him, but he grabs first one arm, then the other. He holds her by the wrists as she struggles.

CHAMBERS

You're under arrest, girly. You have the right to remain silent. You have the—

Cat throws herself right up against him, face to face, and BITES him on the nose. Chambers SCREAMS and grabs his face. BLOOD seeps between his fingers. Cat scrambles away.

Sanchez cuts off her exit. Tom is on his knees, unsteady, gasping for breath.

Cat backs off and SPITS a piece of the cop's nose onto the floor. There's a smear of blood around her mouth.

She snatches up a metal IV stand and holds it in front of her like a quarterstaff, ready for anyone.

Sanchez draws his gun.

TOM

NO!
(panting a little)
    Put that . . . put that away. This is . . . a hospital.

SANCHEZ

She's psycho.

Tom pulls himself unsteadily to his feet.

TOM

She's scared. Look at her.

CHAMBERS

My nose . . .

> TOM
> It's around here somewhere. We can fix it. Madge, find the officer's nose.

(to Cat)

> Don't be afraid. No one will hurt you. Promise.

She's watching him now, warily. She says nothing. Tom edges closer. Cat gives a short, threatening swing of the pole.

> SANCHEZ
> I wouldn't go any closer if I was you, Doc.

> MADGE
> Tom, be careful. I don't think she understands English.

Tom keeps all his attention on Cat.

> TOM
> That's a nasty cut there.

Cat touches her face. Her fingers come away wet with blood.

> TOM
> Can I take a look at it? Put that down, why don't you? I won't hurt you.

TIGHT ON TOM AND CAT

A tense moment. He is right beside her now. He lifts a hand to her face. No sudden movements. Cat is taut, poised. Tom turns her face to one side to examine the gash.

> TOM
> Not as bad as it looks. Still, we better get an X-ray. Will you come with me?

Tom offers her his hand. Cat hesitates a long moment. Then she FLINGS AWAY the pole. It falls with a clatter.

> SANCHEZ
> Real good. We'll take her now, Doc.

Tom faces him down. The nurse is visible in E.G., on her hands and knees, searching for the missing bit of nose.

> TOM
> I'm admitting this patient overnight for observation.

> SANCHEZ
> She's under arrest. We'll observe her down in lockup.

> TOM
> You want the responsibility of removing her against medical advice?
> (off his hesitation)
>   I didn't think so.

Madge triumphantly holds up something we cannot see.

> MADGE
> I found it!

DISSOLVE TO

INT.—HOSPITAL ROOM—LATER THAT NIGHT A semi-private room with two beds.

CLOSE ON CAT

She stands by the window, dressed in a hospital gown now, looking out over the city lights like one entranced. The gash over her eye has been stitched and bandaged.

Cat pushes back her sleeve to expose the bracelet clasped around her forearm. She raises her arm, palm down, points it toward the window and the city beyond.

TIGHT ON CAT'S ARM

as she makes a fist. Inset deeply into the coiling metal are three matte black SLASHES, roughly parallel, sinuous, suggestive.

Now those slashes begin to GLOW: very faint at first, a dim BLUE. Slowly, deliberately, Cat moves her arm from right to left and back again. The blue glow BRIGHTENS when she swings toward the east, DIMS when her fist points west again.

CLOSE ON CAT

Her face solemn, her concentration fierce. She sweeps her arm back and forth again; the glow BRIGHTENS and FADES.

She turns her arm over, opening her fingers.

TIGHT ON CAT'S HAND

As a HOLOGRAM springs to vivid life in her palm: a small, three-dimensional EARTH, turning slowly. She holds a miniature world in her hand. Strange swirling SYMBOLS run across its face, like stock quotations on an electronic ticker.

Behind her, we HEAR the sound of a door OPENING.

RESUME CAT

She WHIRLS. The globe WINKS OUT at once.

REVERSE ANGLE—ON TOM

A uniformed POLICEMAN opens the door for him. Tom is carrying her clothing, neatly folded. He can see how jumpy she is.

                              TOM
    Did I startle you? I'm sorry. I just wanted to see how you were
    doing.

He closes the door behind him. Cat seems to relax.

                              TOM
    I brought your clothes. We washed them for you.

Tom places the pile of clothing on the bed.

                              TOM
    There's a new pair of jeans in there. Your pants were, ah, be-
    yond salvage.

ANGLE ON CAT

Cat crosses the room and snatches up the clothing. She clutches it tight
against her chest.

ANGLE PAST CAT ON TOM

A little taken aback by the fierce possessiveness.

                              TOM
    I know how you feel. My girlfriend is always throwing out my
    favorite shirts.

Cat slips out of the hospital gown, letting it puddle on the floor at her
legs. She is naked underneath. We see her bare back as Cat starts to
dress.

She does it without a trace of self-consciousness or shame. Tom turns
his back, more embarrassed than she is.

She pulls on the silvery undershirt, SNIFFS at the jeans, steps into
them. Tom keeps up a stream of talk.

                              TOM
            I didn't catch your name. I'm Dr. Lake. Thomas.
(nothing)
            We've got you down as a Jane Doe. For the paperwork. The
            office wants to know if you have any medical insurance, Jane.

CAT

is dressed now. She crosses the room to the door, tries to open it. It's
locked.

                              TOM
            It's locked. I don't think the cops want you going anywhere
            right now.

Cat SLAMS a fist against the door.

                              TOM
            Look, I know the food's not great, but there are worse places to
            spend the night.

Cat moves to the window. She looks down. She starts to push at the
glass, looking for a way to open it.

                              TOM
            Don't get any ideas. We're four floors up. Besides, this is a mod-
            ern hospital. None of the windows open.

Cat gives up, turns away angrily.

CLOSE ON TOM

A dawning suspicion in his eyes.

RESUME

Cat retreats to a corner of the room, sinks down to the floor. Her stare
is sullen, angry. Tom looks at her thoughtfully.

                              TOM
        You knew what I was saying. About the window.

Cat watches him. Her face gives nothing away. Tom moves closer,
smiling despite himself.

                              TOM
        You little con artist. You hear me.

Cat turns her head away from him.

                              TOM
        This would be a lot easier if you'd talk to me.

She ignores him.

                              TOM
        Come on. Say something. Anything. Name, rank, phone num-
        ber, I don't care. What's your sign? What's your favorite color?
        You like anchovies on your pizza?
(nothing)
        Fine. I don't need to waste my time.

Scowling, Tom KNOCKS on the door.

ANGLE ON THE DOOR

The POLICEMAN opens the door from outside.

                            POLICEMAN
        All through in here, Dr. Lake?

                              TOM
        I guess we are.

He is about to exit when . . .

                            CAT

(soft)
        Cat.

                            TOM

        She talks . . .
(to policeman)
        Maybe you better give us a few more minutes.

The policeman closes the door, leaving them alone.

                            TOM

        Did you say something?

                            CAT

(a beat, then:)
        Cat.

                            TOM

        Cat? Like in Catherine?

                            CAT

        Cat. Name.
(shy smile)
        Toe Mas.

Cat speaks with a slight ACCENT. Nothing we can easily put a finger
on, nothing that suggests any known country or region, but a musical
lilt to her words that hints that somehow she is a stranger in this place.

                            TOM

        Bingo. Toe Mas. Toe Mas Lake.
(beat)
        How about an address? Do you have a family? A boyfriend?
        Anyone we can contact?
(no response)
        Where did you come from?

Cat gets up from the floor.

                    CAT
        Earth.

                    TOM
        That clarifies things. What part of Earth?

                    CAT
        Angels.

                    TOM
        Angels . . . you mean LA? Los Angeles? Here?

                    CAT
        Not here. There. Angels.

                    TOM
        Okay. How did you get from there to here?

                    CAT
        Door.

Now it's his turn to look blank.

                    TOM
        On the freeway? A car door?

                    CAT
        Door between.
    (impatient)
        Leaving now, Toe Mas. Going now. Getting out.

She gets up, strides to the door, pulls at it. It's locked. She looks at Tom,
expecting him to help.

                    TOM
        That door only opens for me right now. Sorry.

Firmly, but gently, he moves her away from the door, KNOCKS. The policeman in the hall opens for him.

> TOM
>
> Look, my girlfriend's a lawyer. I'll talk to her. That's all I can do for you right now.

> CAT
>
> Not knowing lawyer.

> TOM
>
> You really must be from another country.

He EXITS, the door closes, and Cat throws herself on the bed, frustrated and trapped.

DISSOLVE TO

EXT.—BEACHFRONT APARTMENT—NEAR DAWN

Tom's car, a little Mazda Miata, pulls up in front of a ramshackle old wooden apartment building by the beach.

INT.—TOM'S BEDROOM—DAWN

A woman is asleep in a big brass bed, under a rumpled sheet. In b.g. are lots of bookcases crammed with medical texts, law books, and paperbacks. Right over the bed, very prominent, is Tom's framed antique poster for a performance featuring HARRY HOUDINI.

The woman in the bed is in her late twenties, pretty, with long red hair. Her name is LAURA.

Tom sits on the bed beside her. He touches her shoulder, gently. Laura rolls over, muttering a protest. Tom shakes her a little harder. Her eyes open.

LAURA

(sleepy)

Tom? Is that you? What time is it? You just get home?

(glances at clock)

Oh, God, it's too early. Go away. Leave me alone.

Laura rolls over and pulls the sheet back over her head. Tom gently tugs it down again.

TOM

Wake up. Coffee's on. Jump in the shower and put on your shyster hat. I need help.

Tom moves off. Laura SIGHS, stirs. She sits up in bed, grumpy but awake.

INT.—TOM'S KITCHEN—DAWN

Laura sits at the kitchen table. She has slipped into a terrycloth robe. Her hair is still tousled from sleep. She cradles a steaming mug of coffee and listens. Tom paces the kitchen floor, restless, angry.

TOM

I tell you, there's something very strange about this girl.

LAURA

She obviously made quite a first impression. Normally you don't get so involved with people who knee you in the groin.

TOM

It wasn't a knee. Look, can you help her?

LAURA

I'll see what I can do. Did she really bite off his nose?

TOM

(glumly)

Just the end bit.

Laura can't help but smile.

> LAURA
>
> That's something. If you bite off the whole nose they really throw the book at you.

She finishes her coffee and gets up. Tom grabs her, pulls her close for a kiss.

> TOM
>
> I'll owe you one.

TIGHT ON TOM AND LAURA

as he puts his arms around her.

> LAURA
> (playful)
>
> So, is she cute? Should I be jealous?

> TOM
>
> What is this, cross-examination?

> LAURA
>
> The witness is instructed to answer the question.

> TOM
>
> Not guilty.

Their lips move together.

> LAURA
>
> Good. Otherwise...

Laura changes direction. Instead of kissing, she snaps her teeth together and lightly nips at the end of his nose. Tom breaks up. They laugh together, then kiss.

CUT TO

EXT.—FREEWAY—DAWN

The burned wreckage of the semi still blocks part of one lane and spills across most of the shoulder. A road crew with a CRANE and a FLATBED TRUCK works to remove the wreck. The predawn traffic is light.

> WORKER
>
> Last year it was just freeway shootings. Now they're using missiles.

> FOREMAN
>
> From now on, I stick to surface streets.

Suddenly we hear a CRACK, as loud as a clap of thunder, as sharp as a sonic boom.

> FOREMAN
>
> What the hell...

The crane stops; its lights, its engine, everything. The big flatbed truck dies simultaneously. All the other lights in b.g. also go off: houses, cars, streetlamps.

ANGLE DOWN FREEWAY—FOREMAN'S POV

Only two or three cars are in sight. All of them are dead or dying: headlights out, engines giving up the ghost, slowly coasting to a halt, drivers climbing out.

RESUME

The worker is banging a big emergency flashlight against the heel of his hand, flicking the switch on and off.

WORKER
I don't get this, I just put in new batteries.

But the foreman isn't listening. We HEAR slow, ominous footsteps.

FOREMAN'S POV

Six figures fan out across the freeway. They were not there a moment ago. Now they are. There are three men, three women. The women are as lean and tough and hard-looking as the men. They wear high black boots, black uniforms with silver metallic trim. Their hair is cropped close to their skulls.

Behind them comes a strange vehicle, a PALANQUIN or open sedan chair of black metal, as big as a Caddy, with long OUTRIDERS on either side, as on an outrigger canoe. It FLOATS three feet above the roadway, moving in utter silence, its line alien, suggestive, almost organic. A single passenger rides inside, surrounded by a roiling grayness: the DARKFIELD, a cloud that drinks light, making everything within vague and mysterious, like shapes half-seen in fog. All we can tell is that the passenger inside is hunched and massive, altogether huge by human standards.

REVERSE ANGLE

The foreman and his road crew stare at these apparitions before them. A few have the sense to be afraid.

REVERSE ANGLE—TIGHT ON THANE

The leader of the six on foot is THANE. His collar displays the insignia of rank: a silver pin in the shape of a hound's head. He is in his thirties, awesomely fit, with eyes like ice. A hunter's eyes. A warrior's eyes.

His eyes meet the foreman's for a second.

One by one, the hunters step aboard the palanquin, taking up position on the outriders like footmen on a carriage.

Thane boards last. The palanquin vanishes into the darkness.

THE ROAD CREW

stands in a stunned silence for a moment.

> WORKER
> What the hell just happened?

> FOREMAN
> I don't think I want to know.

All at once, the power returns: headlights, streetlamps, flashlight, everything.

FADE OUT

END OF ACT I

ACT II

FADE IN

INT.—HOSPITAL CORRIDOR—AFTERNOON

Tom strides down the corridor, whistling. Then he notices something odd: no cop by Cat's door. He stops whistling, moves to the door, opens it.

ANGLE INTO ROOM—TOM'S POV

Cat's room is EMPTY, spotless, the bed freshly made. No one has been here for hours.

RESUME

People are coming and going: nurses, patients, a NUTRITIONIST with a food tray, an ORDERLY.

> TOM
>
> Pete, what happened to the girl in this room? Did they move her somewhere?

> ORDERLY
>
> Room was empty when I came on shift, man.

> NUTRITIONIST
>
> That patient was discharged last night, Doctor.

> TOM
>
> By who? I didn't authorize any discharge. Did anyone see the police leave?

Shrugs. No one knows, no one cares. Except one OLD WOMAN struggling down the hall, leaning on a walker.

> OLD WOMAN
>
> They took her. Men in suits. It was three in the morning. She woke me up, the way she was screaming and kicking.

> TOM
>
> God *damn* it!

He goes striding off angrily.

CUT TO

INT.—ER NURSE'S STATION—MOMENTS LATER

TIGHT ON TOM

He is on the phone, still furious. INTERCUT with shots of Laura, behind her desk in a legal office.

TOM

What do you mean she wasn't arrested?

LAURA

I mean there's no arrest report. No paper of any kind. Your little feline friend was never arraigned. The incident was never logged. Officers Sanchez and Chambers are mysteriously unavailable.

TOM

They can't just pretend it never happened. There must have been a hundred witnesses.

LAURA

You didn't happen to get the names of any, did you?

CLOSE ON A HAND

Before Tom can answer, a hand ENTERS FRAME and depresses the button on the receiver.

ANGLE PAST TOM

Still holding the dead phone, he turns to face an imposing man in a dark gray suit: TRAGER. About fifty, his suit impeccable, his hair carefully combed, Trager is a man of ice and iron.

TRAGER

Dr. Thomas John Lake?

Tom just glares at him. Trager flashes a badge.

TRAGER

Special agent Trager, federal intelligence unit. Would you come with me, please?

Tom makes the connection. He's suspicious and angry.

TOM

Why?

(beat)

You removed a patient of mine from this hospital last night. Illegally. Who the hell do you think you are? What have you done with Cat?

TRAGER

Is that her name? She's in good care, Doctor. She'd like to see you.

TOM

I'm not going anywhere with you until I've talked to my lawyer.

Trager has had enough; his patience runs out.

TRAGER

Fine. You get one phone call. Tell her you're under arrest.

TOM

You can't do that!

TRAGER

You'd be astonished at what we can do, Doctor.

(beat)

On the other hand, if you'll give us your cooperation...

TOM

(reconsidering)

I'll call someone to fill in for me.

CUT TO

EXT.—HOSPITAL—NIGHT

Trager escorts Tom out of the hospital. A long black limo with tinted windows waits by the curb. They get in.

INT.—LIMOUSINE—CONTINUOUS

Trager climbs in after Tom and closes the door. The car moves off without a word. A second man sits across from them: thirtyish, sandy-haired, muscular.

> TRAGER
>
> This is agent Cameron.

Agent Cameron wears a blue suit and a large white BANDAGE over his nose that covers the center of his face. He looks unhappy.

> TOM
>
> I see you've met Cat.

Cameron gives him a foul-tempered stare. Tom turns his head away and fakes a COUGH, covering his mouth to hide the smile he cannot quite suppress.

DISSOLVE TO

EXT.—DESERT BASE—NIGHT

The high desert of California. A uniformed GUARD waves the limo through a gate in a high chain-link fence. On one side of the gate a sign says AUTHORIZED PERSONNEL ONLY; on the other DANGER HIGH VOLTAGE. Beyond the fence are the quonset huts and ugly cinder-block buildings of an abandoned army base.

INT.—DESERT BASE—NIGHT—TRACKING

Trager and Cameron escort Tom down a long windowless corridor. They pass one section where the wall has been BLOWN OUT; through a jagged blackened hole we glimpse a long interior room GUTTED by fire, its ceiling collapsed.

                    TOM

You have a fire?

                  TRAGER

Our shooting range. One of our bright boys decided to test fire
your girlfriend's gun.

                    TOM

She's not my girlfriend.

                  TRAGER

Whatever. In here, please. There are some things I want you to
see.

He opens a door. Tom steps through.

INT.—TRAGER'S OFFICE—NIGHT—TIGHT ON A WALL
SAFE

A high-tech, electronic safe with a card slot and numerical keyboard.
Trager's HAND inserts a plastic security card into a slot. The keypad
LIGHTS Trager punches in a sequence of numbers. The safe swings
open; Trager begins to remove the contents.

ANGLE DOWN ON DESK

as Trager spreads out Cat's weapon, her bracelet, three BLACK
CYLINDERS. A hundred-odd BLACK PLASTIC NEEDLES are
scattered across the desktop.

ANGLE UP

Trager and Tom have been joined by MATSUMOTO, a government
scientist, Asian, forty, wearing a lab coat.

                    TOM

She blew up a semi with that?

                              TRAGER

Correct. Go on, pick it up.

Tom lifts the weapon, sights down the barrel.

                                TOM

I used to have a water pistol that looked like this.

                              TRAGER

Close. Try a beebee gun.

                            MATSUMOTO

An air gun, more precisely. Quite sophisticated. I doubt we
could duplicate it. It uses a high-velocity jet of pressurized air
to spit out . . .

Matsumoto lifts a thin black needle with tweezers.

                            MATSUMOTO

. . . these.

                                TOM

Needles?

                            MATSUMOTO

Needles with the explosive power of a bazooka round.

                              TRAGER

This beebee gun has teeth.

Matsumoto picks up a cylinder: black, long as a finger.

                            MATSUMOTO

The police found three of these magazines in her pockets. Each
one holds one hundred forty-four needles, and . . .

He pulls a cap off the back. Inside, built-in, is a POWER CELL; it
pulses with RED LIGHT.

MATSUMOTO

(continuous)

...its own power cell. So you recharge every time you reload. If Detroit had battery technology this good, we'd all be driving electric cars.

Tom is still hefting the weapon.

TOM

Awkward grip. I can barely reach the trigger.

TRAGER

The girl had to use both hands to fire it.

TOM

Bad design...

MATSUMOTO

Unless the gun was designed for someone with bigger hands.

TOM

You'd need fingers like a squid.

Tom puts down the weapon, picks up the bracelet.

TOM

She was wearing this when the paramedics brought her in.

TRAGER

It seems to be very important to her.

TOM

What is it?

MATSUMOTO

The metal is a superconductive alloy. I've never seen anything like it. Inside it's solid microcircuitry. Very odd microcircuitry. Parts of it seem almost organic.

TOM

But what does it do?

MATSUMOTO

At a guess . . . it detects certain unusual subatomic particles.

Tom looks blankly over at Trager. He's lost.

TOM

I don't understand any of this.

TRAGER

Neither do we. That's why you're here. We need answers, Doctor. And the girl won't talk to anyone but you.

OFF Tom's silent, reluctant agreement, we

CUT TO

INT.—CORRIDOR—NIGHT

A uniformed MATRON is seated outside a locked door, beside a window of one-way glass. Cat is visible inside, curled up on a bed, listless, in prison grays. The matron fans herself with a small HAND FAN, its accordion folds alternately red and black.

TRAGER

How's our guest?

MATRON

Quiet. She just lays there, staring off. I don't blame her, in this heat.

TRAGER

Let him in.

He gives the bracelet over to Tom.

                    TRAGER
Your conversation will be monitored and recorded.

The matron unlocks the door. Tom enters.

INT.—CAT'S CELL—CONTINUOUS

Cat looks up slowly.

                    CAT
        Toe Mas.

Cat gets up. She sees the bracelet. Her eyes WIDEN. She moves across
the room, reaching for it.

                    CAT
        Mine! Give it, Toe Mas.

                    TOM
        First we need to talk.

Cat doesn't take no for an answer. She reaches for the bracelet. Tom
holds it out of her reach.

                    CAT
        Give it now. Needing it now. Coming soon. Coming after.

                    TOM
        Who is coming after?

                    CAT
        Darklords! Manhounds! *Give!*

                    TOM
        Tell me what it is and you can have it back.

Cat almost spits the word at him.

CAT

Geon. Give it now!

Tom TOSSES it to her. Cat snatches it out of the air, slides it back onto her arm. It seems to calm her.

TOM

What does it do, Cat? What's it for?

CAT

Finding doors. Doors *between.* Doors away.

Backing away from Tom, Cat extends her arm, hand tight in a fist. She turns in a slow circle, sweeping the room.

TOM

What kind of doors? Cat, what are you doing?

She ignores him, concentrating. The device can't find a reading in this enclosed place. It stays dark.

CAT

No good, no good, *no good.*

TOM

Cat, where did you get that? And the gun, the air gun...
(off her blank look)
The weapon, the...

Frustrated, Tom does a pantomime of lifting the gun with both hands, firing, with appropriate sound effects.

TOM

You know...*phut*...*BOOM!*

He shapes an EXPLOSION with his hands. Cat giggles.

CAT

Phut BOOM?

TOM

Right. The phut boom. Where did you get the phut boom?

She looks at him as though he were a moron.

CAT

Hand cannon, Toe Mas. Stealing it. Not-for-men, hand cannon.
(beat)
Needing it, taking it.

TOM

What did you need the hand cannon for?

CAT

Shooting. Killing.
(off his reaction)
Getting *away,* Toe Mas.

Cat is getting more and more agitated. She looks around the sealed room desperately, searching for a way out.

CAT

Lights out! Darklords coming soon.

TOM

The . . . darklords. Is that a gang?

CAT

Darklords *masters.* Darklords *owners.*

TOM

And the . . . manhounds?

CAT

(whisper)
> Thane . . .

Tom can see the fear on her face now. This conversation is getting to her. She tries the door to the room. It's locked, of course. Cat spins away in frustration.

TOM

> Hey, take it easy. I don't know who these people are, but they can't get to you here. You're safe.

Instead of calming her, that just drives her WILD. Grabbing up a CHAIR, she swings at the mirrored window with all her strength. It bounces off the glass. Cat swings it again and again. The mirror begins to BREAK. A spiderweb of CRACKS fissures out.

CAT

(screaming)
> Not safe! Not safe! Not safe!

The mirror SHATTERS, showering the hall outside with pieces of one-way glass. Cat is about to leap through the broken window when Tom grabs her, restrains her.

TOM

> *Cat, stop.* Don't . . .

He holds her tight, trying to comfort her, as the door opens and Cameron and the Matron come running in.

DISSOLVE TO

EXT.—CANYONS—NIGHT

A densely wooded canyon outside Los Angeles. Thane stands on a precipice, looking down at the city lights. His face is a mask. A woman comes up beside him: DYANA. He senses her presence.

THANE

So many men, Dyana. Their lights go on forever.

DYANA

This is but a shadow of the trueworld, the master says.

THANE

Perhaps the masters of this world say the same thing of our own.

Thane turns his head very slowly toward the east, as if he is listening to something no one else can hear.

DYANA

What is it? Do you have a reading? Is she using the geosyncronator?

When Thane speaks, it is not to Dyana.

THANE

I hear you, Cat. Even now, you call to me

He turns sharply back to Dyana, all business.

THANE

East, northeast, three hundred hexes.

CUT TO

INT. TRAGER'S OFFICE—NIGHT

Trager behind a desk. Tom is pacing. Cameron sits in the visitor's chair, snapping a rubber band.

CAMERON

Pentathol.

TOM

No. She's my patient. I won't allow you to drug her.

TRAGER

We gave you a chance to do it your way, Doctor.

Tom leans over Trager's desk.

TOM

Give me one more shot at it. Let me hypnotize her.

Trager steeples his fingers, thinks, NODS.

CUT TO

INT.—TRAGER'S OFFICE—LATER

The lights have been turned down low. Cat sits in the visitor's chair, Tom close to her side. Trager is behind his desk, watching, Cameron stands.

TOM

...deeper. You hear nothing but my voice now. There are no other sounds, no other voices. Only me. You are relaxed. So relaxed. Floating. All the fear has gone away.

Cat is deep in a trance.

TOM

Tell us your name. Your whole name.

CAT

Cat.

Tom frowns. Trager and Cameron exchange glances.

TOM

All right. Cat, tell us about the place you come from.

                         CAT

All dark. Lights out.

                         TOM

Does it have a name?

                         CAT

Angels.

                         TOM

Where is it?

                         CAT

Behind. Other side.

                         TOM

The other side of . . . the door?

Cat NODS agreement. Tom continues, his voice gentle.

                         TOM

I am going to ask you something else now. You will not be
afraid. All the fear is gone.
(beat)

Cat, who are the darklords?

                         CAT

Owners. Masters.

                         TOM

What do they own?

                         CAT

Earths.

Behind him, Cameron ROLLS HIS EYES in scorn. Trager's face is
impassive, a mask. Only Tom picks up on the plural.

TOM

Earths . . . more than one Earth?

CAT

Not all. Some. Many.

TOM

And your world, from . . .

CAT

Darklords came. Long ago. Lights out. Mommy saying. No cars, no guns, no air-o-planes. Ashes, ashes. All fall down.

TOM

All fall down . . .

CAT

Cities. Soldier men. All fall down. Lights out. Long ago.

TOM

How long ago? How many years?

CAT

Before Cat.

TOM

Cat, where did the darklords come from?
(nothing)
From another country?
(no reply)
Another planet? Did they come in ships? Where?

CAT

The doors.

Silence. Trager leans forward.

TRAGER

Ask her about the weapon.

TOM

Cat, the hand cannon ... you took that from your owner.

CAT

(vehement)

His owner. Owning Thane.

TOM

Thane. Thane was a ... a manhound?

CAT

(echoing)

Let her live, saying. Give to me, saying. Served you well, saying. Little animal, wanting her, saying.

TOM

You were given to Thane ...

CAT

(vehement denial)

Not his. Never his. Pretending. Watching. Listening. Knowing.

TOM

Learning ...

CAT

Waiting. Long waiting. Then taking, running, killing.

TOM

Cat, who did you kill?

CAT

Darklord. Master.

TOM

You learned their secrets, stole the weapon, and escaped through a door, didn't you?

Cat NODS slowly. Cameron looks at Trager.

CAMERON

What the hell is he talking about?

Trager does not reply. He's listening, intent.

TOM

One last question, Cat.

(beat)

How many fingers do the darklords have?

Cat does not respond. Tom holds up a hand in front of her face, his fingers spread wide.

TOM

If this was a darklord's hand, how many fingers would you count?

TIGHT ON CAT—ANGLE THROUGH TOM'S FINGERS

Long hesitation. Finally Cat raises her hand, touching each of Tom's fingers as she counts, SLOWLY.

CAT

One. Two. Three. Four.

(beat)

Five.

"Five" is the thumb. There's a long beat. Cat is still staring at the hand, seeing something else, remembering. Just when we think she's done, her finger moves over PAST Tom's thumb, counting a "finger" that is not there.

CAT

Six.

Now she is done. Tom closes his fingers into a FIST. In the strained silence that follows that moment, we

FADE OUT

END OF ACT II

ACT III

FADE IN

INT.—TRAGER'S OFFICE—NEAR DAWN

Trager leans forward, presses his intercom.

TRAGER

Griggs, summon the matron, and tell Matsumoto to prepare an injection of pentathol.
(to Tom)
Bring her out of it.

Trager heads for the door. Tom bolts after him.

TOM

You can't.

Trager EXITS, followed by Tom. Cameron remains with Cat.

CUT TO

INT.—CORRIDOR—CONTINUOUS

Tom catches Trager by the shoulder, spins him around.

                              TOM
What do you want from her?

                            TRAGER
A story that makes sense.

Matsumoto comes up to them in the hall. He's carrying an instrument
case. Tom is still intent on Trager.

                              TOM
You refuse to see the truth when it's right in front of your face.
How many fingers, Trager?

Tom holds up both hands, fingers spread.

                            TRAGER
What is it with you and fingers?

                              TOM
I learned to count on my fingers. So did you. It's universal. We
have ten fingers, so we count in units of ten. One hundred is
ten times ten. One thousand is ten times ten times ten.

                            TRAGER
What's your point?

                              TOM
That gun you took from Cat. Matsumoto said the magazines
hold one hundred forty-four rounds. Didn't that strike you as
an odd number?

In b.g., the matron approaches down the hall, FANNING herself.

                            TRAGER
Maybe.

                              TOM
Twelve times twelve is one hundred forty-four.

Matsumoto gets it, even if Trager does not.

> MATSUMOTO
>
> Base twelve mathematics. Of course.

> TOM
>
> A race with *twelve* fingers would count in twelves, Trager. How much evidence do you need? Face it. That woman in there is *not* a twentieth-century American.

> TRAGER
>
> What are you saying, that she came down from another planet?

> MATSUMOTO
>
> Not likely. We've run DNA samples. Her genetic structure is completely human.

> TOM
>
> She told you where she came from. Earth. But not our Earth.

> MATSUMOTO
>
> A parallel world?

> TOM
>
> Exactly.

The matron reaches them and stands fanning herself.

> TRAGER
>
> Excuse me?

> MATSUMOTO
>
> A neighbor universe. Certain mathematicians have theorized about the existence of... well, a layman would call them other dimensions. The proofs suggest that an infinite number of these other timelines may co-exist with our own.

TRAGER

What the hell is a timeline?

TOM

Remember the last World Series?

TRAGER

The Braves lost in seven. Cameron was out a week's pay.

TOM

Let me borrow that.
(grabs fan)
What if there was another world where the Braves won? Look, we think of history as a straight line. Past leads to present.

He holds up the fan, folded: a straight line.

TOM

But if more than one result is possible . . . maybe they both happen. New worlds are created at each nexus.

Tom unfolds the fan, just one notch. Now one red fold and one black diverge from the axis pin.

TOM

So you have one world where the Braves won and one world where the Twins won.
(opens the fan more)
Then you have the world where the Pirates and the Bluejays played instead.

TOM

(still spreading)
The world where the Dodgers won the pennant. The world where the Dodgers are still in Brooklyn. The world where baseball was never invented and everybody bets on cricket in October.
(the fan spreads wide)

An infinite number of worlds, embracing all the possibilities, all the alternatives. Not a universe. A multiverse.

Trager looks at the fan, then at Matsumoto.

TRAGER

And these other worlds *exist?*

MATSUMOTO

The math would seem to suggest that. Travel *between* universes, however, is flatly impossible.

(shrugs)

In any case, it's all theory.

Trager scowls, takes the fan from Tom, folds it up.

TRAGER

Theory.

(beat)

Here's a fact, Dr. Lake. I'm sorry I ever involved you in this matter. It's time you went home. I'll arrange transport.

(to matron)

Take her to a holding cell.

TOM

Trager, wait...

Tom GRASPS Trager by the arm, holds him for a moment.

TOM

At least give me a few moments alone with her. I want to say good-bye.

ECU—TOM'S OTHER HAND

While one hand is clutching Trager's arm, the other is dipping into his pocket and lifting his wallet

RESUME

as Trager, unsuspecting, NODS his assent.

> TRAGER
>
> Five minutes. No more.

Trager walks off with Matsumoto. Tom artfully conceals the wallet he's lifted.

CUT TO

INT.—TRAGER'S OFFICE—CONTINUOUS

Tom re-enters Trager's office. Cat is still in her trance. Cameron is playing with his rubber band again.

> TOM
>
> Trager wants you.

> CAMERON
> (hesitant)
>
> Who's going to watch her?

> TOM
>
> Watch her do what? Sleep?

Cameron shrugs, and EXITS. Tom LOCKS the office door behind him, sits beside Cat.

> TOM
>
> I'm going to count to five. When I reach five, you'll wake, re-freshed, relaxed, unafraid. But you'll be very, very quiet. One. Two. Three. Four. Five.

Tom SNAPS his fingers. Cat's eyes open. He puts a finger to her lips.

                    TOM
    No talking. Just nod.
(she nods)
        There's another door, isn't there? A door out. That's where you
        want to go.

                    CAT
(softly)
        Time to go, Toe Mas. Leaving here now.

A long beat; Tom hesitates, his eyes search her face. He reaches a decision, with vast reluctance.

                    TOM
        I'm probably going to regret this, but . . . watch the door, Cat. If
        anyone comes through, bite 'em.

Cat nods eagerly and scrambles to her feet. Tom moves to the wall safe.
He fishes the security card from Trager's wallet, inserts it into the slot,
punches some buttons.

CUT TO

INT.—CORRIDOR—MOMENTS LATER

The matron waits by the door as Cameron and Trager come striding
up. Cameron tries the door. It's locked.

                    CAMERON
    Open up in there. What the hell you trying to pull?

Trager motions him aside.

                    TRAGER
    Doctor, this is very stupid.

He takes out his keys, unlocks the door, and enters the office with
Cameron right behind him.

TRAGER'S POV

He finds himself face-to-face with Tom . . . and the hand cannon. Cat is sliding the bracelet onto her arm. Trager keeps his cool.

> TRAGER
> You really don't want to do this, Dr. Lake. If you fire that in here, you'll kill all of us. Including your girlfriend.

> TOM
> She's not my girlfriend. We need a car.

> TRAGER
> Shall I tell you how many felonies you're committing?

> TOM
> I'd just as soon you didn't, thanks. That limo will do fine.

> TRAGER
> Cameron, bring the limousine around to the front.

CUT TO

INT. ENTRANCE—DAWN—ANGLE OUT THE DOOR

Trager stands at the exit with Tom and Cat. All the other guards are face-down on the floor. Cameron pulls up in the limo.

> TOM
> Let her idle. Okay. Climb out nice and easy and back off. That's it. A little more. Cat, make sure nobody's hiding in the back-seat.

Cat scrambles out to the limo, checks inside.

> CAT
> Not hiding, Toe Mas.

> TOM

I didn't plan this, Trager. It's just happening. Don't take it personally.

Trager just looks at him. Tom makes his break for it.

INT.—LIMOUSINE—CONTINUOUS

Tom jumps in and slams the door. Cat is squirming anxiously beside him in the passenger seat. He tosses the hand cannon into her lap as he revs the engine, pops the clutch, and takes off.

The limo speeds across the compound. Tom drives with his left hand, fumbles in his pocket with his right, pulls out three black cylinders. He tosses those at Cat too.

> TOM

Here. See if you can figure out how to load the phut-boom.

Cat GRINS at him, and slides one of the cylinders into the weapon with an audible CLICK.

> CAT

Hand cannon, Toe Mas. Hand cannon.

Then the high electrified fence and the guardhouse loom up in front of them. Tom floors it.

> TOM

Hold on. I always wanted to see how fast one of these big mothers could go.

EXT.—DESERT BASE—CONTINUOUS

The guards leap out of the way as the limo CRASHES THROUGH the fence in a shower of SPARKS. They bring up their guns and FIRE as the car speeds off. To no effect...

INT.—LIMOUSINE—CONTINUOUS

Tom turns the wheel hard. The limo fishtails, turns, and roars off down the road. Tom risks a quick look at Cat.

TOM

You know, if you turn out to be a runaway from Boise, I'm going to feel really stupid.
(smiles at Cat)
We'll need to lose the limo soon. Every cop west of the Mississippi is going to be looking for it. Where are we going, anyway?

In answer, Cat lifts the bracelet, closes her hand into a fist. The insets GLOW BLUE once more. They are brightest when she points straight ahead: due east.

CAT

That way, Toe Mas.

Tom is impressed.

TOM

I guess you're not from Boise after all.

DISSOLVE TO

EXT.—UNDERPASS—LATER THAT MORNING

Cat helps Tom roll the limo into a weed-choked underpass beneath the highway. It's well hidden when they're done.

TOM

That should do. They'll find it eventually. By then we should be long gone.

CAT

(echoing)
Long gone.

She turns her hand up, opens her fingers. The HOLO appears; the WORLD in her hand. Tom is suitably astonished.

TOM
You know more tricks than Houdini.

TIGHT ON THE HOLO—TOM'S POV

The Earth turns slowly, a transparent ghost in brown and green and blue, but down in what we would call southern New Mexico, a WHITE LIGHT is FLASHING on and off.

CAT
There, Toe Mas. Long gone.

RESUME

as Tom studies the display, makes sense of it.

TOM
New Mexico. Eight hundred miles, at least. We can be there in a day.

Alien SYMBOLS crawl across the face of the globe. Cat understands them, even if Tom does not.

CAT
No good. Too late. Door opening, door closing. Quick quick.
Be there sooner.
(glance at sun)
Before new light. Before...
(searching for word)
...before dawning.

TOM

Tomorrow at dawn? What happens if we don't make it?

CAT

No door.

CUT TO

EXT.—HIGHWAY—DAY

Tom tries to hitch a ride. The traffic shoots past, ignoring him.

DISSOLVE TO

EXT.—HIGHWAY—LATER

Tom coaching Cat on how to hold her thumb.

DISSOLVE TO

EXT.—HIGHWAY—STILL LATER

A car pulls over to pick her up. The DRIVER grins when Cat slides into the passenger seat ... until Tom appears from nowhere and gets in back.

DISSOLVE TO

EXT.—PICKUP TRUCK—SUNSET

Several rides and several hours later. Cat and Tom sit on a bale of HAY in the back of a battered pickup, bouncing down a rough dirt road. The sun is going down. Cat scans with the bracelet. The glow is BRIGHTER now.

TOM

It's brighter.

                    CAT

Closer now.

Tom is in a pensive mood as he watches her scan.

                    TOM

Cat . . . do you know where this door is going to take you?

                    CAT

Someplace.

She sits beside Tom. The bracelet goes dark again.

                    TOM

Someplace worse, maybe. Can you come back?

                    CAT

No coming back.

                    TOM

The doors open only from one side, is that it?
(off her nod)
And you'd go through, not knowing what might wait on the
other side?

                    CAT

Going through.

                    TOM

You might not like where you wind up, Cat.

                    CAT

Is always a next door, Toe Mas.

                    TOM

You can't just keep running. What's the point?

Cat FROWNS, puzzled. The point seems obvious to her. She notices the sunset: the gorgeous red and orange splendor of the evening sky. She points.

                              CAT
        There.

Tom follows her finger, and seems to understand.

DISSOLVE TO

EXT.—ROADSIDE DINER—NIGHT

A big rig slows with a HISS of air brakes on a dark mountain road, Tom and Cat climb down from the cab in front of a roadside diner. The truck rolls on.

INT.—ROADSIDE DINER—CONTINUOUS

Tom parks Cat in a booth, slides in opposite her. It's late. The place is almost deserted. Signs over the counter advertise Mexican food specials.

                        WAITRESS
        What can I get you?

                          TOM
        Let's have a couple of the cheeseburgers.

                          CAT
        Couple of cheeseburgers.

                        WAITRESS
        You want four cheeseburgers?

In b.g., a COWBOY in jeans and denim shirt enters the diner and slides into a booth near the window.

TOM
(firmly)

Two. And two coffees.

CAT

Not knowing coffee.

TOM

Make that one coffee and one milk. You have a pay phone?

WAITRESS

Over by the men's room.

She goes off to place the order. Tom gets up.

TOM

I'll be right back. Don't bite anything but the food.

Cat NODS. Her interest has been captured by a squeeze bottle of ketchup. She SNIFFS at it, squeezes a little on the back of her hand, tastes it, looks an inquiry at Tom.

CAT

Not knowing...

TOM

Ketchup. It's a kind of Republican vegetable. Eat all you want.

He leaves Cat with the ketchup as he crosses to the phone.

ANGLE ON THE PHONE

The phone RINGS. We HEAR Laura's voice.

LAURA

Hello?

TOM

Laura? It's Tom. You're not going to believe—

LAURA

Don't say anything more. There are police here. They've been questioning me about you.

TOM

Damn it. Is it Trager?

LAURA

No. They're very upset with you. Tom, what's this all about?

TOM

Cat. Listen, tell them I'll give myself up in . . .
(looks at watch)
. . . four hours. Just as soon as I get Cat to her door. I don't care what they do to me then.

LAURA

I do.

TOM

It won't be so bad. I know a real good lawyer.
(beat)
I better get off before they trace this. I just wanted to hear your voice. You okay?

LAURA

I will be once you're home.

TOM

Me too. I love you.

Tom HANGS UP. For a moment he seems sad and tired as he walks back to the booth.

CUT TO

INT.—DINER—LATER

ANGLE ON THE REGISTER

The waitress is giving Tom his change.

> TOM
> Thanks. Hey, where are we? What town is this?

> WAITRESS
> T-or-C.
> (off his look)
> Truth or Consequences, New Mexico.

Tom pockets his change and GRINS.

> TOM
> Yeah. Figures.

He EXITS, with Cat right behind him.

ANGLE ON THE COWBOY

Nursing a cup of coffee. He watches them through the window, then produces a PALM-SIZED RADIO. He cups it, speaks into it in a whisper.

> COWBOY
> Subjects have just left the diner. Heading south along the road, on foot.

OFF his watchful eyes, we

CUT TO

EXT.—TWO-LANE ROAD—NIGHT

The night is warm and still. It's very late now, around three in the morning. Cat and Tom walk slowly down the shoulder of a road on the outskirts of T-or-C. There's no traffic at this hour. Cat raises her arm to SCAN. The blue GLOW is VERY BRIGHT now.

>   TOM
>   We must be close.

Cat brings her arm around in a slow SWEEP . . . and the bracelet begins to STROBE, the triple insets FLASHING on and off in sequence, one two three, one two three, one two three, faster and faster.

>   CAT
>   There.

>   TOM
>   That?

REVERSE ANGLE—TOM'S POV

Cat is pointing at an old GAS STATION, a two-pump mom-and-pop operation that looks as though it's been shut for twenty years. The windows are boarded up, the pumps are gone.

Cat crosses the empty highway at a run. Tom comes after, slowly. She does another sweep. The silent STROBING indicates one particular door. Tom is bemused.

>   CAT
>   Door.

>   TOM
>   Of course. What else?

REVERSE ANGLE—ON THE DOOR

The Men's Room. It's BOARDED SHUT.

> TOM
>
> This one doesn't need Houdini.

Tom RIPS OFF the boards, tosses them aside. He opens the door cautiously, peeks inside.

> TOM
>
> I hate to tell you this, but it's a men's room.

> CAT
>
> Too soon.

> TOM
>
> So we wait.

> CAT
>
> (echoing)
> So we wait.
> (shyly)
> Toe Mas...leaving here? Going with?

> TOM
>
> I'm sorry, Cat. This is as far as I go. Whatever's on the other side of that door, it's not for me. I've got a life here. A career. Friends, family.
> (gently)
> A woman I love.
> (beat)
> Do you understand?

Cat looks up, NODS briskly.

> CAT
>
> Understand.

She sits on the ground, crosses her legs. Her face gives nothing away. After a moment, Tom sits beside her. Cat looks at him. Tom, feeling awkward, says nothing. She moves closer, then curls up beside him, and closes her eyes. Finally, Tom puts an arm around her. Cat stirs faintly, and nuzzles closer.

MATCH DISSOLVE TO

EXT.—GAS STATION—NEAR DAWN

Tom and Cat are both asleep.

Suddenly a BLINDING LIGHT hits them straight in the face. Cat wakes instantaneously, Tom more groggily. He holds up a hand in front of his face.

REVERSE ANGLE—TOM'S POV

He is staring into two sets of HEADLIGHTS. Dark figures move out in front of the light, silhouetted in the glare. They have guns in hand. Tom hears a familiar voice.

>   TRAGER
>   You're under arrest.

RESUME

Cat is not about to go meekly. She reaches for her weapon, Tom grabs her arm before she can get it up.

>   TOM
>   Cat, don't.

Cat won't fight Tom. He takes the hand cannon from her.

>   TOM
>   Here. We're unarmed. Don't shoot.

CAMERON

Smart move, Doctor.

Cameron relieves Tom of the weapon and slides it through his belt. Behind him are Trager and two other agents, GRIGGS and MON-DRAGON.

TOM

How did you find us?

TRAGER

Please, Doctor. We never lost you. We played out the line a little to see where she'd go.

Cat struggles as Griggs and Mondragon pull her arms back, handcuff her wrists. Cameron cuffs an unresisting Tom.

TOM

Trager, please, don't do this.

Cat and Tom are forcibly walked toward the waiting cars.

TOM

A few minutes, that's all I ask. The door is about to open. What have you got to lose? For God's sakes, man—

They are about to force Tom inside the car when the headlights of both cars suddenly GO OUT.

TIGHT ON CAT

She is the first to realize what it means. She goes wild, kicking and fighting, anything to be free.

RESUME

Trager has his first serious moments of doubt.

                         TRAGER
Get her under control, damn it.

Tom, staring over Trager's shoulder, is the first to see them.

                          TOM
Trager, we've got company.

REVERSE ANGLE

Silent as ghosts, three black-clad manhounds walk out of the predawn
darkness: Thane, Dyana, ICE.

The palanquin appears a moment later, blocking out the moon. The
other three manhounds are riding atop it, guarding their master. Its
SHADOW drifts across the upturned faces of the agents, and the alien,
distorted voice of the darklord booms down.

                       DARKLORD
Give us the female.

                       MONDRAGON
I'm not seeing this.

                         TRAGER
Cat, who are these people?

                          TOM
Look at them, Trager. You know who they are.

He does; but he still cannot admit it.

                         TRAGER
The girl is a federal prisoner. What's your business with her?

Dyana and Ice move forward toward the feds.

> CAMERON

Hold it right there.

The manhounds keep coming. They're not even armed. Griggs lifts his gun with both hands.

> TRAGER

Griggs, fire a warning shot.

Griggs squeezes off a round. The gun CLICKS. Then Dyana is on him. She grabs his head on both sides. She TWISTS. We hear the SNAP as his neck breaks. Then everything happens at once.

MONDRAGON

pulls the trigger. The gun CLICKS. Ice curls his hands into fists. Six-inch STEEL CLAWS spring from his knuckles. He SLAMS his fist hard into Mondragon's gut.

A BOLT OF ENERGY

crackles down from the palanquin, touching first one car, and then the other. The vehicles EXPLODE and BURN.

THANE

strides through the carnage, straight for Cat. She backs up, looks behind her. We see her REACT.

CAMERON

tries to face Dyana hand to hand. She blocks his karate blow, pulls him off balance, and slams him down across her knee, snapping his spine like a dry stick.

TRAGER

unlocks Tom's cuffs, gives him the keys.

TRAGER

Get her out of here.

Tom runs toward Cat. Trager turns, and...

A BOLT OF ENERGY

from the palanquin FRIES HIM where he stands.

ANGLE ON THE MEN'S ROOM

A pale blue GLOW shines through the crack beneath the men's room door. Cat throws herself against the door. But with her hands cuffed, she can't open it. Tom reaches her at a run. He has the keys.

TOM

Turn around. Hold still.
(unlocks cuffs)
We've got to...

Too late. Thane is there. He grabs Tom contemptuously, and FLINGS him aside like a child. Cat tries to claw out his eye. Thane catches her hand, holds her prisoner by her wrist. She glares at him defiantly.

THANE

Look. Look at he who gave you mercy, and was repaid in shame.

Tom RABBIT PUNCHES Thane from behind.

TOM

Let go of her, you son of a—

Thane whirls, and tears into Tom, a brutal barehand attack. Blow after blow drives Tom back across the lot, staggering.

ANGLE ON THE DOOR (SFX)

Cat OPENS the men's room door. Beyond is chaos, a portal of strobing light. The light is a brilliant BLUE-WHITE. Somehow it hurts the eye to look at it.

Within the light, images flicker past too fast to follow, almost subliminal. For just an instant, the path is clear. Cat could step through at will. But she hesitates . . .

RESUME TOM

Thane is murdering him with his bare hands. Tom FALLS to his knees beside Cameron's corpse. Thane grabs him by the hair, lifts his fist for the killing blow . . . and Cat comes hurtling through the air and lands on his back, pummeling him with blows.

QUICK CUT—THE DOOR

The light has faded to a DEEP MIDNIGHT BLUE. We sense the portal is closing.

RESUME

Thane pulls Cat off his back, and hits her a single terrible backhand blow across the face. She falls.

TIGHT ON TOM

On the ground. Dazed. He wipes blood from his mouth. Then he sees Cameron lying there, still and dead. He crawls to the body, fumbles in the agent's jacket, and pulls out the hand cannon.

ANGLE ALONG THE HAND CANNON

Tom aims at Thane, but he's too close to Cat. Instead he swings the cannon UP at the palanquin, and FIRES.

THE PALANQUIN

is rocked by a tremendous EXPLOSION. The darkfield protects the rider, but we see one of the manhounds FALL, screaming, wreathed in flame. A moment later, the massive palanquin itself CRASHES DOWNWARD.

QUICK CUTS

The manhounds stare in horror.

Ice and Dyana are both directly under the palanquin. They look up in shock as it falls. Dyana drops and ROLLS out. Ice isn't quite quick enough. He SCREAMS as the palanquin crushes him.

Thane moves to help his master.

TOM

staggers over to Cat, sliding the cannon away. She is unconscious on the ground. Beyond her, the door has faded to a DEEP PURPLE GLOW. It's almost closed. Tom scoops up Cat in his arms, and RUNS.

THANE

sees, and comes after them. But too late. Tom LEAPS through the door. Thane lunges after him . . . and finds himself in a gas station men's room. Alone.

SMASH CUT TO

EXT.—BLIZZARD—DAY

as Tom emerges, cradling Cat, into knee-deep SNOW, in the midst of a HOWLING STORM.

FADE OUT

END OF ACT III

ACT IV

EXT.—BLIZZARD—DAY

Tom cradles Cat in his arms as the storm HOWLS around them. It's day, but the sky is DARK, the sun hidden from sight. The wind drives the snow into Tom's bruised, battered face. In b.g., we glimpse the mountains. Tom SHIVERS. He's not dressed for this kind of cold.

TOM'S POV

as he turns, slowly. The world is a stark white wilderness of ice and snow and rock, with no shelter in sight.

RESUME

Already frost is forming on Tom's eyebrows. He picks a direction at random, and begins to WALK, carrying Cat.

DISSOLVE TO

SERIES OF SHOTS—TIGHT ON TOM'S LEGS

as he struggles through knee-high snowdrifts, up ice-slick slopes, over rocks, sometimes staggering, fighting for every yard as the storm rages around him.

DISSOLVE TO

INT.—CAVE—DAY

As caves go, it isn't much: a hole, half hidden by an overhang of rock, a dead tree near its entrance. But it's shelter. Wearily, Tom carries Cat inside, lays her down on the hard-packed earth floor, out of the wind.

He's covered with caked snow, trembling. He picks up some fallen branches from the dead tree near the cave mouth, begins to gather wood for a fire.

DISSOLVE TO

INT.—CAVE—HOURS LATER

Flames crackle and dance near the mouth of the cave. Outside, the snow has finally stopped falling. Tom washes the blood off Cat's face with a handkerchief wet with melted snow.

ANGLE DOWN ON CAT—TOM'S POV

Cat's eyes are open. She's looking up at him.

> TOM
> Good morning. How's the head feel?

> CAT
> Hurts.

> TOM
> Yeah. My face feels like chopmeat. Your friend Thane's got quite a punch.

> CAT
> Not my friend.

She struggles to rise.

RESUME

Tom helps Cat to her feet. She crosses to the mouth of the cave, looks out. Beyond is a white wilderness of snow and ice. Cat SHIVERS, hugs herself.

> TOM
> Grim, isn't it? You're sure the doors don't open in both directions?

> CAT
> Sure.

> TOM
> I was afraid you'd say that.
> (beat, weary)
> Maybe I traded us a quick death for a slow one.

> CAT
> Slow is better. More living.

> TOM
> Even if it's only for a few days? A few hours?

> CAT
> Even if.

She cocks her head sideways, regards him curiously.

> CAT
> Why?

> TOM
> The door was closing.

> CAT
> Still. Why?

> TOM
> Some things you have to do.

Cat thinks about that. Then she moves closer, HUGS him with all her strength.

We can see TEARS in her eyes. Tom can't.

CLOSE ON CAT

Her arms wrapped around Tom, holding him tight.

RESUME

Cat finally breaks the embrace, steps back. Tom looks as awkward as he feels. Maybe he doesn't know what that hug means. Maybe he's thinking of Laura.

> CAT
> Some things you have to do.

That brings a SMILE to Tom's face.

> TOM
> What we need to do is make plans. The firewood won't last long, and we're not dressed for skiing.

> CAT
> Not knowing *skiing*.

> TOM
> It's where you pay a lot of money to strap boards on your feet and slide down a mountain.

He moves to the cave mouth, studies the outside world. The black, overcast sky. The howling wind. The deep drifts of snow and overhangs of ice.

> TOM
> I don't like the look of that sky. Darkness at—

(glances at watch)

 —ten twenty-seven. Blizzards in September.

ANGLE ON TOM

Tom moves away from the wind and the cold, picks up a stick, prods the fire.

> TOM
>
> Maybe there was a geographical shift. Maybe we're in Greenland . . . Antarctica . . .

> SERGEANT (O.S.)
>
> Try Wyoming.

REVERSE ANGLE

as Tom whirls at the sound of the voice. Just inside the cave stand FIVE ARMED SOLDIERS; gaunt, ragged men in ragged uniforms, ice in their beards, hunger and fear in their eyes, snow caking their boots. Their RIFLES cover Tom and Cat.

The SERGEANT is a tall black woman with a rough, earthy voice. She warms her hands over the fire.

> SERGEANT
>
> Nice. Warm. And you know, you can see it for miles.

ANGLE ON CAT

Backing up. She looks sideways at the hand cannon on the ground nearby, tenses to make a dive for it.

RESUME

The sergeant knows exactly what she's doing.

                              SERGEANT
Girl, if you're going to try for that gun over there, you're going
to be real dead real soon.

Cat FREEZES.

                              SOLDIER
What are we going to do with them, Sarge?

                              SERGEANT
March them back to camp and let the Captain have a look.
(to Tom)
    Gather up whatever food you've got and get into your snow
    gear.

                              TOM
We don't have any.

                              SERGEANT
(incredulous)
    In that case, you two are going to have a long, cold walk.

OFF Tom's dismay, we

CUT TO

EXT.—BASE CAMP—THAT AFTERNOON—ESTABLISHING

A small military camp has been dug in against the side of a mountain.
There are tents, crudely built hutches, a firepit in the center of camp.
Around the perimeter, like snowbreaks, are an ancient yellow
SCHOOL BUS, a JEEP, and an ARMORED PERSONNEL CAR-
RIER, all in sorry condition. More striking—and in better repair—are
two larger and more futuristic vehicles: a huge HOVER TANK (designed to ride on a cushion of compressed air, it has no treads), and an
even larger transport FLOATER, an eighteen-wheeler without the
wheels.

ANGLE ON TOM AND CAT

The soldiers stare, curious, as the captives are marched in. Counting the squad that captured Cat and Tom, there are twenty of them. We glimpse a few women and three times as many men.

Their "uniforms" are worn, much patched, and not very uniform. It looks as though they came from two or three different armies. A few have heavy, hooded parkas; one man wears a moth-eaten fur coat; the others bundle up under layers of clothing.

ANGLE ON THE JEEP

as Tom and Cat are marched past. A MACHINE GUN is mounted on the jeep. It's half in pieces now. WALSH, a private with a heavy dark beard wearing a fur-trimmed parka, is cleaning and repairing it. When he sees Cat, he stops, and jumps off the jeep to inspect her.

> WALSH
> Well, look at this. Maybe those snow patrols aren't useless after all.

He blocks Cat's path, touches her under the chin to raise her face. She stares at him impassively.

> WALSH
> You have a name, pretty thing?

> SERGEANT
> Knock it off, Walsh. And get back to work. You were supposed to have that gun cleaned and serviced an hour ago.

> WALSH
> I'd like to clean and service her.

> TOM
> I wouldn't touch her if I were you. She bites.

SERGEANT

Listen to the man. I want that gun back in one piece by mess.

Walsh turns on the sergeant, defiant.

WALSH

Why? You think it matters? What the hell we going to shoot? Snowmen?

SERGEANT

I gave you an order.

Other soldiers gather to watch the confrontation. Among the spectators is a woman, WHITMORE, very PREGNANT. A minority make it clear they agree with Walsh.

WALSH

Stuff your orders.

CRONY

You tell her, Walsh.

WALSH

All this patrolling and drilling and cleaning our guns, what does it prove?

THE CAPTAIN (O.S.)

It proves we can survive, Walsh.

REVERSE ANGLE—ON THE HUTCH

A tall, grim, powerful man has emerged from the command hutch. THE CAPTAIN wears a heavy parka with a hood that shadows his face.

THE CAPTAIN

The snow is the enemy. The cold is the enemy. And despair is the greatest enemy of all. Are you tired of living, Walsh?

CLOSE ON TOM

He is looking at the Captain hard, with a strange expression on his face, almost as if he recognizes him.

RESUME

Walsh is cowed and a little frightened by the Captain.

WALSH

No, sir.

THE CAPTAIN

Death is easy. Lie down in the snow, that's all it takes. Life is harder. It requires courage, work, discipline. Do you want to live?

WALSH

Yes, sir.

THE CAPTAIN

Then get back to work.

Walsh SALUTES and gets back into the jeep. The Captain turns to his sergeant.

THE CAPTAIN

Sergeant, who are these people?

SERGEANT

We found them in a cave by the south ridge, Captain.

THE CAPTAIN

Bring them inside.

CUT TO

INT.—CAPTAIN'S HUTCH—CONTINUOUS

The furniture is crude and well-worn. A wood-burning stove warms the hutch to a comfortable temperature.

The sergeant and one of her men escort Tom and Cat into the hutch. The Captain pulls down his hood. We see his face for the first time. His hair is shoulder length, tangled, but the same iron-gray color. He sports a dark beard shot through with gray, but beneath it the face is the same. Tom recognizes him; so does Cat.

> TOM
> (stunned)
>
> Trager.

CLOSE ON THE CAPTAIN

He frowns, off-balance for a second.

> THE CAPTAIN
> Where did you hear that name?

> TOM
> I . . . knew you.

> THE CAPTAIN
> Before the war?
> (thoughtful)
> No. You're not old enough.
> (beat)
> Names are for peacetime. I'm the Captain.
> (to the sergeant)
> Were they armed?

SERGEANT

We found these in the cave.

She deposits Cat's weapon and TWO spare magazines in front of the Captain, who inspects them carefully.

CAT

Mine! Give it!

The soldiers restrain her as she starts forward.

THE CAPTAIN

Curious. Is this what the enemy is carrying these days?

TOM

We're not the enemy.

THE CAPTAIN

That remains to be seen.

TOM

Your sergeant said this was Wyoming.

That draws a long, curious stare from the Captain.

THE CAPTAIN

This is the Mountain Free State. Or what remains of it.

TOM

The Mountain . . . Captain, what's *happened*?

Cat has figured it out; it's obvious.

CAT

Warring.

THE CAPTAIN

Twenty-nine years of it.

TOM

(shocked)

    Twenty-nine . . .

THE CAPTAIN

    You heard me.

(beat, brusque)

    My turn. I would like some answers. What's your purpose here? Where did you come from?

TOM

    Los Angeles.

THE CAPTAIN

    Do I look like a fool to you? There is no Los Angeles.

(to sergeant)

    Did you find their supplies?

SERGEANT

    The only clothing they've got is what they're wearing, and they had no food at all.

THE CAPTAIN

    How about a vehicle?

CAT

    Walked.

The Captain looks at Tom, who SHRUGS.

TOM

    Ah . . . I hate to say it, but we did.

THE CAPTAIN

(rising)

    You're either a madman or a liar. We don't have food for either. Sergeant, take this man and—

The Captain breaks off as a WOMAN SOLDIER bursts inside the hutch, breathless and scared.

> WOMAN SOLDIER
>
> Captain, it's Barbara. She's gone into labor. Something's gone wrong.

> TOM
>
> Take me there.

(no one moves)

> I'm a doctor. I can help . . .

The Captain studies Tom a moment, uncertain. We hear a SCREAM. It makes up his mind. He NODS. Tom rushes from the hutch with the woman soldier.

CUT TO

INT.—WOMEN'S HUTCH—LATER

Candles and a smoking torch provide the only light. The hutch houses the army's five women. On one cot, Whitmore shudders and pants in the agony of labor.

The sergeant and the other women have gathered to help, but Tom is the only man in the hutch. He kneels between Whitmore's legs. Cat watches from the door, curious as her namesake.

> WHITMORE
>
> It hurts . . . oh, please . . . it hurts . . .

> TOM
>
> Bear down. That's it. Go on, scream if you have to.

She does. Tom ignores it, concentrating.

                                TOM

Barbara, listen to me. It's a breech birth. I'm going to have to
reach in and try and turn the baby around. It's going to hurt.
Are you ready?

Biting her lip, face damp with sweat, Whitmore NODS.

                                TOM

        Here we go.

CLOSE ON CAT

Wide-eyed, watching. Whitmore's next scream is SHATTERING.
Cat pales, whirls, and flees the hutch.

EXT.—WOMEN'S HUTCH—CONTINUOUS

In headlong flight, Cat runs right into the Captain, waiting with a few
other men outside the hutch. The Captain catches her by her arms,
holds her a moment.

                        THE CAPTAIN
        What's happening?

Cat shakes her head wildly; she's the wrong one to ask. She wrenches
free of the Captain, and runs.

DISSOLVE TO

EXT.—WOMEN'S HUTCH—LATER

The Captain and the other men are still waiting. It has grown quiet in
the hutch. Finally the sergeant emerges.

                        SERGEANT
        It's a little girl.

The Captain nods. He shows no visible emotion.

> THE CAPTAIN
>
> And Whitmore?

> SERGEANT
>
> The doc says she'll make it. She wants to see you, Captain.

The Captain enters the hutch.

INT.—WOMEN'S HUTCH—CONTINUOUS

The mother is cradling a tiny newborn to her breast. She looks exhausted and weak, but happy. Tom is drying his hands.

> WHITMORE
>
> Look at her, John. Isn't she beautiful? Would you like to hold her?

The Captain looks uncomfortable. He doesn't know what to say. Whitmore pulls the child closer.

> WHITMORE
>
> She's going to be all right, isn't she?

> THE CAPTAIN
>
> She's going to be fine. We'll be going south as soon as the weather breaks. It's still warm down there south of Mexico. The oceans are full of fish, and there are green valleys where the food grows right out of the ground.

INTERCUT

with reaction shots from Tom, listening. The Captain gently touches the baby's head as she nurses.

THE CAPTAIN

I promise you, Whitmore. She's going to grow up under blue skies. She's going to taste honey and ride a horse and play in the sun. I promise you.

CLOSE ON WHITMORE

There are tears in her eyes. Tears of joy, tears of sorrow? Maybe both. She bites her lip, and nods.

WHITMORE

I want to name her Eve. It will be a new world, won't it? And she's the first...

THE CAPTAIN

It's a good name.

Whitmore SMILES.

RESUME

as the Captain gets up. He looks at Tom.

THE CAPTAIN

Doctor, if I could have a word with you outside.

Tom follows him out.

EXT.—WOMEN'S HUTCH—CONTINUOUS

Outside the hutch, the Captain turns to face Tom. The sergeant, standing nearby, listens to their exchange.

THE CAPTAIN

So you really are a doctor.

TOM

Not a liar or a madman?

Cat, hiding around the corner of the hutch, hears Tom's voice and comes creeping back into view. She listens.

THE CAPTAIN

Maybe all three. It doesn't matter.
(sees Cat, in hiding)
Come out of there.

Cat emerges, shyly.

TOM

Cat, are you all right? Why did you run away?

CAT

Too much hurting. Dying.

TOM

Childbirth doesn't have to be fatal, Cat.

CAT

No dying?

TOM

No dying.

THE CAPTAIN

You had a lot to do with that, it seems. We need a doctor. And we always need women. You're both drafted. Sergeant, explain the terms of enlistment to our new recruits.

The Captain walks off. The sergeant takes over.

SERGEANT

Three articles. First, you obey orders. Second, you serve as long as we want you. Third...the penalty for desertion is death.

OFF the look on Tom's face, we

FADE OUT

END OF ACT IV

ACT V

FADE IN

EXT.—FLOATER—DAY

Inside are crates of canned food, stacks of wood and faded yellow newspaper, bundles of old clothing. The QUARTERMASTER, jowly and unshaven, tosses down a bundle of clothing from the tailgate.

> QUARTERMASTER
> Here you go. You put on six, eight shirts, hey, who needs a coat, right?

Cat pokes her finger through a hole, SNIFFS at the stain around the hole.

> QUARTERMASTER
> That's good luck, you know. I mean, what's the odds on another bullet hitting that same spot, right?

Cat starts pulling on the shirts, layer on layer. A little blood does not bother her at all.

> TOM
> We need warm socks.

> QUARTERMASTER
> Try the five-and-dime.

The quartermaster hands down a couple of rifles.

QUARTERMASTER
This here is your rifle. Make sure you don't lose it. If the enemy shows up, you can hit him with it.

Cat grabs her rifle eagerly, checking the action.

TOM
You mean there's no ammunition?

The quartermaster LAUGHS like that's the funniest thing he's heard in years.

TOM
What good is a rifle without ammunition?

The sergeant gives him a wry, bemused smile.

SERGEANT
Good enough to capture you.

OFF Tom's reaction, we

DISSOLVE TO

INT.—MESS TENT—EVENING

Tom and Cat, wearing their new "uniforms" and looking as ragtag as the rest of this army, accept tin plates of canned beans and mystery meat from the COOK, and carry them to empty places on the mess hall bench.

Cat picks up the meat with her fingers, tears at it with her teeth. She's hungry.

CAT

(her mouth full)

Good. Hot. Eat, Toe Mas.

There's a smear of GREASE around her lips as she grins at him over a ragged piece of meat. She wipes it away with the back of her sleeve. Tom holds up a FORK.

TOM

Remind me to teach you how to use a fork.

He picks up his knife, tries to cut his meat. It's hard. Now it's Cat's turn to grin.

CAT

Use teeth. Better than forks.

Her smile fades as the quartermaster seats himself on the bench beside her. She tries to ignore him.

QUARTERMASTER

Your girlfriend's hungry.

TOM

She's not my girlfriend.

QUARTERMASTER

Your loss. Nice-looking girl like her, nobody to keep her snug at night.

(to Cat)

You come out and visit me tonight, I'll keep you nice and warm. Maybe I can even find you a pair of socks.

He slides close to Cat.

TIGHT ON CAT'S LEG

Under the bench. The quartermaster puts his hand on her knee, slides it slowly up her thigh, his fingers groping.

ANGLE ON CAT

Her eyes flick sideways. That's all the warning he gets. He has one hand on the table and the other under it.

> QUARTERMASTER
> I used to give roses to the girls. When there *were* roses. Hey, roses, socks, what's the difference? They both smell.

He starts to LAUGH at his own joke. Cat picks up a FORK and drives it down brutally into the quartermaster's hand. The man SHRIEKS in sudden agony, and leaps up, clutching his bleeding hand.

> QUARTERMASTER
> My hand . . .

Cat grins at Tom, her eyes sparkling.

> CAT
> Knowing how to use forks. See.

> QUARTERMASTER
> You filthy little . . .

> TOM
> (rising)
> Don't touch her.

The sergeant puts a hand on Tom to cool him.

> SERGEANT
> At ease, Lake. Timms, get back to the floater.

QUARTERMASTER
I was just trying to be nice to her.

The other soldiers don't have much sympathy.

WOMAN SOLDIER
Next time maybe she'll stick it between your legs.

The quartermaster GLARES at them all, and EXITS the mess tent, angry. Tom sits back down.

SERGEANT
He was a good man once.
(shrugs)
Things'll be better once we're moving again. Heading south.

Behind her, Walsh LAUGHS derisively.

WALSH
Yeah? When will that be, sarge? Tomorrow? Day after, you think?
(beat)
Face it. We're never moving south. We been here eighteen months. We'll die here.

WOMAN SOLDIER
The Captain says as soon as the weather breaks...

WALSH
Nothing's going to break around here but us. We're out of ammo, out of fuel, and sooner or later we're going to run out of food. We're all dead men.

He EXITS the mess tent, followed by two other men who obviously agree. A grim silence settles.

                          TOM
        Your vehicles...that tank, the hovercraft...

                       SERGEANT
(wearily)
        The big floater died eighteen months ago. That was the last.
        We have thousands of miles to go, and no transport.

                          CAT
        Walk.

                       SERGEANT
        Even if we could make it through the blizzards on foot without
        freezing to death, there's no way to carry all the food we'd
        need.

No one has the heart to say anything more. The faces in the mess tent
reflect resignation and despair. The sergeant gets to her feet.

                       SERGEANT
        Lake, you're on sentry duty tonight.

                          TOM
        How do you know I won't just run off?

                       SERGEANT
(bitter laugh)
        And where the hell do you think you're going to run to?

DISSOLVE TO

EXT.—BASE CAMP—NIGHT

Tom, huddled up in his ragged clothes, rifle slung over a shoulder,
walks his rounds as sentry. Tom's breath STEAMS in the chill night air.
He looks cold, miserable, lonely.

The night is cold and still. The wind howls through the camp. Tom, gloveless, tries warming his hands in his armpits. It doesn't work. He fumbles in his pockets, takes out his wallet.

TIGHT ON TOM'S HAND

as he opens the wallet to a PHOTO of Laura.

RESUME

Tom looks at the photograph for a long time. He has come a long way, and there may be no way back. For the first time, Tom is thinking about that. We see the pain on his face.

Then we HEAR a noise. The sound of motion.

                              TOM
        Hello? Who goes there?

No answer. Hurriedly, he tucks away the photograph and unslings his rifle.

TRACKING WITH TOM

as he moves in the direction of the noise. We HEAR it again. A stealthy footfall, from the direction of the snowbound vehicles. Tom creeps along past the old yellow school bus, stops. We HEAR a MUF-FLED THUD, a GROAN.

Tom screws up his courage, RUNS toward the cab of the big floater. Outside, he finds the quartermaster lying in the snow, out cold. He gapes at the unconscious man for a moment. Cat sticks her head out of the cab.

                              CAT
        Quiet now, Toe Mas. Making noise loud. Too much.

                              TOM
(surprised)
        Cat, what are you—

She opens the door, grabs him, pulls him in.

                              CAT
        No talk. Inside now.

INT.—FLOATER CAB—CONTINUOUS

It looks like the cab of a semi. Cat slides down under the dash, lights a
MATCH. She's inspecting something.

                              TOM
(whisper)
        What are you doing here?

                              CAT
        Looking. Seeing.

She blows out the match, pulls herself up beside him

                              CAT
        Leaving now.

Cat pushes up her sleeves, shirt after shirt, opens her hand.

The HOLOGRAM winks on. The world spins slowly between her
fingers; alien symbols squirm across the globe; a light flashes in
Montana.

                              TOM
        Another door? To where?

                              CAT
        Out.

                              TOM

(frustrated)
        Out. Out where? How do you know where it leads?

                              CAT

        Go through. Find out.

                              TOM

        Cat, is there a door that leads back the way we came? Can I get
        home again?

                              CAT

        Not knowing. Maybe. Maybe this door.

Tom studies the position of the light.

                              TOM

        That's got to be somewhere in Montana. When does it open?

She lowers her arm. The holo WINKS OUT.

                              CAT

        Two days. Going now.

                              TOM

(disappointed)
        It's too far, Cat. A hundred miles, at least. We'll be lucky to
        make ten miles a day on foot.

                              CAT

        Not feet. Taking this.

She touches the controls of the floater.

                              TOM

        There's no power, remember?

                              CAT

Fixing it.

                              TOM

Who? You?

                              CAT

Knowing how. Thane teaching. Power cells.

It takes Tom a moment to comprehend. Then it hits him.

                              TOM

Power cells—God, yes!
(grins)
            Cat, I could kiss you.

                              CAT

Not knowing *kiss*. Going now, kissing later.

                              TOM

(sudden doubt)
            Wait a minute. The food . . .
(beat)
            All the food is on the truck. If we take it, these people will die.

                              CAT

Dying anyway. Fast, slow. No matter.

                              TOM

That's not what you said back in the cave. Remember? You
thought life was worth something then, even if it was only a
few more days, a few more hours . . .

Cat gets a stubborn look on her face. She doesn't like having her own
words thrown back at her.

>   CAT

> Different then. Talking us then. Talking them now.

Tom stares at her, aghast, realizing maybe for the first time how strong her drive for survival is.

>   TOM

> They're people, Cat. Just like us. There's a baby in that camp not six hours old. A baby I delivered. I'm not going to sentence her to death.

Cat does not understand.

>   CAT

> Leaving now! Going fast!

>   TOM

> Then go.

>   CAT

> You too.

>   TOM

> I'm not going, Cat.

Cat is furious. Her mouth is set in a grim line.

>   CAT
>   *Yes!*

>   TOM

> (quiet but firm)
>   No.

They stare each other down. Finally Cat lowers her eyes.

                              CAT

(surrender)
        Not going too.

CUT TO

EXT.—CAPTAIN'S HUTCH—NIGHT

Tom leads Cat inside the captain's hutch. The windows are all dark, as
if the captain were asleep.

INT.—CAPTAIN'S HUTCH—CONTINUOUS

The interior of the hutch is PITCH DARK. We can barely discern the
figures of Tom and Cat as they pass the windows. Cat is nervous.

                              CAT
        Too dark.

                              TOM
        Captain? Are you . . .

Behind him, a match FLARES to sudden light. The Captain is not
asleep. He is sitting up, behind his desk. He has a service revolver in
one hand. He lights a candle with the other. The hutch fills with flickering light.

                          THE CAPTAIN
        Stay right there. I promise you, *this* gun is loaded.

                              TOM
        We thought you were asleep.

                          THE CAPTAIN
        You thought wrong.

The Captain leans back in his chair. He keeps the pistol pointed at Tom
and Cat. Cat's hand cannon is on the table in front of him.

THE CAPTAIN

You two. Odd. I had rather expected Walsh and his friends.

TOM

Expected Walsh to . . . ?

THE CAPTAIN

To try and kill me, of course. The surest way to promotion.

TOM

We're not here to kill you. We want to talk.

THE CAPTAIN

Yes. You strike me as the sort of man who is much better at talking than at killing. Now your girlfriend here . . .

CAT

Not my girlfriend.

Tom is momentarily bemused by the echo.

TOM

Close, Cat. But we need to have a talk about pronouns.
(to Captain)
    Captain, is it true? About the warm place down south . . .

THE CAPTAIN

I knew a man who knew a man who had seen it with his own eyes.
(shrugs)
    A man needs hope if he wants to keep on living.

TOM

Can I show you something?

The Captain NODS. Tom crosses to the table, picks up one of the spare cylinders, rips the cap off the end.

ANGLE ON TOM'S HAND

as he holds up the magazine for the Captain to see. Inside is the red
GLOW of the power cell, PULSING with energy. The Captain leans
forward, puzzled and curious.

> THE CAPTAIN
>
> What is it?

> TOM
>
> Hope...

The Captain looks at Tom's face. He puts down his gun.

> THE CAPTAIN
>
> I'm listening.

CUT TO

EXT.—THE MOUNTAINS—NIGHT

Black sky over still, silent snows. Nothing moves but the wind
Suddenly we hear a CRACK, as loud as a clap of thunder, as sharp as a
sonic boom.

The darklord's palanquin is suddenly THERE, where there was nothing an instant before. Three surviving manhounds—Thane, Dyana,
and the second woman, JAELE—cling to the battered vehicle. The
palanquin is visibly damaged.

Thane leaps down to the snow, light as a panther. The hunt has resumed.

FADE OUT

END OF ACT V

ACT VI

FADE IN

EXT.—BASE CAMP—MORNING

The camp is feverish with activity. Soldiers are digging out the snowbound bus, securing the load in the floater, cannibalizing parts from the jeep and APC for the bus and the floater. A new animation and energy seems to have taken possession of the Captain's listless little army.

TIGHT ON CAT

Upside down under the raised hood of the floater, face and clothing covered with oil, cables running through her hands, her face as intent as a doctor in surgery. She holds out a hand, wordless. The woman soldier, assisting, puts a power cell in her palm. Cat solders it in place.

RESUME

The quartermaster, his head wrapped in a makeshift bandage to match the one on his hand, sticks his face out the driver's side window. He's excited.

> QUARTERMASTER
> She's showing a charge! Mother of God, look at it, the needle's halfway off the scale.

Cat climbs out, wipes her hands on a rag, NODS.

> SERGEANT
> Try the fans.
> (shouts)
> Stand clear! We're going to try and lift . . .

Soldiers SCRAMBLE out of the way. The quartermaster takes a deep breath, crosses himself, and turns the ignition. There's a high-pitched WHINE as the floater's electric turbines catch hold...and then the ROAR of the great fans under the floater as they start to turn.

LONG SHOT—THE FLOATER

The floater ROCKS back and forth for a moment. Snow comes SPRAYING out all around it, sending the spectators running. Then, slowly, majestically, the hovertruck begins to LIFT off the ground.

The soldiers break into a ragged CHEER.

CAT

All of a sudden, she's surrounded by people. They slap her on the back, grab her hand and pump it. She looks lost at first. Then she gets the idea and slowly begins to smile.

> SERGEANT
> One down. Now let's see what she can do with the tank.

CUT TO

EXT.—SCHOOL BUS—HOURS LATER

The soldiers are filing aboard the school bus, carrying rifles and duffle bags. A crew is at work chaining the bus to the floater. Cat and Tom wait while the Captain talks to the sergeant.

> THE CAPTAIN
> Take the old interstate as far as you can, but stay well clear of Denver. It's still too hot for safety.

> THE SERGEANT
> Yes, sir.

THE CAPTAIN

I should catch up to you by Sunday at the latest. If I'm not at
the rendezvous within the week, go on without me. Is that understood?

SERGEANT

Captain, we'd rather...

THE CAPTAIN

Is that understood?
(off her nod)
You keep on going. No matter what. Those turbines could
burn out any time. You get as far south as you can.

Whitmore is about to board the school bus. Her little girl is cradled in her arms, swathed in layers of clothing. She stops to say
good-bye.

WHITMORE

Doctor...thank you...for everything.

TOM

Take good care of her, you hear?

She KISSES him lightly. Cat watches, frowning.

WHITMORE

You too, Cat. Thank you.
(to Captain)
I...I wish you were going with us.

THE CAPTAIN

I won't be long. The sergeant will get you through.

Whitmore nods. She seems awkward, shy. She turns to board
the bus...and the Captain speaks up.

THE CAPTAIN
Barbara . . .
(she stops)
Could I . . . hold her?

She gives him the baby. The Captain takes the infant tenderly, holds her.

WHITMORE
She has your eyes.

The Captain gives her back the infant, and KISSES her. The kiss is tender and affectionate; it lasts a long time. Cat stares openly, curiously.

TOM
That's a kiss, Cat. They're kissing.

Whitmore is crying. Even the Captain's eyes are damp. They break apart with an effort.

THE CAPTAIN
Take her someplace warm, love.

Choked up, unable to speak, Barbara NODS and boards the bus. Tears are rolling down her face.

CAT
Kissing hurts.

TOM
(smiling)
Oh, I don't know about that.

CUT TO

THE TOW CHAINS

The turbines WHINE. The fans ROAR. The floater lifts off the snow. The chains rattle and clank as the slack is pulled tight.

THE FLOATER

starts forward. Hovering a foot above the snow on a cushion of air, it begins the long journey south. The chains grow taut. For a moment, the bus refuses to move.

THE TIRES

of the bus are frozen into the snow, rimed in ice.

THE FLOATER

The whine of the turbines grows higher and faster as it strains against its load. Nothing. Until finally

THE ICE ON THE TIRES

cracks, and the big tires begin to roll.

TOM AND CAT

watch as the vehicles start to move, very slowly. A window in the bus opens. Walsh sticks his head out.

> WALSH
>
> Hey, Cat...
>
> (off her glare)
>
> You made a liar out of me, pretty lady. I owe you one.

He tosses his warm, heavy, fur-collared parka out of the window at Cat. She catches it, astonished.

> WALSH
>
> Keep it. It's warm where I'm going.

And then the bus is past. Cat stares after it.

> TOM
> Let's go. The Captain is waiting.

REVERSE ANGLE—OVER TOM'S SHOULDER

to where the huge, battle-scarred tank waits, its own turbines slowly starting to rev. They walk toward it, Cat shrugging into the parka as she goes.

MATCH DISSOLVE TO

EXT.—BASE CAMP—HOURS LATER

The empty hutches and abandoned vehicles sit forlorn in the snow. The floater, the school bus, and the tank are all gone. Dyana strides over a rise, to where the darklord waits in its palanquin, looking down over the camp. She bows her head to report. Jaele and a sullen Thane listen.

> DYANA
> A military encampment, my lord. Recently deserted. I found these.

CLOSE ON DYANA'S HAND

as she opens her fist. Inside are two black cylinders.

> THANE
> Cylinders from the hand cannon.

> DYANA
> They've been stripped of their power cells. Useless.

> THANE
> But they prove she was here.

RESUME

Within the shadowed darkfield, the alien STIRS angrily.

> DARKLORD
>
> And she is gone again!

> DYANA
>
> One group went north, another south.

> THANE
>
> The next door is north. Cat will run to it.

> DARKLORD
>
> Then those who went south are nothing to us. Dyana, take us north.

She BOWS her head in acknowledgment. Thane speaks up.

> THANE
>
> My lord, your vehicle is damaged. Travel will be slow. She may reach the door first.

> DARKLORD
>
> Pray that she does not, Thane, disgraced, twice-failed. I will have her, or I will have you in her stead.

> THANE
>
> Send me ahead, lord. She must go around the mountains. I can take a more direct road, and secure the door.

> DARKLORD
>
> Make it so. And do not harm her. She will serve my pleasure, not your empty human pride.

> THANE
>
> To hear is to obey.

Thane climbs onto the OUTRIDER on one side of the palanquin, straddling it like a motorcycle. He works a control. The front section of the outrider slides forward and DETACHES from the main vehicle.

DARKLORD

Be warned, dog. There must be no third failure. My mercy is not without limit.

Thane BOWS his head. The outrider takes off across the snow, swift and silent.

CUT TO

EXT.—THE MOUNTAINS—DAY

The tank, hovering on its cushion of air, makes its way north over the wasteland of snow and ice toward the mountains.

INT.—THE TANK—DAY

The interior of the tank is cramped and cold. The vehicle is obviously in bad shape; in b.g. are circuit boards seared by fire, panels torn out, evidence of makeshift repair. The sound of the fans is loud.

The Captain drives. Tom is seated in the turret gunner's position, Cat huddled at his feet.

TOM

I've been thinking. You said it had been twenty-nine years. That would mean your war started in—

THE CAPTAIN

October, 1962. But it was never my war.

TOM

(figures it out)

The Cuban missile crisis . . . the Soviets never backed down, did they?

The Captain gives a weary shake of his head.

                    TOM
How bad was it?

                THE CAPTAIN
We lost a few cities. Boston, Denver, Washington...but we won.
The new president—McNamara, I think it was—he said so.
People were dancing in the streets. Flags flying everywhere, vic-
tory parades, the second baby boom...God, what fools we were.

                    TOM
Afterwards...the fallout.

                THE CAPTAIN
Poison rains. Crop failures. The survivors swarmed out of the
cities, starving. There was no place for them to go. The lights
went out all over America.

                    CAT
Darklords...

                    TOM
Not here. They did it themselves here. Just men and
women...

                THE CAPTAIN
The food wars were the worst of it. Once they started there
was no stopping them. And all the time the winters were getting longer and colder.

He shakes his head, as if to shake off the memories.

Then, suddenly, a CLAXON sounds. The tank SHAKES. Smoke starts
to pour out of an instrument panel. Cat covers her ears against the
noise.

The Captain grabs a fire extinguisher, rips off a panel cover, and starts to spray. The fans GRIND and fall silent, and the tank crashes to earth, jarringly. The smoke is thick.

THE CAPTAIN

Lake, pop the hatch. *Move it!* Before we all suffocate...

EXT.—THE TANK—CONTINUOUS

Smoke POURS from the open hatch as Tom climbs out. He pulls Cat out after him. The Captain comes last, holding a cloth over his face and COUGHING.

TOM

What happened?

CAT

Firc, Toc Mas.

TOM

I figured out that much.

THE CAPTAIN

Some kind of overload. This thing should have been put out of its misery years ago.

TOM

Can we repair it?

The Captain looks around. There's nothing but mountains, as far as the eye can see. Snow and ice everywhere.

THE CAPTAIN

Do we have a choice?

CUT TO

EXT.—ANOTHER PART OF THE MOUNTAINS—SIMULTA-
NEOUS

Thane rides the outrider through the foothills. His face is grim and implacable. He is moving very fast, eating up the miles. The mountains
loom large ahead of him.

DISSOLVE TO

EXT.—THE TANK—EVENING

The Captain has been working on the tank for hours. Cat sits perched
on top of the turret, their sentry. When the Captain emerges, she
comes vaulting down to hear.

                          TOM
        How does it look?

The Captain's face is grim.

                      THE CAPTAIN
        I can jerry-rig something to replace the burnt-out circuit
        boards. The real problem is this.

He TOSSES something at Tom, who snatches it from the air.

TIGHT ON TOM'S HAND

He's holding a power cell. It's dead, blackened.

RESUME

Cat moves close. Tom gives her the dead power cell with a sour look
on his face.

THE CAPTAIN

The faulty board caused an overload. We're going to need another power cell.

TOM

We don't *have* another power cell. There were only two spare cartridges.

Tom looks helplessly out over the barren winterscape.

TOM

Where the hell is the Energizer bunny when you really need him?

THE CAPTAIN

Excuse me?

TOM

Never mind. What do we do now?

They look at each other helplessly.

THE CAPTAIN

We die.

Tom is startled by the sudden despair in the Captain's tone. If this man is giving up, then the situation must be truly hopeless. The Captain's voice is weary.

THE CAPTAIN

Funny way to end it, though. I always thought I'd die in battle. A soldier's death . . .

(beat)

My father was a soldier, and his father before him. For them it was all about honor and courage, about defending your country from its enemies. Then the war came, and there was no more country, and the enemies I was killing one year turned out to be the people I'd been defending the year before.

(beat)

Nothing was ever right in this war. Not even the dying.

Tom doesn't know what to say, but Cat does.

CAT

No dying now.

She draws the hand cannon, pops out the cartridge. The last cartridge. She offers it to the Captain. He takes it from her hand solemnly, realizing what it means.

THE CAPTAIN

Without this, your weapon is useless.

TOM

Cat, are you sure?

CAT

Sure.

THE CAPTAIN

You're leaving yourself defenseless. If your enemies find you . . . these darklords you've told me about . . . you'll have no way to fight them.

CAT

Lots of ways. Kicking. Biting. Throwing rocks.

The Captain draws his revolver from its holster, presses it into Cat's hand.

THE CAPTAIN

Here. There are only four bullets left, but it's something. Take it.

Cat takes the gun, examines it.

                              CAT
          Something. Better than rocks.
(tucks it away)
          Fixing now. Going now.

The Captain turns back to the tank to resume work.

DISSOLVE TO EXT.—CLIFF FACE—NIGHT—ANGLE DOWN

A bitter wind HOWLS across a sheer cliff of rock and ice. The ground
is a long way down, the top of the precipice a long way up. A HAND
enters frame, grabs a precarious fingerhold. Then Thane pulls himself
up into view. His fingers are BLOODY from clawing at the rock, and
there is FROST on his face, yet he pushes himself on.

As Thane CLIMBS out of sight, we

DISSOLVE TO

EXT.—MOUNTAIN PASS—THE NEXT DAY

The tank climbs slowly up a steep slope, and STOPS where a narrow
pass opens between two high, ice-covered walls of stone. After a moment the hatch opens. Cat scrambles out first. Tom and the Captain are
right behind.

Cat stands on top of the tank, exposes the bracelet, and SCANS. The
BLUE GLOW is brightest when her fist points straight ahead, through
the pass and up the mountain.

                              CAT
          There. That way.

THE CAPTAIN

The pass is too narrow.

He glances up above them, at the looming mountains.

THE CAPTAIN

I don't like the look of that snow up there. If I try to get the tank through, I could bring down half the mountain.

TOM

Cat, how close is the door?

CAT

Close. Two hex, three hex.

TOM

I think we can make it the rest of the way on foot.

THE CAPTAIN

Then this is it. I need to get back to my people.

TOM

You can come with us.

THE CAPTAIN

This is my world. Besides...
(smiling)
I still think you're mad.

Tom SMILES. They CLASP hands. Then Tom and Cat jump off into the snow. Their feet drive DEEP FOOTPRINTS as they land. Tom slips and goes down. Cat pulls him to his feet. The Captain watches them walk off up the slope, then shuts the hatch.

MATCH DISSOLVE TO

THE SAME SPOT—AN HOUR LATER—ANGLE ON DYANA

She kneels beside the deep footprints that Cat and Tom left in the snow. She stands.

THE PALANQUIN

floats close behind her. The creature in the darkfield leans forward eagerly.

> DYANA
>
> They left their vehicle here and continued on foot. Not more than an hour ago.

> DARKLORD
>
> Then she is ours.

> DYANA
>
> What will you do with her, my lord?

> DARKLORD
>
> To you, pain is as short and sharp as a scream. You cannot hear its music. But I can write a symphony with those notes, manhound.

Dyana doesn't want to hear any more. She vaults aboard the palanquin. They push on, through the pass.

CUT TO

EXT.—MINE ENTRANCE—DAY

Tom is breathing hard. Even Cat is flushed by the exertion of the climb, but when she sees the dark hole of the MINE ENTRANCE up ahead, she RUNS. Pushing up her sleeve, she exposes the bracelet, makes a fist. The insets begin to STROBE, one two three, one two three.

TOM

(breathing hard)

Bingo. We found it.

Thane steps out of the darkness inside the mine.

THANE

So you did.

Cat SHRINKS back away from him. She whips out the battered old revolver the Captain gave her, swings it up with both hands, and FIRES without a moment's hesitation.

The bullet catches Thane in the shoulder. He staggers, then straightens himself, smiling.

THANE

The child has a new toy to play with.

BLOOD is seeping from his shoulder wound, but Thane seems to feel very little pain. Tom is horrified.

THANE

That which does not kill me makes me stronger.

Cat SNARLS at him, and FIRES again. The second shot is a clean miss. We hear it RICOCHET off the rocks.

THANE

Afraid? You should be. She is coming, little animal. She is close now. Do you know what she will do with you?

Cat FIRES. The bullet catches Thane square in the stomach. He GRUNTS, bends, clutches at the wound—but only for a moment. Slowly, he straightens, his hands falling back to his sides.

THANE

That one almost hurt.

Only one shot left. Cat is about to use it when Tom catches her wrist.

TOM

Cat, *enough*.

THANE

Cat. Yes. I gave her that name, shadow man. Did she tell you that?
(with mounting rage)
I taught her to speak. To read. To use machines. I gave her life. Food. Honor. I took her as my mate.

TOM

(realizing)
You *loved* her...
(beat)
Let her *go,* Thane. What kind of man are you?

THANE

Not a man. A manhound.

Behind him, suddenly, the mine entrance LIGHTS with a BRIL-
LIANT BLUE LIGHT as the door opens.

CAT

The door...

THANE

There it is. All you need to do is get past me.

At his sides, his hands coil into fists, and six-inch STEEL SPIKES slide
from his knuckles. OFF that moment, we

CUT TO

EXT.—IN THE PASS—SIMULTANEOUS

The darklord drives the palanquin upward.

> DARKLORD
> Faster! Faster! The door is opening. She must not escape. *Faster!*

A half-mile in front of them, the HOVER TANK slowly lifts into view.

> DARKLORD
> What is that? That is a weapons system. Stop it.

The turret of the tank slowly swings around.

INT.—THE TANK

The Captain works the controls, a grim smile on his face.

> THE CAPTAIN
> Welcome to my world, you son-of-a-bitch.

He presses the firing switch.

EXT.—THE TANK

The turret gun belches FLAME. The noise is a hammer blow.

THE PALANQUIN

veers off wildly as a shell EXPLODES directly underneath it. Both manhounds are THROWN OFF. The darkfield absorbs most of the damage, but the darklord SHRIEKS in fury, a torrent of unintelligible alien sounds.

The palanquin returns fire. A LIGHTNING BOLT flies down the pass, smashing into the tank. Then another. Another. The bolts CRACK through the air, and the pass rolls with THUNDER.

INT.—THE TANK—TIGHT ON THE CAPTAIN

He's thrown sideways as the tank is hit. His lights go dark. The vehicle loses power and CRASHES, jarring him.

> THE CAPTAIN
> Hit me again. Hit me again. Come on, *again*.
> (another hit)
> Yes!

Smoke is pouring from his bulkheads now, but the Captain SMILES. He hears something else: a deep, ominous RUMBLING from above.

ANGLE THROUGH THE DARKFIELD

The darklord on her palanquin hears it too. Inside the darkfield, the great distorted form twists in fear, and tries to shelter itself with its arms.

> DARKLORD
> Nooooooo.

The word disintegrates into a SHRILL ALIEN SCREAM, and

AN AVALANCHE

thunders down and buries tank, palanquin, and all.

CUT TO

EXT.—MINE ENTRANCE—ON THANE

His head SNAPS sideways at the sound of the avalanche. In that brief moment of distraction, Cat breaks free of Tom, snaps up the gun, and FIRES her last shot.

The bullet catches Thane in the head, a grazing shot that bloodies his temple. He spins and goes down. Cat flings away the empty gun and scrambles past him to the door.

The BLUE GLOW of the door is fading, growing darker. Thane is already moving, rolling over, hand on his bloody temple. Tom stands frozen.

> CAT
>
> (to Tom)
> Coming *on*!

He doesn't need a second hint. Tom runs, jumping over Thane. Cat takes him by the hand. Together, they LEAP through the door, and we

SMASH CUT TO

EXT.—THE GREENWOOD—DAY

as Tom and Cat LAND in a pile of fallen leaves. The sky is a deep blue overhead. They are in an autumn forest, the foliage brilliant all around. In the distance, perched high on a mountain beside a glittering waterfall, is a CASTLE. Tom stares at it.

An ARROW thunks into the tree trunk an inch from Tom's head, he jerks back, and looks at Cat.

> TOM
> Here we go again.

CAT

Bingo.

And OFF Cat's GRIN, we

FADE OUT

THE END

EIGHT

DOING THE WILD CARD SHUFFLE

YOU CAN TAKE THE BOY OUT OF BAYONNE, BUT YOU CAN'T TAKE BAYONNE OUT OF THE boy. The same is true of funny books. I admit it. Cut me and I still bleed four-colored ink.

Maybe I don't know the name of the current Green Lantern, but I can still recite Hal Jordan's oath, and tell you how it differed from the one that Alan Scott once swore when he recharged his ring. I can name all of the Challengers of the Unknown for you and give you the original line-up of the Avengers, the X-Men, and the Justice League of America (do I really have to include Snapper Carr?). I have no doubt that in some alternate universe Marvel Comics *did* hire me when I applied in 1971, and right now in that world I am sitting at home muttering and gnawing at my wrists as I watch blockbuster movies based on my characters and stories rake in hundreds of millions of dollars while I receive exactly nothing.

In this world I was spared that fate. In this world I wrote short stories and novellas and novels instead of funny books, and later on screenplays and teleplays as well. Yet that love of superheroes never left me, even when I was well-established as a pro. I still had one more good "text story" in me, I figured. Maybe more than one, but one for sure; a gritty, hard-nosed tale about what might befall a would-be superhero in the real world.

The germ of the notion went back years and years, but for most of that time it remained no more than a few lines in my files. A kid like me, raised on comic books, finds himself blessed (or is it cursed?) with an actual super-power. What would he do with it? Ignore it? Exploit it? Try to don a spandex costume and fight crime? How would it change his life? How would the real world react to someone who actually did possess powers and abilities far be-yond those of mortal men?

(That was my working title: "With Powers and Abilities Far Beyond Those of Mortal Men." The phrase is from the old *Superman* TV show, of course, and I later learned that DC Comics had trademarked it, so it was just as well that I never used it.)

Precisely what those powers and abilities should be I never did work out, which may be why I never wrote the story. For a long time I leaned toward pyrokinesis, until Stephen King came out with *Firestarter* in 1980. Not only did King's novel feature a girl who could ignite fires with her mind, but it also gave her father a superpower of his own, a kind of mind control. Though my handling of the theme would have been very different, I could not help feeling as though King had beaten me to the punch.

My life was changing in more important ways in 1980, though. At the end of 1979, I had left my teaching job at Clarke College and moved from Iowa to New Mexico to try and make a go of it as a full-time writer. My marriage had ended in the course of the move, so I arrived in the Land of Enchantment a single man again. Santa Fe has remained my home ever since. Though I ended up spending years in Los Angeles working in television and film, I never truly *moved* there. Instead I would rent a furnished apartment in one of the sprawling Oakwood complexes, or a guest house in someone's backyard, but the moment my current project wrapped I would be on the road again, headed home to New Mexico. Santa Fe was the place where I hung my hats and paid my taxes, the place where I kept my books and my funny books and the old double-breasted pin-striped mustard-yellow sports jacket that had not fit me for a decade.

And Santa Fe was where Parris was too, holding down the fort. We'd met at a convention in 1975, a few months before I entered into my ill-considered marriage. I knew I liked her the moment she told me that "A Song for Lya" made her cry (well, she was a stone fox too, and we were both naked when we met, but never mind about that, it's none of your business). Parris and I stayed in touch after that con, exchanging occasional letters through all the years when I was teaching Catholic girls and she was selling sno-cones and shoveling elephant dung for Ringling Brothers. In 1981 we got together at another convention, and she came to Santa Fe to stay with me a while. That "while" will have lasted twenty-two years by the time you read this. Now and again one of my readers will ask me why I don't write sad stories of unrequited love any longer, the way I did so often in the '70s.

Parris is to blame for that. You can only write that stuff when your heart is broken.

When I first moved to Santa Fe in the wake of my divorce, I knew no one in the city but Roger Zelazny, and him only slightly. Roger took me under his wing. On the first Friday of every month we would drive down to Albuquerque to lunch with Tony Hillerman, Norm Zollinger, Fred Saberhagen, and the other New Mexico writers. I also dropped in on the Albuquerque SF club, where I met the local fans and still more writers and aspiring writers. Before very long, I found myself gaming with some of them.

Though I had been a serious chess player from seventh grade through college, and enjoyed *Risk* and *Diplomacy* and other board games, I had never played *Dungeons & Dragons* or any other role-playing game until I moved to New Mexico. Parris had, however, and she convinced me to give it a try. The bunch that we fell in with were mostly hardcore fans, and half of them were writers. At the time Parris and I joined the group, they were playing Chaosium's *Call of Cthulhu,* based on the works of H. P. Lovecraft, so I felt right at home. Since the rest of the party were all intrepid adventurers determined to save the world from the Cthulhu cults, I played a journalist who was yellow in both senses of the word. As my friends died screaming or went insane, I would run away to cable my story to the *Herald.* Our sessions were like some madcap improv theater, with shuggoths.

Before the year was out, I had become so enamored of gaming that I was running a *Call of Cthulhu* campaign of my own. I'd found that I enjoyed being a gamemaster even more than being a player.

Which brings us to September 1983, when Vic Milan presented me with a new game for my birthday. *SuperWorld* reawakened the frustrated comic book writer inside me, and soon replaced *Call of Cthulhu* as the group's favorite game. We played it obsessively for more than a year, two or three times a week, and no one became more obsessed than me. As gamemaster, I found myself dusting off old characters like Manta Ray and coming up with new ones, villains chiefly...plus one hero who floated around in an iron shell, and called himself the Great and Powerful Turtle. My players, half of whom were writers, created some unforgettable characters of their own; Yeoman, Crypt Kicker, Peregrine, Elephant Girl, Modular Man, Cap'n Trips, Straight Arrow, Black Shadow, Topper, and the Harlem Hammer were only a few of the strange and wondrous folks who first made their appearance in our *SuperWorld* sessions.

The tale of how *SuperWorld* ultimately begat *Wild Cards* is one that I've told numerous times before, most notably in my afterwords for the iBooks reissues of the early volumes of the series. I won't repeat myself here; the reissues are easily available, for those who would like to read the grisly details. Suffice it to say that a number of us fell in love with our characters, and began to think they might have possibilities beyond the game.

Shared worlds were all the rage in the early '80s, thanks to the tremendous success of the *Thieves World* anthologies edited by Bob Asprin and Lynn Abbey. The format was perfect for what we wanted to do with our *SuperWorld* characters, so I pitched the idea to my fellow gamers, filled out our ranks by recruiting Roger Zelazny, Howard Waldrop, Lew Shiner, Stephen Leigh, and half a dozen other writers from all across the country, and drew up a formal proposal for a three-volume anthology series called *Wild Cards*. Shawna McCarthy bought it, her first day on the job as an editor at Bantam Books.

All shared worlds are collaborations, to a greater or a lesser extent. Looking over *Thieves World* and its imitators, I realized that the shared worlds that worked the best were those that shared the most, where the story lines and characters were the most tightly intertwined. Right from the first, therefore, we resolved that *Wild Cards* would be more than just a collection of loosely connected stories set against a common background. We wanted to take the art of collaboration to a whole new level. To signal our intent, we called the books "mosaic novels" rather than anthologies.

I do think we succeeded for the most part... but as with any new form, there were bumps in the road, and lessons that we had to learn the hard way. Editing the series, I often felt like the ringmaster at a nine-ring circus, trying to keep order with a whip made out of spaghetti. Some days it was fun and some days it was frustrating, but it was never ever tedious. When everything was going smoothly, I liked to compare us to a symphony orchestra, with me as the conductor, but a better metaphor might be a herd of cats. We all know how easy it is to herd cats, don't we?

So here's to all the members of the Wild Cards Consortium, as zany and talented a bunch of cats as any editor could ever hope to herd: Roger

Zelazny, Howard Waldrop, Walter Jon Williams, Stephen Leigh, Gail Gerstner Miller, Lewis Shiner, John J. Miller, Victor Milan, Walton (Bud) Simons, Arthur Byron Cover, William F. Wu, Laura J. Mixon, Michael Cassutt, Sage Walker, Edward Bryant, Leanne C. Harper, Kevin Andrew Murphy, Steve Perrin, Parris, Royce Wideman, Pat Cadigan, Chris Claremont, Bob Wayne, and Daniel Abraham. And most of all, here's to Melinda M. Snodgrass, my tireless assistant editor, without whose diplomatic intercessions I would surely have killed and butchered at least four of the aforementioned.

Wild Cards was a hit right from the first, and not only by anthology standards. The sales of the first volume exceeded the sales of any of my novels to that date, save *Fevre Dream* alone, and the later books would be almost as successful. The reviews were excellent, by and large. Walter Jon Williams' story in the first book was a finalist for the Nebula, one of the few shared-world stories ever accorded that honor, and the series as a whole was nominated for the Hugo Award, losing in 1988 at New Orleans to Alan Moore's splendid graphic novel *Watchmen*.

Bantam was only too pleased to make an offer for three more volumes after the first three had been delivered. Our advances rose and rose again. The series became a popular topic for worldcon panels, and two regional conventions chose *Wild Cards* themes, and brought all the authors in as Guests of Honor. Marvel Comics did a *Wild Cards* miniseries under its Epic imprint, and Steve Jackson Games issued a role-playing game, bringing us full circle. Hollywood was heard from too. Disney Studios optioned the film rights to the books, and Melinda Snodgrass and I wrote several drafts of a *Wild Cards* screenplay in the early '90s.

The series began at virtually the same time as my association with *The Twilight Zone*, and continued my three seasons on *Beauty and the Beast*, through all my feature assignments and television pilots. That steady stream of books with my name on the covers undoubtedly helped to keep me alive in the worlds of science fiction and fantasy. Just as I had to return to Santa Fe from time to time during my Hollywood years, to remind myself of who I was and where I lived, I had to keep publishing books and short stories as well. If I hadn't…well, readers have short memories, I fear, and in recent years they have only grown shorter.

Given the long hours and high stress levels so typical of Hollywood, the last thing any television producer needs is a second job, but I had one, courtesy of *Wild Cards*. Not only did I edit the books, but I wrote for them, as often as I could find the time.

"Shell Games," my principal contribution to volume one, had antecedents that went way back. The bones of the story were ones I'd been gnawing on for years before I ever heard of *SuperWorld*; this was "With Powers and Abilities Far Beyond Those of Mortal Men," reworked to fit our new shared universe. (Never throw anything away.) I'd intended to use pyrokinesis for my hero's power, until *Firestarter*, but telekinesis worked just as well. The Great and Powerful Turtle began life as a minor character in our *SuperWorld* campaign, but would soon become quite a major one in *Wild Cards*. Mind you, a story and a game have very different needs, and what works splendidly for one may not work at all for the other, so the Turtle changed quite a bit before he hit the page.

"Shell Games" was not his tale alone, though; he shared the stage with Dr. Tachyon, a character created by Melinda Snodgrass. Working with other people's characters is one of the challenges of doing a shared world. It is often a lot of fun, and often a huge headache. Sometimes it is both at once. In her story "Degradation Rites," which preceded mine in *Wild Cards*, Melinda told how Dr. Tachyon had inadvertently destroyed the mind of a woman he loved in an effort to protect the identity of his ace patients from HUAC. The experience had destroyed Dr. Tachyon as well, and thereafter he had collapsed into a decade-long orgy of guilt, self-recrimination, and alcoholism. It was my job to drag him out of his funk in "Shell Games," and set him back on the path to recovery ... while also introducing my own characters.

If you have read this far, you will soon realize that Thomas Tudbury is far and away the most autobiographical of all the characters I've ever created. That being said, there are important differences as well. Though I cannibalized many elements of my own childhood for Tom's, I also changed some crucial things. In real life I never had a friend like Junkyard Joey DiAngelis, though many was the time I wished for one. (Especially one like the Joey of the screenplay, who Melinda and I changed into a girl.) I had two terrific sisters, while Tom was an only child. Oh, and the real me never developed kickass telekinesis either, more's the pity.

Not all of the characters in *Wild Cards* had antecedents in our *SuperWorld* campaigns. Many were entirely original. Among those were Howard Waldrop's Jetboy, Lew Shiner's heroic pimp Fortunato, Steve Leigh's sinister Puppetman, and Roger Zelazny's Sleeper, Croyd Crenson, who drew the wild card during a long walk home from school one day, and never learned algebra. Jay Ackroyd (aka Popinjay), my other major character in the series, was one of those as well. Jay was first mentioned in *Aces High*, our second volume, but did not come on stage until the third, *Jokers Wild*, where he teams up with Hiram Worchester for most of my story line. As the series went on, Ackroyd came more and more to the fore, and starred in several stories of his own. By the end of our Bantam run, Jay had become almost as popular as the Turtle.

Tom and Jay were not the only arrows in my quiver. From time to time I would choose to tell a story from the viewpoint of one of my myriad lesser characters. The focus of my interstitial narrative in *Aces High* was Jube the Walrus, an alien in a Hawaiian shirt and porkpie hat. In *Jokers Wild* my story featured Hiram Worchester, the urbane and portly proprietor of the restaurant atop the Empire State Building. For *Dealer's Choice* I used a character created by Bud Simons, the bodysnatcher Zelda, to give the readers a better picture of what the bad guys were up to on the Rox.

"The Journal of Xavier Desmond" is the story of another of my secondary players, a joker activist who had first appeared in "Shell Games" as the maître d' of the Funhouse. Des had risen in the world since then, and as the de facto "mayor of Jokertown" he seemed a natural choice to become one of the joker delegates on the global fact-finding tour that provided the spine for our fourth volume, *Aces Abroad*. The Turtle could not very well go, since he never left his shell. Nor was Jay Ackroyd likely to be invited. Hiram Worchester would be, of course, and I could have chosen him to be my protagonist...but I had just done Hiram in the third book, and I wanted to try a joker perspective.

The interstitial narrative was one of the toughest assignments in any *Wild Cards* book. In a mosaic novel, you want the whole to be more than the sum of its parts. If each story was a brick, the interstitial was the mortar that made them a wall. Whoever wrote the interstitial had to wait until the other stories were done, read the first drafts to see where the holes were, and then try to patch them over...while also telling a good story of his own. If the interstitial was just filler, the book would fall apart.

Later in the history of *Wild Cards*, other writers would step forward to do the interstitials. Bud Simons took a crack at it, and Steve Leigh let himself be drafted more than once. In the early volumes, however, the task usually fell to me as editor. "The Journal of Xavier Desmond" is my favorite of those interstitial stories, and represents some of the best work I did for *Wild Cards*. This is the first time it has been presented by itself, shorn of the stories it originally wove around and through.

Nothing goes on forever. After a good long run the *Wild Cards* series began to lose steam. The books had gotten darker (and they had been pretty dark to begin with), and sales were declining with each volume, slowly but steadily. Some of our best writers had gone on to other projects; popular characters had died or retired. The books were still outselling most paperbacks by a healthy margin, but we were definitely on the downslope. When our contract came up for renewal, Bantam offered us the same terms for the next triad that we had received for the last two.

Foolishly, perhaps, we rejected that offer, and took the series to a smaller publisher for a substantial raise. It was a bad mistake. Though we got more money in the short run, our new publisher lacked both Bantam's resources and Bantam's commitment to the series. Without new titles in the pipeline, Bantam soon allowed the first twelve books to go out of print. Not only did our backlist sales dry up, but new readers no longer had an easy entry to the world by way of volume one. We tried to get around that by scrapping the old numbering and promoting volume thirteen as "book one of a new series," but *Card Sharks* remained a confusing read for readers not familiar with all that had gone before. Sales dropped precipitously, and after the publication of the fifteenth volume in 1995, we found ourselves without a publisher.

And that was the end of that.

Or was it? With strange aeons even death may die, said H. P. Lovecraft. As of 2001, *Wild Cards* returned with a brand-new publisher, iBooks. After a seven-year hiatus, *Deuces Down*, the sixteenth volume in the series, was released in 2002 with all new stories. Our seventeenth volume is in the pipeline, and the old books are being re-released for a new generation of readers. Once more we're hearing talk of games and comic books and movie options.

Will any of this come to pass? Will there be an eighteenth book, a nineteenth, a twentieth? Damned if I know.

I wouldn't bet against us, though. There's a certain turtle that I know who has already had more lives than any cat.

SHELL GAMES

WHEN HE'D MOVED INTO THE DORM BACK IN SEPTEMBER, THE FIRST thing that Thomas Tudbury had done was tack up his signed photograph of President Kennedy, and the tattered 1944 *Time* cover with Jetboy as Man of the Year.

By November, the picture of Kennedy was riddled with holes from Rodney's darts. Rod had decorated his side of the room with a Confederate flag and a dozen *Playboy* centerfolds. He hated Jews, niggers, jokers, and Kennedy, and didn't like Tom much either. All through the fall semester, he had fun; covering Tom's bed with shaving cream, short-sheeting him, hiding his eyeglasses, filling his desk drawer with dog turds.

On the day that Kennedy was killed in Dallas, Tom came back to his room fighting to hold the tears. Rod had left him a present. He'd used a red pen. The whole top of Kennedy's head was dripping blood now, and over his eyes Rod had drawn little red X's. His tongue was sticking out of the corner of his mouth.

Thomas Tudbury stared at that for a long, long time. He did not cry; he would not allow himself to cry. He began to pack his suitcases.

The freshman parking lot was halfway across campus. The trunk on his '54 Mercury had a broken lock, so he tossed the bags into the seat. He let the car warm up for a long time in the November chill. He must have looked funny sitting there; a short, overweight guy with a crew cut and horn-rim glasses, pressing his head against the top of the steering wheel like he was going to be sick.

As he was driving out of the lot, he spied Rodney's shiny Olds Cutlass.

Tom shifted to neutral and idled for a moment, considering. He looked around. There was no one in sight; everybody was inside watching the news. He licked his lips nervously, then looked back at the Oldsmobile. His knuckles whitened around the wheel. He stared hard, furrowed his brow, and *squeezed*.

The door panels gave first, bending inward slowly under the pressure. The headlights exploded with small pops, one after the other. Chrome trim clattered to the ground, and the rear windshield shattered suddenly, glass flying everywhere. Fenders buckled and collapsed, metal squealing in protest. Both rear tires blew at once, the side panels caved in, then the hood; the windshield disintegrated entirely. The crankcase gave, and then the walls of the gas tank; oil, gasoline, and transmission fluid pooled under the car. By then Tom Tudbury was more confident, and that made it easier. He imagined he had the Olds caught in a huge invisible fist, a *strong* fist, and he squeezed all the harder. The crunch of breaking glass and the scream of tortured metal filled the parking lot, but there was no one to hear. He methodically mashed the Oldsmobile into a ball of crushed metal.

When it was over, he shifted into gear and left college, Rodney, and childhood behind forever.

SOMEWHERE A GIANT WAS CRYING.

Tachyon woke disoriented and sick, his hangover throbbing in time to the mammoth sobs. The shapes in the dark room were strange and unfamiliar. Had the assassins come in the night again, was the family under attack? He had to find his father. He lurched dizzily to his feet, head swimming, and put a hand against the wall to steady himself.

The wall was too close. These weren't his chambers, this was all wrong, the smell . . . and then the memories came back. He would have preferred the assassins.

He had dreamed of Takis again, he realized. His head hurt, and his throat was raw and dry. Fumbling in the darkness, he found the chain-pull for the overhead light. The bulb swung wildly when he yanked, making the shadows dance. He closed his eyes to still the lurching in his gut. There was a foul taste at the back of his mouth. His hair was matted and filthy, his clothing rumpled. And worst of all, the bottle was empty. Tachyon looked around helplessly. A six-by-ten on the second floor of a lodging house named ROOMS, on a street called the Bowery. Confusingly, the surrounding neighborhood had once been called the Bowery too— Angelface had told him that. But that was before; the area had a different name now. He went to the window, pulling up the shade. The yellow light of a streetlamp filled the room. Across the street, the giant was reaching for the moon, and weeping because he could not grasp it.

Tiny, they called him. Tachyon supposed that was human wit. Tiny would have been fourteen feet tall if only he could stand up. His face was unlined and innocent, crowned with a tangle of soft dark hair. His legs were slender, and perfectly proportioned. And that was the joke: slender, perfectly proportioned legs could not begin to support the weight of a fourteen-foot-tall man. Tiny sat in a wooden wheelchair, a great mechanized thing that rolled through the streets of Jokertown on four bald tires from a wrecked semi. When he saw Tach in the window, he screamed incoherently, almost as though he recognized him. Tachyon turned away from the window, shaking. It was another Jokertown night. He needed a drink.

His room smelled of mildew and vomit, and it was very cold. ROOMS was not as well heated as the hotels he had frequented in the old days. Unbidden, he remembered the Mayflower down in Washington, where he and Blythe...but no, better not to think of that. What time was it anyway? Late enough. The sun was down, and Jokertown came to life at night.

He plucked his overcoat from the floor and slipped it on. Soiled as it was, it was still a marvelous coat, a lovely rich rose color, with fringed golden epaulets on the shoulders and loops of golden braid to fasten the long row of buttons. A musician's coat, the man at the Goodwill had told him. He sat on the edge of his sagging mattress to pull on his boots.

The washroom was down at the end of the hall. Steam rose from his urine as it splashed against the rim of the toilet; his hands shook so badly that he couldn't even aim right. He slapped cold, rust-colored water on his face, and dried his hands on a filthy towel.

Outside, Tach stood for a moment beneath the creaking ROOMS sign, staring at Tiny. He felt bitter and ashamed. And much too sober. There was nothing to be done about Tiny, but he could deal with his sobriety. He turned his back on the weeping giant, slid his hands deep into the pockets of his coat, and walked off briskly down the Bowery.

In the alleys, jokers and winos passed brown paper bags from hand to hand, and stared with dull eyes at the passersby. Taverns, pawnbrokers, and mask shops were all doing a brisk trade. The Famous Bowery Wild Card Dime Museum (they still called it that, but admission was a quarter now) was closing for the day. Tachyon had gone through it once, two years ago, on a day when he was feeling especially guilt-ridden; along with a half-dozen particularly freakish jokers, twenty jars of "monstrous joker babies" floating in formaldehyde, and a sensational little newsreel about the Day of the Wild Card, the museum had a waxworks display whose dioramas featured Jetboy, the Four Aces, a Jokertown Orgy...and him.

A tour bus rolled past, pink faces pressed to the windows. Beneath the neon light of a neighborhood pizza parlor, four youths in black leather jackets and rubber facemasks eyed Tachyon with open hostility. They made him uneasy. He averted his eyes and dipped into the mind of the nearest: *mincing pansy looka that hair dye-job fershure thinks he's inna marching band like to beat his fuckin' drums but no wait shit there's better we'll find us a good one tonight yeah wanna get one that squishes when we hit it.* Tach broke the contact with distaste and hurried on. It was old news, and a new sport: come down to the Bowery, buy some masks, beat up a joker. The police didn't seem to care.

The Chaos Club and its famous All-Joker Revue had the usual big crowd. As Tachyon approached, a long gray limo pulled up to the curb. The doorman, wearing a black tuxedo over luxuriant white fur, opened the door with his tail and helped out a fat man in a dinner jacket. His date was a buxom teenager in a strapless evening gown and pearls, her blonde hair piled high in a bouffant hairdo.

A block farther on, a snake-lady called out a proposition from the top of a nearby stoop. Her scales were rainbow-colored, glistening. "Don't be scared, Red," she said, "it's still soft inside." He shook his head.

The Funhouse was housed in a long building with giant picture windows fronting the street, but the glass had been replaced with one-way mirrors. Randall stood out front, shivering in tails and domino.

He looked perfectly normal—until you noticed that he never took his right hand out of his pocket. "Hey, Tacky," he called out. "Whattaya make of Ruby?"

"Sorry, I don't know her," Tachyon said.

Randall scowled. "No, the guy who killed Oswald."

"Oswald?" Tach said, confused. "Oswald who?"

"Lee Oswald, the guy who shot Kennedy. He got killed on TV this afternoon."

"Kennedy's dead?" Tachyon said. It was Kennedy who'd permitted his return to the United States, and Tach admired the Kennedys; they seemed almost Takisian. But assassination was part of leadership. "His brothers will avenge him," he said. Then he recalled that they didn't do things that way on Earth, and besides, this man Ruby had already avenged him, it seemed. How strange that he had dreamed of assassins.

"They got Ruby in jail," Randall was saying. "If it was me, I'd give the fucker a medal." He paused. "He shook my hand once," he added. "When he was running against Nixon, he came through to give a speech at the Chaos Club. Afterward, when he was leaving, he was shaking hands with everybody." The doorman took his right hand out of his pocket. It was hard and chitinous, insectile, and in the middle was a cluster of swollen blind eyes. "He didn't even flinch," Randall said. "Smiled and said he hoped I'd remember to vote."

Tachyon had known Randall for a year, but he had never seen his hand before. He wanted to do what Kennedy had done, to grasp that twisted claw, embrace it, shake it. He tried to slide his hand out of the pocket of his coat, but the bile rose in the back of his throat, and somehow all he could do was look away, and say, "He was a good man."

Randall hid his hand again. "Go on inside, Tacky," he said, not unkindly. "Angelface had to go and see a man, but she told Des to keep your table open."

Tachyon nodded and let Randall open the door for him. Inside, he gave his coat and shoes to the girl in the checkroom, a joker with a trim little body whose feathered owl mask concealed whatever the wild card had done to her face. Then he pushed through the interior doors, his stockinged feet sliding with smooth familiarity over the mirrored floor. When he looked down, another Tachyon was staring back up at him, framed by his feet; a grossly fat Tachyon with a head like a beach ball.

Suspended from the mirrored ceiling, a crystal chandelier glittered with a hundred pinpoint lights, its reflections sparkling off the floor tiles and walls and mirrored alcoves, the silvered goblets and mugs, and even the waiters' trays. Some of the mirrors reflected true; the others were distorting mirrors, funhouse mirrors. When you looked over your shoulder in the Funhouse, you could never tell what you'd find looking back. It was the only establishment in Jokertown that attracted jokers and normals in equal numbers. In the Funhouse the normals could see themselves twisted and malformed, and giggle, and play at being jokers; and a joker, if he was very lucky, might glance in the right mirror and see himself as he once had been.

"Your booth is waiting, Doctor Tachyon," said Desmond, the maître d'. Des was a large, florid man; his thick trunk, pink and wrinkled, curled around a wine list. He lifted it, and beckoned for Tachyon to follow with one of the fingers that dangled from its end. "Will you be having your usual brand of cognac tonight?"

"Yes," Tach said, wishing he had some money for a tip.

That night he had his first drink for Blythe, as always, but his second was for John Fitzgerald Kennedy.

The rest were for himself.

———

AT THE END OF HOOK ROAD, PAST THE ABANDONED REFINERY AND the import/export warehouses, past the railroad sidings with their forlorn red boxcars, beneath the highway underpass, past the empty lots full of weeds and garbage, past the huge soybean-oil tanks, Tom found his refuge. It was almost dark by the time he arrived, and the engine in the Merc was thumping ominously. But Joey would know what to do about that.

The junkyard stood hard on the oily polluted waters of New York Bay. Behind a ten-foot-high chain-link fence topped with three curly strands of barbed wire, a pack of junkyard dogs kept pace with his car, barking a raucous welcome that would have terrified anyone who knew the dogs less well. The sunset gave a strange bronze cast to the mountains of shattered, twisted, rusted automobiles, the acres of scrap metal, the hills and valleys of junk and trash. Finally Tom came to the wide double gate. On one side a metal sign warned TRESPASSERS

KEEP OUT; on the other side another sign told them to BEWARE OF THE DOGS. The gate was chained and locked.

Tom stopped and honked his horn.

Just beyond the fence he could see the four-room shack that Joey called home. A huge sign was mounted on top of the corrugated tin roof, with yellow spotlights stuck up there to illuminate the letters. It said DI ANGELIS SCRAP METAL & AUTO PARTS. The paint was faded and blistered by two decades of sun and rain; the wood itself had cracked, and one of the spots had burned out. Next to the house was parked an ancient yellow dump truck, a tow truck, and Joey's pride and joy, a blood-red 1959 Cadillac coupe with tail fins like a shark and a monster of a hopped-up engine poking right up through its cutaway hood.

Tom honked again. This time he gave it their special signal, tooting out the *Here-he-comes-to-save-the-daaaay!* theme from the *Mighty Mouse* cartoons they'd watched as kids.

A square of yellow light spilled across the junkyard as Joey came out with a beer in either hand.

They were nothing alike, him and Joey. They came from different stock, lived in different worlds, but they'd been best friends since the day of the third-grade pet show. That was the day he'd found out that turtles couldn't fly; the day he realized what he was, and what he could do.

Stevie Bruder and Josh Jones had caught him out in the school-yard. They played catch with his turtles, tossing them back and forth while Tommy ran between them, red-faced and crying. When they got bored, they bounced them off the punchball square chalked on the wall. Stevie's German shepherd ate one. When Tommy tried to grab the dog, Stevie laid into him and left him on the ground with broken glasses and a split lip.

They would have done worse, except for Junkyard Joey, a scrawny kid with shaggy black hair, two years older than his classmates, but he'd already been left back twice, couldn't hardly read, and they always said he smelled bad on account of his father, Dom, owned the junkyard. Joey wasn't as big as Stevie Bruder, but he didn't care, that day or any day. He just grabbed Stevie by the back of his shirt and yanked him around and kicked him in the balls. Then he kicked the dog too, and he would have kicked Josh Jones, except Josh ran away. As he fled, a dead turtle floated off the ground and flew across the schoolyard to smack him in the back of his fat red neck.

Joey had seen it happen. "How'd you do that?" he said, astonished. Until that moment, even Tommy hadn't realized that *he* was the reason his turtles could fly.

It became their shared secret, the glue that held their odd friendship together. Tommy helped Joey with his homework and quizzed him for tests. Joey became Tommy's protector against the random brutality of playground and schoolyard. Tommy read comic books to Joey, until Joey's own reading got so much better that he didn't need Tommy. Dom, a grizzled man with salt-and-pepper hair, a beer belly, and a gentle heart, was proud of that; he couldn't read himself, not even Italian. The friendship lasted through grammar school and high school and Joey's dropping out. It survived their discovery of girls, weathered the death of Dom DiAngelis and Tom's family moving off to Perth Amboy. Joey DiAngelis was still the only one who knew what Tom was.

Joey popped the cap on another Rheingold with the church key that hung around his neck. Under his sleeveless white undershirt a beer belly like his father's was growing. "You're too fucking smart to be doing shitwork in a TV repair shop," he was saying.

"It's a job," Tom said. "I did it last summer, I can do it full time. It's not important what kind of job I have. What's important is what I do with my, uh, talent."

"Talent?" Joey mocked.

"You know what I mean, you dumb wop." Tom set his empty bottle down on the top of the orange crate next to the armchair. Most of Joey's furnishings weren't what you'd call lavish; he scavenged them from the junkyard. "I been thinking about what Jetboy said at the end, trying to think what it meant. I figure he was saying that there were things he hadn't done yet. Well, shit, I haven't done *anything*. All the way back I asked what I could do for the country, y'know? Well, fuck, we both know the answer to that one."

Joey rocked back in his chair, sucking on his Rheingold and shaking his head. Behind him, the wall was lined with the bookshelves that Dom had built for the kids almost ten years ago. The bottom row was all men's magazines. The rest were comic books. Their comic books. *Superman*s and *Batman*s, *Action Comics* and *Detective,* the *Classics*

*Illustrated*s that Joey had mined for all his book reports, horror comics and crime comics and air-war comics, and best of all, their treasure—an almost complete run of *Jetboy Comics.*

Joey saw what he was looking at. "Don't even think it," he said, "you're no fuckin' Jetboy, Tuds."

"No," said Tom, "I'm more than he was. I'm—"

"A dork," Joey suggested.

"An ace," he said gravely. "Like the Four Aces."

"They were a colored doo-wop group, weren't they?"

Tom flushed. "You dumb wop, they weren't singers, they—"

Joey cut him off with a sharp gesture. "I know who the fuck they were, Tuds. Gimme a break. They were dumb shits, like you. They all went to jail or got shot or something, didn't they? Except for the fuckin' snitch, whatsisname." He snapped his fingers. "You know, the guy in *Tarzan.*"

"Jack Braun," Tom said. He'd done a term paper on the Four Aces once. "And I bet there are others, hiding out there. Like me. I've been hiding. But no more."

"So you figure you're going to go to the *Bayonne Times* and give a fucking show? You asshole. You might as well tell 'em you're a commie. They'll make you move to Jokertown and they'll break all the goddamned windows in your dad's house. They might even draft you, asswipe."

"No," said Tom. "I've got it scoped out. The Four Aces were easy targets. I'm not going to let them know who I am or where I live." He used the beer bottle in his hand to gesture vaguely at the bookshelves. "I'm going to keep my name secret. Like in the comics."

Joey laughed out loud. "Fuckin' A. You gonna wear long johns too, you dumb shit?"

"Goddamn it," Tom said. He was getting pissed off. "Shut the fuck up." Joey just sat there, rocking and laughing. "Come on, big mouth," Tom snapped, rising. "Get off your fat ass and come outside, and I'll show you just how dumb I am. C'mon, you know so damned much."

Joey DiAngelis got to his feet. "This I gotta see."

Outside, Tom waited impatiently, shifting his weight from foot to foot, breath steaming in the cold November air, while Joey went to the big metal box on the side of the house and threw a switch. High atop their poles, the junkyard lights blazed to life. The dogs gathered around, sniffing, and followed them when they began to walk. Joey had a beer bottle poking out of a pocket of his black leather jacket.

It was only a junkyard, full of garbage and scrap metal and wrecked cars, but tonight it seemed as magical as when Tommy was ten. On a rise overlooking the black waters of New York Bay, an ancient white Packard loomed like a ghostly fort. That was just what it had been, when Joey and he had been kids; their sanctum, their stronghold, their cavalry outpost and space station and castle rolled all in one. It shone in the moonlight, and the waters beyond were full of promise as they lapped against the shore. Darkness and shadows lay heavy in the yard, changing the piles of trash and metal into mysterious black hills, with a maze of gray alleys between them. Tom led them into that labyrinth, past the big trash heap where they'd played king-of-the-mountain and dueled with scrap-iron swords, past the treasure troves where they'd found so many busted toys and hunks of colored glass and deposit bottles, and once even a whole cardboard carton full of comic books.

They walked between rows of twisted, rusty cars stacked one on another; Fords and Chevys, Hudsons and DeSotos, a Corvette with a shattered accordion hood, a litter of dead Beetles, a dignified black hearse as dead as the passengers it had carried. Tom looked at them all carefully. Finally he stopped. "That one," he said, pointing to the remains of a gutted old Studebaker Hawk. Its engine was gone, as were its tires; the windshield was a spiderweb of broken glass, and even in the darkness they could see where rust had chewed away at the fenders and side panels. "Not worth anything, right?"

Joey opened his beer. "Go ahead, it's all yours."

Tom took a deep breath and faced the car. His hands became fists at his sides. He stared hard, concentrating. The car rocked slightly. Its front grille lifted an unsteady couple of inches from the ground.

"Whooo-eeee," Joey said derisively, punching Tom lightly in the shoulder. The Studebaker dropped with a clang, and a bumper fell off. "Shit, I'm impressed," Joey said.

"Damn it, keep quiet and leave me alone," Tom said. "I can do it, I'll show you, just shut your fuckin' mouth for a minute. I've been practicing. You don't know the things I can do."

"Won't say a fuckin' word," Joey promised, grinning. He took a swig of his beer.

Tom turned back to the Studebaker. He tried to blot out everything, forget about Joey, the dogs, the junkyard; the Studebaker filled
his world. His stomach was a hard little ball. He told it to relax, took
several deep breaths, let his fists uncurl. *Come on, come on, take it easy,
don't get upset, do it, you've done more than this, this is easy, easy.*

The car rose slowly, drifting upward in a shower of rust. Tom turned
it around and around, faster and faster. Then, with a triumphant smile,
Tom threw it fifty feet across the junkyard. It crashed into a stack of dead
Chevys and brought the whole thing down in an avalanche of metal.

Joey finished his Rheingold. "Not bad. A few years ago, you could
barely lift me over a fence."

"I'm getting stronger all the time," Tom said.

Joey DiAngelis nodded, and tossed his empty bottle to the side.
"Good," he said, "then you won't have any problem with me, willya?"
He gave Tom a hard push with both hands.

Tom staggered back a step, frowning. "Cut it out, Joey."

"Make me," Joey said. He shoved him again, harder. This time
Tom almost lost his footing.

"Damn it, *stop* it," Tom said. "It's not funny, Joey."

"No?" Joey said. He grinned. "I think it's fuckin' hilarious. But hey,
you can stop me, can't you? Use your damn power." He moved right up
in Tom's face and slapped him lightly across the cheek. "Stop me, ace,"
he said. He slapped him harder. "C'mon, Jetboy, stop me." The third slap
was the hardest yet. "Let's go, supes, whatcha waitin' for?" The fourth
blow had a sharp sting; the fifth snapped Tom's head half around. Joey
stopped smiling; Tom could smell the beer on his breath.

Tom tried to grab his hand, but Joey was too strong, too fast; he
evaded Tom's grasp and landed another slap. "You wanna box, ace? I'll
turn you into fuckin' dogmeat. Dork. Asshole." The slap almost tore
Tom's head off, and brought stinging tears to his eyes. "*Stop me,* jagoff,"
Joey screamed. He closed his hand, and buried his fist in Tom's stomach so hard it doubled him over and took his breath away.

Tom tried to summon his concentration, to grab and push, but it
was the schoolyard all over again, Joey was everywhere, fists raining
down on him, and it was all he could do to get his hands up and try to
block the blows, and it was no good anyway, Joey was much stronger,
he pounded him, pushed him, screaming all the while, and Tom

couldn't think, couldn't focus, couldn't do anything but hurt, and he was retreating, staggering back, and Joey came after him, fists cocked, and caught him with an uppercut that landed right on his mouth with a crack that made his teeth hurt. All of a sudden Tom was lying on his back on the ground, with a mouth full of blood.

Joey stood over him frowning. "Fuck," he said. "I didn't mean to bust your lip." He reached down, took Tom by the hand, and yanked him roughly to his feet.

Tom wiped blood from his lip with the back of his hand. There was blood on the front of his shirt too. "Look at me, I'm all messed up," he said with disgust. He glared at Joey. "That wasn't fair. You can't expect me to do anything when you're pounding on me, damn it."

"Uh-huh," Joey said. "And while you're concentrating and squinting your eyes, you figure the fuckin' bad guys are just gonna leave you alone, right?" He clapped Tom across the back. "They'll knock out all your fuckin' teeth. That's if you're lucky, if they don't just shoot you. You ain't no Jetboy, Tuds." He shivered. "C'mon. It's fuckin' cold out here."

WHEN HE WOKE IN WARM DARKNESS, TACH REMEMBERED ONLY A little of the binge, but that was how he liked it. He struggled to sit up. The sheets he was lying on were satin, smooth and sensual, and beneath the odor of stale vomit he could still smell a faint trace of some flowery perfume.

Unsteady, he tossed off the bedclothes and pulled himself to the edge of the four-poster bed. The floor beneath his bare feet was carpeted. He was naked, the air uncomfortably warm on his bare skin. He reached out a hand, found the light switch, and whimpered a little at the brightness. The room was pink-and-white clutter with Victorian furnishings and thick, soundproofed walls. An oil painting of John F. Kennedy smiled down from above the hearth; in one corner stood a three-foot-tall plaster statue of the Virgin Mary.

Angelface was seated in a pink wingback chair by the cold fireplace, blinking at him sleepily and covering her yawn with the back of her hand.

Tach felt sick and ashamed. "I put you out of your own bed again, didn't I?" he said.

"It's all right," she replied. Her feet were resting on a tiny footstool. Her soles were ugly and bruised, black and swollen despite the special padded shoes she wore. Otherwise she was lovely. Unbound, her black hair fell to her waist, and her skin had a flushed, radiant quality to it, a warm glow of life. Her eyes were dark and liquid, but the most amazing thing, the thing that never failed to astonish Tachyon, was the warmth in them, the affection he felt so unworthy of. With all he had done to her, and to all the rest of them, somehow this woman called Angelface forgave, and cared.

Tach raised a hand to his temple. Someone with a buzz saw was trying to remove the back of his skull. "My head," he groaned. "At your prices, the least you could do is take the resins and poisons out of the drinks you sell. On Takis, we—"

"I know," Angelface said. "On Takis you've bred hangovers out of your wines. You told me that one already."

Tachyon gave her a weary smile. She looked impossibly fresh, wearing nothing but a short satin tunic that left her legs bare to the thigh. It was a deep, wine red, lovely against her skin. But when she rose, he glimpsed the side of her face, where her cheek had rested against the chair as she slept. The bruise was darkening already, a purple blossom on her cheek. "Angel . . ." he began.

"It's nothing," she said. She pushed her hair forward to cover the blemish. "Your clothes were filthy. Mal took them out to be cleaned. So you're my prisoner for a while."

"How long have I slept?" Tachyon asked.

"All day," Angelface replied. "Don't worry about it. Once I had a customer get so drunk he slept for five months." She sat down at her dressing table, lifted a phone, and ordered breakfast: toast and tea for herself, eggs and bacon and strong coffee with brandy for Tachyon. With aspirin on the side.

"No," he protested. "All that food. I'll get sick."

"You have to eat. Even spacemen can't live on cognac alone."

"Please . . ."

"If you want to drink, you'll eat," she said brusquely. "That's the deal, remember?"

The deal, yes. He remembered. Angelface provided him with rent money, food, and an unlimited bar tab, as much drink as he'd ever need to wash away his memories. All he had to do was eat and tell her stories. She loved to listen to him talk. He told her family anecdotes, lectured about Takisian customs, filled her with history and legends and romances, with tales of balls and intrigues and beauty far removed from the squalor of Jokertown.

Sometimes, after closing, he would dance for her, tracing the ancient, intricate pavanes of Takis across the nightclub's mirrored floors while she watched and urged him on. Once, when both of them had drunk far too much wine, she talked him into demonstrating the Wedding Pattern, an erotic ballet that most Takisians danced but once, on their wedding night. That was the only time she had ever danced with him, echoing the steps, hesitantly at first, and then faster and faster, swaying and spinning across the floor until her bare feet were raw and cracked and left wet red smears upon the mirror tiles. In the Wedding Pattern, the dancing couple came together at the end, collapsing into a long triumphant embrace. But that was on Takis; here, when the moment came, she broke the pattern and shied away from him, and he was reminded once again that Takis was far away.

Two years before, Desmond had found him unconscious and naked in a Jokertown alley. Someone had stolen his clothing while he slept, and he was fevered and delirious. Des had summoned help to carry him to the Funhouse. When he came to, he was lying on a cot in a back room, surrounded by beer kegs and wine racks. "Do you know what you were drinking?" Angelface had asked him when they'd brought him to her office. He hadn't known; all he recalled was that he'd needed a drink so badly it was an ache inside him, and the old black man in the alley had generously offered to share. "It's called Sterno," Angelface told him. She had Des bring in a bottle of her finest brandy. "If a man wants to drink, that's his business, but at least you can kill yourself with a little class." The brandy spread thin tendrils of warmth through his chest and stopped his hands from shaking. When he'd emptied the snifter, Tach had thanked her effusively, but she drew back when he tried to touch her. He asked her why. "I'll show you," she had said, offering her hand. "Lightly," she told him. His kiss had been the merest brush of his lips, not on the back of her hand but against the inside of her wrist, to feel her pulse, the life current inside her, because she was so very lovely, and kind, and because he wanted her.

A moment later he'd watched with sick dismay as her skin darkened to purple and then black. *Another one of mine,* he'd thought.

Yet somehow they had become friends. Not lovers, of course, except sometimes in his dreams; her capillaries ruptured at the slightest pressure, and to her hypersensitive nervous system even the lightest touch was painful. A gentle caress turned her black and blue; lovemaking would probably kill her. But friends, yes. She never asked him for anything he could not give, and so he could never fail her.

Breakfast was served by a hunchbacked black woman named Ruth who had pale blue feathers instead of hair. "The man brought this for you this morning," she told Angelface after she'd set the table, handing across a thick, square packet wrapped in brown paper. Angelface accepted it without comment while Tachyon drank his brandy-laced coffee and lifted knife and fork to stare with sick dismay at the implacable bacon and eggs.

"Don't look so stricken," Angelface said.

"I don't think I've told you about the time the Network starship came to Takis, and what my great-grandmother Amurath had to say to the Ly'bahr envoy," he began.

"No," she said. "Go on. I like your great-grandmother."

"That's one of us. She terrifies me," Tachyon said, and launched into the story.

———

TOM WOKE WELL BEFORE DAWN, WHILE JOEY WAS SNORING IN THE back room. He brewed a pot of coffee in a battered percolator and popped a Thomas' English muffin into the toaster. While the coffee perked, he folded the hide-a-bed back into a couch. He covered his muffins with butter and strawberry preserves, and looked around for something to read. The comics beckoned.

He remembered the day they'd saved them. Most had been his, originally, including the run of *Jetboy* he got from his dad. He'd loved those comics. And then one day in 1954 he'd come home from school and found them gone, a full bookcase and two orange crates of funny books vanished. His mother said some women from the PTA had come by to tell her what awful things comic books were. They'd shown her a copy of a book by a Dr. Wertham about how comics turned kids into juvenile delinquents and homos, and how they glorified aces and jokers, and so his mother had let them take Tom's collection. He screamed and yelled and threw a tantrum, but it did no good.

The PTA had gathered up comic books from every kid in school. They were going to burn them all Saturday, in the schoolyard. It was happening all over the country; there was even talk of a law banning comic books, or at least the kinds about horror and crime and people with strange powers.

Wertham and the PTA turned out to be right: that Friday night, on account of comic books, Tommy Tudbury and Joey DiAngelis became criminals.

Tom was nine; Joey was eleven, but he'd been driving his pop's truck since he was seven. In the middle of the night, he swiped the truck and Tom snuck out to meet him. When they got to the school, Joey jimmied open a window, and Tom climbed on his shoulders and looked into the dark classroom and concentrated and grabbed the carton with his collection in it and lifted it up and floated it out into the bed of the truck. Then he snatched four or five other cartons for good measure. The PTA never noticed; they still had plenty to burn. If Dom DiAngelis wondered where all the comics had come from, he never said a word; he just built the shelves to hold them, proud as punch of his son who could read. From that day on, it was their collection, jointly.

Setting his coffee and muffin on the orange crate, Tom went to the bookcase and took down a couple of issues of *Jetboy Comics*. He reread them as he ate, *Jetboy on Dinosaur Island, Jetboy and the Fourth Reich,* and his favorite, the final issue, the true one, *Jetboy and the Aliens*. Inside the cover, the title was "Thirty Minutes Over Broadway." Tom read it twice as he sipped his cooling coffee. He lingered over some of the best panels. On the last page, they had a picture of the alien, Tachyon, weeping. Tom didn't know if that had happened or not. He closed the comic book and finished his English muffin. For a long time he sat there thinking.

Jetboy was a hero. And what was he? Nothing. A wimp, a chickenshit. A fuck of a lot of good his wild card power did anybody. It was useless, just like him.

Dispiritedly, he shrugged into his coat and went outside. The junkyard looked raw and ugly in the dawn, and a cold wind was blowing. A few hundred yards to the east, the bay was green and choppy. Tom climbed up to the old Packard on its little hill. The door creaked when he yanked it open. Inside, the seats were cracked and smelled of rot, but at least he was out of that wind. Tom slouched back with his knees up against the dash, staring out at sunrise. He sat unmoving for a long time; across the yard, hubcaps and old tires floated up in the air and went screaming off to splash into the choppy green waters of New York Bay. He could see the Statue of Liberty on her island, and the hazy outlines of the towers of Manhattan off to the northeast.

It was nearly seven-thirty, his limbs were stiff, and he'd lost count of the number of hubcaps he'd flung, when Tom Tudbury sat up with a strange expression on his face. The icebox he'd been juggling forty feet from the ground came down with a crash. He ran his fingers through his hair and lifted the icebox again, moved it over twenty yards or so, and dropped it right on Joey's corrugated tin roof. Then he did the same with a tire, a twisted bicycle, six hubcaps, and a little red wagon.

The door to the house flew open with a bang, and Joey came charging out into the cold wearing nothing but boxer shorts and a sleeveless undershirt. He looked real pissed. Tom snatched his bare feet, pulled them out from under him, and dumped him on his butt, hard. Joey cursed.

Tom grabbed him and yanked him into the air, upside down. "Where the fuck are you, Tudbury?" Joey screamed. "Cut it out, you dork. Lemme down."

Tom imagined two huge invisible hands, and tossed Joey from one to the other. "When I get down, I'm going to punch you so fuckin' hard you'll eat through a straw for the rest of your life," Joey promised.

The crank was stiff from years of disuse, but Tom finally managed to roll down the Packard's window. He stuck his head out. "Hiya, kids, hiya, hiya, hiya," he croaked, chortling.

Suspended twelve feet from the ground, Joey dangled and made a fist. "I'll pluck your fuckin' magic twanger, shithead," he shouted. Tom yanked off his boxer shorts and hung them from a telephone pole. "You're gonna die, Tudbury," Joey said.

Tom took a big breath and set Joey on the ground, very gently. The moment of truth. Joey came running at him, screaming obsceni-ties. Tom closed his eyes, put his hands on the steering wheel, and *lifted*.

The Packard shifted beneath him. Sweat dotted his brow. He shut out the world, concentrated, counted to ten, slowly, backward.

When he finally opened his eyes, half expecting to see Joey's fist smashing into his nose, there was nothing to behold but a seagull perched on the hood of the Packard, its head cocked as it peered through the cracked windshield. He was floating. He was flying.

Tom stuck his head out of the window. Joey stood twenty feet below him, glaring, hands on his hips and a disgusted look on his face. "Now," Tom yelled down, smiling, "what was it you were saying last night?"

"I hope you can stay up there all day, you son of a bitch," Joey said. He made an ineffectual fist, and waved it. Lank black hair fell across his eyes. "Ah, shit, what does this prove? If I had a gun, you'd still be dead meat."

"If you had a gun, I wouldn't be sticking my head out the window," Tom said. "In fact, it'd be better if I didn't have a window." He considered that for a second, but it was hard to think while he was up here. The Packard was heavy. "I'm coming down," he said to Joey. "You, uh, you calmed down?"

Joey grinned. "Try me and see, Tuds."

"Move out of the way. I don't want to squash you with this damn thing."

Joey shuffled to one side, bare-ass and goose-pimpled, and Tom let the Packard settle as gently as an autumn leaf on a still day. He had the door half open when Joey reached in, grabbed him, yanked him up, and pushed him back against the side of the car, his other hand cocked into a fist. "I oughtta—" he began. Then he shook his head, snorted, and punched Tom lightly in the shoulder. "Gimme back my fuckin' drawers, ace," he said.

Back inside the house, Tom reheated the leftover coffee. "I'll need you to do the work," he said as he made himself some scrambled eggs and ham and a couple more English muffins. Using his teke always gave him quite an appetite. "You took auto shop and welding and all that shit. I'll do the wiring."

"Wiring?" Joey said, warming his hands over his cup. "What the fuck for?"

"The lights and the TV cameras. I don't want any windows people can shoot through. I know where we can get some cameras cheap, and you got lots of old sets around here, I'll just fix them up." He sat down and attacked his eggs wolfishly. "I'll need loudspeakers too. Some kind of PA system. A generator. Wonder if I'll have room for a refrigerator in there?"

"That Packard's a big motherfucker," Joey said. "Take out the seats and you'll have room for three of the fuckers."

"Not the Packard," Tom said. "I'll find a lighter car. We can cover up the windows with old body panels or something."

Joey pushed hair out of his eyes. "Fuck the body panels. I got armor plate. From the war. They scrapped a bunch of ships at the Navy base in '46 and '47, and Dom put in a bid for the metal, and bought us twenty goddamn tons. Fuckin' waste a money—who the fuck wants to buy battleship armor? I still got it all, sitting way out back rusting. You need a fuckin' sixteen-inch gun to punch through that shit, Tuds. You'll be safe as—fuck, I dunno. Safe, anyhow."

Tom knew. "Safe," he said loudly, "as a turtle in its shell!"

———

ONLY TEN SHOPPING DAYS WERE LEFT UNTIL CHRISTMAS, AND Tach sat in one of the window alcoves, nursing an Irish coffee against the December cold and gazing through the one-way glass at the Bowery. The Funhouse wouldn't open for another hour yet, but the back door was always unlocked for Angelface's friends. Up on stage, a pair of joker jugglers who called themselves Cosmos and Chaos were tossing bowling balls around. Cosmos floated three feet above the stage in the lotus position, his eyeless face serene. He was totally blind, but he never missed a beat or dropped a ball. His partner, six-armed Chaos, capered around like a lunatic, chortling and telling bad jokes and keeping a cascade of flaming clubs going behind his back with two arms while the other four flung bowling balls at Cosmos. Tach spared them only a glance. As talented as they were, their deformities pained him.

Mal slid into his booth. "How many of those you had?" the bouncer demanded, glaring at the Irish coffee. The tendrils that hung from his lower lip expanded and contracted in a blind wormlike pulsing, and his huge, malformed blue-black jaw gave his face a look of belligerent contempt.

"I don't see that it's any of your business."

"You're no damn use at all, are you?"

"I never claimed I was."

Mal grunted. "You're worth 'bout as much as a sack of shit. I don't see why the hell Angel needs no damn pantywaist spaceman hanging round the place sopping up her booze...."

"She doesn't. I told her that."

"You can't tell that woman nothin'," Mal agreed. He made a fist. A very large fist. Before the Day of the Wild Card, he'd been the eighth-ranked heavyweight contender. Afterward, he had climbed as high as third... until they'd banned wild cards from professional sports, and wiped out his dreams in a stroke. The measure was aimed at aces, they said, to keep the games competitive, but there had been no exceptions made for jokers. Mal was older now, sparse hair turned iron gray, but he still looked strong enough to break Floyd Patterson over his knee and mean enough to stare down Sonny Liston. "Look at that," he growled in disgust, glaring out the window. Tiny was outside in his chair. "What the hell is he doing here? I told him not to come by here no more." Mal started for the door.

"Can't you just leave him alone?" Tachyon called after him. "He's harmless."

"Harmless?" Mal rounded on him. "His screamin' scares off all the fuckin' tourists, and who the hell's gonna pay for all your free booze?"

But then the door pushed open, and Desmond stood there, over-coat folded over one arm, his trunk half-raised. "Let him be, Mal," the maître d' said wearily. "Go on, now." Muttering, Mal stalked off.

Desmond came over and seated himself in Tachyon's booth. "Good morning, Doctor," he said.

Tachyon nodded and finished his drink. The whiskey had all gone to the bottom of the cup, and it warmed him on the way down. He found himself staring at the face in the mirrored tabletop: a worn, dissipated, *coarse* face, eyes reddened and puffy, long red hair tangled and greasy, features distorted by alcoholic bloat. That wasn't him, that couldn't be him, he was handsome, clean-featured, distinguished, his face was—

Desmond's trunk snaked out, its fingers locking around his wrist roughly, yanking him forward. "You haven't heard a word I've said, have you?" Des said, his voice low and urgent with anger. Blearily,

Tach realized that Desmond had been talking to him. He began to mutter apologies.

"Never mind about that," Des said, releasing his grip. "Listen to me. I was asking for your help, Doctor. I may be a joker, but I'm not an uneducated man. I've read about you. You have certain—abilities, let us say."

"No," Tach interrupted. "Not the way you're thinking."

"Your powers are quite well documented," Des said.

"I don't..." Tach began awkwardly. He spread his hands. "That was then. I've lost—I mean, I can't, not anymore." He stared down at his own wasted features, wanting to look Des in the eye, to make him understand, but unable to bear the sight of the joker's deformity.

"You mean you won't," Des said. He stood up. "I thought that if I spoke to you before we opened, I might actually find you sober. I see I was mistaken. Forget everything I said."

"I'd help you if I could," Tach began to say.

"I wasn't asking for me," Des said sharply.

When he was gone, Tachyon went to the long silver-chrome bar and got down a full bottle of cognac. The first glass made him feel better; the second stopped his hands from shaking. By the third he had begun to weep. Mal came over and looked down at him in disgust. "Never knew no man cried as much as you do," he said, thrusting a dirty handkerchief at Tachyon roughly before he left to help them open.

HE HAD BEEN ALOFT FOR FOUR AND A HALF HOURS WHEN THE NEWS of the fire came crackling over the police-band radio down by his right foot. Not very *far* aloft, true, only about six feet from the ground, but that was enough—six feet or sixty, it didn't make all that much difference, Tom had found. Four and a half hours, and he didn't feel the least bit tired yet. In fact, he felt *sensational*.

He was strapped securely into a bucket seat Joey had pulled from a mashed-up Triumph TR-3 and mounted on a low pivot right in the center of the VW. The only light was the wan phosphor glow from an array of mismatched television screens that surrounded him on all sides. Between the cameras and their tracking motors, the generator, the ventilation system, the sound equipment, the control panels, the spare box of vacuum tubes, and the little refrigerator, he hardly had space to swing around. But that was okay. Tom was more a claustrophile than a claustrophobe anyway; he liked it in here. Around the exterior of the gutted Beetle, Joey had mounted two overlapping layers of thick battleship armor. It was better than a goddamned tank. Joey had already pinged a few shots off it with the Luger that Dom had taken off a German officer during the war. A lucky shot might be able to take out one of his cameras or lights, but there was no way to get to Tom himself inside the shell. He was better than safe, he was *invulnerable,* and when he felt this secure and sure of himself, there was no limit on what he might be able to do.

The shell was heavier than the Packard by the time they'd gotten finished with it, but it didn't seem to matter. Four and a half hours, never touching ground, sliding around silently and almost effortlessly through the junkyard, and Tom hadn't even worked up a sweat.

When he heard the report over the radio, a jolt of excitement went through him. *This is it!* he thought. He ought to wait for Joey, but Joey had driven to Pompeii Pizza to pick up dinner (pepperoni, onion, and extra cheese) and there was no time to waste; this was his chance.

The ring of lights on the bottom of the shell threw stark shadows over the hills of twisted metal and trash as Tom pushed the shell higher into the air, eight feet up, ten, twelve. His eyes flicked nervously from one screen to the next, watching the ground recede. One set, its picture tube filched from an old Sylvania, began a slow vertical roll. Tom played with a knob and stopped it. His palms were sweaty. Fifteen feet up, he began to creep forward, until the shell reached the shoreline. In front of him was darkness; it was too thick a night to see New York, but he knew it was there, if he could reach it. On his small black-and-white screens, the waters of New York Bay seemed even darker than usual, an endless choppy ocean of ink looming before him. He'd have to grope his way across, until the city lights came into sight. And if he lost it out there, over the water, he'd be joining Jetboy and J.F.K. a lot sooner than he planned; even if he could unscrew the hatch quick enough to avoid drowning, he couldn't swim.

But he *wasn't* going to lose it, Tom thought suddenly. Why the fuck was he hesitating? He wasn't going to lose it ever again, was he? He had to believe that.

He pressed his lips together, pushed off with his mind, and the shell slid smoothly out over the water. The salt waves beneath him rose and fell. He'd never had to push against water before; it felt different. Tom had an instant of panic; the shell rocked and dropped three feet before he caught hold of himself and adjusted. He calmed himself with an effort, shoved upward, and rose. *High,* he thought, he'd come in high, he'd *fly* in, like Jetboy, like Black Eagle, like a fucking *ace.* The shell moved out, faster and faster, gliding across the bay with swift serenity as Tom gained confidence. He'd never felt so incredibly powerful, so good, so goddamned *right.*

The compass worked fine; in less than ten minutes, the lights of the Battery and the Wall Street district loomed up before him. Tom pushed still higher, and floated uptown, hugging the shoreline of the Hudson. Jetboy's Tomb came and went beneath him. He'd stood in front of it a dozen times, gazing up at the face of the big metal statue out front. He wondered what that statue might think if it could look up and see him tonight.

He had a New York street map, but tonight he didn't need it; the flames could be seen almost a mile off. Even inside his armor Tom could feel the heat waves licking up at him when he made a pass overhead. He carefully began a descent. His fans whirred, and his cameras tracked at his command; below was chaos and cacophony, sirens and shouting, the crowd, the hurrying firemen, the police barricades, and the ambulances, big hook-and-ladder trucks spraying water into the inferno. At first no one noticed him, hovering fifty feet above the sidewalk—until he came in low enough for his lights to play on the walls of the building. Then he saw them looking up, pointing; he felt giddy with excitement.

But he had only an instant to relish the feeling. Then, from the corner of an eye, he saw her in one of his screens. She appeared suddenly in a fifth-floor window, bent over and coughing, her dress already afire. Before he could act, the flames licked at her; she screamed and jumped.

He caught her in midair, without thinking, without hesitating, without wondering whether he could do it. He just *did* it, caught her and held her and lowered her gently to the ground. The firemen surrounded her, put out her dress, and hustled her into an ambulance. And now, Tom saw, *everyone* was looking up at him, at the strange dark shape floating high in the night, with its ring of shining lights. The police band was crackling; they were reporting him as a flying saucer, he heard. He grinned.

A cop climbed up on top of his police car, holding a bullhorn, and began to hail him. Tom turned off the radio to hear better over the roar of the flames. He was telling Tom to land and identify himself, asking who he was, what he was.

That was easy. Tom turned on his microphone. "I'm the Turtle," he said. The VW had no tires; in the wheel wells, Joey had rigged the most humongous speakers they could find, powered by the largest amp on the market. For the first time, the voice of the Turtle was heard in the land, a booming "I'M THE TURTLE" echoing down the streets and alleys, a rolling thunder crackling with distortion. Except what he said didn't sound quite right. Tom cranked the volume up even higher, injected a little more bass into his voice. "*I AM THE GREAT AND POWERFUL TURTLE,*" he announced to them all.

Then he flew a block west, to the dark polluted waters of the Hudson, and imagined two huge invisible hands forty feet across. He lowered them into the river, cupped them full, and lifted. Rivulets of water dribbled to the street all the way back. When he dropped the first cascade on the flames, a ragged cheering went up from the crowd below.

———

"MERRY CHRISTMAS," TACH DECLARED DRUNKENLY WHEN THE clock struck midnight and the record Christmas Eve crowd began to whoop and shout and pound on the tables. On stage, Humphrey Bogart cracked a lame joke in an unfamiliar voice. All the lights in the house dimmed briefly; when they came back up, Bogart had been replaced by a portly, round-faced man with a red nose. "Who is he now?" Tach asked the twin on his left.

"W. C. Fields," she whispered. She slid her tongue around the inside of his ear. The twin on the right was doing something even more interesting under the table, where her hand had somehow found a way into his trousers. The twins were his Christmas gift from Angelface. "You can pretend they're me," she'd told him, though of course they were nothing like her. Nice kids, both of them, buxom and cheerful and absolutely uninhibited, if a bit simpleminded; they reminded him of Takisian sex toys. The one on the right had drawn the wild card, but she wore her cat mask even in bed, and there was no visible deformity to disturb the sweet pleasure of his erection.

W. C. Fields, whoever he was, offered some cynical observation, about Christmas and small children. The crowd hooted him off the stage. The Projectionist had an astonishing array of faces, but he couldn't tell a joke. Tach didn't mind; he had all the diversion he needed.

"Paper, Doc?" The vendor thrust a copy of the *Herald Tribune* across the table with a thick three-fingered hand. His flesh was blue-black and oily-looking. "All the Christmas news," he said, shifting the clumsy stack of papers under his arm. Two small curving tusks protruded from the corners of his wide, grinning mouth. Beneath a porkpie hat, the great bulge of his skull was covered with tufts of bristly red hair. On the streets they called him the Walrus.

"No thank you, Jube," Tach said with drunken dignity. "I have no desire to wallow in human folly tonight."

"Hey, look," said the twin on the right. "The Turtle!"

Tachyon looked around, momentarily befuddled, wondering how that huge armored shell could possibly have gotten inside the Funhouse, but of course she was referring to the newspaper.

"You better buy it for her, Tacky," the twin on the left said, giggling. "If you don't she'll pout."

Tachyon sighed. "I'll take one. But only if I don't have to listen to any of your jokes, Jube."

"Heard a new one about a joker, a Polack, and an Irishman stuck on a desert island, but just for that I'm not going to tell it," the Walrus replied with a rubbery grin.

Tachyon dug for some coins, found nothing in his pockets but a small, feminine hand. Jube winked. "I'll get it from Des," he said. Tachyon spread the newspaper out on the table, while the club erupted in applause as Cosmos and Chaos made their entrance.

A grainy photograph of the Turtle was spread across two columns. Tachyon thought it looked like a flying pickle, a big lumpy dill covered with little bumps. The Turtle had apprehended a hit-and-run driver who had killed a nine-year-old boy in Harlem, intercepting his flight and lifting the car twenty feet off the ground, where it floated with its engine roaring and its tires spinning madly until the police finally caught up. In a related sidebar, the rumor that the shell was an experimental robot flying tank had been denied by an Air Force spokesman.

"You'd think they'd have found something more important to write about by now," Tachyon said. It was the third big story about the

Turtle this week. The letter columns, the editorial pages, everything was Turtle, Turtle, Turtle. Even television was rabid with Turtle speculation. Who was he? What was he? How did he do it?

One reporter had even sought out Tach to ask that question. "Telekinesis," Tachyon told him. "It's nothing new. Almost common, in fact." Teke had been the single ability most frequently manifested by virus victims back in '46. He'd seen a dozen patients who could move paper clips and pencils, and one woman who could lift her own body weight for ten minutes at a time. Even Earl Sanderson's flight had been telekinetic in origin. What he did not tell them was that teke on *this* scale was unprecedented. Of course, when the story ran, they got half of it wrong.

"He's a joker, you know," whispered the twin on the right, the one in the silver-gray cat mask. She was leaning against his shoulder, reading about the Turtle.

"A joker?" Tach said.

"He hides inside a shell, doesn't he? Why would he do that unless he was really awful to look at?" She had taken her hand out of his trousers. "Could I have that paper?"

Tach pushed it toward her. "They're cheering him now," he said sharply. "They cheered the Four Aces too."

"That was a colored group, right?" she said, turning her attention to the headlines.

"She's keeping a scrapbook," her sister said. "All the jokers think he's one of them. Stupid, huh? I bet it's just a machine, some kind of Air Force flying saucer."

"He is not," her twin said. "It says so right here." She pointed to the sidebar with a long, red-painted nail.

"Never mind about her," the twin on the left said. She moved closer to Tachyon, nibbling on his neck as her hand went under the table. "Hey, what's wrong? You're all soft."

"My pardons," Tachyon said gloomily. Cosmos and Chaos were flinging axes, machetes, and knives across the stage, the glittering cascade multiplied into infinity by the mirrors around them. He had a bottle of fine cognac at hand, and lovely, willing women on either side of him, but suddenly, for some reason he could not have named, it did not feel like such a good night after all. He filled his glass almost to the brim and inhaled the heady alcoholic fumes. "Merry Christmas," he muttered to no one in particular.

CONSCIOUSNESS RETURNED WITH THE ANGRY TONES OF MAL'S voice. Tach lifted his head groggily from the mirrored tabletop, blinking down at his puffy red reflection. The jugglers, the twins, and the crowd were long gone. His cheek was sticky from lying in a puddle of spilled liquor. The twins had jollied him and fondled him and one of them had even gone under the table, for all the good it did. Then Angelface had come to the tableside and sent them away. "Go to sleep, Tacky," she'd said. Mal had come up to ask if he should lug him back to bed. "Not today," she'd said, "you know what day this is. Let him sleep it off here." He couldn't recall when he'd gone to sleep.

His head was about to explode, and Mal's shouting wasn't making things any better. "I don't give a flyin' fuck *what* you were promised, scumbag, you're not seeing her," the bouncer yelled. A softer voice said something in reply. "You'll get your fuckin' money, but that's all you'll get," Mal snapped.

Tach raised his eyes. In the mirrors he saw their reflections darkly: odd twisted shapes outlined in the wan dawn light, reflections of reflections, hundreds of them, beautiful, monstrous, uncountable, his children, his heirs, the offspring of his failures, a living sea of jokers. The soft voice said something else. "Ah, kiss my joker ass," Mal said. He had a body like a twisted stick and a head like a pumpkin; it made Tach smile. Mal shoved someone and reached behind his back, groping for his gun.

The reflections and the reflections of the reflections, the gaunt shadows and the bloated ones, the round-faced ones and the knife-thin ones, the black and the white, they moved all at once, filling the club with noise; a hoarse shout from Mal, the crack of gunfire. Instinctively Tach dove for cover, cracking his forehead hard on the edge of the table as he slid down. He blinked back tears of pain and lay curled up on the floor, peering out at the reflections of feet while the world disintegrated into a sharp-edged cacophony. Glass was shattering and falling, mirrors breaking on all sides, silvered knives flying through the air, too many for even Cosmos and Chaos to catch, dark splinters eating into the reflections, taking bites out of all the twisted shadow-shapes, blood spattering against the cracked mirrors.

It ended as suddenly as it had begun. The soft voice said something and there was the sound of footsteps, the crunch of glass underfoot. A moment later, a muffled scream from off behind him. Tach lay under the table, drunk and terrified. His finger hurt: bleeding, he saw, sliced open by a sliver of mirror. All he could think of were the stupid human superstitions about broken mirrors and bad luck. He cradled his head in his arms so the awful nightmare would go away. When he woke again, a policeman was shaking him roughly.

———————

MAL WAS DEAD, ONE DETECTIVE TOLD HIM; THEY SHOWED HIM A morgue photo of the bouncer lying in a pool of blood and a welter of broken glass. Ruth was dead too, and one of the janitors, a dim-witted cyclops who had never hurt anyone. They showed him a newspaper. The Santa Claus Slaughter, that was what they called it, and the lead was about three jokers who'd found death waiting under the tree on Christmas morning.

Miss Fascetti was gone, the other detective told him, did he know anything about that? Did he think she was involved? Was she a culprit or a victim? What could he tell them about her? He said he didn't know any such person, until they explained that they were asking about Angela Fascetti and maybe he knew her better as Angelface. She was gone and Mal was shot dead, and the most frightening thing of all was that Tach did not know where his next drink was coming from.

They held him for four days, questioning him relentlessly, going over the same ground again and again, until Tachyon was screaming at them, pleading with them, demanding his rights, demanding a lawyer, demanding a drink. They gave him only the lawyer. The lawyer said they couldn't hold him without charging him, so they charged him with being a material witness, with vagrancy, with resisting arrest, and questioned him again.

By the third day, his hands were shaking and he was having waking hallucinations. One of the detectives, the kindly one, promised him a bottle in return for his cooperation, but somehow his answers never quite satisfied them, and the bottle was not forthcoming. The bad-tempered one threatened to hold him forever unless he told the truth. I thought it was a nightmare, Tach told him, weeping. I was drunk, I'd been asleep. No, I couldn't see them, just the reflections, distorted, multiplied. I don't know how many there were. I don't know what it was about. No, she had no enemies, everyone loved Angelface. No, she didn't kill Mal, that didn't make sense, Mal loved her. One of them had a soft voice. No, I don't know which one. No, I can't remember what they said. No, I don't know if they were jokers or not, they looked like jokers, but the mirrors distort, some of them, not all of them, don't you see? No, I couldn't possibly pick them out of a lineup, I never really saw them. I had to hide under the table, do you see, the assassins had come, that's what my father always told me, there wasn't anything I could do.

When they realized that he was telling them all he knew, they dropped the charges and released him. To the dark streets of Jokertown and the cold of the night.

HE WALKED DOWN THE BOWERY ALONE, SHIVERING. THE WALRUS was hawking the evening papers from his newsstand on the corner of Hester. "Read all about it," he called out. "Turtle Terror in Jokertown." Tachyon paused to stare dully at the headlines. POLICE SEEK TUR-TLE, the *Post* reported. TURTLE CHARGED WITH ASSAULT, announced the *World-Telegram*. So the cheering had stopped already. He glanced at the text. The Turtle had been prowling Jokertown the past two nights, lifting people a hundred feet in the air to question them, threatening to drop them if he didn't like their answers. When police tried to make an arrest last night, the Turtle had deposited two of their black-and-whites on the roof of Freakers at Chatham Square. CURB THE TURTLE, the editorial in the *World-Telegram* said.

"You all right, Doc?" the Walrus asked.

"No," said Tachyon, putting down the paper. He couldn't afford to pay for it anyway.

Police barriers blocked the entrance to the Funhouse, and a padlock secured the door. CLOSED INDEFINITELY, the sign said. He needed a drink, but the pockets of his bandleader's coat were empty.

He thought of Des and Randall, and realized that he had no idea where they lived, or what their last names might be.

Trudging back to ROOMS, Tach climbed wearily up the stairs. When he stepped into the darkness, he had just enough time to notice that the room was frigidly cold; the window was open and a bitter wind was scouring out the old smells of urine, mildew, and drink. Had he done that? Confused, he stepped toward it, and someone came out from behind the door and grabbed him.

It happened so fast he scarcely had time to react. The forearm across his windpipe was an iron bar, choking off his scream, and a hand wrenched his right arm up behind his back, hard. He was choking, his arm close to breaking, and then he was being shoved toward the open window, running at it, and Tachyon could only thrash feebly in a grip much stronger than his own. The windowsill caught him square in the stomach, knocking the last of his breath right out of him, and suddenly he was falling, head over heels, locked helplessly in the steel embrace of his attacker, both of them plunging toward the sidewalk below.

They jerked to a stop five feet above the cement, with a wrench that elicited a grunt from the man behind him.

Tach had closed his eyes before the instant of impact. He opened them as they began to float upward. Above the yellow halo of the streetlamp was a ring of much brighter lights, set in a hovering darkness that blotted out the winter stars.

The arm across his throat had loosened enough for Tachyon to groan. "You," he said hoarsely, as they curved around the shell and came to rest gently on top of it. The metal was icy cold, its chill biting right through the fabric of Tachyon's pants. As the Turtle began to rise straight up into the night, Tachyon's captor released him. He drew in a shuddering breath of cold air, and rolled over to face a man in a zippered leather jacket, black dungarees, and a rubbery green frog mask. "Who . . . ?" he gasped.

"I'm the Great and Powerful Turtle's mean-ass sidekick," the man in the frog mask said, rather cheerfully.

"DOCTOR TACHYON, I PRESUME," boomed the shell's speakers, far above the alleys of Jokertown. "I'VE ALWAYS WANTED TO MEET YOU. I READ ABOUT YOU WHEN I WAS JUST A KID."

"Turn it down," Tach croaked weakly.

"OH. SURE. Is that better?" The volume diminished sharply. "It's noisy in here, and behind all this armor I can't always tell how loud I sound. I'm sorry if we scared you, but we couldn't take the chance of you saying no. We need you."

Tach stayed just where he was, shivering, shaken. "What do you want?" he asked wearily.

"Help," the Turtle declared. They were still rising; the lights of Manhattan spread out all around them, and the spires of the Empire State Building and the Chrysler Building rose uptown. They were higher than either. The wind was cold and gusting; Tach clung to the shell for dear life.

"Leave me alone," Tachyon said. "I have no help to give you. I have no help to give anybody."

"Fuck, he's crying," the man in the frog mask said.

"You don't understand," the Turtle said. The shell began to drift west, its motion silent and steady. There was something awesome and eerie about the flight. "You have to help. I've tried on my own, but I'm getting nowhere. But you, your powers, they can make the difference."

Tachyon was lost in his own self-pity, too cold and exhausted and despairing to reply. "I want a drink," he said.

"Fuck it," said Frog-face. "Dumbo was right about this guy, he's nothing but a goddamned wino."

"He doesn't understand," said the Turtle. "Once we explain, he'll come around. Doctor Tachyon, we're talking about your friend Angelface."

He needed a drink so badly it hurt. "She was good to me," he said, remembering the sweet perfume of her satin sheets, and her bloody footprints on the mirror tiles. "But there's nothing I can do. I told the police everything I know."

"Chickenshit asshole," said Frog-face.

"When I was a kid, I read about you in *Jetboy Comics*," the Turtle said. "'Thirty Minutes Over Broadway,' remember? You were supposed to be as smart as Einstein. I might be able to save your friend Angelface, but I can't without your powers."

"I don't do that any longer. I *can't*. There was someone I hurt, someone I cared for, but I seized her mind, just for an instant, for a good reason, or at least I thought it was for a good reason, but it . . . destroyed her. I can't do it again."

"Boohoo," said Frog-face mockingly. "Let's toss 'im, Turtle, he's not worth a bucket of warm piss." He took something out of one of the pockets of his leather jacket; Tach was astonished to see that it was a bottle of beer.

"Please," Tachyon said, as the man popped off the cap with a bottle-opener hung round his neck. "A sip," Tach said. "Just a sip." He hated the taste of beer, but he needed something, anything. It had been days. "Please."

"Fuck off," Frog-face said.

"Tachyon," said the Turtle, "you can make him."

"No I can't," Tach said. The man raised the bottle up to green rubber lips. "I can't," Tach repeated. Frog-face continued to drink. "No." He could hear it gurgling. "Please, just a little."

The man lowered the beer bottle, sloshed it thoughtfully. "Just a swallow left," he said.

"Please." He reached out, hands trembling.

"Nah," said Frog-face. He began to turn the bottle upside down. "Course, if you're really thirsty, you could just grab my mind, right? *Make* me give you the fuckin' bottle." He tipped the bottle a little more. "Go on, I dare ya, try it."

Tach watched the last mouthful of beer dribble down onto the Turtle's shell and run off into empty air.

"Fuck," said the man in the frog mask. "You got it bad, don't you?" He pulled another bottle from his pocket, opened it, and handed it across. Tach cradled it with both hands. The beer was cold and sour, but he had never tasted anything half so sweet. He drained it all in one long swallow.

"Got any other smart ideas?" Frog-face asked the Turtle.

Ahead of them was the blackness of the Hudson River, the lights of Jersey off to the west. They were descending. Beneath them, overlooking the Hudson, was a sprawling edifice of steel and glass and marble that Tachyon suddenly recognized, though he had never set foot inside it: Jetboy's Tomb. "Where are we going?" he asked.

"We're going to see a man about a rescue," the Turtle said.

Jetboy's Tomb filled the entire block, on the site where the pieces of his plane had come raining down. It filled Tom's screens too, as he sat in the warm darkness of his shell, bathed in a phosphor glow. Motors whirred as the cameras moved in their tracks. The huge flanged wings of the tomb curved upward, as if the building itself was about to take flight. Through tall, narrow windows, he could see glimpses of the full-size replica of the JB-1 suspended from the ceiling, its scarlet flanks aglow from hidden lights. Above the doors, the hero's last words had been carved, each letter chiseled into the black Italian marble and filled in stainless steel. The metal flashed as the shell's white-hot spots slid across the legend:

> I CANT DIE YET,
> I HAVEN'T SEEN *THE JOLSON STORY*

Tom brought the shell down in front of the monument, to hover five feet above the broad marble plaza at the top of the stairs. Nearby, a twenty-foot-tall steel Jetboy looked out over the West Side Highway and the Hudson beyond, his fists cocked. The metal used for the sculpture had come from the wreckage of crashed planes, Tom knew. He knew that statue's face better than he knew his father's.

The man they'd come to meet emerged from the shadows at the base of the statue, a chunky dark shape huddled in a thick overcoat, hands shoved deep into his pockets. Tom shone a light on him; a camera tracked to give him a better view. The joker was a portly man, round-shouldered and well-dressed. His coat had a fur collar and his fedora was pulled low. Instead of a nose, he had an elephant's trunk in the middle of his face. The end of it was fringed with fingers, snug in a little leather glove.

Dr. Tachyon slid off the top of the shell, lost his footing and landed on his ass. Tom heard Joey laugh. Then Joey jumped down too and pulled Tachyon to his feet.

The joker glanced down at the alien. "So you convinced him to come after all. I'm surprised."

"We were real fuckin' persuasive," Joey said.

"Des," Tachyon said, sounding confused. "What are you doing here? Do you know these people?"

Elephant-face twitched his trunk. "Since the day before yesterday, yes, in a manner of speaking. They came to me. The hour was late, but a phone call from the Great and Powerful Turtle does pique one's interest. He offered his help, and I accepted. I even told them where you lived."

Tachyon ran a hand through his tangled, filthy hair. "I'm sorry about Mal. Do you know anything about Angelface? You know how much she meant to me."

"In dollars and cents, I know quite precisely," Des said.

Tachyon's mouth gaped open. He looked hurt. Tom felt sorry for him. "I wanted to go to you," he said. "I didn't know where to find you."

Joey laughed. "He's listed in the fuckin' phone book, dork. Ain't that many guys named Xavier Desmond." He looked at the shell. "How the fuck is he gonna find the lady if he couldn't even find his buddy here?"

Desmond nodded. "An excellent point. This isn't going to work. Just look at him!" His trunk pointed. "What good is he? We're wasting precious time."

"We did it your way," Tom replied. "We're getting nowhere. No one's talking. He can get the information we need."

"I don't understand any of this," Tachyon interrupted.

Joey made a disgusted sound. He had found a beer somewhere and was cracking the cap.

"What's happening?" Tach asked.

"If you had been the least bit interested in anything besides cognac and cheap tarts, you might know," Des said icily.

"Tell him what you told us," Tom commanded. When he knew, Tachyon would surely help, he thought. He *had* to.

Des gave a heavy sigh. "Angelface had a heroin habit. She hurt, you know. Perhaps you noticed that from time to time, Doctor? The drug was the only thing that got her through the day. Without it, the pain would have driven her insane. Nor was hers an ordinary junkie's habit. She used uncut heroin in quantities that would have killed any normal user. You saw how minimally it affected her. The joker metabolism is a curious thing. Do you have any idea how expensive heroin is, Doctor Tachyon? Never mind, I see that you don't. Angelface made quite a bit of money from the Funhouse, but it was never enough. Her source gave her credit until she was in far over her head, then demanded . . . call it a promissory note. Or a Christmas present. She had no choice. It was that or be cut off. She hoped to come up with the money, being an eternal optimist. She failed. On Christmas morning her source came by to collect. Mal wasn't about to let them have her. They insisted."

Tachyon was squinting in the glare of the lights. His image began to roll upward. "Why didn't she tell me?" he said.

"I suppose she didn't want to burden you, Doctor. It might have taken the fun out of your self-pitying binges."

"Have you told the police?"

"The police? Ah, yes. New York's finest. The ones who seem so curiously uninterested whenever a joker is beaten or killed, yet ever so diligent if a tourist is robbed. The ones who so regularly arrest, harass, and brutalize any joker who has the poor taste to live anywhere outside of Jokertown. Perhaps we might consult the officer who commented that raping a joker woman is more a lapse in taste than a crime." Des snorted. "Doctor Tachyon, where do you think Angelface bought her drugs? Do you think any ordinary street pusher would have access to uncut heroin in the quantities she needed? The police *were* her source. The head of the Jokertown narcotics squad, if you care to be precise. Oh, I'll grant you that it's unlikely the whole department is involved. Homicide may be conducting a legitimate investigation. What do you think they'd say if we told them that Bannister was the murderer? You think they'd arrest one of their own? On the strength of my testimony, or the testimony of any joker?"

"We'll make good her note," Tachyon blurted. "We'll give this man his money or the Funhouse or whatever it is he wants."

"The promissory note," Desmond said wearily, "was not for the Funhouse."

"Whatever it was, give it to him!"

"She promised him the only thing she still had that he wanted," Desmond said. "Herself. Her beauty and her pain. The word's out on the street, if you know how to listen. There's going to be a very special New Year's Eve party somewhere in the city. Invitation only. Expensive. A unique thrill. Bannister will have her first. He's wanted that for a long time. But the other guests will have their turn. Jokertown hospitality."

Tachyon's mouth worked soundlessly for a moment. "The *police*?"

he finally managed. He looked as shocked as Tom had been when Desmond told him and Joey.

"Do you think they love us, Doctor? We're freaks. We're *diseased*. Jokertown is a hell, a dead end, and the Jokertown police are the most brutal, corrupt, and incompetent in the city. I don't think anyone planned what happened at the Funhouse, but it happened, and Angelface knows too much. They can't let her live, so they're going to have some fun with the joker cunt."

Tom Tudbury leaned toward his microphone. "I can rescue her," he said. "These fuckers haven't seen anything like the Great and Powerful Turtle. But I can't *find* her."

Des said, "She has a lot of friends. But none of us can read minds, or make a man do something he doesn't want to."

"I *can't*," Tachyon protested. He seemed to shrink into himself, to edge away from them, and for an instant Tom thought the little man was going to run away. "You don't understand."

"What a fuckin' candy-ass," Joey said loudly.

Watching Tachyon crumble on his screens, Tom Tudbury finally ran out of patience. "If you fail, you fail," he said. "And if you don't try, you fail too, so what the fuck difference does it make? Jetboy failed, but at least he *tried*. He wasn't an ace, he wasn't a goddamned *Takisian*, he was just a guy with a jet, but he did what he could."

"I want to. I . . . just . . . *can't*."

Des trumpeted his disgust. Joey shrugged.

Inside his shell, Tom sat in stunned disbelief. He wasn't going to help. He hadn't believed it, not really. Joey had warned him, Desmond too, but Tom had insisted, he'd been sure, this was *Doctor Tachyon,* of course he'd help, maybe he was having some problems, but once they explained the situation to him, once they made it clear what was at stake and how much they needed him—he *had* to help. But he was saying no. It was the last goddamned straw.

He twisted the volume knob up all the way. "YOU SON OF A BITCH," he boomed, and the sound hammered out over the plaza. Tachyon flinched away. "YOU NO-GOOD FUCKING LITTLE ALIEN CHICKENSHIT!" Tachyon stumbled backward down the stairs, but the Turtle drifted after him, loudspeakers blaring. "IT WAS ALL A LIE, WASN'T IT? EVERYTHING IN THE COMIC

BOOKS, EVERYTHING IN THE PAPERS, IT WAS ALL A STU-
PID LIE. ALL MY LIFE THEY BEAT ME UP AND THEY
CALLED ME A FUCKING WIMP AND A COWARD BUT
YOU'RE THE COWARD, YOU ASSHOLE, YOU SHITTY LIT-
TLE WHINER, YOU WON'T EVEN TRY, YOU DON'T GIVE
A DAMN ABOUT ANYBODY, ABOUT YOUR FRIEND AN-
GELFACE OR ABOUT KENNEDY OR JETBOY OR ANY-
BODY, YOU HAVE ALL THESE FUCKING POWERS AND
YOU'RE *NOTHING,* YOU WON'T DO ANYTHING, YOU'RE
WORSE THAN OSWALD OR BRAUN OR ANY OF THEM."
Tachyon staggered down the steps, hands over his ears, shouting some-
thing unintelligible, but Tom was past listening. His anger had a life of its
own now. He lashed out, and the alien's head snapped around and red-
dened with the force of the slap. *"ASSHOLE!"* Tom was shrieking.
"YOU'RE THE ONE IN A SHELL." Invisible blows rained down on
Tachyon in a fury. He reeled, fell, rolled a third of the way down the
stairs, tried to get back to his feet, was bowled over again, and bounced
down to the street head over heels. "ASSHOLE!" the Turtle thundered.
"RUN, YOU SHITHEAD. GET OUT OF HERE, OR I'LL
THROW YOU IN THE DAMNED RIVER! RUN, YOU LIT-
TLE WIMP, BEFORE THE GREAT AND POWERFUL TURTLE
REALLY GETS UPSET! RUN, DAMN IT! YOU'RE THE ONE
IN THE SHELL! YOU'RE THE ONE IN THE SHELL!"

And he ran, dashing blindly from one streetlight to the next, until
he was lost in the shadows. Tom Tudbury watched him vanish on the
shell's array of television screens. He felt sick and beaten. His head was
throbbing. He needed a beer, or an aspirin, or both. When he heard
the sirens coming, he scooped up Joey and Desmond and set them on
top of his shell, killed his lights, and rose straight up into the night,
high, high up, into darkness and cold and silence.

————

THAT NIGHT TACH SLEPT THE SLEEP OF THE DAMNED, THRASHING
about like a man in a fever dream, crying out, weeping, waking again
and again from nightmares, only to drift back into them. He dreamt he
was back on Takis, and his hated cousin Zabb was boasting about a new
sex toy, but when he brought her out it was Blythe, and he raped her

right there in front of him. Tach watched it all, powerless to intervene; her body writhed beneath his and blood flowed from her mouth and ears and vagina. She began to change, into a thousand joker shapes each more horrible than the last, and Zabb went right on raping them all as they screamed and struggled. But afterward, when Zabb rose from the corpse covered with blood, it wasn't his cousin's face at all, it was his own, worn and dissipated, a *coarse* face, eyes reddened and puffy, long red hair tangled and greasy, features distorted by alcoholic bloat or perhaps by a Funhouse mirror.

He woke around noon, to the terrible sound of Tiny weeping outside his window. It was more than he could stand. It was all more than he could stand. He stumbled to the window and threw it open and screamed at the giant to be quiet, to stop, to leave him alone, to give him peace, please, but Tiny went on and on, so much pain, so much guilt, so much shame, why couldn't they let him be, he couldn't take it anymore, no, shut up, shut up, *please shut up,* and suddenly Tach shrieked and reached out with his mind and plunged into Tiny's head and shut him up.

The silence was thunderous.

———

The nearest phone booth was in a candy store a block down. Vandals had ripped the phone book to shreds. He dialed information and got the listing for Xavier Desmond on Christie Street, only a short walk away. The apartment was a fourth-floor walkup above a mask shop. Tachyon was out of breath by the time he got to the top.

Des opened the door on the fifth knock. "You," he said.

"The Turtle," Tach said. His throat was dry. "Did he get anything last night?"

"No," Desmond replied. His trunk twitched. "The same story as before. They're wise to him now, they know he won't really drop them. They call his bluff. Short of actually killing someone, there's nothing to do."

"Tell me who to ask," Tach said.

"You?" Des said.

Tach could not look the joker in the eye. He nodded.

"Let me get my coat," Des said. He emerged from the apartment bundled up for the cold, carrying a fur cap and a frayed beige raincoat.

"Put your hair up in the hat," he told Tachyon, "and leave that ridiculous coat here. You don't want to be recognized." Tach did as he said. On the way out, Des went into the mask shop for the final touch.

"A chicken?" Tach said when Des handed him the mask. It had bright yellow feathers, a prominent orange beak, a floppy red coxcomb on top.

"I saw it and I knew it was you," said Des. "Put it on."

A large crane was moving into position at Chatham Square, to get the police cars off Freakers' roof. The club was open. The doorman was a seven-foot-tall hairless joker with fangs. He grabbed Des by the arm as they tried to pass under the neon thighs of the six-breasted dancer who writhed on the marquee. "No jokers allowed," he said brusquely. "Get lost, Tusker."

Reach out and grab his mind, Tachyon thought. Once, before Blythe, he would have done it instinctively. But now he hesitated, and hesitating, he was lost.

Des reached into his back pocket, pulled out a wallet, extracted a fifty-dollar bill. "You were watching them lower the police cars," he said. "You never saw me pass."

"Oh, yeah," the doorman said. The bill vanished in a clawed hand. "Real interesting, them cranes."

"Sometimes money is the most potent power of all," Des said as they walked into the cavernous dimness within. A sparse noontime crowd sat eating the free lunch and watching a stripper gyrate down a long runway behind a barbed-wire barrier. She was covered with silky gray hair, except for her breasts, which had been shaved bare. Desmond scanned the booths along the far wall. He took Tach's elbow and led him to a dark corner, where a man in a peacoat was sitting with a stein of beer. "They lettin' jokers in here now?" the man asked gruffly as they approached. He was saturnine and pockmarked.

Tach went into his mind. *Fuck what's this now the elephant man's from the Funhouse who's the other one damned jokers anyhow gotta lotta nerve.*

"Where's Bannister keeping Angelface?" Des asked.

"Angelface is the slit at the Funhouse, right? Don't know no Bannister. Is this a game? Fuck off, joker, I ain't playing." In his thoughts, images came tumbling: Tach saw mirrors shattering, silver knives flying through the air, felt Mal's shove and saw him reach for a gun, watched him shudder and spin as the bullets hit, heard Bannister's soft voice as he told them to kill Ruth, saw the warehouse over on the Hudson where they were keeping her, the livid bruises on her arm when they'd grabbed her, tasted the man's fear, fear of jokers, fear of discovery, fear of Bannister, the fear of *them*. Tach reached out and squeezed Desmond's arm.

Des turned to go. "Hey, hold it right there," the man with the pockmarked face said. He flashed a badge as he unfolded from the booth. "Undercover narcotics," he said, "and you been using, mister, asking asshole junkie questions like that." Des stood still as the man frisked him down. "Well, looka this," he said, producing a bag of white powder from one of Desmond's pockets. "Wonder what this is? You're under arrest, freak-face."

"That's not mine," Desmond said calmly.

"The hell it ain't," the man said, and in his mind the thoughts ran one after another *little accident resisting arrest what could i do huh? jokers'll scream but who listens to a fuckin' joker only whatymi gonna do with the other one?* and he glanced at Tachyon. *Jeez looka the chickenman's shaking maybe the fucker IS using that'd be great.*

Trembling, Tach realized the moment of truth was at hand.

He was not sure he could do it. It was different than with Tiny; that had been blind instinct, but he was awake now, and he knew what he was doing. It had been so easy once, as easy as using his hands. But now those hands trembled, and there was blood on them, and on his mind as well . . . he thought of Blythe and the way her mind had shattered under his touch, like the mirrors in the Funhouse, and for a terrible, long second nothing happened, until the fear was rank in his throat, and the familiar taste of failure filled his mouth.

Then the pockfaced man smiled an idiot's smile, sat back down in his booth, laid his head on the table, and went to sleep as sweetly as a child.

Des took it in stride. "Your doing?"

Tachyon nodded.

"You're shaking," Des asked. "Are you all right, Doctor?"

"I think so," Tachyon said. The policeman had begun to snore loudly. "I think maybe I am all right, Des. For the first time in years." He looked at the joker's face, looked past the deformity to the man beneath. "I know where she is," he said. They started toward the exit. In the cage, a full-breasted, bearded hermaphrodite had started into a bump-and-grind. "We have to move quickly."

"In an hour I can get together twenty men."

"No," Tachyon said. "The place they're holding her isn't in Jokertown."

Des stopped with his hand on the door. "I see," he said. "And outside of Jokertown, jokers and masked men are rather conspicuous, aren't they?"

"Exactly," Tach said. He did not voice his other fear, of the retribution that would surely be enacted should jokers dare to confront police, even police as corrupt as Bannister and his cohorts. He would take the risk himself, he had nothing left to lose, but he could not permit them to take it. "Can you reach the Turtle?" he asked.

"I can take you to him," Des replied. "When?"

"Now," Tach said. In an hour or two, the sleeping policeman would awaken and go straight to Bannister. And say what? That Des and a man in a chicken mask had been asking questions, that he'd been about to arrest them but suddenly he'd gotten very sleepy? Would he dare admit to that? If so, what would Bannister make of it? Enough to move Angelface? Enough to kill her? They could not chance it.

When they emerged from the dimness of Freakers, the crane had just lowered the second police car to the sidewalk. A cold wind was blowing, but behind his chicken feathers, Doctor Tachyon had begun to sweat.

———

TOM TUDBURY WOKE TO THE DIM, MUFFLED SOUND OF SOMEONE pounding on his shell.

He pushed aside the frayed blanket and bashed his head sitting up. "Ow, goddamn it," he cursed, fumbling in the darkness until he found the map light. The pounding continued, a hollow *boom boom boom* against the armor, echoing. Tom felt a stab of panic. The police, he thought, they've found me, they've come to drag me out and haul me up on charges. His head hurt. It was cold and stuffy in here. He turned on the space heater, the fans, the cameras. His screens came to life.

Outside was a bright cold December day, the sunlight painting every grimy brick with stark clarity. Joey had taken the train back to Bayonne, but Tom had remained; they were running out of time, he had no other choice. Des found him a safe place, an interior courtyard in the depths of Jokertown, surrounded by decaying five-story tenements, its cobblestones redolent with the smell of sewage, wholly hidden from the street. When he'd landed, just before dawn, lights had blinked on in a few of the dark windows, and faces had come to peer cautiously around the shades; wary, frightened, not-quite-human faces, briefly seen and gone as quickly, when they decided that the thing outside was none of their concern.

Yawning, Tom pulled himself into his seat and panned his cameras until he found the source of the commotion. Des was standing by an open cellar door, arms crossed, while Doctor Tachyon hammered on the shell with a length of broom handle.

Astonished, Tom flipped open his microphones. "YOU."

Tachyon winced. "Please."

He lowered the volume. "Sorry. You took me by surprise. I never expected to see you again. After last night, I mean. I didn't hurt you, did I? I didn't mean to, I just—"

"I understand," Tachyon said. "But we've got no time for recriminations or apologies now."

Des began to roll upward. Damn that vertical hold. "We know where they have her," the joker said as his image flipped. "That is, if Doctor Tachyon can indeed read minds as advertised."

"Where?" Tom said. Des continued to flip, flip, flip.

"A warehouse on the Hudson," Tachyon replied. "Near the foot of a pier. I can't tell you an address, but I saw it clearly in his thoughts. I'll recognize it."

"Great!" Tom enthused. He gave up on his efforts to adjust the vertical hold and whapped the screen. The picture steadied. "Then we've got them. Let's go." The look on Tachyon's face took him aback. "You are coming, aren't you?"

Tachyon swallowed. "Yes," he said. He had a mask in his hand. He slipped it on.

That was a relief, Tom thought; for a second there, he'd thought he'd have to go it alone. "Climb on," he said.

With a deep sigh of resignation, the alien scrambled on top of the shell, his boots scrabbling at the armor. Tom gripped his armrests tightly and pushed up. The shell rose as easily as a soap bubble. He felt elated. This was what he was meant to do, Tom thought; Jetboy must have felt like this.

Joey had installed a monster of a horn in the shell. Tom let it rip as they floated clear of the rooftops, startling a coop of pigeons, a few winos, and Tachyon with the distinctive blare of *Here-I-come-to-save-the-daaaaaay.*

"It might be wise to be a bit more subtle about this," Tachyon said diplomatically.

Tom laughed. "I don't believe it, I got a man from outer space who mostly dresses like Pinky Lee riding on my back, and he's telling me I ought to be subtle." He laughed again as the streets of Jokertown spread out all around them.

THEY MADE THEIR FINAL APPROACH THROUGH A MAZE OF WATER-front alleys. The last was a dead end, terminating in a brick wall scrawled over with the names of gangs and young lovers. The Turtle rose above it, and they emerged in the loading area behind the warehouse. A man in a short leather jacket sat on the edge of the loading dock. He jumped to his feet when they hove into view. His jump took him a lot higher than he'd anticipated, about ten feet higher. He opened his mouth, but before he could shout, Tach had him; he went to sleep in midair. The Turtle stashed him atop a nearby roof.

Four wide loading bays opened onto the dock, all chained and pad-locked, their corrugated metal doors marked with wide brown streaks of rust. TRESPASSERS WILL BE PROSECUTED said the lettering on the narrow door to the side.

Tach hopped down, landing easily on the balls of his feet, his nerves tingling. "I'll go through," he told the Turtle. "Give me a minute, and then follow."

"A minute," the speakers said. "You got it."

Tach pulled off his boots, opened the door just a crack, and slid into the warehouse on purple-stockinged feet, summoning up all the stealth and fluid grace they'd once taught him on Takis. Inside, bales of shred-ded paper, bound tightly in thin wire, were stacked twenty and thirty feet high. Tachyon crept down a crooked aisle toward the sound of voices. A huge yellow forklift blocked his path. He dropped flat and squirmed underneath it, to peer around one massive tire.

He counted five altogether. Two of them were playing cards, sitting in folding chairs and using a stack of coverless paperbacks for a table. A grossly fat man was adjusting a gigantic paper-shredding machine against the far wall. The last two stood over a long table, bags of white powder piled in neat rows in front of them. The tall man in the flannel shirt was weighing something on a small set of scales. Next to him, supervising, was a slender balding man in an expensive raincoat. He had a cigarette in his hand, and his voice was smooth and soft. Tachyon couldn't quite make out what he was saying. There was no sign of Angelface.

He dipped into the sewer that was Bannister's mind, and saw her. Between the shredder and the baling machine. He couldn't see it from under the forklift; the machinery blocked the line of sight, but she was there. A filthy mattress had been tossed on the concrete floor, and she lay atop it, her ankles swollen and raw where the handcuffs chafed against her skin.

———

"... FIFTY-EIGHT HIPPOPOTAMI, FIFTY-NINE HIPPOPOTAMI, *SIXTY* hippopotami," Tom counted.

The loading bays were big enough. He squeezed, and the padlock disintegrated into shards of rust and twisted metal. The chains came clanking down, and the door rattled upward, rusty tracks screeching protest. Tom turned on all his lights as the shell slid forward. Inside, towering stacks of paper blocked his way. There wasn't room to go between them. He shoved them, *hard,* but even as they started to collapse, it occurred to him that he could go above them. He pushed up toward the ceiling.

———

"WHAT THE FUCK," ONE OF THE CARDPLAYERS SAID, WHEN THEY heard the loading gate screech open.

A heartbeat later, they were all moving. Both cardplayers scrambled to their feet; one of them produced a gun. The man in the flannel shirt looked up from his scales. The fat man turned away from the shredder, shouting something, but it was impossible to make out what he was saying. Against the far wall, bales of paper came crashing down, knocking into neighboring stacks and sending them down too, in a chain reaction that spread across the warehouse.

Without an instant's hesitation, Bannister went for Angelface. Tach took his mind and stopped him in mid-stride, with his revolver half-drawn.

And then a dozen bales of shredded paper slammed down against the rear of the forklift. The vehicle shifted, just a little, crushing Tachyon's left hand under a huge black tire. He cried out in shock and pain, and lost Bannister.

———————

DOWN BELOW, TWO LITTLE MEN WERE SHOOTING AT HIM. THE first shot startled him so badly that Tom lost his concentration for a split second, and the shell dropped four feet before he got it back. Then the bullets were *ping*ing harmlessly off his armor and ricocheting around the warehouse. Tom smiled. "I AM THE GREAT AND POWER-FUL TURTLE," he announced at full volume, as stacks of paper crashed down all around. "YOU ASSHOLES ARE UP SHIT CREEK. SURRENDER NOW."

The nearest asshole didn't surrender. He fired again, and one of Tom's screens went black. "OH, FUCK," Tom said, forgetting to kill his mike. He grabbed the guy's arm and pulled the gun away, and from the way the jerk screamed he'd probably dislocated his shoulder too, goddammit. He'd have to watch that. The other guy started running, jumping over a collapsed pile of paper. Tom caught him in mid-jump, took him straight up to the ceiling, and hung him from a rafter. His eyes flicked from screen to screen, but one screen was dark now and the damned vertical hold had gone again on the one next to it, so he couldn't make out a fucking thing to that side. He didn't have time to fix it. Some guy in a flannel shirt was loading bags into a suitcase, he saw on the big screen, and from the corner of his eye, he spied a fat guy climbing into a forklift....

———————

HIS HAND CRUSHED BENEATH THE TIRE, TACHYON WRITHED IN EX-cruciating pain and tried not to scream. Bannister—had to stop

Bannister before he got to Angelface. He ground his teeth together and tried to will away the pain, to gather it into a ball and push it from him the way he'd been taught, but it was hard, he'd lost the discipline, he could feel the shattered bones in his hand, his eyes were blurry with tears, and then he heard the forklift's motor turn over, and suddenly it was surging forward, rolling right up his arm, coming straight at his head, the tread of the massive tire a black wall of death rushing toward him . . . and passing an inch over the top of his skull, as it took to the air.

The forklift flew nicely across the warehouse and embedded itself in the far wall, with a little push from the Great and Powerful Turtle. The fat man dove off in midair and landed on a pile of coverless paperbacks. It wasn't until then that Tom happened to notice Tachyon lying on the floor under the place the forklift had been. He was holding his hand funny and his chicken mask was all smashed up and dirty, Tom saw, and as he staggered to his feet he was shouting something. He went running across the floor, reeling, unsteady. Where the fuck was he going in such a hurry?

Frowning, Tom smacked the malfunctioning screen with the back of his hand, and the vertical roll stopped suddenly. For an instant, the image on the television was clear and sharp. A man in a raincoat stood over a woman on a mattress. She was real pretty, and there was a funny smile on her face, sad but almost accepting, as he pressed the revolver right up to her forehead.

Tach came reeling around the shredding machine, his ankles all rubber, the world a red blur, his shattered bones jabbing against each other with every step, and found them there, Bannister touching her lightly with his pistol, her skin already darkening where the bullet would go in, and through his tears and his fears and a haze of pain, he reached out for Bannister's mind and seized it . . . just in time to feel him squeeze the trigger, and wince as the gun kicked back in his mind. He heard the explosion from two sets of ears.

"Nooooooooooooooooooo!" he shrieked. He closed his eyes, sunk to his knees. He made Bannister fling the gun away, for what good it would

do, none at all, too late, again he'd come too late, *failed, failed,* again, Angelface, Blythe, his sister, everyone he loved, all of them gone. He doubled over on the floor, and his mind filled with images of broken mirrors, of the Wedding Pattern danced in blood and pain, and that was the last thing he knew before the darkness took him.

He woke to the astringent smell of a hospital room and the feel of a pillow under his head, the pillowcase crisp with starch. He opened his eyes. "Des," he said weakly. He tried to sit, but he was bound up somehow. The world was blurry and unfocused.

"You're in traction, Doctor," Des said. "Your right arm was broken in two places, and your hand is worse than that."

"I'm sorry," Tach said. He would have wept, but he had run out of tears. "I'm so sorry. We tried, I...I'm so sorry, I—"

"Tacky," she said in that soft, husky voice.

And she was there, standing over him, dressed in a hospital gown, black hair framing a wry smile. She had combed it forward to cover her forehead; beneath her bangs was a hideous purple-green bruise, and the skin around her eyes was red and raw. For a moment he thought he was dead, or mad, or dreaming. "It's all right, Tacky. I'm okay. I'm here."

He stared up at her numbly. "You're dead," he said dully. "I was too late. I heard the shot, I had him by then but it was too late, I felt the gun recoil in his hand."

"Did you feel it jerk?" she asked him.

"Jerk?"

"A couple of inches, no more. Just as he fired. Just enough. I got some nasty powder burns, but the bullet went into the mattress a foot from my head."

"The Turtle," Tach said hoarsely.

She nodded. "He pushed aside the gun just as Bannister squeezed the trigger. And you made the son of a bitch throw away the revolver before he could get off a second shot."

"You got them," Des said. "A couple of men escaped in the confusion, but the Turtle delivered three of them, including Bannister. Plus a suitcase packed with twenty pounds of pure heroin. And it turns out that warehouse is owned by the mafia."

"The mafia?" Tachyon said.

"The mob," Des explained. "Criminals, Doctor Tachyon."

"One of the men captured in the warehouse has already turned state's evidence," Angelface said. "He'll testify to everything—the bribes, the drug operation, the murders at the Funhouse."

"Maybe we'll even get some decent police in Jokertown," Des added.

The feelings that rushed through Tachyon went far beyond relief. He wanted to thank them, wanted to cry for them, but neither the tears nor the words would come. He was weak and happy. "I didn't fail," he managed at last.

"No," Angelface said. She looked at Des. "Would you wait outside?" When they were alone, she sat on the edge of the bed. "I want to show you something. Something I wish I'd shown you a long time ago." She held it up in front of him. It was a gold locket. "Open it."

It was hard to do with only one hand, but he managed. Inside was a small round photograph of an elderly woman in bed. Her limbs were skeletal and withered, sticks draped in mottled flesh, and her face was horribly twisted. "What's wrong with her?" Tach asked, afraid of the answer. Another joker, he thought, another victim of his failures.

Angelface looked down at the twisted old woman, sighed, and closed the locket with a snap. "When she was four, in Little Italy, she was run over while playing in the street. A horse stepped on her face, and the wagon wheel crushed her spine. That was in, oh, 1886. She was completely paralyzed, but she lived. If you could call it living. That little girl spent the next sixty years in a bed, being fed, washed, and read to, with no company except the holy sisters. Sometimes all she wanted was to die. She dreamed about what it would be like to be beautiful, to be loved and desired, to be able to dance, to be able to *feel* things. Oh, how she wanted to *feel* things." She smiled. "I should have said thank you long ago, Tacky, but it's hard for me to show that picture to anyone. But I am grateful, and now I owe you doubly. You'll never pay for a drink at the Funhouse."

He stared at her. "I don't want a drink," he said. "No more. That's done." And it was, he knew; if she could live with her pain, what excuse could he possibly have to waste his life and talents? "Angelface," he said suddenly, "I can make you something better than heroin. I was . . .

I *am* a biochemist, there are drugs on Takis, I can synthesize them, painkillers, nerve blocks. If you'll let me run some tests on you, maybe I can tailor something to your metabolism. I'll need a lab, of course. Setting things up will be expensive, but the drug could be made for pennies."

"I'll have some money," she said. "I'm selling the Funhouse to Des. But what you're talking about is illegal."

"To hell with their stupid laws," Tach blazed. "I won't tell if you won't." Then words came tumbling out one after the other, a torrent: plans, dreams, hopes, all of the things he'd lost or drowned in cognac and Sterno, and Angelface was looking at him, astonished, smiling, and when the drugs they had given him finally began to wear off, and his arm began to throb again, Doctor Tachyon remembered the old disciplines and sent the pain away, and somehow it seemed as though part of his guilt and his grief went with it, and he was whole again, and alive.

THE HEADLINE SAID TURTLE, TACHYON SMASH HEROIN RING. Tom was gluing the article into the scrapbook when Joey returned with the beers. "They left out the Great and Powerful part," Joey observed, setting down a bottle by Tom's elbow.

"At least I got first billing," Tom said. He wiped thick white paste off his fingers with a napkin, and shoved the scrapbook aside. Underneath were some crude drawings he'd made of the shell. "Now," he said, "where the fuck are we going to put the record player, huh?"

From the Journal of Xavier Desmond

———————— ❖ ————————

NOVEMBER 30/JOKERTOWN

MY NAME IS XAVIER DESMOND, AND I AM A JOKER.

Jokers are always strangers, even on the street where they were born, and this one is about to visit a number of strange lands. In the next five months I will see veldts and mountains, Rio and Cairo, the Khyber Pass and the Straits of Gibraltar, the Outback and the Champs-Élysées— all very far from home for a man who has often been called the mayor of Jokertown. Jokertown, of course, has no mayor. It is a neighborhood, a ghetto neighborhood at that, and not a city. Jokertown is more than a place though. It is a condition, a state of mind. Perhaps in that sense my title is not undeserved.

I have been a joker since the beginning. Forty years ago, when Jetboy died in the skies over Manhattan and loosed the wild card upon the world, I was twenty-nine years of age, an investment banker with a lovely wife, a two-year-old daughter, and a bright future ahead of me. A month later, when I was finally released from the hospital, I was a monstrosity with a pink elephantine trunk growing from the center of my face where my nose had been. There are seven perfectly functional fingers at the end of my trunk, and over the years I have become quite adept with this "third hand." Were I suddenly restored to so-called normal humanity, I believe it would be as traumatic as if one of my limbs were amputated. With my trunk I am ironically somewhat more than human . . . and infinitely less.

My lovely wife left me within two weeks of my release from the hospital, at approximately the same time that Chase Manhattan informed me that my services would no longer be required. I moved to Jokertown nine months later, following my eviction from my Riverside Drive apartment for "health reasons." I last saw my daughter in 1948. She was married in June of 1964, divorced in 1969, remarried in June of 1972. She has a fondness for June weddings, it seems. I was invited to neither of them. The private detective I hired informs me that she and her husband now live in Salem, Oregon, and that I have two grandchildren, a boy and a girl, one from each marriage. I sincerely doubt that either knows that their grandfather is the mayor of Jokertown.

I am the founder and president emeritus of the Jokers' Anti-Defamation League, or JADL, the oldest and largest organization dedicated to the preservation of civil rights for the victims of the wild card virus. The JADL has had its failures, but overall it has accomplished great good. I am also a moderately successful businessman. I own one of New York's most storied and elegant nightclubs, the Funhouse, where jokers and nats and aces have enjoyed all the top joker cabaret acts for more than two decades. The Funhouse has been losing money steadily for the last five years, but no one knows that except me and my accountant. I keep it open because it is, after all, the Funhouse, and were it to close, Jokertown would seem a poorer place.

Next month I will be seventy years of age.

My doctor tells me that I will not live to be seventy-one. The cancer had already metastasized before it was diagnosed. Even jokers cling stubbornly to life, and I have been doing the chemotherapy and the radiation treatments for half a year now, but the cancer shows no sign of remission.

My doctor tells me the trip I am about to embark on will probably take months off my life. I have my prescriptions and will dutifully continue to take the pills, but when one is globe-hopping, radiation therapy must be forgone. I have accepted this.

Mary and I often talked of a trip around the world, in those days before the wild card when we were young and in love. I could never have dreamt that I would finally take that trip without her, in the twilight of my life, and at government expense, as a delegate on a fact-finding mission organized and funded by the Senate Committee on Ace Resources and Endeavors, under the official sponsorship of the United Nations and the World Health Organization. We will visit every continent but Antarctica and call upon thirty-nine different countries (some only for a few hours), and our official charge is to investigate the treatment of wild card victims in cultures around the world.

There are twenty-one delegates, only five of whom are jokers. I suppose my selection is a great honor, recognition of my achievements and my status as a community leader. I believe I have my good friend Dr. Tachyon to thank for it.

But then, I have my good friend Dr. Tachyon to thank for a great many things.

DECEMBER 1/NEW YORK CITY

The journey is off to an inauspicious start. For the last hour we have been holding on the runway at Tomlin International, waiting for clearance for takeoff. The problem, we are informed, is not here, but down in Havana. So we wait.

Our plane is a custom 747 that the press has dubbed the *Stacked Deck*. The entire central cabin has been converted to our requirements, the seats replaced with a small medical laboratory, a press room for the print journalists, and a miniature television studio for their electronic counterparts. The newsmen themselves have been segregated in the tail. Already they've made it their own. I was back there twenty minutes ago and found a poker game in progress. The business-class cabin is full of aides, assistants, secretaries, publicists, and security personnel. First class is supposedly reserved exclusively for the delegates.

As there are only twenty-one delegates, we rattle around like peas in a pod. Even here the ghettoes persist—jokers tend to sit with jokers, nats with nats, aces with aces.

Hartmann is the only man aboard who seems entirely comfortable with all three groups. He greeted me warmly at the press conference and sat with Howard and myself for a few moments after boarding, talking earnestly about his hopes for the trip. It is difficult not to like the senator. Jokertown has delivered him huge majorities in each of his campaigns as far back as his term as mayor, and no wonder—no other politician has worked so long and hard to defend jokers' rights. Hartmann gives me hope; he's living proof that there can indeed be trust and mutual respect between joker and nat. He's a decent, honorable man, and in these days when fanatics such as Leo Barnett are inflaming the old hatreds and prejudices, jokers need all the friends they can get in the halls of power.

Dr. Tachyon and Senator Hartmann co-chair the delegation. Tachyon arrived dressed like a foreign correspondent from some film noir classic, in a trench coat covered with belts, buttons, and epaulettes, a snap-brim fedora rakishly tilted to one side. The fedora sports a foot-long red feather, however, and I cannot begin to imagine where one goes to purchase a powder-blue crushed-velvet trench coat. A pity that those foreign-correspondent films were all in black and white.

Tachyon would like to think that he shares Hartmann's lack of prejudice toward jokers, but that's not strictly true. He labors unceasingly in his clinic, and one cannot doubt that he cares, and cares deeply . . . many jokers think of him as a saint, a hero . . . yet, when one has known the doctor as long as I have, deeper truths become apparent. On some unspoken level he thinks of his good works in Jokertown as a penance. He does his best to hide it, but even after all these years you can see the revulsion in his eyes. Dr. Tachyon and I are "friends," we have known each other for decades now, and I believe with all my heart that he sincerely cares for me . . . but not for a second have I ever felt that he considers me an equal, as Hartmann does. The senator treats me like a man, even an important man, courting me as he might any political leader with votes to deliver. To Dr. Tachyon, I will always be a joker.

Is that his tragedy, or mine?

Tachyon knows nothing of the cancer. A symptom that our friendship is as diseased as my body? Perhaps. He has not been my personal physician for many years now. My doctor is a joker, as are my accountant, my attorney, my broker, and even my banker—the world changed since Chase dismissed me, and as mayor of Jokertown I am obliged to practice my own personal brand of affirmative action.

WE HAVE JUST BEEN CLEARED FOR TAKEOFF. THE SEAT-HOPPING IS over; people are belting themselves in. It seems I carry Jokertown with me wherever I go—Howard Mueller sits closest to me, his seat customized to accommodate his nine-foot-tall form and the immense length of his arms. He's better known as Troll, and he works as chief of security at Tachyon's clinic, but I note that he does not sit with Tachyon among the aces. The other three joker delegates—Father Squid, Chrysalis, and the poet Dorian Wilde—are also here in the center section of first class. Is it coincidence, prejudice, or shame that puts us here, in the seats furthest from the windows? Being a joker makes one a tad paranoid about these things, I fear. The politicians, of both the domestic and UN varieties, have clustered to our right, the aces forward of us (aces up front, of course, of course) and to our left. Must stop now, the stewardess has asked me to put my tray table back up.

Airborne. New York and Robert Tomlin International Airport are far behind us, and Cuba waits ahead. From what I've heard, it will be an easy and pleasant first stop. Havana is almost as American as Las Vegas or Miami Beach, albeit considerably more decadent and wicked. I may actually have friends there—some of the top joker entertainers go on to the Havana casinos after getting their starts in the Funhouse and the Chaos Club. I must remind myself to stay away from the gaming tables, however; joker luck is notoriously bad.

_____

AS SOON AS THE SEAT BELT SIGN WENT OFF, A NUMBER OF THE ACES ascended to the first-class lounge. I can hear their laughter drifting down the spiral stairway—Peregrine, pretty young Mistral—who looks just like the college student she is when not in her flying gear— boisterous Hiram Worchester, and Asta Lenser, the ballerina from the ABT whose ace name is Fantasy. Already they are a tight little clique, a "fun bunch" for whom nothing could possibly go wrong. The golden people, and Tachyon very much in their midst. Is it the aces or the women that draw him? I wonder. Even my dear friend Angela, who still loves the man deeply after twenty-odd years, admits that Dr. Tachyon thinks mainly with his penis where women are concerned.

Yet even among the aces there are the odd men out. Jones, the black strongman from Harlem (like Troll and Hiram W. and Peregrine, he requires a custom seat, in his case to support his extraordinary weight), is nursing a beer and reading a copy of *Sports Illustrated*. Radha O'Reilly is just as solitary, gazing out the window. She seems very quiet. Billy Ray and Joanne Jefferson, the two Justice Department aces who head up our security contingent, are not delegates and thus are seated back in the second section.

And then there is Jack Braun. The tensions that swirl around him are almost palpable. Most of the other delegates are polite to him, but no one is truly friendly, and he's being openly shunned by some, such as Hiram Worchester. For Dr. Tachyon, clearly Braun does not even exist. I wonder whose idea it was to bring him on this trip. Certainly not Tachyon's, and it seems too politically dangerous for Hartmann to be responsible. A gesture to appease the conservatives on SCARE perhaps? Or are there ramifications that I have not considered?

Braun glances up at the stairway from time to time, as if he would love nothing so much as to join the happy group upstairs, but remains firmly in his seat. It is hard to credit that this smooth-faced, blond-haired boy in the tailored safari jacket is really the notorious Judas Ace of the fifties. He's my age or close to it, but he looks barely twenty... the kind of boy who might have taken pretty young Mistral to her senior prom a few years back and gotten her home well before midnight.

One of the reporters, a man named Downs from *Aces* magazine, was up here earlier, trying to get Braun to consent to an interview. He was persistent, but Braun's refusal was firm, and Downs finally gave up. Instead he handed out copies of the latest issue of *Aces* and then sauntered up to the lounge, no doubt to pester someone else. I am not a regular reader of *Aces,* but I accepted a copy and suggested to Downs that his publisher consider a companion periodical, to be called *Jokers*. He was not overly enthused about the idea.

The issue features a rather striking cover photograph of the Turtle's shell outlined against the oranges and reds of sunset, blurbed with "The Turtle—Dead or Alive?" The Turtle has not been seen since Wild Card Day, back in September, when he was napalmed and crashed into the Hudson. Twisted and burnt pieces of his shell were found on the riverbed, though no body has ever been recovered. Several hundred people claim to have seen the Turtle near dawn the following day, flying an older shell in the sky over Jokertown, but since he has not reappeared since, some are putting that sighting down to hysteria and wishful thinking.

I have no opinion on the Turtle, though I would hate to think that he was truly dead. Many jokers believe that he is one of us, that his shell conceals some unspeakable joker deformity. Whether that is true or not, he has been a good friend to Jokertown for a long, long time.

There is, however, an aspect to this trip that no one ever speaks of, although Downs' article brings it to mind. Perhaps it falls to me to mention the unmentionable then. The truth is, all that laughter up in the lounge has a slightly nervous ring to it, and it is no coincidence that this junket, under discussion for so many years, was put together so swiftly in the past two months. They want to get us out of town for a while—not just the jokers, the aces too. The aces *especially,* one might even say.

This last Wild Card Day was a catastrophe for the city, and for every victim of the virus everywhere. The level of violence was shocking and made headlines across the nation. The still-unsolved murder of the Howler, the dismemberment of a child ace in the midst of a huge crowd at Jetboy's Tomb, the attack on Aces High, the destruction of the Turtle (or at least his shell), the wholesale slaughter at the Cloisters, where a dozen bodies were brought out in pieces, the predawn aerial battle that lit up the entire East Side...days and even weeks later the authorities were still not certain that they had an accurate death toll.

One old man was found literally embedded in a solid brick wall, and when they began to chip him out, they found they could not tell where his flesh ended and the wall began. The autopsy revealed a ghastly mess inside, where his internal organs were fused with the bricks that penetrated them.

A *Post* photographer snapped a picture of that old man trapped in his wall. He looks so gentle and sweet. The police subsequently announced that the old man was an ace himself, and moreover a notorious criminal, that he was responsible for the murders of Kid Dinosaur and the Howler, the attempted murder of the Turtle, the attack on Aces High, the battle over the East River, the ghastly blood rites performed at the Cloisters, and a whole range of lesser crimes. A number of aces came forward to support this explanation, but the public does not seem convinced. According to the polls, more people believe the conspiracy theory put forward in the *National Informer*—that the killings were independent, caused by powerful aces known and un-known carrying out personal vendettas, using their powers in utter dis-regard for law and public safety, and that afterward those aces conspired with each other and the police to cover up their atrocities, blaming everything on one crippled old man who happened to be conveniently dead, clearly at the hands of some ace.

Already several books have been announced, each purporting to explain what really happened—the immoral opportunism of the pub-lishing industry knows no bounds. Koch, ever aware of the prevailing winds, has ordered several cases reopened and has instructed the IAD to investigate the police role.

Jokers are pitiful and loathed. Aces have great power, and for the first time in many years a sizable segment of the public has begun to distrust those aces and fear that power. No wonder that demagogues like Leo Barnett have swelled so vastly in the public mind of late.

So I'm convinced that our tour has a hidden agenda; to wash the blood with some "good ink," as they say, to defuse the fear, to win back trust and take everyone's mind off Wild Card Day.

I admit to mixed feelings about aces, some of whom definitely abuse their power. Nonetheless, as a joker, I find myself desperately hoping that we succeed . . . and desperately fearing the consequences if we do not.

DECEMBER 8, 1986/MEXICO CITY

Another state dinner this evening, but I've begged off with a plea of ill-ness. A few hours to relax in my hotel room and write in the journal are most welcome. And my regrets were anything but fabricated—the tight schedule and pressures of the trip have begun to take their toll, I fear. I have not been keeping down all of my meals, although I've done my utmost to see that my distress remains unnoticed. If Tachyon sus-pected, he would insist on an examination, and once the truth was dis-covered, I might be sent home.

I will not permit that. I wanted to see all the fabled, far-off lands that Mary and I had once dreamed of together, but already it is clear that what we are engaged in here is far more important than any pleasure trip. Cuba was no Miami Beach, not for anyone who cared to look outside Havana; there are more jokers dying in the cane fields than cavorting on cabaret stages. And Haiti and the Dominican Republic were infinitely worse, as I've already noted in these pages.

A joker presence, a strong joker voice—we desperately need these things if we are to accomplish any good at all. I will not allow myself to be disqualified on medical grounds. Already our numbers are down by one—Dorian Wilde returned to New York rather than continue on to Mexico. I confess to mixed feelings about that. When we began, I had little respect for the "poet laureate of Jokertown," whose title is as dubious as my own mayoralty, though his Pulitzer is not. He seems to get a perverse glee from waving those wet, slimy tendrils of his in people's faces, flaunting his deformity in a deliberate attempt to draw a reaction. I suspect this aggressive nonchalance is in fact motivated by the same self-loathing that makes so many jokers take to masks, and a few sad cases actually attempt to amputate the deformed parts of their bodies. Also, he dresses almost as badly as Tachyon with his ridiculous Edwardian affectation, and his unstated preference for perfume over baths makes his company a trial to anyone with a sense of smell. Mine, alas, is quite acute.

Were it not for the legitimacy conferred on him by the Pulitzer, I doubt that he would ever have been named for this tour, but there are very few jokers who have achieved that kind of worldly recognition. I find precious little to admire in his poetry either, and much that is repugnant in his endless mincing recitations.

All that being said, I confess to a certain admiration for his impromptu performance before the Duvaliers. I suspect he received a severe dressing-down from the politicians. Hartmann had a long private conversation with "The Divine Wilde" as we were leaving Haiti, and after that Dorian seemed much subdued.

While I don't agree with much that Wilde has to say, I do nonetheless think he ought to have the right to say it. He will be missed. I wish I knew why he was leaving. I asked him that very question and tried to convince him to go on for the benefit of all his fellow jokers. His reply was an offensive suggestion about the sexual uses of my trunk, couched in the form of a vile little poem. A curious man.

With Wilde gone, Father Squid and myself are the only true representatives of the joker point of view, I feel. Howard M. (Troll, to the world) is an imposing presence, nine feet tall, incredibly strong, his green-tinged skin as tough and hard as horn, and I also know him to be a profoundly decent and competent man, and a very intelligent one, but...he is by nature a follower, not a leader, and there is a shyness in him, a reticence, that prevents him from speaking out. His height makes it impossible for him to blend with the crowd, but sometimes I think that is what he desires most profoundly.

As for Chrysalis, she is none of those things, and she has her own unique charisma. I cannot deny that she is a respected community leader, one of the most visible (no pun intended) and powerful of jokers. Yet I have never much liked Chrysalis. Perhaps this is my own prejudice and self-interest. The rise of the Crystal Palace has had much to do with the decline of the Funhouse. But there are deeper issues. Chrysalis wields considerable power in Jokertown, but she has never used it to benefit anyone but herself. She has been aggressively apolitical, carefully distancing herself from the JADL and all joker rights agitation. When the times called for passion and commitment, she remained cool and uninvolved, hidden behind her cigarette holders, liqueurs, and upper-class British accent.

Chrysalis speaks only for Chrysalis, and Troll seldom speaks at all, which leaves it to Father Squid and myself to speak for the jokers. I would do it gladly, but I am so tired....

I FELL ASLEEP EARLY AND WAS WAKENED BY THE SOUNDS OF MY FELLOW delegates returning from the dinner. It went rather well, I understand. Excellent. We need some triumphs. Howard tells me that Hartmann gave a splendid speech and seemed to captivate President de la Madrid Hurtado throughout the meal. Peregrine captivated all the other males in the room, according to reports. I wonder if the other women are envious. Mistral is quite pretty, Fantasy is mesmerizing when she dances, and Radha O'Reilly is arresting, her mixed Irish and Indian heritage giving her features a truly exotic cast. But Peregrine overshadows all of them. What do they make of her?

The male aces certainly approve. The *Stacked Deck* is close quarters, and gossip travels quickly up and down the aisles. Word is that Dr. Tachyon and Jack Braun have both made passes and have been firmly rebuffed. If anything, Peregrine seems closest with her cameraman, a nat who travels back with the rest of the reporters. She's making a documentary of this trip. Hiram is also close to Peregrine, but while there's a certain flirtatiousness to their constant banter, their friendship is more platonic in nature. Worchester has only one true love, and that's food. To that, his commitment is extraordinary. He seems to know all the best restaurants in every city we visit. His privacy is constantly being invaded by local chefs, who sneak up to his hotel room at all hours, carrying their specialties and begging for just a moment, just a taste, just a little approval. Far from objecting, Hiram delights in it.

In Haiti he found a cook he liked so much that he hired him on the spot and prevailed upon Hartmann to make a few calls to the INS and expedite the visa and work permit. We saw the man briefly at the Port-au-Prince airport, struggling with a huge trunk full of cast-iron cookware. Hiram made the trunk light enough for his new employee (who speaks no English, but Hiram insists that spices are a universal language) to carry on one shoulder. At tonight's dinner, Howard tells me, Worchester insisted on visiting the kitchen to get the chef's recipe for *chicken mole,* but while he was back there he concocted some sort of flaming dessert in honor of our hosts.

By rights I ought to object to Hiram Worchester, who revels in his acedom more than any other man I know, but I find it hard to dislike anyone who enjoys life so much and brings such enjoyment to those around him. Besides, I am well aware of his various anonymous charities in Jokertown, though he does his best to conceal them. Hiram is no more comfortable around my kind than Tachyon is, but his heart is as large as the rest of him.

Tomorrow the group will fragment yet again. Senators Hartmann and Lyons, Congressman Rabinowitz, and Ericsson from WHO will meet with the leaders of the PRI, Mexico's ruling party, while Tachyon and our medical staff visit a clinic that has claimed extraordinary success in treating the virus with laetrile. Our aces are scheduled to lunch with three of their Mexican counterparts. I'm pleased to say that Troll has been invited to join them. In some quarters, at least, his superhuman strength and near invulnerability have qualified him as an ace. A small breakthrough, of course, but a breakthrough nonetheless.

The rest of us will be traveling down to Yucatán and the Quintana Roo to look at Mayan ruins and the sites of several reported antijoker atrocities. Rural Mexico, it seems, is not as enlightened as Mexico City. The others will join us in Chichén Itzá the following day, and our last day in Mexico will be given over to tourism.

And then it will be on to Guatemala . . . perhaps. The daily press has been full of reports on an insurrection down there, an Indian uprising against the central government, and several of our journalists have gone ahead already, sensing a bigger story than this tour. If the situation seems too unstable, we may be forced to skip that stop.

December 15, 1986/En Route to Lima, Peru

I have been dilatory about keeping up my journal—no entry yesterday or the day before. I can only plead exhaustion and a certain amount of despondence.

Guatemala took its toll on my spirit, I'm afraid. We are, of course, stringently neutral, but when I saw the televised news reports of the insurrection and heard some of the rhetoric being attributed to the Mayan revolutionaries, I dared to hope. When we actually met with the Indian leaders, I was even briefly elated. They considered my presence in the room an honor, an auspicious omen, seemed to treat me with the same sort of respect (or lack of respect) they gave Hartmann and Tachyon, and the way they treated their own jokers gave me heart.

Well, I am an old man—an old *joker* in fact—and I tend to clutch at straws. Now the Mayan revolutionaries have proclaimed a new nation, an Amerindian homeland, where their jokers will be welcomed and honored. The rest of us need not apply. Not that I would care much to live in the jungles of Guatemala—even an autonomous joker homeland down here would scarcely cause a ripple in Jokertown, let alone any kind of significant exodus. Still, there are so few places in the world where jokers are welcome, where we can make our homes in peace . . . the more we travel on, the more we see, the more I am forced to conclude that Jokertown is the best place for us, our only true home. I cannot express how much that conclusion saddens and terrifies me.

Why must we draw these lines, these fine distinctions, these labels and barriers that set us apart? Ace and nat and joker, capitalist and communist, Catholic and Protestant, Arab and Jew, Indian and *Latino,* and on and on everywhere, and of course true humanity is to be found only on *our* side of the line and we feel free to oppress and rape and kill the "other," whoever he might be.

There are those on the *Stacked Deck* who charge that the Guatemalans were engaged in conscious genocide against their own Indian populations, and who see this new nation as a very good thing. But I wonder.

THE MAYAS THINK JOKERS ARE TOUCHED BY THE GODS, SPECIALLY blessed. No doubt it is better to be honored than reviled for our various handicaps and deformities. No doubt.

But...

We have the Islamic nations still ahead of us ... a third of the world, someone told me. Some Muslims are more tolerant than others, but virtually all of them consider deformity a sign of Allah's displeasure. The attitudes of the true fanatics such as the Shiites in Iran and the Nur sect in Syria are terrifying, Hitlerian. How many jokers were slaughtered when the Ayatollah displaced the Shah? To some Iranians the tolerance he extended to jokers and women was the Shah's greatest sin.

And are we so very much better in the enlightened USA, where fundamentalists like Leo Barnett preach that jokers are being punished for their sins? Oh, yes, there is a distinction; I must remember that. Barnett says he hates the sins but loves the sinners, and if we will only repent and have faith and love Jesus, surely we will be cured.

No, I'm afraid that ultimately Barnett and the Ayatollah and the Mayan priests are all preaching the same creed—that our bodies in some sense reflect our souls, that some divine being has taken a direct hand and twisted us into these shapes to signify his pleasure (the Mayas) or displeasure (Nur al-Allah, the Ayatollah, the Fire-breather). Most of all, each of them is saying that jokers are *different.*

My own creed is distressingly simple—I believe that jokers and aces and nats are all just men and women and ought to be treated as such. During my dark nights of the soul I wonder if I am the only one left who still believes this.

STILL BROODING ABOUT GUATEMALA AND THE MAYAS. A POINT I failed to make earlier—I could not help noticing that this glorious idealistic revolution of theirs was led by two aces and a nat. Even down here, where jokers are supposedly kissed by the gods, the aces lead and the jokers follow.

A few days ago—it was during our visit to the Panama Canal, I believe—Digger Downs asked me if I thought the US would ever have a joker president. I told him I'd settle for a joker congressman (I'm afraid Nathan Rabinowitz, whose district includes Jokertown, heard the comment and took it for some sort of criticism of his representation). Then Digger wanted to know if I thought an ace could be elected president. A more interesting question, I must admit. Downs always looks half asleep, but he is sharper than he appears, though not in a class with some of the other reporters aboard the *Stacked Deck,* like Herrmann of the AP or Morgenstern of the *Washington Post.*

I told Downs that before this last Wild Card Day it might have been possible... barely. Certain aces, like the Turtle (still missing, the latest NY papers confirm), Peregrine, Cyclone, and a handful of others are first-rank celebrities, commanding considerable public affection. How much of that could translate to the public arena, and how well it might survive the rough give-and-take of a presidential campaign, that's a more difficult question. Heroism is a perishable commodity.

Jack Braun was standing close enough to hear Digger's question and my reply. Before I could conclude—I wanted to say that the whole equation had changed this September, that among the casualties of Wild Card Day was any faint chance that an ace might be a viable presidential candidate—Braun interrupted. "They'd tear him apart," he told us.

What if it was someone they loved? Digger wanted to know.

"They loved the Four Aces," Braun said.

Braun is no longer quite the exile he was at the beginning of the tour. Tachyon still refuses to acknowledge his existence and Hiram is barely polite, but the other aces don't seem to know or care who he is. In Panama he was often in Fantasy's company, squiring her here and there, and I've heard rumors of a liaison between Golden Boy and Senator Lyons' press secretary, an attractive young blonde. Undoubtedly, of the male aces, Braun is by far the most attractive in the conventional sense, although Mordecai Jones has a certain brooding presence. Downs has been struck by those two also. The next issue of *Aces* will feature a piece comparing Golden Boy and the Harlem Hammer, he informs me.

DECEMBER 29, 1986/BUENOS AIRES

Don't cry for Jack, Argentina. . . .

Evita's bane has come back to Buenos Aires. When the musical first played Broadway, I wondered what Jack Braun must have thought, listening to Lupone sing of the Four Aces. Now that question has even more poignance. Braun has been very calm, almost stoic, in the face of his reception here, but what must he be feeling inside?

Perón is dead, Evita even deader, even Isabel just a memory, but the Perónistas are still very much a part of the Argentine political scene. They have not forgotten. Everywhere the signs taunt Braun and invite him to go home. He is the ultimate *gringo* (do they use that word in Argentina, I wonder), the ugly but awesomely powerful American who came to the Argentine uninvited and toppled a sovereign government because he disapproved of its politics. The United States has been doing such things for as long as there has been a Latin America, and I have no doubt that these same resentments fester in many other places. The United States and even the dread "secret aces" of the CIA are abstract concepts, however, faceless and difficult to get a fix on—Golden Boy is flesh and blood, real and very visible, and *here*.

Someone inside the hotel leaked our room assignments, and when Jack stepped out onto his balcony the first day, he was showered with dung and rotten fruit. He has stayed inside ever since, except for official functions, but even there he is not safe. Last night as we stood in a receiving line at the Casa Rosada, the wife of a union official—a beautiful young woman, her small dark face framed by masses of lustrous black hair—stepped up to him with a sweet smile, looked straight into his eyes, and spit in his face.

It caused quite a stir, and Senators Hartmann and Lyons have filed some sort of protest, I believe. Braun himself was remarkably restrained, almost gallant. Digger was hounding him ruthlessly after the reception; he's cabling a write-up on the incident back to *Aces* and wanted a quote. Braun finally gave him something. "I've done things I'm not proud of," he said, "but getting rid of Juan Perón isn't one of them."

"Yeah, yeah," I heard Digger tell him, "but how did you feel when she spit on you?"

Jack just looked disgusted. "I don't hit women," he said. Then he walked off and sat by himself.

Downs turned to me when Braun was gone. "I don't hit women," he echoed in a singsong imitation of Golden Boy's voice, then added, "What a weenie...."

The world is too ready to read cowardice and betrayal into anything Jack Braun says and does, but the truth, I suspect, is more complex. Given his youthful appearance, it's hard to recall at times how old the Golden Boy really is—his formative years were during the Depression and World War II, and he grew up listening to the NBC Blue Network, not MTV. No wonder some of his values seem quaintly old-fashioned.

In many ways the Judas Ace seems almost an innocent, a bit lost in a world that has grown too complicated for him. I think he is more troubled than he admits by his reception here in Argentina. Braun is the last representative of a lost dream that flourished briefly in the aftermath of World War II and died in Korea and the HUAC hearings and the Cold War. They thought they could reshape the world, Archibald Holmes and his Four Aces. They had no doubts, no more than their country did. Power existed to be used, and they were supremely confident in their ability to tell the good guys from the bad guys. Their own democratic ideals and the shining purity of their intentions were all the justification they needed. For those few early aces it must have been a golden age, and how appropriate that a golden boy be at its center.

Golden ages give way to dark ages, as any student of history knows, and as all of us are currently finding out.

Braun and his colleagues could do things no one else had ever done—they could fly and lift tanks and absorb a man's mind and memories, and so they bought the illusion that they could make a real difference on a global scale, and when that illusion dissolved beneath them, they fell a very long way indeed. Since then no other ace has dared to dream as big.

Even in the face of imprisonment, despair, insanity, disgrace, and death, the Four Aces had triumphs to cling to, and Argentina was perhaps the brightest of those triumphs. What a bitter homecoming this must be for Jack Braun.

As if this was not enough, our mail caught up with us just before we left Brazil, and the pouch included a dozen copies of the new issue of *Aces* with Digger's promised feature story. The cover has Jack Braun and Mordecai Jones in profile, scowling at each other (All cleverly doctored, of course. I don't believe the two had ever met before we all got together at Tomlin) over a blurb that reads, "The Strongest Man in the World."

The article itself is a lengthy discussion of the two men and their public careers, enlivened by numerous anecdotes about their feats of strength and much speculation about which of the two is, indeed, the strongest man in the world.

Both of the principals seem embarrassed by the piece, Braun perhaps more acutely. Neither much wants to discuss it, and they certainly don't seem likely to settle the matter anytime soon. I understand that there has been considerable argument and even wagering back in the press compartment since Digger's piece came out (for once, Downs seems to have had an impact on his journalistic colleagues), but the bets are likely to remain unresolved for a long time to come. I told Downs that the story was spurious and offensive as soon as I read it. He seemed startled. "I don't get it," he said to me. "What's your beef?"

My beef, as I explained to him, was simple. Braun and Jones are scarcely the only people to manifest superhuman strength since the advent of the wild card; in fact, that particular power is a fairly common one, ranking close behind telekinesis and telepathy in Tachyon's incidence-of-occurrence charts. It has something to do with maximizing the contractile strength of the muscles, I believe. My point is, a number of prominent jokers display augmented strength as well—just off the top of my head, I cited Elmo (the dwarf bouncer at the Crystal Palace), Ernie of Ernie's Bar & Grill, the Oddity, Quasiman...and, most notably, Howard Mueller. The Troll's strength does not perhaps equal that of Golden Boy and the Harlem Hammer, but assuredly it approaches it. None of these jokers were so much as mentioned in passing in Digger's story, although the names of a dozen other superstrong aces were dropped here and there. Why was that? I wanted to know.

I can't claim to have made much of an impression unfortunately. When I was through, Downs simply rolled his eyes and said, "You people are so damned *touchy*." He tried to be accommodating by telling me that if this story went over big, maybe he'd write up a sequel on the strongest joker in the world, and he couldn't comprehend why that "concession" made me even angrier. And they wonder why we people are touchy...

Howard thought the whole argument was vastly amusing. Sometimes I wonder about him.

Actually my fit of pique was nothing compared to the reaction the magazine drew from Billy Ray, our security chief. Ray was one of the other aces mentioned in passing, his strength dismissed as not being truly "major league." Afterward he could be heard the length of the plane, suggesting that maybe Downs would like to step outside with him, seeing as how he was so minor league. Digger declined the offer. From the smile on his face I doubt that Carnifex will be getting any good press in *Aces* anytime soon.

Since then, Ray has been grousing about the story to anyone who will listen. The crux of his argument is that strength isn't everything; he may not be as strong as Braun or Jones, but he's strong enough to take either of them in a fight, and he'd be glad to put his money where his mouth is.

Personally I have gotten a certain perverse satisfaction out of this tempest in a teapot. The irony is, they are arguing about who has the most of what is essentially a minor power. I seem to recall that there was some sort of demonstration in the early seventies, when the battleship *New Jersey* was being refitted at the Bayonne Naval Supply Center over in New Jersey. The Turtle lifted the battleship telekinetically, got it out of the water by several feet, and held it there for almost half a

minute. Braun and Jones lift tanks and toss automobiles about, but neither could come remotely close to what the Turtle did that day.

The simple truth is, the contractile strength of the human muscula-
ture can be increased only so much. Physical limits apply. Dr. Tachyon
says there may also be limits to what the human mind can accomplish,
but so far they have not been reached.

If the Turtle is indeed a joker, as many believe, I would find this
irony especially satisfying.

I suppose I am, at base, as small a man as any.

January 16/Addis Ababa, Ethiopia

A hard day in a stricken land. The local Red Cross representatives took
some of us out to see some of their famine relief efforts. Of course we'd
all been aware of the drought and the starvation long before we got
here, but seeing it on television is one thing, and being here amidst it is
quite another.

A day like this makes me acutely aware of my own failures and
shortcomings. Since the cancer took hold of me, I've lost a good deal of
weight (some unsuspecting friends have even told me how good I
look), but moving among these people made me very self-conscious of
the small paunch that remains. They were starving before my eyes,
while our plane waited to take us back to Addis Ababa... to our hotel,
another reception, and no doubt a gourmet Ethiopian meal. The guilt
was overwhelming, as was the sense of helplessness.

I believe we all felt it. I cannot conceive of how Hiram Worchester
must have felt. To his credit he looked sick as he moved among the
victims, and at one point he was trembling so badly he had to sit in
the shade for a while by himself. The sweat was just pouring off him. But
he got up again afterward, his face white and grim, and used his gravity
power to help them unload the relief provisions we had brought with us.

So many people have contributed so much and worked so hard for
the relief effort, but here it seems like nothing. The only realities in the
relief camps are the skeletal bodies with their massive swollen bellies,
the dead eyes of the children, and the endless heat pouring down from
above onto this baked, parched landscape.

Parts of this day will linger in my memory for a long time—or at least as long a time as I have left to me. Father Squid gave the last rites to a dying woman who had a Coptic cross around her neck. Peregrine and her cameraman recorded much of the scene on film for her documentary, but after a short time she had had enough and returned to the plane to wait for us. I've heard that she was so sick she lost her breakfast.

And there was a young mother, no more than seventeen or eighteen surely, so gaunt that you could count every rib, with eyes incredibly ancient. She was holding her baby to a withered, empty breast. The child had been dead long enough to begin to smell, but she would not let them take it from her. Dr. Tachyon took control of her mind and held her still while he gently pried the child's body from her grasp and carried it away. He handed it to one of the relief workers and then sat on the ground and began to weep, his body shaking with each sob.

Mistral ended the day in tears as well. En route to the refugee camp, she had changed into her blue-and-white flying costume. The girl is young, an ace, and a powerful one; no doubt she thought she could help. When she called the winds to her, the huge cape she wears fastened at wrist and ankle ballooned out like a parachute and pulled her up into the sky. Even the strangeness of the jokers walking between them had not awakened much interest in the inward-looking eyes of the refugees, but when Mistral took flight, most of them—not all, but most—turned to watch, and their gaze followed her upward into that high, hot blueness until finally they sank back into the lethargy of despair. I think Mistral had dreamed that somehow her wind powers could push the clouds around and make the rains come to heal this land. And what a dutiful, vainglorious dream it was. . . .

She flew for almost two hours, sometimes so high and far that she vanished from our sight, but for all her ace powers, all she could raise was a dust devil. When she gave up at last, she was exhausted, her sweet young face grimy with dust and sand, her eyes red and swollen.

Just before we left, an atrocity underscored the depth of the despair here. A tall youth with acne scars on his cheeks attacked a fellow refugee—went berserk, gouged out a woman's eye, and actually ate it while the people watched without comprehension. Ironically we'd met the boy briefly when we'd first arrived—he'd spent a year in a

Christian school and had a few words of English. He seemed stronger and healthier than most of the others we saw. When Mistral flew, he jumped to his feet and called out after her. "Jetboy!" he said in a very clear, strong voice. Father Squid and Senator Hartmann tried to talk to him, but his English-language skills were limited to a few nouns, including "chocolate," "television," and "Jesus Christ." Still, the boy was more alive than most—his eyes went wide at Father Squid, and he put out a hand and touched his facial tendrils wonderingly and actually smiled when the senator patted his shoulder and told him that we were here to help, though I don't think he understood a word. We were all shocked when we saw them carrying him away, still screaming, those gaunt brown cheeks smeared with blood.

A hideous day all around. This evening back in Addis Ababa our driver swung us by the docks, where relief shipments stand two stories high in some places. Hartmann was in a cold rage. If anyone can make this criminal government take action and feed its starving people, he is the one. I pray for him, or would, if I believed in a god...but what kind of god would permit the obscenities we have seen on this trip....

———

AFRICA IS AS BEAUTIFUL A LAND AS ANY ON THE FACE OF THE earth. I should write of all the beauty we have seen this past month. Victoria Falls, the snows of Kilimanjaro, a thousand zebra moving through the tall grass as if the wind had stripes. I've walked among the ruins of proud ancient kingdoms whose very names were unknown to me, held pygmy artifacts in my hand, seen the face of a bushman light up with curiosity instead of horror when he beheld me for the first time. Once during a visit to a game preserve I woke early, and when I looked out of my window at the dawn, I saw that two huge African elephants had come to the very building, and Radha stood between them, naked in the early morning light, while they touched her with their trunks. I turned away then; it seemed somehow a private moment.

Beauty, yes—in the land and in so many of the people, whose faces are full of warmth and compassion.

Still, for all that beauty, Africa has depressed and saddened me considerably, and I will be glad to leave. The camp was only part of it.

Before Ethiopia there was Kenya and South Africa. It is the wrong time of year for Thanksgiving, but the scenes we have witnessed these past few weeks have put me more in the mood for giving thanks than I've ever felt during America's smug November celebration of football and gluttony. Even jokers have things to give thanks for. I knew that already, but Africa has brought it home to me forcefully.

South Africa was a grim way to begin this leg of the trip. The same hatreds and prejudices exist at home of course, but whatever our faults we are at least civilized enough to maintain a facade of tolerance, brotherhood, and equality under the law. Once I might have called that mere sophistry, but that was before I tasted the reality of Capetown and Pretoria, where all the ugliness is out in the open, enshrined by law, enforced by an iron fist whose velvet glove has grown thin and worn indeed. It is argued that at least South Africa hates openly, while America hides behind a hypocritical facade. Perhaps, perhaps...but if so, I will take the hypocrisy and thank you for it.

I suppose that was Africa's first lesson, that there are worse places in the world than Jokertown. The second was that there are worse things than repression, and Kenya taught us that.

Like most of the other nations of Central and East Africa, Kenya was spared the worst of the wild card. Some spores would have reached these lands through airborne diffusion, more through the seaports, arriving via contaminated cargo in holds that had been poorly sterilized or never sterilized at all. CARE packages are looked on with deep suspicion in much of the world, and with good reason, and many captains have become quite adept at concealing the fact that their last port of call was New York City.

When one moves inland, wild card cases become almost nonexistent. There are those who say that the late Idi Amin was some kind of insane joker-ace, with strength as great as Troll or the Harlem Hammer, and the ability to transform into some kind of were-creature, a leopard or a lion or a hawk. Amin himself claimed to be able to ferret out his enemies telepathically, and those few enemies who survived say that he was a cannibal who felt human flesh was necessary to maintain his powers. All this is the stuff of rumor and propaganda, however, and whether Amin was a joker, an ace, or a pathetically deluded nat madman, he is assuredly dead, and in this corner of the world, documented cases of the wild card virus are vanishingly hard to locate.

But Kenya and the surrounding nations have their own viral nightmare. If the wild card is a chimera here, AIDS is an epidemic. While the president was hosting Senator Hartmann and most of the tour, a few of us were on an exhausting visit to a half-dozen clinics in rural Kenya, hopping from one village to another by helicopter. They assigned us only one battered chopper, and that at Tachyon's insistence. The government would have much preferred that we spend our time lecturing at the university, meeting with educators and political leaders, touring game preserves and museums.

Most of my fellow delegates were only too glad to comply. The wild card is forty years old, and we have grown used to it—but AIDS, that is a new terror in the world, and one that we have only begun to understand. At home it is thought of as a homosexual affliction, and I confess that I am guilty of thinking of it that way myself, but here in Africa, that belief is given the lie. Already there are more AIDS victims on this continent alone than have ever been infected by the Takisian xenovirus since its release over Manhattan forty years ago.

And AIDS seems a crueler demon somehow. The wild card kills ninety percent of those who draw it, often in ways that are terrible and painful, but the distance between ninety percent and one hundred is not insignificant if you are among the ten who live. It is the distance between life and death, between hope and despair. Some claim that it's better to die than to live as a joker, but you will not find me among their number. If my own life has not always been happy, nonetheless I have memories I cherish and accomplishments I am proud of. I am glad to have lived, and I do not want to die. I've accepted my death, but that does not mean I welcome it. I have too much unfinished business. Like Robert Tomlin, I have not yet seen *The Jolson Story*. None of us have.

In Kenya we saw whole villages that are dying. Alive, smiling, talking, capable of eating and defecating and making love and even babies, alive to all practical purposes—and yet dead. Those who draw the Black Queen may die in the agony of unspeakable transformations, but there are drugs for pain, and at least they die quickly. AIDS is less merciful.

We have much in common, jokers and AIDS victims. Before I left

Jokertown, we had been planning for a JADL fund-raising benefit at the Funhouse in late May—a major event with as much big-name entertainment as we could book. After Kenya I cabled instructions back to New York to arrange for the proceeds of the benefit to be split with a suitable AIDS victims' group. We pariahs need to stick together. Perhaps I can still erect a few necessary bridges before my own Black Queen lies faceup on the table.

JANUARY 30/JERUSALEM

The open city of Jerusalem, they call it. An international metropolis, jointly governed by commissioners from Israel, Jordan, Palestine, and Great Britain under a United Nations mandate, sacred to three of the world's great religions.

Alas, the apt phrase is not "open city" but "open sore." Jerusalem bleeds as it has for almost four decades. If this city is sacred, I should hate to visit one that was profane.

Senators Hartmann and Lyons and the other political delegates lunched with the city commissioners today, but the rest of us spent the afternoon touring this free international city in closed limousines with bulletproof windshields and special underbody armor to withstand bomb blasts. Jerusalem, it seems, likes to welcome distinguished international visitors by blowing them up. It does not seem to matter who the visitors are, where they come from, what religion they practice, how their politics lean—there are enough factions in this city so that everyone can count on being hated by someone.

Two days ago we were in Beirut. From Beirut to Jerusalem, that is a voyage from day to night. Lebanon is a beautiful country, and Beirut is so lovely and peaceful it seems almost serene. Its various regions appear to have solved the problem of living in comparative harmony, although there are of course incidents—nowhere in the Middle East (or the world, for that matter) is completely safe.

But Jerusalem—the outbreaks of violence have been endemic for thirty years, each worse than the one before. Entire blocks resemble nothing so much as London during the Blitz, and the population that remains has grown so used to the distant sound of machine-gun fire that they scarcely seem to pay it any mind.

We stopped briefly at what remains of the Wailing Wall (largely destroyed in 1967 by Palestinian terrorists in reprisal for the assassination of al-Haziz by Israeli terrorists the year before) and actually dared to get out of our vehicles. Hiram looked around fiercely and made a fist, as if daring anyone to start trouble. He has been in a strange state of late; irritable, quick to anger, moody. The things we witnessed in Africa have affected us all, however. One shard of the wall is still fairly imposing. I touched it and tried to feel the history. Instead I felt the pocks left in the stone by bullets.

Most of our party returned to the hotel afterward, but Father Squid and I took a detour to visit the Jokers' Quarter. I'm told that it is the second-largest joker community in the world, after Jokertown itself... a distant second, but second nonetheless. It does not surprise me. Islam does not view my people kindly, and so jokers come here from all over the Middle East for whatever meager protection is offered by UN sovereignty and a small, outmanned, outgunned, and demoralized international peacekeeping force.

The Quarter is unspeakably squalid, and the weight of human misery within its walls is almost palpable. Yet ironically the streets of the Quarter are reputed safer than any other place in Jerusalem. The Quarter has its own walls, built in living memory, originally to spare the feelings of decent people by hiding living obscenities from their sight, but those same walls have given a measure of security to those who dwell within. Once inside I saw no nats at all, only jokers—jokers of all races and religions, all living in relative peace. Once they might have been Muslims or Jews or Christians, zealots or Zionists or followers of the Nur, but after their hand had been dealt, they were only jokers. The joker is the great equalizer, cutting through all other hatreds and prejudices, uniting all mankind in a new brotherhood of pain. A joker is a joker is a joker, and anything else he is, is unimportant.

Would that it worked the same way with aces.

The sect of Jesus Christ, Joker has a church in Jerusalem, and Father Squid took me there. The building looked more like a mosque than a Christian church, at least on the outside, but inside it was not so terribly different from the church I'd visited in Jokertown, though much older and in greater disrepair. Father Squid lit a candle and said a prayer, and then we went back to the cramped, tumbledown rectory where Father Squid conversed with the pastor in halting Latin while we shared a bottle of sour red wine. As they were talking, I heard the sound of automatic weaponry chattering off in the night somewhere a few blocks away. A typical Jerusalem evening, I suppose.

———

No one will read this book until after my death, by which time I will be safely immune from prosecution. I've thought long and hard about whether or not I should record what happened tonight, and finally decided that I should. The world needs to remember the lessons of 1976 and be reminded from time to time that the JADL does not speak for all jokers.

An old joker woman pressed a note into my hand as Father Squid and I were leaving the church. I suppose someone recognized me.

When I read the note, I begged off the official reception, pleading illness once again, but this time it was a ruse. I dined in my room with a wanted criminal, a man I can only describe as a notorious international joker terrorist, although he is a hero inside the Jokers' Quarter. I will not give his real name, even in these pages, since I understand that he still visits his family in Tel Aviv from time to time. He wears a black canine mask on his "missions" and to the press, Interpol, and the sundry factions that police Jerusalem, he is variously known as the Black Dog and the Hound of Hell. Tonight he wore a completely different mask, a butterfly-shaped hood covered with silver glitter, and had no problem crossing the city.

"What you've got to remember," he told me, "is that nats are fundamentally stupid. You wear the same mask twice and let your picture get taken with it, and they start thinking it's your face."

The Hound, as I'll call him, was born in Brooklyn but emigrated to Israel with his family at age nine and became an Israeli citizen. He was twenty when he became a joker. "I traveled halfway around the world to draw the wild card," he told me. "I could have stayed in Brooklyn."

We spent several hours discussing Jerusalem, the Middle East, and the politics of the wild card. The Hound heads what honesty forces me to call a joker terrorist organization, the Twisted Fists. They are illegal in both Israel and Palestine, no mean trick. He was evasive about how many members they had, but not at all shy about confessing that virtually all of their financial support comes from New York's Jokertown. "You may not like us, Mr. Mayor," the Hound told me, "but your people do." He even hinted slyly that one of the joker delegates on our tour was among their supporters, although of course he refused to supply a name.

The Hound is convinced that war is coming to the Middle East, and soon. "It's overdue," he said. "Neither Israel nor Palestine have ever had defensible borders, and neither one is an economically viable nation. Each is convinced that the other one is guilty of all sorts of terrorist atrocities, and they're both right. Israel wants the Negev and the West Bank, Palestine wants a port on the Mediterranean, and both countries are still full of refugees from the 1948 partition who want their homes back. Everyone wants Jerusalem except the UN, which has it. Shit, they *need* a good war. The Israelis looked like they were winning in '48 until the *Nasr* kicked their asses. I know that Bernadotte won the Nobel Peace Prize for the Treaty of Jerusalem, but just between you and me, it might have been better if they'd fought it out to the bitter end...any kind of end."

I asked him about all the people who would have died, but he just shrugged. "They'd be dead. But maybe if it was over, really *over*, some of the wounds would start to heal. Instead we got two pissed-off half-countries that share the same little desert and won't even recognize each other, we've got four decades of hatred and terrorism and fear, and we're still going to get the war, and soon. It beats me how Bernadotte pulled off the Peace of Jerusalem anyway, though I'm not surprised that he got assassinated for his troubles. The only ones who hate the terms worse than the Israelis are the Palestinians."

I pointed out that, unpopular as it might be, the Peace of Jerusalem had lasted almost forty years. He dismissed that as "a forty-year stalemate, not real peace. Mutual fear was what made it work. The Israelis have always had military superiority. But the Arabs had the Port Said aces, and you think the Israelis don't remember? Every time the Arabs put up a memorial to the *Nasr*, anywhere from Baghdad to Marrakesh, the Israelis blow it up. Believe me, they remember. Only now the whole thing's coming unbalanced. I got sources say Israel has been running its own wild card experiments on volunteers from their armed forces, and they've come up with a few aces of their own. Now that's fanaticism for you, to volunteer for the wild card. And on the Arab side, you've got Nur al-Allah, who calls Israel a 'bastard joker nation' and has vowed to destroy it utterly. The Port Said aces were pussycats compared to his bunch, even old Khôf. No, it's coming, and soon."

"And when it comes?" I asked him.

He was carrying a gun, some kind of small semiautomatic machine pistol with a long Russian name. He took it out and laid it on the table between us. "When it comes," he said, "they can kill each other all they want, but they damn well better leave the Quarter alone, or they'll have us to deal with. We've already given the Nur a few lessons. Every time they kill a joker, we kill five of them. You'd think they'd get the idea, but the Nur's a slow learner."

I told him that Senator Hartmann was hoping to set up a meeting with the Nur al-Allah to begin discussions that might lead to a peaceful solution to this area's problems. He laughed. We talked for a long time, about jokers and aces and nats, and violence and nonviolence and war and peace, about brotherhood and revenge and turning the other cheek and taking care of your own, and in the end we settled nothing. "Why did you come?" I finally asked him.

"I thought we should meet. We could use your help. Your knowledge of Jokertown, your contacts in nat society, the money you could raise."

"You won't get my help," I told him. "I've seen where your road leads. Tom Miller walked that road ten years ago."

"Gimli?" He shrugged. "First, Gimli was crazy as a bedbug, I'm not. Gimli wants the world to kiss it and make it all better. I just fight to protect my own. To protect you, Des. Pray that your Jokertown never needs the Twisted Fists, but if you do, we'll be there. I read *Time*'s cover story on Leo Barnett. Could be the Nur isn't the only slow learner. If that's how it is, maybe the Black Dog will go home and find that tree that grows in Brooklyn, right? I haven't been to a Dodgers game since I was eight."

My heart stopped in my throat as I looked at the gun on the table, but I reached out and put my hand on the phone. "I could call down to our security right now and make certain that won't happen, that you won't kill any more innocent people."

"But you won't," the Hound said. "Because we have so much in common."

I told him we had nothing in common.

"We're both jokers," he said. "What else matters?" Then he holstered his gun, adjusted his mask, and walked calmly from my room.

And God help me, I sat there alone for several endless minutes, until I heard the elevator doors open down the hall—and finally took my hand off the phone.

February 7/Kabul, Afghanistan

I am in a good deal of pain today. Most of the delegates have gone on a day trip to various historic sights, but I elected to stay at the hotel once again.

Our tour...what can I say? Syria has made headlines around the world. Our press contingent has doubled in size, all of them eager to get the inside story of what happened out in the desert. For once, I am not unhappy to have been excluded. Peri has told me what it was like....

Syria has touched all of us, myself included. Not all of my pain is caused by the cancer. There are times when I grow profoundly weary, looking back over my life and wondering whether I have done any good at all, or if all my life's work has been for nothing. I have tried to speak out on behalf of my people, to appeal to reason and decency and the common humanity that unites us all, and I have always been convinced that quiet strength, perseverance, and nonviolence would get us further in the long run. Syria makes me wonder...how do you reason with a man like the Nur al-Allah, compromise with him, talk to him? How do you appeal to his humanity when he does not consider you human at all? If there is a God, I pray that He forgives me, but I find myself wishing they had killed the Nur.

Hiram has left the tour, albeit temporarily. He promises to rejoin in India, but by now he is back in New York City, after jetting from Damascus to Rome and then catching a Concorde back to America. He told us that an emergency had arisen at Aces High that demanded his personal attention, but I suspect the truth is that Syria shook him more than he cared to admit. The rumor has swept round the plane that Hiram lost control in the desert, that he hit General Sayyid with far more weight than was necessary to stop him. Billy Ray, of course, doesn't think Hiram went far enough. "If it'd been me, I would have piled it on till he was just a brown and red stain on the floor," he told me.

Worchester himself refused to talk about it and insisted that he was taking this brief leave of us simply because he was "sick unto death of stuffed grape leaves," but even as he made the joke, I noticed beads of sweat on his broad, bald forehead and a slight tremor in his hand. I hope a short respite restores him; the more we have traveled together, the more I have come to respect Hiram Worchester.

If clouds do indeed have a silver lining, however, then perhaps one good did come out of the monstrous incident in Syria: Gregg Hartmann's stature seems to have been vastly enhanced by his near brush with death. For a decade now his political fortunes have been haunted by the specter of the Great Jokertown Riot in 1976, when he "lost his head" in public. To me his reaction was only human—he had just witnessed a woman being torn to pieces by a mob, after all. But presidential candidates are not allowed to weep or grieve or rage like the rest of us, as Muskie proved in '72 and Hartmann confirmed in '76.

Syria may finally have put that tragic incident to rest. Everyone who was there agrees that Hartmann's behavior was exemplary—he was firm, cool-headed, courageous, a pillar of strength in the face of the Nur's barbarous threats. Every paper in America has run the AP photo that was taken as they pulled out: Hiram helping Tachyon into the helicopter in the background, while in the foreground Senator Hartmann waited, his face streaked with dust, yet still grim and strong, his blood soaking through the sleeve of his white shirt.

Gregg still claims that he is not going to be a presidential candidate in 1988, and indeed all the polls show that Gary Hart has an over-whelming lead for the Democratic nomination, but Syria and the pho-tograph will surely do wonders for his name recognition and his standing. I find myself desperately hoping that he will reconsider. I have nothing against Gary Hart, but Gregg Hartmann is something special, and perhaps for those of us touched by the wild card, he is our last best hope.

If Hartmann fails, all my hopes fail with him, and then what choice will we have but to turn to the Black Dog?

I SUPPOSE I SHOULD WRITE SOMETHING ABOUT AFGHANISTAN, BUT there is little to record. I don't have the strength to see what sights Kabul has to offer. The Soviets are much in evidence here, but they are being very correct and courteous. The war is being kept at arm's length for the duration of our short stopover. Two Afghan jokers have been produced for our approval, both of whom swear (through Soviet interpreters) that a joker's life is idyllic here. Somehow I am not convinced. If I understand correctly, they are the only two jokers in all of Afghanistan.

The *Stacked Deck* flew directly from Baghdad to Kabul. Iran was out of the question. The Ayatollah shares many of the Nur's views on wild cards, and he rules his nation in name as well as fact, so even the UN could not secure us permission to land. At least the Ayatollah makes no distinctions between aces and jokers—we are all the demon children of the Great Satan, according to him. Obviously he has not forgotten Jimmy Carter's ill-fated attempt to free the hostages, when a half-dozen government aces were sent in on a secret mission that turned into a horrid botch. The rumor is that Carnifex was one of the aces involved, but Billy Ray emphatically denies it. "If I'd been along, we would have gotten our people out and kicked the old man's ass for good measure," he says. His colleague from Justice, Lady Black, just pulls her black cloak more tightly about herself and smiles enigmatically. Mistral's father, Cyclone, has often been linked to that doomed mission as well, but it's not something she'll talk about.

Tomorrow morning we'll fly over the Khyber Pass and cross into India, a different world entirely, a whole sprawling subcontinent, with the largest joker population anywhere outside the United States.

FEBRUARY 12/CALCUTTA

India is as strange and fabulous a land as any we have seen on this trip...if indeed it is correct to call it a land at all. It seems more like a hundred lands in one. I find it hard to connect the Himalayas and the palaces of the Moguls to the slums of Calcutta and Bengali jungles. The Indians themselves live in a dozen different worlds, from the aging Britishers who try to pretend that the Viceroy still rules in their little enclaves of the Raj, to the maharajas and nawabs who are kings in all but name, to the beggars on the streets of this sprawling filthy city.

There is so *much* of India.

In Calcutta you see jokers on the streets everywhere you go. They are as common as beggars, naked children, and corpses, and too frequently one and the same. In this quasi-nation of Hindu and Muslim and Sikh, the vast majority of jokers seems to be Hindu, but given Islam's attitudes, that can hardly be a surprise. The orthodox Hindu has invented a new caste for the joker, far below even the untouchable, but at least they are allowed to live.

Interestingly enough, we have found no jokertowns in India. This culture is sharply divided along racial and ethnic grounds, and the enmities run very deep, as was clearly shown in the Calcutta wild card riots of 1947, and the wholesale nationwide carnage that accompanied the partition of the subcontinent that same year. Despite that, today you find Hindu and Muslim and Sikh living side by side on the same street, and jokers and nats and even a few pathetic deuces sharing the same hideous slums. It does not seem to have made them love each other any more, alas.

India also boasts a number of native aces, including a few of considerable power. Digger is having a grand time dashing about the country interviewing them all, or as many as will consent to meet with him.

Radha O'Reilly, on the other hand, is obviously very unhappy here. She is Indian royalty herself, it appears, at least on her mother's side...her father was some sort of Irish adventurer. Her people practice a variety of Hinduism built around Gonesh, the elephant god, and the black mother Kali, and to them her wild card ability makes her the destined bride of Gonesh, or something along those lines. At any rate she seems firmly convinced that she is in imminent danger of being kidnapped and forcibly returned to her homeland, so except for the official receptions in New Delhi and Bombay, she has remained closely closeted in the various hotels, with Carnifex, Lady Black, and the rest of our security close at hand. I believe she will be very happy to leave India once again.

Dr. Tachyon, Peregrine, Mistral, Fantasy, Troll, and the Harlem Hammer have just returned from a tiger hunt in the Bengal. Their host was one of the Indian aces, a maharaja blessed with a form of the Midas touch. I understand that the gold he creates is inherently unstable and reverts to its original state within twenty-four hours, although the process of transmutation is still sufficient to kill any living thing he touches. Still, his palace is reputed to be quite a spectacular place. He's solved the traditional mythic dilemma by having his servants feed him.

Tachyon returned from the expedition in as good a spirit as I've seen him since Syria, wearing a golden Nehru jacket and matching turban, fastened by a ruby the size of my thumb. The maharaja was lavish with his gifts, it seems. Even the prospect of the jacket and turban reverting to common cloth in a few hours does not seem to have dampened our alien's enthusiasm for the day's activities. The glittering pageant of the hunt, the splendors of the palace, and the maharaja's harem all seem to have reminded Tach of the pleasures and prerogatives he once enjoyed as a prince of the Ilkazam on his home world. He admitted that even on Takis there was no sight to compare to the end of the hunt, when the maneater had been brought to bay and the maharaja calmly approached it, removed one golden glove, and transmuted the huge beast to solid gold with a touch.

While our aces were accepting their presents of fairy gold and hunting tigers, I spent the day in humbler pursuits, in the unexpected company of Jack Braun, who was invited to the hunt with the others but declined. Instead Braun and I made our way across Calcutta to visit the monument the Indians erected to Earl Sanderson on the site where he saved Mahatma Gandhi from assassination.

The memorial resembles a Hindu temple and the statue inside looks more like some minor Indian deity than an American black who played football for Rutgers, but still... Sanderson has indeed become some sort of god to these people; various offerings left by worshipers were strewn about the feet of his statue. It was very crowded, and we had to wait for a long time before we were admitted. The Mahatma is still universally revered in India, and some of his popularity seems to have rubbed off on the memory of the American ace who stepped between him and an assassin's bullet.

Braun said very little when we were inside, just stared up at the statue as if somehow willing it to come to life. It was a moving visit, but not entirely a comfortable one. My obvious deformity drew hard looks from some of the higher-caste Hindus in the press of the people. And whenever someone brushed against Braun too tightly—as happened frequently among such a tightly packed mass of people—his biological force field would begin to shimmer, surrounding him with a ghostly golden glow. I'm afraid my nervousness got the better of me, and I interrupted Braun's reveries and got us out of there hastily. Perhaps I overreacted, but if even one person in that crowd had realized who Jack Braun was, it might have triggered a vastly ugly scene. Braun was very moody and quiet on the way back to our hotel.

Gandhi is a personal hero of mine, and for all my mixed feelings about aces I must admit that I am grateful to Earl Sanderson for the intervention that saved Gandhi's life. For the great prophet of nonviolence to die by an assassin's bullet would have been too grotesque, and I think India would have torn itself apart in the wake of such a death, in a fratricidal bloodbath the likes of which the world has never seen.

If Gandhi had not lived to lead the reunification of the subcontinent after the death of Jinnah in 1948, would that strange two-headed nation called Pakistan actually have endured? Would the All-India Congress have displaced all the petty rulers and absorbed their domains, as it threatened to do? The very shape of this decentralized, endlessly diverse patchwork country is an expression of the Mahatma's dreams. I find it inconceivable to imagine what course Indian history might have taken without him. So in that respect, at least, the Four Aces left a real mark on the world and perhaps demonstrated that one determined man can indeed change the course of history for the better.

I pointed all this out to Jack Braun on our ride home, when he seemed so withdrawn. I'm afraid it did not help much. He listened to me patiently and when I was finished, he said, "It was Earl who saved him, not me," and lapsed back into silence.

———

TRUE TO HIS PROMISE, HIRAM WORCHESTER RETURNED TO THE tour today, via Concorde from London. His brief sojourn in New York seems to have done him a world of good. His old ebullience was back, and he promptly convinced Tachyon, Mordecai Jones, and Fantasy to join him on an expedition to find the hottest vindaloo in Calcutta. He pressed Peregrine to join the foraging party as well, but the thought seemed to make her turn green.

Tomorrow morning Father Squid, Troll, and I will visit the Ganges, where legend has it a joker can bathe in the sacred waters and be cured of his afflictions. Our guides tell us there are hundreds of documented cases, but I am frankly dubious, although Father Squid insists that there have been miraculous joker cures in Lourdes as well. Perhaps I shall succumb and leap into the sacred waters after all. A man dying of cancer can ill afford the luxury of skepticism, I suppose.

Chrysalis was invited to join us, but declined. These days she seems most comfortable in the hotel bars, drinking amaretto and playing endless games of solitaire. She has become quite friendly with two of our reporters, Sara Morgenstern and the ubiquitous Digger Downs, and I've even heard talk that she and Digger are sleeping together.

Back from the Ganges. I must make my confession. I took off my shoe and sock, rolled up my pants leg, and put my foot in the sacred waters. Afterward, I was still a joker, alas... a joker with a wet foot.

The sacred waters are filthy, by the way, and while I was fishing for my miracle, someone stole my shoe.

MARCH 14/HONG KONG

I have been feeling better of late, I'm pleased to say. Perhaps it was our brief sojourn in Australia and New Zealand. Coming close upon the heels of Singapore and Jakarta, Sydney seemed almost like home, and I was strangely taken with Auckland and the comparative prosperity and cleanliness of its little toy jokertown. Aside from a distressing tendency to call themselves "uglies," an even more offensive term than "joker," my Kiwi brethren seem to live as decently as any jokers anywhere. I was even able to purchase a week-old copy of the *Jokertown Cry* at my hotel. It did my soul good to read the news of home, even though too many of the headlines seem to be concerned with a gang war being fought in our streets.

Hong Kong has its jokertown too, as relentlessly mercantile as the rest of the city. I understand that mainland China dumps most of its jokers here, in the Crown Colony. In fact a delegation of leading joker merchants have invited Chrysalis and me to lunch with them tomorrow and discuss "possible commercial ties between jokers in Hong Kong and New York City." I'm looking forward to it.

Frankly it will be good to get away from my fellow delegates for a few hours. The mood aboard the *Stacked Deck* is testy at best at present, chiefly thanks to Thomas Downs and his rather overdeveloped journalistic instincts.

Our mail caught up with us in Christchurch, just as we were taking off for Hong Kong, and the packet included advance copies of the latest issue of *Aces.* Digger went up and down the aisles after we were airborne, distributing complimentary copies as is his wont. He ought to have read them first. He and his execrable magazine hit a new low this time out, I'm afraid.

The issue features his cover story of Peregrine's pregnancy. I was amused to note that the magazine obviously feels that Peri's baby is the big news of the trip, since they devoted twice as much space to it as they have to any of Digger's previous stories, even the hideous incident in Syria, though perhaps that was only to justify the glossy four-page footspread of Peregrine past and present, in various costumes and states of undress.

The whispers about her pregnancy started as early as India and were officially confirmed while we were in Thailand, so Digger could hardly be blamed for filing a story. It's just the sort of thing that *Aces* thrives on. Unfortunately for his own health and our sense of camaraderie aboard the *Stacked Deck,* Digger clearly did not agree with Peri that her "delicate condition" was a private matter. Digger dug too far.

The cover asks, "Who Fathered Peri's Baby?" Inside, the piece opens with a double-page spread illustrated by an artist's conception of Peregrine holding an infant in her arms, except that the child is a black silhouette with a question mark instead of a face. "Daddy's an Ace, Tachyon Says," reads the subhead, leading into a much larger orange banner that claims, "Friends Beg Her to Abort Monstrous Joker Baby." Gossip has it that Digger plied Tachyon with brandy while the two of them were inspecting the raunchier side of Singapore's nightlife, managing to elicit a few choice indiscretions. He did not get the name of the father of Peregrine's baby, but once drunk enough, Tachyon displayed no reticence in sounding off about all the reasons why he believes Peregrine ought to abort this child, the foremost of which is the nine percent chance that the baby will be born a joker.

I confess that reading the story filled me with a cold rage and made me doubly glad that Dr. Tachyon is not my personal physician. It is at moments such as this that I find myself wondering how Tachyon can possibly pretend to be my friend, or the friend of any joker. *In vino veritas*, they say; Tachyon's comments make it quite clear that he thinks abortion is the only choice for any woman in Peregrine's position. The Takisians abhor deformity and customarily "cull" (such a polite word) their own deformed children (very few in number, since they have not yet been blessed with the virus that they so generously decided to share with Earth) shortly after birth. Call me oversensitive if you will, but the clear implication of what Tachyon is saying is that death is preferable to jokerhood, that it is better that this child never live at all than live the life of a joker.

When I set the magazine aside I was so livid that I knew I could not possibly speak to Tachyon himself in any rational manner, so I got up and went back to the press compartment to give Downs a piece of my mind. At the very least I wanted to point out rather forcefully that it was grammatically permissible to omit the adjective "monstrous" before the phrase "joker baby," though clearly the copy editors at *Aces* feel it compulsory.

Digger saw me coming, however, and met me halfway. I've managed to raise his consciousness at least enough so that he knew how upset I'd be, because he started right in with excuses. "Hey, I just wrote the article," he began. "They do the headlines back in New York, that and the art, I've got no control over it. Look, Des, next time I'll talk to them—"

He never had a chance to finish whatever promise he was about to make, because just then Josh McCoy stepped up behind him and tapped him on the shoulder with a rolled-up copy of *Aces*. When Downs turned around, McCoy started swinging. The first punch broke Digger's nose with a sickening noise that made me feel rather faint. McCoy went on to split Digger's lips and loosen a few teeth. I grabbed McCoy with my arms and wrapped my trunk around his neck to try to hold him still, but he was crazy strong with rage and brushed me off easily, I'm afraid. I've never been the physical sort, and in my present condition I fear that I'm pitifully weak. Fortunately Billy Ray came along in time to break them up before McCoy could do serious damage.

Digger spent the rest of the flight back in the rear of the plane stoked up with painkillers. He managed to offend Billy Ray as well by dripping blood on the front of his white Carnifex costume. Billy is nothing if not obsessive about his appearance, and as he kept telling us, "those fucking bloodstains don't come out." McCoy went up front, where he helped Hiram, Mistral, and Mr. Jayewardene console Peri, who was considerably upset by the story. While McCoy was assaulting Digger in the rear of the plane, she was tearing into Dr. Tachyon up front. Their confrontation was less physical but equally dramatic, Howard tells me. Tachyon kept apologizing over and over again, but no amount of apologies seemed to stay Peregrine's fury. Howard says it was a good thing that her talons were packed away safely with the luggage.

Tachyon finished out the flight alone in the first-class lounge with a bottle of Remy Martin and the forlorn look of a puppy dog who has just piddled on the Persian rug. If I had been a crueler man, I might have gone upstairs and explained my own grievances to him, but I found that I did not have the heart. I find that very curious, but there is something about Dr. Tachyon that makes it difficult to stay angry with him for very long, no matter how insensitive and egregious his behavior.

No matter. I am looking forward to this part of the trip. From Hong Kong we travel to the mainland, Canton and Shanghai and Peking and other stops equally exotic. I plan to walk upon the Great Wall and see the Forbidden City. During World War II I'd chosen to serve in the navy in hopes of seeing the world, and the Far East always had a special glamour for me, but I wound up assigned to a desk in Bayonne, New Jersey. Mary and I were going to make up for that afterward, when the baby was a little older and we had a little more in the way of financial security.

Well, we made our plans, and meanwhile the Takisians made theirs.

Over the years China came to represent all the things I'd never done, all the far places I meant to visit and never did, my own personal Jolson story. And now it looms on my horizon, at last. It's enough to make one believe the end is truly near.

March 21/En Route to Seoul

A face out of my past confronted me in Tokyo and has preyed on my mind ever since. Two days ago I decided that I would ignore him and the issues raised by his presence, that I would make no mention of him in this journal.

I've made plans to have this volume offered for publication after my death. I do not expect a bestseller, but I would think the number of celebrities aboard the *Stacked Deck* and the various newsworthy events we've generated will stir up at least a little interest in the great American public, so my volume may find its own audience. Whatever modest royalties it earns will be welcomed by the JADL, to which I've willed my entire estate.

Yet, even though I will be safely dead and buried before anyone reads these words, and therefore in no position to be harmed by any personal admissions I might make, I find myself reluctant to write of Fortunato. Call it cowardice, if you will. Jokers are notorious cowards, if one listens to the jests, the cruel sort that they do not allow on television. I can easily justify my decision to say nothing of Fortunato. My dealings with him over the years have been private matters, having little to do with politics or world affairs or the issues that I've tried to address in this journal, and nothing at all to do with this tour.

Yet I have felt free, in these pages, to repeat the gossip that has inevitably swirled about the airplane, to report on the various foibles and indiscretions of Dr. Tachyon and Peregrine and Jack Braun and Digger Downs and all the rest. Can I truly pretend that their weaknesses are of public interest and my own are not? Perhaps I could... the public has always been fascinated by aces and repelled by jokers... but I will not. I want this journal to be an honest one, a true one. And I want the readers to understand a little of what it has been like to live forty years as a joker. And to do that I must talk of Fortunato, no matter how deeply it may shame me.

Fortunato now lives in Japan. He helped Hiram in some obscure way after Hiram had suddenly and quite mysteriously left the tour in Tokyo. I don't pretend to know the details of that; it was all carefully hushed up. Hiram seemed almost himself when he returned to us in Calcutta, but he has deteriorated rapidly again, and he looks worse every day. He has become volatile and unpleasant, and secretive. But this is not about Hiram, of whose woes I know nothing. The point is, Fortunato was embroiled in the business somehow and came to our hotel, where I spoke to him briefly in the corridor. That was all there was to it . . . now. But in years past Fortunato and I have had other dealings.

FORGIVE ME. THIS IS HARD. I AM AN OLD MAN AND A JOKER, AND age and deformity alike have made me sensitive. My dignity is all I have left, and I am about to surrender it.

I was writing about self-loathing.

This is a time for hard truths, and the first of those is that many nats are disgusted by jokers. Some of these are bigots, always ready to hate anything different. In that regard we jokers are no different from any other oppressed minority; we are all hated with the same honest venom by those predisposed to hate.

There are other normals, however, who are more predisposed to tolerance, who try to see beyond the surface to the human being beneath. People of good will, not haters, well-meaning generous people like . . . well, like Dr. Tachyon and Hiram Worchester to choose two examples close to hand. Both of these gentlemen have proven over the years that they care deeply about jokers in the abstract, Hiram through his anonymous charities, Tachyon through his work at the clinic. And yet both of them, I am convinced, are just as sickened by the simple physical deformity of most jokers as the Nur al-Allah or Leo Barnett. You can see it in their eyes, no matter how nonchalant and cosmopolitan they strive to be. Some of their best friends are jokers, but they wouldn't want their sister to marry one.

This is the first unspeakable truth of jokerhood.

How easy it would be to rail against this, to condemn men like Tach and Hiram for hypocrisy and "formism" (a hideous word coined by a particularly moronic joker activist and taken up by Tom Miller's Jokers for a Just Society in their heyday). Easy, and wrong. They are decent men, but still only men, and cannot be thought less because they have normal human feelings.

Because, you see, the second unspeakable truth of jokerhood is that no matter how much jokers offend nats, we offend ourselves even more.

Self-loathing is the particular psychological pestilence of Jokertown, a disease that is often fatal. The leading cause of death among jokers under the age of fifty is, and always has been, suicide. This despite the fact that virtually every disease known to man is more serious when contracted by a joker, because our body chemistries and very shapes vary so widely and unpredictably that no course of treatment is truly safe.

In Jokertown you'll search long and hard before you'll find a place to buy a mirror, but there are mask shops on every block.

If that was not proof enough, consider the issue of names. Nick-flames, they call them. They are more than that. They are spotlights on the true depths of joker self-loathing.

If this journal is to be published, I intend to insist that it be titled *The Journal of Xavier Desmond,* not *A Joker's Journal* or any such variant. I am a man, a particular man, not just a generic joker. Names are important; they are more than just words, they shape and color the things they name. The feminists realized this long ago, but jokers still have not grasped it.

I have made it a point over the years to answer to no name but my own, yet I know a joker dentist who calls himself Fishface, an accomplished ragtime pianist who answers to Catbox, and a brilliant joker mathematician who signs his papers "Slimer." Even on this tour I find myself accompanied by three people named Chrysalis, Troll, and Father Squid.

We are, of course, not the first minority to experience this particular form of oppression. Certainly black people have been there—entire generations were raised with the belief that the "prettiest" black girls were the ones with the lightest skins whose features most closely approximated the Caucasian ideal. Finally some of them saw through that lie and proclaimed that black was beautiful.

From time to time various well-meaning but foolish jokers have attempted to do the same thing. Freakers, one of the more debauched institutions of Jokertown, has what it calls a "Twisted Miss" contest every year on Valentine's Day. However sincere or cynical these efforts are, they are surely misguided. Our friends the Takisians took care of that by putting a clever little twist on the prank they played on us.

The problem is, every joker is unique.

Even before my transformation I was never a handsome man. Even after the change I am by no means hideous. My "nose" is a trunk, about two feet long, with fingers at its end. My experience has been that most people get used to the way I look if they are around me for a few days. I like to tell myself that after a week or so you scarcely notice that I'm any different, and maybe there's even a grain of truth in that.

If the virus had only been so kind as to give all jokers trunks where their noses had been, the adjustment might have been a good deal easier, and a "Trunks Are Beautiful" campaign might have done some real good.

But to the best of my knowledge I am the only joker with a trunk. I might work very hard to disregard the aesthetics of the nat culture I live in, to convince myself that I am one handsome devil and that the rest of them are the funny-looking ones, but none of that will help the next time I find that pathetic creature they call Snotman sleeping in the dumpster behind the Funhouse. The horrible reality is, my stomach is as thoroughly turned by the more extreme cases of joker deformity as I imagine Dr. Tachyon's must be—but if anything, I am even more guilty about it.

Which brings me, in a roundabout way, back to Fortunato. Fortunato is . . . or was at least . . . a procurer. He ran a high-priced call girl ring. All of his girls were exquisite; beautiful, sensual, skilled in every erotic art, and by and large pleasant people, as much a delight out of bed as in it. He called them geishas.

For more than two decades I was one of his best customers.

I believe he did a lot of business in Jokertown. I know for a fact that Chrysalis often trades information for sex, upstairs in her Crystal Palace, whenever a man who needs her services happens to strike her fancy. I know a handful of truly wealthy jokers, none of whom are married, but almost all of whom have nat mistresses. The hometown papers we've seen tell us that the Five Families and the Shadow Fists are warring in the streets, and I know why—because in Jokertown prostitution is big business, along with drugs and gambling.

The first thing a joker loses is his sexuality. Some lose it totally, becoming incapable or asexual. But even those whose genitalia and sexual drives remain unaffected by the wild card find themselves bereft of sexual identity. From the instant one stabilizes, one is no longer a man or a woman, only a joker.

A normal sex drive, abnormal self-loathing, and a yearning for the thing that's been lost...manhood, femininity, beauty, whatever. They are common demons in Jokertown, and I know them well. The onset of my cancer and the chemotherapy have combined to kill all my interest in sex, but my memories and my shame remain intact. It shames me to be reminded of Fortunato. Not because I patronized a prostitute or broke their silly laws—I have contempt for those laws. It shames me because, try as I did over the years, I could never find it in me to desire a joker woman. I knew several who were worthy of love; kind, gentle, caring women, who needed commitment and tenderness and yes, sex, as much as I did. Some of them became my cherished friends. Yet I could never respond to them sexually. They remained as unattractive in my eyes as I must have been in theirs.

So it goes, in Jokertown.

The seat belt light has just come on, and I'm not feeling very well at present, so I will sign off here.

APRIL 10/STOCKHOLM

Very tired. I fear my doctor was correct—this trip may have been a drastic mistake, insofar as my health is concerned. I feel I held up remarkably well during the first few months, when everything was fresh and new and exciting, but during this last month a cumulative exhaustion has set in, and the day-to-day grind has become almost unbearable. The flights, the dinners, the endless receiving lines, the visits to hospitals and joker ghettos and research institutions, it is all threatening to become one great blur of dignitaries and airports and translators and buses and hotel dining rooms.

I am not keeping my food down well, and I know I have lost weight. The cancer, the strain of travel, my age...who can say? All of these, I suspect.

Fortunately the trip is almost over now. We are scheduled to return to Tomlin on April 29, and only a handful of stops remain. I confess that I am looking forward to my return home, and I do not think I am alone in that. We are all tired.

Still, despite the toll it has taken, I would not have forfeited this trip for anything. I have seen the Pyramids and the Great Wall, walked the streets of Rio and Marrakesh and Moscow, and soon will add Rome and Paris and London to that list. I have seen and experienced the stuff of dreams and nightmares, and I have learned much, I think. I can only pray that I survive long enough to use some of that knowledge.

Sweden is a bracing change from the Soviet Union and the other Warsaw Pact nations we have visited. I have no strong feelings about socialism one way or the other, but grew very weary of the model joker "medical hostels" we were constantly being shown and the model jokers who occupied them. Socialist medicine and socialist science would undoubtedly conquer the wild card, and great strides were already being made, we were repeatedly told, but even if one credits these claims, the price is a lifetime of "treatment" for the handful of jokers the Soviets admit to having.

Billy Ray insists that the Russians actually have thousands of jokers locked away safely out of sight in huge gray "joker warehouses," nominally hospitals but actually prisons in all but name, staffed by a lot of guards and precious few doctors and nurses. Ray also says there are a dozen Soviet aces, all of them secretly employed by the government, the military, the police, or the party. If these things exist—the Soviet Union denies all such allegations, of course—we got nowhere close to any of them, with Intourist and the KGB carefully managing every aspect of our visit, despite the government's assurance to the United Nations that this UN-sanctioned tour would receive "every cooperation."

To say that Dr. Tachyon did not get along well with his socialist colleagues would be a considerable understatement. His disdain for Soviet medicine is exceeded only by Hiram's disdain for Soviet cooking. Both of them do seem to approve of Soviet vodka, however, and have consumed a great deal of it.

There was an amusing little debate in the Winter Palace, when one of our hosts explained the dialectic of history to Dr. Tachyon, telling him feudalism must inevitably give way to capitalism, and capitalism to socialism, as a civilization matures. Tachyon listened with remarkable politeness and then said, "My dear man, there are two great star-faring civilizations in this small sector of the galaxy. My own people, by your lights, must be considered feudal, and the Network is a form of capitalism more rapacious and virulent than anything you've ever dreamed of. Neither of us show any signs of maturing into socialism, thank you." Then he paused for a moment and added, "Although, if you think of it in the right light, perhaps the Swarm might be considered communist, though scarcely civilized."

It was a clever little speech, I must admit, although I think it might have impressed the Soviets more if Tachyon had not been dressed in full cossack regalia when he delivered it. Where does he get these outfits?

OF THE OTHER WARSAW BLOC NATIONS THERE IS LITTLE TO REPORT. Yugoslavia was the warmest, Poland the grimmest, Czechoslovakia seemed the most like home. Downs wrote a marvelously engrossing piece for *Aces*, speculating that the widespread peasant accounts of active contemporary vampires in Hungary and Romania were actually manifestations of the wild card. It was his best work, actually, some really excellent writing, and all the more remarkable when you consider that he based the whole thing on a five-minute conversation with a pastry chef in Budapest. We found a small joker ghetto in Warsaw and a widespread belief in a hidden "solidarity ace" who will shortly come forth to lead that outlawed trade union to victory. He did not, alas, come forth during our two days in Poland. Senator Hartmann, with greatest difficulty, managed to arrange a meeting with Lech Walesa, and I believe that the AP news photo of their meeting has enhanced his stature back home. Hiram left us briefly in Hungary—another "emergency" back in New York, he said—and returned just as we arrived in Sweden, in somewhat better spirits.

Stockholm is a most congenial city, after many of the places we have been. Virtually all the Swedes we have met speak excellent English, we are free to come and go as we please (within the confines of our merciless schedule, of course), and the king was gracious to all of us. Jokers are quite rare here, this far north, but he greeted us with complete equanimity, as if he'd been hosting jokers all of his life.

Still, as enjoyable as our brief visit has been, there is only one incident that is worth recording for posterity. I believe we have unearthed something that will make the historians around the world sit up and take notice, a hitherto-unknown fact that puts much of recent Middle Eastern history into a new and startling perspective.

It occurred during an otherwise unremarkable afternoon a number of the delegates spent with the Nobel trustees. I believe it was Senator Hartmann they actually wanted to meet. Although it ended in violence, his attempt to meet and negotiate with the Nur al-Allah in Syria is correctly seen here for what it was—a sincere and courageous effort on behalf of peace and understanding, and one that makes him to my mind a legitimate candidate for next year's Nobel Peace Prize.

At any rate, several of the other delegates accompanied Gregg to the meeting, which was cordial but hardly stimulating. One of our hosts, it turned out, had been a secretary to Count Folke Bernadotte when he negotiated the Peace of Jerusalem, and sadly enough had also been with Bernadotte when he was gunned down by Israeli terrorists two years later. He told us several fascinating anecdotes about Bernadotte, for whom he clearly had great admiration, and also showed us some of his personal memorabilia of those difficult negotiations. Among the notes, journals, and interim drafts was a photo book.

I gave the book a cursory glance and then passed it on, as did most of my companions. Dr. Tachyon, who was seated beside me on the couch, seemed bored by the proceedings and leafed through the photographs with rather more care. Bernadotte figured in most of them, of course—standing with his negotiating team, talking with David Ben-Gurion in one photo and King Faisal in the next. The various aides, including our host, were seen in less formal poses, shaking hands with Israeli soldiers, eating with a tentful of Bedouin, and so on. The usual sort of thing. By far the single most interesting picture showed Bernadotte surrounded by the *Nasr*, the Port Said aces who so dramatically reversed the tide of battle when they joined with Jordan's crack Arab Legion. Khôf sits beside Bernadotte in the center of the photograph, all in black, looking like death incarnate, surrounded by the younger aces. Ironically enough, of all the faces in that photo, only three are still alive, the ageless Khôf among them. Even an undeclared war takes its toll.

That was not the photograph that caught Tachyon's attention, however. It was another, a very informal snapshot, showing Bernadotte and various members of his team in some hotel room, the table in front of them littered with papers. In one corner of the photograph was a young man I had not noticed in any of the other pictures—slim, dark-haired, with a certain intense look around the eyes, and a rather ingratiating grin. He was pouring a cup of coffee. All very innocent, but Tachyon stared at the photograph for a long time and then called our host over and said to him privately, "Forgive me if I tax your memory, but I would be very interested to know if you remember this man." He pointed him out. "Was he a member of your team?"

Our Swedish friend leaned over, studied the photograph, and chuckled. "Oh, him," he said in excellent English. "He was... what is the slang word you use, for a boy who runs errands and does odd jobs? An animal of some sort..."

"A gofer," I supplied.

"Yes, he was a *gopher,* as you put it. Actually a young journalism student. Joshua, that was his name. Joshua... something. He said he wanted to observe the negotiations from within so he could write about them afterward. Bernadotte thought the idea was ridiculous when it was first put to him, rejected it out of hand in fact, but the young man was persistent. He finally managed to corner the count and put his case to him personally, and somehow he talked him around. So he was not officially a member of the team, but he was with us constantly from that point through the end. He was not a very efficient gopher, as I recall, but he was such a pleasant young man that everyone liked him regardless. I don't believe he ever wrote his article."

"No," Tachyon said. "He wouldn't have. He was a chess player, not a writer."

Our host lit up with remembrance. "Why, yes! He played incessantly, now that I recall. He was quite good. Do you know him, Dr. Tachyon? I've often wondered whatever became of him."

"So have I," Tachyon replied very simply and very sadly. Then he closed the book and changed the topic.

I have known Dr. Tachyon for more years than I care to contemplate. That evening, spurred by my own curiosity, I managed to seat myself near to Jack Braun and ask him a few innocent questions while we ate. I'm certain that he suspected nothing, but he was willing enough to reminisce about the Four Aces, the things they did and tried to do, the places they went, and more importantly, the places they did not go. At least not officially.

Afterward, I found Dr. Tachyon drinking alone in his room. He invited me in, and it was clear that he was feeling quite morose, lost in his damnable memories. He lives as much in the past as any man I have ever known. I asked him who the young man in the photograph had been.

"No one," Tachyon said. "Just a boy I used to play chess with." I'm not sure why he felt he had to lie to me.

"His name was not Joshua," I told him, and he seemed startled. I wonder, does he think my deformity affects my mind, my memory? "His name was David, and he was not supposed to be there. The Four Aces were never officially involved in the Mideast, and Jack Braun says that by late 1948 the members of the group had gone their own ways. Braun was making movies."

"Bad movies," Tachyon said with a certain venom.

"Meanwhile," I said, "the Envoy was making peace."

"He was gone for two months. He told Blythe and me that he was going on a vacation. I remember. It never occurred to me that he was involved."

No more has it ever occurred to the rest of the world, though perhaps it should have. David Harstein was not particularly religious, from what little I know of him, but he was Jewish, and when the Port Said aces and the Arab armies threatened the very existence of the new state of Israel, he acted all on his own.

His was a power for peace, not war; not fear or sandstorms or lightning from a clear sky, but pheromones that made people like him and want desperately to please him and agree with him, that made the mere presence of the ace called Envoy a virtual guarantee of a successful negotiation. But those who knew who and what he was showed a distressing tendency to repudiate their agreements once Harstein and his pheromones had left their presence. He must have pondered that, and with the stakes so high, he must have decided to find out what might happen if his role in the process was carefully kept secret. The Peace of Jerusalem was his answer.

I wonder if even Folke Bernadotte knew who his gopher really was. I wonder where Harstein is now, and what he thinks of the peace that he so carefully and secretly wrought. And I find myself reflecting on what the Black Dog said in Jerusalem.

What would it do to the fragile Peace of Jerusalem if its origins were revealed to the world? The more I reflect on that, the more certain I grow that I ought to tear these pages from my journal before I offer it for publication. If no one gets Dr. Tachyon drunk, perhaps this secret can even be kept.

Did he ever do it again, I wonder? After HUAC, after prison and disgrace and his celebrated conscription and equally celebrated disappearance, did the Envoy ever sit in on any other negotiations with the world's being none the wiser? I wonder if we'll ever know.

I think it unlikely and wish it were not. From what I have seen on this tour, in Guatemala and South Africa, in Ethiopia and Syria and Jerusalem, in India and Indonesia and Poland, the world today needs the Envoy more than ever.

APRIL 27/SOMEWHERE OVER THE ATLANTIC

The interior lights were turned out several hours ago, and most of my fellow travelers are long asleep, but the pain has kept me awake. I've taken some pills, and they are helping, but still I cannot sleep. Nonetheless, I feel curiously elated...almost serene. The end of my journey is near, in both the larger and smaller senses. I've come a long way, yes, and for once I feel good about it.

We still have one more stop—a brief sojourn in Canada, whirlwind visits to Montreal and Toronto, a government reception in Ottawa. And then home. Tomlin International, Manhattan, Jokertown. It will be good to see the Funhouse again.

I wish I could say that the tour had accomplished everything we set out to do, but that's scarcely the case. We began well, perhaps, but the violence in Syria, West Germany, and France undid our unspoken dream of making the public forget the carnage of Wild Card Day. I can only hope that the majority will realize that terrorism is a bleak and ugly part of the world we live in, that it would exist with or without the wild card. The bloodbath in Berlin was instigated by a group that included jokers, aces, and nats, and we would do well to remember that and remind the world of it forcefully. To lay that carnage at the door of Gimli and his pathetic followers, or the two fugitive aces still being sought by the German police, is to play into the hands of men like Leo Barnett and the Nur al-Allah. Even if the Takisians had never brought their curse to us, the world would have no shortage of desperate, insane, and evil men.

For me, there is a grim irony in the fact that it was Gregg's courage and compassion that put his life at risk, and hatred that saved him, by turning his captors against each other in that fratricidal holocaust.

Truly, this is a strange world.

I pray that we have seen the last of Gimli, but meanwhile I can rejoice. After Syria it seems unlikely that anyone could still doubt Gregg Hartmann's coolness under fire, but if that was indeed the case, surely all such fears have now been firmly laid to rest by Berlin. After Sara Morgenstern's exclusive interview was published in the *Post,* I understand Hartmann shot up ten points in the polls. He's almost neck and neck with Hart now. The feeling aboard the plane is that Gregg is definitely going to run.

I said as much to Digger back in Dublin, over a Guinness and some fine Irish soda bread in our hotel, and he agreed. In fact, he went further and predicted that Hartmann would get the nomination. I wasn't quite so certain and reminded him that Gary Hart still seems a formidable obstacle, but Downs grinned in that maddeningly cryptic way of his beneath his broken nose and said, "Yeah, well, I got this hunch that Gary is going to fuck up and do something really stupid, don't ask me why."

If my health permits, I will do everything I can to rally Jokertown behind a Hartmann candidacy. I don't think I'm alone in my commitment either. After the things we have seen, both at home and abroad, a growing number of prominent aces and jokers are likely to throw their weight behind the senator. Hiram Worchester, Peregrine, Mistral, Father Squid, Jack Braun...perhaps even Dr. Tachyon, despite his notorious distaste for politics and politicians.

Terrorism and bloodshed notwithstanding, I do believe we accomplished some good on this journey. Our report will open some official eyes, I can only hope, and the press spotlight that has shone on us everywhere has greatly increased public awareness of the plight of jokers in the Third World.

On a more personal level, Jack Braun did much to redeem himself and even buried his thirty-year enmity with Tachyon; Peri seems positively radiant in her pregnancy; and we did manage, however belatedly, to free poor Jeremiah Strauss from twenty years of simian bondage. I remember Strauss from the old days, when Angela owned the Funhouse and I was only the maître d', and I offered him a booking if and when he resumes his theatrical career as the Projectionist. He was appreciative, but noncommittal. I don't envy him his period of adjustment. For all practical purposes, he is a time traveler.

And Dr. Tachyon...well, his new punk haircut is ugly in the extreme, he still favors his wounded leg, and by now the entire plane knows of his sexual dysfunction, but none of this seems to bother him since young Blaise came aboard in France. Tachyon has been evasive about the boy in his public statements, but of course everyone knows the truth. The years he spent in Paris are scarcely a state secret, and if the boy's hair was not a sufficient clue, his mind control power makes his lineage abundantly clear.

Blaise is a strange child. He seemed a little awed by the jokers when he first joined us, particularly Chrysalis, whose transparent skin clearly fascinated him. On the other hand, he has all of the natural cruelty of an unschooled child (and believe me, any joker knows how cruel a child can be). One day in London, Tachyon got a phone call and had to leave for a few hours. While he was gone, Blaise grew bored, and to amuse himself he seized control of Mordecai Jones and made him climb onto a table and recite "I'm a Little Teapot," which Blaise had just learned as part of an English lesson. The table collapsed under the Hammer's weight, and I don't think Jones is likely to forget the humiliation. He didn't much like Dr. Tachyon to begin with.

Of course not everyone will look back on this tour fondly. The trip was very hard on a number of us, there's no gainsaying that. Sara Morgenstern has filed several major stories and done some of the best writing of her career, but nonetheless the woman is edgier and more neurotic with every passing day. As for her colleagues in the back of the plane, Josh McCoy seems alternately madly in love with Peregrine and absolutely furious with her, and it cannot be easy for him with the whole world knowing that he is not the father of her child. Meanwhile, Digger's profile will never be the same.

Downs is, at least, as irrepressible as he is irresponsible. Just the other day he was telling Tachyon that if he got an exclusive on Blaise, maybe he would be able to keep Tach's impotence off the record. This gambit was not well received. Digger has also been thick as thieves with Chrysalis of late. I overheard them having a very curious conversation in the bar one night in London. "I know he is," Digger was saying. Chrysalis told him that knowing it and proving it were two different things. Digger said something about how they smelled different to him, how he'd known ever since they met, and Chrysalis just laughed and said that was fine, but smells that no one else could detect weren't much good as proof, and even if they were, he'd have to blow his own cover to go public. They were still going at it when I left the bar.

I think even Chrysalis will be delighted to return to Jokertown. Clearly she loved England, but given her Anglophile tendencies, that was hardly a surprise. There was one tense moment when she was introduced to Churchill during a reception, and he gruffly inquired as to exactly what she was trying to prove with her affected British accent. It is quite difficult to read expressions on her unique features, but for a moment I was sure she was going to kill the old man right there in front of the Queen, Prime Minister, and a dozen British aces. Thankfully she gritted her teeth and put it down to Lord Winston's advanced age. Even when he was younger, he was never precisely reticent about expressing his thoughts.

Hiram Worchester has perhaps suffered more on this trip than any of us. Whatever reserves of strength were left to him burned out in Germany, and since then he has seemed exhausted. He shattered his special custom seat as we were leaving Paris—some sort of miscalculation with his gravity control, I believe, but it delayed us nearly three hours while repairs were made. His temper has been fraying too. During the business with the seat, Billy Ray made one too many fat jokes, and Hiram finally snapped and turned on him in a white rage, calling him (among other things) an "incompetent little guttermouth." That was all it took. Carnifex just grinned that ugly little grin of his, said, "For that you get your ass kicked, fat man," and started to get out of his seat. "I didn't say you could get up," Hiram replied; he made a fist and trebled Billy's weight, slamming him right back into the seat cushion. Billy was still straining to get up and Hiram was making him heavier and heavier, and I don't know where it might have ended if Dr. Tachyon hadn't broken it up by putting both of them to sleep with his mind control.

I don't know whether to be disgusted or amused when I see these world-famous aces squabbling like petty children, but Hiram at least has the excuse of ill health. He looks terrible these days: white-faced, puffy, perspiring, short of breath. He has a huge, hideous scab on his neck, just below the collar line, that he picks at when he thinks no one is watching. I would strongly advise him to seek out medical attention, but he is so surly of late that I doubt my counsel would be welcomed. His short visits to New York during the tour always seemed to do him a world of good, however, so we can only hope that homecoming restores his health and spirits.

AND LASTLY, ME.

Observing and commenting on my fellow travelers and what they've gained or lost, that's the easy part. Summing up my own experience is harder. I'm older and, I hope, wiser than when we left Tomlin International, and undeniably I am five months closer to death.

Whether this journal is published or not after my passing, Mr. Ackroyd assures me that he will personally deliver copies to my grandchildren and do everything in his power to make sure that they are read. So perhaps it is to them that I write these last, concluding words . . . to them, and all the others like them. . . .

Robert, Cassie . . . we never met, you and I, and the blame for that falls as much on me as on your mother and your grandmother. If you wonder why, remember what I wrote about self-loathing and please understand that I was not exempt. Don't think too harshly of me . . . or of your mother or grandmother. Joanna was far too young to understand what was happening when her daddy changed, and as for Mary . . . we loved each other once, and I cannot go to my grave hating her. The truth is, had our roles been reversed, I might well have done the same thing. We're all only human, and we do the best we can with the hand that fate has dealt us.

Your grandfather was a joker, yes. But I hope as you read this book you'll realize that he was something else as well—that he accomplished a few things, spoke up for his people, did some good. The JADL is perhaps as good a legacy as most men leave behind them, a better monument to my mind than the Pyramids, the Taj Mahal, or Jetboy's Tomb. All in all, I haven't done so badly. I'll leave behind some friends who loved me, many treasured memories, much unfinished business. I've wet my foot in the Ganges, heard Big Ben sound the hour, and walked on the Great Wall of China. I've seen my daughter born and held her in my arms, and I've dined with aces and TV stars, with presidents and kings.

Most important, I think I leave the world a slightly better place for my having been in it. And that's really all that can be asked of any of us.

Remember me to your children, if you will.

My name was Xavier Desmond, and I was a man.

NINE

The Heart in Conflict

OLD-TIMERS AND TRUEFEN STILL CHERISH THEIR MEMORIES OF BAT DURSTON, THAT FEARless scourge of the spaceways whose adventures appeared so often in *Galaxy* in the early '50s.

Bat always got the cover in those days. The *back* cover. Under the legend "YOU'LL NEVER SEE IT IN GALAXY" ran twin columns:

Hoofs drumming, Bat Durston came galloping down through the narrow pass at Eagle Gulch, a tiny gold colony 400 miles north of Tombstone. He spurred hard for a low overhang of rim-rock...and at that point, a tall, lean wrangler stepped out from behind a high boulder, six-shooter in a sun-tanned hand. "Rear back and dismount, Bat Durston," the stranger lipped thinly. "You don't know it, but this is your last saddle-jaunt through these here parts."

Jets blasting, Bat Durston came screeching down through the atmosphere of Bbllzznaj, a tiny planet seven billion light-years from Sol. He cut out his super-hyper-drive for the landing... and at that point a tall, lean spaceman stepped out of the tail assembly, proton gun blaster in a space-tanned hand "Get back from those controls, Bat Durston," the tall stranger lipped thinly. "You don't know it, but this is your last space trip through this particular section of the universe."

"Sound alike?" editor H. L. Gold would write, beneath the twin columns. "They should—one is merely a western transplanted to some alien and impossible planet. If this is your idea of science fiction, you're welcome to it. YOU'LL NEVER FIND IT IN GALAXY! What you will find in *Galaxy* is the finest science fiction...authentic, plausible, thoughtful...written by authors who do not automatically switch over from crime waves to earth invasions; by people who know and love science fiction...for people who also know and love it."

The ad appeared on the premiere issue of *Galaxy* in September, 1950, and turned up again on many subsequent issues. This was back when I was a wee lad of two (I have pictures to prove it). Even *Rocky Jones* was in my future at that point (Rocky and Bat had surely palled around in space ranger school), along with Heinlein, Howard, Tolkien, Lovecraft, and the Fantastic Four.

By the time I reached the point where I was writing SF myself, *Galaxy* was well past its H. L. Golden age. Gold gave up the reins (the helm? the starship controls?) in 1961 after an auto accident, and Frederik Pohl stepped in for a distinguished stint as editor. Toward the end of the decade Ejler Jakobsson succeeded Pohl and hired Gardner Dozois to read his slush. The rest is history, as you know if you've read my earlier commentaries.

I never sold another story to *Galaxy* while Jakobsson was editor, though I did come close once or twice. I did sell many more stories to Ted White, though after "Exit to San Breta" most of my stuff appeared in *Amazing,* not *Fantastic.* But the market where I made my reputation, where all my early award nominees appeared, and ultimately my first Hugo winner, was *Analog,* the leading magazine in the field, which for decades had come to epitomize "hard science fiction" under its legendary editor, John W. Campbell, Jr.

JWC passed away just as I was breaking in, and Ben Bova succeeded him at *Analog.* Campbell is rightly regarded as a great editor. He remade the field when he took over *Astounding* in the '30s, and gave science fiction its Golden Age. He was famous for developing new writers as well, but somehow I doubt that he would have responded as favorably as Bova did to the melancholy, romantic, downbeat stories I was writing in the early '70s. Had Campbell lived for another ten years, my career would have taken a much different path, I suspect, along with many other careers.

Bova came to the editor's chair as a science fiction writer of impeccable credentials. Ben was known for hard SF, *real* SF, and that was important in those vanished days of yesteryear, when the war between the Old Wave and the New Wave still raged. Nonetheless, the moment he was enthroned, Ben began to open up the magazine, and stories soon appeared within the hallowed pages of *Analog* that would never have appeared under JWC...mine own among them.

This was not an entirely painless process, as a glance at any letter column of that period would tell you. Every new issue contained one or two "cancel my subscription" letters from old subscribers outraged by the appearance of a profane word, a sex scene, or a less-than-competent man. Fortunately, they were a minority. The reborn *Analog* became the best short fiction market of the '70s, and Ben Bova won the Hugo for Best Editor five years in a row from 1973 to 1977, and once again in 1979.

The first sale I made to Bova—my third sale overall, and the first one that wasn't lost before being bought—was actually a "science fact" article about computer chess. I had been captain of my college chess team at Northwestern, where some friends of mine had written a chess-playing program for the big campus mainframe, a giant CDC 6400 that lived in its own sealed, temperature-controlled building. When Chess 4.0 defeated rival programs from a half-dozen other colleges to win the world's first computer chess championship, I knew I had an article, and indeed I did.

It was the only science fact article I ever sold to *Analog,* the only one I ever *wrote.* I was a journalist, not a scientist. But once I'd sold a science fact article to *Analog,* no one could question my bona fides, the way they were then questioning all those squishy-soft New Wave writers who were selling to *Orbit* and *New Dimensions.* Though Bova had broadened *Analog*'s horizons, the magazine still had the reputation of being hard-nosed, steel-clad, scientifically rigorous, and perhaps a bit puritanical. Gardner Dozois once told a woman I was chasing that there was no point in going to bed with me, since when you sold to *Analog* a white van pulled up in front of your house, and two guys in silver jumpsuits confiscated your penis. (I will not comment on the truth of this, except to note that Gardner himself later sold to *Analog,* and presently shares an office with its editor. I have never asked to see what is in the large locked cabinet behind Stan Schmidt's desk.)

"The Computer Was a Fish," my science fact article about David Slate and his champion chess-playing program, was shortly followed by "With Morning Comes Mistfall" and "The Second Kind of Loneliness" and "A Song for Lya" and all the rest. I had other markets besides *Analog,* of course. Ted White bought as many stories from me as did Bova; *Amazing* and *Fantastic* under White were terrific magazines. I also sold to *The Magazine of Fantasy and Science Fiction,* and managed to hit many of the original anthologies series of the day.

But I got my share of rejections as well. No writer likes being rejected, though it comes with the territory, and you need to get used to it. A few of mine were especially galling, though. Those were the ones where the editors had no problems with my plot or characterization or style, and even went out of their way to say that they'd enjoyed reading the stories. They rejected them nonetheless ... because *they weren't real science fiction.*

"Night Shift" was about the night shift at a busy spaceport, as the spaceships come and go. They could have just as easily been trucks, an editor said. Another said that "With Morning Comes Mistfall" put him in mind of attempts to find the Loch Ness monster. Even "Second Kind of Loneliness" took its lumps. This could be a story about a lighthouse keeper, one rejection said. The focus is not on the star ring or the nullspace vortex so much as on the "rather pathetic" protagonist, with his hopes and dreams and fears.

I mean, really. What were these guys trying to tell me? I was an *Analog* writer, I'd sold a science fact article...*and they were claiming that I wrote Bat Durston stories!*

Of course, it was true that I had based "Night Shift" on my father's experiences as a longshoreman and a few weeks I once spent working in a truck dispatch office...

And it was true that the seed for "With Morning Comes Mistfall" had been planted when I read an article in the paper about a scientist who was taking a fleet of sonar-equipped boats to Loch Ness, intending to flush out Nessie or disprove him...

And it was true that "Second Kind of Loneliness" was peopled by my own personal demons, and based on incidents and characters from my own life, as was "A Song for Lya."

And even "Sandkings," a few years later, started with that guy I knew in college and his aquarium of piranha.

But so what? When I wrote the stories I moved them to other planets, and put aliens in them, and spaceships. How much more bloody science-fictional could they *get*?

All those years when I'd been growing up and reading fantasy and horror and science fiction, I'd never once worried about which was what and what was which or where the boundaries were drawn or whether this was *real* science fiction and *real* fantasy and *real* horror. My staple fare in the '50s was made up of paperbacks and comic books. I knew the SF magazines were out there somewhere, but seldom saw one, so I remained blissfully unaware of Bat Durston and Horace Gold's fulminations against him. As a kid I did not even know the proper names for all the genres and subgenres. To me they were monster stories and space stuff and sword & sorcery. Or "weird stuff." That was my father's term for all of it. He liked westerns, you see, but his son liked "weird stuff."

But now that I was a published professional writer, and an *Analog* writer at that (with penis, thank you very much), it behooved me to find out what *real* science fiction was. So I reread Damon Knight's *In Search of Wonder*, James Blish's *The Issue at Hand*, and L. Sprague de Camp's *Science Fiction Handbook*, and looked into *Locus* and *Science Fiction Review*. I paid careful attention to Alexei Panshin's "SF in Dimension" columns in *Amazing*. I followed the debate between the Old Wave and New Wave with interest, since that New Wave crap wasn't real SF science fiction either, according to the Old Wave guys. And of course I paid careful attention to the various definitions of science fiction.

There were a lot of those about, many of them mutually contradictory. L. Sprague de Camp defined SF in *The Science Fiction Handbook*, and Kingsley Amis defined it differently in *New Maps of Hell*. Ted Sturgeon had a definition, Fred Pohl had a definition, Reginald Bretnor had a definition, David G. Hartwell had a definition, Alexei Panshin had a definition, and over in the corner stood Damon Knight pointing at something. The Old Wave and the New Wave each championed its own view of what the genre ought to be. H. L. Gold must surely have had a definition, since he knew Bat Durston did not fit it. I absorbed all of this as best I could, and finally discerned the shape of a *real* science fiction story, as opposed to the stuff that I was writing.

The ultimate template for the True Science Fiction Story was Isaac Asimov's first sale, "Marooned Off Vesta," published in *Amazing* in 1939. Asimov would later write more famous stories, and better stories—well, to tell the truth, pretty much *everything* he wrote after that was a better story—but "Marooned Off Vesta" was sure-enough pure-quill science fiction, in which everything hinges on the fact that water boils at a lower temperature in a vacuum.

This was a sobering realization for me. For although I had pages of scribbled notes for the stories I wanted to tell next year and the year after and the year after that, not one of them had anything to do with the boiling point of water. If truth be told, it seemed to me that Asimov had said just about all there was to say on that particular subject, leaving nothing for the rest of us except, well...Bat Durston.

The thing is, though, the more I considered old Bat, and Asimov, and Heinlein and Campbell, and Wells and Verne, and Vance and Anderson and Le Guin and Brackett and Williamson and de Camp and Kuttner and Moore and

Cordwainer Smith and Doc Smith and George O. Smith and Northwest Smith, and all the rest of the Smiths and the Joneses too, the more I realized something that H. L. Gold did not.

Boys and girls, they're *all* Bat Durston stories.

All of mine, and all of yours, and all of his, and all of hers. *The Space Merchants* (which Gold serialized in *Galaxy* as *Gravy Planet*) is about Madison Avenue in the '50s, *The Forever War* is about Vietnam, *Neuromancer* is a caper novel tricked up in fancy prose, and Asimov's *Galactic Empire* bears a suspicious likeness to one the Romans had a while back. Why else would Bel Riose remind us so much of this guy Belisarius? And when you look really really hard at "Marooned Off Vesta," it turns out that it's not about the boiling point of water after all. It's about some desperate men trying to survive.

Step back and squint hard at the back cover of that first issue of *Galaxy*, if you will, and you will realize how easily those two columns might have been reversed. The same advertisement could just as well have been run on a western magazine, with only minor changes. "YOU'LL NEVER SEE IT IN SIX-GUN STORIES," the editor might well have trumpeted. "Sound alike? They should— one is merely a sci-fi story transplanted to the range. If this is your idea of western fiction, you're welcome to it. YOU'LL NEVER FIND IT IN SIX-GUN STORIES! What you will find here is the finest western fiction...authentic, plausible, thoughtful...written by people who know and love the Old West... for people who also know and love it."

So I will see your Bat Durston, Mr. Gold. And I'll raise you William Faulkner, *Casablanca,* and the Bard.

In the film *The Goodbye Girl* Richard Dreyfuss plays an actor forced to portray Richard III as a lisping effeminate poof by a "genius" director. These days that no longer seems quite as much like a parody as it once did. The London stage has given us Derek Jarman's notorious modern-dress version of Marlowe's *Edward II,* wherein Piers Gaveston's chief item of wardrobe is a studded leather jock strap. When I was last in the West End, they were presenting a *Coriolanus* set against the Terror of Revolutionary France. The most recent filmed version of *Romeo and Juliet* made it a tale of warring urban street gangs, complete with automobiles, helicopters, and television reporters. And if you have not seen Ian McClellan's film of *Richard III,* set in a fascist England during the 1930s, you've missed some fabulous art direction and cinematography, and a mesmerizing performance by McClellan, whose portrayal of Dickie Crookback is equal to Olivier's.

One might argue that *Richard III* is rightfully about the Wars of the Roses, not the fascist movements of the '30s. One might also insist that *Coriolanus* should be set in Rome, not Paris. One might point out rather forcefully that Mercutio was *not*, in fact, a black drag queen. All that is true, as far as it goes.

And yet...sometimes...more often than not...the Bard's plays still work, no matter how bizarrely the genius directors decide to trick them out. Once in the while, as in Ian McClellan's film of *Richard III*, they work rather magnificently.

And for that matter, my favorite science fiction film of all time is not *2001: A Space Odyssey* or *Alien*, or *Star Wars*, or *Bladerunner*, or (ugh) *The Matrix*, but rather *Forbidden Planet*, better known to us cognoscenti as *The Tempest on Altair-4*, and starring Leslie Nielsen, Anne Francis, Walter Pidgeon, and Bat Durston.

But how could this be? How could critics and theatergoers and Shakespeareans possibly applaud these Bat Durston productions, rip'd untimely as they are from their natural and proper settings?

The answer is simple. Motor cars or horses, tricorns or togas, ray-guns or six-shooters, none of it matters, so long as the people remain. Sometimes we get so busy drawing boundaries and making labels that we lose track of that truth.

Casablanca put it most succinctly. "It's still the same old story, a fight for love and glory, a case of do or die."

William Faulkner said much the same thing while accepting the Nobel Prize for Literature, when he spoke of "the old verities and truths of the heart, the universal truths lacking which any story is ephemeral and doomed—love and honor and pity and pride and compassion and sacrifice." The "human heart in conflict with itself," Faulkner said, "alone can make good writing, because only that is worth writing about."

We can make up all the definitions of science fiction and fantasy and horror that we want. We can draw our boundaries and make our labels, but in the end it's still the same old story, the one about the human heart in conflict with itself.

The rest, my friends, is furniture.

The House of Fantasy is built of stone and wood and furnished in High Medieval. Its people travel by horse and galley, fight with sword and spell and battle-axe, communicate by palantir or raven, and break bread with elves and dragons.

The House of Science Fiction is built of duralloy and plastic and furnished in Faux Future. Its people travel by starship and aircar, fight with nukes and tailored germs, communicate by ansible and laser, and break protein bars with aliens.

The House of Horror is built of bone and cobwebs and furnished in Ghastly Gothick. Its people travel only by night, fight with anything that will kill messily, communicate in screams and shrieks and gibbers, and sip blood with vampires and werewolves.

The Furniture Rule, I call it.

Forget the definitions. Furniture Rules.

Ask Phyllis Eisenstein, who has written a series of fine stories about a minstrel named Alaric, traveling through a medieval realm she never names ... but if you corner her at a con she may whisper the name of this far kingdom. "Germany." The only fantastic element in the Alaric stories is teleportation, a psi ability generally classed as a trope of SF. Ah, but Alaric carries a lute, and sleeps in castles, and around him are lords with swords, so ninety-nine readers out of every hundred, and most publishers as well, see the series as fantasy. The Furniture Rules.

Ask Walter Jon Williams. In *Metropolitan* and *City on Fire* he gives us a secondary world as fully imagined as Tolkien's Middle Earth, a world powered entirely by magic, which Walter calls "plasm." But because the world is a single huge decaying city, rife with corrupt politics and racial tensions, and the plasm is piped and metered by the plasm authority, and the sorcerers live in high-rises instead of castles, critics and reviewers and readers alike keep calling the books science fiction. The Furniture Rules.

Peter Nicholls writes, "... SF and fantasy, if genres at all, are impure genres ... their fruit may be SF, but the roots are fantasy, and the flowers and leaves perhaps something else again." If anything, Nicholls does not go far enough, for westerns and mysteries and romances and historicals and all the rest are impure as well. What we really have, when we get right down to the nitty-gritty, are *stories*. Just stories.

And that's what we have in this final section of the book. Some stories that I wrote. A little of this with a little of that. Weird stuff, folks, just weird stuff.

"Under Siege," for instance. It's a time travel story. By definition that makes it science fiction (though, come to think of it, isn't time travel actually a rather unscientific fantasy?), yet it began life as a mainstream historical. If you started reading this book at the beginning *(as you should have!)* and didn't skip over my juvenalia, certain aspects of this story will seem oddly familiar to you. Yes indeed, it's our old friend "The Fortress," which earned me an A and my first rejection, courtesy of Franklin D. Scott and Erik J. Friis. In 1968 "The Fortress" went into the drawer to hibernate. In 1984 I took it out again, added a dwarf and some time travel, called it "Under Siege," and sold it to Ellen Datlow for *Omni*. (Never throw *anything* away.)

Then there's "The Skin Trade," the first (and only) story in my series about PI Randi Wade and Willie the werewolf collection agent. I wrote that one for the 1988 installment of Dark Harvest's annual horror anthology, while I was out in L.A. working on *Beauty and the Beast*. I shared *Night Visions 5* with Stephen King and Dan Simmons. To play on the same field as those two, I knew I'd need to bring my game. Hunched over my computer at the old Seward offices of *Beauty and the Beast* long after everyone else had left, I would drink whole pots of coffee to keep myself awake, and stagger home so wired that I *couldn't* sleep even when I tumbled into bed. It is a wonder that Willie Flambeaux didn't come out talking like Vincent, or vice versa. My deadline came and went, and on I wrote, months after King and Simmons had delivered. I have no doubt that Paul Mikol of Dark Harvest was sorely tempted to give my place to someone faster. But when I finally got the story in, Paul wrote to say, "All right, it kills me, but it was worth the wait." In 1989 "The Skin Trade" won the World Fantasy Award for Best Novella, and I took home one of Gahan Wilson's wonderfully gloomy busts of H. P. Lovecraft to adorn my mantel. Sometimes I put a little hat on him.

"Unsound Variations" is my chess story. It's got some time travel too, sure, but mostly it's my chess story. Not long after moving to Santa Fe, I had this swell idea for an anthology of science fiction and fantasy stories about chess. I could reprint "Midnight by the Morphy Watch" by Fritz Leiber, "The Marvelous Brass Chessplaying Automaton" by Gene Wolfe, and "Von Goom's Gambit," a wonderfully weird Lovecraftian short originally published in *Chess Review*. The rest of the book I would fill out with originals. I knew lots of writers who loved chess.

Fred Saberhagen was one of them. Unfortunately, when I wrote him about my book, he wrote back to tell me he'd just sold a chess anthology to Ace, and would be reprinting "Midnight by the Morphy Watch" and "The Marvelous Brass Chessplaying Automaton" and "Von Goom's Gambit." So instead of him writing a story for my anthology, I wrote a story for his *Pawn to*

Infinity, drawing on my experiences as the captain of Northwestern's chess team. The story is fiction, to be sure, and any resemblance to actual persons living or dead is coincidental... but I would like to point out that I myself once actually fielded six teams for the Pan-American Intercollegiate Team Championships, a record that endured for close to thirty years.

"The Glass Flower" has a sadder distinction. It marked the last time I ever returned to my old SF future history. Kleronomas was one of the touchstone names of that history, along with Stephan Cobalt Northstar, Erika Stormjones, and Tomo and Walberg. I thought it was past time that I brought one of my mythic figures onto the stage. "The Glass Flower" appeared in *Asimov's* in September, 1986. Except for *Avalon,* the abortive novel I began before getting caught up by *A Game of Thrones* and *Doorways,* I have not since visited any of my thousand worlds. Will I ever return to them? I make no promises. Maybe. That's the best that I can do. Definitely maybe.

"The Hedge Knight" is a prequel to my epic fantasy series *A Song of Ice and Fire,* set amongst the Seven Kingdoms of Westeros about ninety years prior to *A Game of Thrones.* Since the epic itself is far from finished, it would never have occurred to me to write a prequel had not Robert Silverberg phoned me to invite me to contribute to *Legends,* his gigantic new fantasy anthology. Big fantasy anthologies had been done before, of course, but Silverberg had put together an all-star roster of contributors for *Legends,* including Stephen King, Terry Pratchett, Ursula K. Le Guin, and most of the world's other leading fantasists. It was plain that this book was going to be huge, and I knew I had to be a part of it. I did not want to give away anything about the end of *A Song of Ice and Fire* or the fate of its principal characters, so a prequel seemed the way to go. (Several of the other *Legends* contributors took the same route, as it turned out.)

"The Hedge Knight" is high fantasy, nothing could be plainer. Or could it? Doesn't fantasy require, well... *magic*? I have dragons in "The Hedge Knight," yes indeed... on helmet crests and banners. Plus one stuffed with sawdust, dancing on its strings. Oh, and Dunk remembers old Ser Arlan talking about seeing a real live dragon once, perhaps that should suffice. If not, well... you can say "The Hedge Knight" is more of a historical adventure than a true fantasy, except that all the history is imaginary. So what does that make it? Don't ask me, I just wrote it. I have since written a sequel, "The Sworn Sword." Look for it come Christmas, in Silverberg's *LEGENDS II*. More tales of Dunk and Egg will follow in the years to come, unless I'm run down by a bus or a better idea.

The last story in the book is "Portraits of His Children," a novelette for which I won the Nebula and lost the Hugo back in 1986. This is a story about writing, and the price we writers pay when we mine our dreams and fears and memories. Back when "Portraits" was nominated for those awards, there was some spirited debate about whether or not it should actually be eligible. Is it a fantasy story, or just a tale of madness? Is it neither, is it both? You be the judge. So long as it's a good story, that's enough for me.

Stories of the human heart in conflict with itself transcend time, place, and setting. So long as love and honor and pity and pride and compassion and sacrifice are present, it matters not a whit whether that tall, lean stranger has a proton pistol or a six-shooter in his hand. Or a sword—

Armor clinking, Lord Durston rode toward the crumbling old castle, hard by the waters of the Dire Lake, a drear land a thousand leagues beyond the realms of men. He reined up as he drew near... and at that point a tall, lean elven lord stepped out from the mouth of a cave, a glowing longsword in one moon-pale hand. "Throw down your blade, Lord Durston," the tall stranger lipped thinly. "You know it not, but you shall ride no more through the land of faery."

Fantasy? Science fiction? Horror?
I say it's a story, and I say the hell with it.

UNDER SIEGE

───────────── ✥ ─────────────

ON THE HIGH RAMPARTS OF VARGÖN, COLONEL BENGT ANTTONEN
stood alone and watched phantasms race across the ice.

The world was snow and wind and bitter, burning cold. The winter sea had frozen hard around Helsinki, and in its icy grip it held the
six island citadels of the great fortress called Sveaborg. The wind was a
knife drawn from a sheath of ice. It cut through Anttonen's uniform,
chafed at his cheeks, brought tears to his eyes and froze them as they
trickled down his face. The wind howled around the towering gray
granite walls, forced its way through doors and cracks and gun em-
placements, insinuated itself everywhere. Out upon the frozen sea, it
snapped and shrieked at the Russian artillery, and sent puffs of snow
from the drifts running and swirling over the ice like strange white
beasts, ghostly animals all asparkle, wearing first one shape and then another, changing constantly as they ran.

They were creatures as malleable as Anttonen's thoughts. He wondered what form they would take next and where they were running
to so swiftly, these misty children of snow and wind. Perhaps they
could be taught to attack the Russians. He smiled, savoring the fancy of
the snow beasts unleashed upon the enemy. It was a strange, wild
thought. Colonel Bengt Anttonen had never been an imaginative man
before, but of late his mind had often been taken by such whimsies.

Anttonen turned his face into the wind again, welcoming the chill, the numbing cold. He wanted it to cool his fury, to cut into the heart of him and freeze the passions that seethed there. He wanted to be numb. The cold had turned even the turbulent sea into still and silent ice; now let it conquer the turbulence within Bengt Anttonen. He opened his mouth, exhaled a long plume of breath that rose from his reddened cheeks like steam, inhaled a draught of frigid air that went down like liquid oxygen.

But panic came in the wake of that thought. Again, it was happening again. What was liquid oxygen? Cold, he knew somehow; colder than the ice, colder than this wind. Liquid oxygen was bitter and white, and it steamed and flowed. He knew it, knew it as certainly as he knew his own name. But *how*?

Anttonen turned from the ramparts. He walked with long swift strides, his hand touching the hilt of his sword as if it could provide some protection against the demons that had invaded his mind. The other officers were right; he was going mad, surely. He had proved it this afternoon at the staff meeting.

The meeting had gone very badly, as they all had of late. As always, Anttonen had raised his voice against the others, hopelessly, stupidly. He was right, he *knew* that. Yet he knew also that he could not convince them, and that each word further undermined his status, further damaged his career.

Jägerhorn had brought it on once again. Colonel F. A. Jägerhorn was everything that Anttonen was not; dark and handsome, polished and politic, an aristocrat with an aristocrat's control. Jägerhorn had important connections, had influential relatives, had a charmed career. And, most importantly, Jägerhorn had the confidence of Vice-Admiral Carl Olof Cronstedt, commandant of Sveaborg.

At the meeting, Jägerhorn had had a sheaf of reports.

"The reports are wrong," Anttonen had insisted. "The Russians do not outnumber us. And they have barely forty guns, sir. Sveaborg mounts ten times that number."

Cronstedt seemed shocked by Anttonen's tone, his certainty, his insistence. Jägerhorn simply smiled. "Might I ask how you come by this intelligence, Colonel Anttonen?" he asked.

That was the question Bengt Anttonen could never answer. "I know," he said stubbornly.

Jägerhorn rattled the papers in his hand. "My own intelligence comes from Lieutenant Klick, who is in Helsinki and has direct access to reliable reports of enemy plans, movements, and numbers." He looked to Vice-Admiral Cronstedt. "I submit, sir, that this information is a good deal more reliable than Colonel Anttonen's mysterious certainties. According to Klick, the Russians outnumber us already, and General Suchtelen will soon be receiving sufficient reinforcements to enable him to launch a major assault. Furthermore, they have a formidable amount of artillery on hand. Certainly more than the forty pieces that Colonel Anttonen would have us believe to be the extent of their armament."

Cronstedt was nodding, agreeing. Even then Anttonen could not be silent. "Sir," he insisted, "Klick's reports must be discounted. The man cannot be trusted. Either he is in the pay of the enemy or they are deluding him."

Cronstedt frowned. "That is a grave charge, Colonel."

"Klick is a fool and a damned Anjala traitor!"

Jägerhorn bristled at that, and Cronstedt and a number of junior officers looked plainly aghast. "Colonel," the commandant said, "it is well known that Colonel Jägerhorn has relatives in the Anjala League. Your comments are offensive. Our situation here is perilous enough without my officers fighting among themselves over petty political differences. You will offer an apology at once."

Given no choice, Anttonen had tendered an awkward apology. Jägerhorn accepted with a patronizing nod.

Cronstedt went back to the papers. "Very persuasive," he said, "and very alarming. It is as I have feared. We have come to a hard place." Plainly his mind was made up. It was futile to argue further. It was at times like this that Bengt Anttonen most wondered what madness had possessed him. He would go to staff meetings determined to be circumspect and politic, and no sooner would he be seated than a strange arrogance would seize him. He argued long past the point of wisdom; he denied obvious facts, confirmed in written reports from reliable sources; he spoke out of turn and made enemies on every side.

"No, sir," he said, "I beg of you, disregard Klick's intelligence. Sveaborg is vital to the spring counteroffensive. We have nothing to fear if we can hold out until the ice melts. Once the sea lanes are open, Sweden will send help."

Vice-Admiral Cronstedt's face was drawn and weary, an old man's face. "How many times must we go over this? I grow tired of your argumentative attitude, and I am quite aware of Sveaborg's importance to the spring offensive. The facts are plain. Our defenses are flawed, and the ice makes our walls accessible from all sides. Sweden's armies are being routed—"

"We know that only from the newspapers the Russians allow us, sir," Anttonen blurted. "French and Russian papers. Such news is unreliable."

Cronstedt's patience was exhausted. "Quiet!" he said, slapping the table with an open palm. "I have had enough of your intransigence, Colonel Anttonen. I respect your patriotic fervor, but not your judgment. In the future, when I require your opinion, I shall ask for it. Is that clear?"

"Yes, sir," Anttonen had said.

Jägerhorn smiled. "If I may proceed?"

The rebuke had been as smarting as the cold winter wind. It was no wonder Anttonen had felt driven to the cold solitude of the battlements afterwards.

By the time he returned to his quarters, Bengt Anttonen's mood was bleak and confused. Darkness was falling, he knew. Over the frozen sea, over Sveaborg, over Sweden and Finland. And over America, he thought. Yet the afterthought left him sick and dizzy. He sat heavily on his cot, cradling his head in his hands. America, America, what madness was that, what possible difference could the struggle between Sweden and Russia make to that infant nation so far away?

Rising, he lit a lamp, as if light would drive the troubling thoughts away, and splashed some stale water on his face from the basin atop the modest dresser. Behind the basin was the mirror he used for shaving; slightly warped and dulled by corrosion, but serviceable. As he dried his big, bony hands, he found himself staring at his own face, the features at once so familiar and so oddly, frighteningly strange. He had unruly graying hair, dark gray eyes, a narrow straight nose, slightly sunken cheeks, a square chin. He was too thin, almost gaunt. It was a stubborn, common, plain face. The face he had worn all his life. Long ago, Bengt Anttonen had grown resigned to the way he looked. Until recently, he scarcely gave his appearance any thought. Yet now he stared at himself, unblinking, and felt a disturbing fascination welling up inside him, a sense of satisfaction, a pleasure in the cast of his image that was alien and troubling.

Such vanity was sick, unmanly, another sign of madness. Anttonen wrenched his gaze from the mirror. He lay himself down with a will.

For long moments he could not sleep. Fancies and visions danced against his closed eyelids, sights as fantastic as the phantom animals fashioned by the wind: flags he did not recognize, walls of polished metal, great storms of fire, men and women as hideous as demons asleep in beds of burning liquid. And then, suddenly, the thoughts were gone, peeled off like a layer of burned skin. Bengt Anttonen sighed uneasily, and turned in his sleep . . .

. . . BEFORE THE AWARENESS IS ALWAYS THE PAIN, AND THE PAIN comes first, the only reality in a still quiet empty world beyond sensation. For a second, an hour I do not know where I am and I am afraid. And then the knowledge comes to me; returning, I am returning, in the return is always pain, I do not want to return, but I must. I want the sweet clean purity of ice and snow, the bracing touch of the winter wind, the healthy lines of Bengt's face. But it fades, fades though I scream and clutch for it, crying, wailing. It fades, fades, and then is gone.

I sense motion, a stirring all around me as the immersion fluid ebbs away. My face is exposed first. I suck in air through my wide nostrils, spit the tubes out of my bleeding mouth. When the fluid falls below my ears, I hear a gurgling, a greedy sucking sound. The vampire machines feed on the juices of my womb, the black blood of my second life. The cold touch of air on my skin pains me. I try not to scream, manage to hold the noise down to a whimper.

Above, the top of my tank is coated by a thin ebony film that has clung to the polished metal. I can see my reflection. I'm a stirring sight, nostril hairs aquiver on my noseless face, my right cheek bulging with a swollen greenish tumor. Such a handsome devil. I smile, showing a triple row of rotten teeth, fresh new incisors pushing up among them like sharpened stakes in a field of yellow toadstools. I wait for release. The tank is too damned small, a coffin. I am buried alive, and the fear is a palpable weight upon me. They do not like me. What if they just leave me in here to suffocate and die? "Out!" I whisper, but no one hears.

Finally the lid lifts and the orderlies are there. Rafael and Slim. Big strapping fellows, blurred white colossi with flags sewn above the pockets of their uniforms. I cannot focus on their faces. My eyes are not so good at the best of times, and especially bad just after a return. I know the dark one is Rafe, though, and it is he who reaches down and unhooks the IV tubes and the telemetry, while Slim gives me my injection. Ahhh. Good. The hurt fades. I force my hands to grasp the sides of the tank. The metal feels strange; the motion is clumsy, deliberate, my body slow to respond. "What took you so long?" I ask.

"Emergency," says Slim. "Rollins." He is a testy, laconic sort, and he doesn't like me. To learn more, I would have to ask question after question. I don't have the strength. I concentrate instead on pulling myself to a sitting position. The room is awash with a bright blue-white fluorescent light. My eyes water after so long in darkness. Maybe the orderlies think I'm crying with joy to be back. They're big but not too bright. The air has an astringent, sanitized smell and the hard coolness of air conditioning. Rafe lifts me up from the coffin, the fifth silvery casket in a row of six, each hooked up to the computer banks that loom around us. The other coffins are all empty now. I am the last vampire to rise this night, I think. Then I remember. Four of them are gone, have been gone for a long time. There is only Rollins and myself, and something has happened to Rollins.

They set me in my chair and Slim moves behind me, rolls me past the empty caskets and up the ramps to debriefing. "Rollins," I ask him.

"We lost him."

I didn't like Rollins. He was even uglier than me, a wizened little homunculus with a swollen, oversized cranium and a distorted torso without arms or legs. He had real big eyes, lidless, so he could never close them.

Even asleep, he looked like he was staring at you. And he had no sense of humor. No goddamned sense of humor at all. When you're a geek, you got to have a sense of humor. But whatever his faults, Rollins was the only one left, besides me. Gone now. I feel no grief, only a numbness.

The debriefing room is cluttered but somehow impersonal. They wait for me on the other side of the table. The orderlies roll me up opposite them and depart. The table is a long Formica barrier between me and my superiors, maybe a *cordon sanitaire*. They cannot let me get too close, after all, I might be contagious. They are normals. I am... what am I? When they conscripted me, I was classified as an HM3. Human Mutation, third category. Or a hum-three, in the vernacular. The hum-ones are the nonviables, stillborns and infant deaths and living veggies. We got millions of 'em. The hum-twos are viable but useless, all the guys with extra toes and webbed hands and funny eyes. Got thousands of them. But us hum-threes are a fucking *elite,* so they tell us. That's when they draft us. Down here, inside the Graham Project bunker, we get new names. Old Charlie Graham himself used to call us his "timeriders" before he croaked, but that's too romantic for Major Salazar. Salazar prefers the official government term: G. C., for Graham Chrononaut. The orderlies and grunts turned G. C. into "geek," of course, and we turned it right back on 'em, me and Nan and Creeper, when they were still with us. *They* had a terrific sense of humor, now. The killer geeks, we called ourselves. Six little killer geeks riding the timestream biting the heads off vast chickens of probability. Heigh-ho.

And then there was one.

Salazar is pushing papers around on the table. He looks sick. Under his dark complexion I can see an unhealthy greenish tinge, and the blood vessels in his nose have burst beneath the skin. None of us are in good shape down here, but Salazar looks worse than most. He's been gaining weight, and it looks bad on him. His uniforms are all too tight now, and there won't be any fresh ones. They've closed down the commissaries and the mills, and in a few years we'll all be wearing rags. I've told Salazar he ought to diet, but no one will listen to a geek, except when the subject is chickens. "Well," Salazar says to me, his voice snapping. A hell of a way to start a debriefing. Three years ago, when it began, he was full of starch and vinegar, very correct and military, but even the Maje has no time left for decorum now.

"What happened to Rollins?" I ask.

Doctor Veronica Jacobi is seated next to Salazar. She used to be chief headshrinker down here, but since Graham Crackers went and expired she's been heading up the whole scientific side of the show.

"Death trauma," she says, professionally. "Most likely, his host was killed in action."

I nod. Old story. Sometimes the chickens bite back. "He accomplish anything?"

"Not that we've noticed," Salazar says glumly.

The answer I expected. Rollins had gotten rapport with some ignorant grunt of a footsoldier in the army of Charles XII. I had this droll mental picture of him marching the guy up to his loon of a teenaged king and trying to tell the boy to stay away from Poltava. Charles probably hanged him on the spot—though, come to think of it, it had to be something quicker, or else Rollins would have had time to disengage.

"Your report," prompts Salazar.

"Right, Maje," I say lazily. He hates to be called Maje, though not so much as he hated Sally, which was what Creeper used to call him. Us killer geeks are an insolent lot. "It's no good," I tell them. "Cronstedt is going to meet with General Suchtelen and negotiate for surrender. Nothing Bengt says sways him one damned bit. I been pushing too hard. Bengt thinks he's going crazy. I'm afraid he may crack."

"All timeriders take that risk," Jacobi says. "The longer you stay in rapport, the stronger your influence grows on the host, and the more likely it becomes that your presence will be felt. Few hosts can deal with that perception." Ronnie has a nice voice, and she's always polite to me. Well-scrubbed and tall and calm and even friendly, and above all ineffably polite. I wonder if she'd be as polite if she knew that she'd figured prominently in my masturbation fantasies ever since we'd been down here? They only put five women into the Cracker Box, with thirty-two men and six geeks, and she's by far the most pleasant to contemplate.

Creeper liked to contemplate her, too. He even bugged her bedroom, to watch her in action. She never knew. Creeper had a talent for that stuff, and he'd rig up these tiny little audio-video units on his workbench and plant them everywhere. He said that if he couldn't live life, at least he was going to watch it. One night he invited me into his room, when Ronnie was entertaining big, red-haired Captain Halliburton, the head of the base security, and her fella in those early days. I watched, yeah; got to confess that I watched. But afterward I got angry. Told Creeper he had no right to spy on Ronnie, or on any of them. "They make us spy on our hosts," he said, "right inside their fucking *heads,* you geek. Turnabout is fair play." I told him it was different, but I got so mad I couldn't explain why.

It was the only fight Creeper and me ever had. In the long run, it didn't mean much. He went on watching, without me. They never caught the little sneak, but it didn't matter, one day he went timeriding and didn't come back. Big strong Captain Halliburton died too, caught too many rads on those security sweeps, I guess. As far as I know, Creeper's hook-up is still in place; from time to time I've thought about going in and taking a peek, to see if Ronnie has herself a new lover. But I haven't. I really don't want to know. Leave me with my fantasies and my wet dreams; they're a lot better anyway.

Salazar's fat fingers drum upon the table. "Give us a full report on your activities," he says curtly.

I sigh and give them what they want, everything in boring detail. When I'm done, I say, "Jägerhorn is the key to the problem. He's got Cronstedt's ear. Anttonen don't."

Salazar is frowning. "If only you could establish rapport with Jägerhorn," he grumbles. What a futile whiner. He knows that's impossible.

"You takes what you gets," I tell him. "If you're going to wish impossible wishes, why stop at Jägerhorn? Why not Cronstedt? Hell, why not the goddamned *Czar?*"

"He's right, Major," Veronica says. "We ought to be grateful that we've got a link with Anttonen. At least he's a colonel. That's better than we did in any of the other target periods."

Salazar is still unhappy. He's a military historian by trade. He thought this would be easy when they transferred him out from West Point, or what was left of it. "Anttonen is peripheral," he declares. "We must reach the key figures. Your chrononauts are giving me footnotes, bystanders, the wrong men in the wrong place at the wrong time. It is impossible."

"You knew the job was dangerous when you took it," I say. A killer geek quoting Superchicken; I'd get thrown out of the union if they knew. "We don't get to pick and choose."

The Maje scowls at me. I yawn. "I'm tired of this," I say. "I want something to eat. Some ice cream. I want some rocky road ice cream.

Seems funny, don't it? All that goddamned ice, and I come back want-ing ice cream." There is no ice cream, of course. There hasn't been any ice cream for half a generation, anywhere in the godforsaken mess they call a world. But Nan used to tell me about it. Nan was the oldest geek, the only one born before the big crash, and she had lots of stories about the way things used to be. I liked it best when she talked about ice cream. It was smooth and cold and sweet, she said. It melted on your tongue, and filled your mouth with liquid, delicious cold. Sometimes she would recite the flavors for us, as solemnly as Chaplain Todd read-ing his Bible: vanilla and strawberry and chocolate, fudge swirl and pra-line, rum raisin and heavenly hash, banana and orange sherbet and mint chocolate chip, pistachio and butterscotch and coffee and cinnamon and butter pecan. Creeper used to make up flavors to poke fun at her, but there was no getting to Nan. She just added his inventions to her list, and spoke fondly thereafter of anchovy almond and liver chip and radiation ripple, until I couldn't tell the real flavors from the made-up ones anymore, and didn't really care.

Nan was the first we lost. Did they have ice cream in St. Petersburg back in 1917? I hope they did. I hope she got a bowl or two before she died.

Major Salazar is still talking, I realize. He has been talking for some time. ". . . our last chance now," he is saying. He begins to babble about Sveaborg, about the importance of what we are doing here, about the urgent need to *change* something somehow, to prevent the Soviet Union from ever coming into existence, and thus forestall the war that has laid the world to waste. I've heard it all before, I know it all by heart. The Maje has terminal verbal diarrhea, and I'm not so dumb as I look.

It was all Graham Crackers' idea, the last chance to win the war or maybe just save ourselves from the plagues and bombs and the poisoned winds. But the Maje was the historian, so he got to pick all the targets, when the computers had done their probability analysis. He had six geeks and he got six tries. "Nexus points," he called 'em. Critical points in history. Of course, some were better than others. Rollins got the Great Northern War, Nan got the Revolution, Creeper got to go all the way back to Ivan the Terrible, and I got Sveaborg. Impregnable, invincible Sveaborg. Gibraltar of the North.

"There is no reason for Sveaborg to surrender," the Maje is saying. It is his own ice cream litany. History and tactics give him the sort of comfort that butter brickle gave to Nan. "The garrison is seven thousand strong, vastly outnumbering the besieging Russians. The artillery inside the fortress is much superior. There is plenty of ammunition, plenty of food. If Sveaborg only holds out until the sea lanes are open, Sweden will launch its counteroffensive and the siege will be broken easily. The entire course of the war may change! You must make Cronstedt listen to reason."

"If I could just lug back a history text and let him read what they say about him, I'm sure he'd jump through flaming hoops," I say. I've had enough of this. "I'm tired," I announce. "I want some food." Suddenly, for no apparent reason, I feel like crying. "I want something to eat, damn it, I don't want to talk anymore, you hear, I want *something to eat.*"

Salazar glares, but Veronica hears the stress in my voice, and she is up and moving around the table. "Easy enough to arrange," she says to me, and to the Maje. "We've accomplished all we can for now. Let me get him some food." Salazar grunts, but he dares not object. Veronica wheels me away, toward the commissary.

Over stale coffee and a plate of mystery meat and overcooked vegetables, she consoles me. She's not half bad at it; a pro, after all. Maybe, in the old days, she wouldn't have been considered especially striking—I've seen the old magazines, after all, even down here we have our old *Playboys*, our old videotapes, our old novels, our old record albums, our old funny books, nothing *new* of course, nothing recent, but lots and lots of the old junk. I ought to know, I practically mainline the stuff, when I'm not flailing around inside Bengt's cranium, I'm planted in front of my tube, running some old TV show or a movie, maybe reading a paperback at the same time, trying to imagine what it would be like to live back then, before they screwed up everything. So I know all about the old standards, and maybe it's true that Ronnie ain't up to, say, Bo or Marilyn or Brigitte or Garbo. Still, she's nicer to look at than anybody else down in this damned septic tank. And the rest of us don't quite measure up either. Creeper wasn't no Groucho, no matter how hard he tried; me, I look just like Jimmy Cagney, but the big green tumor and all the extra yellow teeth and the want of a nose spoil the effect, just a little.

I push my fork away with the meal half-eaten. "It has no taste. Back then, food had *taste*."

Veronica laughs. "You're lucky. You get to taste it. For the rest of us, this is all there is."

"Lucky? Ha-ha. I know the difference, Ronnie. You don't. Can you miss something you never had?" I'm sick of talking about it, though; I'm sick of it all. "You want to play chess?"

She smiles and gets up in search of our set. An hour later, she's won the first game and we're starting the second. There are about a dozen chess players down here in the Cracker Box; now that Graham and Creeper are gone, I can beat all of them except Ronnie. The funny thing is, back in 1808 I could probably be world champion. Chess has come a long way in the last two hundred years, and I've memorized openings that those old guys never even dreamed of.

"There's more to the game than book openings," Veronica says, and I realize I've been talking aloud.

"I'd still win," I insist. "Hell, those guys have been dead for centuries, how much fight can they put up?"

She smiles, and moves a knight. "Check," she says.

I realize that I've lost again. "Some day I've got to learn to play this game," I say. "Some world champion."

Veronica begins to put the pieces back in the box. "This Sveaborg business is a kind of chess game too," she says conversationally, "a chess game across time, us and the Swedes against the Russians and the Finnish nationalists. What move do you think we should make against Cronstedt?"

"Why did I know that the conversation was going to come back to that?" I say. "Damned if I know. I suppose the Maje has an idea."

She nods. Her face is serious now. Pale soft face, framed by dark hair. "A desperate idea. These are desperate times."

What would it be like if I did succeed, I wonder? If I changed something? What would happen to Veronica and the Maje and Rafe and Slim and all the rest of them? What would happen to *me,* lying there in my coffin full of darkness? There are theories, of course, but no one really knows. "I'm a desperate man, ma'am," I say to her, "ready for any desperate measures. Being subtle sure hasn't done diddly-squat. Let's hear it. What do I gotta get Bengt to do now? Invent the machine gun? Defect to the Russkis? Expose his privates on the battlements? What?"

She tells me.

I'm dubious. "Maybe it'll work," I say. "More likely, it'll get Bengt slung into the deepest goddamned dungeon that place has. They'll really think he's nuts. Jägerhorn might just shoot him outright."

"No," she says. "In his own way, Jägerhorn is an idealist. A man of principle. I agree, it is a chancy move. But you don't win chess games without taking chances. Will you do it?"

She has such a nice smile; I think she likes me. I shrug. "Might as well," I say. "Can't dance."

"... SHALL BE ALLOWED TO DISPATCH TWO COURIERS TO THE KING, the one by the northern, the other by the southern road. They shall be furnished with passports and safeguards, and every possible facility shall be given them for accomplishing their journey. Done at the island of Lonan, 6 April, 1808."

The droning voice of the officer reading the agreement stopped suddenly, and the staff meeting was deathly quiet. A few of the Swedish officers stirred uneasily in their seats, but no one spoke.

Vice-Admiral Cronstedt rose slowly. "This is the agreement," he said. "In view of our perilous position, it is better than we could have hoped for. We have used a third of our powder already, our defenses are exposed to attack from all sides because of the ice, we are outnumbered and forced to support a large number of fugitives who rapidly consume our provisions. General Suchtelen might have demanded our immediate surrender. By the grace of God, he did not. Instead we have been allowed to retain three of Sveaborg's six islands, and will regain two of the others, should five Swedish ships-of-the-line arrive to aid us before the third of May. If Sweden fails us, we must surrender. Yet the fleet shall be restored to Sweden at the conclusion of the war, and this immediate truce will prevent any further loss of life."

Cronstedt sat down. At his side, Colonel Jägerhorn came crisply to his feet. "In the event the Swedish ships do not arrive on time, we must make plans for an orderly surrender of the garrison." He launched into a discussion of the details.

Bengt Anttonen sat quietly. He had expected the news, had somehow known it was coming, but it was no less dismaying for all that. Cronstedt and Jägerhorn had negotiated a disaster. It was foolish. It was craven. It was hopelessly doomed. Immediate surrender of Wester-Svartö, Langorn, and Oster-Lilla-Svartö, the rest of the garrison to come later, capitulation deferred for a meaningless month. History would revile them. Schoolchildren would curse their names. And he was helpless.

When the meeting at last ended, the others rose to depart. Anttonen rose with them, determined to be silent, to leave the room quietly for once, to let them sell Sveaborg for thirty pieces of silver if they would. But as he tried to turn, the compulsion seized him, and he went instead to where Cronstedt and Jägerhorn lingered. They both watched him approach. In their eyes, Anttonen thought he could see a weary resignation.

"You must not do this," he said heavily.

"It is done," Cronstedt replied. "The subject is not open for further discussion, Colonel. You have been warned. Go about your duties." He climbed to his feet, turned to go.

"The Russians are cheating you," Anttonen blurted.

Cronstedt stopped and looked at him.

"Admiral, please, you must listen to me. This provision, this agreement that we will retain the fortress if five ships-of-the-line reach us by the third of May, it is a fraud. The ice will not have melted by the third of May. No ship will be able to reach us. The armistice agreement provides that the ships must have entered Sveaborg's harbor by noon on the third of May. General Suchtelen will use the time afforded by the truce to move his guns and gain control of the sea approaches. Any ship attempting to reach Sveaborg will come under heavy attack. And there is more. The messengers you are sending to the King, sir, they—"

Cronstedt's face was ice and granite. He held up a hand. "I have heard enough. Colonel Jägerhorn, arrest this madman." He gathered up his papers, refusing to look Anttonen in the face, and strode angrily from the room.

"Colonel Anttonen, you are under arrest," Jägerhorn said, with surprising gentleness in his voice. "Don't resist, I warn you, that will only make it worse."

Anttonen turned to face the other colonel. His heart was sick. "You will not listen. None of you will listen. Do you know what you are doing?"

"I think I do," Jägerhorn said.

Anttonen reached out and grabbed him by the front of his uniform. "You do *not*. You think I don't know what you are, Jägerhorn? You're a nationalist, damn you. This is the great age of nationalism. You and your Anjala League, your damned Finnlander noblemen, you're all Finnish nationalists. You resent Sweden's domination. The Czar has promised you that Finland will be an autonomous state under his protection, so you have thrown off your loyalty to the Swedish crown."

Colonel F. A. Jägerhorn blinked. A strange expression flickered across his face before he regained his composure. "You cannot know that," he said. "No one knows the terms—I—"

Anttonen shook him bodily. "History is going to laugh at you, Jägerhorn. Sweden will lose this war, because of you, because of Sveaborg's surrender, and you'll get your wish, Finland will become an autonomous state under the Czar. But it will be no freer than it is now, under Sweden. You'll swap your King like a secondhand chair at a flea market, for the butchers of the Great Wrath, and gain nothing by the transaction."

"Like a . . . a market for fleas? What is that?"

Anttonen scowled. "A flea market, a flea . . . I don't know," he said. He released Jägerhorn, turned away. "Dear God, I do know. It is a place where . . . where things are sold and traded. A fair. It has nothing to do with fleas, but it is full of strange machines, strange smells." He ran his fingers through his hair, fighting not to scream. "Jägerhorn, my head is full of demons. Dear God, I must confess. Voices, I hear voices day and night, even as the French girl, Joan, the warrior maid. I know things that will come to pass." He looked into Jägerhorn's eyes, saw the fear there, and held his hands up, entreating now. "It is no choice of mine, you must believe that. I pray for silence, for release, but the whispering continues, and these strange fits seize me. They are not of my doing, yet they must be sent for a reason, they must be true, or why would God torture me so? Have mercy, Jägerhorn. Have mercy on me, and listen!"

Colonel Jägerhorn looked past Anttonen, his eyes searching for help, but the two of them were quite alone. "Yes," he said. "Voices, like the French girl. I did not understand."

Anttonen shook his head. "You hear, but you will not believe. You are a patriot, you dream you will be a hero. You will be no hero. The common folk of Finland do not share your dreams. They remember the Great Wrath. They know the Russians only as ancient enemies, and they hate. They will hate you as well. And Cronstedt, ah, poor Admiral Cronstedt. He will be reviled by every Finn, every Swede, for generations to come. He will live out his life in this new Grand Duchy of Finland on a Russian stipend, and he will die a broken man on April 7, 1820, twelve years and one day after he met with Suchtelen on Lonan and gave Sveaborg to Russia. Later, years later, a man named Runeberg will write a series of poems about this war. Do you know what he will say of Cronstedt?"

"No," Jägerhorn said. He smiled uneasily. "Have your voices told you?"

"They have taught me the words by heart," said Bengt Anttonen. He recited:

Call him the arm we trusted in,
that shrank in time of stress,
call him Affliction, Scorn, and Sin,
and Death and Bitterness,
but mention not his former name,
lest they should blush who bear the same.

"That is the glory you and Cronstedt are winning here, Jägerhorn," Anttonen said bitterly. "That is your place in history. Do you like it?"

Colonel Jägerhorn had been carefully edging around Anttonen; there was a clear path between him and the door. But now he hesitated. "You are speaking madness," he said. "And yet—and yet—how could you have known of the Czar's promises? You would almost have me believe you. Voices? Like the French girl? The voice of God, you say?"

Anttonen sighed. "God? I do not know. Voices, Jägerhorn, that is all I hear. Perhaps I am mad."

Jägerhorn grimaced. "They will revile us, you say? They will call us traitors and denounce us in poems?"

Anttonen said nothing. The madness had ebbed; he was filled with a helpless despair.

"No," Jägerhorn insisted. "It is too late. The agreement is signed. We have staked our honor on it. And Vice-Admiral Cronstedt, he is so uncertain. His family is here, and he fears for them. Suchtelen has played him masterfully and we have done our part. It cannot be undone. I do not believe this madness of yours, yet even if I believed, there is no hope for it, nothing to be done. The ships will not come in time. Sveaborg must yield, and the war must end with Sweden's defeat. How could it be otherwise? The Czar is allied with Bonaparte himself, he cannot be resisted!"

"The alliance will not last," Anttonen said, with a rueful smile. "The French will march on Moscow and it will destroy them as it destroyed Charles XII. The winter will be their Poltava. All of this will come too late for Finland, too late for Sveaborg."

"It is too late even now," Jägerhorn said. "Nothing can be changed."

For the first time, Bengt Anttonen felt the tiniest glimmer of hope. "It is not too late."

"What course do you urge upon us, then? Cronstedt has made his decision. Should we mutiny?"

"There will be a mutiny in Sveaborg, whether we take part or not. It will fail."

"What then?"

Bengt Anttonen lifted his head, stared Jägerhorn in the eyes. "The agreement stipulates that we may send two couriers to the King, to inform him of the terms, so the Swedish ships may be dispatched on time."

"Yes. Cronstedt will choose our couriers tonight, and they will leave tomorrow, with papers and safe passage furnished by Suchtelen."

"You have Cronstedt's ear. See that I am chosen as one of the couriers."

"You?" Jägerhorn looked doubtful. "What good will that serve?" He frowned. "Perhaps this voice you hear is the voice of your own fear. Perhaps you have been under siege too long, and it has broken you, and now you hope to run free."

"I can prove my voices speak true," Anttonen said.

"How?" snapped Jägerhorn.

"I will meet you tomorrow at dawn at Ehrensvard's tomb, and I will tell you the names of the couriers that Cronstedt has chosen. If I am right, you will convince him to send me in the place of one of those chosen. He will agree, gladly. He is anxious to be rid of me."

Colonel Jägerhorn rubbed his jaw, considering. "No one could know the choices but Cronstedt. It is a fair test." He put out his hand. "Done."

They shook. Jägerhorn turned to go. But at the doorway he turned back. "Colonel Anttonen," he said, "I have forgotten my duty. You are in my custody. Go to your own quarters and remain there, until the dawn."

"Gladly," said Anttonen. "At dawn, you will see that I am right."

"Perhaps," said Jägerhorn, "but for all our sakes, I shall hope very much that you are wrong."

――――――――――

... AND THE MACHINES SUCK AWAY THE LIQUID NIGHT THAT EN-folds me, and I'm screaming, screaming so loudly that Slim draws back, a wary look on his face. I give him a broad geekish smile, rows on rows of yellow rotten teeth. "Get me out of here, turkey," I shout. The pain is a web around me, but this time it doesn't seem as bad, this time I can almost stand it, this time the pain is *for* something.

They give me my shot, and lift me into my chair, but this time I'm eager for the debriefing. I grab the wheels and give myself a push, breaking free of Rafe, rolling down the corridors like I used to do in the old days, when Creeper was around to race me. There's a bit of a problem with one ramp, and they catch me there, the strong silent guys in their ice cream suits (that's what Nan called 'em, anyhow), but I scream at them to leave me alone. They do. Surprises the hell out of me.

The Maje is a little startled when I come rolling into the room all by my lonesome. He starts to get up. "Are you..."

"Sit down, Sally," I say. "It's good news. Bengt psyched out Jägerhorn good. I thought the kid was gonna wet his pants, believe me. I think we got it socked. I'm meeting Jägerhorn tomorrow at dawn to clinch the sale." I'm grinning, listening to myself. Tomorrow, hey, I'm talking about 1808, but tomorrow is how it feels. "Now here's the sixty-four-thousand-dollar question. I need to know the names of the two guys that Cronstedt is going to try and send to the Swedish king. Proof, y'know?

"Jägerhorn says he'll get me sent if I can convince him. So you look up those names for me, Maje, and once I say the magic words, the duck will come down and give us Sveaborg."

"This is very obscure information," Salazar complains. "The couriers were detained for weeks, and did not even arrive in Stockholm until the day of the surrender. Their names may be lost to history." What a whiner, I'm thinking; the man is never satisfied.

Ronnie speaks up for me, though. "Major Salazar, those names had better not be lost to history, or to us. You were our military historian. It was your job to research each of the target periods *thoroughly*." The way she's talking to him, you'd never guess he was the boss. "The Graham Project has every priority. You have our computer files, our dossiers on the personnel of Sveaborg, and you have access to the war college at New West Point. Maybe you can even get through to someone in what remains of Sweden. I don't care how you do it, but it must be done. The entire project could rest on this piece of information. The entire world. Our past and our future. I shouldn't need to tell you that." She turns to me. I applaud. She smiles. "You've done well," she says. "Would you give us the details?"

"Sure," I say. "It was a piece of cake. With ice cream on top. What'd they used to call that?"

"A la mode."

"Sveaborg a la mode," I say, and I serve it up to them. I talk and talk. When I finally finish, even the Maje looks grudgingly pleased. Pretty damn good for a geek, I think. "OK," I say when I'm done with the report. "What's next? Bengt gets the courier job, right? And I get the message through somehow. Avoid Suchtelen, don't get detained, the Swedes send in the cavalry."

"Cavalry?" Sally looks confused.

"It's a figure of speech," I say, with unusual patience.

The Maje nods. "No," he says. "The couriers—it's true that General Suchtelen lied, and held them up as an extra form of insurance. The ice might have melted, after all. The ships might have come through in time. But it was an unnecessary precaution. That year, the ice around Helsinki did not melt until well after the deadline date." He gives me a solemn stare. He has never looked sicker, and the greenish tinge of his skin undermines the effect he's trying to achieve. "We must make a bold stroke. You will be sent out as a courier, under the terms of the truce. You and the other courier will be brought before General Suchtelen to receive your safe conducts through Russian lines. That is the point at which you will strike. The affair is settled, and war in those days was an honorable affair. No one will expect treachery."

"Treachery?" I say. I don't like the sound of what I'm hearing.

For a second, the Maje's smile looks almost genuine; he's finally lit on something that pleases him. "Kill Suchtelen," he says.

"Kill Suchtelen?" I repeat.

"Use Anttonen. Fill him with rage. Have him draw his weapon. Kill Suchtelen."

I see. A new move in our crosstime chess game. The geek gambit.

"They'll kill Bengt," I say.

"You can disengage," Salazar says.

"Maybe they'll kill him fast," I point out. "Right there, on the spot, y'know."

"You take that risk. Other men have given their lives for our nation. This is war." The Maje frowns. "Your success may doom us all. When you change the past, the present as it now exists may simply cease to exist, and us with it. But our nation will live, and millions we have lost will be restored to us. Healthier, happier versions of ourselves will enjoy the rich lives that were denied us. You yourself will be born whole, without sickness or deformity."

"Or talent," I say. "In which case I won't be able to go back to do this, in which case the past stays unchanged."

"The paradox does not apply. You have been briefed on this. The past and the present and future are not contemporaneous. And it will be Anttonen who effects the change, not yourself. He is of that time." The Maje is impatient. His thick, dark fingers drum on the tabletop. "Are you a coward?"

"Fuck you and the horse you rode in on," I tell him. "You don't get it. I could give a shit about me. I'm better off dead. But they'll kill *Bengt.*"

He frowns. "What of it?"

Veronica has been listening intently. Now she leans across the table and touches my hand, gently. "I understand. You identify with him, don't you?"

"He's a good man," I say. Do I sound defensive? Very well, then; I *am* defensive. "I feel bad enough that I'm driving him around the bend, I don't want to get him killed. I'm a freak, a geek, I've lived my whole life under siege and I'm going to die here, but Bengt has people who love him, a life ahead of him. Once he gets out of Sveaborg, there's a whole world out there."

"He has been dead for almost two centuries," Salazar says.

"I was inside his head this afternoon," I snap.

"He will be a casualty of war," the Maje says. "In war, soldiers die. It is a fact of life, then as now."

Something else is bothering me. "Yeah, maybe, he's a soldier, I'll buy that. He knew the job was dangerous when he took it. But he cares about *honor,* Sally. A little thing we've forgotten. To die in battle, sure, but you want me to make him a goddamned *assassin,* have him violate a flag of truce. He's an honorable man. They'll revile him."

"The ends justify the means," says Salazar bluntly. "Kill Suchtelen, kill him under the flag of truce, yes. It will kill the truce as well. Suchtelen's second-in-command is far less wily, more prone to outbursts of temper, more eager for a spectacular victory. You will tell him that Cronstedt *ordered* you to cut down Suchtelen. He will shatter the truce, will launch a furious attack against the fortress, an attack that Sveaborg, impregnable as it is, will easily repulse. Russian casualties will be heavy, and Swedish determination will be fired by what they will see as Russian treachery. Jägerhorn, with proof before him that the Russian promises are meaningless, will change sides. Cronstedt, the hero of Ruotsinsalmi, will become the hero of Sveaborg as well. The fortress will hold. With the spring the Swedish fleet will land an army at Sveaborg, behind Russian lines, while a second Swedish army sweeps down from the north. The entire course of the war will change. When Napoleon marches on Moscow, a Swedish army will already hold St. Petersburg. The Czar will be caught in Moscow, deposed, executed. Napoleon will install a puppet government, and when his retreat comes, it will be north, to link up with his Swedish allies at St. Petersburg. The new Russian regime will not survive Bonaparte's fall, but the Czarist restoration will be as short-lived as the French restoration, and Russia will evolve toward a liberal parliamentary democracy. The Soviet Union will never come into being to war against the United States." He emphasizes his final words by pounding his fist on the conference table.

"Sez you," I say mildly.

Salazar gets red in the face. "That is the computer projection," he insists. He looks away from me, though. Just a quick little averting of the eyes, but I catch it. Funny. He can't look me in the eyes.

Veronica squeezes my hand. "The projection may be off," she admits. "A little or a lot. But it is all we have. And this is our last chance. I understand your concern for Anttonen, really I do. It's only natural. You've been part of him for months now, living his life, sharing his thoughts and feelings. Your reservations do you credit. But now millions of lives are in the balance, against the life of this one man. This one, dead man. It's your decision. The most important decision in all of human history, perhaps, and it rests with you alone." She smiles. "Think about it carefully, at least."

When she puts it like that, and holds my little hand all the while, I'm powerless to resist. Ah, Bengt. I look away from them, sigh. "Break out the booze tonight," I say wearily to Salazar, "the last of that old pre-war stuff you been saving."

The Maje looks startled, discomfited; the jerk thought his little cache of prewar Glenlivet and Irish Mist and Remy Martin was a well-kept secret. And so it was until Creeper planted one of his little bugs, heigh-ho. "I do not think drunken revelry is in order," Sally says. Defending his treasure. He's homely and mean-spirited, but nobody ever said he wasn't selfish.

"Shut up and come across," I say. Tonight I ain't gonna be denied. I'm giving up Bengt, the Maje can give up some booze. "I want to get shit-faced," I tell them. "It's time to drink to the goddamned dead and toast the living, past and present. It's in the rules, damn you. The geek always gets a bottle before he goes out to meet the chickens."

WITHIN THE CENTRAL COURTYARD OF THE VARGÖN CITADEL, Bengt Anttonen waited in the predawn chill. Behind him stood Ehrensvard's tomb, the final resting place of the man who had built Sveaborg, and now slept securely within the bosom of his creation, his bones safe behind her guns and her thick granite walls, guarded by all her daunting might. He had built her impregnable, and impregnable she stood, so none would come to disturb his rest. But now they wanted to give her away.

The wind was blowing. It came howling down out of a black empty sky, stirred the barren branches of the trees that stood in the empty courtyard, and cut through Anttonen's warmest coat. Or perhaps it was another sort of chill that lay upon him; the chill of fear. Dawn was almost at hand. Above, the stars were fading. And his head was empty, echoing, mocking. Light would soon break over the horizon, and with the light would come Colonel Jägerhorn, hard-faced, imperious, demanding, and Anttonen would have nothing to say to him.

He heard footsteps. Jägerhorn's boots rang on the stones. Anttonen turned to face him, watching him climb the few small steps up to Ehrensvard's memorial. They stood a foot apart, conspirators huddled against the cold and darkness. Jägerhorn gave him a curt, short nod. "I have met with Cronstedt."

Anttonen opened his mouth. His breath steamed in the frigid air. And just as he was about to succumb to the emptiness, about to admit that his voices had failed him, something whispered deep inside him. He spoke two names.

There was such a long silence that Anttonen once again began to fear. Was it madness after all, and not the voice of God? Had he been wrong? But then Jägerhorn looked down, frowning, and clapped his gloved hands together in a gesture that spoke of finality. "God help us all," he said, "but I believe you."

"I will be the courier?"

"I have already broached the subject with Vice-Admiral Cronstedt," Jägerhorn said. "I have reminded him of your years of service, your excellent record. You are a good soldier and a man of honor, damaged only by your own patriotism and the pressure of the siege. You are that sort of warrior who cannot bear inaction, who must always be doing something. You deserve more than arrest and disgrace, I have argued. As a courier, you will redeem yourself, I have told him I have no doubt of it. And by removing you from Sveaborg, we will remove also a source of tension and dissent around which mutiny might grow. The Vice-Admiral is well aware that a good many of the men are most unwilling to honor our pact with Suchtelen. He is convinced." Jägerhorn smiled wanly. "I am nothing if not convincing, Anttonen. I can marshal an argument as Bonaparte marshals his armies. So this victory is ours. You are named courier."

"Good," said Anttonen. Why did he feel so sick at heart? He should have been full of jubilation.

"What will you do?" Jägerhorn asked. "For what purpose do we conspire?"

"I will not burden you with that knowledge," Anttonen replied. It was knowledge he lacked himself. He must be the courier, he had known that since yesterday, but the why of it still eluded him, and the future was cold as the stone of Ehrensvard's tomb, as misty as Jägerhorn's breath. He was full of a strange foreboding, a sense of approaching doom.

"Very well," said Jägerhorn. "I pray that I have acted wisely in this." He removed his glove, offered his hand. "I will count on you, on your wisdom and your honor."

"My honor," Bengt repeated. Slowly, too slowly, he took off his own glove to shake the hand of the dead man standing there before him. Dead man? He was no dead man; he was live, warm flesh. But it was frigid there under those bare trees, and when Anttonen clasped Jägerhorn's hand, the other's skin felt cold to the touch.

"We have had our differences," said Jägerhorn, "but we are both Finns, after all, and patriots, and men of honor, and now too we are friends."

"Friends," Anttonen repeated. And in his head, louder than it had ever been before, so clear and strong it seemed almost as if someone had spoken behind him, came a whisper, sad somehow, and bitter. *C'mon, Chicken Little,* it said, *shake hands with your pal, the geek.*

Gather ye Four Roses while ye may, for time is still aflying, and this same geek what smiles today tomorrow may be dying. Heigh-ho, drunk again, second night inna row, chugging all the Maje's good booze, but what does it matter, he won't be needing it. After this next little timeride, he won't even exist, or that's what they tell me. In fact, he'll never have existed, which is a real weird thought. Old Major Sally Salazar, his big thick fingers, his greenish tinge, the endearing way he had of whining and bitching, he sure seemed real this afternoon at that last debriefing, but now it turns out there never was any such person. Never was a Creeper, never a Rafe or a Slim, Nan never ever told us about ice cream and reeled off the names of all those flavors, butter pecan and rum raisin are one with Ninevah and Tyre, heigh-ho. Never happened, nope, and I slug down another shot, drinking alone, in my room, in my cubicle, the savior at this last liquid supper, where the hell are all my fucking apostles? Ah, drinking, drinking, but not with me.

They ain't s'posed to know, nobody's s'posed to know but me and the Maje and Ronnie, but the word's out, yes it is, and out there in the corridors it's turned into a big wild party, boozing and singing and fighting, a little bit of screwing for those lucky enough to have a partner, of which number I am not one, alas. I want to go out and join in, hoist a few with the boys, but no, the Maje says no, too dangerous, one of the motley horde might decide that even this kind of has-been life is better than a never-was nonlife, and therefore off the geek, ruining everybody's plans for a good time. So here I sit on geek row, in my little room boozing alone, surrounded by five other little rooms, and down at the end of the corridor is a most surly guard, pissed off that he isn't out there getting a last taste, who's got to keep me in and the rest of them out.

I was sort of hoping Ronnie might come by, you know, to share a final drink and beat me in one last game of chess and maybe even play a little kissy-face, which is a ridiculous fantasy on the face of it, but somehow I don't wanna die a virgin, even though I'm not really going to die, since once the trick is done, I won't ever have lived at all. It's goddamned noble of me if you ask me and you got to 'cause there ain't nobody else around to ask. Another drink now but the bottle's almost empty, I'll have to ring the Maje and ask for another. Why won't Ronnie come by? I'll never be seeing her again, after tomorrow, tomorrow-tomorrow and two-hundred-years-ago-tomorrow. I could refuse to go, stay here and keep the happy lil' family alive, but I don't think she'd like that. She's a lot more sure than me. I asked her this afternoon if Sally's projections could tell us about the side effects. I mean, we're changing this war, and we're keeping Sveaborg and (we hope) losing the Czar and (we hope) losing the Soviet Union and (we sure as hell hope) maybe losing the big war and all, the bombs and the rads and the plagues and all that good stuff, even radiation ripple ice cream which was the Creeper's favorite flavor, but what if we lose other stuff? I mean, with Russia so changed and all, are we going to lose Alaska? Are we gonna lose vodka? Are we going to lose George Orwell? Are we going to lose Karl Marx? We tried to lose Karl Marx, actually, one of the other geeks, Blind Jeffey, he went back to take care of Karlie, but it didn't work out. Maybe vision was too damn much for him. So we got to keep Karl, although come to think of it, who cares about Karl Marx, are we gonna lose Groucho? No Groucho, no Groucho ever, I don't like that concept, last night I shot a geek in my pajamas and how he got in my pajamas I'll never know, but maybe, who the hell knows how us geeks get anyplace, all these damn dominoes falling every which way, knocking over other dominoes, dominoes was never my game, I'm a chess player, world chess champion in temporal exile, that's me, dominoes is a dumb damn game. What if it don't work, I asked Ronnie, what if we take out Russia, and, well, Hitler wins World War II so we wind up swapping missiles and germs and biotoxins with Nazi Germany? Or England? Or fucking Austria-Hungary, maybe, who can say? The superpower Austria-Hungary, what a thought, last night I shot a Hapsburg in my pajamas, the geeks put him there, heigh-ho.

Ronnie didn't make me no promises, kiddies. Best she could do was shrug and tell me this story about a horse. This guy was going to get his head cut off by some old-timey king, y'see, so he pipes up and tells the king that if he's given a year, he'll teach the king's horse to talk. The king likes this idea, for some reason, maybe he's a Mister Ed fan, I dunno, but he gives the guy a year. And afterwards, the guy's friends say, hey, what is this, you can't get no horse to talk. So the guy says, well, I got a year now, that's a long time, all kinds of things could happen. Maybe the king will die. Maybe I'll die. Maybe the horse will die. Or maybe the horse will talk.

I'm too damn drunk, I am I am, and my head's full of geeks and talking horses and falling dominoes and unrequited love, and all of a sudden I got to see her. I set down the bottle, oh so carefully, even though it's empty, don't want no broken glass on geek row, and I wheel myself out into the corridor, going slow, I'm not too coordinated right now. The guard is at the end of the hall, looking wistful. I know him a little bit. Security guy, big black fellow, name of Dex. "Hey, Dex," I say as I come wheeling up, "screw this shit, let's us go party, I want to see lil' Ronnie." He just looks at me, shakes his head. "C'mon," I say. I bat my baby-blues at him. Does he let me by? Does the Pope shit in the woods? Hell no, old Dex says, "I got my orders, you stay right here." All of a sudden I'm mad as hell, this ain't fair, I want to see Ronnie. I gather up all my strength and try to wheel right by him. No cigar; Dex turns, blocks my way, grabs the wheelchair and pushes. I go backwards fast, spin around when a wheel jams, flip over and out of the chair. It hurts. Goddamn it hurts. If I had a nose, I woulda bloodied it, I bet. "You stay where you are, you fucking freak," Dex tells me. I start to cry, damn him anyhow, and he watches me as I get my chair upright and pull myself into it. I sit there staring at him. He stands there staring at me. "Please," I say finally. He shakes his head. "Go get her then," I say. "Tell her I want to see her." Dex grins. "She's busy," he tells me. "Her and Major Salazar. She don't want to see you."

I stare at him some more. A real withering, intimidating stare. He doesn't wither or look intimidated. It can't be, can it? Her and the Maje? Her and old Sally Greenface? No way, he's not her type, she's got better taste than that, I know she has. Say it ain't so, Joe. I turn around, start back to my cubicle. Dex looks away. Heigh-ho, fooled him.

Creeper's room is the one beyond mine, the last one at the end of the hall. Everything's just like he left it. I turn on the set, play with the damn switches, trying to figure out how it works. My mind isn't at its sharpest right at this particular minute, it takes me a while, but finally I get it, and I jump from scene to scene down in the Cracker Box, savoring all these little vignettes of life in these United States as served up by Creeper's clever ghost. Each scene has its own individual charm. There's a gang bang going on in the commissary, right on top of one of the tables where Ronnie and I used to play chess. Two huge security men are fighting up in the airlock area; they've been at it a long time, their faces are so bloody I can't tell who the hell they are, but they keep at it, staggering at each other blindly, swinging huge awkward fists, grunting, while a few others stand around and egg them on. Slim and Rafe are sharing a joint, leaning up against my coffin. Slim thinks they ought to rip out all the wires, fuck up everything so I can't go time-riding. Rafe thinks it'd be easier to just bash my head in. Somehow I don't think he loves me no more. Maybe I'll cross him off my Christmas list. Fortunately for the geek, both of them are too stoned and screwed up to do anything at all. I watch a half-dozen other scenes, and finally, a little reluctantly, I go to Ronnie's room, where I watch her screwing Major Salazar.

Heigh-ho, as Creeper would say, what'd you expect, really?

I could not love thee, dear, so much, loved I not honor more. She walks in beauty like the night. But she's not so pretty, not really, back in 1808 there were lovelier women, and Bengt's just the man to land 'em too, although Jägerhorn probably does even better. My Veronica's just the queen bee of a corrupt poisoned hive, that's all. They're done now. They're talking. Or rather the Maje is talking, bless his soul, he's into his ice cream litany, he's just been making love to Ronnie and now he's lying there in bed talking about Sveaborg, damn him. "...only a thirty percent chance that the massacre will take place," he's saying, "the fortress is very strong, formidably strong, but the Russians have the numbers, and if they do bring up sufficient reinforcements, Cronstedt's fears may prove to be substantial. But even that will work out. The assassination, well, the rules will be suspended, they'll slaughter everyone inside, but Sveaborg will become a sort of Swedish Alamo, and the branching paths ought to come together again. Good probability. The end results will be the same." Ronnie isn't listening to him, though; there's a look on her face I've never seen, drunken, hungry, scared, and now she's moving lower on him and doing something I've only seen in my fantasies, and now I don't want to watch anymore, no, oh no, no, oh no.

————

GENERAL SUCHTELEN HAD ESTABLISHED HIS COMMAND POST ON the outskirts of Helsinki, another clever ploy. When Sveaborg turned its cannon on him, every third shot told upon the city the fortress was supposed to protect, until Cronstedt finally ordered the firing stopped. Suchtelen took advantage of that concession as he had all the rest. His apartments were large and comfortable; from his windows, across the white expanse of ice and snow, the gray form of Sveaborg loomed large. Colonel Bengt Anttonen stared at it morosely as he waited in the anteroom with Cronstedt's other courier and the Russians who had escorted them to Suchtelen. Finally the inner doors opened and the dark Russian captain emerged. "The general will see you now," he said.

General Suchtelen sat behind a wide wooden desk. An aide stood by his right arm. A guard was posted at the door, and the captain entered with the Swedish couriers. On the broad, bare expanse of the desk was an inkwell, a blotter, and two signed safe conducts, the passes that would take them through the Russian lines to Stockholm and the Swedish king, one by the southern and the other by the northern route. Suchtelen said something, in Russian, the aide provided a translation. Horses had been provided, and fresh mounts would be available for them along the way, orders had been given. Anttonen listened to the discussion with a curiously empty feeling and a vague sense of disorientation. Suchtelen was going to let them go. Why did that surprise him? Those were the terms of the agreement, after all, those were the conditions of the truce. As the translator droned on, Anttonen felt increasingly lost and listless. He had conspired to get himself here, the voices had told him to, and now here he was, and he did not know why, nor did he know what he was to do.

They handed him one of the safe conducts, placed it in his outstretched hand. Perhaps it was the touch of the paper; perhaps it was something else. A sudden red rage filled him, an anger so fierce and blind and all-consuming that for an instant the world seemed to flicker and vanish and he was somewhere else, seeing naked bodies twining in a room whose walls were made of pale green blocks. And then he was back, the rage still hot within him, but cooling now, cooling quickly. They were staring at him, all of them. With a sudden start, Anttonen realized that he had let the safe conduct fall to the floor, that his hand had gone to the hilt of his sword instead, and the blade was now half-drawn, the metal shining dully in the sunlight that streamed through Suchtelen's window. Had they acted more quickly, they might have stopped him, but he had caught them all by surprise. Suchtelen began to rise from his chair, moving as if in slow motion. Slow motion, Bengt wondered briefly, what was that? But he knew, he knew. The sword was all the way out now. He heard the captain shout something behind him, the aide began to go for his pistol, but Quick Draw McGraw he wasn't, Bengt had the drop on them all, heigh-ho. He grinned, spun the sword in his hand, and offered it, hilt first, to General Suchtelen.

"My sword, sir, and Colonel Jägerhorn's compliments," Bengt Anttonen heard himself say with something approaching awe. "The fortress is in your grasp. Colonel Jägerhorn suggests that you hold up our passage for a month. I concur. Detain us here, and you are certain of victory. Let us go, and who knows what chance misfortune might occur to bring the Swedish fleet? It is a long time until the third of May. In such a time, the king might die, or the horse might die, or you or I might die. Or the horse might talk."

The translator put away his pistol and began to translate; the other courier began to protest, ineffectually. Bengt Anttonen found himself possessed of an eloquence that even his good friend might envy. He spoke on and on. He had one moment of strange weakness, when his stomach churned and his head swam, but somehow he knew it was nothing to be alarmed at, it was just the pills taking effect, it was just a monster dying far away in a metal coffin full of night, and then there were none, heigh-ho, one siege was ending and another would go on and on, and what did it matter to Bengt, the world was a big, crisp, cold, jeweled oyster. He thought this was the beginning of a beautiful friendship, and what the hell, maybe he'd save their asses after all, if he happened to feel like it, but he'd do it his way.

After a time, General Suchtelen, nodding, reached out and accepted the proffered sword.

COLONEL BENGT ANTTONEN REACHED STOCKHOLM ON THE THIRD of May, in the Year of Our Lord Eighteen Hundred and Eight, with a message for Gustavus Adolphus IV, King of Sweden. On the same date, Sveaborg, impregnable Sveaborg, Gibraltar of the North, surrendered to the inferior Russian forces.

At the conclusion of hostilities, Colonel Anttonen resigned his commission in the Swedish army and became an émigré, first to England, and later to America. He took up residence in New York City, where he married, fathered nine children, and became a well-known and influential journalist, widely respected for his canny ability to sense coming trends. When events proved him wrong, as happened infrequently, Anttonen was always surprised. He was a founder of the Republican Party, and his writings were instrumental in the election of John Charles Fremont to the Presidency in 1856.

In 1857, a year before his death, Anttonen played Paul Morphy in a New York chess tournament, and lost a celebrated game. Afterward, his only comment was, "I could have beat him at dominoes," a phrase that Morphy's biographers are fond of quoting.

THE SKIN TRADE

WILLIE SMELLED THE BLOOD A BLOCK AWAY FROM HER APARTMENT.

He hesitated and sniffed at the cool night air again. It was autumn, with the wind off the river and the smell of rain in the air, but the scent, *that* scent, was copper and spice and fire, unmistakable. He knew the smell of human blood.

A jogger bounced past, his orange sweats bright under the light of the full moon. Willie moved deeper into the shadows. What kind of fool ran at this hour of the night? *Asshole,* Willie thought, and the sentiment emerged in a low growl. The man looked around, startled. Willie crept back further into the foliage. After a long moment, the jogger continued up the bicycle path, moving a little faster now.

Taking a chance, Willie moved to the edge of the park, where he could stare down her street from the bushes. Two police cruisers were parked outside her building, lights flashing. What the hell had she gone and done?

When he heard the distant sirens and saw another set of lights approaching, flashing red and blue, Willie felt close to panic. The blood scent was heavy in the air and set his skull to pounding. It was too much. He turned and ran deep into the park, for once not caring who might see him, anxious only to get away. He ran south, swift and silent, until he was panting for breath, his tongue lolling out of his mouth. He wasn't in shape for this kind of shit. He yearned for the safety of his own apartment, for his La-Z-Boy and a good shot of Primatene Mist.

Down near the riverfront, he finally came to a stop, wheezing and trembling, half-drunk with blood and fear. He crouched near a bridge abutment, staring at the headlights of passing cars and listening to the sound of traffic to soothe his ragged nerves.

Finally, when he was feeling a little stronger, he ran down a squirrel. The blood was hot and rich in his mouth, and the flesh made him feel ever so much stronger, but afterwards he got a hairball from all the goddamned fur.

————

"WILLIE," RANDI WADE SAID SUSPICIOUSLY, "IF THIS IS JUST SOME crazy scheme to get into my pants, it's not going to work."

The small man studied his reflection in the antique oval mirror over her couch, tried out several faces until he found a wounded look he seemed to like, then turned back to let her see it. "You'd think that? You'd think that of *me*? I come to you, I need your help, and what do I get, cheap sexual innuendo. You ought to know me better than that, Wade, I mean, Jesus, how long we been friends?"

"Nearly as long as you've been trying to get into my pants," Randi said. "Face it, Flambeaux, you're a horny little bastard."

Willie deftly changed the subject. "It's very amateur hour, you know, doing business out of your apartment."

He sat in one of her red velvet wingback chairs. "I mean, it's a nice place, don't get me wrong, I love this Victorian stuff, can't wait to see the bedroom, but isn't a private eye supposed to have a sleazy little office in the bad part of town? You know, frosted glass on the door, a bottle in the drawer, lots of dust on the filing cabinets..."

Randi smiled. "You know what they charge for those sleazy little offices in the bad part of town? I've got a phone machine, I'm listed in the Yellow Pages..."

"AAA-Wade Investigations," Willie said sourly. "How do you expect people to find you? Wade, it should be under W, if God had meant everybody to be listed under A, He wouldn't have invented all those other letters." He coughed. "I'm coming down with something," he complained, as if it were her fault. "Are you going to help me, or what?"

"Not until you tell me what this is all about," Randi said, but she'd already decided to do it. She liked Willie, and she owed him. He'd given her work when she needed it, with his friendship thrown into the bargain. Even his constant, futile attempts to jump her bones were somehow endearing, although she'd never admit it to Willie. "You want to hear about my rates?"

"Rates?" Willie sounded pained. "What about friendship? What about old times' sake? What about all the times I bought you lunch?"

"You never bought me lunch," Randi said accusingly.

"Is it my fault you kept turning me down?"

"Taking a bucket of Popeye's extra spicy to an adult motel for a snack and a quickie does not constitute a lunch invitation in my book," Randi said.

Willie had a long, morose face, with broad rubbery features capable of an astonishing variety of expressions. Right now he looked as though someone had just run over his puppy. "It would not have been a quickie," he said with vast wounded dignity. He coughed, and pushed himself back in the chair, looking oddly childlike against the red velvet cushions. "Randi," he said, his voice suddenly gone scared and weary, "this is for real."

She'd first met Willie Flambeaux when his collection agency had come after her for the unpaid bills left by her ex. She'd been out of work, broke, and desperate, and Willie had taken pity on her and given her work at the agency. As much as she'd hated hassling people for money, the job had been a godsend, and she'd stayed long enough to wipe out her debt. Willie's lopsided smile, endless propositions, and mordant intelligence had somehow kept her sane. They'd kept in touch, off and on, even after Randi had left the hounds of hell, as Willie liked to call the collection agency.

All that time, Randi had never heard him sound scared, not even when discoursing on the prospect of imminent death from one of his many grisly and undiagnosed maladies. She sat down on the couch. "Then I'm listening," she said. "What's the problem?"

"You see this morning's *Courier*?" he asked. "The woman that was murdered over on Parkway?"

"I glanced at it," Randi said.

"She was a friend of mine."

"Oh, Jesus." Suddenly Randi felt guilty for giving him a hard time. "Willie, I'm so sorry."

"She was just a kid," Willie said. "Twenty-three. You would have liked her. Lots of spunk. Bright too. She'd been in a wheelchair since high school. The night of her senior prom, her date drank too much and got pissed when she wouldn't go all the way. On the way home he floored it and ran head-on into a semi. Really showed her. The boy was killed instantly. Joanie lived through it, but her spine was severed, she was paralyzed from the waist down. She never let it stop her. She went on to college and graduated with honors, had a good job."

"You knew her through all this?"

Willie shook his head. "Nah. Met her about a year ago. She'd been a little overenthusiastic with her credit cards, you know the tune. So I showed up on her doorstep one day, introduced her to Mr. Scissors, one thing led to another and we got to be friends. Like you and me, kind of." He looked up into her eyes. "The body was mutilated. Who'd do something like that? Bad enough to kill her, but . . ." Willie was beginning to wheeze. His asthma. He stopped, took a deep breath. "And what the fuck does it mean? *Mutilated,* Jesus, what a nasty word, but mutilated *how*? I mean, are we talking Jack the Ripper here?"

"I don't know. Does it matter?"

"It matters to me." He wet his lips. "I phoned the cops today, tried to get more details. It was a draw. I wouldn't tell them my name and they wouldn't give me any information. I tried the funeral home too. A closed-casket wake, then the body is going to be cremated. Sounds to me like something getting covered up."

"Like what?" she said.

Willie sighed. "You're going to think this is real weird, but what if . . ." He ran his fingers through his hair. He looked very agitated. "What if Joanie was . . . well, savaged . . . ripped up, maybe even . . . well, partially eaten . . . you know, like by . . . some kind of animal."

Willie was going on, but Randi was no longer listening.

A coldness settled over her. It was old and gray, full of fear, and suddenly she was twelve years old again, standing in the kitchen door listening to her mother make that sound, that terrible high thin wailing sound. The men were still trying to talk to her, to make her understand . . . *some kind of animal,* one of them said. Her mother didn't seem to hear or understand, but Randi did. She'd repeated the words aloud, and all the eyes had gone to her, and one of the cops had said, *Jesus, the kid,* and they'd all stared until her mother had finally gotten up and put her to bed. She began to weep uncontrollably as she tucked in the sheets...her mother, not Randi. Randi hadn't cried. Not then, not at the funeral, not ever in all the years since.

"Hey. Hey! Are you okay?" Willie was asking.

"I'm fine," she said sharply.

"Jesus, don't scare me like that, I got problems of my own, you know? You looked like...hell, I don't know what you looked like, but I wouldn't want to meet it in a dark alley."

Randi gave him a hard look. "The paper said Joan Sorenson was murdered. An animal attack isn't murder."

"Don't get legal on me, Wade. I don't know, I don't even know that an animal was involved, maybe I'm just nuts, paranoid, you name it. The paper left out the grisly details. The fucking paper left out a lot." Willie was breathing rapidly, twisting around in his chair, his fingers drumming on the arm.

"Willie, I'll do whatever I can, but the police are going to go all out on something like this, I don't know how much I'll be able to add."

"The police," he said in a morose tone. "I don't trust the police." He shook his head. "Randi, if the cops go through her things, my name will come up, you know, on her Rolodex and stuff."

"So you're afraid you might be a suspect, is that it?"

"Hell, I don't know, maybe so."

"You have an alibi?"

Willie looked very unhappy. "No. Not really. I mean, not anything you could use in court. I was supposed to...to see her that night. Shit, I mean, she might have written my name on her fucking *calendar* for all I know. I just don't want them nosing around, you know?"

"Why not?"

He made a face. "Even us turnip-squeezers have our dirty little secrets. Hell, they might find all those nude photos of you." She didn't laugh. Willie shook his head. "I mean, God, you'd think the cops would have better things to do than go around solving murders—I haven't gotten a parking ticket in over a year. Makes you wonder what the hell this town is coming to." He had begun to wheeze again. "Now

I'm getting too worked up again, damn it. It's you, Wade. I'll bet you're wearing crotchless panties under those jeans, right?" Glaring at her accusingly, Willie pulled a bottle of Primatene Mist from his coat pocket, stuck the plastic snout in his mouth, and gave himself a blast, sucking it down greedily.

"You must be feeling better," Randi said.

"When you said you'd do anything you could to help, did that include taking off all of your clothes?" Willie said hopefully.

"No," Randi said firmly. "But I'll take the case."

RIVER STREET WAS NOT EXACTLY A PRESTIGE ADDRESS, BUT WILLIE liked it just fine. The rich folks up on the bluffs had "river views" from the gables and widow's walks of their old Victorian houses, but Willie had the river itself flowing by just beneath his windows. He had the sound of it, night and day, the slap of water against the pilings, the foghorns when the mists grew thick, the shouts of pleasure-boaters on sunny afternoons. He had moonlight on the black water, and his very own rotting pier to sit on, any midnight when he had a taste for solitude. He had eleven rooms that used to be offices, a men's room (with urinal) *and* a ladies' room (with Tampax dispenser), hardwood floors, lovely old skylights, and if he ever got that loan, he was definitely going to put in a kitchen. He also had an abandoned brewery down on the ground floor, should he ever decide to make his own beer. The drafty red brick building had been built a hundred years ago, which was about how long the flats had been considered the bad part of town. These days what wasn't boarded up was industrial, so Willie didn't have many neighbors, and that was the best part of all.

Parking was no problem either. Willie had a monstrous old lime-green Cadillac, all chrome and fins, that he left by the foot of the pier, two feet from his door. It took him five minutes to undo all his locks. Willie believed in locks, especially on River Street. The brewery was dark and quiet. He locked and bolted the doors behind him and trudged upstairs to his living quarters.

He was more scared than he'd let on to Randi. He'd been upset enough last night, when he'd caught the scent of blood and figured that Joanie had done something really dumb, but when he'd gotten the morning paper and read that she'd been the victim, that she'd been tortured and killed and mutilated... *mutilated,* dear God, what the hell did that *mean,* had one of the others... no, he couldn't even think about that, it made him sick.

His living room had been the president's office back when the brewery was a going concern. It fronted on the river, and Willie thought it was nicely furnished, all things considered. None of it matched, but that was all right. He'd picked it up piece by piece over the years, the new stuff usually straight repossession deals, the antiques taken in lieu of cash on hopeless and long-overdue debts. Willie nearly always managed to get *something,* even on the accounts that everyone else had written off as a dead loss. If it was something he liked, he paid off the client out of his own pocket, ten or twenty cents on the dollar, and kept the furniture. He got some great bargains that way.

He had just started to boil some water on his hotplate when the phone began to ring.

Willie turned and stared at it, frowning. He was almost afraid to answer. It could be the police... but it could be Randi or some other friend, something totally innocent. Grimacing, he went over and picked it up. "Hello."

"Good evening, William." Willie felt as though someone was running a cold finger up his spine. Jonathan Harmon's voice was rich and mellow; it gave him the creeps. "We've been trying to reach you."

I'll bet you have, Willie thought, but what he said was, "Yeah, well, I been out."

"You've heard about the crippled girl, of course."

"Joan," Willie said sharply. "Her name was Joan. Yeah, I heard. All I know is what I read in the paper."

"I own the paper," Jonathan reminded him. "William, some of us are getting together at Blackstone to talk. Zoe and Amy are here right now, and I'm expecting Michael any moment. Steven drove down to pick up Lawrence. He can swing by for you as well, if you're free."

"No," Willie blurted. "I may be cheap, but I'm never free." His laugh was edged with panic.

"William, your life may be at stake."

"Yeah, I'll bet, you sonofabitch. Is that a threat? Let me tell you, I wrote down everything I know, *everything,* and gave copies to a couple of friends of mine." He hadn't, but come to think of it, it sounded like a good idea. "If I wind up like Joanie, they'll make sure those letters get to the police, you hear me?"

He almost expected Jonathan to say, calmly, "I *own* the police," but there was only silence and static on the line, then a sigh. "I realize you're upset about Joan—"

"Shut the fuck up about Joanie," Willie interrupted. "You got no right to say jack shit about her; I know how you felt about her. You listen up good, Harmon, if it turns out that you or that twisted kid of yours had anything to do with what happened, I'm going to come up to Blackstone one night and kill you myself, see if I don't. She was a good kid, she...she..." Suddenly, for the first time since it had happened, his mind was full of her—her face, her laugh, the smell of her when she was hot and bothered, the graceful way her muscles moved when she ran beside him, the noises she made when their bodies joined together. They all came back to him, and Willie felt tears on his face. There was a tightness in his chest as if iron bands were closing around his lungs. Jonathan was saying something, but Willie slammed down the receiver without bothering to listen, then pulled the jack. His water was boiling merrily away on the hotplate. He fumbled in his pocket and gave himself a good belt of his inhaler, then stuck his head in the steam until he could breathe again. The tears dried up, but not the pain.

Afterwards he thought about the things he'd said, the threats he made, and he got so shaky that he went back downstairs to double-check all his locks.

COURIER SQUARE WAS FAR GONE IN DECAY. THE BIG DEPARTMENT stores had moved to suburban malls, the grandiose old movie palaces had been chopped up into multi-screens or given over to porno, once-fashionable storefronts now housed palm readers and adult bookstores. If Randi had really wanted a seedy little office in the bad part of town, she could find one on Courier Square. What little vitality the Square had left came from the newspaper.

The Courier Building was a legacy of another time, when downtown was still the heart of the city and the newspaper its soul. Old

Douglas Harmon, who'd liked to tell anyone who'd listen that he was cut from the same cloth as Hearst and Pulitzer, had always viewed journalism as something akin to a religious vocation, and the "gothic deco" edifice he built to house his newspaper looked like the result of some unfortunate mating between the Chrysler Building and some especially grotesque cathedral. Five decades of smog had blackened its granite facade and acid rain had eaten away at the wolf's head gargoyles that snarled down from its walls, but you could still set your watch by the monstrous old presses in the basement and a Harmon still looked down on the city from the publisher's office high atop the Iron Spire. It gave a certain sense of continuity to the Square, and the city.

The black marble floors in the lobby were slick and wet when Randi came in out of the rain, wearing a Burberry raincoat a couple sizes too big for her, a souvenir of her final fight with her ex-husband. She'd paid for it, so she was damn well going to wear it. A security guard sat behind the big horseshoe-shaped reception desk, beneath a wall of clocks that once had given the time all over the world. Most were broken now, hands frozen into a chronological cacophony. The lobby was a gloomy place on a dark afternoon like this, full of drafts as cold as the guard's face. Randi took off her hat, shook out her hair, and gave him a nice smile. "I'm here to see Barry Schumacher."

"Editorial. Third floor." The guard barely gave her a glance before he went back to the bondage magazine spread across his lap. Randi grimaced and walked past, heels clicking against the marble.

The elevator was an open grillwork of black iron; it rattled and shook and took forever to deliver her to the city room on the third floor. She found Schumacher alone at his desk, smoking and staring out his window at the rain-slick streets. "Look at that," he said when Randi came up behind him. A streetwalker in a leather miniskirt was standing under the darkened marquee of the Castle. The rain had soaked her thin white blouse and plastered it to her breasts. "She might as well be topless," Barry said. "Right in front of the Castle too. First theater in the state to show *Gone with the Wind,* you know that? All the big movies used to open there." He grimaced, swung his chair around, ground out his cigarette. "Hell of a thing," he said.

"I cried when Bambi's mother died," Randi said.

"In the Castle?"

She nodded. "My father took me, but he didn't cry. I only saw him cry once, but that was later, much later, and it wasn't a movie that did it."

"Frank was a good man," Schumacher said dutifully. He was pushing retirement age, overweight and balding, but he still dressed impeccably, and Randi remembered a young dandy of a reporter who'd been quite a rake in his day. He'd been a regular in her father's Wednesday night poker game for years. He used to pretend that she was his girlfriend, that he was waiting for her to grow up so they could get married. It always made her giggle. But that had been a different Barry Schumacher; this one looked as if he hadn't laughed since Kennedy was president. "So what can I do for you?" he asked.

"You can tell me everything that got left out of the story on that Parkway murder," she said. She sat down across from him.

Barry hardly reacted. She hadn't seen him much since her father died; each time she did, he seemed grayer and more exhausted, like a man who'd been bled dry of passion, laughter, anger, everything. "What makes you think anything was left out?"

"My father was a cop, remember? I know how this city works. Sometimes the cops ask you to leave something out."

"They ask," Barry agreed. "Them asking and us doing, that's two different things. Once in a while we'll omit a key piece of evidence, to help them weed out fake confessions. You know the routine." He paused to light another cigarette.

"How about this time?"

Barry shrugged. "Hell of a thing. Ugly. But we printed it, didn't we?"

"Your story said the victim was mutilated. What does that mean, exactly?"

"We got a dictionary over by the copy editors' desk, you want to look it up."

"I don't want to look it up," Randi said, a little too sharply. Barry was being an asshole; she hadn't expected that. "I know what the word means."

"So you are saying we should have printed all the juicy details?" Barry leaned back, took a long drag on his cigarette. "You know what Jack the Ripper did to his last victim? Among other things, he cut off her breasts. Sliced them up neat as you please, like he was carving white meat off a turkey, and piled the slices on top of each other, beside the bed. He was very tidy, put the nipples on top and everything." He exhaled smoke. "Is that the sort of detail you want? You know how many kids read the *Courier* every day?"

"I don't care what you print in the *Courier,*" Randi said. "I just want to know the truth. Am I supposed to infer that Joan Sorenson's breasts were cut off?"

"I didn't say that," Schumacher said.

"No. You didn't say much of anything. Was she killed by some kind of animal?"

That did draw a reaction. Schumacher looked up, his eyes met hers, and for a moment she saw a hint of the friend he had been in those tired eyes behind their wire-rim glasses. "An animal?" he said softly. "Is that what you think? This isn't about Joan Sorenson at all, is it? This is about your father." Barry got up and came around his desk. He put his hands on her shoulders and looked into her eyes. "Randi, honey, let go of it. I loved Frank too, but he's dead, he's been dead for . . . hell, it's almost twenty years now. The coroner said he got killed by some kind of rabid dog, and that's all there is to it."

"There was no trace of rabies, you know that as well as I do. My father emptied his gun. What kind of rabid dog takes six shots from a police .38 and keeps on coming, huh?"

"Maybe he missed," Barry said.

"He didn't miss!" Randi said sharply. She turned away from him. "We couldn't even have an open casket, too much of the body had been . . ." Even now, it was hard to say without gagging, but she was a big girl now and she forced it out. ". . . eaten," she finished softly. "No animal was ever found."

"Frank must have put some bullets in it, and after it killed him the damned thing crawled off somewhere and died," Barry said. His voice was not unkind. He turned her around to face him again. "Maybe that's how it was and maybe not. It was a hell of a thing, but it happened eighteen years ago, honey, and it's got nothing to do with Joan Sorenson."

"Then tell me what happened to her," Randi said.

"Look, I'm not supposed to . . ." He hesitated, and the tip of his tongue flicked nervously across his lips. "It was a knife," he said softly. "She was killed with a knife, it's all in the police report, just some psycho with a sharp knife." He sat down on the edge of his desk, and his voice took on its familiar cynicism again. "Some weirdo seen too many of those damn sick holiday movies, you know the sort, *Halloween, Friday the 13th,* they got one for every holiday."

"All right." She could tell from his tone that she wouldn't be getting any more out of him. "Thanks."

He nodded, not looking at her. "I don't know where these rumors come from. All we need, folks thinking there's some kind of wild animal running around, killing people." He patted her shoulder. "Don't be such a stranger, you hear? Come by for dinner some night. Adele is always asking about you."

"Give her my best." She paused at the door. "Barry." He looked up, forced a smile. "When they found the body, there wasn't anything missing?"

He hesitated briefly. "No," he said.

Barry had always been the big loser at her father's poker games. He wasn't a bad player, she recalled her father saying, but his eyes gave him away when he tried to bluff... like they gave him away right now.

Barry Schumacher was lying.

THE DOORBELL WAS BROKEN, SO HE HAD TO KNOCK. NO ONE ANswered, but Willie didn't buy that for a minute. "I know you're there, Mrs. Juddiker," he shouted through the window. "I could hear the TV a block off. You turned it off when you saw me coming up the walk. Gimme a break, okay?" He knocked again. "Open up, I'm not going away."

Inside, a child started to say something, and was quickly shushed. Willie sighed. He hated this. Why did they always put him through this? He took out a credit card, opened the door, and stepped into a darkened living room, half-expecting a scream. Instead he got shocked silence.

They were gaping at him, the woman and two kids. The shades

had been pulled down and the curtains drawn. The woman wore a white terry cloth robe, and she looked even younger than she'd sounded on the phone. "You can't just walk in here," she said.

"I just did," Willie said. When he shut the door, the room was awfully dark. It made him nervous. "Mind if I put on a light?" She didn't say anything, so he did. The furniture was all ratty Salvation Army stuff, except for the gigantic big-screen projection TV in the far corner of the room. The oldest child, a little girl who looked about four, stood in front of it protectively. Willie smiled at her. She didn't smile back.

He turned back to her mother. She looked maybe twenty, maybe younger, dark, maybe ten pounds overweight but still pretty. She had a spray of brown freckles across the bridge of her nose. "Get yourself a chain for the door and use it," Willie told her. "And don't try the no-one's-home game on us hounds of hell, okay?" He sat down in a black vinyl recliner held together by electrical tape. "I'd love a drink. Coke, juice, milk, anything, it's been one of those days." No one moved, no one spoke. "Aw, come on," Willie said, "cut it out. I'm not going to make you sell the kids for medical experiments, I just want to talk about the money you owe, okay?"

"You're going to take the television," the mother said.

Willie glanced at the monstrosity and shuddered. "It's a year old and it weighs a million pounds. How'm I going to move something like that, with my bad back? I've got asthma too." He took the inhaler out of his pocket, showed it to her. "You want to kill me, making me take the damned TV would do the trick."

That seemed to help a little. "Bobby, get him a can of soda," the mother said. The boy ran off. She held the front of her robe closed as she sat down on the couch, and Willie could see that she wasn't wearing anything underneath. He wondered if she had freckles on her breasts too; sometimes they did. "I told you on the phone, we don't have no money. My husband run off. He was out of work anyway, ever since the pack shut down."

"I know," Willie said. The pack was short for meatpacking plant, which is what everyone liked to call the south side slaughterhouse that had been the city's largest employer until it shut its doors two years back. Willie took a notepad out of his pocket, flipped a few pages.

"Okay, you bought the thing on time, made two payments, then moved, left no forwarding address. You still owe two thousand eight hundred sixteen dollars. And thirty-one cents. We'll forget the interest and late charges." Bobby returned and handed him a can of Diet Chocolate Ginger Beer. Willie repressed a shudder and cracked the pop-top.

"Go play in the backyard," she said to the children. "Us grown-ups have to talk." She didn't sound very grown-up after they had left, however; Willie was half-afraid she was going to cry. He hated it when they cried. "It was Ed bought the set," she said, her voice trembling. "It wasn't his fault. The card came in the mail."

Willie knew that tune. A credit card comes in the mail, so the next day you run right out and buy the biggest item you can find. "Look, I can see you got plenty of troubles. You tell me where to find Ed, and I'll get the money out of him."

She laughed bitterly. "You don't know Ed. He used to lug around those big sides of beef at the pack, you ought to see the arms on him. You go bother him and he'll just rip your face off and shove it up your asshole, mister."

"What a lovely turn of phrase," Willie said. "I can't wait to make his acquaintance."

"You won't tell him it was me that told you where to find him?" she asked nervously.

"Scout's honor," Willie said. He raised his right hand in a gesture that he thought was vaguely Boy Scoutish, although the can of Diet Chocolate Ginger Beer spoiled the effect a little.

"Were you a Scout?" she asked.

"No," he admitted. "But there was one troop that used to beat me up regularly when I was young."

That actually got a smile out of her. "It's your funeral. He's living with some slut now, I don't know where. But weekends he tends bar down at Squeaky's."

"I know the place."

"It's not real work," she added thoughtfully. "He don't report it or nothing. That way he still gets the unemployment. You think he ever sends anything over for the kids? No way!"

"How much you figure he owes you?" Willie said.

"Plenty," she said.

Willie got up. "Look, none of my business, but it is my business, if you know what I mean. You want, after I've talked to Ed about this television, I'll see what I can collect for you. Strictly professional, I mean, I'll take a little cut off the top, give the rest to you. It may not be much, but a little bit is better than nothing, right?"

She stared at him, astonished. "You'd do that?"

"Shit, yeah. Why not?" He took out his wallet, found a twenty. "Here," he said. "An advance payment. Ed will pay me back." She looked at him incredulously, but did not refuse the bill. Willie fumbled in the pocket of his coat. "I want you to meet someone," he said. He always carried a few cheap pairs of scissors in the pocket of his coat. He found one and put it in her hand. "Here, this is Mr. Scissors. From now on, he's your best friend."

She looked at him like he'd gone insane.

"Introduce Mr. Scissors to the next credit card that comes in the mail," Willie told her, "and then you won't have to deal with assholes like me."

He was opening the door when she caught up to him. "Hey, what did you say your name was?"

"Willie," he told her.

"I'm Betsy." She leaned forward to kiss him on the cheek, and the white robe opened just enough to give him a quick peek at her small breasts. Her chest was lightly freckled, her nipples wide and brown. She closed the robe tight again as she stepped back. "You're no asshole, Willie," she said as she closed the door.

He went down the walk feeling almost human, better than he'd felt since Joanie's death. His Caddy was waiting at the curb, the ragtop up to keep out the off-again on-again rain that had been following him around the city all morning. Willie got in and started her, then glanced into the rearview mirror just as the man in the back seat sat up.

The eyes in the mirror were pale blue. Sometimes, after the spring runoff was over and the river had settled back between its banks, you could find stagnant pools along the shore, backwaters cut off from the flow, foul-smelling places, still and cold, and you wondered how deep they were and whether there was anything living down there in that darkness. Those were the kind of eyes he had, deep-set in a dark, hollow-cheeked face and framed by brown hair that fell long and straight to his shoulders.

Willie swiveled around to face him. "What the hell were you doing back there, catching forty winks? Hate to point this out, Steven, but this vehicle is actually one of the few things in the city that the Harmons do not own. Guess you got confused, huh? Or did you just mistake it for a bench in the park? Tell you what, no hard feelings, I'll drive you to the park, even buy you a newspaper to keep you warm while you finish your little nap."

"Jonathan wants to see you," Steven said, in that flat, chill tone of his. His voice, like his face, was still and dead.

"Yeah, good for him, but maybe I don't want to see Jonathan, you ever think of that?" He was dogmeat, Willie thought; he had to suppress the urge to bolt and run.

"Jonathan wants to see you," Steven repeated, as if Willie hadn't understood. He reached forward. A hand closed on Willie's shoulder. Steven had a woman's fingers, long and delicate, his skin pale and fine. But his palm was crisscrossed by burn scars that lay across the flesh like brands, and his fingertips were bloody and scabbed, the flesh red and raw. The fingers dug into Willie's shoulder with ferocious, inhuman strength. "Drive," he said, and Willie drove.

"I'M SORRY," THE POLICE RECEPTIONIST SAID. "THE CHIEF HAS A full calendar today. I can give you an appointment on Thursday."

"I don't want to see him on Thursday. I want to see him now." Randi hated the cophouse. It was always full of cops. As far as she was concerned, cops came in three flavors: those who saw an attractive woman they could hit on, those who saw a private investigator and resented her, and the old ones who saw Frank Wade's little girl and felt sorry for her. Types one and two annoyed her; the third kind really pissed her off.

The receptionist pressed her lips together, disapproving. "As I've explained, that simply isn't possible."

"Just tell him I'm here," Randi said. "He'll see me."

"He's with someone at the moment, and I'm quite sure that he doesn't want to be interrupted."

Randi had about had it. The day was pretty well shot, and she'd found out next to nothing. "Why don't I just see for myself?" she said sweetly. She walked briskly around the desk, and pushed through the waist-high wooden gate.

"You can't go in there!" the receptionist squeaked in outrage, but by then Randi was opening the door. Police Chief Joseph Urquhart sat behind an old wooden desk cluttered with files, talking to the coroner. Both of them looked up when the door opened. Urquhart was a tall, powerful man in his early sixties. His hair had thinned considerably, but what remained of it was still red, though his eyebrows had gone completely gray. "What the hell—" he started.

"Sorry to barge in, but Miss Congeniality wouldn't give me the time of day," Randi said as the receptionist came rushing up behind her.

"Young lady, this is the police department, and I'm going to throw you out on your ass," Urquhart said gruffly as he stood up and came around the desk, "unless you come over here right now and give your Uncle Joe a big hug."

Smiling, Randi crossed the bearskin rug, wrapped her arms around him, and laid her head against his chest as the chief tried to crush her. The door closed behind them, too loudly. Randi broke the embrace. "I miss you," she said.

"Sure you do," he said, in a faintly chiding tone. "That's why we see so much of you."

Joe Urquhart had been her father's partner for years, back when they were both in uniform. They'd been tight, and the Urquharts had been like an aunt and uncle to her. His older daughter had babysat for her, and Randi had returned the favor for the younger girl. After her father's death, Joe had looked out for them, helped her mother through the funeral and all the legalities, made sure the pension fund got Randi through college. Still, it hadn't been the same, and the families drifted apart, even more so after her mother had finally passed away. These days Randi saw him only once or twice a year, and felt guilty about it. "I'm sorry," she said. "You know I mean to keep in touch, but—"

"There's never enough time, is there?" he said.

The coroner cleared her throat. Sylvia Cooney was a local institution, a big brusque woman of indeterminate age, built like a cement mixer, her iron-gray hair tied in a tight bun at the back of her smooth, square face. She'd been coroner as long as Randi could remember. "Maybe I should excuse myself," she said.

Randi stopped her. "I need to ask you about Joan Sorenson. When will autopsy results be available?"

Cooney's eyes went quickly to the chief, then back to Randi. "Nothing I can tell you," she said. She left the office and closed the door with a soft click behind her.

"That hasn't been released to the public yet," Joe Urquhart said. He walked back behind his desk, gestured. "Sit down."

Randi settled into a seat, let her gaze wander around the office. One wall was covered by commendations, certificates, and framed photographs. She saw her father there with Joe, both of them looking so achingly young, two grinning kids in uniform standing in front of their black-and-white. A moose head was mounted above the photographs, peering down at her with its glassy eyes. More trophies hung from the other walls. "Do you still hunt?" she asked him.

"Not in years," Urquhart said. "No time. Your dad used to kid me about it all the time. Always said that if I ever killed anyone on duty, I'd want the head stuffed and mounted. Then one day it happened, and the joke wasn't so funny anymore." He frowned. "What's your interest in Joan Sorenson?"

"Professional," Randi said.

"Little out of your line, isn't it?"

Randi shrugged. "I don't pick my cases."

"You're too good to waste your life snooping around motels," Urquhart said. It was a sore point between them. "It's not too late to join the force."

"No," Randi said. She didn't try to explain; she knew from past experience that there was no way to make him understand. "I went out to the precinct house this morning to look at the report on Sorenson. It's missing from the file; no one knows where it is. I got the names of the cops who were at the scene, but none of them had time to talk to me. Now I'm told the autopsy results aren't being made public either. You mind telling me what's going on?"

Joe glanced out the windows behind him. The panes were wet with rain. "This is a sensitive case," he said. "I don't want the media blowing this thing all out of proportion."

"I'm not the media," Randi said.

Urquhart swiveled back around. "You're not a cop either. That's your choice. Randi, I don't want you involved in this, do you hear?"

"I'm involved whether you like it or not," she said. She didn't give him time to argue. "How did Joan Sorenson die? Was it an animal attack?"

"No," he said. "It was not. And that's the last question I'm going to answer." He sighed. "Randi," he said, "I know how hard you got hit by Frank's death. It was pretty rough on me too, remember? He phoned me for backup. I didn't get there in time. You think I'll ever forget that?" He shook his head. "Put it behind you. Stop imagining things."

"I'm not imagining anything," Randi snapped. "Most of the time I don't even think about it. This is different."

"Have it your way," Joe said. There was a small stack of files on the corner of the desk near Randi. Urquhart leaned forward and picked them up, tapped them against his blotter to straighten them. "I wish I could help you." He slid open a drawer, put the file folders away. Randi caught a glimpse of the name on the top folder: *Helander.* "I'm sorry," Joe was saying. He started to rise. "Now, if you'll excuse—"

"Are you just rereading the Helander file for old times' sake, or is there some connection to Sorenson?" Randi asked.

Urquhart sat back down. "Shit," he said.

"Or maybe I just imagined that was the name on the file."

Joe looked pained. "We have reason to think the Helander boy might be back in the city."

"Hardly a boy anymore," Randi said. "Roy Helander was three years older than me. You're looking at him for Sorenson?"

"We have to, with his history. The state released him two months ago, it turns out. The shrinks said he was cured." Urquhart made a face. "Maybe, maybe not. Anyway, he's just a name. We're looking at a hundred names."

"Where is he?"

"I wouldn't tell you if I knew. He's a bad piece of business, like the rest of his family. I don't like you getting mixed up with his sort, Randi. Your father wouldn't either."

Randi stood up. "My father's dead," she said, "and I'm a big girl now."

WILLIE PARKED THE CAR WHERE 13TH STREET DEAD-ENDED, AT THE foot of the bluffs. Blackstone sat high above the river, surrounded by a ten-foot-high wrought iron fence with a row of forbidding spikes along its top. You could drive to the gatehouse easily enough, but you had to go all the way down Central, past downtown, then around on Grandview and Harmon Drive, up and down the hills and all along the bluffs where aging steamboat Gothic mansions stood like so many dowagers staring out over the flats and river beyond, remembering better days. It was a long, tiresome drive.

Back before the automobile, it had been even longer and more tiresome. Faced with having to travel to Courier Square on a daily basis, Douglas Harmon made things easy for himself. He built a private cable car: a two-car funicular railway that crept up the gray stone face of the bluffs from the foot of 13th below to Blackstone above.

Internal combustion, limousines, chauffeurs, and paved roads had all conspired to wean the Harmons away from Douglas' folly, making the cable car something of a back door in more recent years, but that suited Willie well enough. Jonathan Harmon always made him feel like he ought to come in by the servant's entrance anyway.

Willie climbed out of the Caddy and stuck his hands in the sagging pockets of his raincoat. He looked up. The incline was precipitous, the rock wet and dark. Steven took his elbow roughly and propelled him forward. The cable car was wooden, badly in need of a whitewash, with bench space for six. Steven pulled the bell cord; the car jerked as they began to ascend. The second car came down to meet them, and they crossed halfway up the bluff. The car shook and Willie spotted rust on the rails. Even here at the gate of Blackstone, things were falling apart.

Near the top of the bluff, they passed through a gap in the wrought iron fence, and the New House came into view, gabled and turreted and covered with Victorian gingerbread. The Harmons had lived there for almost a century, but it was still the New House, and always would be. Behind the house the estate was densely forested, the narrow driveway winding through thick stands of old growth. Where the other founding families had long ago sold off or parceled out their lands to developers, the Harmons had held tight, and Blackstone remained intact, a piece of the forest primeval in the middle of the city.

Against the western sky, Willie glimpsed the broken silhouette of the tower, part of the Old House whose soot-dark stone walls gave Blackstone its name. The house was set well back among the trees, its lawns and courts overgrown, but even when you couldn't see it you knew it was there somehow. The tower was a jagged black presence outlined against the red-stained gray of the western horizon, crooked and forbidding. It had been Douglas Harmon, the journalist and builder of funicular railways, who had erected the New House and closed the Old, immense and gloomy even by Victorian standards; but neither Douglas, his son Thomas, nor his grandson Jonathan had ever found the will to tear it down. Local legend said the Old House was haunted. Willie could just about believe it. Blackstone, like its owner, gave him the creeps.

The cable car shuddered to a stop, and they climbed out onto a wooden deck, its paint weathered and peeling. A pair of wide French doors led into the New House. Jonathan Harmon was waiting for them, leaning on a walking stick, his gaunt figure outlined by the light that spilled through the door. "Hello, William," he said. Harmon was barely past sixty, Willie knew, but long snow-white hair and a body wracked by arthritis made him look much older. "I'm so glad that you could join us," he said.

"Yeah, well, I was in the neighborhood, just thought I'd drop by," Willie said. "Only thing is, I just remembered, I left the windows open in the brewery. I better run home and close them, or my dust bunnies are going to get soaked."

"No," said Jonathan Harmon. "I don't think so."

Willie felt the bands constricting across his chest. He wheezed, found his inhaler, and took two long hits. He figured he'd need it. "Okay, you talked me into it, I'll stay," he told Harmon, "but I damn well better get a drink out of it. My mouth still tastes like Diet Chocolate Ginger Beer."

"Steven, be a good boy and get our friend William a snifter of Remy Martin, if you'd be so kind. I'll join him. The chill is on my bones." Steven, silent as ever, went inside to do as he was told. Willie made to follow, but Jonathan touched his arm lightly. "A moment," he said. He gestured. "Look."

Willie turned and looked. He wasn't quite so frightened anymore. If Jonathan wanted him dead, Steven would have tried already, and maybe succeeded. Steven was a dreadful mistake by his father's standards, but there was a freakish strength in those scarred hands. No, this was some other kind of deal.

They looked east over the city and the river. Dusk had begun to settle, and the streetlights were coming on down below, strings of luminescent pearls that spread out in all directions as far as the eye could see and leapt across the river on three great bridges. The clouds were gone to the east, and the horizon was a deep cobalt blue. The moon had begun to rise.

"There were no lights out there when the foundations of the Old House were dug," Jonathan Harmon said. "This was all wilderness. A wild river coursing through the forest primeval, and if you stood on high at dusk, it must have seemed as though the blackness went on forever. The water was pure, the air was clean, and the woods were thick with game . . . deer, beaver, bear . . . but no people, or at least no white men. John Harmon and his son James both wrote of seeing Indian campfires from the tower from time to time, but the tribes avoided this place, especially after John had begun to build the Old House."

"Maybe the Indians weren't so dumb after all," Willie said.

Jonathan glanced at Willie, and his mouth twitched. "We built this city out of nothing," he said. "Blood and iron built this city, blood and iron nurtured it and fed its people. The old families knew the power of blood and iron, they knew how to make this city great. The Rochmonts hammered and shaped the metal in smithies and foundries and steel mills, the Anders family moved it on their flatboats and steamers and railroads, and your own people found it and pried it from the earth. You come from iron stock, William Flambeaux, but we Harmons were always blood. We had the stockyards and the slaughterhouse, but long before that, before this city or this nation existed, the Old House was a center of the skin trade. Trappers and hunters would come here every season with furs and skins and beaver pelts to sell to the Harmons, and from here the skins would move downriver. On rafts, at first, and then on flatboats. Steam came later, much later."

"Is there going to be a pop quiz on this?" Willie asked.

"We've fallen a long way," he said, looking pointedly at Willie. "We need to remember how we started. Black iron and red, red blood. You need to remember. Your grandfather had the Flambeaux blood, the old pure strain."

Willie knew when he was being insulted. "And my mother was a Pankowski," he said, "which makes me half-frog, half-Polack, and all mongrel. Not that I give a shit. I mean, it's terrific that my great-grandfather owned half the state, but the mines gave out around the turn of the century, the Depression took the rest, my father was a drunk, and I'm in collections, if that's okay with you." He was feeling pissed off and rash by then. "Did you have any particular reason for sending Steven to kidnap me, or was it just a yen to discuss the French and Indian War?"

Jonathan said, "Come. We'll be more comfortable inside, the wind is cold." The words were polite enough, but his tone had lost all faint trace of warmth. He led Willie inside, walking slowly, leaning heavily on the cane. "You must forgive me," he said. "It's the damp. It aggravates the arthritis, inflames my old war wounds." He looked back at Willie. "You were unconscionably rude to hang up on me. Granted, we have our differences, but simple respect for my position—"

"I been having a lot of trouble with my phone lately," Willie said. "Ever since they deregulated, service has turned to shit." Jonathan led him into a small sitting room. There was a fire burning in the hearth; the heat felt good after a long day tramping through the cold and the rain. The furnishings were antique, or maybe just old; Willie wasn't too clear on the difference.

Steven had preceded them. Two brandy snifters, half-full of amber liquid, sat on a low table. Steven squatted by the fire, his tall, lean body folded up like a jackknife. He looked up as they entered and stared at Willie a moment too long, as if he'd suddenly forgotten who he was or what he was doing there. Then his flat blue eyes went back to the fire, and he took no more notice of them or their conversation.

Willie looked around for the most comfortable chair and sat in it. The style reminded him of Randi Wade, but that just made him feel guilty. He picked up his cognac. Willie was couth enough to know that he was supposed to sip but cold and tired and pissed-off enough so that he didn't care. He emptied it in one long swallow, put it down on the floor, and relaxed back into the chair as the heat spread through his chest.

Jonathan, obviously in some pain, lowered himself carefully onto the edge of the couch, his hands closed round the head of his walking stick. Willie found himself staring. Jonathan noticed. "A wolf's head," he said. He moved his hands aside to give Willie a clear view. The firelight reflected off the rich yellow metal. The beast was snarling, snapping.

Its eyes were red. "Garnets?" Willie guessed.

Jonathan smiled the way you might smile at a particularly doltish child. "Rubies," he said, "set in 18-karat gold." His hands, large and heavily veined, twisted by arthritis, closed round the stick again, hiding the wolf from sight.

"Stupid," Willie said. "There's guys in this city would kill you as soon as look at you for a stick like that."

Jonathan's smile was humorless. "I will not die on account of gold, William." He glanced at the window. The moon was well above the horizon. "A good hunter's moon," he said. He looked back at Willie. "Last night you all but accused me of complicity in the death of the crippled girl." His voice was dangerously soft. "Why would you say such a thing?"

"I can't imagine," Willie said. He felt light-headed. The brandy had rushed right to his mouth. "Maybe the fact that you can't remember her name had something to do with it. Or maybe it was because you always hated Joanie, right from the moment you heard about her. My pathetic little mongrel bitch, I believe that was what you called her. Isn't it funny the way that little turns of phrase stick in the mind? I don't know, maybe it was just me, but somehow I got this impression that you didn't exactly wish her well. I haven't even mentioned Steven yet."

"Please don't," Jonathan said icily. "You've said quite enough. Look at me, William. Tell me what you see."

"You," said Willie. He wasn't in the mood for asshole games, but Jonathan Harmon did things at his own pace.

"An old man," Jonathan corrected. "Perhaps not so old in years alone, but old nonetheless. The arthritis grows worse every year, and there are days when the pain is so bad I can scarcely move. My family is all gone but for Steven, and Steven, let us be frank, is not all that I might have hoped for in a son." He spoke in firm, crisp tones, but Steven did not even look up from the flames. "I'm tired, William. It's true, I did not approve of your crippled girl, or even particularly of you. We live in a time of corruption and degeneracy, when the old truths of blood and iron have been forgotten. Nonetheless, however much I may have loathed your Joan Sorenson and what she represented, I had no taste of her blood. All I want is to live out my last years in peace."

Willie stood up. "Do me a favor and spare me the old sick man act. Yeah, I know all about your arthritis and your war wounds. I also know who you are and what you're capable of. Okay, you didn't kill Joanie. So who did? Him?" He jerked a thumb toward Steven.

"Steven was here with me."

"Maybe he was and maybe he wasn't," Willie said.

"Don't flatter yourself, Flambeaux, you're not important enough for me to lie to you. Even if your suspicion was correct, my son is not capable of such an act. Must I remind you that Steven is crippled as well, in his own way?"

Willie gave Steven a quick glance. "I remember once when I was just a kid, my father had to come see you, and he brought me along. I used to love to ride your little cable car. Him and you went inside to talk, but it was a nice day, so you let me play outside. I found Steven in the woods, playing with some poor sick mutt that had gotten past your fence. He was holding it down with his foot, and pulling off its legs, one by one, just ripping them out with his bare hands like a normal kid might pull petals off a flower. When I walked up behind him, he had two off and was working on the third. There was blood all over his face. He couldn't have been more than eight."

Jonathan Harmon sighed. "My son is...disturbed. We both know that, so there is no sense in my denying it. He is also dysfunctional, as you know full well. And whatever residual strength remains is controlled by his medication. He has not had a truly violent episode in years. Have you, Steven?"

Steven Harmon looked back at them. The silence went on too long as he stared, unblinking, at Willie. "No," he finally said.

Jonathan nodded with satisfaction, as if something had been settled.

"So you see, William, you do us a great injustice. What you took for a threat was only an offer of protection. I was going to suggest that you move to one of our guest rooms for a time. I've made the same suggestion to Zoe and Amy."

Willie laughed. "I'll bet. Do I have to fuck Steven too or is that just for the girls?"

Jonathan flushed, but kept his temper. His futile efforts to marry off Steven to one of the Anders sisters was a sore spot. "I regret to say they declined my offer. I hope you will not be so unwise. Blackstone has certain . . . protections . . . but I cannot vouch for your safety beyond these walls."

"Safety?" Willie said. "From what?"

"I do not know, but I can tell you this—in the dark of night, there are things that hunt the hunters."

"Things that hunt the hunters," Willie repeated. "That's good, has a nice beat, but can you dance to it?" He'd had enough. He started for the door. "Thanks but no thanks. I'll take my chances behind my own walls." Steven made no move to stop him.

Jonathan Harmon leaned more heavily on his cane. "I can tell you how she was really killed," he said quietly.

Willie stopped and stared into the old man's eyes. Then he sat back down.

———

IT WAS ON THE SOUTH SIDE IN A NEIGHBORHOOD THAT MADE THE flats look classy, on an elbow of land between the river and that old canal that ran past the pack. Algae and raw sewage choked the canal and gave off a smell that drifted for blocks. The houses were single-story clapboard affairs, hardly more than shacks. Randi hadn't been down here since the pack had closed its doors. Every third house had a sign on the lawn, flapping forlornly in the wind, advertising a property for sale or for rent, and at least half of those were dark. Weeds grew waist-high around the weathered rural mailboxes, and they saw at least two burned-out lots.

Years had passed, and Randi didn't remember the number, but it was the last house on the left, she knew, next to a Sinclair station on the corner. The cabbie cruised until they found it. The gas station was boarded up; even the pumps were gone, but the house stood there much as she recalled. It had a For Rent sign on the lawn, but she saw a light moving around inside. A flashlight, maybe? It was gone before she could be sure.

The cabbie offered to wait. "No," she said. "I don't know how long I'll be." After he was gone, she stood on the barren lawn for a long time, staring at the front door, before she finally went up the walk.

She'd decided not to knock, but the door opened as she was reaching for the knob. "Can I help you, miss?"

He loomed over her, a big man, thick-bodied but muscular. His face was unfamiliar, but he was no Helander. They'd been a short, wiry family, all with the same limp, dirty blond hair. This one had hair black as wrought iron, and shaggier than the department usually liked. Five o'clock shadow gave his jaw a distinct blue-black cast. His hands were large, with short blunt fingers. Everything about him said cop.

"I was looking for the people who used to live here."

"The family moved away when the pack closed," he told her. "Why don't you come inside?" He opened the door wider. Randi saw bare floors, dust, and his partner, a beer-bellied black man standing by the door to the kitchen.

"I don't think so," she said.

"I insist," he replied. He showed her a gold badge pinned to the inside of his cheap gray suit.

"Does that mean I'm under arrest?"

He looked taken aback. "No. Of course not. We'd just like to ask you a few questions." He tried to sound friendlier. "I'm Rogoff."

"Homicide," she said.

His eyes narrowed. "How—?"

"You're in charge of the Sorenson investigation," she said. She'd been given his name at the cophouse that morning. "You must not have much of a case if you've got nothing better to do than hang around here waiting for Roy Helander to show."

"We were just leaving. Thought maybe he'd get nostalgic, hole up at the old house, but there's no sign of it." He looked at her hard and frowned. "Mind telling me your name?"

"Why?" she asked. "Is this a bust or a come-on?"

He smiled. "I haven't decided yet."

"I'm Randi Wade." She showed him her license.

"Private detective," he said, his tone carefully neutral. He handed the license back to her. "You working?"

She nodded.

"Interesting. I don't suppose you'd care to tell me the name of your client."

"No."

"I could haul you into court, make you tell the judge. You can get that license lifted, you know. Obstructing an ongoing police investigation, withholding evidence."

"Professional privilege," she said.

Rogoff shook his head. "PIs don't have privilege. Not in this state."

"This one does," Randi said. "Attorney-client relationship. I've got a law degree too." She smiled at him sweetly. "Leave my client out of it. I know a few interesting things about Roy Helander I might be willing to share."

Rogoff digested that. "I'm listening."

Randi shook her head. "Not here. You know the automat on Courier Square?" He nodded. "Eight o'clock," she told him. "Come alone. Bring a copy of the coroner's report on Sorenson."

"Most girls want candy or flowers," he said.

"The coroner's report," she repeated firmly. "They still keep the old case records downtown?"

"Yeah," he said. "Basement of the courthouse."

"Good. You can stop by and do a little remedial reading on the way. It was eighteen years ago. Some kids had been turning up missing. One of them was Roy's little sister. There were others—Stanski, Jones, I forget all the names. A cop named Frank Wade was in charge of the investigation. A gold badge, like you. He died."

"You saying there's a connection?"

"You're the cop. You decide." She left him standing in the doorway and walked briskly down the block.

———

STEVEN DIDN'T BOTHER TO SEE HIM DOWN TO THE FOOT OF THE bluffs. Willie rode the little funicular railway alone, morose and lost in thought. His joints ached like nobody's business and his nose was running. Every time he got upset his body fell to pieces, and Jonathan Harmon had certainly upset him. That was probably better than killing him, which he'd half expected when he found Steven in his car, but still. . . .

He was driving home along 13th Street when he saw the bar's neon sign on his right. Without thinking, he pulled over and parked. Maybe Harmon was right and maybe Harmon had his ass screwed on backwards, but in any case Willie still had to make a living. He locked up the Caddy and went inside.

It was a slow Tuesday night, and Squeaky's was empty. It was a workingman's tavern. Two pool tables, a shuffleboard machine in back, booths along one wall. Willie took a bar stool. The bartender was an old guy, hard and dry as a stick of wood. He looked mean. Willie considered ordering a banana daiquiri, just to see what the guy would say, but one look at that sour, twisted old face cured the impulse, and he asked for a boilermaker instead. "Ed working tonight?" he asked when the bartender brought the drinks.

"Only works weekends," the man said, "but he comes in most nights, plays a little pool."

"I'll wait," Willie said. The shot made his eyes water. He chased it down with a gulp of beer. He saw a pay phone back by the men's room. When the bartender gave him his change, he walked back, put in a quarter, and dialed Randi. She wasn't home; he got her damned machine. Willie hated phone machines. They'd made life a hell of a lot more difficult for collection agents, that was for sure. He waited for the tone, left Randi an obscene message, and hung up.

The men's room had a condom dispenser mounted over the urinals. Willie read the instructions as he took a leak. The condoms were intended for prevention of disease only, of course, even though the one dispensed by the left-hand slot was a French tickler. Maybe he ought to install one of these at home, he thought. He zipped up, flushed, washed his hands.

When he walked back out into the taproom, two new customers stood over the pool table, chalking up cues. Willie looked at the bartender, who nodded. "One of you Ed Juddiker?" Willie asked.

Ed wasn't the biggest—his buddy was as large and pale as Moby Dick—but he was big enough, with a real stupid-mean look on his face. "Yeah?"

"We need to talk about some money you owe." Willie offered him one of his cards.

Ed looked at the hand, but made no effort to take the card. He laughed. "Get lost," he said. He turned back to the pool table. Moby Dick racked up the balls and Ed broke.

That was all right, if that was the way he wanted to play it. Willie sat back on the bar stool and ordered another beer. He'd get his money one way or the other. Sooner or later Ed would have to leave, and then it would be his turn.

———

WILLIE STILL WASN'T ANSWERING HIS PHONE. RANDI HUNG UP THE pay phone and frowned. He didn't have an answering machine either, not Willie Flambeaux, that would be too sensible. She knew she shouldn't worry. The hounds of hell don't punch time clocks, as he'd told her more than once. He was probably out running down some deadbeat. She'd try again when she got home. If he still didn't answer, then she'd start to worry.

The automat was almost empty. Her heels made hollow clicks on the old linoleum as she walked back to her booth and sat down. Her coffee had gone cold. She looked idly out the window. The digital clock on the State National Bank said 8:13. Randi decided to give him ten more minutes.

The red vinyl of the booth was old and cracking, but she felt strangely comfortable here, sipping her cold coffee and staring off at the Iron Spire across the Square. The automat had been her favorite restaurant when she was a little girl. Every year on her birthday she would demand a movie at the Castle and dinner at the automat, and every year her father would laugh and oblige. She loved to put the nickels in the coin slots and make the windows pop open, and fill her father's cup out of the old brass coffee machine with all its knobs and levers.

Sometimes you could see disembodied hands through the glass, sticking a sandwich or a piece of pie into one of the slots, like something from an old horror movie. You never saw any people working at the automat, just hands; the hands of people who hadn't paid their bills, her father once told her, teasing. That gave her the shivers, but somehow made her annual visits even more delicious, in a creepy kind of way. The truth, when she learned it, was much less interesting. Of course, that was true of most everything in life.

These days, the automat was always empty, which made Randi wonder how the floor could possibly stay so filthy, and you had to put quarters into the coin slots beside the little windows instead of nickels. But the banana cream pie was still the best she'd ever had, and the coffee that came out of those worn brass spigots was better than anything she'd ever brewed at home.

She was thinking of getting a fresh cup when the door opened and Rogoff finally came in out of the rain. He wore a heavy wool coat. His hair was wet. Randi looked out at the clock as he approached the booth. It said 8:17. "You're late," she said.

"I'm a slow reader," he said. He excused himself and went to get some food. Randi watched him as he fed dollar bills into the change machine. He wasn't bad-looking if you liked the type, she decided, but the type was definitely cop.

Rogoff returned with a cup of coffee, the hot beef sandwich with mashed potatoes, gravy, and overcooked carrots, and a big slice of apple pie.

"The banana cream is better," Randi told him as he slid in opposite her.

"I like apple," he said, shaking out a paper napkin.

"Did you bring the coroner's report?"

"In my pocket." He started cutting up the sandwich. He was very methodical, slicing the whole thing into small bite-sized portions before he took his first taste. "I'm sorry about your father."

"So was I. It was a long time ago. Can I see the report?"

"Maybe. Tell me something I don't already know about Roy Helander."

Randi sat back. "We were kids together. He was older, but he'd been left back a couple of times, till he wound up in my class. He was a bad kid from the wrong side of the tracks and I was a cop's daughter, so we didn't have much in common...until his little sister disappeared."

"He was with her," Rogoff said.

"Yes he was. No one disputed that, least of all Roy. He was fifteen, she was eight. They were walking the tracks. They went off together, and Roy came back alone. He had blood on his dungarees and all over his hands. His sister's blood."

Rogoff nodded. "All that's in the file. They found blood on the tracks too."

"Three kids had already vanished. Jessie Helander made four. The way most people looked at it, Roy had always been a little strange. He was solitary, inarticulate, used to hook school and run off to some secret hideout he had in the woods. He liked to play with the younger kids instead of boys his own age. A degenerate from a bad family, a child molester who had actually raped and killed his own sister, that was what they said. They gave him all kinds of tests, decided he was deeply disturbed, and sent him away to some kiddy snakepit. He was still a juvenile, after all. Case closed, and the city breathed easier."

"If you don't have any more than that, the coroner's report stays in my pocket," Rogoff said.

"Roy said he didn't do it. He cried and screamed a lot, and his story wasn't coherent, but he stuck to it. He said he was walking along ten feet or so behind his sister, balancing on the rails and listening for a train, when a monster came out of a drainage culvert and attacked her."

"A monster," Rogoff said.

"Some kind of big shaggy dog, that was what Roy said. He was describing a wolf. Everybody knew it."

"There hasn't been a wolf in this part of the country for over a century."

"He described how Jessie screamed as the thing began to rip her apart. He said he grabbed her leg, tried to pull her out of its jaws, which would explain why he had her blood all over him. The wolf turned and looked at him and growled. It had red eyes, burning red eyes, Roy said, and he was real scared, so he let go. By then Jessie was almost certainly dead. It gave him one last snarl and ran off, carrying the body in its jaws." Randi paused, took a sip of coffee. "That was his story. He told it over and over, to his mother, the police, the psychologists, the judge, everyone. No one ever believed him."

"Not even you?"

"Not even me. We all whispered about Roy in school, about what he'd done to his sister and those other kids. We couldn't quite imagine it, but we knew it had to be horrible. The only thing was, my father never quite bought it."

"Why not?"

She shrugged. "Instincts, maybe. He was always talking about how a cop had to go with his instincts. It was his case, he'd spent more time with Roy than anyone else, and something about the way the boy told the story had affected him. But it was nothing that could be proved. The evidence was overwhelming. So Roy was locked up." She watched his eyes as she told him. "A month later, Eileen Stanski vanished. She was six."

Rogoff paused with a forkful of the mashed potatoes, and studied her thoughtfully. "Inconvenient," he said.

"Dad wanted Roy released, but no one supported him. The official line was that the Stanski girl was unconnected to the others. Roy had done four, and some other child molester had done the fifth."

"It's possible."

"It's bullshit," Randi said. "Dad knew it and he said it. That didn't make him any friends in the department, but he didn't care. He could be a very stubborn man. You read the file on his death?"

Rogoff nodded. He looked uncomfortable.

"My father was savaged by an animal. A dog, the coroner said. If you want to believe that, go ahead." This was the hard part. She'd picked at it like an old scab for years, and then she'd tried to forget it, but nothing ever made it easier. "He got a phone call in the middle of the night, some kind of lead about the missing kids. Before he left he phoned Joe Urquhart to ask for backup."

"Chief Urquhart?"

Randi nodded. "He wasn't chief then. Joe had been his partner when he was still in uniform. He said Dad told him he had a hot tip, but not the details, not even the name of the caller."

"Maybe he didn't know the name."

"He knew. My father wasn't the kind of cop who goes off alone in the middle of the night on an anonymous tip. He drove down to the stockyards by himself. It was waiting for him there. Whatever it was took six rounds and kept coming. It tore out his throat, and after he was dead it ate him. What was left by the time Urquhart got there . . .

Joe testified that when he first found the body he wasn't even sure it was human."

She told the story in a cool, steady voice, but her stomach was churning. When she finished Rogoff was staring at her. He set down his fork and pushed his plate away. "Suddenly I'm not very hungry anymore."

Randi's smile was humorless. "I love our local press. There was a case a few years ago when a woman was kidnapped by a gang, held for two weeks. She was beaten, tortured, sodomized, raped hundreds of times. When the story broke, the paper said she'd been quote *assaulted* unquote. It said my father's body had been mutilated. It said the same thing about Joan Sorenson. I've been told her body was intact." She leaned forward, looked hard into his dark brown eyes. "That's a lie."

"Yes," he admitted. He took a sheet of paper from his breast pocket, unfolded it, passed it across to her. "But it's not the way you think."

Randi snatched the coroner's report from his hand, and scanned quickly down the page. The words blurred, refused to register. It wasn't adding up the way it was supposed to.

Cause of death: exsanguination.

Somewhere far away, Rogoff was talking. "It's a security building, her apartment's on the fourteenth floor. No balconies, no fire escapes, and the doorman didn't see a thing. The door was locked. It was a cheap spring lock, easy to jimmy, but there was no sign of forced entry."

The instrument of death was a blade at least twelve inches long, extremely sharp, slender and flexible, perhaps a surgical instrument.

"Her clothing was all over the apartment, just ripped to hell, in tatters. In her condition, you wouldn't think she'd put up much of a struggle, but it looks like she did. None of the neighbors heard anything, of course. The killer chained her to her bed, naked, and went to work. He worked fast, knew what he was doing, but it still must have taken her a long time to die. The bed was soaked with her blood, through the sheets and mattress, right down to the box spring."

Randi looked back up at him, and the coroner's report slid from her fingers onto the Formica table. Rogoff reached over and took her hand.

"Joan Sorenson wasn't devoured by any animal, Miss Wade. She was flayed alive, and left to bleed to death. And the part of her that's missing is her skin."

IT WAS A QUARTER PAST MIDNIGHT WHEN WILLIE GOT HOME. HE parked the Caddy by the pier. Ed Juddiker's wallet was on the seat beside him. Willie opened it, took out the money, counted. Seventy-nine bucks. Not much, but it was a start. He'd give half to Betsy this first time, credit the rest to Ed's account. Willie pocketed the money and locked the empty wallet in the glovebox. Ed might need the driver's license. He'd bring it by Squeaky's over the weekend, when Ed was on, and talk to him about a payment schedule.

Willie locked up the car and trudged wearily across the rain-slick cobbles to his front door. The sky above the river was dark and starless. The moon was up by now, he knew, hidden somewhere behind those black cotton clouds. He fumbled for his keys, buried down under his inhaler, his pillbox, a half-dozen pairs of scissors, a handkerchief, and the miscellaneous other junk that made his coat pocket sag. After a long minute, he tried his pants pocket, found them, and started in on his locks. He slid the first key into his double deadbolt.

The door opened slowly, silently.

The pale yellow light from a streetlamp filtered through the brewery's high, dusty windows, patterning the floor with faint squares and twisted lines. The hulks of rusting machines crouched in the dimness like great dark beasts. Willie stood in the doorway, keys in hand, his heart pounding like a triphammer. He put the keys in his pocket, found his Primatene, took a hit. The hiss of the inhaler seemed obscenely loud in the stillness.

He thought of Joanie, of what happened to her.

He could run, he thought. The Cadillac was only a few feet behind him, just a few steps; whatever was waiting in there couldn't possibly be fast enough to get him before he reached the car. Yeah, hit the road, drive all night, he had enough gas to make Chicago, it wouldn't follow him there. Willie took the first step back, then stopped, and giggled nervously. He had a sudden picture of himself sitting behind the wheel of his big lime-green chromeboat, grinding the ignition, grinding and grinding and flooding the engine as something dark and terrible emerged from inside the brewery and crossed the cobblestones behind him. That was silly; it was only in bad horror movies that the ignition didn't turn over, wasn't it? Wasn't it?

Maybe he had just forgotten to lock up when he'd left for work that morning. He'd had a lot on his mind, a full day's work ahead of him and a night of bad dreams behind; maybe he'd just closed the fucking door behind him and forgotten about his locks.

He never forgot about his locks.

But maybe he had, just this once.

Willie thought about changing. Then he remembered Joanie, and put the thought aside. He stood on one leg, pulled off his shoe. Then the other. Water soaked through his socks. He edged forward, took a deep breath, moved into the darkened brewery as silently as he could, pulling the door shut behind him. Nothing moved. Willie reached down into his pocket, pulled out Mr. Scissors. It wasn't much, but it was better than bare hands. Hugging the thick shadows along the wall, he crossed the room and began to creep upstairs on stockinged feet.

The streetlight shone through the window at the end of the hall. Willie paused on the steps when his head came up to the level of the second-story landing. He could look up and down the hallway. All the office doors were shut. No light leaking underneath or through the frosted-glass transoms. Whatever waited for him waited in darkness.

He could feel his chest constricting again. In another moment he'd need his inhaler. Suddenly he just wanted to get it over with. He climbed the final steps and crossed the hall in two long strides, threw open the door to his living room, and slammed on the lights.

Randi Wade was sitting in his beanbag chair. She looked up blinking as he hit the lights. "You startled me," she said.

"I startled *you!*" Willie crossed the room and collapsed into his La-Z-Boy. The scissors fell from his sweaty palm and bounced on the hardwood floor. "Jesus H. Christ on a crutch, you almost made me lose control of my personal hygiene. What the hell are you doing here? Did I forget to lock the door?"

Randi smiled. "You locked the door and you locked the door and then you locked the door some more. You're world class when it comes to locking doors, Flambeaux. It took me twenty minutes to get in."

Willie massaged his throbbing temples. "Yeah, well, with all the women who want this body, I got to have some protection, don't I?" He noticed his wet socks, pulled one off, grimaced. "Look at this," he said. "My shoes are out in the street getting rained on, and my feet are soaking. If I get pneumonia, you get the doctor bills, Wade. You could have waited."

"It was raining," she pointed out. "You wouldn't have wanted me to wait in the rain, Willie. It would have pissed me off, and I'm in a foul mood already."

Something in her voice made Willie stop rubbing his toes to look up at her. The rain had plastered loose strands of light brown hair across her forehead, and her eyes were grim. "You look like a mess," he admitted.

"I tried to make myself presentable, but the mirror in your ladies' room is missing."

"It broke. There's one in the men's room."

"I'm not that kind of a girl," Randi said. Her voice was hard and flat. "Willie, your friend Joan wasn't killed by an animal. She was flayed. The killer took her skin."

"I know," Willie said, without thinking.

Her eyes narrowed. They were gray-green, large and pretty, but right now they looked as cold as marbles. "You *know*?" she echoed. Her voice had gone very soft, almost to a whisper, and Willie knew he was in trouble. "You give me some bullshit story and send me running all around town, and you *know*? Do you know what happened to my father too, is that it? It was just your clever little way of getting my attention?"

Willie gaped at her. His second sock was in his hand. He let it drop to the floor. "Hey, Randi, gimme a break, okay? It wasn't like that at all. I just found out a few hours ago, honest. How could I know? I wasn't there, it wasn't in the paper." He was feeling confused and guilty. "What the hell am I supposed to know about your father? I don't know jack shit about your father. All the time you worked for me, you mentioned your family maybe twice."

Her eyes searched his face for signs of deception. Willie tried to give his warmest, most trustworthy smile. Randi grimaced. "Stop it," she said wearily. "You look like a used car salesman. All right, you didn't know about my father. I'm sorry. I'm a little wrought up right now, and I thought..." She paused thoughtfully. "Who told you about Sorenson?"

Willie hesitated. "I can't tell you," he said. "I wish I could, I really do. I can't. You wouldn't believe me anyway." Randi looked very unhappy. Willie kept talking. "Did you find out whether I'm a suspect? The police haven't called."

"They've probably been calling all day. By now they may have an APB out on you. If you won't get a machine, you ought to try coming home occasionally." She frowned. "I talked to Rogoff from Homicide." Willie's heart stopped, but she saw the look on his face and held up a hand. "No, your name wasn't mentioned. By either of us. They'll be calling everyone who knew her, probably, but it's just routine questioning. I don't think they'll be singling you out."

"Good," Willie said. "Well, look, I owe you one, but there's no reason for you to go on with this. I know it's not paying the rent, so—"

"So what?" Randi was looking at him suspiciously. "Are you trying to get rid of me now? After you got me involved in the first place?" She frowned. "Are you holding out on me?"

"I think you've got that reversed," Willie said lightly. Maybe he could joke his way out of it. "You're the one who gets bent out of shape whenever I offer to help you shop for lingerie."

"Cut the shit," Randi said sharply. She was not amused in the least, he could see that. "We're talking about the torture and murder of a girl who was supposed to be a friend of yours. Or has that slipped your mind somehow?"

"No," he said, abashed. Willie was very uncomfortable. He got up and crossed the room, plugged in the hotplate. "Hey, listen, you want a cup of tea? I got Earl Grey, Red Zinger, Morning Thunder—"

"The police think they have a suspect," Randi said.

Willie turned to look at her. "Who?"

"Roy Helander," Randi said.

"Oh, boy," Willie said. He'd been a PFC in Hamburg when the Helander thing went down, but he'd had a subscription to the *Courier* to keep up on the old hometown, and the headlines had made him ill. "Are you sure?"

"No," she said. "They're just rounding up the usual suspects. Roy was a great scapegoat last time, why not use him again? First they have to find him, though. No one's really sure that he's still in the state, let alone the city."

Willie turned away, busied himself with hotplate and kettle. All of a sudden he found it difficult to look Randi in the eye. "You don't think Helander was the one who grabbed those kids."

"Including his own sister? Hell no. Jessie was the last person he'd ever have hurt, she actually *liked* him. Not to mention that he was safely locked away when number five disappeared. I knew Roy Helander. He had bad teeth and he didn't bathe often enough, but that doesn't make him a child molester. He hung out with younger kids because the older ones made fun of him. I don't think he had any friends. He had some kind of secret place in the woods where he'd go to hide when things got too rough, he—"

She stopped suddenly, and Willie turned toward her, a teabag dangling from his fingers. "You thinking what I'm thinking?"

The kettle began to scream.

RANDI TOSSED AND TURNED FOR OVER AN HOUR AFTER SHE GOT home, but there was no way she could sleep. Every time she closed her eyes she would see her father's face, or imagine poor Joan Sorenson, tied to that bed as the killer came closer, knife in hand. She kept coming back to Roy Helander, to Roy Helander and his secret refuge. In her mind, Roy was still the gawky adolescent she remembered, his blond hair lank and unwashed, his eyes frightened and confused as they made him tell the story over and over again. She wondered what had become of that secret place of his during all the years he'd been locked up and drugged in the state mental home, and she wondered if maybe sometimes he hadn't dreamt of it as he lay there in his cell. She thought maybe he had. If Roy Helander had indeed come home, Randi figured she knew just where he was.

Knowing about it and finding it were two different things, however. She and Willie had kicked it around without narrowing it down any. Randi tried to remember, but it had been so long ago, a whispered conversation in the schoolyard. A secret place in the woods, he'd said, a place where no one ever came that was his and his alone, hidden and full of magic. That could be anything, a cave by the river, a treehouse, even something as simple as a cardboard lean-to. But where were these woods? Outside the city were suburbs and industrial parks and farms; the nearest state forest was forty miles north along the river road. If this secret place was in one of the city parks, you'd think someone would have stumbled on it years ago. Without more to go on, Randi didn't have a prayer of finding it. But her mind worried it like a pit bull with a small child.

Finally her digital alarm clock read 2:13, and Randi gave up on sleep altogether. She got out of bed, turned on the light, and went back to the kitchen. The refrigerator was pretty dismal, but she found a couple of bottles of Pabst. Maybe a beer would help put her to sleep. She opened a bottle and carried it back to bed.

Her bedroom furnishings were a hodgepodge. The carpet was a remnant, the blond chest-of-drawers was boring and functional, and the four-poster queen-sized bed was a replica, but she did own a few genuine antiques—the massive oak wardrobe, the full-length clawfoot dressing mirror in its ornate wooden frame, and the cedar chest at the foot of the bed. Her mother always used to call it a hope chest. Did little girls still keep hope chests? She didn't think so, at least not around here. Maybe there were still places where hope didn't seem so terribly unrealistic, but this city wasn't one of them.

Randi sat on the floor, put the beer on the carpet, and opened the chest.

Hope chests were where you kept your future, all the little things that were part of the dreams they taught you to dream when you were a child. She hadn't been a child since she was twelve, since the night her mother woke her with that terrible inhuman sound. Her chest was full of memories now.

She took them out, one by one. Yearbooks from high school and college, bundles of love letters from old boyfriends and even that asshole she'd married, her school ring and her wedding ring, her diplomas, the letters she'd won in track and girls' softball, a framed picture of her and her date at the senior prom.

Way, way down at the bottom, buried under all the other layers of her life, was a police .38. Her father's gun, the gun he emptied the night he died. Randi took it out and carefully put it aside. Beneath it was the book, an old three-ring binder with a blue cloth cover. She opened it across her lap.

The yellowed *Courier* story on her father's death was Scotch-taped to the first sheet of paper, and Randi stared at that familiar photograph for a long time before she flipped the page. There were other clippings: stories about the missing children that she'd torn furtively from *Courier* back issues in the public library, magazine articles about animal attacks, serial killers, and monsters, all sandwiched between the lined pages she'd filled with her meticulous twelve-year-old's script. The handwriting grew broader and sloppier as she turned the pages; she'd kept up the book for years, until she'd gone away to college and tried to forget. She'd thought she'd done a pretty good job of that, but now, turning the pages, she knew that was a lie. You never forget. She only had to glance at the headlines, and it all came back to her in a sickening rush.

Eileen Stanski, Jessie Helander, Diane Jones, Gregory Torio, Erwin Weiss. None of them had ever been found, not so much as a bone or a piece of clothing. The police said her father's death was accidental, unrelated to the case he was working on. They'd all accepted that, the chief, the mayor, the newspaper, even her mother, who only wanted to get it all behind them and go on with their lives. Barry Schumacher and Joe Urquhart were the last to buy in, but in the end even they came around, and Randi was the only one left. Mere mention of the subject upset her mother so much that she finally stopped talking about it, but she didn't forget. She just asked her questions quietly, kept up her binder, and hid it every night at the bottom of the hope chest.

For all the good it had done.

The last twenty-odd pages in the back of the binder were still blank, the blue lines on the paper faint with age. The pages were stiff as she turned them. When she reached the final page, she hesitated. Maybe it wouldn't be there, she thought. Maybe she had just imagined it. It made no sense anyway. He would have known about her father, yes, but their mail was censored, wasn't it? They'd never let him send such a thing.

Randi turned the last page. It was there, just as she'd known it would be.

She'd been a junior in college when it arrived. She'd put it all behind her. Her father had been dead for seven years, and she hadn't even looked at her binder for three. She was busy with her classes and her sorority and her boyfriends, and sometimes she had bad dreams but mostly it was okay, she'd grown up, she'd gotten real. If she thought about it at all, she thought that maybe the adults had been right all along, it had just been some kind of an animal.

. . . some kind of animal . . .

Then one day the letter had come. She'd opened it on the way to class, read it with her friends chattering beside her, laughed and made a joke and stuck it away, all very grown-up. But that night, when her roommate had gone to sleep, she took it out and turned on her Tensor to read it again, and felt sick. She was going to throw it away, she remembered. It was just trash, a twisted product of a sick mind.

Instead she'd put it in the binder.

The Scotch tape had turned yellow and brittle, but the envelope was still white, with the name of the institution printed neatly in the left-hand corner. Someone had probably smuggled it out for him. The letter itself was scrawled on a sheet of cheap typing paper in block letters. It wasn't signed, but she'd known who it was from.

Randi slid the letter out of the envelope, hesitated for a moment, and opened it.

IT WAS A WEREWOLF

She looked at it and looked at it and looked at it, and suddenly she didn't feel very grown-up anymore. When the phone rang she nearly jumped a foot.

Her heart was pounding in her chest. She folded up the letter and stared at the phone, feeling strangely guilty, as if she'd been caught doing something shameful. It was 2:53 in the morning. Who the hell would be calling now? If it was Roy Helander, she thought she might just scream. She let the phone ring.

On the fourth ring, her machine cut in. "This is AAA-Wade Investigations, Randi Wade speaking. I can't talk right now, but you can leave a message at the tone, and I'll get back to you."

The tone sounded. "Uh, hello," said a deep male voice that was definitely not Roy Helander.

Randi put down the binder, snatched up the receiver. "Rogoff? Is that you?"

"Yeah," he said. "Sorry if I woke you. Listen, this isn't by the book and I can't figure out a good excuse for why I'm calling you, except that I thought you ought to know."

Cold fingers crept down Randi's spine. "Know what?"

"We've got another one," he said.

WILLIE WOKE IN A COLD SWEAT.

What was that?

A noise, he thought. Somewhere down the hall.

Or maybe just a dream? Willie sat up in bed and tried to get a grip on himself. The night was full of noises. It could have been a towboat on the river, a car passing by underneath his windows, anything. He still felt sheepish about the way he'd let his fear take over when he found his door open. He was just lucky he hadn't stabbed Randi with those scissors. He couldn't let his imagination eat him alive. He slid back down under the covers, rolled over on his stomach, closed his eyes.

Down the hall, a door opened and closed.

His eyes opened wide. He lay very still, listening. He'd locked all the locks, he told himself, he'd walked Randi to the door and locked all his locks, the springlock, the chain, the double deadbolt, he'd even lowered the police bar. No one could get in once the bar was in place, it could only be lifted from inside, the door was solid steel. And the back door might as well be welded shut, it was so corroded and un-movable. If they broke a window he would have heard the noise, there was no way, no way. He was just dreaming.

The knob on his bedroom door turned slowly, clicked. There was a small metallic rattle as someone pushed at the door. The lock held. The second push was slightly harder, the noise louder.

By then Willie was out of bed. It was a cold night, his jockey shorts and undershirt small protection against the chill, but Willie had other things on his mind. He could see the key still sticking out of the key-hole. An antique key for a hundred-year-old lock. The office keyholes were big enough to peek through. Willie kept the keys inside them, just to plug up the drafts, but he never turned them . . . except tonight. Tonight for some reason he'd turned that key before he went to bed and somehow felt a little more secure when he heard the tumblers click. And now that was all that stood between him and whatever was out there.

He backed up against the window, glanced out at the cobbled alley behind the brewery. The shadows lay thick and black beneath him. He seemed to recall a big green metal dumpster down below, directly under the window, but it was too dark to make it out.

Something hammered at the door. The room shook.

Willie couldn't breathe. His inhaler was on the dresser across the room, over by the door. He was caught in a giant's fist and it was squeezing all the breath right out of him. He sucked at the air.

The thing outside hit the door again. The wood began to splinter. Solid wood, a hundred years old, but it split like one of your cheap-ass hollow-core modern doors.

Willie was starting to get dizzy. It was going to be real pissed off, he thought giddily, when it finally got in here and found that his asthma had already killed him. Willie peeled off his undershirt, dropped it to the floor, hooked a thumb in the elastic of his shorts.

The door shook and shattered, falling half away from its hinges. The next blow snapped it in two. His head swam from lack of oxygen. Willie forgot all about his shorts and gave himself over to the change.

Bones and flesh and muscles shrieked in the agony of transformation, but the oxygen rushed into his lungs, sweet and cold, and he could breathe again. Relief shuddered through him and he threw back his head and gave it voice. It was a sound to chill the blood, but the dark shape picking its way through the splinters of his door did not hesitate, and neither did Willie. He gathered his feet up under him, and leapt. Glass shattered all around him as he threw himself through the window, and the shards spun outward into the darkness. Willie missed the dumpster, landed on all fours, lost his footing, and slid three feet across the cobbles.

When he looked up, he could see the shape above him, filling his window. Its hands moved, and he caught the terrible glint of silver, and that was all it took. Willie was on his feet again, running down the street faster than he had ever run before.

THE CAB LET HER OFF TWO HOUSES DOWN. POLICE BARRICADES HAD gone up all around the house, a dignified old Victorian manor badly in need of fresh paint. Curious neighbors, heavy coats thrown on over pajamas and bathrobes, lined Grandview, whispering to each other and glancing back at the house. The flashers on the police cars lent a morbid avidity to their faces.

Randi walked past them briskly. A patrolman she didn't know stopped her at the police barrier. "I'm Randi Wade," she told him. "Rogoff asked me to come down."

"Oh," he said. He jerked a thumb back at the house. "He's inside, talking to the sister."

Randi found them in the living room. Rogoff saw her, nodded, waved her off, and went back to his questioning.

The other cops looked at her curiously, but no one said anything. The sister was a young-looking forty, slender and dark, with pale skin and a wild mane of black hair that fell half down her back. She sat on the edge of a sectional in a white silk teddy that left little to the imagination, seemingly just as indifferent to the cold air coming through the open door as she was to the lingering glances of the policemen.

One of the cops was taking some fingerprints off a shiny black grand piano in the corner of the room. Randi wandered over as he finished. The top of the piano was covered with framed photographs. One was a summer scene, taken somewhere along the river, two pretty girls in matching bikinis standing on either side of an intense young man. The girls were dappled with moisture, laughing for the photographer, long black hair hanging wetly down across wide smiles. The man, or boy, or whatever he was, was in a swimsuit, but you could tell he was bone dry. He was gaunt and sallow, and his blue eyes stared into the lens with a vacancy that was oddly disturbing. The girls could have been as young as eighteen or as old as twenty. One of them was the woman Rogoff was questioning, but Randi could not have told you which one. Twins. She glanced at the other photos, half-afraid she'd find a picture of Willie. Most of the faces she didn't recognize, but she was still looking them over when Rogoff came up behind her.

"Coroner's upstairs with the body," he said. "You can come up if you've got the stomach."

Randi turned away from the piano and nodded. "You learn anything from the sister?"

"She had a nightmare," he said. He started up the narrow staircase, Randi close behind him. "She says that as far back as she can remember, whenever she had bad dreams, she'd just cross the hall and crawl in bed with Zoe." They reached the landing. Rogoff put his hand on a glass doorknob, then paused. "What she found when she crossed the hall this time is going to keep her in nightmares for years to come."

He opened the door. Randi followed him inside.

The only light was a small bedside lamp, but the police photographer was moving around the room, snapping pictures of the red twisted thing on the bed. The light of his flash made the shadows leap and writhe, and Randi's stomach writhed with them. The smell of blood was overwhelming. She remembered summers long ago, hot July days when the wind blew from the south and the stink of the slaughterhouse settled over the city. But this was a thousand times worse.

The photographer was moving, flashing, moving, flashing. The world went from gray to red, then back to gray again. The coroner was bent over the corpse, her motions turned jerky and unreal by the strobing of the big flash gun. The white light blazed off the ceiling, and Randi looked up and saw the mirrors there. The dead woman's mouth gaped open, round and wide in a silent scream. He'd cut off her lips with her skin, and the inside of her mouth was no redder than the outside. Her face was gone, nothing left but the glistening wet ropes of muscle and here and there the pale glint of bone, but he'd left her her eyes. Large dark eyes, pretty eyes, sensuous, like her sister's downstairs. They were wide open, staring up in terror at the mirror on the ceiling. She'd been able to see every detail of what was being done to her. What had she found in the eyes of her reflection? Pain, terror, despair? A twin all her life, perhaps she'd found some strange comfort in her mirror image, even as her face and her flesh and her humanity had been cut away from her.

The flash went off again, and Randi caught the glint of metal at wrist and ankle. She closed her eyes for a second, steadied her breathing, and moved to the foot of the bed, where Rogoff was talking to the coroner.

"Same kind of chains?" he asked.

"You got it. And look at this." Coroner Cooney took the unlit cigar out of her mouth and pointed.

The chain looped tightly around the victim's ankle. When the flash went off again, Randi saw the other circles, dark, black lines, scored across the raw flesh and exposed nerves. It made her hurt just to look.

"She struggled," Rogoff suggested. "The chain chafed against her flesh."

"Chafing leaves you raw and bloody," Cooney replied. "What was done to her, you'd never notice chafing. That's a burn, Rogoff, a third-degree burn. Both wrists, both ankles, wherever the metal touched her. Sorenson had the same burn marks. Like the killer heated the chains until they were white-hot. Only the metal is cold now. Go on, touch it."

"No thanks," Rogoff said. "I'll take your word for it."

"Wait a minute," Randi said.

The coroner seemed to notice her for the first time. "What's she doing here?" she asked.

"It's a long story," Rogoff replied. "Randi, this is official police business, you'd better keep—"

Randi ignored him. "Joan Sorenson had the same kind of burn marks?" she asked Cooney. "At wrist and ankle, where the chains touched her skin?"

"That's right," Cooney said. "So what?"

"What are you trying to say?" Rogoff asked her.

She looked at him. "Joan Sorenson was a cripple. She had no use of her legs, no sensation at all below the waist. So why bother to chain her ankles?"

Rogoff stared at her for a long moment, then shook his head. He looked over to Cooney. The coroner shrugged. "Yeah. So. An interesting point, but what does it mean?"

She had no answer for them. She looked away, back at the bed, at the skinned, twisted, mutilated thing that had once been a pretty woman.

The photographer moved to a different angle, pressed his shutter. The flash went off again. The chain glittered in the light. Softly, Randi brushed a fingertip across the metal. She felt no heat. Only the cold, pale touch of silver.

The night was full of sounds and smells.

Willie had run wildly, blindly, a gray shadow streaking down black rain-slick streets, pushing himself harder and faster than he had ever pushed before, paying no attention to where he went, anywhere, nowhere, everywhere, just so it was far away from his apartment and the thing that waited there with death shining bright in its hand. He darted along grimy alleys, under loading docks, bounded over low chain-link fences. There was a cinder-block wall somewhere that almost stopped him, three leaps and he failed to clear it, but on the fourth try he got his front paws over the top, and his back legs kicked and scrabbled and pushed him over. He fell onto damp grass, rolled in the dirt, and then he was up and running again. The streets were almost empty of traffic, but as he streaked across one wide boulevard, a pickup truck appeared out of nowhere, speeding, and caught him in its lights. The sudden glare startled him; he froze for a long instant in the center of the street, and saw shock and terror on the driver's face. A horn blared as the pickup began to brake, went into a skid, and fishtailed across the divider.

By then Willie was gone.

He was moving through a residential section now, down quiet streets lined by neat two-story houses. Parked cars filled the narrow driveways, realtors' signs flapped in the wind, but the only lights were the streetlamps . . . and sometimes, when the clouds parted for a second, the pale circle of the moon. He caught the scent of dogs from some of the backyards, and from time to time he heard a wild, frenzied barking, and knew that they had smelled him too. Sometimes the barking woke owners and neighbors, and then lights would come on in the silent houses, and doors would open in the backyards, but by then Willie would be blocks away, still running.

Finally, when his legs were aching and his heart was thundering and his tongue lolled redly from his mouth, Willie crossed the railroad tracks, climbed a steep embankment, and came hard up against a ten-foot chain-link fence with barbed wire strung along the top. Beyond the fence was a wide, empty yard and a low brick building, windowless and vast, dark beneath the light of the moon. The smell of old blood was faint but unmistakable, and abruptly Willie knew where he was.

The old slaughterhouse. The pack, they'd called it, bankrupt and abandoned now for almost two years. He'd run a long way. At last he let himself stop and catch his breath. He was panting, and as he dropped to the ground by the fence, he began to shiver, cold despite his ragged coat of fur.

He was still wearing jockey shorts, Willie noticed after he'd rested a moment. He would have laughed, if he'd had the throat for it. He thought of the man in the pickup and wondered what he'd thought when Willie appeared in his headlights, a gaunt gray specter in a pair of white briefs, with glowing eyes as red as the pits of hell.

Willie twisted himself around and caught the elastic in his jaws. He tore at them, growling low in his throat, and after a brief struggle managed to rip them away. He slung them aside and lowered himself to the damp ground, his legs resting on his paws, his mouth half-open, his eyes wary, watchful. He let himself rest. He could hear distant traffic, a dog barking wildly a half-mile away, could smell rust and mold, the stench of diesel fumes, the cold scent of metal. Under it all was the slaughterhouse smell, faded but not gone, lingering, whispering to him of blood and death. It woke things inside him that were better left sleeping, and Willie could feel the hunger churning in his gut.

He could not ignore it, not wholly, but tonight he had other concerns, fears that were more important than his hunger. Dawn was only a few hours away, and he had nowhere to go. He could not go home, not until he knew it was safe again, until he had taken steps to protect himself. Without keys and clothes and money, the agency was closed to him too. He had to go somewhere, trust someone.

He thought of Blackstone, thought of Jonathan Harmon sitting by his fire, of Steven's dead blue eyes and scarred hands, of the old tower jutting up like a rotten black stake. Jonathan might be able to protect him, Jonathan with his strong walls and his spiked fence and all his talk of blood and iron.

But when he saw Jonathan in his mind's eye, the long white hair, the gold wolf's head cane, the veined arthritic hands twisting and grasping, then the growl rose unbidden in Willie's throat, and he knew Blackstone was not the answer.

Joanie was dead, and he did not know the others well enough, hardly knew all their names, didn't want to know them better.

So, in the end, like it or not, there was only Randi.

Willie got to his feet, weary now, unsteady. The wind shifted, sweeping across the yards and the runs, whispering to him of blood until his nostrils quivered. Willie threw back his head and howled, a long shuddering lonely call that rose and fell and went out through the cold night air until the dogs began to bark for blocks around. Then, once again, he began to run.

———

ROGOFF GAVE HER A LIFT HOME. DAWN WAS JUST STARTING TO break when he pulled his old black Ford up to the front of her six-flat. As she opened the door, he shifted into neutral and looked over at her. "I'm not going to insist right now," he said, "but it might be that I need to know the name of your client. Sleep on it. Maybe you'll decide to tell me."

"Maybe I can't," Randi said. "Attorney-client privilege, remember?"

Rogoff gave her a tired smile. "When you sent me to the courthouse, I had a look at your file too. You never went to law school."

"No?" She smiled back. "Well, I meant to. Doesn't that count for something?" She shrugged. "I'll sleep on it, we can talk tomorrow." She got out, closed the door, moved away from the car. Rogoff shifted into drive, but Randi turned back before he could pull away. "Hey, Rogoff, you have a first name?"

"Mike," he said.

"See you tomorrow, Mike."

He nodded and pulled away just as the streetlamps began to go out. Randi walked up the stoop, fumbling for her key.

"Randi!"

She stopped, looked around. "Who's there?"

"Willie." The voice was louder this time. "Down here by the garbage cans."

Randi leaned over the stoop and saw him. He was crouched down low, surrounded by trash bins, shivering in the morning chill. "You're naked," she said.

"Somebody tried to kill me last night. I made it out. My clothes didn't. I've been here an hour, not that I'm complaining mind you, but

I think I have pneumonia and my balls are frozen solid. I'll never be able to have children now. Where the fuck have you been?"

"There was another murder. Same m.o."

Willie shook so violently that the garbage cans rattled together. "Jesus," he said, his voice gone weak. "Who?"

"Her name was Zoe Anders."

Willie flinched. "Fuck fuck fuck," he said. He looked back up at Randi. She could see the fear in his eyes, but he asked anyway. "What about Amy?"

"Her sister?" Randi said. He nodded. "In shock, but fine. She had a nightmare." She paused a moment. "So you knew Zoe too. Like Sorenson?"

"No. Not like Joanie." He looked at her wearily. "Can we go in?"

She nodded and opened the door. Willie looked so grateful she thought he was about to lick her hand.

THE UNDERWEAR WAS HER EX-HUSBAND'S, AND IT WAS TOO BIG. The pink bathrobe was Randi's, and it was too small. But the coffee was just right, and it was warm in here, and Willie felt bone-tired and nervous but glad to be alive, especially when Randi put the plate down in front of him. She'd scrambled the eggs up with cheddar cheese and onion and done up a rasher of bacon on the side, and it smelled like nirvana. He fell to eagerly.

"I think I've figured out something," she said. She sat down across from him.

"Good," he said. "The eggs, I mean. That is, whatever you figured out, that's good too, but Jesus, I *needed* these eggs. You wouldn't believe how hungry you get—" He stopped suddenly, stared down at the scrambled eggs, and reflected on what an idiot he was, but Randi hadn't noticed. Willie reached for a slice of bacon, bit off the end. "Crisp," he said. "Good."

"I'm going to tell you," Randi said, as if he hadn't spoken at all. "I've got to tell somebody, and you've known me long enough so I don't think you'll have me committed. You may laugh." She scowled at him. "If you laugh, you're back out in the street, minus the boxer shorts and the bathrobe."

"I won't laugh," Willie said. He didn't think he'd have much difficulty not laughing. He felt rather apprehensive. He stopped eating.

Randi took a deep breath and looked him in the eye. She had very lovely eyes, Willie thought. "I think my father was killed by a werewolf," she said seriously, without blinking.

"Oh, Jesus," Willie said. He didn't laugh. A very large invisible anaconda wrapped itself around his chest and began to squeeze. "I," he said, "I, I, I." Nothing was coming in or out. He pushed back from the table, knocking over the chair, and ran for the bathroom. He locked himself in and turned on the shower full blast, twisting the hot tap all the way around. The bathroom began to fill up with steam. It wasn't nearly as good as a blast from his inhaler, but it did beat suffocating. By the time the steam was really going good, Willie was on his knees, gasping like a man trying to suck an elephant through a straw. Finally he began to breathe again.

He stayed on his knees for a long time, until the spray from the shower had soaked through his robe and his underwear and his face was flushed and red. Then he crawled across the tiled floor, turned off the shower, and got unsteadily to his feet. The mirror above the sink was all fogged up. Willie wiped it off with a towel and peered in at himself. He looked like shit. Wet shit. Hot wet shit. He felt worse. He tried to dry himself off, but the steam and the shower spray had gone everywhere and the towels were as damp as he was. He heard Randi moving around outside, opening and closing drawers. He wanted to go out and face her, but not like this. A man has to have some pride. For a moment he just wanted to be home in bed with his Primatene on the end table, until he remembered that his bedroom had been occupied the last time he'd been there.

"Are you ever coming out?" Randi asked.

"Yeah," Willie said, but it was so weak that he doubted she heard him. He straightened and adjusted the frilly pink robe. Underneath the undershirt looked as though he'd been competing in a wet T-shirt contest. He sighed, unlocked the door, and exited. The cold air gave him goose pimples.

Randi was seated at the table again. Willie went back to his place. "Sorry," he said. "Asthma attack."

"I noticed," Randi replied. "Stress related, aren't they?"

"Sometimes."

"Finish your eggs," she urged. "They're getting cold."

"Yeah," Willie said, figuring he might as well, since it would give him something to do while he figured out what to tell her. He picked up his fork.

It was like the time he'd grabbed a dirty pot that had been sitting on top of his hotplate since the night before and realized too late that he'd never turned the hotplate off. Willie shrieked and the fork clattered to the table and bounced, once, twice, three times. It landed in front of Randi. He sucked on his fingers. They were already starting to turn red. Randi looked at him very calmly and picked up the fork. She held it, stroked it with her thumb, touched its prongs thoughtfully to her lip. "I brought out the good silver while you were in the bathroom," she said. "Solid sterling. It's been in the family for generations."

His fingers hurt like hell. "Oh, Jesus. You got any butter? Oleo, lard, I don't care, anything will..." He stopped when her hand went under the table and came out again holding a gun. From where Willie sat, it looked like a very big gun.

"Pay attention, Willie. Your fingers are the least of your worries. I realize you're in pain, so I'll give you a minute or two to collect your thoughts and try to tell me why I shouldn't blow off your fucking head right here and now." She cocked the hammer with her thumb.

Willie just stared at her. He looked pathetic, like a half-drowned puppy. For one terrible moment Randi thought he was going to have another asthma attack. She felt curiously calm, not angry or afraid or even nervous, but she didn't think she had it in her to shoot a man in the back as he ran for the bathroom, even if he was a werewolf.

Thankfully, Willie spared her that decision. "You don't want to shoot me," he said, with remarkable aplomb under the circumstances. "It's bad manners to shoot your friends. You'll make a hole in the bathrobe."

"I never liked that bathrobe anyway. I hate pink."

"If you're really so hot to kill me, you'd stand a better chance with the fork," Willie said.

"So you admit that you're a werewolf?"

"A lycanthrope," Willie corrected. He sucked at his burnt fingers again and looked at her sideways. "So sue me. It's a medical condition.

I got allergies, I got asthma, I got a bad back, and I got lycanthropy, is it my fault? I didn't kill your father. I never killed anyone. I ate half a pit bull once, but can you blame me?" His voice turned querulous. "If you want to shoot me, go ahead and try. Since when do you carry a gun anyway? I thought all that shit about private eyes stuffing heat was strictly television."

"The phrase is *packing* heat, and it is. I only bring mine out for special occasions. My father was carrying it when he died."

"Didn't do him much good, did it?" Willie said softly.

Randi considered that for a moment. "What would happen if I pulled the trigger?" The gun was getting heavy, but her hand was steady.

"I'd try to change. I don't think I'd make it, but I'd have to try. A couple bullets in the head at this range, while I'm still human, yeah, that'd probably do the job. But you don't want to miss and you *really* don't want to wound me. Once I'm changed, it's a whole different ball game."

"My father emptied his gun on the night he was killed," Randi said thoughtfully.

Willie studied his hand and winced. "Oh fuck," he said. "I'm getting a blister."

Randi put the gun on the table and went to the kitchen to get him a stick of butter. He accepted it from her gratefully. She glanced toward the window as he treated his burns. "The sun's up," she said, "I thought werewolves only changed at night, during the full moon?"

"Lycanthropes," Willie said. He flexed his fingers, sighed. "That full-moon shit was all invented by some screenwriter for Universal; go look at your literature, we change at will, day, night, full moon, new moon, makes no difference. Sometimes I *feel* more like changing during the full moon, some kind of hormonal thing, but more like getting horny than going on the rag, if you know what I mean." He grabbed his coffee. It was cold by now, but that didn't stop Willie from emptying the cup. "I shouldn't be telling you all this, fuck, Randi, I like you, you're a friend, I care about you, you should only forget this whole morning, believe me, it's healthier."

"Why?" she said bluntly. She wasn't about to forget anything. "What's going to happen to me if I don't? Are you going to rip my throat out? Should I forget Joan Sorenson and Zoe Anders too? How about Roy Helander and all those missing kids? *Am I supposed to forget what happened to my father?*" She stopped for a moment, lowered her voice. "You came to me for help, Willie, and pardon, but you sure as hell look as though you still need it."

Willie looked at her across the table with a morose hangdog expression on his long face. "I don't know whether I want to kiss you or slap you," he finally admitted. "Shit, you're right, you know too much already." He stood up. "I got to get into my own clothes, this wet underwear is giving me pneumonia. Call a cab, we'll go check out my place, talk. You got a coat?"

"Take the Burberry," Randi said. "It's in the closet." The coat was even bigger on him than it had been on Randi, but it beat the pink bathrobe. He looked almost human as he emerged from the closet, fussing with the belt. Randi was rummaging in the silver drawer. She found a large carving knife, the one her grandfather used to use on Thanksgiving, and slid it through the belt of her jeans. Willie looked at it nervously. "Good idea," he finally said, "but take the gun too."

THE CAB DRIVER WAS THE QUIET TYPE. THE DRIVE ACROSS TOWN passed in awkward silence. Randi paid him while Willie climbed out to check the doors. It was a blustery overcast day, and the river looked gray and choppy as it slapped against the pier.

Willie kicked his front door in a fit of pique, and vanished down the alley. Randi waited by the pier and watched the cab drive off. A few minutes later Willie was back, looking disgusted. "This is ridiculous," he said. "The back door hasn't been opened in years, you'd need a hammer and chisel just to knock through the rust. The loading docks are bolted down and chained with the mother of all padlocks on the chains. And the front door... there's a spare set of keys in my car, but even if we got those the police bar can only be lifted from inside. So how the hell did it get in, I ask you?"

Randi looked at the brewery's weathered brick walls appraisingly. They looked pretty solid to her, and the second-floor windows were a good twenty feet off street level. She walked around the side to take a look down the alley. "There's a window broken," she said.

"That was me getting out," Willie said, "not my nocturnal caller getting in."

Randi had already figured out that much from the broken glass all over the cobblestones. "Right now I'm more concerned about how *we're* going to get in." She pointed. "If we move that dumpster a few feet to the left and climb on top, and you climb on my shoulders, I think you might be able to hoist yourself in."

Willie considered that. "What if it's still in there?"

"What?" Randi said.

"Whatever was after me last night. If I hadn't jumped through that window, it'd be me without a skin this morning, and believe me, I'm cold enough as is." He looked at the window, at the dumpster, and back at the window. "Fuck," he said, "we can't stand here all day. But I've got a better idea. Help me roll the dumpster away from the wall a little."

Randi didn't understand, but she did as Willie suggested. They left the dumpster in the center of the alley, directly opposite the broken window. Willie nodded and began unbelting the coat she'd lent him. "Turn around," he told her. "I don't want you freaking out. I've got to get naked and your carnal appetites might get the best of you."

Randi turned around. The temptation to glance over her shoulder was irresistible. She heard the coat fall to the ground. Then she heard something else . . . soft padding steps, like a dog. She turned. He'd circled all the way down to the end of the alley. Her ex-husband's old underwear lay puddled across the cobblestones atop the Burberry coat. Willie came streaking back toward the brewery building speed. He was, Randi noticed, not a very prepossessing wolf. His fur was a dirty gray-brown color, kind of mangy, his rear looked too large and his legs too thin, and there was something ungainly about the way he ran. He put on a final burst of speed, leapt on top of the dumpster, bounded off the metal lid, and flew through the shattered window, breaking more glass as he went. Randi heard a loud *thump* from inside the bedroom.

She went around to the front. A few moments later, the locks began to unlock, one by one, and Willie opened the heavy steel door. He was wearing his own bathrobe, a red tartan flannel, and his hand was full of keys. "Come on," he said. "No sign of night visitors. I put on some water for tea."

"The fucker must have crawled out of the toilet," Willie said. "I don't see any other way he could have gotten in."

Randi stood in front of what remained of his bedroom door. She studied the shattered wood, ran her finger lightly across one long, jagged splinter, then knelt to look at the floor. "Whatever it was, it was strong. Look at these gouges in the wood, look at how sharp and clean they are. You don't do that with a fist. Claws, maybe. More likely some kind of knife. And take a look at this." She gestured toward the brass doorknob, which lay on the floor amidst a bunch of kindling.

Willie bent to pick it up.

"Don't touch," she said, grabbing his arm. "Just look."

He got down on one knee. At first he didn't notice anything. But when he leaned close, he saw how the brass was scored and scraped.

"Something sharp," Randi said, "and hard." She stood. "When you first heard the sounds, what direction were they coming from?"

Willie thought for a moment. "It was hard to tell," he said. "Toward the back, I think."

Randi walked back. All along the hall, the doors were closed. She studied the banister at the top of the stairs, then moved on, and began opening and closing doors. "Come here," she said, at the fourth door.

Willie trotted down the hall. Randi had the door ajar. The knob on the hall side was fine; the knob on the inside displayed the same kind of scoring they'd seen on his bedroom door. Willie was aghast. "But this is the *men's room*," he said. "You mean it *did* come out of the toilet? I'll never shit again."

"It came out of this room," Randi said. "I don't know about the toilet." She went in and looked around. There wasn't much to look at. Two toilet stalls, two urinals, two sinks with a long mirror above them and antique brass soap dispensers beside the water taps, a paper towel dispenser, Willie's towels and toiletries. No window. Not even a small frosted-glass window. No window at all.

Down the hall the teakettle began to whistle. Randi looked thoughtful as they walked back to the living room.

"Joan Sorenson died behind a locked door, and the killer got to Zoe Anders without waking her sister right across the hall."

"The fucking thing can come and go as it pleases," Willie said. The idea gave him the creeps. He glanced around nervously as he got out the teabags, but there was nobody there but him and Randi.

"Except it can't," Randi said. "With Sorenson and Anders, there was no damage, no sign of a break-in, nothing but a corpse. But with you, the killer was stopped by something as simple as a locked door."

"Not stopped," Willie said, "just slowed down a little." He repressed a shudder and brought the tea over to his coffee table.

"Did he get the right Anders sister?" she asked.

Willie stood there stupidly for a moment holding the kettle poised over the cups. "What do you mean?"

"You've got identical twins sharing the same house. Let's presume it's a house the killer's never visited before. Somehow he gains entry, and he chains, murders, and flays only *one* of them, without even waking the other." Randi smiled up at him sweetly. "You can't tell them apart by sight, he probably didn't know which room was which, so the question is, did he get the werewolf?"

It was nice to know that she wasn't infallible. "Yes," he said, "and no. They were twins, Randi. Both lycanthropes." She looked honestly surprised. "How did you know?" he asked her.

"Oh, the chains," she said negligently. Her mind was far away, gnawing at the puzzle. "Silver chains. She was burned wherever they'd touched her flesh. And Joan Sorenson was a werewolf too, of course. She was crippled, yes . . . but only as a human, not after her transformation. That's why her legs were chained, to hold her if she changed." She looked at Willie with a baffled expression on her face. "It doesn't make sense, to kill one and leave the other untouched. Are you sure that Amy Anders is a werewolf too?"

"A lycanthrope," he said. "Yes. Definitely. They were even harder to tell apart as wolves. At least when they were human they dressed differently. Amy likes white lace, frills, that kind of stuff, and Zoe was into leather." There was a cut-glass ashtray in the center of the coffee table filled with Willie's private party mix: aspirin, Allerest, and Tums. He took a handful of pills and swallowed them.

"Look, before we go on with this, I want one card on the table," Randi said.

For once he was ahead of her. "If I knew who killed your father, I'd tell you, but I don't, I was in the service, overseas. I vaguely remember something in the *Courier,* but to tell the truth I'd forgotten all about it until you threw it at me last night. What can I tell you?" He shrugged.

"Don't bullshit me, Willie. My father was killed by a werewolf. You're a werewolf. You must know something."

"Hey, try substituting *Jew* or *diabetic* or *bald man* for werewolf in that statement, and see how much sense it makes. I'm not saying you're wrong about your father because you're not; it fits, it all fits, everything from the condition of the body to the empty gun, but even if you buy that much, then you got to ask *which* werewolf."

"How many of you *are* there?" Randi asked incredulously.

"Damned if I know," Willie said. "What do you think, we get together for a lodge meeting every time the moon is full? The purebloods, hell, not many, the pack's been getting pretty thin these last few generations. But there's lots of mongrels like me, half-breeds, quarter-breeds, what have you, the old families had their share of bastards. Some can work the change, some can't. I've heard of a few who change one day and never do manage to change back. And that's just from the old bloodlines, never mind the ones like Joanie."

"You mean Joanie was different?"

Willie gave her a reluctant nod. "You've seen the movies. You get bitten by a werewolf, you turn into a werewolf; that is, assuming there's enough of you left to turn into anything except a cadaver." She nodded, and he went on. "Well, that part's true, or partly true, it doesn't happen as often as it once did. Guy gets bit nowadays, he runs to a doctor, gets the wound cleaned and treated with antiseptic, gets his rabies shots and his tetanus shots and his penicillin and fuck-all knows what else, and he's fine. The wonders of modern medicine."

Willie hesitated briefly, looking in her eyes, those lovely eyes, wondering if she'd understand, and finally he plunged ahead. "Joanie was such a good kid, it broke my heart to see her in that chair. One night she told me that the hardest thing of all was realizing that she'd never know what it felt like to make love. She'd been a virgin when they hit that truck. We'd had a few drinks, she was crying, and... well, I couldn't take it. I told her what I was and what I could do for her, she didn't believe a word of it, so I had to show her. I bit her leg, she couldn't feel a damned thing down there anyway, I bit her and I held the bite for a long time, worried it around good. Afterwards I nursed her myself. No doctors, no antiseptic, no rabies vaccine. We're talking major-league infection here, there was a day or two when her fever was running so high I thought maybe I'd killed her; her leg had turned nearly black, you could see the stuff going up her veins. I got to admit it was pretty gross, I'm in no hurry to try it again, but it worked. The fever broke and Joanie changed."

"You weren't just friends," Randi said with certainty. "You were lovers."

"Yeah," he said. "As wolves. I guess I look sexier in fur. I couldn't even begin to keep up with her, though. Joanie was a pretty active wolf. We're talking almost every night here."

"As a human, she was still crippled," Randi said.

Willie nodded, held up his hand. "See." The burns were still there, and a blood blister had formed on his index finger. "Once or twice the change has saved my life, when my asthma got so bad I thought I was going to suffocate. That kind of thing doesn't cross over, but it's sure as hell waiting for you when you cross back. Sometimes you even get nasty surprises. Catch a bullet as a wolf and it's nothing, a sting and a slap, heals up right away, but you can pay for it when you change into human form, especially if you change too soon and the damn thing gets infected. And silver will burn the shit out of you no matter what form you're in. LBJ was my favorite president, just *loved* them cupro-nickel-sandwich quarters."

Randi stood up. "This is all a little overwhelming. Do you *like* being a werewolf?"

"A lycanthrope." Willie shrugged. "I don't know, do you like being a woman? It's what I am."

Randi crossed the room and stared out his window at the river.

"I'm very confused," she said. "I look at you and you're my friend Willie. I've known you for years. Only you're a werewolf too. I've been telling myself that werewolves don't exist since I was twelve, and now I find out the city is full of them. Only someone or something is killing them, flaying them. Should I care? Why should I care?" She ran a hand through her tangled hair. "We both know that Roy Helander didn't kill those kids. My father knew it too. He kept pressing, and one night he was lured to the stockyards and some kind of animal tore out his throat. Every time I think of that I think maybe I ought to find this werewolf-killer and sign up to help him. Then I look at you again." She turned and looked at him. "And damn it, you're *still* my friend."

She looked as though she was going to cry. Willie had never seen her cry and he didn't want to. He hated it when they cried. "Remember when I first offered you a job, and you wouldn't take it, because you thought all collection agents were pricks?"

She nodded.

"Lycanthropes are skinchangers. We turn into wolves. Yeah, we're carnivores, you got it, you don't meet many vegetarians in the pack, but there's meat and there's meat. You won't find nearly as many rats around here as you will in other cities this size. What I'm saying is the skin may change, but what you do is still up to the person inside. So stop thinking about werewolves and werewolf-killers and start thinking about murderers, 'cause that's what we're talking about."

Randi crossed the room and sat back down. "I hate to admit it, but you're making sense."

"I'm good in bed too," Willie said with a grin. The ghost of a smile crossed her face.

"Fuck you."

"Exactly my suggestion. What kind of underwear are you wearing?"

"Never mind my underwear," she said. "Do you have any ideas about these murderers? Past *or* present?"

Sometimes Randi had a one-track mind, Willie thought; unfortunately, it never seemed to be the track that led under the sheets. "Jonathan told me about an old legend," he said.

"Jonathan?" she said.

"Jonathan Harmon, yeah, that one, old blood and iron, the *Courier,* Blackstone, the pack, the founding family, all of it."

"Wait a minute. He's a were—a lycanthrope?"

Willie nodded. "Yeah, leader of the pack, he—"

Randi leapt ahead of him. "And it's hereditary?"

He saw where she was going. "Yes, but—"

"Steven Harmon is mentally disturbed," Randi interrupted. "His family keeps it out of the papers, but they can't stop the whispering. Violent episodes, strange doctors coming and going at Blackstone, shock treatments. He's some kind of pain freak, isn't he?"

Willie sighed. "Yeah. Ever see his hands? The palms and fingers are covered with silver burns. Once I saw him close his hand around a silver cartwheel and hold it there until smoke started to come out between his fingers. It burned a big round hole right in the center of his palm." He shuddered. "Yeah, Steven's a freak all right, and he's strong enough to rip your arm out of your socket and beat you to death with it, but he didn't kill your father, he couldn't have."

"Says you," she said.

"He didn't kill Joanie or Zoe either. They weren't just murdered, Randi. They were skinned. That's where the legend comes in. The word is *skinchangers,* remember? What if the power was *in* the skin? So you catch a werewolf, flay it, slip into the bloody skin...and change."

Randi was staring at him with a sick look on her face. "Does it really work that way?"

"Someone thinks so."

"Who?"

"Someone who's been thinking about werewolves for a long time. Someone who's gone way past obsession into full-fledged psychopathy. Someone who thinks he saw a werewolf once, who thinks werewolves done him wrong, who hates them, wants to hurt them, wants revenge...but maybe also, down deep, someone who wants to know what's it like."

"Roy Helander," she said.

"Maybe if we could find this damned secret hideout in the woods, we'd know for sure."

Randi stood up. "I wracked my brains for hours. We could poke around a few of the city parks some, but I'm not sanguine on our prospects. No. I want to know more about these legends, and I want to look at Steven with my own eyes. Get your car, Willie. We're going to pay a visit to Blackstone."

He'd been afraid she was going to say something like that. He reached out and grabbed another handful of his party mix. "Oh, Jesus," he said, crunching down on a mouthful of pills. "This isn't *The Addams Family,* you know. Jonathan is for real."

"So am I," said Randi, and Willie knew the cause was lost.

IT WAS RAINING AGAIN BY THE TIME THEY REACHED COURIER Square. Willie waited in the car while Randi went inside the gun-smith's. Twenty minutes later, when she came back out, she found him snoring behind the wheel. At least he'd had the sense to lock the doors of his mammoth old Cadillac. She tapped on the glass, and he sat right up and stared at her for a moment without recognition. Then he woke up, leaned over, and unlocked the door on the passenger side. Randi slid beside him.

"How'd it go?"

"They don't get much call for silver bullets, but they know some-one upstate who does custom work for collectors," Randi said in a disgusted tone of voice.

"You don't sound too happy about it."

"I'm not. You wouldn't believe what they're going to charge me for a box of silver bullets, never mind that it's going to take two weeks. It was going to take a month, but I raised the ante." She looked glumly out the rain-streaked window. A torrent of gray water rushed down the gutter, carrying its flotilla of cigarette butts and scraps of yesterday's newspaper.

"Two weeks?" Willie turned the ignition and put the barge in gear. "Hell, we'll both probably be dead in two weeks. Just as well, the whole idea of silver bullets makes me nervous."

They crossed the Square, past the Castle marquee and the Courier Building, and headed up Central, the windshield wipers clicking back and forth rhythmically. Willie hung a left on 13th and headed toward the bluff while Randi took out her father's revolver, opened the cylinder, and checked to see that it was fully loaded. Willie watched her out of the corner of his eye as he drove. "Waste of time," he said. "Guns don't kill werewolves, werewolves kill werewolves."

"Lycanthropes," Randi reminded him.

He grinned and for a moment looked almost like the man she'd shared an office with, a long time ago.

Both of them grew visibly more intense as they drove down 13th, the Caddy's big wheels splashing through the puddles. They were still a block away when she saw the little car crawling down the bluff, white against the dark stone. A moment later, she saw the lights, flashing red-and-blue.

Willie saw them too. He slammed on the brakes, lost traction, and had to steer wildly to avoid slamming into a parked car as he fishtailed. His forehead was beading with sweat when he finally brought the car to a stop, and Randi didn't think it was from the near collision. "Oh, Jesus," he said, "oh, Jesus, not Harmon too, I don't *believe* it." He began to wheeze, and fumbled in his pocket for an inhaler.

"Wait here, I'll check it out," Randi told him. She got out, turned up the collar of her coat, and walked the rest of the way, to where 13th dead-ended flush against the bluff. The coroner's wagon was parked amidst three police cruisers. Randi arrived at the same time as the cable car. Rogoff was the first one out. Behind him she saw Cooney, the police photographer, and two uniforms carrying a body bag. It must have gotten pretty crowded on the way down.

"You." Rogoff seemed surprised to see her. Strands of black hair were plastered to his forehead by the rain.

"Me," Randi agreed. The plastic of the body bag was wet, and the uniforms were having trouble with it. One of them lost his footing as he stepped down, and Randi thought she saw something shift inside the bag. "It doesn't fit the pattern," she said to Rogoff. "The other killings have all been at night."

Rogoff took her by the arm and drew her away, gently but firmly. "You don't want to look at this one, Randi."

There was something in his tone that made her look at him hard. "Why not? It can't be any worse than Zoe Anders, can it? Who's in the bag, Rogoff? The father or the son?"

"Neither one," he said. He glanced back behind them, up toward the top of the bluff, and Randi found herself following his gaze. Nothing was visible of Blackstone but the high wrought iron fence that surrounded the estate. "This time his luck ran out on him. The dogs got to him first. Cooney says the scent of blood off of... of what he was wearing...well, it must have driven them wild. They tore him to pieces, Randi." He put his hand on her shoulder, as if to comfort her.

"No," Randi said. She felt numb, dazed.

"Yes," he insisted. "It's over. And believe me, it's not something you want to see."

She backed away from him. They were loading the body in the rear of the coroner's wagon while Sylvia Cooney supervised the operation, smoking her cigar in the rain. Rogoff tried to touch her again, but she whirled away from him, and ran to the wagon. "Hey!" Cooney said.

The body was on the tailgate, half in and half out of the wagon. Randi reached for the zipper on the body bag. One of the cops grabbed her arm. She shoved him aside and unzipped the bag. His face was half gone. His right cheek and ear and part of his jaw had been torn away, devoured right down to the bone. What features he had left were obscured by blood.

Someone tried to pull her away from the tailgate. She spun and kicked him in the balls, then turned back to the body and grabbed it under the arms and pulled. The inside of the body bag was slick with blood. The corpse slid loose of the plastic sheath like a banana squirting out of its skin and fell into the street. Rain washed down over it, and the runoff in the gutter turned pink, then red. A hand, or part of a hand, fell out of the bag almost like an afterthought. Most of the arm was gone, and Randi could see bones peeking through, and places where huge hunks of flesh had been torn out of his thigh, shoulder, and torso. He was naked, but between his legs was nothing but a raw red wound where his genitalia had been.

Something was fastened around his neck, and knotted beneath his chin. Randi leaned forward to touch it, and drew back when she saw his face. The rain had washed it clean. He had one eye left, a green eye, open and staring. The rain pooled in the socket and ran down his cheek. Roy had grown gaunt to the point of emaciation, with a week's growth of beard, but his long hair was still the same color, the color he'd shared with all his brothers and sisters, that muddy Helander blond.

Something was knotted under his chin, a long twisted cloak of some kind; it had gotten all tangled when he fell. Randi was trying to straighten it when they caught her by both arms and dragged her away bodily. "No," she said wildly. "What was he wearing? What was he wearing, damn you! I have to see!" No one answered. Rogoff had her right arm prisoned in a grip that felt like steel. She fought him wildly, kicking and shouting, but he held her until the hysteria had passed, and then held her some more as she leaned against his chest, sobbing.

She didn't quite know when Willie had come up, but suddenly there he was. He took her away from Rogoff and led her back to his Cadillac, and they sat inside, silent, as first the coroner's wagon and then the police cruisers drove off one by one. She was covered with blood. Willie gave her some aspirin from a bottle he kept in his glove compartment. She tried to swallow it, but her throat was raw and she wound up gagging it back up. "It's all right," he told her, over and over. "It wasn't your father, Randi. Listen to me, please, it *wasn't your father*!"

"It was Roy Helander," Randi said to him at last. "And he was wearing Joanie's skin."

WILLIE DROVE HER HOME; SHE WAS IN NO SHAPE TO CONFRONT Jonathan Harmon or anybody. She'd calmed down, but the hysteria was still there, just under the surface, he could see it in the eyes, hear it in her voice. If that wasn't enough, she kept telling him the same thing, over and over. "It was Roy Helander," she'd say, like he didn't know, "and he was wearing Joanie's skin."

Willie found her keys and helped her upstairs to her apartment. Inside, he made her take a couple of sleeping pills from the all-purpose pharmaceutical in his glove box, then turned down the bed and undressed her. He figured if anything would snap her back to herself, it would be his fingers on the buttons of her blouse, but she just smiled at him, vacant and dreamy, and told him that it was Roy Helander and he was wearing Joanie's skin. The big silver knife jammed through her belt loops gave him pause. He finally unzipped her fly, undid her buckle, and yanked off the jeans, knife and all. She didn't wear panties. He'd always suspected as much.

When Randi was finally in bed asleep, Willie went back to her bathroom and threw up.

Afterward he made himself a gin-and-tonic to wash the taste of vomit out of his mouth, and went and sat alone in her living room in one of her red velvet chairs. He'd had even less sleep than Randi these past few nights, and he felt as though he might drift off at any moment, but he knew somehow that it was important not to. It was Roy Helander and he was wearing Joanie's skin. So it was over, he was safe.

He remembered the way his door shook last night, a solid wood door, and it split like so much cheap paneling. Behind it was something dark and powerful, something that left scars on brass doorknobs and showed up in places it had no right to be. Willie didn't know what had been on the other side of his door, but somehow he didn't think that the gaunt, wasted, half-eaten travesty of a man he'd seen on 13th Street quite fit the bill. He'd believe that his nocturnal visitor had been Roy Helander, with or without Joanie's skin, about the same time he'd believe that the man had been eaten by dogs. *Dogs!* How long did Jonathan expect to get away with that shit? Still, he couldn't blame him, not with Zoe and Joanie dead, and Helander trying to sneak into Blackstone dressed in a human skin.

. . . there are things that hunt the hunters.

Willie picked up the phone and dialed Blackstone.

"Hello." The voice was flat, affectless, the voice of someone who cared about nothing and no one, not even himself.

"Hello, Steven," Willie said quietly. He was about to ask for Jonathan when a strange sort of madness took hold of him, and he heard himself say, "Did you watch? Did you see what Jonathan did to him, Steven? Did it get you off?"

The silence on the other end of the line went on for ages. Sometimes Steven Harmon simply forgot how to talk. But not this time. "Jonathan didn't do him. I did. It was easy. I could smell him coming through the woods. He never even saw me. I came around behind him and pinned him down and bit off his ear. He wasn't very strong at all. After a while he changed into a man, and then he was all slippery, but it didn't matter, I—"

Someone took the phone away. "Hello, who is this?" Jonathan's voice said from the receiver.

Willie hung up. He could always call back later. Let Jonathan sweat awhile, wondering who it had been on the other end of the line. "After a while he changed into a man," Willie repeated aloud. Steven did it himself. Steven couldn't do it himself. Could he? "Oh Jesus," Willie said.

Somewhere far away, a phone was ringing.

Randi rolled over in her bed. "Joanie's skin," she muttered groggily in low, half-intelligible syllables. She was naked, with the blankets tangled around her. The room was pitch dark. The phone rang again. She sat up, a sheet curled around her neck. The room was cold, and her head pounded. She ripped loose the sheet, threw it aside. Why was she naked? What the hell was going on? The phone rang again and her machine cut in. "This is AAA–Wade Investigations, Randi Wade speaking. I can't talk right now, but you can leave a message at the tone, and I'll get back to you."

Randi reached out and speared the phone just in time for the *beep* to sound in her ear. She winced. "It's me," she said. "I'm here. What time is it? Who's this?"

"Randi, are you all right? It's Uncle Joe." Joe Urquhart's gruff voice was a welcome relief. "Rogoff told me what happened, and I was very concerned about you. I've been trying to reach you for hours."

"Hours?" She looked at the clock. It was past midnight. "I've been asleep. I think." The last she remembered, it had been daylight and she and Willie had been driving down 13th on their way to Blackstone to . . .

It was Roy Helander and he was wearing Joanie's skin.

"Randi, what's wrong? You sure you're okay? You sound wretched. Damn it, *say* something."

"I'm here," she said. She pushed hair back out of her eyes. Someone had opened her window, and the air was frigid on her bare skin. "I'm fine," she said. "I just...I was asleep. It shook me up, that's all. I'll be fine."

"If you say so." Urquhart sounded dubious.

Willie must have brought her home and put her to bed, she thought. So where was he? She couldn't imagine that he'd just dump her and then take off, that wasn't like Willie.

"Pay attention," Urquhart said gruffly. "Have you heard a word I've said?"

She hadn't. "I'm sorry. I'm just...disoriented, that's all. It's been a strange day."

"I need to see you," Urquhart said. His voice had taken on a sudden urgency. "Right away. I've been going over the reports on Roy Helander and his victims. There's something out of place, something disturbing. And the more I look at these case files and Cooney's autopsy report, the more I keep thinking about Frank, about what happened that night." He hesitated. "I don't know how to say this. All these years...I only wanted the best for you, but I wasn't...wasn't completely honest with you."

"Tell me," she said. Suddenly she was a lot more awake.

"Not over the phone. I need to see you face-to-face, to show it to you. I'll swing by and get you. Can you be ready in fifteen minutes?"

"Ten," Randi said.

She hung up, hopped out of bed and opened the bedroom door. "Willie?" she called out. There was no answer. "Willie!" she repeated more loudly. Nothing. She turned on the lights, padded barefoot down the hall, expecting to find him snoring away on her sofa. But the living room was empty.

Her hands were sandpaper dry, and when she looked down she saw that they were covered with old blood. Her stomach heaved. She found the clothes she'd been wearing in a heap on the bedroom floor. They were brown and crusty with dried blood as well. Randi started the shower and stood under the water for a good five minutes, running it so hot that it burned the way that silver fork must have burned in Willie's hand. The blood washed off, the water turning faintly pink as it whirled away and down. She toweled off thoroughly, and found a warm flannel shirt and a fresh pair of jeans. She didn't bother with her hair; the rain would wet it down again soon enough. But she made a point of finding her father's gun and sliding the long silver carving knife through the belt loop of her jeans.

As she bent to pick up the knife, Randi saw the square of white paper on the floor by her end table. She must have knocked it off when she'd reached for the phone.

She picked it up, opened it. It was covered with Willie's familiar scrawl, a page of hurried, dense scribbling. *I got to go, you're in no condition,* it began. *Don't go anywhere or talk to anyone. Roy Helander wasn't sneaking in to kill Harmon, I finally figured it out. The damned Harmon family secret that's no secret at all, I should have twigged, Steven—*

That was as far as she'd gotten when the doorbell rang.

WILLIE HUGGED THE GROUND TWO-THIRDS OF THE WAY UP THE bluff, the rain coming down around him and his heart pounding in his chest as he clung to the tracks. Somehow the grade didn't seem nearly as steep when you were riding the cable car as it did now. He glanced behind him, and saw 13th Street far below. It made him dizzy. He wouldn't even have gotten this far if it hadn't been for the tracks. Where the slope grew almost vertical, he'd been able to scrabble up from tie to tie, using them like rungs on a ladder. His hands were full of splinters, but it beat trying to crawl up the wet rock, clinging to ferns for dear life.

Of course, he could have changed, and bounded up the tracks in no time at all. But somehow he didn't think that would have been such a good idea. *I could smell him coming,* Steven had said. The human scent was fainter, in a city full of people. He had to hope that Steven and Jonathan were inside the New House, locked up for the night. But if they were out prowling around, at least this way Willie thought he had a ghost of a chance.

He'd rested long enough. He craned his head back, looking up at the high black iron fence that ran along the top of the bluff, trying to measure how much further he had to go. Then he took a good long shot off his inhaler, gritted his teeth, and scrambled for the next tie up.

THE WINDSHIELD WIPERS SWEPT BACK AND FORTH ALMOST SI-lently as the long dark car nosed through the night. The windows were tinted a gray so dark it was almost black. Urquhart was in civvies, a red-and-black lumberjack shirt, dark woolen slacks, and bulky down jacket. His police cap was his only concession to uniform. He stared straight out into the darkness as he drove. "You look terrible," she told him.

"I feel worse." They swept under an overpass and around a long ramp onto the river road. "I feel old, Randi. Like this city. This whole damn city is old and rotten."

"Where are we going?" she asked him. At this hour of night, there was no other traffic on the road. The river was a black emptiness off to their left. Streetlamps swam in haloes of rain to the right as they sailed past block after cold, empty block stretching away toward the bluffs.

"To the pack," Urquhart said. "To where it happened."

The car's heater was pouring out a steady blast of warm air, but suddenly Randi felt deathly cold. Her hand went inside her coat, and closed around the hilt of the knife. The silver felt comfortable and comforting. "All right," she said. She slid the knife out of her belt and put it on the seat between them.

Urquhart glanced over. She watched him carefully. "What's that?" he said.

"Silver," Randi said. "Pick it up."

He looked at her. "What?"

"You heard me," she said. "Pick it up."

He looked at the road, at her face, back out at the road. He made no move to touch the knife.

"I'm not kidding," Randi said. She slid away from him, to the far side of the seat, and braced her back against the door. When Urquhart looked over again, she had the gun out, aimed right between his eyes. "Pick it up," she said very clearly.

The color left his face. He started to say something, but Randi shook her head curtly. Urquhart licked his lips, took his hand off the wheel, and picked up the knife. "There," he said, holding it up awkwardly while he drove with one hand. "I picked it up. Now what am I supposed to do with it?"

Randi slumped back against the seat. "Put it down," she said with relief.

Joe looked at her.

He rested for a long time in the shrubs on top of the bluff, listening to the rain fall around him and dreading what other sounds he might hear. He kept imagining soft footfalls stealing up behind him, and once he thought he heard a low growl somewhere off to his right. He could feel his hackles rise, and until that moment he hadn't even known he *had* hackles, but it was nothing, just his nerves working on him; Willie had always had bad nerves. The night was cold and black and empty.

When he finally had his breath back, Willie began to edge past the New House, keeping to the bushes as much as he could, well away from the windows. There were a few lights on, but no other sign of life. Maybe they'd all gone to bed. He hoped so.

He moved slowly and carefully, trying to be as quiet as possible. He watched where his feet came down, and every few steps he'd stop, look around, listen. He could change in an instant if he heard anyone . . . or any*thing* . . . coming toward him. He didn't know how much good that would do, but maybe, just maybe, it would give him a chance.

His raincoat dragged at him, a waterlogged second skin as heavy as lead. His shoes had soaked through, and the leather squished when he moved. Willie pushed away from the house, further back into the trees, until a bend in the road hid the lights from view. Only then, after a careful glance in both directions to make sure nothing was coming, did he dare risk a dash across the road.

Once across he plunged deeper into the woods, moving faster now, a little more heedless. He wondered where Roy Helander had been when Steven had caught him. Somewhere around here, Willie thought, somewhere in this dark primal forest, surrounded by old growth, with centuries of leaves and moss and dead things rotting in the earth beneath his feet.

As he moved away from the bluff and the city, the forest grew denser, until finally the trees pressed so close together that he lost sight of the sky, and the raindrops stopped pounding against his head. It was almost dry here. Overhead, the rain drummed relentlessly against a canopy of leaves. Willie's skin felt clammy, and for a moment he was lost, as if he'd wandered into some terrible cavern far beneath the earth, a dismal cold place where no light ever shone.

Then he stumbled between two huge, twisted old oaks, and felt air and rain against his face again, and raised his head, and there it was ahead of him, broken windows gaping down like so many blind eyes from walls carved from rock that shone like midnight and drank all light and hope. The tower loomed up to his right, some monstrous erection against the storm clouds, leaning crazily.

Willie stopped breathing, groped for his inhaler, found it, dropped it, picked it up. The mouthpiece was slimy with humus. He cleaned it on his sleeve, shoved it in his mouth, took a hit, two, three, and finally his throat opened up again.

He glanced around, heard only the rain, saw nothing. He stepped forward toward the tower. Toward Roy Helander's secret refuge.

THE BIG DOUBLE GATE IN THE HIGH CHAIN-LINK FENCE HAD BEEN padlocked for two years, but it was open tonight, and Urquhart drove straight through. Randi wondered if the gate had been opened for her father as well. She thought maybe it had.

Joe pulled up near one of the loading docks, in the shadow of the old brick slaughterhouse. The building gave them some shelter from the rain, but Randi still trembled in the cold as she climbed out. "Here?" she asked. "This is where you found him?"

Urquhart was staring off into the stockyard. It was a huge area, subdivided into a dozen pens along the railroad siding. There was a maze of chest-high fencing they called the "runs" between the slaughterhouse and the pens, to force the cows into a single line and herd them along inside, where a man in a blood-splattered apron waited with a hammer in his hand. "Here," Joe said, without looking back at her.

There was a long silence. Somewhere far off, Randi thought she heard a faint, wild howl, but maybe that was just the wind and the rain. "Do you believe in ghosts?" she asked Joe.

"Ghosts?" The chief sounded distracted.

She shivered. "It's like . . . I can feel him, Joe. Like he's still here, after all this time, still watching over me."

Joe Urquhart turned toward her. His face was wet with rain or maybe tears. "I watched over you," he said. "He asked me to watch over you, and I did, I did my best."

Randi heard a sound somewhere off in the night. She turned her head, frowning, listening. Tires crunched across gravel and she saw headlights outside the fence. Another car coming.

"You and your father, you're a lot alike," Joe said wearily. "Stubborn. Won't listen to nobody. I took good care of you, didn't I take good care of you? I got my own kids, you know, but you never wanted nothing, did you? So why the hell didn't you listen to me?"

By then Randi knew. She wasn't surprised. Somehow she felt as though she'd known for a long time. "There was only one phone call that night," she said. "You were the one who phoned for backup, not Dad."

Urquhart nodded. He was caught for a moment in the headlights of the oncoming car, and Randi saw the way his jaw trembled as he worked to get out the words. "Look in the glove box," he said.

Randi opened the car door, sat on the edge of the seat, and did as he said. The glove compartment was unlocked. Inside was a bottle of aspirin, a tire pressure gauge, some maps, and a box of cartridges. Randi opened the box and poured some bullets out into her palm. They glimmered pale and cold in the car's faint dome light. She left the box on the seat, climbed out, kicked the door shut. "My silver bullets," she said. "I hadn't expected them quite so soon."

"Those are the ones Frank ordered made up, eighteen years ago," Joe said. "After he was buried, I went by the gunsmith and picked them up. Like I said, you and him were a lot alike."

The second car pulled to a stop, pinning her in its high beams. Randi threw a hand across her eyes against the glare. She heard a car door opening and closing.

Urquhart's voice was anguished. "I told you to stay away from this thing, damn it. I *told* you! Don't you understand? They *own* this city!"

"He's right. You should have listened," Rogoff said, as he stepped into the light.

WILLIE GROPED HIS WAY DOWN THE LONG DARK HALL WITH ONE hand on the wall, placing each foot carefully in front of the last. The stone was so thick that even the sound of the rain did not reach him. There was only the echo of his careful footsteps, and the rush of blood inside his ears. The silence within the Old House was profound and unnerving, and there was something about the walls that bothered him as well. It was cold, but the stones under his fingers were moist and curiously warm to the touch, and Willie was glad for the darkness.

Finally he reached the base of the tower, where shafts of dim light fell across crabbed, narrow stone steps that spiraled up and up and up. Willie began to climb. He counted the steps at first, but somewhere around two hundred he lost the count, and the rest was a grim ordeal that he endured in silence. More than once he thought of changing. He resisted the impulse.

His legs ached from the effort when he reached the top. He sat down on the steps for a moment, his back to a slick stone wall. He was breathing hard, but when he groped for his inhaler, it was gone. He'd probably lost it in the woods. He could feel his lungs constricting in panic, but there was no help for it.

Willie got up.

The room smelled of blood and urine and something else, a scent he did not place, but somehow it made him tremble. There was no roof. Willie realized that the rain had stopped while he'd been inside. He looked up as the clouds parted, and a pale white moon stared down.

And all around other moons shimmered into life, reflected in the tall empty mirrors that lined the chamber. They reflected the sky above and each other, moon after moon after moon, until the room swam in silvered moonlight and reflections of reflections of reflections.

Willie turned around in a slow circle and a dozen other Willies turned with him. The moonstruck mirrors were streaked with dried blood, and above them a ring of cruel iron hooks curved up from the stone walls. A human skin hung from one of them, twisting slowly in some wind he could not feel, and as the moonlight hit it, it seemed to writhe and change, from woman to wolf to woman, both and neither.

That was when Willie heard the footsteps on the stairs.

"THE SILVER BULLETS WERE A BAD IDEA," ROGOFF SAID. "WE HAVE a local ordinance here. The police get immediate notice any time someone places an order for custom ammunition. Your father made the same mistake. The pack takes a dim view of silver bullets."

Randi felt strangely relieved. For a moment she'd been afraid that Willie had betrayed her, that he'd been one of them after all, and that thought had been like poison in her soul. Her fingers were still curled tight around a dozen of the bullets. She glanced down at them, so close and yet so far.

"Even if they're still good, you'll never get them loaded in time," Rogoff said.

"You don't need the bullets," Urquhart told her. "He just wants to talk. They promised me, honey, no one needs to get hurt."

Randi opened her hand. The bullets fell to the ground. She turned to Joe Urquhart. "You were my father's best friend. He said you had more guts than any man he ever knew."

"They don't give you any choice," Urquhart said. "I had kids of my own. They said if Roy Helander took the fall, no more kids would vanish, they promised they'd take care of it, but if we kept pressing, one of my kids would be the next to go. That's how it works in this town. Everything would have been all right, but Frank just wouldn't let it alone."

"We only kill in self-defense," Rogoff said. "There's a sweetness to human flesh, yes, a power that's undeniable, but it's not worth the risk."

"What about the children?" Randi said. "Did you kill them in self-defense too?"

"That was a long time ago," Rogoff said.

Joe stood with his head downcast. He was beaten, Randi saw, and she realized that he'd been beaten for a long time. All those trophies on his walls, but somehow she knew that he had given up hunting forever on the night her father died. "It was his son," Joe muttered quietly, in a voice full of shame. "Steven's never been right in the head, everyone knows that, he was the one who killed the kids, *ate* them. It was horrible, Harmon told me so himself, but he still wasn't going to let us have Steven. He said he'd...he'd control Steven's...appetites...if we closed the case. He was good as his word too, he put Steven on medication, and it stopped, the murders stopped."

She ought to hate Joe Urquhart, she realized, but instead she pitied him. After all this time, he still didn't understand. "Joe, he lied. It was never Steven."

"It was Steven," Joe insisted, "it had to be, he's insane. The rest of them . . . you can do business with them, Randi, listen to me now, you can talk to them."

"Like you did," she said. "Like Barry Schumacher."

Urquhart nodded. "That's right. They're just like us, they got some crazies, but not all of them are bad. You can't blame them for taking care of their own, we do the same thing, don't we? Look at Mike here, he's a good cop."

"A good cop who's going to change into a wolf in a minute or two and tear out my throat," Randi said.

"Randi, honey, listen to me," Urquhart said. "It doesn't have to be like that. You can walk out of here, just say the word. I'll get you onto the force, you can work with us, help us to . . . to keep the peace. Your father's dead, you won't bring him back, and the Helander boy, he deserved what he got, he was *killing* them, skinning them alive; it was self-defense. Steven is sick, he's always been sick—"

Rogoff was watching her from beneath his tangle of black hair. "He still doesn't get it," she said. She turned back to Joe. "Steven is sicker than you think. Something is missing. Too inbred, maybe. Think about it. Anders and Rochmonts, Flambeauxes and Harmons, the four great founding families, all werewolves, marrying each other generation after generation to keep the lines pure, for how many centuries? They kept the lines pure all right. They bred themselves Steven. He didn't kill those children. Roy Helander saw a *wolf* carry off his sister, and Steven can't change into a wolf. He got the bloodlust, he got inhuman strength, he burns at the touch of silver, but that's all. The last of the purebloods *can't work the change!*"

"She's right," Rogoff said quietly.

"Why do you think you never found any remains?" Randi put in. "Steven didn't kill those kids. His father carried them off, up to Blackstone."

"The old man had some crazy idea that if Steven ate enough human flesh, it might fix him, make him whole," Rogoff said.

"It didn't work," Randi said. She took Willie's note out of her pocket, let the pages flutter to the ground. It was all there. She'd finished reading it before she'd gone down to meet Joe. Frank Wade's little girl was nobody's fool.

"It didn't work," Rogoff echoed, "but by then Jonathan had got the taste. Once you get started, it's hard to stop." He looked at Randi for a long time, as if he were weighing something. Then he began . . .

. . . TO CHANGE. SWEET COLD AIR FILLED HIS LUNGS, AND HIS MUScles and bones ran with fire as the transformation took hold. He'd shrugged out of pants and coat, and he heard the rest of his clothing ripping apart as his body writhed, his flesh ran like hot wax, and he reformed, born anew.

Now he could see and hear and smell. The tower room shimmered with moonlight, every detail clear and sharp as noon, and the night was alive with sound, the wind and the rain and the rustle of bats in the forest around them, and traffic sounds and sirens from the city beyond. He was alive and full of power, and something was coming up the steps. It climbed slowly, untiring, and its smells filled the air. The scent of blood hung all around it, and beneath he sensed an aftershave that masked an unwashed body, sweat and dried semen on its skin, a heavy tang of wood smoke in its hair, and under it all the scent of sickness, sweetly rotten as a grave.

Willie backed all the way across the room, staring at the arched door, the growl rising in his throat. He bared long yellowed teeth, and slaver ran between them.

Steven stopped in the doorway and looked at him. He was naked. The wolf's hot red eyes met his cold blue ones, and it was hard to tell which were more inhuman. For a moment Willie thought that Steven didn't quite comprehend. Until he smiled and reached for the skin that twisted above him, on an iron hook.

Willie leapt.

He took Steven high in the back and bore him down, with his

hand still clutched around Zoe's skin. For a second Willie had a clear shot at his throat, but he hesitated and the moment passed. Steven caught Willie's foreleg in a pale scarred fist, and snapped it in half like a normal man might break a stick. The pain was excruciating. Then Steven was lifting him, flinging him away. He smashed up hard against one of the mirrors, and felt it shatter at the impact. Jagged shards of glass flew like knives, and one of them lanced through his side.

Willie rolled away; the glass spear broke under him, and he whimpered. Across the room, Steven was getting to his feet. He put out a hand to steady himself.

Willie scrambled up. His broken leg was knitting already, though it hurt when he put his weight on it. Glass fragments clawed inside him with every step. He could barely move. Some fucking werewolf he turned out to be.

Steven was adjusting his ghastly cloak, pulling flaps of skin down over his own face. The skin trade, Willie thought giddily, yeah, that was it, and in a moment Steven would use that damn flayed skin to do what he could never manage on his own, he would *change,* and then Willie would be meat.

Willie came at him, jaws gaping, but too slow. Steven's foot pistoned down, caught him hard enough to take his breath away, pinned him to the floor. Willie tried to squirm free, but Steven was too strong. He was bearing down, crushing him. All of a sudden Willie remembered that dog, so many years ago.

Willie bent himself almost double and took a bite out of the back of Steven's calf.

The blood filled his mouth, exploding inside him. Steven reeled back. Willie jumped up, darted forward, bit him again. This time he sank his teeth in good and held, worrying at the flesh. The pounding in his head was thunderous. He was full of power, he could feel it swelling within him. Suddenly he knew that he could tear Steven apart; he could taste the fine sweet flesh close to the bone, could hear the music of his screams, could imagine the way it would feel when he held him in his jaws and shook him like a rag doll and felt the life go out of him in a sudden giddy rush. It swept over him, and Willie bit and bit and bit again, ripping away chunks of meat, drunk on blood.

And then, dimly, he heard Steven screaming, screaming in a high shrill thin voice, a little boy's voice. "No, Daddy," he was whining, over and over again. "No, please, don't bite me, Daddy, don't bite me anymore."

Willie let him go and backed away.

Steven sat on the floor, sobbing. He was bleeding like a sonofabitch. Pieces were missing from thigh, calf, shoulder, and foot. His legs were drenched in blood. Three fingers were gone off his right hand. His cheeks were slimy with gore.

Suddenly Willie was scared.

For a moment he didn't understand. Steven was beaten, he could see that; he could rip out his throat or let him live, it didn't matter, it was over. But something was wrong, something was terribly, sickeningly wrong. It felt as though the temperature had dropped a hundred degrees, and every hair on his body was prickling and standing on end. What the hell was going on? He growled low in his throat and backed away, toward the door, keeping a careful eye on Steven.

Steven giggled. "You'll get it now," he said. "You called it. You got blood on the mirrors. You called it back again."

The room seemed to spin. Moonlight ran from mirror to mirror to mirror, dizzyingly. Or maybe it wasn't moonlight.

Willie looked into the mirrors.

The reflections were gone. Willie, Steven, the moon, all gone. There was blood on the mirrors and they were full of fog, a silvery pale fog that shimmered as it moved.

Something was moving through the fog, sliding from mirror to mirror to mirror, around and around. Something hungry that wanted to get out.

He saw it, lost it, saw it again. It was in front of him, behind him, off to the side. It was a hound, gaunt and terrible; it was a snake, scaled and foul; it was a man, with eyes like pits and knives for its fingers. It wouldn't hold still, every time he looked its shape seemed to change, and each shape was worse than the last, more twisted and obscene. Everything about it was lean and cruel. Its fingers were sharp, so sharp, and he looked at them and felt their caress sliding beneath his skin, tingling along the nerves, pain and blood and fire trailing behind them. It was black, blacker than black, a black that drank all light forever, and it was all shining silver too. It was a nightmare that lived in a funhouse mirror, the thing that hunts the hunters.

He could feel the evil throbbing through the glass.

"Skinner," Steven called.

The surface of the mirrors seemed to ripple and bulge, like a wave cresting on some quicksilver sea. The fog was thinning, Willie realized with sudden terror; he could see it clearer now, and he knew it could see him. And suddenly Willie Flambeaux knew what was happening, knew that when the fog cleared the mirrors wouldn't be mirrors anymore; they'd be doors, *doors,* and the skinner would come . . .

. . . SLIDING FORWARD, THROUGH THE RUINS OF HIS CLOTHING, SLITted eyes glowing like embers from a muzzle black as coal. He was half again as large as Willie had been, his fur thick and black and shaggy, and when he opened his mouth, his teeth gleamed like ivory daggers.

Randi edged backward, along the side of the car. The knife was in her hand, moonlight running off the silver blade, but somehow it didn't seem like very much. The huge black wolf advanced on her, his tongue lolling between his teeth, and she put her back up against the car door and braced herself for his leap.

Joe Urquhart stepped between them.

"No," he said. "Not her too, you owe me, talk to her, give her a chance, I'll make her see how it is."

The wolf growled a warning.

Urquhart stood his ground, and all of a sudden he had his revolver out, and he was holding it in two shaky hands, drawing a bead. "Stop. I mean it. She didn't have time to load the goddamned silver bullets, but I've had eighteen fucking years. I'm the fucking police chief in this fucking city, and you're under arrest."

Randi put her hand on the door handle, eased it open. For a moment the wolf stood frozen, baleful red eyes fixed on Joe, and she thought it was actually going to work. She remembered her father's old Wednesday night poker games; he'd always said Joe, unlike Barry Schumacher, ran one hell of a bluff.

Then the wolf threw back his head and howled, and all the blood went out of her. She knew that sound. She'd heard it in her dreams a thousand times. It was in her blood, that sound, an echo from far off and long ago, when the world had been a forest and humans had run naked in fear before the hunting pack. It echoed off the side of the old slaughterhouse and trembled out over the city, and they must have heard it all over the flats, heard it and glanced outside nervously and checked their locks before they turned up the volumes on their TVs.

Randi opened the door wider and slid one leg inside the car as the wolf leapt.

She heard Urquhart fire, and fire again, and then the wolf slammed into his chest and smashed him back against the car door. Randi was half into the car, but the door swung shut hard, crunching down on her left foot with awful force. She heard a bone break under the impact, and shrieked at the sudden flare of pain. Outside Urquhart fired again, and then he was screaming. There were ripping sounds and more screams and something wet spattered against her ankle.

Her foot was trapped, and the struggle outside slammed her open door against it again and again and again. Each impact was a small explosion as the shattered bones grated together and ripped against raw nerves. Joe was screaming and droplets of blood covered the tinted window like rain. Her head swam, and for a moment Randi thought she'd faint from the pain, but she threw all her weight against the door and moved it just enough and drew her foot inside and when the next impact came it slapped the door shut *hard* and Randi pressed the lock.

She leaned against the wheel and almost threw up. Joe had stopped screaming, but she could hear the wolf tearing at him, ripping off chunks of flesh. *Once you get started it's hard to stop,* she thought hysterically. She got out the .38, cracked the cylinder with shaking hands, flicked out the shells. Then she was fumbling around on the front seat. She found the box, tipped it over, snatched up a handful of silver.

It was silent outside. Randi stopped, looked up.

He was on the hood of the car.

WILLIE *CHANGED.*

He was running on instinct now; he didn't know why he did it, he just did. The pain was there waiting for him along with his humanity, as he'd known it would be. It shrieked through him like a gale wind, and sent him whimpering to the floor. He could feel the glass shard under his ribs, dangerously close to a lung, and his left arm bent sickeningly downward at a place it was never meant to bend, and when he tried to move it, he screamed and bit his tongue and felt his mouth fill with blood.

The fog was a pale thin haze now, and the mirror closest to him bulged outward, throbbing like something alive.

Steven sat against the wall, his blue eyes bright and avid, sucking his own blood from the stumps of his fingers. "Changing won't help," he said in that weird flat tone of his. "Skinner don't care. It knows what you are. Once it's called, it's got to have a skin." Willie's vision was blurry with tears, but he saw it again then, in the mirror behind Steven, pushing at the fading fog, pushing, pushing, trying to get through.

He staggered to his feet. Pain roared through his head. He cradled his broken arm against his body, took a step toward the stairs, and felt broken glass grind against his bare feet. He looked down. Pieces of the shattered mirror were everywhere.

Willie's head snapped up. He looked around wildly, dizzy, counting. Six, seven, eight, nine . . . the tenth was broken. Nine then. He threw himself forward, slammed all his body weight into the nearest mirror. It shattered under the impact, disintegrated into a thousand pieces. Willie crunched the biggest shards underfoot, stamped on them until his heels ran wet with blood. He was moving without thought. He caromed around the room, using his own body as a weapon, hearing the sweet tinkling music of breaking glass. The world turned into a red fog of pain and a thousand little knives sliced at him everywhere, and he wondered, if the skinner came through and got him, whether he'd even be able to tell the difference.

Then he was staggering away from another mirror, and white-hot needles were stabbing through his feet with every step, turning into fire as they lanced up his calves. He stumbled and fell, hard. Flying glass had cut his face to ribbons, and the blood ran down into his eyes.

Willie blinked, and wiped the blood away with his good hand. His old raincoat was underneath him, blood-soaked and covered with ground glass and shards of mirror. Steven stood over him, staring down. Behind him was a mirror. Or was it a door?

"You missed one," Steven said flatly.

Something hard was digging into his gut, Willie realized. His hand fumbled around beneath him, slid into the pocket of his raincoat, closed on cold metal.

"Skinner's coming for you now," Steven said.

Willie couldn't see. The blood had filled his eyes again. But he could still feel. He got his fingers through the loops and rolled and brought his hand up fast and hard, with all the strength he had left, and put Mr. Scissors right through the meat of Steven's groin.

The last thing he heard was a scream, and the sound of breaking glass.

CALM, RANDI THOUGHT, *CALM*, BUT THE DREAD THAT FILLED HER was more than simple fear. Blood matted his jaws, and his eyes stared at her through the windshield, glowing that hideous baleful red. She looked away quickly, tried to chamber a bullet. Her hands shook, and it slid out of her grip, onto the floor of the car. She ignored it, tried again.

The wolf howled, turned, fled. For a moment she lost sight of him. Randi craned her head around, peering nervously out through the darkness. She glanced into the rearview mirror, but it was fogged up, useless. She shivered, as much from cold as from fear. *Where was he?* she thought wildly.

Then she saw him, running toward the car.

Randi looked down, chambered a bullet, and had a second in her fingers when he came flying over the hood and smashed against the glass. Cracks spiderwebbed out from the center of the windshield. The wolf snarled at her. Slaver and blood smeared the glass. Then he hit the glass again. Again. Again. Randi jumped with every impact. The windshield cracked and cracked again, then a big section in the center went milky and opaque.

She had the second bullet in the cylinder. She slid in a third. It was freezing inside the car. She looked out into the darkness through a haze of cracks and blood smears, loaded a fourth bullet, and was closing the cylinder when he hit the windshield again and it all caved in on her.

One moment she had the gun and the next it was gone. The weight was on her chest and the safety glass, broken into a million milky pieces but still clinging together, fell across her face like a shroud. Then it ripped away, and the blood-soaked jaws and hot red eyes were right there in front of her.

The wolf opened his mouth and she was feeling the furnace heat of his breath, smelling awful carnivore stench.

"You fucker!" she screamed, and almost laughed, because it wasn't much as last words go.

Something sharp and silvery bright came sliding down through the back of his throat.

It went so quickly Randi didn't understand what was happening, no more than he did. Suddenly the bloodlust went out of the dark red eyes, and they were full of pain and shock and finally fear, and she saw more silver knives sliding through his throat before his mouth filled with blood. And then the great black-furred body shuddered, and struggled, as something pulled it back off her, front paws beating a tattoo against the seat. There was a smell of burning hair in the air. When the wolf began to scream, it sounded almost human.

Randi choked back her own pain, slammed her shoulder against the door, and knocked what was left of Joe Urquhart aside. Halfway out the door, she glanced back.

The hand was twisted and cruel, and its fingers were long bright silver razors, pale and cold and sharp as sin. Like five long jointed knives the fingers had sunk through the back of the wolf's neck, and grabbed hold, and pulled, and the blood was coming out between his teeth in great gouts now and his legs were kicking feebly. It yanked at him then, and she heard a sickening wet *crunching* as the thing began to *pull* the wolf through the rearview mirror with inexorable, unimaginable force, to whatever was on the other side. The great black-furred body seemed to waver and shift for a second, and the wolf's face took on an almost human cast.

When his eyes met hers, the red light had gone out of them; there was nothing there but pain and pleading.

His first name was Mike, she remembered.

Randi looked down. Her gun was on the floor.

She picked it up, checked the cylinder, closed it, jammed the barrel up against his head, and fired four times.

When she got out of the car and put her weight on her ankle, the pain washed over her in great waves. Randi collapsed to her hands and knees. She was throwing up when she heard the sirens.

". . . SOME KIND OF ANIMAL," SHE SAID.

The detective gave her a long, sour look, and closed his notebook. "That's all you can tell me?" he said. "That Chief Urquhart was killed by some kind of animal?"

Randi wanted to say something sharp, but she was all fucked up on painkillers. They'd had to put two pins in her and it still hurt like hell, and the doctors said she'd have to stay another week. "What do you want me to tell you?" she said weakly. "That's what I saw, some kind of animal. A wolf."

The detective shook his head. "Fine. So the chief was killed by some kind of animal, probably a wolf. So where's Rogoff? His car was there, his blood was all over the inside of the chief's car, so tell me . . . *where the fuck is Rogoff?*"

Randi closed her eyes, and pretended it was the pain. "I don't know," she said.

"I'll be back," the detective said when he left.

She lay with her eyes closed for a moment, thinking maybe she could drift back to sleep, until she heard the door open and close. "He won't be," a soft voice told her. "We'll see to it."

Randi opened her eyes. At the foot of the bed was an old man with long white hair leaning on a gold wolf's head cane. He wore a black suit, a mourning suit, and his hair fell to his shoulders. "My name is Jonathan Harmon," he said.

"I've seen your picture. I know who you are. And what you are." Her voice was hoarse. "A lycanthrope."

"Please," he said. "A werewolf."

"Willie . . . what happened to Willie?"

"Steven is dead," Jonathan Harmon said.

"Good," Randi spat. "Steven and Roy, they were doing it together, Willie said. For the skins. Steven hated the others, because they could work the change and he couldn't. But once your son had his skin, he didn't need Helander anymore, did he?"

"I can't say I will mourn greatly. To be frank, Steven was never the sort of heir I might have wished for." He went to the window, opened the curtains, and looked out. "This was once a great city, you know, a city of blood and iron. Now it's all turned to rust."

"Fuck your city," Randi said. "What about Willie?"

"It was a pity about Zoe, but once the skinner has been summoned, it keeps hunting until it takes a skin, from mirror to mirror to mirror. It knows our scent, but it doesn't like to wander far from its gates. I don't know how your mongrel friend managed to evade it twice, but he did . . . to Zoe's misfortune, and Michael's." He turned and looked at her. "You will not be so lucky. Don't congratulate yourself too vigorously, child. The pack takes care of its own. The doctor who writes your next prescription, the pharmacist who fills it, the boy who delivers it . . . any of them could be one of us. We don't forget our enemies, Miss Wade. Your family would do well to remember that."

"You were the one," she said with a certainty. "In the stockyards, the night my father . . ."

Jonathan nodded curtly. "He was a crack shot, I'll grant him that. He put six bullets in me. My war wounds, I call them. They still show up on X-rays, but my doctors have learned not to be curious."

"I'll kill you," Randi said.

"I think not." He leaned over the bed. "Perhaps I'll come for you myself some night. You ought to see me, Miss Wade. My fur is white now, pale as snow, but the stature, the majesty, the power, those have not left me. Michael was a half-breed, and your Willie, he was hardly more than a dog. The pureblood is rather more. We are the dire wolves, the nightmares who haunt your racial memories, the dark shapes circling endlessly beyond the light of your fires."

He smiled down at her, then turned and walked away. At the door he paused. "Sleep well," he said.

Randi did not sleep at all, not even when night fell and the nurse came in and turned out the lights, despite all her pleading. She lay there in the dark staring up at the ceiling, feeling more alone than she'd ever been. He was dead, she thought. Willie was dead and she'd better start getting used to the idea. Very softly, alone in the darkness of the private room, she began to cry.

She cried for a long time, for Willie and Joan Sorenson and Joe Urquhart and finally, after all this time, for Frank Wade. She ran out of tears and kept crying, her body shaking with dry sobs. She was still shaking when the door opened softly, and a thin knife of light from the hall cut across the room.

"Who's there?" she said hoarsely. "Answer, or I'll scream."

The door closed quietly. "Ssssh. Quiet, or they'll hear." It was a woman's voice, young, a little scared. "The nurse said I couldn't come in, that it was after visiting hours, but he told me to get to you right away." She moved close to the bed.

Randi turned on her reading light. Her visitor looked nervously toward the door. She was dark, pretty, no more than twenty, with a spray of freckles across her nose. "I'm Betsy Juddiker," she whispered. "Willie said I was to give you a message, but it's all crazy stuff..."

Randi's heart skipped a beat. "Willie...tell me! I don't care how crazy it sounds, just tell me."

"He said that he couldn't phone you hisself because the pack might be listening in, that he got hurt bad but he's okay, that he's up north, and he's found this vet who's taking care of him good. I know, it sounds funny, but that's what he said, a vet."

"Go on."

Betsy nodded. "He sounded hurt on the phone, and he said he couldn't...couldn't *change* right now, except for a few minutes to call, because he was hurt and the pain was always waiting for him, but to say that the vet had gotten most of the glass out and set his leg and he was going to be fine. And then he said that on the night he'd gone, he'd come by *my* house and left something for you, and I was to find it and bring it here." She opened her purse and rummaged around. "It was in the bushes by the mailbox, my little boy found it." She gave it over.

It was a piece of some broken mirror, Randi saw, a shard as long and slender as her finger. She held it in her hand for a moment, confused and uncertain. The glass was cold to the touch, and it seemed to grow colder as she held it.

"Careful, it's real sharp," Betsy said. "There was one more thing, I don't understand it at all, but Willie said it was important. He said to tell you that there were no mirrors where he was, not a one, but last he'd seen, there were plenty up in Blackstone."

Randi nodded, not quite grasping it, not yet. She ran a finger thoughtfully along the shiny sliver of glass.

"Oh, look," Betsy said. "I told you. Now you've gone and cut yourself."

Unsound Variations

———————— ❖ ————————

AFTER THEY SWUNG OFF THE INTERSTATE, THE ROAD BECAME A narrow two-lane that wound a tortuous path through the mountains in a series of switchbacks, each steeper than the last. Peaks rose all around them, pine-covered and crowned by snow and ice, while swift cold waterfalls flashed by, barely seen, on either side. The sky was a bright and brilliant blue. It was exhilarating scenery, but it did nothing to lighten Peter's mood. He concentrated blindly on the road, losing himself in the mindless reflexes of driving.

As the mountains grew higher, the radio reception grew poorer, stations fading in and out with every twist in the road, until at last they could get nothing at all. Kathy went from one end of the band to the other, searching, and then back again. Finally she snapped off the radio in disgust. "I guess you'll just have to talk to me," she said.

Peter didn't need to look at her to hear the sharpness in her tone, the bitter edge of sarcasm that had long ago replaced fondness in her voice. She was looking for an argument, he knew. She was angry about the radio, and she resented him dragging her on this trip, and most of all she resented being married to him. At times, when he was feeling very sorry for himself, he did not even blame her. He had not turned out to be much of a bargain as a husband; a failed writer, failed journalist, failing businessman, depressed and depressing. He was still a lively sparring partner, however. Perhaps that was why she tried to provoke fights so often. After all the blood had been let, one or both of them would start crying, and then they would usually make love, and life would be pleasant for an hour or two. It was about all they had left.

Not today, though. Peter lacked the energy, and his mind was on other things. "What do you want to talk about?" he asked her. He kept his tone amicable and his eyes on the road.

"Tell me about these clowns we're going to visit," she said.

"I did. They were my teammates on the chess team, back when I was at Northwestern."

"Since when is chess a team sport anyway?" Kathy said. "What'd you do, vote on each move?"

"No. In chess, a team match is really a bunch of individual matches. Usually four or five boards, at least in college play. There's no consultation or anything. The team that wins the most individual games wins the match point. The way it works—"

"I get it," she said sharply. "I may not be a chess player, but I'm not stupid. So you and these other three were the Northwestern team?"

"Yes and no," Peter said. The Toyota was straining; it wasn't used to grades this steep, and it hadn't been adjusted for altitude before they took off from Chicago. He drove carefully. They were up high enough now to come across icy patches, and snow drifting across the road.

"Yes and no," Kathy said sarcastically. "What does that mean?"

"Northwestern had a big chess club back then. We played in a lot of tournaments—local, state, national. Sometimes we fielded more than one team, so the line-up was a bit different every tournament. It depended on who could play and who couldn't, who had a midterm, who'd played in the last match—lots of things. We four were Northwestern's B team in the North American Intercollegiate Team Championships, ten years ago this week. Northwestern hosted that tournament, and I ran it, as well as playing."

"What do you mean *B team*?"

Peter cleared his throat and eased the Toyota around a sharp curve, gravel rattling against the underside of the car as one wheel brushed the shoulder. "A school wasn't limited to just one team," he said. "If you had the money and a lot of people who wanted to play, you could enter several. Your best four players would make up your A team, the real contender. The second four would be the B team, and so on." He paused briefly, and continued with a faint note of pride in his voice. "The nationals at Northwestern were the biggest ever held, up to that time, although of course that record has since been broken. We set a second record, though, that still stands. Since the tournament was on our home grounds, we had lots of players on hand. We entered six teams. No other school has ever had more than four in the nationals, before or after." The record still brought a smile to his face. Maybe it wasn't much of a record, but it was the only one he had, and it was *his*. Some people lived and died without ever setting a record of any kind, he reflected silently. Maybe he ought to tell Kathy to put his on his tombstone: HERE LIES PETER K. NORTEN. HE FIELDED SIX TEAMS. He chuckled.

"What's so funny?"

"Nothing."

She didn't pursue it. "So you ran this tournament, you say?"

"I was the club president and the chairman of the local committee. I didn't direct, but I put together the bid that brought the nationals to Evanston, made all the preliminary arrangements. And I organized all six of our teams, decided who would play on each one, appointed the team captains. But during the tournament itself I was only the captain of the B team."

She laughed. "So you were a big deal on the second-string. It figures. The story of your life."

Peter bit back a sharp reply, and said nothing. The Toyota swerved around another hairpin, and a vast Colorado mountain panorama opened up in front of them. It left him strangely unmoved.

After a while Kathy said, "When did you stop playing chess?"

"I sort of gave it up after college. Not a conscious decision, really. I just kind of drifted out of it. I haven't played a game of tournament chess in almost nine years. I'm probably pretty rusty by now. But back then I was fairly good."

"How good is fairly good?"

"I was rated as a Class A player, like everyone else on our B team."

"What does that mean?"

"It means my USCF rating was substantially higher than that of the vast majority of tournament chess players in the country," he said. "And the tournament players are generally much better than the unrated wood-pushers you encounter in bars and coffeehouses. The ratings went all the way down to Class E. Above Class A you had Experts, and Masters, and Senior Masters at the top, but there weren't many of them."

"Three classes above you?"

"Yes."

"So you might say, at your very best, you were a fourth-class chess player."

At that Peter did look over at her. She was leaning back in her seat, a faint smirk on her face. "Bitch," he said. He was suddenly angry.

"Keep your eyes on the road!" Kathy snapped.

He wrenched the car around the next turn hard as he could, and pressed down on the gas. She hated it when he drove fast. "I don't know why the hell I try to talk to you," he said.

"My husband, the big deal," she said. She laughed. "A fourth-class chess player playing on the junior varsity team. And a fifth-rate driver too."

"Shut up," Peter said furiously. "You don't know what the hell you're talking about. Maybe we were only the B team, but we were good. We finished better than anyone had any right to expect, only a half-point behind Northwestern A. And we almost scored one of the biggest upsets in history."

"Do tell."

Peter hesitated, already regretting his words. The memory was important to him, almost as important as his silly little record. *He* knew what it meant, how close they had come. But she'd never understand; it would only be another failure for her to laugh at. He should never have mentioned it.

"Well?" she prodded. "What about this great upset, dear? Tell me."

It was too late, Peter realized. She'd never let him drop it now. She'd needle him and needle him until he told her. He sighed and said, "It was ten years ago this week. The nationals were always held between Christmas and New Year's, when everyone was on break. An eight-round team tournament, two rounds a day. All of our teams did moderately well. Our A team finished seventh overall."

"You were on the B team, sweetie."

Peter grimaced. "Yes. And we were doing best of all, up to a point.

Scored a couple nice upsets late in the tournament. It put us in a strange position. Going into the last round, the University of Chicago was in first place, alone, with a 6-1 match record. They'd beaten our A team, among their other victims, and they were defending national champions. Behind them were three other schools at 5½-½. Berkeley, the University of Massachusetts, and—I don't know, someone else, it doesn't matter. What mattered was that all three of those teams had already played U of C. Then you had a whole bunch of teams at 5-2, including both Northwestern A and B. One of the 5-2 teams had to be paired up against Chicago in the final round. By some freak, it turned out to be us. Everyone thought that cinched the tournament for them.

"It was really a mismatch. They were the defending champions, and they had an awesome team. Three Masters and an Expert, if I recall. They outrated us by hundreds of points on every board. It should have been easy. It wasn't.

"It was never easy between U of C and Northwestern. All through my college years, we were the two big Midwestern chess powers, and we were archrivals. The Chicago captain, Hal Winslow, became a good friend of mine, but I gave him a lot of headaches. Chicago *always* had a stronger team than we did, but we gave them fits nonetheless. We met in the Chicago Intercollegiate League, in state tournaments, in regional tournaments, and several times in the nationals. Chicago won most of those, but not all. We took the city championship away from them once, and racked up a couple other big upsets too. And that year, in the nationals, we came *this* close"—he held up two fingers, barely apart—"to the biggest upset of all." He put his hand back on the wheel, and scowled.

"Go on," she said. "I'm breathless to know what comes next."

Peter ignored the sarcasm. "An hour into the match, we had half the tournament gathered around our tables, watching. Everyone could see that Chicago was in trouble. We clearly had superior positions on two boards, and we were even on the other two.

"It got better. I was playing Hal Winslow on third board. We had a dull, even position, and we agreed to a draw. And on fourth board, E.C. gradually got outplayed and finally resigned in a dead lost position."

"E.C.?"

"Edward Colin Stuart. We all called him E.C. Quite a character. You'll meet him up at Bunnish's place."

"He lost?"

"Yes."

"This doesn't sound like such a thrilling upset to me," she said drily. "Though maybe by your standards, it's a triumph."

"E.C. lost," Peter said, "but by that time, Delmario had clearly busted his man on board two. The guy dragged it out, but finally we got the point, which tied the score at 1½–1½, with one game in progress. And we were winning that one. It was incredible. Bruce Bunnish was our first board. A real turkey, but a half-decent player. He was another A player, but he had a trick memory. Photographic. Knew every opening backwards and forwards. He was playing Chicago's big man." Peter smiled wryly. "In more ways than one. A Master name of Robinson Vesselere. Damn strong chess player, but he must have weighed four hundred pounds. He'd sit there absolutely immobile as you played him, his hands folded on top of his stomach, little eyes squinting at the board. And he'd crush you. He should have crushed Bunnish easily. Hell, he was rated four hundred points higher. But that wasn't what had gone down. With that trick memory of his, Bunnish had somehow outplayed Vesselere in an obscure variation of the Sicilian. He was swarming all over him. An incredible attack. The position was as complicated as anything I'd ever seen, very sharp and tactical. Vesselere was counterattacking on the queenside, and he had some pressure, but nothing like the threats Bunnish had on the kingside. It was a won game. We were all sure of that."

"So you almost won the championship?"

"No," Peter said. "No, it wasn't that. If we'd won the match, we would have tied Chicago and a few other teams at 6–2, but the championship would have gone to someone else, some team with 6½ match points. Berkeley maybe, or Mass. It was just the upset itself we wanted. It would have been *incredible*. They were the best college chess team in the country. We weren't even the best at our school. If we had beaten them, it would have caused a sensation. And we came so close."

"What happened?"

"Bunnish blew it," Peter said sourly. "There was a critical position. Bunnish had a sac. A sacrifice, you know? A double piece sac. Very sharp, but it would have busted up Vesselere's kingside and driven his king out into the open. But Bunnish was too timid for that. Instead he kept looking at Vesselere's queenside attack, and finally he made some feeble defensive move. Vesselere shifted another piece to the queenside, and Bunnish defended again. Instead of following up his advantage, he made a whole series of cautious little adjustments to the position, and before long his attack had dissipated. After that, of course, Vesselere overwhelmed him." Even now, after ten years, Peter felt the disappointment building inside him as he spoke. "We lost the match 2½-1½, and Chicago won another national championship. Afterwards, even Vesselere admitted that he was busted if Brucie had played knight takes pawn at the critical point. *Damn.*"

"You lost. That's what this amounts to. You lost."

"We came close."

"Close only counts in horseshoes and grenades," Kathy said. "You lost. Even then you were a loser, dear. I wish I'd known."

"*Bunnish* lost, damn it," Peter said. "It was just like him. He had a Class A rating, and that trick memory, but as a team player he was worthless. You don't know how many matches he blew for us. When the pressure was on, we could always count on Bunnish to fold. But that time was the worst, that game against Vesselere. I could have killed him. He was an arrogant asshole, too."

Kathy laughed. "Isn't this arrogant asshole the one we are now speeding to visit?"

"It's been ten years. Maybe he's changed. Even if he hasn't, well, he's a multimillionaire asshole now. Electronics. Besides, I want to see E.C. and Steve again, and Bunnish said they'd be there."

"Delightful," said Kathy. "Well, rush on, then. I wouldn't want to miss this. It might be my only opportunity to spend four days with an asshole millionaire and three losers."

Peter said nothing, but he pressed down on the accelerator, and the Toyota plunged down the mountain road, faster and faster, rattling as it picked up speed. Down and down, he thought, down and down. Just like my goddamned life.

Four miles up Bunnish's private road, they finally came within sight of the house. Peter, who still dreamed of buying his own house after a decade of living in cheap apartments, took one look and knew he was gazing at a three-million-dollar piece of property. There were three levels, all blending into the mountainside so well you hardly noticed them, built of natural wood and native stone and tinted glass. A huge solar greenhouse was the most conspicuous feature. Beneath the house, a four-car garage was sunk right into the mountain itself.

Peter pulled into the last empty spot, between a brand-new silver Cadillac Seville that was obviously Bunnish's and an ancient rusted VW Beetle that was obviously not. As he pulled the key from the ignition, the garage doors shut automatically behind them, blocking out daylight and the gorgeous mountain vistas. The door closed with a resounding metallic clang.

"Someone knows we're here," Kathy observed.

"Get the suitcases," Peter snapped.

To the rear of the garage they found the elevator, and Peter jabbed the topmost of the two buttons. When the elevator doors opened again, it was on a huge living room. Peter stepped out and stared at a wilderness of potted plants beneath a vaulting skylight, at thick brown carpets, fine wood paneling, bookcases packed with leatherbound volumes, a large fireplace, and Edward Colin Stuart, who rose from a leather-clad armchair across the room when the elevator arrived.

"E.C.," Peter said, setting down his suitcase. He smiled.

"Hello, Peter," E.C. said, coming toward them quickly. They shook hands.

"You haven't changed a goddamned bit in ten years," Peter said. It was true. E.C. was still slender and compact, with a bushy head of sandy blond hair and a magnificent handlebar mustache. He was wearing jeans and a tapered purple shirt with a black vest, and he seemed just as he had a decade ago: brisk, trim, efficient. "Not a damn bit," Peter repeated.

"More's the pity," E.C. said. "One is supposed to change, I believe." His blue eyes were as unreadable as ever. He turned to Kathy, and said, "I'm E.C. Stuart."

"Oh, pardon," Peter said. "This is my wife, Kathy."

"Delighted," she said, taking his hand and smiling at him.

"Where's Steve?" Peter asked. "I saw his VW down in the garage. Gave me a start. How long has he been driving that thing now? Fifteen years?"

"Not quite," E.C. said. "He's around somewhere, probably having a drink." His mouth shifted subtly when he said it, telling Peter a good deal more than his words did.

"And Bunnish?"

"Brucie has not yet made his appearance. I think he was waiting for you to arrive. You probably want to settle in to your rooms."

"How do we find them, if our host is missing?" Kathy asked drily.

"Ah," said E.C., "you haven't been acquainted with the wonders of Bunnishland yet. Look." He pointed to the fireplace.

Peter would have sworn that there had been a painting above the mantel when they had entered, some sort of surreal landscape. Now there was a large rectangular screen, with words on it, vivid red against black. WELCOME, PETER. WELCOME, KATHY. YOUR SUITE IS ON THE SECOND LEVEL, FIRST DOOR. PLEASE MAKE YOURSELF COMFORTABLE.

Peter turned. "How...?"

"No doubt triggered by the elevator," E.C. said. "I was greeted the same way. Brucie is an electronics genius, remember. The house is full of gadgets and toys. I've explored a bit." He shrugged. "Why don't you two unpack and then wander back? I won't go anywhere."

They found their rooms easily enough. The huge, tiled bath featured an outside patio with a hot tub, and the suite had its own sitting room and fireplace. Above it was an abstract painting, but when Kathy closed the room door it faded away and was replaced by another message: I HOPE YOU FIND THIS SATISFACTORY.

"Cute guy, this host of ours," Kathy said, sitting on the edge of the bed. "Those TV screens or whatever they are better not be two-way. I don't intend to put on any show for any electronic voyeur."

Peter frowned. "Wouldn't be surprised if the house *was* bugged. Bunnish was always a strange sort."

"How strange?"

"He was hard to like," Peter said. "Boastful, always bragging about how good he was as a chess player, how smart he was, that sort of thing.

No one really believed him. His grades were good, I guess, but the rest of the time he seemed close to dense. E.C. has a wicked way with hoaxes and practical jokes, and Bunnish was his favorite victim. I don't know how many laughs we had at his expense. Bunnish was kind of a goon in person, too. Pudgy, round-faced with big cheeks like some kind of chipmunk, wore his hair in a crew cut. He was in ROTC. I've never seen anyone who looked more ridiculous in a uniform. He never dated."

"Gay?"

"No, not hardly. Asexual is closer to it." Peter looked around the room and shook his head. "I can't imagine how Bunnish made it this big. Him of all people." He sighed, opened his suitcase, and started to unpack. "I might have believed it of Delmario," he continued. "Steve and Bunnish were both in Tech, but Steve always seemed much brighter. We all thought he was a real whiz-kid. Bunnish just seemed like an arrogant mediocrity."

"Fooled you," Kathy said. She smiled sweetly. "Of course, he's not the only one to fool you, is he? Though perhaps he was the first."

"Enough," Peter said, hanging the last of his shirts in the closet. "Come on, let's get back downstairs. I want to talk to E.C."

They had no sooner stepped out of their suite when a voice hailed them. *"Pete?"*

Peter turned, and the big man standing in the doorway down the hall smiled a blurry smile at him. "Don't you recognize me, Peter?"

"Steve?" Peter said wonderingly.

"Sure, hey, who'd you think?" He stepped out of his own room, a bit unsteadily, and closed the door behind him. "This must be the wife, eh? Am I right?"

"Yes," Peter said. "Kathy, this is Steve Delmario. Steve, Kathy." Delmario came over and pumped her hand enthusiastically, after clapping Peter roundly on the back. Peter found himself staring. If E.C. had scarcely changed at all in the past ten years, Steve had made up for it. Peter would never have recognized his old teammate on the street.

The old Steve Delmario had lived for chess and electronics. He was a fierce competitor, and he loved to tinker things together, but he was frustratingly uninterested in anything outside his narrow passions. He had been a tall, gaunt youth with incredibly intense eyes held captive behind Coke-bottle lenses in heavy black frames. His black hair had al-ways been either ruffled and unkempt or—when he treated himself to one of his do-it-yourself haircuts—grotesquely butchered. He was equally careless about his clothing, most of which was Salvation Army chic minus the chic: baggy brown pants with cuffs, ten-year-old shirts with frayed collars, a zippered and shapeless gray sweater he wore everywhere. Once E.C. had observed that Steve Delmario looked like the last man left alive on earth after a nuclear holocaust, and for almost a semester thereafter the whole club had called Delmario, "the last man on earth." He took it with good humor. For all his quirks, Delmario had been well-liked.

The years had been cruel to him, however. The Coke-bottle glasses in the black frames were the same, and the clothes were equally haphazard—shabby brown cords, a short-sleeved white shirt with three felt-tip pens in the pocket, a faded sweater-vest with every button buttoned, scuffed Hush Puppies—but the rest had all changed. Steve had gained about fifty pounds, and he had a bloated, puffy look about him. He was almost entirely bald, nothing left of the wild black hair but a few sickly strands around his ears. And his eyes had lost their feverish intensity, and were filled instead with a fuzziness that Peter found terri-bly disturbing. Most shocking of all was the smell of alcohol on his breath. E.C. had hinted at it, but Peter still found it difficult to accept. In college, Steve Delmario had never touched anything but an infre-quent beer.

"It is good to see you again," Peter said, though he was no longer quite sure that was true. "Shall we go on downstairs? E.C. is waiting."

Delmario nodded. "Sure, sure, let's do it." He clapped Peter on the back again. "Have you seen Bunnish yet? Damn, this is some place he's got, isn't it? You seen those message screens? Clever, real clever. Never would have figured Bunnish to go as far as this, not our old Funny Bunny, eh?" He chuckled. "I've looked at some of his patents over the years, you know. Real ingenious. Real fine work. And from *Bunnish*. I guess you just never know, do you?"

The living room was awash with classical music when they de-scended the spiral stair. Peter didn't recognize the composition; his own tastes had always run to rock. But classical music had been one of E.C.'s passions, and he was sitting in an armchair now, eyes closed, listening.

"Drinks," Delmario was saying. "I'll fix us all some drinks. You folks must be thirsty. Bunny's got a wet bar right behind the stair here. What do you want?"

"What are the choices?" Kathy asked.

"Hell, he's got anything you could think of," said Delmario.

"A Beefeater martini, then," she said. "Very dry."

Delmario nodded. "Pete?"

"Oh," said Peter. He shrugged. "A beer, I guess."

Delmario went behind the stair to fix up their drinks, and Kathy arched her eyebrows at him. "Such refined tastes," she said. "A *beer!*"

Peter ignored her and went over to sit beside E.C. Stuart. "How the hell did you find the stereo?" he asked. "I don't see it anywhere." The music seemed to be coming right out of the walls.

E.C. opened his eyes, gave a quirkish little smile, and brushed one end of his mustache with a finger. "The message screen blabbed the secret to me," he said. "The controls are built into the wall back over there," nodding, "and the whole system is concealed. It's voice-activated, too. Computerized. I *told* it what album I wanted to hear."

"Impressive," Peter admitted. He scratched his head. "Didn't Steve put together a voice-activated stereo back in college?"

"Your beer," Delmario said. He was standing over them, holding out a cold bottle of Heineken. Peter took it, and Delmario—with a drink in hand—seated himself on the ornate tiled coffee table. "I had a system," he said. "Real crude, though. Remember, you guys used to kid me about it."

"You bought a good cartridge, as I recall," E.C. said, "but you had it held by a tone-arm you made out of a bent coat hanger."

"It worked," Delmario protested. "It was voice-activated too, like you said, but real primitive. Just on and off, that's all, and you had to speak real loud. I figured I could improve on it after I got out of school, but I never did." He shrugged. "Nothing like this. This is real sophisticated."

"I've noticed," E.C. said. He craned up his head slightly and said, in a very loud clear voice, "I've had enough music now, thank you." The silence that followed was briefly startling. Peter couldn't think of a thing to say.

Finally E.C. turned to him and said, all seriously, "How did Bunnish get you here, Peter?"

Peter was puzzled. "Get me here? He just invited us. What do you mean?"

"He paid Steve's way, you know," E.C. said. "As for me, I turned down this invitation. Brucie was never one of my favorite people, you know that. He pulled strings to change my mind. I'm with an ad agency in New York. He dangled a big account in front of them, and I was told to come here or lose my job. Interesting, eh?"

Kathy had been sitting on the sofa, sipping her martini and looking bored. "It sounds as though this reunion is important to him," she observed.

E.C. stood up. "Come here," he said. "I want to show you something." The rest of them rose obediently, and followed him across the room. In a shadowy corner surrounded by bookcases, a chessboard had been set up, with a game in progress. The board was made of squares of light and dark wood, painstakingly inlaid into a gorgeous Victorian table. The pieces were ivory and onyx. "Take a look at that," E.C. said.

"That's a beautiful set," Peter said, admiringly. He reached down to lift the Black queen for a closer inspection, and grunted in surprise. The piece wouldn't move.

"Tug away," E.C. said. "It won't do you any good. I've tried. The pieces are glued into position. Every one of them."

Steve Delmario moved around the board, his eyes blinking behind his thick glasses. He set his drink on the table and sank into the chair behind the White pieces. "The position," he said, his voice a bit blurry with drink. "I know it."

E.C. Stuart smiled thinly and brushed his mustache. "Peter," he said, nodding toward the chessboard. "Take a good look."

Peter stared, and all of a sudden it came clear to him, the position on the board became as familiar as his own features in a mirror. "The game," he said. "From the nationals. This is the critical position from Bunnish's game with Vesselere."

E.C. nodded. "I thought so. I wasn't sure."

"Oh, *I'm* sure," Delmario said loudly. "How the hell could I *not* be sure? This is right where Bunny blew it, remember? He played king to knight one, instead of the sac. Cost us the match. Me, I was sitting right next to him, playing the best damned game of chess I ever played. Beat a Master, and what good did it do? Not a damn bit of good, thanks to Bunnish." He looked at the board and glowered. "Knight takes pawn, that's all he's got to play, busts Vesselere wide open. Check, check, check, check, got to be a mate there somewhere."

"You were never able to find it, though, Delmario," Bruce Bunnish said from behind them.

None of them had heard him enter. Peter started like a burglar surprised while copping the family silver.

Their host stood in the doorway a few yards distant. Bunnish had changed, too. He had lost weight since college, and his body looked hard and fit now, though he still had the big round cheeks that Peter remembered. His crew cut had grown out into a healthy head of brown hair, carefully styled and blow-dried. He wore large, tinted glasses and expensive clothes. But he was still Bunnish. His voice was loud and grating, just as Peter remembered it.

Bunnish strolled over to the chessboard almost casually. "You analyzed that position for weeks afterward, Delmario," he said. "You never found the mate."

Delmario stood up. "I found a dozen mates," he said.

"Yes," Bunnish said, "but none of them were forced. Vesselere was a Master. He wouldn't have played into any of your so-called mating lines."

Delmario frowned and took a drink. He was going to say something else—Peter could see him fumbling for the words—but E.C. stood up and took away his chance. "Bruce," he said, holding out his hand. "Good to see you again. How long has it been?"

Bunnish turned and smiled superciliously. "Is that another of your jokes, E.C.? You know how long it has been, and I know how long it has been, so why do you ask? Norten knows, and Delmario knows. Maybe you're asking for Mrs. Norten." He looked at Kathy. "Do you know how long it has been?"

She laughed. "I've heard."

"Ah," said Bunnish. He swung back to face E.C. "Then we all know, so it must be another of your jokes, and I'm not going to answer. Do you remember how you used to phone me at three in the morning, and ask me what time it was? Then I'd tell you, and you'd ask me what I was doing calling you at that hour?"

E.C. frowned and lowered his hand.

"Well," said Bunnish, into the awkward silence that followed, "no sense standing here around this stupid chessboard. Why don't we all go sit down by the fireplace, and talk." He gestured. "Please."

But when they were seated, the silence fell again. Peter took a swallow of beer and realized that he was more than just ill at ease. A palpable tension hung in the air. "Nice place you've got here, Bruce," he said, hoping to lighten the atmosphere.

Bunnish looked around smugly. "I know," he said. "I've done awfully well, you know. Awfully well. You wouldn't believe how much money I have. I hardly know what to do with it all." He smiled broadly and fatuously. "And how about you, my friends? Here I am boasting once again, when I ought to be listening to all of you recount your own triumphs." Bunnish looked at Peter. "You first, Norten. You're the captain, after all. How have you done?"

"All right," Peter said, uncomfortably. "I've done fine. I own a bookstore."

"A *bookstore*! How wonderful! I recall that you always wanted to be in publishing, though I rather thought you'd be writing books instead of selling them. Whatever happened to those novels you were going to write, Peter? Your literary career?"

Peter's mouth was very dry. "I . . . things change, Bruce. I haven't had much time for writing." It sounded so feeble, Peter thought. All at once, he was desperately wishing he was elsewhere.

"No time for writing," echoed Bunnish. "A pity, Norten. You had such promise."

"He's still promising," Kathy put in sharply. "You ought to hear him promise. He's been promising as long as I've known him. He never writes, but he does promise."

Bunnish laughed. "Your wife is very witty," he said to Peter. "She's almost as funny as E.C. was, back in college. You must enjoy being married to her a great deal. I recall how fond you were of E.C.'s little jokes." He looked at E.C. "Are you still a funny man, Stuart?"

E.C. looked annoyed. "I'm hysterical," he said, in a flat voice.

"Good," said Bunnish. He turned to Kathy and said, "I don't know if Peter has told you all the stories about old E.C., but he really played some amazing pranks. Hilarious man, that's our E.C. Stuart. Once, when our chess team had won the city championship, he had a girl-friend of his call up Peter and pretend to be an AP reporter. She interviewed him for an hour before he caught on."

Kathy laughed. "Peter is sometimes a bit slow," she said.

"Oh, that was nothing. Normally I was the one E.C. liked to play tricks on. I didn't go out much, you know. Deathly afraid of girls. But E.C. had a hundred girlfriends, all of them gorgeous. One time he took pity on me and offered to fix me up on a blind date. I accepted eagerly, and when the girl arrived on the corner where we were supposed to meet, she was wearing dark glasses and carrying a cane. Tapping. You know."

Steve Delmario guffawed, tried to stifle his laughter, and nearly choked on his drink. "Sorry," he wheezed, "sorry."

Bunnish waved casually. "Oh, go ahead, laugh. It *was* funny. The girl wasn't really blind, you know, she was a drama student who was re-hearsing a part in a play. But it took me all night to find that out. I was such a fool. And that was only one joke. There were hundreds of others."

E.C. looked somber. "That was a long time ago. We were kids. It's all behind us now, Bruce."

"Bruce?" Bunnish sounded surprised. "Why, Stuart, that's the first time you've ever called me *Bruce*. You *have* changed. You were the one who started calling me Brucie. God, how I hated that name! Brucie, Brucie, Brucie, I *loathed* it. How many times did I ask you to call me Bruce? How many times? Why, I don't recall. I do recall, though, that after three years you finally came up to me at one meeting and said that you'd thought it over, and now you agreed that I was right, that Brucie was not an appropriate name for a Class A chess player, a twenty-year-old, an officer in ROTC. Your exact words. I remember the whole speech, E.C. It took me so by surprise that I didn't know what to say, so I said, *'Good, it's about time!'* And then you grinned, and said that Brucie was out, that you'd never call me Brucie again. From now on, you said, you'd call me *Bunny*."

Kathy laughed, and Delmario choked down an explosive outburst, but Peter only felt cold all over. Bunnish's smile was genial enough, but his tone was pure iced venom as he recounted the incident. E.C. did not look amused either. Peter took a swallow of his beer, casting about for some ploy to get the conversation onto a different track. "Do any of you still play?" he heard himself blurt out.

They all looked at him. Delmario seemed almost befuddled. "Play?" he said. He blinked down at his empty glass.

"Help yourself to a refill," Bunnish told him. "You know where it is." He smiled at Peter as Delmario moved off to the bar. "You mean chess, of course."

"Chess," Peter said. "You remember chess. Odd little pastime played with black and white pieces and lots of two-faced clocks." He looked around. "Don't tell me we've *all* given it up?"

E.C. shrugged. "I'm too busy. I haven't played a rated game since college."

Delmario had returned, ice cubes clinking softly in a tumbler full of bourbon. "I played a little after college," he said, "but not for the last five years." He sat down heavily, and stared into the cold fireplace. "Those were my bad years. Wife left me, I lost a couple jobs. Bunny here was way ahead of me. Every goddamn idea I came up with, he had a patent on it already. Got so I was useless. That was when I started to drink." He smiled, and took a sip. "Yeah," he said. "Just then. And I stopped playing chess. It all comes out, you know, it all comes out over the board. I was losing, losing lots. To all these *fish,* God, I tell you, I couldn't take it. Rating went down to Class B." Delmario took another drink, and looked at Peter. "You need something to play good chess, you know what I'm saying? A kind of... hell, I don't know... a kind of arrogance. Self-confidence. It's all wrapped up with ego, that kind of stuff, and I didn't have it anymore, whatever it was. I used to have it, but I lost it all. I had bad luck, and I looked around one day and it was gone, and my chess was gone with it. So I quit." He lifted the tumbler to his lips, hesitated, and drained it all. Then he smiled for them. "Quit," he repeated. "Gave it up. Chucked it away. Bailed out." He chuckled, and stood up, and went off to the bar again.

"I play," Bunnish said forcefully. "I'm a Master now."

Delmario stopped in midstride, and fixed Bunnish with such a look of total loathing that it could have killed. Peter saw that Steve's hand was shaking.

"I'm very happy for you, Bruce," E.C. Stuart said. "Please do enjoy your Mastership, and your money, and Bunnishland." He stood and straightened his vest, frowning. "Meanwhile, I'm going to be going."

"Going?" said Bunnish. "Really, E.C., so soon? Must you?"

"Bunnish," E.C. said, "you can spend the next four days playing your little ego games with Steve and Peter, if you like, but I'm afraid I am not amused. You always were a pimple-brain, and I have better things to do with my life than to sit here and watch you squeeze out ten-year-old pus. Am I making myself clear?"

"Oh, perfectly," Bunnish said.

"Good," said E.C. He looked at the others. "Kathy, it was nice meeting you. I'm sorry it wasn't under better circumstances. Peter, Steve, if either of you comes to New York in the near future, I hope you'll look me up. I'm in the book."

"E.C., don't you . . ." Peter began, but he knew it was useless. Even in the old days, E.C. Stuart was headstrong. You could never talk him into or out of anything.

"Good-bye," he said, interrupting Peter. He went briskly to the elevator, and they watched the wood-paneled doors close on him.

"He'll be back," Bunnish said after the elevator had gone.

"I don't think so," Peter replied.

Bunnish got up, smiling broadly. Deep dimples appeared in his large, round cheeks. "Oh, but he will, Norten. You see, it's my turn to play the little jokes now, and E.C. will soon find that out."

"What?" Delmario said.

"Don't you fret about it, you'll understand soon enough," Bunnish said. "Meanwhile, please do excuse me. I have to see about dinner. You all must be ravenous. I'm making dinner myself, you know. I sent my servants away, so we could have a nice private reunion." He looked at his watch, a heavy gold Swiss. "Let's all meet in the dining room in, say, an hour. Everything should be ready by then. We can talk some more. About life. About chess." He smiled, and left.

Kathy was smiling too. "Well," she said to Peter after Bunnish had left the room, "this is all vastly more entertaining than I would have imagined. I feel as if I just walked into a Harold Pinter play."

"Who's that?" Delmario asked, resuming his seat.

Peter ignored him. "I don't like any of this," he said. "What the hell did Bunnish mean about playing a joke on us?"

He didn't have to wait long for an answer. While Kathy went to fix herself another martini, they heard the elevator again, and turned expectantly toward the doors. E.C. stepped out frowning. "Where is he?" he said in a hard voice.

"He went to cook dinner," Peter said. "What is it? He said something about a joke. . . ."

"Those garage doors won't open," E.C. said. "I can't get my car out. There's no place to go without it. We must be fifty miles from the nearest civilization."

"I'll go down and ram out with my VW," Delmario said helpfully. "Like in the movies."

"Don't be absurd," E.C. said. "That door is stainless steel. There's no way you're going to batter it down." He scowled and brushed back one end of his mustache. "Battering down Brucie, however, is a much more viable proposition. Where the hell is the kitchen?"

Peter sighed. "I wouldn't if I were you, E.C.," he said. "From the way he's been acting, he'd just love a chance to clap you in jail. If you touch him, it's assault, you know that."

"Phone the police," Kathy suggested.

Peter looked around. "Now that you mention it, I don't see a phone anywhere in this room. Do you?" Silence. "There was no phone in our suite, either, that I recall."

"Hey!" Delmario said. "That's right, Pete, you're right."

E.C. sat down. "He appears to have us checkmated," he said.

"The exact word," said Peter. "Bunnish is playing some kind of game with us. He said so himself. A joke."

"Ha, ha," said E.C. "What do you suggest we do, then? Laugh?"

Peter shrugged. "Eat dinner, talk, have our reunion, find out what the hell Bunnish wants with us."

"Win the game, guys, that's what we do," Delmario said.

E.C. stared at him. "What the hell does that mean?"

Delmario sipped his bourbon and grinned. "Peter said Bunny was playing some kind of game with us, right? OK, fine. Let's play. Let's beat him at this goddamned game, whatever the hell it is." He chuckled. "Hell, guys, this is the Funny Bunny we're playing. Maybe he is a Master, I don't give a good goddamn, he'll still find a way to blow it in the end. You know how it was. Bunnish *always* lost the big games. He'll lose this one, too."

"I wonder," said Peter. "I wonder."

Peter brought another bottle of Heineken back to the suite with him, and sat in a deck chair on the patio drinking it while Kathy tried out the hot tub.

"This is nice," she said from the tub. "Relaxing. Sensuous, even. Why don't you come on in?"

"No, thanks," Peter said.

"We ought to get one of these."

"Right. We could put it in our living room. The people in the apartment downstairs would love it." He took a swallow of beer and shook his head.

"What are you thinking about?" Kathy asked.

Peter smiled grimly. "Chess, believe it or not."

"Oh? Do tell."

"Life is a lot like chess," he said.

She laughed. "Really? I'd never noticed, somehow."

Peter refused to let her needling get to him. "All a matter of choices. Every move you face choices, and every choice leads to different variations. It branches and then branches again, and sometimes the variation you pick isn't as good as it looked, isn't sound at all. But you don't know that until your game is over."

"I hope you'll repeat this when I'm out of the tub," Kathy said. "I want to write it all down for posterity."

"I remember, back in college, how many possibilities life seemed to hold. Variations. I knew, of course, that I'd only live one of my fantasy lives, but for a few years there, I had them all, all the branches, all the variations. One day I could dream of being a novelist, one day I would be a journalist covering Washington, the next—oh, I don't know, a politician, a teacher, whatever. My dream lives. Full of dream wealth and dream women. All the things I was going to do, all the places I was going to live. They were mutually exclusive, of course, but since I didn't have any of them, in a sense I had them all. Like when you sit down at a chessboard to begin a game, and you don't know what the opening will be. Maybe it will be a Sicilian, or a French, or a Ruy Lopez. They all coexist, all the variations, until you start making the moves. You always dream of winning, no matter what line you choose, but the variations are still...different." He drank some more beer. "Once the game begins, the possibilities narrow and narrow and narrow, the other variations fade, and you're left with what you've got—a position half of your own making, and half chance, as embodied by that stranger across the board. Maybe you've got a good game, or maybe you're in trouble, but in any case there's just that one position to work from. The might-have-beens are gone."

Kathy climbed out of the hot tub and began toweling herself off. Steam rose from the water, and moved gently around her. Peter found himself looking at her almost with tenderness, something he had not felt in a long time. Then she spoke, and ruined it. "You missed your calling," she said, rubbing briskly with the towel. "You should have taken up poster-writing. You have a knack for poster profundity. You know, like, *I am not in this world to live up to your expect—*"

"Enough," Peter said. "How much blood do you have to draw, damn it?"

Kathy stopped and looked at him. She frowned. "You're really down, aren't you?" she said.

Peter stared off at the mountains, and did not bother to reply.

The concern left her voice as quickly as it had come. "Another depression, huh? Drink another beer, why don't you? Feel sorry for yourself some more. By midnight you'll have worked yourself up to a good crying jag. Go on."

"I keep thinking of that match," Peter said.

"Match?"

"In the nationals," he said. "Against Chicago. It's weird, but I keep having this funny feeling, like...like it was right there that it all started to go bad. We had a chance to do something big, something special. But it slipped away from us, and nothing has been right since. A losing variation, Kathy. We picked a losing variation, and we've been losing ever since. All of us."

Kathy sat down on the edge of the tub. "All of you?"

Peter nodded. "Look at us. I failed as a novelist, failed as a journal-ist, and now I've got a failing bookstore. Not to mention a bitch wife. Steve is a drunk who couldn't even get together enough money to pay his way out here. E.C. is an aging account executive with an indiffer-ent track record, going nowhere. Losers. You said it, in the car."

She smiled. "Ah, but what about our host? Bunnish lost bigger than any of you, and he seems to have won everything since."

"Hmmmm," said Peter. He sipped thoughtfully at his beer. "I wonder. Oh, he's rich enough, I'll give you that. But he's got a chess-board in his living room with the pieces glued into position, so he can stare every day at the place he went wrong in a game played ten years ago. That doesn't sound like a winner to me."

She stood up, and shook loose her hair. It was long and auburn and it fell around her shoulders gorgeously, and Peter remembered the sweet lady he had married eight years ago, when he was a bright young writer working hard on his first novel. He smiled. "You look nice," he said.

Kathy seemed startled. "You *are* feeling morose," she said. "Are you sure you don't have a fever?"

"No fever. Just a memory, and a lot of regrets."

"Ah," she said. She walked back toward their bedroom, and snapped the towel at him in passing. "C'mon, captain. Your team is go-ing to be waiting, and all this heavy philosophy has given me quite an appetite."

————

The food was fine, but the dinner was awful.

They ate thick slabs of rare prime rib, with big baked potatoes and lots of fresh vegetables. The wine looked expensive and tasted wonder-ful. Afterwards, they had their choice of three desserts, plus fresh-ground coffee and several delicious liqueurs. Yet the meal was strained and unpleasant, Peter thought. Steve Delmario was in pretty bad shape even before he came to the table, and while he was there he drank wine as if it were water, getting louder and fuzzier in the process. E.C. Stuart was coldly quiet, his fury barely held in check behind an icy, aloof demeanor. And Bunnish thwarted every one of Peter's attempts to move conversation to safe neutral ground.

His genial expansiveness was a poor mask for gloating, and he insisted on opening old wounds from their college years. Every time Peter recounted an anecdote that was amusing or harmless, Bunnish smiled and countered with one that stank of hurt and rejection.

Finally, over coffee, E.C. could stand no more of it. "Pus," he said loudly, interrupting Bunnish. It was about the third word he'd permitted himself the entire meal. "Pus and more pus. Bunnish, what's the point? You've brought us here. You've got us trapped here, with you. Why? So you can prove that we treated you shabbily back in college? Is that the idea? If so, fine. You've made your point. You were treated shabbily. I am ashamed, I am guilty. Mea culpa, mea culpa, mea maxima culpa. Now let's end it. It's over."

"Over?" said Bunnish, smiling. "Perhaps it is. But you've changed, E.C. Back when I was the butt of your jokes, you'd recount them for weeks. *Over* wasn't so final then, was it? And what about my game with Vesselere in the nationals? When that was over, did we forget it? Oh, no, we did not. That game was played in December, you'll recall. I heard about it until I graduated in May. At every meeting. That game was *never* over for me. Delmario liked to show me a different checkmate every time I saw him. Our dear captain refrained from playing me in any league matches for the rest of the year. And you, E.C., you liked to greet me with, 'Say, Bunny, lost any big ones lately?' You even reprinted that game in the club newsletter, and mailed it in to *Chess Life*. No doubt all this seems like ancient history to you. I have this trick memory, though. I can't forget things quite so easily. I remember it all. I remember the way Vesselere sat there, with his hands folded on his stomach, never moving, staring at me out of those itty-bitty eyes of his. I remember the way he moved his pieces, very carefully, very daintily, lifting each one between thumb and forefinger. I remember wandering into the halls between moves to get a drink of water, and seeing Norten over by the wall charts, talking to Mavora from the A team. You know what he was saying? He was gesturing with his hands, all worked up, and he was telling him, *He's going to blow it, damn it, he's going to blow it!* Isn't that right, Peter? And Les looked over at me as I passed, and said, *Lose this one and your ass is grass, Bunny!* He was another endearing soul. I remember all the people who kept coming to look at my game. I remember Norten standing in the corner with Hal

Winslow, the two mighty captains, talking heatedly. Winslow was all rumpled and needed a shave and he had his clipboard, and he was trying to figure out who'd finish where if we won, or tied, or lost. I remember how it felt when I tipped over my king, too. I remember the way Delmario started kicking the wall, the way E.C. shrugged and glanced up at the ceiling, and the way Peter came over and just said *Bunnish!* and shook his head. You see? My trick memory is as tricky as ever, and I haven't forgotten a thing. And especially I haven't forgotten that game. I can recite all the moves to you right now, if you'd like."

"Shit," said Steve Delmario. "Only one important move to recite, Bunny. Knight takes pawn, that's the move you ought to recite. The sac, the winning sac, the one you didn't play. I forget what kind of feeble thing you did instead."

Bunnish smiled. "My move was king to knight one," he said. "To protect my rook pawn. I'd castled long, and Vesselere was threatening to snatch it."

"Pawn, shmawn," said Delmario. "You had him busted. The sac would have gutted that whale like nobody's goddamned business. What a laugh that would have been. The bunny rabbit beating the whale. Old Hal Winslow would have been so shocked he would have dropped his clipboard. But you blew it, guarding some diddly-squat little pawn. You blew it."

"So you told me," said Bunnish. "And told me, and told me."

"Look," Peter said, "I don't see the sense in rehashing all of this. Steve is drunk, Bruce. You can see that. He doesn't know what he's saying."

"He knows exactly what he's saying, Norten," Bunnish replied. He smiled thinly and removed his glasses. Peter was startled by his eyes. The hatred there was almost tangible, and there was something else as well, something old and bitter and somehow *trapped*. The eyes passed lightly over Kathy, who was sitting quietly amidst all the old hostility, and touched Steve Delmario, Peter Norten, and E.C. Stuart each in turn, with vast loathing and vast amusement.

"Enough," Peter said, almost pleadingly.

"NO!" said Delmario. The drink had made him belligerent. "It's not enough, it'll never be enough, goddamn it. Get out a set, Bunny! I

dare you! We'll analyze it right now, go over the whole thing again, I'll show you how you pissed it all away." He pulled himself to his feet.

"I have a better idea," said Bunnish. "Sit down, Delmario."

Delmario blinked uncertainly, and then fell back into his chair.

"Good," said Bunnish. "We'll get to my idea in a moment, but first I'm going to tell you all a story. As Archie Bunker once said, revenge is the best way to get even. But it isn't revenge unless the victim knows. So I'm going to tell you. I'm going to tell you exactly how I've ruined your lives."

"Oh, come off it!" E.C. said.

"You never did like stories, E.C.," Bunnish said. "Know why? Because when someone tells a story, they become the center of attention. And you always needed to be the center of attention, wherever you were. Now you're not the center of anything, though. How does it feel to be insignificant?"

E.C. gave a disgusted shake of his head and poured himself more coffee. "Go on, Bunnish," he said. "Tell your story. You have a captive audience."

"I do, don't I?" Bunnish smiled. "All right. It all begins with that game. Me and Vesselere. I did *not* blow that game. It was never won."

Delmario made a rude noise.

"I know," Bunnish continued, unperturbed, "now, but I did not know then. I thought that you were right. I'd thrown it all away, I thought. It ate at me. For years and years, more years than you would believe. Every night I went to sleep replaying that game in my head. That game blighted my entire life. It became an obsession. I wanted only one thing—another chance. I wanted to go back, somehow, to choose another line, to make different moves, to come out a winner. I'd picked the wrong variation, that was all. I knew that if I had another chance, I'd do better. For more than fifty years, I worked toward that end, and that end alone."

Peter swallowed a mouthful of cold coffee hastily and said, "What? Fifty years? You mean five, don't you?"

"Fifty," Bunnish repeated.

"You are insane," said E.C.

"No," said Bunnish. "I am a genius. Have you ever heard of time travel, any of you?"

"It doesn't exist," said Peter. "The paradoxes..."

Bunnish waved him quiet. "You're right and you're wrong, Norten. It exists, but only in a sort of limited fashion. Yet that is enough. I won't bore you with mathematics none of you can understand. Analogy is easier. Time is said to be the fourth dimension, but it differs from the other three in one conspicuous way—our consciousness moves along it. From past to present only, alas. Time itself does not flow, no more than, say, width can flow. Our minds flicker from one instant of time to the next. This analogy was my starting point. I reasoned that if consciousness can move in one direction, it can move in the other direction as well. It took me fifty years to work out the details, however, and make what I call a *flashback* possible.

"That was in my first life, gentlemen, a life of failure and ridicule and poverty. I tended my obsession and did what I had to so as to keep myself fed. And I hated you, each of you, for every moment of those fifty years. My bitterness was inflamed as I watched each of you succeed, while I struggled and failed. I met Norten once, twenty years after college, at an autographing party. You were so patronizing. It was then that I determined to ruin you, all of you.

"And I did. What is there to say? I perfected my device at the age of seventy-one. There is no way to move matter through time, but *mind,* mind is a different issue. My device would send my mind back to any point in my own lifetime that I chose, superimpose my consciousness with all of its memories on the consciousness of my earlier self. I could take nothing with me, of course." Bunnish smiled and tapped his temple significantly. "But I still had my photographic memory. It was more than enough. I memorized things I would need to know in my new life, and I flashed back to my youth. I was given another chance, a chance to make some different moves in the game of life. I did."

Steve Delmario blinked. "Your body," he said blurrily. "What happened to your body, huh?"

"An interesting question. The kick of the flashback kills the would-be time-traveler. The body, that is. The timeline itself goes on, however. At least my equations indicate that it should. I've never been around to witness it. Meanwhile, changes in the past create a new, variant timeline."

"Oh, alternate tracks," Delmario said. He nodded. "Yeah."

Kathy laughed. "I can't believe I'm sitting here listening to all this," she said. "And that *he*"—she pointed to Delmario—"is taking it seriously."

E.C. Stuart had been looking idly at the ceiling, with a disdainful, faintly tolerant smile on his face. Now he straightened. "I agree," he said to Kathy. "I am not so gullible as you were, Bruce," he told Bunnish, "and if you are trying to get some laughs by having us swallow this crock of shit, it isn't going to work."

Bunnish turned to Peter. "Captain, what's your vote?"

"Well," said Peter carefully, "all this is a little hard to credit, Bruce. You spoke of the game becoming an obsession with you, and I think that's true. I think you ought to be talking to a professional about this, not to us."

"A professional what?" Bunnish said.

Peter fidgeted uncomfortably. "You know. A shrink or a counselor."

Bunnish chuckled. "Failure hasn't made you any less patronizing," he said. "You were just as bad in the bookstore, in that line where you turned out to be a successful novelist."

Peter sighed, "Bruce, can't you see how pathetic these delusions of yours are? I mean, you've obviously been quite a success, and none of us have done as well, but even that wasn't enough for you, so you've constructed all these elaborate fantasies about how *you* have been the one behind our various failures. Vicarious, imaginary revenge."

"Neither vicarious nor imaginary, Norten," Bunnish snapped. "I can tell you exactly how I did it."

"Let him tell his stories, Peter," E.C. said. "Then maybe he'll let us out of this funny farm."

"Why, thank you, E.C.," Bunnish said. He looked around the table with smug satisfaction, like a man about to live out a dream he has cherished for a long, long time. Finally he fastened on Steve Delmario. "I'll start with you," he said, "because in fact, I *did* start with you. You were easy to destroy, Delmario, because you were always so limited. In the original timeline, you were as wealthy as I am in this one. While I spent my life perfecting my flashback device, you made vast fortunes in the wide world out there. Electronic games at first, later more basic stuff, home computers, that sort of thing. You were born for that, and you were the best in the business, inspired and ingenious.

"When I flashed back, I simply took your place. Before using my device, I studied all your early little games, your cleverest ideas, the basic patents that came later and made you so rich. And I memorized all of them, along with the dates on which you'd come up with each and every one. Back in the past, armed with all this foreknowledge, it was child's play to beat you to the punch. Again and again. In those early years, Delmario, didn't it ever strike you as strange the way I anticipated every one of your small brainstorms? I'm living *your* life, Delmario."

Delmario's hand had begun to tremble as he listened. His face looked dead. "God damn you," he said. "God *damn* you."

"Don't let him get to you, Steve," E.C. put in. "He's just making this up to see us squirm. It's all too absurd for words."

"But it's *true*," Delmario wailed, looking from E.C. to Bunnish and then, helpless, at Peter. Behind the thick lenses his eyes seemed wild. "Peter, what he said—all my ideas—he was always ahead of me, he, he, I *told* you, he—"

"Yes," Peter said firmly, "and you told Bruce too, when we were talking earlier. Now he's just using your fears against you."

Delmario opened his mouth, but no words came out.

"Have another drink," Bunnish suggested.

Delmario stared at Bunnish as if he were about to leap up and strangle him. Peter tensed himself to intervene. But then, instead, Delmario reached out for a half-empty wine bottle, and filled his glass sloppily.

"This is contemptible, Bruce," E.C. said.

Bunnish turned to face him. "Delmario's ruin was easy and dramatic," he said. "You were more difficult, Stuart. He had nothing to live for but his work, you see, and when I took that away from him, he just collapsed. I only had to anticipate him a half-dozen times before all of his belief in himself was gone, and he did the rest himself. But you, E.C., you had more resources."

"Go on with the fairy tale, Bunnish," E.C. said in a put-upon tone.

"Delmario's ideas had made me rich," Bunnish said. "I used the money against you. Your fall was less satisfying and less resounding than Delmario's. He went from the heights to the pits. You were only a moderate success to begin with, and I had to settle for turning you into a moderate failure. But I managed. I pulled strings behind the scenes to lose you a number of large accounts. When you were with Foote, Cone I made sure another agency hired away a copywriter named Allerd, just before he came up with a campaign that would have rebounded to your credit. And remember when you left that position to take a better-paying slot at a brand-new agency? Remember how quickly that agency folded, leaving you without an income? That was me. I've given your career twenty or thirty little shoves like that. Haven't you ever wondered at how infallibly wrong most of your professional moves have been, Stuart? At your bad luck?"

"No," said E.C. "I'm doing well enough, thank you."

Bunnish smiled. "I played one other little joke on you, too. You can thank me for that case of herpes you picked up last year. The lady who gave it to you was well paid. I had to search for her for a good number of years until I found the right combination—an out-of-work actress who was young and gorgeous and precisely your type, yet sufficiently desperate to do just about anything, and gifted with an incurable venereal disease as well. How did you like her, Stuart? It's your fault, you know. I just put her in your path, you did the rest yourself. And I thought it was so fitting, after my blind date and all."

E.C.'s expression did not change. "If you think this is going to break me down or make me believe you, you're way off base. All this proves is that you've had me investigated, and managed to dig up some dirt on my life."

"Oh," said Bunnish. "Always so skeptical, Stuart. Scared that if you believe, you'll wind up looking foolish. Tsk." He turned toward Peter. "And you, Norten. You. Our fearless leader. You were the most difficult of all."

Peter met Bunnish's eyes and said nothing.

"I read your novel, you know," Bunnish said casually.

"I've never published a novel."

"Oh, but you have! In the original timeline, that is. Quite a success too. The critics loved it, and it even appeared briefly on the bottom of the *Times* bestseller list."

Peter was not amused. "This is so obvious and pathetic," he said.

"It was called *Beasts in a Cage,* I believe," Bunnish said.

Peter had been sitting and listening with contempt, humoring a sick, sad man. Now, suddenly, he sat upright as if slapped.

He heard Kathy suck in her breath. "My God," she said.

E.C. seemed puzzled. "Peter? What is it? You look..."

"No one knows about that book," Peter said. "How the hell did you find out? My old agent, you must have gotten the title from him. Yes. That's it, isn't it?"

"No," said Bunnish, smiling complacently.

"You're lying!"

"Peter, what is it?" said E.C. "Why are you so upset?"

Peter looked at him. "My book," he said. "I... *Beasts in a Cage* was..."

"There was such a book?"

"Yes," Peter said. He swallowed nervously, feeling confused and angry. "Yes, there was. I... after college. My first novel." He gave a nervous laugh. "I thought it would be the first. I had... had a lot of hopes. It was ambitious. A serious book, but I thought it had commercial possibilities as well. The circus. It was about the circus, you know how I was always fascinated by the circus. A metaphor for life, I thought, a kind of life, but very colorful too, and dying, a dying institution. I thought I could write the great circus novel. After college, I traveled with Ringling Brothers' Blue Show for a year, doing research. I was a butcher, I... that's what they call the vendors in the stands, you see. A year of research, and I took two years to write the novel. The central character was a boy who worked with the big cats. I finally finished it and sent it off to my agent, and less than three weeks after I'd gotten it into the mail, I, I..." He couldn't finish.

But E.C. understood. He frowned. "That circus bestseller? What was the title?"

"Blue Show," Peter said, the words bitter in his mouth. "By Donald Hastings Sullivan, some old hack who'd written fifty gothics and a dozen formula westerns, all under pen names. Such a book, from such a writer. No one could believe it. E.C., *I* couldn't believe it. It was *my*

book, under a different title. Oh, it wasn't word-for-word. *Beasts in a Cage* was a lot better written. But the story, the background, the incidents, even a few of the character names...it was frightening. My agent never marketed my book. He said it was too much like *Blue Show* to be publishable, that no one would touch it. And even if I did get it published, he warned me, I would be labeled derivative at best, and a plagiarist at worst. It looked like a rip-off, he said. Three years of my life, and he called it a rip-off. We had words. He fired me, and I couldn't get another agent to take me on. I never wrote another book. The first one had taken too much out of me." Peter turned to Bunnish. "I destroyed my manuscript, burned every copy. No one knew about that book except my agent, me, and Kathy. How did you find out?"

"I told you," said Bunnish. "I read it."

"You damned liar!" Peter said. He scooped up a glass in a white rage, and flung it down the table at Bunnish's smiling face, wanting to obliterate that complacent grin, to see it dissolve into blood and ruin. But Bunnish ducked and the glass shattered against a wall.

"Easy, Peter," E.C. said. Delmario was blinking in owlish stupidity, lost in an alcoholic haze. Kathy was gripping the edge of the table. Her knuckles had gone white.

"Methinks our captain doth protest too much," Bunnish said, his dimples showing. "You know I'm telling the truth, Norten. I read your novel. I can recite the whole plot to prove it." He shrugged. "In fact, I did recite the whole plot. To Donald Hastings Sullivan, who wrote *Blue Show* while in my employ. I would have done it myself, but I had no aptitude for writing. Sully was glad for the chance. He got a handsome flat fee and we split the royalties, which were considerable."

"You son of a bitch," Peter said, but he said it without force. He felt his rage ebbing away, leaving behind only a terrible sickly feeling, the certainty of defeat. He felt cheated and helpless and, all of a sudden, he realized that he believed Bunnish, believed every word of his preposterous story. "It's true, isn't it?" he said. "It is really true. You did it to me. You. You stole my words, my dreams, all of it."

Bunnish said nothing.

"And the rest of it," Peter said, "the other failures, those were all you too, weren't they? After *Blue Show,* when I went into journalism...that big story that evaporated on me, all my sources suddenly denying everything or vanishing, so it looked like I'd made it all up. The assignments that evaporated, all those lawsuits, plagiarism, invasion of privacy, libel, every time I turned around I was being sued. Two years, and they just about ran me out of the profession. But it wasn't bad luck, was it? It was you. You stole my *life*."

"You ought to be complimented, Norten. I had to break you twice. The first time I managed to kill your literary career with *Blue Show*, but then while my back was turned you managed to become a terribly popular journalist. Prizewinning, well known, all of it, and by then it was too late to do anything. I had to flash back once more to get you, do everything all over."

"I ought to kill you, Bunnish," Peter heard himself say.

E.C. shook his head. "Peter," he said, in the tone of a man explaining something to a high-grade moron, "this is all an elaborate hoax. Don't take Bunny seriously."

Peter stared at his old teammate. "No, E.C. It's true. It's all true. Stop worrying about being the butt of a joke, and think about it. It makes sense. It explains everything that has happened to us."

E.C. Stuart made a disgusted noise, frowned, and fingered the end of his mustache.

"Listen to your captain, Stuart," Bunnish said.

Peter turned back to him. "Why? That's what I want to know. *Why?* Because we played jokes on you? Kidded you? Maybe we were rotten, I don't know, it didn't seem to be so terrible at the time. You brought a lot of it on yourself. But whatever we might have done to you, we never deserved this. We were your teammates, your friends."

Bunnish's smile curdled, and the dimples disappeared. "You were *never* my friends."

Steve Delmario nodded vigorously at that. "You're no friend of mine, Funny Bunny, I tell you that. Know what you are? A *wimp*. You were always a goddamn wimp, that's why nobody ever liked you, you were just a damn wimp loser with a crew cut. Hell, you think you were the only one ever got kidded? What about me, the ol' last man on earth, huh, what about that? What about the jokes E.C. played on Pete, on Les, on all the others?" He took a drink. "Bringing us here like this, that's another damn wimp thing to do. You're the same Bunny you always were. Wasn't enough to *do* something, you had to brag about it, let everybody know. And if somethin' went wrong, was never your fault, was it? You only lost 'cause the room was too noisy, or the lighting was bad, whatever." Delmario stood up. "You make me sick. Well, you screwed up all our lives maybe, and now you told us about it. Good for you. You had your damn wimp fun. Now let us out of here."

"I second that motion," said E.C.

"Why, I wouldn't think of it," Bunnish replied. "Not just yet. We haven't played any chess yet. A few games for old times' sake."

Delmario blinked, and moved slightly as he stood holding the back of his chair. "The *game*," he said, suddenly reminded of his challenge to Bunnish of a few minutes ago. "We were goin' to play over the game."

Bunnish folded his hands neatly in front of him on the table. "We can do better than that," he said. "I am a very fair man, you see. None of you ever gave me a chance, but I'll give one to you, to each of you. I've stolen your lives. Wasn't that what you said, Norten? Well, *friends*, I'll give you a shot at winning those lives back. We'll play a little chess. We'll replay the game, from the critical position. I'll take Vesselere's side and you can have mine. The three of you can consult, if you like, or I'll play you one by one. I don't care. All you have to do is beat me. Win the game you say I should have won, and I'll let you go, and give you anything you like. Money, property, a job, whatever."

"Go t'hell, wimp," Delmario said. "I'm not interested in your damn money."

Bunnish picked up his glasses from the table and donned them, smiling widely. "Or," he said, "if you prefer, you can win a chance to use my flashback device. You can go back then, anticipate me, do it all over, live the lives you were destined to live before I dealt myself in. Just think of it. It's the best opportunity you'll ever have, any of you, and I'm making it so *easy*. All you have to do is win a won game."

"Winning a won game is one of the hardest things in chess," Peter said sullenly. But even as he said it, his mind was racing, excitement stirring deep in his gut. It was a chance, he thought, a chance to re-shape the ruins of his life, to make it come out right. To obliterate the wrong turnings, to taste the wine of success instead of the wormwood of failure, to avoid the mockery that his marriage to Kathy had become. Dead hopes rose like ghosts to dance again in the graveyard of his dreams. He had to take the shot, he knew. He *had* to.

Steve Delmario was there before him. "I can win that goddamned game," he boomed drunkenly. "I could win it with my eyes shut. You're on, Bunny. Get out a set, damn you!"

Bunnish laughed and stood up, putting his big hands flat on the tabletop and using them to push himself to his feet. "Oh no, Delmario. You're not going to have the excuse of being drunk when you lose. I'm going to crush you when you are cold stone sober. Tomorrow. I'll play you tomorrow."

Delmario blinked furiously. "Tomorrow," he echoed.

———

Later, when they were alone in their room, Kathy turned on him. "Peter," she said, "let's get out of here. Tonight. Now."

Peter was sitting before the fire. He had found a small chess set in the top drawer of his bedside table, and had set up the critical position from Vesselere-Bunnish to study it. He scowled at the distraction and said, "Get out? How the hell do you propose we do that, with our car locked up in that garage?"

"There's got to be a phone here somewhere. We could search, find it, call for help. Or just walk."

"It's December, and we're in the mountains miles from anywhere. We try to walk out of here and we could freeze to death. No." He turned his attention back to the chessboard and tried to concentrate.

"Peter," she said angrily.

He looked up again. "What?" he snapped. "Can't you see I'm busy?"

"We have to do *something.* This whole scene is insane. Bunnish needs to be locked up."

"He was telling the truth," Peter said.

Kathy's expression softened, and for an instant there was something like sorrow on her face. "I know," she said softly.

"You know," Peter mimicked savagely. "You know, do you? Well, do you know how it *feels?* That bastard is going to pay. He's responsible for every rotten thing that has happened to me. For all I know, he's probably responsible for you."

Kathy's lips moved only slightly, and her eyes moved not at all, but suddenly the sorrow and sympathy were gone from her face, and instead Peter saw familiar pity, well-honed contempt. "He's just going to crush you again," she said coldly. "He wants you to lust after this chance, because he intends to deny it to you. He's going to beat you, Peter. How are you going to like that? How are you going to live with it, afterwards?"

Peter looked down at the chess pieces. "That's what he intends, yeah. But he's a moron. This is a *won* position. It's only a matter of find-ing the winning line, the right variation. And we've got three shots at it. Steve goes first. If he loses, E.C. and I will be able to learn from his mistakes. I won't lose. I've lost everything else, maybe, but not this. This time I'm going to be a winner. You'll see."

"I'll see, all right," Kathy said. "You pitiful bastard."

Peter ignored her, and moved a piece. Knight takes pawn.

KATHY REMAINED IN THE SUITE THE NEXT MORNING. "GO PLAY your damn games if you like," she told Peter. "I'm going to soak in the hot tub, and read. I want no part of this."

"Suit yourself," Peter said. He slammed the door behind him, and thought once again what a bitch he'd married.

Downstairs, in the huge living room, Bunnish was setting up the board. The set he'd chosen was not ornate and expensive like the one in the corner, with its pieces glued into place. Sets like that looked good for decorative purposes, but were useless in serious play. Instead Bunnish had shifted a plain wooden table to the center of the room, and fetched out a standard tournament set: a vinyl board in green and white that he unrolled carefully, a well-worn set of Drueke pieces of standard Staunton design, cast in black and white plastic with lead weights in the bases, beneath the felt, to give them a nice heft. He placed each piece into position from memory, without once looking at the game frozen on the expensive inlaid board across the room. Then he began to set a double-faced chess clock. "Can't play without the clock, you know," he said, smiling. "I'll set it exactly the same as it stood that day in Evanston."

When everything was finished, Bunnish surveyed the board with satisfaction and seated himself behind Vesselere's Black pieces. "Ready?" he asked.

Steve Delmario sat down opposite him, looking pale and terribly hungover. He was holding a big tumbler full of orange juice, and behind his thick glasses his eyes moved nervously. "Yeah," he said. "Go on."

Bunnish pushed the button that started Delmario's clock.

Very quickly, Delmario reached out, played knight takes pawn—the pieces clicked together softly as he made the capture—and used the pawn he'd taken to punch the clock, stopping his own timer and starting Bunnish's.

"The sac," said Bunnish. "What a surprise." He took the knight.

Delmario played bishop takes pawn, saccing another piece. Bunnish was forced to capture with his king. He seemed unperturbed. He was smiling faintly, his dimples faint creases in his big cheeks, his eyes clear and sharp and cheerful behind his tinted eyeglasses.

Steve Delmario was leaning forward over the board, his dark eyes sweeping back and forth over the position, back and forth, over and over again as if double-checking that everything was really where he thought it was. He crossed and uncrossed his legs. Peter, standing just behind him, could almost feel the tension beating off Delmario in waves, twisting him. Even E.C. Stuart, seated a few feet distant in a big comfortable armchair, was staring at the game intently. The clock ticked softly. Delmario lifted his hand to move his queen, but hesitated with his fingers poised above it. His hand trembled.

"What's the matter, Steve?" Bunnish asked. He steepled his hands just beneath his chin, and smiled when Delmario looked up at him. "You hesitate. Don't you know? He who hesitates is lost. Uncertain, all of a sudden? Surely that can't be. You were always so certain before. How many mates did you show me? How many?"

Delmario blinked, frowned. "I'm going to show you one more, Bunny," he said furiously. His fingers closed on his queen, shifted it across the board. "Check."

"Ah," said Bunnish. Peter studied the position. The double sac had cleared away the pawns in front of the Black king, and the queen check permitted no retreat. Bunnish marched his king up a square, toward the center of the board, toward the waiting White army. Surely he was lost now. His own defenders were all over on the queenside, and the enemy was all around him. But Bunnish did not seem worried.

Delmario's clock was ticking as he examined the position. He sipped his juice, shifted restlessly in his seat. Bunnish yawned, and grinned tauntingly. "You were the winner that day, Delmario. Beat a Master. The only winner. Can't you find the win now? Where are all those mates, eh?"

"There's so many I don't know which one to go with, Bunny," Steve said. "Now shut up, damn you. I'm trying to think."

"Oh," said Bunnish. "Pardon."

Delmario consumed ten minutes on his clock before he reached out and moved his remaining knight. "Check."

Bunnish advanced his king again.

Delmario licked his lips, slid his queen forward a square. "Check."

Bunnish's king went sideways, toward the safety of the queenside.

Delmario flicked a pawn forward. "Check."

Bunnish had to take. He removed the offending pawn with his king, smiling complacently.

With the file open, Delmario could bring his rooks into play. He shifted one over. "Check."

Bunnish's harried king moved again.

Now Delmario moved the rook forward, sliding it right up the file to confront the enemy king face-to-face. "Check!" he said loudly.

Peter sucked in his breath sharply, without meaning to. The rook was hanging! Bunnish could just snatch it off. He stared at the position over Delmario's shoulder. Bunnish could take the rook with his king, all right, but then the other rook came over, the king had to go back, then if the queen shifted just one square...yes...too many mate threats in that variation. Black had lots of resources, but they all ended in disaster. But if Bunnish took with his knight instead of his king, he left that square unguarded...hmmm...queen check, king up, bishop comes in...no, mate was even quicker that way.

Delmario drained his orange juice and set the empty tumbler down with self-satisfied firmness.

Bunnish moved his king diagonally forward. The only possible move, Peter thought. Delmario leaned forward. Behind him, Peter leaned forward too. The White pieces were swarming around Black's isolated king now, but how to tighten the mating net? Steve had three different checks, Peter thought. No, four, he could do that too. He watched and analyzed in silence. The rook check was no good, the king just retreated, and further checks simply drove him to safety. The bishop? No, Bunnish could trade off, take with his rook—he was two pieces up, after all. Several subvariations branched off from the two queen checks. Peter was still trying to figure out where they led, when Delmario reached out suddenly, grabbed a pawn from in front of his king, and moved it up two squares. He slammed it down solidly, and slapped the clock. Then he sat back and crossed his arms. "Your move, Bunny," he said.

Peter studied the board. Delmario's last move didn't give check, but the pawn advance cut off an important escape square. Now that threatened rook check was no longer innocuous. Instead of being chased back to safety, the Black king got mated in three. Of course, Bunnish had a tempo now, it was his move, he could bring up a defender. His queen now, could...no, then queen check, king back, rook check, and the Black queen fell...bishop maybe...no, check there and mate in one, unstoppable. The longer Peter looked at the position, the fewer defensive resources he saw for Black. Bunnish could delay the loss, but he couldn't stop it. He was smashed!

Bunnish did not look smashed. Very calmly he picked up a knight and moved it to queen's knight six. "Check," he said quietly.

Delmario stared. Peter stared. E.C. Stuart got up out of his chair and drifted closer, his finger brushing back his mustache as he considered the game. The check was only a time-waster, Peter thought. Delmario could capture the knight with either of two pawns, or he could simply move his king. Except...Peter scowled...if White took with the bishop pawn, queen came up with check, king moved to the second, queen takes rook pawn with check, king...no, that was no good. White got mated by force. The other way seemed to bring on the mate even faster, after the queen checked from the eighth rank.

Delmario moved his king up.

Bunnish slid a bishop out along a diagonal. "Check."

There was only one move. Steve moved his king forward again. He was being harassed, but his mating net was still intact, once the checks had run their course.

Bunnish flicked his knight backward, with another check.

Delmario was blinking and twisting his legs beneath the table. Peter saw that if he brought his king back, Bunnish had a forced series of checks leading to mate . . . but the Black knight hung now, to both rook and queen, and . . . Delmario captured it with the rook.

Bunnish grabbed White's advanced pawn with his queen, removing the cornerstone of the mating net. Now Delmario could play queen takes queen, but then he lost his queen to a fork, and after the tradeoffs that followed he'd be hopelessly busted. Instead he retreated his king.

Bunnish made a *tsk*ing noise and captured the White knight with his queen, again daring Delmario to take it. With knight and pawn both gone, Delmario's mating threats had all dissipated, and if White snatched that Black queen, there was a check, a pin, take, take, take, and . . . Peter gritted his teeth together . . . and White would suddenly be in the endgame down a piece, hopelessly lost. No. There had to be something better. The position still had a lot of play in it. Peter stared, and analyzed.

Steve Delmario stared too, while his clock ticked. The clock was one of those fancy jobs, with a move counter. It showed that he had to make seven more moves to reach time control. He had just under fifteen minutes remaining. Some time pressure, but nothing serious.

Except that Delmario sat and sat, eyes flicking back and forth across the board, blinking. He took off his thick glasses and cleaned them methodically on his shirttail. When he slid them back on, the position had not changed. He stared at the Black king fixedly, as if he were willing it to fall. Finally he started to get up. "I need a drink," he said.

"I'll get it," Peter snapped. "Sit down. You've only got eight minutes left."

"Yeah," Delmario said. He sat down again. Peter went to the bar and made him a screwdriver. Steve drained half of it in a gulp, never taking his eyes from the chessboard.

Peter happened to glance at E.C. Stuart. E.C. shook his head and cast his eyes up toward the ceiling. Not a word was spoken, but Peter heard the message: *forget it.*

Steve Delmario sat there, growing more and more agitated. With three minutes remaining on his clock, he reached out his hand, thought better of it, and pulled back. He shifted in his seat, gathered his legs up under him, leaned closer to the board, his nose a bare couple inches above the chessmen. His clock ticked.

He was still staring at the board when Bunnish smiled and said, "Your flag is down, Delmario."

Delmario looked up, blinking. His mouth hung open. "Time," he said urgently. "I just need time to find the win, got to be here some-place, got to, all those checks. . . ."

Bunnish rose. "You're out of time, Delmario. Doesn't matter any-way. You're dead lost."

"NO! No I'm not, damn you, there's a win . . ."

Peter put a hand on Steve's shoulder. "Steve, take it easy," he said. "I'm sorry. Bruce is right. You're busted here."

"No," Delmario insisted. "I *know* there's a winning combo, I just got to . . . got to . . . only . . ." His right hand, out over the board, began to shake, and he knocked over his own king.

Bunnish showed his dimples. "Listen to your captain, winner-boy," he said. Then he looked away from Delmario, to where E.C. stood scowling. "You're next, Stuart. Tomorrow. Same time, same place."

"And if I don't care to play?" E.C. said disdainfully.

Bunnish shrugged. "Suit yourself," he said. "I'll be here, and the game will be here. I'll start your clock on time. You can lose over the board or lose by forfeit. You lose either way."

"And me?" Peter said.

"Why, captain," said Bunnish. "I'm saving *you* for last."

STEVE DELMARIO WAS A WRECK. HE REFUSED TO LEAVE THE CHESS-board except to mix himself fresh drinks. For the rest of the morning and most of the afternoon he remained glued to his seat, drinking like a fish and flicking the chess pieces around like a man possessed, playing and replaying the game. Delmario wolfed down a couple sandwiches that Peter made up for him around lunchtime, but there was no talking to him, no calming him. Peter tried. In an hour or so, Delmario would be passed out from the booze he was downing in such alarming quan-tities.

Finally he and E.C. left Delmario alone, and went upstairs to his suite. Peter knocked on the door. "You decent, Kathy? E.C. is with me."

She opened the door. She had on jeans and a T-shirt. "Decent as I ever get," she said. "Come on in. How did the great game come out?"

"Delmario lost," Peter said. "It was a close thing, though. I thought we had him for a moment."

Kathy snorted.

"So what now?" E.C. said.

"You going to play tomorrow?"

E.C. shrugged. "Might as well. I've got nothing to lose."

"Good," Peter said. "You can beat him. Steve almost won, and we both know the shape he's in. We've got to analyze, figure out where he went wrong."

E.C. fingered his mustache. He looked cool and thoughtful. "That pawn move," he suggested. "The one that didn't give check. It left White open for that counterattack."

"It also set up the mating net," Peter said. He looked over his shoulder, saw Kathy standing with her arms crossed. "Could you get the chessboard from the bedroom?" he asked her. When she left, Peter turned back to E.C. "I think Steve was already lost by the time he made that pawn move. That was his only good shot—lots of threats there. Everything else just petered out after a few checks. He went wrong before that, I think."

"All those checks," E.C. said. "One too many, maybe?"

"Exactly," said Peter. "Instead of driving him into a checkmate, Steve drove him into safety. You've got to vary somewhere in there."

"Agreed."

Kathy arrived with the chess set and placed it on the low table between them. As Peter swiftly set up the critical position, she folded her legs beneath her and sat on the floor. But she grew bored very quickly when they began to analyze, and it wasn't long before she got to her feet again with a disgusted noise. "Both of you are crazy," she said. "I'm going to get something to eat."

"Bring us back something, will you?" Peter asked. "And a couple of beers?" But he hardly noticed it when she placed the tray beside them.

They stayed at it well into the night. Kathy was the only one who went down to dine with Bunnish. When she returned, she said, "That man is *disgusting*," so emphatically that it actually distracted Peter from the game. But only for an instant.

"Here, try this," E.C. said, moving a knight, and Peter looked back quickly.

"I SEE YOU DECIDED TO PLAY, STUART," BUNNISH SAID THE NEXT morning.

E.C., looking trim and fresh, his sandy hair carefully combed and brushed, a steaming mug of black coffee in hand, nodded briskly. "You're as sharp as ever, Brucie."

Bunnish chuckled.

"One point, however," E.C. said, holding up a finger. "I still don't believe your cock-and-bull story about time travel. We'll play this out, all right, but we'll play for money, not for one of your flashbacks. Understood?"

"You jokers are such suspicious types," Bunnish said. He sighed. "Anything you say, of course. You want money. Fine."

"One million dollars."

Bunnish smiled broadly. "Small change," he said. "But I agree. Beat me, and you'll leave here with one million. You'll take a check, I hope?"

"A certified check." E.C. turned to Peter. "You're my witness," he said, and Peter nodded. The three of them were alone this morning. Kathy was firm in her disinterest, and Delmario was in his room sleeping off his binge.

"Ready?" Bunnish asked.

"Go on."

Bunnish started the clock. E.C. reached out and played the sacrifice. Knight takes pawn. His motions were crisp and economical. Bunnish captured, and E.C. played the bishop sac without a second's hesitation. Bunnish captured again, pushed the clock.

E.C. Stuart brushed back his mustache, reached down, and moved a pawn. No check.

"Ah," Bunnish said. "An improvement. You have something up

your sleeve, don't you? Of course you do. E.C. Stuart always has something up his sleeve. The hilarious, unpredictable E.C. Stuart. Such a joker. So imaginative."

"Play chess, Brucie," snapped E.C.

"Of course." Peter drifted closer to the board while Bunnish studied the position. They had gone over and over the game last night, and had finally decided that the queen check that Delmario had played following the double sac was unsound. There were several other checks in the position, all tempting, but after hours of analysis he and E.C. had discarded those as well. Each of them offered plenty of traps and checkmates should Black err, but each of them seemed to fail against correct play, and they had to assume Bunnish would play correctly.

E.C.'s pawn move was a more promising line. Subtler. Sounder. It opened lines for White's pieces, and interposed another barrier between Black's king and the safety of the queenside. Suddenly White had threats everywhere. Bunnish had serious troubles to chew on now.

He did not chew on them nearly as long as Peter would have expected. After studying the position for a bare couple minutes, he picked up his queen and snatched off White's queen rook pawn, which was undefended. Bunnish cupped the pawn in his hand, yawned, and slouched back in his chair, looking lazy and unperturbed.

E.C. Stuart permitted himself a brief scowl as he looked over the position. Peter felt uneasy as well. That move ought to have disturbed Bunnish more than it had, he thought. White had so many threats . . . last night they had analyzed the possibilities exhaustively, playing and replaying every variation and subvariation until they were sure that they had found the win. Peter had gone to sleep feeling almost jubilant. Bunnish had a dozen feasible defenses to their pawn thrust. They'd had no way of knowing which one he would choose, so they had satisfied themselves that each and every one ultimately ended in failure.

Only now Bunnish had fooled them. He hadn't played *any* of the likely defenses. He had just ignored E.C.'s mating threats, and gone pawn-snatching as blithely as the rankest patzer. Had they missed something? While E.C. considered the best reply, Peter drew up a chair to the side of the board so he could analyze in comfort.

There was nothing, he thought, nothing. Bunnish had a check

next move, if he wanted it, by pushing his queen to the eighth rank. But it was meaningless. E.C. hadn't weakened his queenside the way Steve had yesterday, in his haste to find a mate. If Bunnish checked, all Stuart had to do was move his king up to queen two. Then the Black queen would be under attack by a rook, and forced to retreat or grab another worthless pawn. Meanwhile, Bunnish would be getting checkmated in the middle of the board. The more Peter went over the variations, the more convinced he became that there was no way Bunnish could possibly work up the kind of counterattack he had used to smash Steve Delmario.

E.C., after a long and cautious appraisal of the board, seemed to reach the same conclusion. He reached out coolly and moved his knight, hemming in Bunnish's lonely king once and for all. Now he threatened a queen check that would lead to mate in one. Bunnish could capture the dominating knight, but then E.C. just recaptured with a rook, and checkmate followed soon thereafter, no matter how Bunnish might wriggle on the hook.

Bunnish smiled across the board at his opponent, and lazily shoved his queen forward a square to the last rank. "Check," he said.

E.C. brushed back his mustache, shrugged, and played his king up. He punched the clock with a flourish. "You're lost," he said flatly.

Peter was inclined to agree. That last check had accomplished nothing; in fact, it seemed to have worsened Black's plight. The mate threats were still there, as unstoppable as ever, and now Black's queen was under attack as well. He could pull it back, of course, but not in time to help with the defense. Bunnish ought to be frantic and miserable.

Instead his smile was so broad that his fat cheeks were threatening to crack in two. "Lost?" he said. "Ah, Stuart, this time the joke is on you!" He giggled like a teenage girl, and brought his queen down the rank to grab off White's rook. "Check!"

Peter Norten had not played a game of tournament chess in a long, long time, but he still remembered the way it had felt when an opponent suddenly made an unexpected move that changed the whole complexion of a game: the brief initial confusion, the *what is that?* feeling, followed by panic when you realized the strength of the unanticipated move, and then the awful swelling gloom that built and built as you followed through one losing variation after another in your head. There was no worse moment in the game of chess.

That was how Peter felt now.

They had missed it totally. Bunnish was giving up his queen for a rook, normally an unthinkable sacrifice, but not in this position. E.C. *had* to take the offered queen. But if he captured with his king, Peter saw with sudden awful clarity, Black had a combination that won the farm, which meant he had to use the other rook, pulling it off its crucial defense of the central knight . . . and then . . . oh, *shit!*

E.C. tried to find another alternative for more than fifteen minutes, but there was no alternative to be found. He played rook takes queen. Bunnish quickly seized his own rook and captured the knight that had moved so menacingly into position only two moves before. With ruthless precision, Bunnish then forced the tradeoff of one piece after another, simplifying every danger off the board. All of a sudden they were in the endgame. E.C. had a queen and five pawns; Bunnish had a rook, two bishops, a knight, and four pawns, and—ironically—his once-imperiled king now occupied a powerful position in the center of the board.

Play went on for hours, as E.C. gamely gave check after check with his rogue queen, fighting to pick up a loose piece or perhaps draw by repetition. But Bunnish was too skilled for such desperation tactics. It was only a matter of technique.

Finally E.C. tipped over his king.

"I thought we looked at every possible defense," Peter said numbly.

"Why, captain," said Bunnish cheerfully. "Every attempt to defend loses. The defending pieces block off escape routes or get in the way. Why should I help mate myself? I'd rather let you try to do that."

"I *will* do that," Peter promised angrily. "Tomorrow."

Bunnish rubbed his hands together. "I can scarcely wait!"

———

THAT NIGHT THE POSTMORTEM WAS HELD IN E.C.'S SUITE; KATHY— who had greeted their glum news with an "I told you so" and a contemptuous smile—had insisted that she didn't want them staying up half the night over a chessboard in *her* presence. She told Peter he was behaving like a child, and they had angry words before he stormed out.

Steve Delmario was going over the morning's loss with E.C. when Peter joined them. Delmario's eyes looked awfully bloodshot, but otherwise he appeared sober, if haggard. He was drinking coffee. "How does it look?" Peter asked when he pulled up a seat.

"Bad," E.C. said.

Delmario nodded. "Hell, worse'n bad, it's starting to look like that damn sac is unsound after all. I can't believe it, I just can't, it all looks so promising, got to be something there. *Got* to. But I'm damned if I can find it."

E.C. added, "The surprise he pulled today is a threat in a number of variations. Don't forget, we gave up two pieces to get to this position. Unfortunately, that means that Brucie can easily afford to give some of that material back to get out of the fix. He still comes out ahead, and wins the endgame. We've found a few improvements on my play this morning—"

"That knight doesn't have to drop," interjected Delmario.

". . . but nothing convincing," E.C. concluded.

"You ever think," Delmario said, "that maybe the Funny Bunny was *right*? That maybe the sac don't work, maybe the game was never won at all?" His voice had a note of glum disbelief in it.

"There's one thing wrong with that," Peter said.

"Oh?"

"Ten years ago, after Bunnish had blown the game and the match, Robinson Vesselere *admitted* that he had been lost."

E.C. looked thoughtful. "That's true. I'd forgotten that."

"Vesselere was almost a Senior Master. He had to know what he was talking about. The win is there. I mean to find it."

Delmario clapped his hands together and whooped gleefully. "Hell yes, Pete, you're right! Let's go!"

⸻

"AT LAST THE PRODIGAL SPOUSE RETURNS," KATHY SAID POINTedly when Peter came in. "Do you have any idea what time it is?"

She was seated in a chair by the fireplace, though the fire had burned down to ashes and embers. She wore a dark robe, and the end of the cigarette she was smoking was a bright point in the darkness. Peter had come in smiling, but now he frowned. Kathy had once been a heavy smoker, but she'd given it up years ago. Now she only lit a cigarette when she was very upset. When she lit up, it usually meant they were headed for a vicious row.

"It's late," Peter said. "I don't know how late. What does it matter?" He'd spent most of the night with E.C. and Steve, but it had been worth it. They'd found what they had been looking for. Peter had returned tired but elated, expecting to find his wife asleep. He was in no mood for grief. "Never mind about the time," he said to her, trying to placate. "We've *got* it, Kath."

She crushed out her cigarette methodically. "Got what? Some new move you think is going to defeat our psychopathic host? Don't you understand that I don't give a damn about this stupid game of yours? Don't you listen to a thing I say? I've been waiting up half the night, Peter. It's almost three in the morning. I want to talk."

"Yeah?" Peter snapped. Her tone had gotten his back up. "Did you ever think that maybe I didn't want to listen? Well, think it. I have a big game tomorrow. I need my sleep. I can't afford to stay up till dawn screaming at you. Understand? Why the hell are you so hot to talk anyway? What could you possibly have to say that I haven't heard before, huh?"

Kathy laughed nastily. "I could tell you a few things about your old friend Bunnish that you haven't heard before."

"I doubt it."

"Do you? Well, did you know that he's been trying to get me into bed for the past two days?"

She said it tauntingly, throwing it at him. Peter felt as if he had been struck. *"What?"*

"Sit down," she snapped, "and listen."

Numbly, he did as she bid him. "Did you?" he asked, staring at her silhouette in the darkness, the vaguely ominous shape that was his wife.

"*Did I?* Sleep with him, you mean? Jesus, Peter, how can you ask that? Do you loathe me that much? I'd sooner sleep with a roach. That's what he reminds me of anyway." She gave a rueful chuckle. "He isn't exactly a sophisticated seducer, either. He actually offered me money."

"Why are you telling me this?"

"To knock some goddamned sense into you! Can't you see that

Bunnish is trying to destroy you, all of you, any way he can? He didn't want me. He just wanted to get at you. And you, you and your moron teammates, are playing right into his hands. You're becoming as obsessed with that idiot chess game as *he* is." She leaned forward. Dimly, Peter could make out the lines of her face. "Peter," she said almost imploringly, "don't play him. He's going to beat you, love, just like he beat the others."

"I don't think so, *love,*" Peter said from between clenched teeth. The endearment became an epithet as he hurled it back at her. "Why the hell are you always so ready to predict defeat for me, huh? Can't you ever be supportive, not even for a goddamned minute? If you won't help, why don't you just bug off? I've had all I can stand of you, damn it. Always belittling me, mocking. You've never believed in me. I don't know why the hell you married me, if all you wanted to do was make my life a hell. *Just leave me alone!*"

For a long moment after Peter's outburst there was silence. Sitting there in the darkened room, he could almost feel her rage building—any instant now he expected to hear her start screaming. Then he would scream back, and she would get up and break something, and he would grab her, and then the knives would come out in earnest. He closed his eyes, trembling, feeling close to tears. He didn't want this, he thought. He really didn't.

But Kathy fooled him. When she spoke, her voice was surprisingly gentle. "Oh, Peter," she said. "I never meant to hurt you. Please. I love you."

He was stunned. "Love me?" he said wonderingly.

"Please listen. If there is anything at all left between us, please just listen to me for a few minutes. Please."

"All right," he said.

"Peter, I *did* believe in you once. Surely you must remember how good things were in the beginning? I was supportive then, wasn't I? The first few years, when you were writing your novel? I worked, I kept food on the table, I gave you the time to write."

"Oh, yes," he said, anger creeping back into his tone. Kathy had thrown that at him before, had reminded him forcefully of how she'd supported them for two years while he wrote a book that turned out to be so much wastepaper. "Spare me your reproaches, huh? It wasn't my fault I couldn't sell the book. You heard what Bunnish said."

"I wasn't reproaching you, damn it!" she snapped. "Why are you always so ready to read criticism into every word I say?" She shook her head, and got her voice back under control. "Please, Peter, don't make this harder than it is. We have so many years of pain to overcome, so many wounds to bind up. Just hear me out.

"I was trying to say that I did believe in you. Even after the book, after you burned it ... even then. You made it hard, though. I didn't think you were a failure, but *you* did, and it changed you, Peter. You let it get to you. You gave up writing, instead of just gritting your teeth and doing another book."

"I wasn't tough enough, I know," he said. "The loser. The weakling."

"*Shut up!*" she said in exasperation. "I didn't say that, *you* did. Then you went into journalism. I still believed. But everything kept going wrong. You got fired, you got sued, you became a disgrace. Our friends started drifting away. And all the time you insisted that none of it was your fault. You lost all the rest of your self-confidence. You didn't dream anymore. You whined, bitterly and incessantly, about your bad luck."

"You never helped."

"Maybe not," Kathy admitted. "I tried to, at the start, but it just got worse and worse and I couldn't deal with it. You weren't the dreamer I'd married. It was hard to remember how I'd admired you, how I'd respected you. Peter, you loathed yourself so much that there was no way to keep the loathing from rubbing off on me."

"So?" Peter said. "What's the point, Kathy?"

"I never left you, Peter," she said. "I could have, you know. I wanted to. I stayed, through all of it, all the failures and all the self-pity. Doesn't that say anything to you?"

"It says you're a masochist," he snapped. "Or maybe a sadist."

That was too much for her. She started to reply, and her voice broke, and she began to weep. Peter sat where he was and listened to her cry. Finally the tears ran out, and she said, quietly, "Damn you. Damn you. I hate you."

"I thought you loved me. Make up your mind."

"You ass. You insensitive creep. Don't you understand, Peter?"

"Understand *what*?" he said impatiently. "You said listen, so I've been listening, and all you've been doing is rehashing all the same old stuff, recounting all my inadequacies. I heard it all before."

"Peter, can't you see that this week has changed *everything*? If you'd only stop hating, stop loathing me and yourself, maybe you could see it. We have a chance again, Peter. If we try. Please."

"I don't see that anything has changed. I'm going to play a big chess game tomorrow, and you know how much it means to me and my self-respect, and you don't care. You don't care if I win or lose. You keep telling me I'm *going* to lose. You're *helping* me to lose by making me argue when I should be sleeping. What the hell has changed? You're the same damn bitch you've been for years."

"I will tell you what has changed," she said. "Peter, up until a few days ago, both of us thought you were a failure. But you aren't! *It hasn't been your fault.* None of it. Not bad luck, like you kept saying, and not personal inadequacy either, like you really thought. Bunnish has done it all. Can't you see what a difference that makes? You've never had a chance, Peter, but you have one now. There's no reason you shouldn't believe in yourself. We *know* you can do great things! Bunnish admitted it. We can leave here, you and I, and start all over again. You could write another book, write plays, do anything you want. You have the talent. You've never lacked it. We can dream again, believe again, love each other again. Don't you see? Bunnish had to gloat to complete his revenge, but by gloating he's *freed* you!"

Peter sat very still in the dark room, his hand clenching and unclenching on the arm of the chair as Kathy's words sunk in. He had been so wrapped up in the chess game, so obsessed with Bunnish's obsession, that he had never seen it, never considered it. *It wasn't me,* he thought wonderingly. *All those years, it was never me.* "It's true," he said in a small voice.

"Peter?" she said, concerned.

He heard the concern, heard more than that, heard love in her voice. So many people, he thought, make such grand promises, promise better or worse, promise rich or poorer, and bail out as soon as things turn the least bit sour in a relationship. But she had stayed, through all of it, the failures, the disgrace, the cruel words and the poisonous thoughts, the weekly fights, the poverty. She had stayed.

"Kathy," he said. The next words were very hard. "I love you, too." He started to get up and move toward her, and began to cry.

They arrived late the next morning. They showered together, and Peter dressed with unusual care. For some reason, he felt it was important to look his best. It was a new beginning, after all. Kathy came with him. They entered the living room holding hands. Bunnish was already behind the board, and Peter's clock was ticking. The others were there too. E.C. was seated patiently in a chair. Delmario was pacing. "Hurry up," he said when Peter came down the stairs. "You've lost five minutes already."

Peter smiled. "Easy, Steve," he said. He went over and took his seat behind the White pieces. Kathy stood behind him. She looked gorgeous this morning, Peter thought.

"It's your move, captain," Bunnish said, with an unpleasant smile.

"I know," Peter said. He made no effort to move, scarcely even looked at the board. "Bruce, why do you hate me? I've been thinking about that, and I'd like to know the answer. I can understand about Steve and E.C. Steve had the presumption to win when you lost, and he rubbed your nose in that defeat afterwards. E.C. made you the butt of his jokes. But why me? What did I ever do to you?"

Bunnish looked briefly confused. Then his face grew hard. "You. You were the worst of them all."

Peter was startled. "I never..."

"The big captain," Bunnish said sarcastically. "That day ten years ago, you never even *tried*. You took a quick grandmaster draw with your old friend Hal Winslow. You could have tried for a win, played on, but you didn't. Oh, no. You never cared how much more pressure you put on the rest of us. And when we lost, you didn't take any of the blame, not a bit of it, even though you gave up half a point. It was all *my* fault. And that wasn't all of it, either. Why was *I* on first board, Norten? All of us on the B team had approximately the same rating. How did I get the honor of being board one?"

Peter thought for a minute, trying to recall the strategies that had motivated him ten years before. Finally he nodded. "You always lost the big games, Bruce. It made sense to put you up on board one, where you'd face the other teams' big guns, the ones who'd probably beat whoever we played there. That way the lower boards would be manned by more reliable players, the ones we could count on in the clutch."

"In other words," Bunnish said, "I was a write-off. You expected me to lose, while you won matches on the lower boards."

"Yes," Peter admitted. "I'm sorry."

"Sorry," mocked Bunnish. "You *made* me lose, expected me to lose, and then tormented me for losing, and now you're sorry. You didn't play chess that day. You never played chess. You were playing a bigger game, a game that lasted for years, between you and Winslow of U.C. And the team members were your pieces and your pawns. Me, I was a sac. A gambit. That was all. And it didn't work anyway. Winslow beat you. You *lost*."

"You're right," Peter admitted. "I lost. I think I understand now. Why you did all the things you've done."

"You're going to lose again now," Bunnish said. "*Move,* before your clock runs out." He nodded down at the checkered wasteland that lay between them, at the complex jumble of Black and White pieces.

Peter glanced at the board with disinterest. "We analyzed until three in the morning last night, the three of us. I had a new variation all set. A single sacrifice, instead of the double sac. I play knight takes pawn, but I hold back from the bishop sac, swing my queen over instead. That was the idea. It looked pretty good. But it's unsound, isn't it?"

Bunnish stared at him. "Play it, and we'll find out!"

"No," said Peter. "I don't want to play."

"*Pete!*" Steve Delmario said in consternation. "You got to, what are you saying, beat this damn bastard."

Peter looked at him. "It's no good, Steve."

There was a silence. Finally Bunnish said, "You're a coward, Norten. A coward and a failure and a weakling. Play the game out."

"I'm not interested in the game, Bruce. Just tell me. The variation is unsound."

Bunnish made a disgusted noise. "Yes, yes," he snapped. "It's unsound. There's a countersac, I give up a rook to break up your mating threats, but I win a piece back a few moves later."

"All the variations are unsound, aren't they?" Peter said.

Bunnish smiled thinly.

"White doesn't have a won game at all," Peter said. "We were wrong, all those years. You never blew the win. You never *had* a win. Just a position that looked good superficially, but led nowhere."

"Wisdom, at last," Bunnish said. "I've had computers print out every possible variation. They take forever, but I've had lifetimes. When I flashed back—you have no idea how many times I have flashed back, trying one new idea after another—that is always my target point, that day in Evanston, the game with Vesselere. I've tried every move there is to be tried in that position, every wild idea. It makes no difference. Vesselere always beats me. All the variations are unsound."

"But," Delmario protested, looking bewildered, "Vesselere *said* he was lost. He *said* so!"

Bunnish looked at him with contempt. "I had made him sweat a lot in a game he should have won easily. He was just getting back. He was a vindictive man, and he knew that by saying that he'd make the loss that much more painful." He smirked. "I've taken care of *him* too, you know."

E.C. Stuart rose up from his chair and straightened his vest. "If we're done now, Brucie, maybe you would be so kind as to let us out of Bunnishland?"

"*You* can go," Bunnish said. "And that drunk, too. But not Peter." He showed his dimples. "Why, Peter has almost won, in a sense. So I'm going to be generous. You know what I'm going to do for you, Captain? I'm going to let you use my flashback device."

"No thank you," Peter said.

Bunnish stared, befuddled. "What do you mean, no? Don't you understand what I'm giving you? You can wipe out all your failures, try again, make some different moves. Be a success in another timeline."

"I know. Of course, that would leave Kathy with a dead body in *this* timeline, wouldn't it? And you with the satisfaction of driving me to something that uncannily resembles suicide. No. I'll take my chances with the future instead of the past. With Kathy."

Bunnish let his mouth droop open. "What do you care about her? She hates you anyway. She'll be better off with you dead. She'll get the insurance money and you'll get somebody better, somebody who cares about you."

"But I do care about him," Kathy said. She put a hand on Peter's shoulder. He reached up and touched it, and smiled.

"Then you're a fool too," Bunnish cried. "He's nothing, he'll *never* be anything. I'll see to that."

Peter stood up. "I don't think so, somehow. I don't think you can hurt us anymore. Any of us." He looked at the others. "What do you think, guys?"

E.C. cocked his head thoughtfully, and ran a finger along the underside of his mustache. "You know," he said, "I think you're right."

Delmario just seemed baffled, until all of a sudden the light broke across his face, and he grinned. "You can't steal ideas I haven't come up with yet, can you?" he said to Bunnish. "Not in this timeline, anyhow." He made a loud whooping sound and stepped up to the chessboard. Reaching down, he stopped the clock. "Checkmate," he said. "Checkmate, checkmate, *checkmate!*"

———————

LESS THAN TWO WEEKS LATER, KATHY KNOCKED SOFTLY ON THE door of his study. "Wait a sec!" Peter shouted. He typed out another sentence, then flicked off the typewriter and swiveled in his chair. "C'mon in."

She opened the door and smiled at him. "I made some tuna salad, if you want to take a break for lunch. How's the book coming?"

"Good," Peter said. "I should finish the second chapter today, if I keep at it." She was holding a newspaper, he noticed. "What's that?"

"I thought you ought to see this," she replied, handing it over.

She'd folded it open to the obits. Peter took it and read. Millionaire electronics genius Bruce Bunnish had been found dead in his Colorado home, hooked up to a strange device that had seemingly electrocuted him. Peter sighed.

"He's going to try again, isn't he?" Kathy said.

Peter put down the newspaper. "The poor bastard. He can't see it."

"See what?"

Peter took her hand and squeezed it. "All the variations are unsound," he said. It made him sad. But after lunch, he soon forgot about it, and went back to work.

THE GLASS FLOWER

ONCE, WHEN I WAS JUST A GIRL IN THE FIRST FLUSH OF MY TRUE youth, a young boy gave me a glass flower as a token of his love.

He was a rare and precious boy, though I confess that I have long forgotten his name. So too was the flower he gave me. On the steel and plastic worlds where I have spent my lives, the ancient glassblower's art is lost and forgotten, but the unknown artisan who had fashioned my flower remembered it well. My flower has a long and delicate stem, curved and graceful, all of fine thin glass, and from that frail support the bloom explodes, as large as my fist, impossibly exact. Every detail is there, caught, frozen in crystal for eternity; petals large and small crowding each other, bursting from the center of the blossom in a slow transparent riot, surrounded by a crown of six wide drooping leaves, each with its tracery of veins intact, each unique. It was as if an alchemist had been wandering through a garden one day, and in a moment of idle play had transmuted an especially large and beautiful flower into glass.

All that it lacks is life.

I kept that flower with me for near two hundred years, long after I had left the boy who gave it to me and the world where he had done the giving. Through all the varied chapters of my lives, the glass flower was always close at hand. It amused me to keep it in a vase of polished wood and set it near a window. Sometimes the leaves and petals would catch the sun and flash brilliantly for an incandescent instant; at other times they would filter and fracture the light, scattering blurred rainbows on my floor. Often towards dusk, when the world was dimmer, the flower would seem to fade entirely from view, and I might sit staring at an empty vase. Yet, when the morning came, the flower would be back again. It never failed me.

The glass flower was terribly fragile, but no harm ever came to it. I cared for it well; better, perhaps, than I have ever cared for anything, or anyone. It outlasted a dozen lovers, more than a dozen professions, and more worlds and friends than I can name. It was with me in my youth on Ash and Erikan and Shamdizar, and later on Rogue's Hope and Vagabond, and still later when I had grown old on Dam Tullian and Lilith and Gulliver. And when I finally left human space entirely, put all my lives and all the worlds of men behind me, and grew young again, the glass flower was still at my side.

And, at very long last, in my castle built on stilts, in my house of pain and rebirth where the game of mind is played, amid the swamps and stinks of Croan'dhenni, far from all humanity save those few lost souls who seek us out—it was there too, my glass flower.

On the day Kleronomas arrived.

"JOACHIM KLERONOMAS," I SAID.

"Yes."

There are cyborgs and then there are cyborgs. So many worlds, so many different cultures, so many sets of values and levels of technologies. Some cyberjacks are half organic, some more, some less; some sport only a single metal hand, the rest of their cyberhalves cleverly concealed beneath the flesh. Some cyborgs wear synthaflesh that is indistinguishable from human skin, though that is no great feat, given the variety of skin to be seen among the thousand worlds. Some hide the metal and flaunt the flesh; with others the reverse is true.

The man who called himself Kleronomas had no flesh to hide or flaunt. A cyborg he called himself, and a cyborg he was in the legends that had grown up around his name, but as he stood before me, he seemed more a robot, insufficiently organic to pass even as android.

He was naked, if a thing of metal and plastic can be naked. His chest was jet; some shining black alloy or smooth plastic, I could not tell. His arms and legs were transparent plasteel. Beneath that false skin, I could see the dark metal of his duralloy bones, the power-bars and flexors that were muscles and tendons, the micromotors and sensing computers, the intricate pattern of lights racing up and down his superconductive neurosystem. His fingers were steel. On his right hand, long silver claws sprang rakishly from his knuckles when he made a fist.

He was looking at me. His eyes were crystalline lenses set in metal sockets, moving back and forth in some green translucent gel. They had no visible pupils; behind each implacable crimson iris burned a dim light that gave his stare an ominous red glow. "Am I that fascinating?" he asked me. His voice was surprisingly natural; deep and resonant, with no metallic echoes to corrode the humanity of his inflections.

"Kleronomas," I said. "Your name is fascinating, certainly. A very long time ago, there was another man of that name, a cyborg, a legend. You know that, of course. He of the Kleronomas Survey. The founder of the Academy of Human Knowledge on Avalon. Your ancestor? Perhaps metal runs in your family."

"No," said the cyborg. "Myself. I am Joachim Kleronomas."

I smiled for him. "And I'm Jesus Christ. Would you care to meet my Apostles?"

"You doubt me, Wisdom?"

"Kleronomas died on Avalon a thousand years ago."

"No," he said. "He stands before you now."

"Cyborg," I said, "this is Croan'dhenni. You would not have come here unless you sought rebirth, unless you sought to win new life in the game of mind. So be warned. In the game of mind, your lies will be stripped away from you. Your flesh and your metal and your illusions, we will take them all, and in the end there will be only you, more naked and alone than you can ever imagine. So do not waste my time. It is the most precious thing I have, time. It is the most precious thing any of us have. Who are you, cyborg?"

"Kleronomas," he said. Was there a mocking note in his voice? I could not tell. His face was not built for smiling. "Do you have a name?" he asked me.

"Several," I said.

"Which do you use?"

"My players call me Wisdom."

"That is a title, not a name," he said.

I smiled. "You are traveled, then. Like the real Kleronomas. Good. My birth name was Cyrain. I suppose, of all my names, I am most used to that one. I wore it for the first fifty years of my life, until I came to Dam Tullian and studied to be a Wisdom and took a new name with the title."

"Cyrain," he repeated. "That alone?"

"Yes."

"On what world were you born, then?"

"Ash."

"Cyrain of Ash," he said. "How old are you?"

"In standard years?"

"Of course."

I shrugged. "Close to two hundred. I've lost count."

"You look like a child, like a girl close to puberty, no more."

"I am older than my body," I said.

"As am I," he said. "The curse of the cyborg, Wisdom, is that parts can be replaced."

"Then you're immortal?" I challenged him.

"In one crude sense, yes."

"Interesting," I said. "Contradictory. You come here to me, to Croan'dhenni and its Artifact, to the game of mind. Why? This is a place where the dying come, cyborg, in hopes of winning life. We don't get many immortals."

"I seek a different prize," the cyborg said.

"Yes?" I prompted.

"Death," he told me. "Life. Death. Life."

"Two different things," I said. "Opposites. Enemies."

"No," said the cyborg. "They are the same."

SIX HUNDRED STANDARD YEARS AGO, A CREATURE KNOWN IN LEG-end as The White landed among the Croan'dhenni in the first starship they had ever seen. If the descriptions in Croan'dhic folklore can be trusted, then The White was of no race I have ever encountered, nor heard of, though I am widely traveled. This does not surprise me. The manrealm and its thousand worlds (perhaps there are twice that number, perhaps less, but who can keep count?), the scattered empires of Fyndii and Damoosh and g'vhern and N'or Talush, and all the other sentients who are known to us or rumored of, all this together, all those lands and stars and lives colored by passion and blood and history, sprawling proudly across the light-years, across the black gulfs that only the *volcryn* ever truly know, all of this, all of our little universe . . . it is only an island of light surrounded by a vastly greater area of grayness and myth that fades ultimately into the black of ignorance. And *this* only in one small galaxy, whose uttermost reaches we shall never know, should we endure a billion years. Ultimately, the sheer size of things will defeat us, however we may strive or scream; that truth I am sure of.

But I do not defeat easily. That is my pride, my last and only pride; it is not much to face the darkness with, but it is something. When the end comes, I will meet it raging.

The White was like me in that. It was a frog from a pond beyond ours, a place lost in the gray where our little lights have not yet shone on the dark waters. Whatever sort of creature it might have been, whatever burdens of history and evolution it carried in its genes, it was nonetheless my kin. Both of us were angry mayflies, moving restlessly from star to star because we, alone among our fellows, knew how short our day. Both of us found a destiny of sorts in these swamps of Croan'dhenni.

The White came utterly alone to this place, set down its little starship (I have seen the remains: a toy, that ship, a trinket, but with lines that are utterly alien to me, and deliciously chilling), and, exploring, found something.

Something older than itself, and stranger.

The Artifact.

Whatever strange instruments it had, whatever secret alien knowledge it possessed, whatever instinct bid it enter; all lost now, and none of it matters. The White knew, knew something the native sentients had never guessed, knew the purpose of the Artifact, knew how it might be activated. For the first time in—a thousand years? A million? For the first time in a long while, the game of mind was played. And The White changed, emerged from the Artifact as something else, as the first. The first mindlord. The first master of life and death. The first painlord. The first lifelord. The titles are born, worn, discarded, forgotten, and none of them matter.

Whatever I am, The White was the first.

HAD THE CYBORG ASKED TO MEET MY APOSTLES, I WOULD NOT have disappointed him. I gathered them when he left me. "The new player," I told them, "calls himself Kleronomas. I want to know who he is, what he is, and what he hopes to gain. Find out for me."

I could feel their greed and fear. The Apostles are a useful tool, but loyalty is not for them. I have gathered to me twelve Judas Iscariots, each of them hungry for that kiss.

"I'll have a full scan worked up," suggested Doctor Lyman, pale weak eyes considering me, flatterer's smile trembling.

"Will he consent to an interface?" asked Deish Green-9, my own cyberjack. His right hand, sunburned red-black flesh, was balled into a fist; his left was a silver ball that cracked open to exude a nest of writhing metallic tendrils. Beneath his heavy beetling brow, where he should have had eyes, a seamless strip of mirrorglass was set into his skull. He had chromed his teeth. His smile was very bright.

"We'll find out," I said.

Sebastian Cayle floated in his tank, a twisted embryo with a massive monstrous head, flippers moving vaguely, huge blind eyes regarding me through turgid greenish fluids as bubbles rose all around his pale naked flesh. *He is a Liar* came the whisper in my head. *I will find the truth for you, Wisdom.*

"Good," I told him.

Tr'k'nn'r, my Fyndii mindmute, sang to me in a high shrill voice at the edge of human hearing. He loomed above them all like a stickman in a child's crude drawing, a stickman three meters tall, excessively jointed, bending in all the wrong places at all the wrong angles, assembled of old bones turned gray as ash by some ancient fire. But the crystalline eyes beneath his brow ridge were fervid as he sang, and fragrant black fluids ran from the bottom of his lipless vertical mouth. His song was of pain and screaming and nerves set afire, of secrets revealed, of truth dragged steaming and raw from all its hidden crevasses.

"No," I said to him. "He is a cyborg. If he feels pain it is only because he wills it. He would shut down his receptors and turn you off, loneling, and your song would turn to silence."

The neurowhore Shayalla Loethen smiled with resignation. "Then there's nothing for me to work on either, Wisdom?"

"I'm not sure," I admitted. "He has no obvious genitalia, but if there's anything organic left inside him, his pleasure centers might be intact. He claims to have been male. The instincts might still be viable. Find out."

She nodded. Her body was soft and white as snow, and sometimes as cold, when she wanted cold, and sometimes white-hot, when that was her desire. Those lips that curled upwards now with anticipation were crimson and alive. The garments that swirled around her changed shape and color even as I watched, and sparks began to play along her fingertips, arcing across her long, painted nails.

"Drugs?" asked Braje, biomed, gengineer, poisoner. She sat thinking, chewing some tranq of her own devising, her swollen body as damp and soft as the swamps outside. "Truetell? Agonine? Esperon?"

"I doubt it," I said.

"Disease," she offered. "Manthrax or gangrene. The slow plague, and we've got the cure?" She giggled.

"No," I said curtly.

And the rest, and on and on. They all had their suggestions, their ways of finding out things I wanted to know, of making themselves useful to me, of earning my gratitude. Such are my Apostles. I listened to them, let myself be carried along by the babble of voices, weighed, considered, handed out orders, and finally I sent them all away, all but one.

Khar Dorian will be the one to kiss me when that day finally comes. I do not have to be a Wisdom to know that truth.

The rest of them want something of me. When they get it, they will be gone. Khar got his desire long ago, and still he comes back and back and back, to my world and my bed. It is not love of me that brings him back, nor the beauty of the young body I wear, nor anything as simple as the riches he earns. He has grander things in mind.

"He rode with you," I said. "All the way from Lilith. Who is he?"

"A player," Dorian said, grinning at me crookedly, taunting me. He is breathtakingly beautiful. Lean and hard and well fit, with the arrogance and rough-hewn masculine sexuality of a thirty-year-old, flush with health and power and hormones. His hair is blond and long and unkempt. His jaw is clean and strong, his nose straight and unbroken, his eyes a hale, vibrant blue. But there is something old living behind those eyes, something old and cynical and sinister.

"Dorian," I warned him, "don't try games with me. He is more than just a player. Who is he?"

Khar Dorian got up, stretched lazily, yawned, grinned. "Who he says he is," my slaver told me. "Kleronomas."

MORALITY IS A CLOSELY KNIT GARMENT THAT BINDS TIGHTLY WHEN it binds at all, but the vastnesses that lie between the stars are prone to unraveling it, to plucking it apart into so many loose threads, each brightly colored, but forming no discernible pattern. The fashionable Vagabonder is a rustic-spectacular on Cathaday, the Ymirian swelters on Vess, the Vessman freezes on Ymir, and the shifting lights the Fellanei wear instead of cloth provoke rape, riot, and murder on half a dozen worlds. So it is with morals. Good is no more constant than the cut of a lapel; the decision to take a sentient life weighs no more heavily than the decision to bare one's breasts, or hide them.

There are worlds on which I am a monster. I stopped caring a long time ago. I came to Croan'dhenni with my own fashion sense, and no concern for the aesthetic judgments of others.

Khar Dorian calls himself a slaver, and points out to me that we do, indeed, deal in human flesh. He can call himself what he likes. I am no slaver; the charge offends me. A slaver sells his clients into bondage and servitude, deprives them of freedom, mobility, and time, all precious commodities. I do no such thing. I am only a thief. Khar and his underlings bring them to me from the swollen cities of Lilith, from the harsh mountains and cold wastes of Dam Tullian, from the rotting tenements along the canals of Vess, from spaceport bars on Fellanora and Cymeranth and Shrike, from wherever he can find them, he takes them and brings them to me, and I steal from them and set them free.

A lot of them refuse to go.

They cluster outside my castle walls in the city they have built, toss gifts to me as I pass, call out my name, beg favors of me. I have left them freedom, mobility, and time, and they squander it all in futility, hoping to win back the one thing I have stolen.

I steal their bodies, but they lose their souls themselves.

And perhaps I am unduly harsh to call myself a thief. These victims Khar brings me are unwilling players in the game of mind, but no less players for all that. Others pay so very dearly and risk so very much for the same privilege. Some we call players and some we call prizes, but when the pain comes and the game of mind begins, we are all the same, all naked and alone without riches or health or status, armed with only the strength that lies within us. Win or lose, live or die, it is up to us and us alone.

I give them a chance. A few have even won. Very few, true, but how many thieves give their victims any chance at all?

The Steel Angels, whose worlds lie far from Croan'dhenni on the other side of human space, teach their children that strength is the only virtue and weakness the only sin, and preach that the truth of their faith is written large on the universe itself. It is a difficult point to argue. By their creed, I have every moral right to the bodies I take, because I am stronger and therefore better and more holy than those born to that flesh.

The little girl born in my present body was not a Steel Angel, un-fortunately.

"AND BABY MAKES THREE," I SAID, "EVEN IF BABY IS MADE OF metal and plastic and names himself a legend."

"Eh?" Rannar looked at me blankly. He is not as widely traveled as me, and the reference, something I have dredged up from my forgotten youth on some world he's never walked, escapes him entirely. His long, sour face wore a look of patient bafflement.

"We have three players now," I told him carefully. "We can play the game of mind."

That much Rannar understood. "Ah yes, of course. I'll see to it at once, Wisdom."

Craimur Delhune was the first. An ancient thing, almost as old as me, though he had done all of his living in the same small body. No wonder it was worn out. He was hairless and shriveled, a wheezing half-blind travesty, his flesh full of alloplas and metal implants that labored day and night just to keep him alive. It was not something they could do much longer, but Craimur Delhune had not had enough living yet, and so he had come to Croan'dhenni to pay for the flesh and begin all over again. He had been waiting nearly half a standard year.

Rieseen Jay was a stranger case. She was under fifty and in decent health, though her flesh bore its own scars. Rieseen was jaded. She had sampled every pleasure Lilith offered, and Lilith offers a good many pleasures. She had tasted every food, flowed with every drug, sexed with males, females, aliens, and animals, risked her life skiing the glaciers, baiting pit-dragons, fighting in the soar-wars for the delectation of holofans everywhere. She thought a new body would be just the thing to add spice to life. Maybe a male body, she thought, or an alien's off-color flesh. We get a few like her.

And Joachim Kleronomas made three.

In the game of mind, there are seats for seven. Three players, three prizes, and me.

Rannar offered me a thick portfolio, full of photographs and reports on the prizes newly arrived on Khar Dorian's ships, on the *Bright Phoenix* and the *Second Chance* and the *New Deal* and the *Fleshpot* (Khar has always had a certain black sense of humor). The majordomo hovered at my elbow, solicitous and helpful, as I turned the pages and made my selections. "She's delicious," he said once, at a picture of a slim Vessgirl with frightened yellow eyes that hinted at a hybrid gene-mix. "Very strong and healthy, that one," he said later, as I considered a hugely muscled youth with green eyes and waist-long braided black hair. I ignored him. I always ignore him.

"Him," I said, taking out the file of a boy as slender as a stiletto, his ruddy skin covered with tattoos. Khar had purchased him from the authorities on Shrike, where he'd been convicted of killing another sixteen-year-old. On most worlds, Khar Dorian, the infamous free trader, smuggler, raider, and slaver, had a name synonymous with evil; parents threatened their children with him. On Shrike he was a solid citizen who did the community great service by buying up the garbage in the prisons.

"Her," I said, setting aside a second photograph, of a pudgy young woman of about thirty standard whose wide green eyes betrayed a certain vacancy. From Cymeranth, her file said. Khar had dropped one of his raiders into a coldsleep facility for the mentally damaged and helped himself to some young, healthy, attractive bodies. This one was soft and fat, but that would change once an active mind wore the flesh again. The original owner had sucked up too much dreamdust.

"And it," I said. The third file was that of a g'vhern hatchling, a grim-looking individual with fierce magenta eye-crests and huge, leathery batwings that glistened with iridescent oils. It was for Rieseen Jay, who thought she might like to try a nonhuman body. If she could win it.

"Very good, Wisdom," said Rannar approvingly. He was always approving. When he had come to Croan'dhenni, his body was grotesque; he'd been caught in bed with the daughter of his employer, a V'lador knight of the blood, and the punishment was extensive ritual mutilation. He did not have the price of a game. But I'd had two players waiting for almost a year, one of whom was dying of manthrax, so when Rannar offered me ten years of faithful service to make up the difference, I accepted.

Sometimes I had my regrets. I could feel his eyes on my body, could sense his mind stripping away the soft armor of my clothes to fasten, leechlike, on my small, budding breasts. The girl he'd been found with was not much younger than the flesh I now wore.

MY CASTLE IS BUILT OF OBSIDIAN.

North of here, far north, in the smoky polar wastelands where eternal fires burn against a purple sky, the black volcanic glass lies upon the ground like common stone. It took thousands of Croan'dhic miners nine standard years to find enough for my purposes and drag it all back to the swamps, over all those barren kilometers. It took hundreds of artisans another six years to cut and polish it and fit it all together into the dark shimmering mosaic that is my home. I judged the effort worthwhile.

My castle stands on four great jagged pillars high up above the smells and damp of the Croan'dhic swampland, ablaze with colored lights whose ghosts glimmer within the black glass. My castle gleams; a thing of beauty, austere and forbidding, supreme and apart from the shantytown that has grown up around it, where the losers and discards and dispossessed huddle hopelessly in floating reed-huts, festering tree-houses, and hovels on half-rotted wooden stilts. The obsidian appeals to my aesthetic sense, and I find its symbolism appropriate to this house of pain and rebirth. Life is born in the heat of sexual passion as obsidian is born in volcanic fire. The clean truth of light can sometimes flow through its blackness, beauty seen dimly through darkness, and like life, it is terribly fragile, with edges that can be dangerously sharp.

Inside my castle are rooms on rooms, some paneled over with fragrant native woods and covered with furs and thick carpets, some left bare and black, ceremonial chambers where dark reflections move through glass walls and footsteps click brittle against glass floors. In the center, at the very apex, rises an onion-shaped obsidian tower, braced by steel. Within the dome, a single chamber.

I ordered the castle built, replacing an older and much shabbier structure, and to that single tower chamber, I caused the Artifact to be moved.

It is there that the game of mind is played.

My own suite is at the base of the tower. The reasons for that were symbolic as well. None achieve rebirth without first passing through me.

I was breaking fast in bed, on butterfruit and raw fish and strong black coffee, with Khar Dorian stretched out languid and insolent beside me, when my scholar Apostle, Alta-k-Nahr, came to me with her report.

She stood at the foot of my bed, her back twisted like a great question mark by her disease, her long features permanently set in a grimace of distaste, her skin shot through with swollen veins like great blue worms, and she told me of her researches on the historical Kleronomas in a voice unnecessarily soft.

"His full name was Joachim Charle Kleronomas," she said, "and he was native to New Alexandria, a first-generation colony less than seventy light-years from Old Earth. Records of his birthdate, childhood, and adolescence are fragmentary and contradictory. The most popular legends indicate his mother was a high-ranking officer on a warship of the 13th Human Fleet, under Stephen Cobalt Northstar, and that Kleronomas met her only twice. He was gestated in a hireling host-mother and reared by his father, a minor scholar at a library on New Alexandria. My opinion is that this tale of his origin explains, a bit too

neatly, how Kleronomas came to combine both the scholastic and martial traditions; therefore I question its reliability.

"More certain is the fact that he joined the military at a very early
age, in those last days of the Thousand Years War. He served initially as
systems tech on a screamer-class raider with the 17th Human Fleet, distinguished himself in deepspace actions off El Dorado and Arturius and
in the raids on Hrag Druun, after which he was promoted to cadet
and given command training. By the time the 17th was shifted from
its original base on Fenris to a minor sector capital called Avalon,
Kleronomas had earned further distinction, and was the third-in-
command of the dropship *Hannibal*. But in the raids on Hruun-
Fourteen, the *Hannibal* took heavy damage from Hrangan defenders,
and was finally abandoned. The screamer in which Kleronomas escaped was disabled by enemy fire and crashed planetside, killing everyone aboard. He was the sole survivor. Another screamer picked up
what was left of him, but he was so near dead and horribly maimed that
they shoved him into cryostorage at once. He was taken back to
Avalon, but resources were few and demands many, and they had no
time to bother reviving him. They kept him under for years.

"Meanwhile, the Collapse was in progress. It had been in progress
all of his lifetime, actually, but communications across the width of the
old Federal Empire were so slow that no one knew it. But a single
decade saw the revolt on Thor, the total disintegration of the 15th
Human Fleet, and Old Earth's attempt to remove Stephen Cobalt
Northstar from command of the 13th, which led inevitably to the se-
cession of Newholme and most of the other first-generation colonies,
to Northstar's obliteration of Wellington, to civil war, breakaway
colonies, lost worlds, the fourth great expansion, the hellfleet legend,
and ultimately the sealing of Old Earth and the effective cessation of
commercial starflight for a generation. Longer than that, far far longer,
on some more remote worlds, many of which devolved to near-
savagery or developed odd variant cultures.

"Out on the front, Avalon had its own first-hand experience of the
Collapse when Rajeen Tober, commanding the 17th Fleet, refused to
submit to the civil authorities and took his ships deep into the
Tempter's Veil to found his own personal empire safe from both

Hrangan and human retaliation. The departure of the 17th left Avalon essentially defenseless. The only warships still in the sector were the ancient hulks of the 5th Human Fleet, which had last seen combat nearly seven centuries earlier, when Avalon was a very distant strikebase against the Hrangans. About a dozen capital-class ships and thirty-odd smaller craft of the 5th remained in orbit around Avalon, most needing extensive repairs, all functionally obsolete. But they were the only defenders left to a frightened world, so Avalon determined to refit and restore them. To crew these museum pieces, Avalon turned to its cryonic wards, and began to thaw every combat veteran on hand, including Joachim Kleronomas. The damage he had sustained was extensive, but Avalon needed every last body. Kleronomas returned more machine than man. A cyborg."

I leaned forward to interrupt Alta's recitation. "Are there any pictures of him as he was then?" I asked her.

"Yes. Both before and after. Kleronomas was a big man, with blue-black skin, a heavy outthrust jaw, gray eyes, long pure white hair. After the operation, the jaw and the bottom half of his face were gone entirely, replaced with seamless metal. No mouth, no nose. He took nourishment intravenously. One eye was lost, replaced by a crystal sensor with IR/UV range. His right arm and the entire right half of his chest was cybered, steel plate, duralloy mesh, plastic. A third of his inner organs were synthetic. And they gave him a jack, of course, and built in a small computer. From the beginning, Kleronomas disdained cosmetics; he looked exactly like what he was."

I smiled. "But what he was, that was still a good deal more fleshy than our new guest?"

"True," said my scholar. "The rest of the history is more well known. There weren't many officers among the revived. Kleronomas was given his own command, a small courier-class ship. He served for a decade, pursuing the scholarly studies in history and anthropology that were his private passion, and rising higher and higher in the ranks while Avalon waited for ships that never came and built more and more ships of its own. There were no trades, no raids; the interregnum had come.

"Finally, a bolder civil leadership decided to risk a few of its ships and find out how the rest of human civilization had fared. Six of the

ancient 5th Fleet dreadnaughts were refitted as science survey craft and
sent out. Kleronomas was given command of one of them. Of those
survey ships, two were lost on their missions, and three others returned
within two years carrying minimal information on a handful of the
closest systems, prompting the Avalonians to reinitiate starflight on a
very limited local basis. Kleronomas was thought lost.

"He was not lost. When the small, limited goals of the original survey were completed, he decided to continue rather than return to
Avalon. He became obsessed with the next star, and the next after that,
and the next after that. He took his ship on and on. There were mu-
tinies, desertions, dangers to be faced and fought, and Kleronomas dealt
with them all. As a cyborg, he was immensely long-lived. The legends
say he became ever more metallic as the voyage went on, and on Eris
discovered the matrix crystal and expanded his intellectual abilities by
orders of magnitude through the addition of the first crystal-matrix
computer. That particular story fits his character; he was obsessed not
only with the acquisition of knowledge, but with its retention. Altered
so, he would never forget.

"When he finally returned to Avalon, more than a hundred standard years had passed. Of the men and women who had left Avalon with
him, Kleronomas alone survived; his ship was manned by the descen-
dants of its original crew, plus those recruits he had gathered on the
worlds he visited. But he had surveyed four hundred and forty-nine
planets, and more asteroids, comets, and satellites than anyone would
have dreamed possible. The information he brought back became the
foundation upon which the Academy of Human Knowledge was built,
and the crystal samples, incorporated into existing systems, became the
medium in which that knowledge was stored, eventually evolving into
the academy's vast Artificial Intelligences and the fabled crystal towers of
Avalon. The resumption of large-scale starflight soon thereafter was the
real end of the interregnum. Kleronomas himself served as the first academy administrator until his death, which supposedly came on Avalon in
ai-42, that is, forty-two standard years after the day of his return."

I laughed. "Excellent," I told Alta-k-Nahr. "He's a fraud, then.
Dead at least seven hundred years." I looked at Khar Dorian, whose
long fine hair was spread across the pillow as he nibbled on a heel of
mead bread. "You are slipping, Khar. He fooled you."

Khar swallowed, grinned. "Whatever you say, Wisdom," he said, in a tone that told me he was anything but contrite. "Shall I kill him for you?"

"No," I said. "He is a player. In the game of mind, there are no imposters. Let him play. Let him play."

DAYS LATER, WHEN THE GAME HAD BEEN SCHEDULED, I CALLED THE cyborg to me. I saw him in my office, a large room with deep scarlet carpeting, where my glass flower sits by the great window that overlooks my battlements and the swamp town below.

His face was without expression. Of course, of course. "You summoned me, Cyrain of Ash."

"The game is set," I told him. "Four days from today."

"I am pleased," he said.

"Would you like to see the prizes?" I offered him the files; the boy, the girl, the hatchling.

He glanced at them briefly, without interest.

"I am told," I said to him, "that you have spent a lot of time wandering these past days. Inside my castle, and outside in the town and the swamps."

"True," he said. "I do not sleep. Knowledge is my diversion, my addiction. I was curious to learn what sort of place this was."

Smiling, I said, "And what sort of place is it, cyborg?"

He could not smile, nor frown. His tone was even, polite. "A vile place," he said. "A place of despair and degradation."

"A place of eternal, undying hope," I said.

"A place of sickness, of the body and the soul."

"A place where the sick grow well," I countered.

"And where the well grow sick," the cyborg said. "A place of death."

"A place of life," I said. "Isn't that why you came? For life?"

"And death," he said. "I have told you, they are the same."

I leaned forward. "And I have told you, they are very different. You make harsh judgments, cyborg. Rigidity is to be expected in a machine, but this fine, precious moral sensitivity is not."

"Only my body is machine," he said.

I picked up his file. "That is not my understanding," I said. "Where is your morality in regard to lying? Especially so transparent a lie?" I opened the file flat on my desk. "I've had a few interesting reports from my Apostles. You've been extraordinarily cooperative."

"If you wish to play the game of mind, you cannot offend the painlord," he said.

I smiled. "I'm not as easily offended as you might think." I searched through the reports. "Doctor Lyman did a full scan on you. He finds you an ingenious construct. And made entirely of plastic and metal. There is nothing organic left inside you, cyborg. Or should I call you robot? Can computers play the game of mind, I wonder? We will certainly find out. You have three of them, I see. A small one in what should be your brain case that attends to motor functions, sensory input and internal monitoring, a much larger library unit occupying most of your lower torso, and a crystal matrix in your chest." I looked up. "Your heart, cyborg?"

"My mind," he said. "Ask your Doctor Lyman, and he will tell of other cases like mine. What is a human mind? Memories. Memories are data. Character, personality, individual volition. Those are programming. It is possible to imprint the whole of a human mind upon a crystal matrix computer."

"And trap the soul in the crystal?" I said. "Do you believe in souls?"

"Do you?" he asked.

"I must. I am mistress of the game of mind. It would seem to be required of me." I turned to the other reports my Apostles had assembled on this construct who called himself Kleronomas. "Deish Green-9 interfaced with you. He says you have a system of incredible sophistication, that the speed of your circuitry greatly exceeds human thought, that your library contains far more accessible information than any single organic brain could retain even were it able to make full use of its capacity, and that the mind and memories locked within that crystal matrix are that of one Joachim Kleronomas. He swears to that."

The cyborg said nothing. Perhaps he might have smiled then, had he the capacity.

"On the other hand," I said, "my scholar Alta-k-Nahr assures me that Kleronomas is dead seven hundred years. Who am I to believe?"

"Whomever you choose," he said indifferently.

"I might hold you here and send to Avalon for confirmation," I said. I grinned. "A thirty-year voyage in, thirty more years back out. Say a year to research the question. Can you wait sixty-one years to play, cyborg?"

"As long as necessary," he said.

"Shayalla says you are thoroughly asexual."

"That capacity was lost from the day they remade me," he said. "My interest in the subject lingered for some centuries afterwards, but finally that too faded. If I choose, I have access to a full range of erotic memories of the days when I wore organic flesh. They remain as fresh as the day they were entered into my computer. Once locked in crystal, memories cannot fade, as with a human brain. They are there, waiting to be tapped. But for centuries now, I have had no inclination to recall them."

I was intrigued. "You cannot forget," I said.

"I can erase," he said. "I can choose not to remember."

"If you are among the winners in our little game of mind, you will regain your sexuality."

"I am aware of that. It will be an interesting experience. Perhaps then I will choose to tap those ancient memories."

"Yes," I said, delighted. "You'll begin to use them, and at precisely the same instant you will begin to forget them. There is a loss there, cyborg, as sharp as your gain."

"Gain or loss. Living and dying. I have told you, Cyrain, they cannot be separated."

"I don't accept that," I said. It was at issue with all I believe, all I am; his repetition of the lie annoyed me. "Braje says you cannot be affected by drugs or disease. Obvious. You could be dismantled, though. Several of my Apostles have offered to dispose of you, at my command. My aliens are especially bloodthirsty, it seems."

"I have no blood," he said. Sardonic? Or was it all the power of suggestion?

"Your lubricants might suffice," I said drily. "Tr'k'nn'r would test your capacity for pain. AanTerg Moonscorer, my g'vhern aerialist, has offered to drop you from a great height."

"That would be an unconscionable crime by nest standards."

"Yes and no," I said. "A nestborn g'vhern would be aghast at the suggestion that flight be thus perverted. My Apostle, on the other hand, would be more aghast at the suggestion of birth control. Flapping those oily leather wings you'll find the mind of a half-sane cripple from New Rome. This is Croan'dhenni. We are not as we seem."

"So it appears."

"Jonas has offered to destroy you too, in a less dramatic but equally effective fashion. He's my largest Apostle. Deformed by runaway glands. The patron saint of advanced automatic weaponry, and my chief of security."

"Obviously you have declined these offers," the cyborg said.

I leaned back. "Obviously," I said, "though I always reserve the right to change my mind."

"I am a player," he said. "I have paid Khar Dorian, have bribed the Croan'dhic port-guards, have paid your majordomo and yourself. Inwards, on Lilith and Cymeranth and Shrike and other worlds where they speak of this black palace and its half-mythical mistress, they say that your players are treated fairly."

"Wrong," I said. "I am never fair, cyborg. Sometimes I am just. When the whim takes me."

"Do you threaten all your players as you have threatened me?" he asked.

"No," I admitted. "I'm making a special exception in your case."

"Why?" he asked.

"Because you're dangerous," I said, smiling. We had come to the heart of it at last. I shuffled through all my Apostolic bulls, and extracted the last of them, the most important. "At least one of my Apostles you have never met, but he knows you, cyborg, knows you better than you would dream."

The cyborg said nothing.

"My pet telepath," I said. "Sebastian Cayle. He's blind and twisted and I keep him in a big jar, but he has his uses. He can probe through walls. He has stroked the crystals of your mind, friend, and tripped the binary synapses of your id. His report is a bit cryptic, but admirably terse." I slid it across the desk for the cyborg to read.

A haunted labyrinth of thought. The steel ghost. The truth within the lie, life in death and death in life. He will take everything from you if he can. Kill him now.

"You are ignoring his advice," the cyborg said.

"I am," I told him.

"Why?"

"Because you're a mystery, one I plan to solve when we play the game of mind. Because you're a challenge, and it has been a long time since I was challenged. Because you dare to judge me and dream of destroying me, and it has been ages since anyone found the courage to do either of those things."

Obsidian makes a dark, distorted mirror, but one that suits me. We take our reflections for granted all our lives, until the hour comes when our eyes search for the familiar features and find instead the image of a stranger. You cannot know the meaning of horror or of fascination until you take that first long gaze from a stranger's eyes, and raise an unfamiliar hand to touch the other's cheek, and feel those fingers, light and cool and afraid, brush against your skin.

I was already a stranger when I came to Croan'dhenni more than a century ago. I knew my face, as well I should, having worn it nearly ninety years. It was the face of a woman who was both hard and strong, with deep lines around her gray eyes from squinting into alien suns, a wide mouth not without its generosity, a nose once broken that had not healed straight, short brown hair in perpetual disarray. A comfortable face, and one that I had a certain affection for. But I lost it somewhere, perhaps during my years on Gulliver, lost it when I was too busy to notice. By the time I reached Lilith, the first stranger had begun to haunt my mirrors. She was an old woman, old and wrinkled. Her eyes were gray and rheumy and starting to dim, her hair white and thin, with patches of pinkish scalp showing through; the edge of her mouth trembled, there were broken capillaries in her nose, and beneath her chin lay several folds of soft gray flesh like the wattles of a hen. Her skin was soft and loose, where mine had always been taut and flush with health, and there was another thing, a thing you could not see in the mirror—a smell of sickness that enveloped her like the cheap perfume of an aged courtesan, a pheromone for death.

I did not know her, this old sick thing, nor did I cherish her company. They say that age and sickness come slowly on worlds like Avalon and Newholme and Prometheus; legends claim death no longer comes at all on Old Earth behind its shining walls. But Avalon and Newholme and Prometheus were far away, and Old Earth is sealed and lost to us, and I was alone on Lilith with a stranger in my mirror. And so I took myself beyond the manrealm, past the furthest reach of human arms, to the wet dimness of Croan'dhenni, where whispers said a new life could be found. I wanted to look into a mirror once more, and find the old friend that I had lost.

Instead I found more strangers.

The first was the painlord itself; mindlord, lifelord, master of life and death. Before my coming, it had ruled here forty-odd standard years. It was Croand'hic, a native, a great bulbous thing with swollen eyes and mottled blue-green skin, a grotesque parody of a toad with slender, double-jointed arms and three long vertical maws like wet black wounds in its fragrant flesh. When I looked upon it, I could taste its weakness; it was vastly fat, a sea of spreading blubber with an odor like rotten eggs, where the Croand'hic guards and servants were well-muscled and hard. But to topple the mindlord, you must become the mindlord. When we played the game of mind I took its life, and woke in that vile body.

It is no easy thing for a human mind to wear an alien skin; for a day and a night I was lost inside that hideous flesh, sorting through sights and sounds and smells that made no more sense than the images in a nightmare, screaming, clawing for control and sanity. I survived. A triumph of spirit over flesh. When I was ready, another game of mind was called, and this time I emerged with the body of my choice.

She was a human. Thirty-nine years of age by her reckoning, healthy, plain of face but strong of body, a professional gambler who had come to Croan'dhenni for the ultimate game. She had long red-brown hair and eyes whose blue-green color reminded me of the seas of Gulliver. She had some strength, but not enough. In those distant days, before the coming of Khar Dorian and his slavers' fleet, few humans found their way to Croan'dhenni. My choice was limited. I took her.

That night I looked into the mirror again. It was still a stranger's face, hair too long, eyes of the wrong hue, a nose as straight as the blade of a knife, a careful guarded mouth that had done too little smiling.

Years afterward, when that body began to cough blood from some infernal pestilence out of the Croan'dhic swamps, I built a room of obsidian mirrors to meet each new stranger. Years pass more swiftly than I care to think while that room remains sealed and inviolate, but always, finally, the day comes when I know I will be visiting it once more, and then my servants climb the stairs and polish the black mirrors to a fine dark sheen, and when the game of mind is done I ascend alone and strip off my clothing and stand and turn in solitude, slow dancing with the images of others.

High, sharp cheekbones and dark eyes sunk in deep hollows beneath her brow. A face shaped like a heart, surrounded by a nimbus of wild black hair, large pale breasts tipped with brown.

Taut lean muscles moving beneath oiled red-brown skin, long fingernails sharp as claws, a narrow pointed chin, brown hair like wire bristles cut in a thin high stripe across her scalp and halfway down her back, the hot scent of rut heavy between her thighs. My thighs? On a thousand worlds, humanity changes in a thousand different ways.

Massive bony head looking down at the world from near three meters' height, beard and hair blending into one leonine mane as bright as beaten gold, strength written large in every bone and sinew, the broad flat chest with its useless red nipples, the strangeness of the long, soft penis between my legs. Too much strangeness for me; the penis stayed soft all the months I wore that body, and that year my mirrored room was opened twice.

A face very like the one that I remember. But how well do I remember? A century was gone to dust, and I kept no likenesses of the faces I had worn. From my first youth long ago, only the glass flower remained. But she had short brown hair, a smile, gray-green eyes. Her neck was too long, her breasts too small, perhaps. But she was close, close, until she grew old, and the day came when I glimpsed another stranger walking beside me inside the castle walls.

And now the haunted child. In the mirrors she looks like a daughter of dreams, the daughter I might have birthed had I been far lovelier than I ever was. Khar brought her to me, a gift he said, a most beautiful gift, to repay me in kind after I had found him gray and impotent, hoarse of voice and scarred of face, and made him young and handsome.

She is perhaps eleven years old, perhaps twelve. Her body is gaunt and awkward, but the beauty is there, locked inside, just beginning to blossom. Her breasts are budding now, and her blood first came less than half a year ago. Her hair is silver-gold, long and straight, a glittering cascade that falls nearly to her heels. Her eyes are large in her small face, and they are the deepest, purest violet. Her face is something sculpted. She was bred to be thus, no doubt of that; genetic tailoring has made the Shrikan trade-lords and the wealthy of Lilith and Fellanora a breathtakingly beautiful folk.

When Khar brought her to me, she was shy of seven, her mind already gone, a whimpering animal thing screaming in a dark locked room within her skull. Khar says she was that way when he bought her, the dispossessed daughter of a Fellanei robber baron toppled and executed for political crimes, his family and friends and retainers slain with him or turned into mindless sexual playthings for his victorious enemies. That is what Khar says. Most of the time I even believe him.

She is younger and prettier than I can ever remember being, even in my lost first youth on Ash, where a nameless boy gave me a glass flower. I hope to wear this sweet flesh for as many years as I wore the body I was born to. If I dwell here long enough, perhaps the day will come when I can look into a dark mirror and see my own face again.

ONE BY ONE THEY ASCENDED UNTO ME; THROUGH WISDOM TO REbirth, or so they hoped.

High above the swamps, locked within my tower, I prepared for them in the changing chamber, hard by my unimpressive throne. The Artifact is not prepossessing; a rudely shaped bowl of some soft alien alloy, charcoal-gray in color and faintly warm to the touch, with six niches spaced evenly around the rim. They are seats; cramped, hard, uncomfortable seats, designed for obviously nonhuman physiognomies, but seats nonetheless. From the floor of the bowl rises a slender column that blossoms into another seat, the awkward cup that enthrones...choose the title you like best. Painlord, mindlord, lifelord, giver and taker, operator, trigger, master. All of them are me. And others before me, the chain rattling back to The White and perhaps earlier, to the makers, the unknowns who fashioned this machine in the dimness of distant eons.

If the chamber has its drama, that is my doing. The walls and ceiling are curved, and fashioned laboriously of a thousand individual pieces of polished obsidian. Some shards are cut very thin, so the gray light of the Croan'dhic sun can force its way through. Some shards are so thick as to be almost opaque. The room is one color, but a thousand shades, and for those who have the wit to see it, it forms a great mosaic of life and death, dreams and nightmares, pain and ecstasy, excess and emptiness, everything and nothing, blending one into the other, around and around unending, a circle, a cycle, the worm that eats its own tail forever, each piece individual and fragile and razor-edged and each part of a greater picture that is vast and black and brittle.

I stripped and handed my clothing to Rannar, who folded each garment neatly. The cup is topless and egg-shaped. I climbed inside and folded my legs beneath me in a lotus, the best possible compromise between the lines of the Artifact and the human physique. The interior walls of the machine began to bleed; glistening red-black fluid beading on the gray metal of the egg, each globule swelling fatter and heavier until it burst. Streams trickled down the smooth, curved walls, and the moisture began to collect at the bottom. My bare skin burned where the fluid touched me. The flow came faster and heavier, the fire creeping up my body, until I was half immersed.

"Send them in," I told Rannar. How many times have I said those words? I have lost count.

The prizes were led in first. Khar Dorian came with the tattooed boy. "There," Khar said offhandedly, gesturing to a seat while smiling lasciviously for me, and the hard youth, this killer, this wild bloody tough, shrank away from his escort and took the place assigned to him. Braje, my biomed, brought the woman. They too are of a kind; pallid, overweight, soft. Braje giggled as she fastened the manacles about her complaisant charge. The hatchling fought, its lean muscles writhing, its great wings beating together in a dramatic but ultimately ineffectual thunderclap as huge, glowering Jonas and his men forced it down into its niche. As they manacled it into place, Khar Dorian grinned and the g'vhern made a high, thin whistling sound that hurt the ears.

Craimur Delhune had to be carried in by his aides and hirelings. "There," I told them, pointing, and they propped him awkwardly into one of the niches. His shrunken, wizened face stared at me, half-blind eyes darting around the chamber like small, feral beasts, his mouth sucking greedily, as if his rebirth was done and he sought a mother's breast. He was blind to the mosaic; for him, it was only a dark room with black glass walls.

Rieseen Jay swaggered in, bored by my chamber before she even entered it. She saw the mosaic but gave it only a cursory glance, as something beneath her notice, too tiresome to study. Instead she made a slow circuit of the niches, inspecting each of the prizes like a butcher examining the meat. She lingered longest in front of the hatchling, seeming to delight in its struggles, its obvious fear, the way it hissed and whistled at her and glared from those fierce, bright eyes. She reached out to touch a wing, and leapt back, laughing, when the hatchling bit at her. Finally she took herself to a seat, where she sprawled languidly, waiting for the game to begin.

Finally Kleronomas.

He saw the mosaic at once, stopped, stared up at it, his crystalline eyes scanning slowly around the room, halting here and there again to study some fine detail. He paused so long that Rieseen Jay grew impatient, and snapped at him to take a seat. The cyborg studied her, metal face unreadable. "Quiet," I said.

He finished his study of the dome, taking his own time, and only then seated himself in the final empty niche. The way he took his place was as if all the seats had been vacant and this was his choice, selected by him alone.

"Clear the room," I commanded. Rannar bowed and gestured them out, Jonas and Braje and the others. Khar Dorian went last, and made a gesture at me as he took his leave. Meaning what? Good luck? Perhaps. I heard Rannar seal the door.

"Well?" demanded Rieseen Jay.

I gave her a look that silenced her. "You are all seated in the Siege Perilous," I said. I always began with those words. No one ever understood. This time...Kleronomas, perhaps. I watched the mask that was his face. Within the crystal of his eyes, I saw a slight shifting motion, and tried to find a meaning in it. "There are no rules in the game of mind. But I have rules, for when it is over, when you are back in my domain.

"Those of you who are here unwillingly, if you are strong enough to hold the flesh you wear, it is yours forever. I give it to you freely. No prize plays more than once. Hold fast to your birthflesh and when it is done, Khar Dorian will take you back to the world he found you on and set you loose with a thousand standards and your freedom.

"Those players who find rebirth this day, who rise in strange flesh when this game is ended, remember that what you have won or lost is your own doing, and spare me your regrets and recriminations. If you are dissatisfied with the outcome of this gaming, you may of course play again. If you have the price.

"One last warning. For all of you. This is going to hurt. This is going to hurt more than anything you ever imagined."

So saying, I began the game of mind.

Once more.

What can you say about pain?

Words can trace only the shadow of the thing itself. The reality of hard, sharp physical pain is like nothing else, and it is beyond language. The world is too much with us, day and night, but when we hurt, when we really hurt, the world melts and fades and becomes a ghost, a dim memory, a silly unimportant thing. Whatever ideals, dreams, loves, fears, and thoughts we might have had become ultimately unimportant. We are alone with our pain, it is the only force in the cosmos, the only thing of substance, the only thing that matters, and if the pain is bad enough and lasts long enough, if it is the sort of agony that goes on and on, then all the things that are our humanity melt before it and the proud sophisticated computer that is the human brain becomes capable of but a single thought:

Make it stop, make it STOP!

And if the pain does eventually stop, afterwards, with the passage of time, even the mind that has experienced it becomes unable to comprehend it, unable to remember how bad it truly was, unable to describe it so as to even approach the terrible truth of what it felt like when it was happening.

In the game of mind, the agony of the painfield is like no other pain, like nothing I have ever experienced.

The painfield does no harm to the body, leaves no marks, no scars, no injuries, no signs to mark its passing. It touches the mind directly with an agony beyond my power to express. How long does it last? A question for relativists. It lasts but the smallest part of a microsecond, and it lasts forever.

The Wisdoms of Dam Tullian are masters of a hundred different disciplines of mind and body, and they teach their acolytes a technique for isolating pain, dissociating from it, pushing it away and thus transcending it. I had been a Wisdom for half my life when I first played the game of mind. I used all I had been taught, all the tricks and truths I had mastered and learned to rely on. They were utterly useless. This was a pain that did not touch the body, a pain that did not race along the nerve paths, a pain that filled the mind so completely and so shatteringly that not even the smallest part of you was free to think or plan or meditate. The pain was you, and you were the pain. There was nothing to dissociate from, no cool sanctum of thought where you might retreat.

The painfield was infinite and eternal, and from that ceaseless and unthinkable agony there was only one sure surcease. It was the old one, the true one, the same balm that has been succor to billions of men and women, and even the smallest of the beasts of the field, since the beginning of time. Pain's dark lord. My enemy, my lover. Again, yet again, wanting only an end to suffering, I rushed to his black embrace.

Death took me, and the pain ended.

On a vast, echoey plain in a place beyond life, I waited for the others.

DIM SHADOWS TAKING FORM FROM THE MISTS. FOUR, FIVE, YES. Have we lost some of them? It would not surprise me. In three games out of four, a player finds his truth in death and seeks no further. This time? No. I see the sixth shape striding out of the writhing fog, we are all here, I look around myself once more, count three, four, five, six, seven, and me, eight.

Eight?

That's wrong, that's very wrong. I am dizzy, disoriented. Nearby someone is screaming. A little girl, sweet-faced, innocent, dressed in pastels and pretty gems. She does not know how she got here, she does not understand, her eyes are lost and childish and far too trusting, and the pain has woken her from a dreamdust languor to a strange land full of fear.

I raise a small, strong hand, gaze at the thick brown fingers, the patch of callous by my thumb, the blunt wide nails trimmed to the quick. I make a fist, a familiar gesture, and in my hand a mirror takes shape from the iron of my will and the quicksilver of my desire. Within its glittering depths I see a face. It is the face of a woman who is both hard and strong, with deep lines around her gray eyes from squinting into alien suns, a wide mouth not without its generosity, a nose once broken that has not healed straight, short brown hair in perpetual disarray. A comfortable face. It gives me comfort now.

The mirror dissolves into smoke. The land, the sky, everything is shifting and uncertain. The sweet little girl is still screaming for her daddy. Some of the others are staring at me, lost. There is a young man, plain of face, his black hair swept back straight and feathered with color in a style that has not been the fashion on Gulliver for a century. His body looks soft, but in his eyes I see a hard edge that reminds me of Khar Dorian. Rieseen Jay seems stunned, wary, frightened, but still she is recognizably Rieseen Jay; whatever else might be said of her, she has a strong sense of who she is. Perhaps that will even be enough. The g'vhern looms near her, far larger here than it seemed before, its body glistening with oil as it spreads demonic wings and begins to whip the fog into long gray ribbons. In the game of mind, it wears no manacles; Rieseen Jay looks long, and cowers away from it. So too does another player, a wispy gray shape covered by a blaze of tattoos, his face a pale blur with neither purpose nor definition. The little girl screams on and on. I turn away from them, leave them to their own devices, and face the final player.

A big man, his skin the color of polished ebony with a dark blue undertone where his long muscles flex as he stretches. He is naked. His jaw is square and heavy, jutting sharply forward. Long hair surrounds his face and falls past his shoulders, hair as white and crisp as fresh bedsheets, as white as the untouched snow of a world that men have never walked. As I watch him, his thick, dark penis stirs against his leg, swells, grows erect. He smiles at me. "Wisdom," he says.

Suddenly I'm naked too.

I frown, and now I wear an ornate suit of armor, overlapping plates of gilded duralloy, filigreed with forbidding runes, and beneath my arm is a matching antique helmet, festooned with a plume of bright feathers. "Joachim Kleronomas," I say. His penis grows and thickens until it is an absurd fat staff that presses hard against the flatness of his stomach. I cover it, and him, in a uniform from a history text, all black and silver, with the blue-green globe of Old Earth sewn on his right sleeve and twin silver galaxies swirling on his collar.

"No," he says, amused, "I never reached that rank," and the galaxies are gone, replaced by a circle of six silver stars. "And for most of my time, Wisdom, my allegiance was to Avalon, not Earth." His uniform is less martial, more functional, a simple gray-green jumpsuit with a black fabric belt and a pocket heavy with pens. Only the silver circle of stars remains. "There," he says.

"Wrong," I tell him. "Wrong still." And when I am done talking, only the uniform remains. Inside the cloth the flesh is gone, replaced by silver-metal mockery, a shining empty thing with a toaster for a head. But only for an instant. Then the man is back, frowning, unhappy. "Cruel," he says to me. The hardness of his penis strains at the fabric of his crotch.

Behind him, the eighth man, the ghost who ought not be here, the misplaced phantom, makes a soft whispery sound, a sound like the rustling of dry dead leaves in a cold autumn wind.

He is a thin, shadowy thing, this intruder. I must look at him very hard to see him at all. He is much smaller than Kleronomas, and he gives the impression of being old and frail, though his flesh is so wispy, so insubstantial, that it is hard to be sure. He is a vision suggested by the random drift of the fog, perhaps, an echo dressed in faded white, but his eyes glow and shimmer and they are trapped and afraid. He reaches out to me. The flesh of his hand is translucent, pulled tightly over gray ancient bones.

I back away, uncertain. In the game of mind, the lightest touch can have a terrible reality.

Behind me I hear more screaming, the terrible wild sound of someone in an ecstasy of fear. I turn.

It has begun in earnest now. The players are seeking their prey. Craimur Delhune, young and vital and far more muscular than he was a moment ago, stands with a flaming sword in one hand, swinging it easily at the tattooed boy. The boy is on his knees, shrieking, trying to cover himself with upraised arms, but Delhune's bright blade passes through the gray shadowflesh unimpeded, and slices at the shining tattoos. He removes them from the boy surgically, swing by swing, and they drift upwards in the misty air, shining images of life cut free of the gray skin on which they were imprisoned. Delhune snatches them as they float by and swallows them whole. Smoke drifts from his nostrils and his open mouth. The boy screams and cringes. Soon there will be nothing left but shadow.

The hatchling has taken to the air. It circles above us, keening at us in its high, thin voice as its wings thunder.

Rieseen Jay has had second thoughts, it seems. She stands above the whimpering little girl, who grows less little with each passing moment. Jay is changing her. She is older now, fatter, her eyes just as frightened but far more vacant. Wherever she turns her head, mirrors appear and sing taunts at her with fat wet lips. Her flesh swells and swells, tearing free of her poor, frayed clothing; thin lines of spittle run down her chin. She wipes at it, crying, but it only flows faster, and now it turns pink with blood. She is enormous, gross, revolting. "That's you," the mirrors say. "Don't look away. Look at yourself. You're not a little girl. Look, look, look. Aren't you pretty? Aren't you sweet? Look at you, look at you." Rieseen Jay folds her arms, smiles with satisfaction.

Kleronomas looks at me with cold judgment on his face. A band of black cloth wraps itself about my eyes. I blink, vanish it, glare at him. "I'm not blind," I say. "I see them. It is not my fight."

The fat woman is as large as a truck, as pale and soft as a maggot. She is naked and immense and with each blink of Jay's eye she grows more monstrous. Huge white breasts burst forth from her face, hands, thighs, and the brown meaty nipples open gaping mouths and began to sing. A thick green penis appears above her vagina, curls down, enters her. Cancers blossom on her skin like a field of dark flowers. And everywhere are the mirrors, blinking in and out, reflecting and distorting and enlarging, relentlessly showing her everything she is, documenting every grotesque fancy that Jay inflicts upon her. The fat woman is hardly human. From a mouth the size of my head, gumless and bleeding, she issues forth a sound like the wailing of the damned. Her flesh begins to smoke and tremble.

The cyborg points. All the mirrors explode.

The mist is full of daggers, shards of slivered glass flying everywhere. One comes at me and I make it gone. But the others, the others . . . they curve like smart missiles, become an aerial flotilla, attack. Rieseen Jay is pierced in a thousand places, and the blood drips from her eyes, her breasts, her open mouth. The monster is a little girl again, crying.

"A moralist," I say to Kleronomas.

He ignores me, turns to look at Craimur Delhune and the shadow boy. Tattoos flame to new life upon the youth's skin, and in his hand a sword appears and takes fire. Delhune takes a step back, unnerved. The boy touches his flesh, mouths some silent oath, rises warily.

"An altruist," I say. "Giving succor to the weak."

Kleronomas turns. "I hold no brief with slaughter."

I laugh at him. "Maybe you're just saving them for yourself, cyborg. If not, you had better grow wings fast, before your prize flies away."

His face is cold. "My prize is in front of me," he says.

"Somehow I knew that," I reply, donning my plumed helmet. My armor is alive with golden highlights; my sword is a spear of light.

My armor is as black as the pit, and the designs worked upon it, black on black, are of spiders and snakes and human skulls and faces a-writhe with pain. My long straight silver sword turns to obsidian, and twists into a grotesquerie of barbs and hooks and cruel spikes. He has a sense of drama, this damned cyborg. "No," I say. "I will not be cast as evil." I am gold and silver once more, shining, and my plumes are red and blue. "Wear the suit yourself if you like it so much."

It stands before me, black and hideous, the helmet open on a grinning skull. Kleronomas sends it away. "I need no props," he says. His gray-and-white ghost flitters at his side, plucking at him. Who is that? I wonder yet again.

"Fine," I say. "Then we'll dispense with the symbols."

My armor is gone.

I hold out my bare, open hand. "Touch me," I say. "Touch me, cyborg."

As his hand reaches out to mine, metal creeps up his long dark fingers.

———————

IN THE GAME OF MIND, EVEN MORE THAN IN LIFE, IMAGE AND metaphor are everything.

The place beyond time, the endless fog-shrouded plain, the cold sky and the uncertain earth beneath us, even that is illusion. It is mine, all of it, a setting—however unearthly, however surreal—against which the players may act out their tawdry dramas of dominance and submission, conquest and despair, death and rebirth, rape and mind-rape. Without my shaping, my vision and the visions of all the other painlords through the eons, they would have no ground below, no sky above, no place to set their feet, no feet to set. The reality offers not even the scant comfort of the barren landscape I give them. The reality is chaos, unendurable, outside of space and time, bereft of matter or energy, without measurement and therefore frighteningly infinite and suffocatingly claustrophobic, terribly eternal and achingly brief. In that reality the players are trapped; seven minds locked into a telepathic gestalt, into a congress so intimate it cannot be borne by most. And therefore they shrink away, and the very first things we create, in a place where we are gods (or devils, or both), are the bodies we have left behind. Within these walls of flesh we take our refuge and try to order chaos.

The blood has the taste of salt; but there is no blood, only illusion. The cup holds a black and bitter drink; but there is no cup, only an image. The wounds are open and raw, dripping anguish; but there are no wounds, no body to be wounded, only metaphor, symbol, conjuring. Nothing is real, and everything can hurt, can kill, can evoke a lasting madness.

To survive, the players must be resilient, disciplined, stable, and ruthless; they must possess a ready imagination, an extensive vocabulary of symbols, a certain amount of psychological insight. They must find the weakness in their opponent, and hide their own phobias thoroughly. The rules are simple. Believe in everything; believe in nothing. Hold tight to yourself and your sanity.

Even when they kill you, it has no meaning, unless you believe that you have died.

Upon this plane of illusion where these all-too-mutable bodies whirl and feint in a trite pavane that I have seen a thousand times before, plucking swords and mirrors and monsters from the air to throw at one another like jugglers gone mad, the most frightening thing of all is a simple touch.

The symbolism is direct, the meaning clear. Flesh upon flesh. Stripped of metaphor, stripped of protection, stripped of masks. Mind upon mind. When we touch, the walls are down.

Even time is illusory in the game of mind; it runs as fast, or as slow, as we desire.

I am Cyrain, I tell myself, born of Ash, far-traveled, a Wisdom of Dam Tullian, master of the game of mind, mistress of the obsidian castle, ruler of Croan'dhenni, mindlord, painlord, lifelord, whole and immortal and invulnerable. Enter me.

His fingers are cool and hard.

I HAVE PLAYED THE GAME OF MIND BEFORE, HAVE CLASPED HANDS with others who thought themselves strong. In their minds, in their souls, in them, I have seen things. In dark gray tunnels I have traced the graffiti of their ancient scars. The quicksand of their insecurities has clutched at my boots. I have smelled the rank odor of their fears, great swollen beasts who dwell in a palpable living darkness. I have burned my fingers on the hot flesh of lusts who will not speak a name. I have ripped the cloaks from their still, quiet secrets. And then I have taken it all, been them, lived their lives, drunk the cold draught of their knowledge, rummaged through their memories. I have been born a dozen times, have suckled at a dozen teats, have lost a dozen virginities, male and female.

Kleronomas was different.

I stood in a great cavern, alive with lights. The walls and floor and ceiling were translucent crystal, and all around me spires and cones and twisted ribbons rose bright and red and hard, cold to the touch yet alive, the soulsparks moving through them everywhere. A crystalline fairy city in a cave. I touched the nearest outcropping, and the memory flooded into me, the knowledge as clear and sharp and certain as the day it had been etched there. I turned and looked around with new eyes, now discerning rigid order where initially I had perceived only chaotic beauty. It was clean. It took my breath away. I looked everywhere for the vulnerability, the door of gangrenous flesh, the pool of blood, the place of weeping, the shuffling unclean thing that must live deep inside him, and I found nothing, nothing, nothing, only perfection, only the clean sharp crystal, so very red, glowing from within, growing, changing, yet eternal. I touched it once again, wrapping my hand about an outcropping that rose in front of me like a stalagmite. The knowledge was mine. I began to walk, touching, touching, drinking everywhere. Glass flowers bloomed on every side, fantastic scarlet blooms, fragile and beautiful. I took one and sniffed at it, but it had no scent. The perfection was daunting. Where was his weakness? Where was the hidden flaw in this diamond that would enable me to crack it with a single sharp blow?

Here within him there was no decay.

Here there was no place for death.

Here nothing lived.

It felt like home.

And then in front of me the ghost took form, gray and gaunt and unsteady. His bare feet sent up thin tendrils of smoke as they trod lightly on the gleaming crystals underneath, and I caught the scent of burning meat. And I smiled. The specter haunted the crystal maze, but every touch meant pain and destruction. "Come here," I said. He looked at me. I could see the lights on the far side of the cavern through the haze of his uncertain flesh. He moved to me and I opened my arms to him, entered him, possessed him.

I seated myself upon a balcony in the highest tower of my castle, and drank from a small cup of fragrant black coffee laced with brandy. The swamps were gone; instead I gazed upon mountains, hard and cold and clean. They rose blue-white all around me, and from the highest peak flew a plume of snow crystals caught in a steady endless wind. The wind cut through me, but I scarcely felt it. I was alone and at peace, and the coffee tasted good, and death was far away.

He walked out upon the balcony, and seated himself upon one of the parapets. His pose was casual, insolent, confident. "I know you," he said. It was the ultimate threat.

I was not afraid. "I know you," I said. "Shall I conjure up your ghost?"

"He will be here soon enough. He is never far from me."

"No," I said. I sipped my coffee, and let him wait. "I am stronger than you," I told him finally. "I can win the game, cyborg. You were wrong to challenge me."

He said nothing.

I set down my cup, drained and empty, passed my hand across it, smiled as my glass flower grew and spread its colorless transparent petals. A broken rainbow crawled across the table.

He frowned. Color crept into my flower. It softened and drooped, the rainbow was banished. "The other was not real," he said. "A glass flower is not alive."

I held up his rose, pointed at the broken stem. "This flower is dying," I said. In my hands, it became glass once again. "A glass flower lasts forever."

He transmuted the glass back to living tissue. He was stubborn, I will say that for him. "Even dying, it lives."

"Look at its imperfections," I said. I pointed them out, one by one. "Here an insect has gnawed upon it. Here a petal has grown malformed, here, these dark splotches, those are blight, here the wind has bent it. And look what I can do." I took the largest, prettiest petal between thumb and forefinger, ripped it off, fed it to the wind. "Beauty is no protection. Life is terribly vulnerable. And ultimately, all of it ends like this." In my hand, the flower turned brown and shriveled and began to rot. Worms festered upon it briefly, and foul black fluids ran from it, and then it was dust. I crumpled it, blew it away, and from behind his ear I plucked another flower. Glass.

"Glass is hard," he said, "and cold."

"Warmth is a byproduct of decay, the stepchild of entropy," I told him.

Perhaps he would have replied, but we were no longer alone. Over the crenellated edge of the parapets the ghost came crawling, pulling himself up with frail gray-white hands that left bloody stains upon the purity of my stone. He stared at us wordlessly, a half-transparent whispering in white. Kleronomas averted his eyes.

"Who is he?" I asked.

The cyborg could not answer.

"Do you even remember his name?" I asked him. He replied with silence, and I laughed at them both. "Cyborg, you judged me, found my morality suspect, my actions tainted, but whatever I might be, I am nothing to you. I steal their bodies. You've taken his mind. Haven't you? *Haven't you?*"

"I never meant to," he said.

"Joachim Kleronomas died on Avalon seven hundred years ago, just as they say he did. Steel and plastic he might wear, but inside he was still rotting flesh, even at the end, and with all flesh there comes a time when the cells die. A thin flat line on a machine, glowing in the darkness, and an empty metal shell. The end of a legend. What did they do then? Scoop out the brain and bury it beneath some oversized monument? No doubt." The coffee was strong and sweet; here it never grew lukewarm, because my will did not permit it. "But they did not bury the machine, did they? That expensive, sophisticated cybernetic organism, the library computer with its wealth of knowledge, the crystal matrix with all its frozen memories. All that was too valuable to discard. The good scientists of Avalon kept it in an interface with the academy's main system, correct? How many centuries passed before one of them decided to don that cyborg body again, and keep his own death at bay?"

"Less than one," the cyborg said. "Less than fifty standard years."

"He should have erased you," I said. "But why? His brain would be riding the machine, after all. Why deny himself access to all that marvelous knowledge, why destroy those crystallized memories? Why, when he could savor them instead? How much better to have a whole second lifetime at his disposal, to be able to access wisdom he had never earned, recollect places he had never been and people he had never met." I shrugged, and looked at the ghost. "Poor stupid thing. If you'd ever played the game of mind, you might have understood."

What can the mind be made of, if not memories? Who are we, after all? Only who we think we are, no more, no less.

Etch your memories on diamond, or on a block of rancid meat, those are the choices. Bit by bit the flesh must die, and give way to steel and metal. Only the diamond memories survive to drive the body. In the end no flesh remains, and the echoes of lost memories are ghostly scratchings on the crystal.

"He forgot who he was," the cyborg said. "I forgot who I was, rather. I began to think . . . he began to think he was me." He looked up at me, his eyes locked on mine. They were red crystal, those eyes, and behind them I could see a glow. His skin was taking on a hard, polished sheen, silvering as I watched. And this time he was doing it himself. "You have your own weaknesses," he said, pointing.

Where it curls about the handle of my coffee cup, my hand has grown black, and spotted with corruption. I could smell the decay. Flesh began to flake off, and beneath I saw the bloody bone, bleaching to grim whiteness. Death crept up my bare arm, inexorably. I suppose it was meant to fill me with horror. It only filled me with disgust.

"No," I said. My arm was whole and healthy. "No," I repeated, and now I was metal, silver-bright and undying, eyes like opals, glass flowers twined through platinum hair. I could see my reflection gleaming upon the polished jet of his chest; I was beautiful. Perhaps he could see himself as well, mirrored in my chrome, for just then he turned his head away.

He seemed so strong, but on Croan'dhenni, in my castle of obsidian, in this house of pain and rebirth where the game of mind is played, things are not always as they seem.

"Cyborg," I said to him, "you are lost."

"The other players," he began.

"No." I pointed. "He will stand between you and any victim you might choose. Your ghost. Your guilt. He will not allow it. You will not allow it."

The cyborg could not look at me. "Yes," in a voice tainted by metal and corroded by despair.

"You will live forever," I said.

"No. I will go on forever. It is different, Wisdom. I can tell you the precise temperature reading of any environment, but I cannot feel heat or cold. I can see into the infrared and the ultraviolet, can magnify my sensors to count every pore on your skin, but I am blind to what I think must be your beauty. I desire life, real life, with the seed of death growing inexorably within it, and therefore giving it meaning."

"Good," I said, satisfied.

He finally looked at me. Trapped in that shining metal face were two pale, lost, human eyes. "Good?"

"I make my own meaning, cyborg, and life is the enemy of death, not its mother. Congratulations. You've won. And so have I." I rose and reached across the table, plunged my hand through the cold black chest, and ripped the crystal heart from his breast. I held it up and it shone, brighter and brighter, its scarlet rays dancing brilliantly upon the cold dark mountains of my mind.

I OPENED MY EYES.

No, incorrect; I activated my sensors once again, and the scene in the chamber of change came into focus with a clarity and sharpness I had never experienced. My obsidian mosaic, black against black, was now a hundred different shades, each distinct from the others, the pattern crisp and clear. I was seated in a niche along the rim; in the center cup, the child-woman stirred and blinked large violet eyes. The door opened and they came to her, Rannar solicitous, Khar Dorian aloof, trying to conceal his curiosity, Braje giggling as she gave her shots.

"No," I announced to them. My voice was too deep, too male. I adjusted it. "No, here," I said, sounding more like myself.

Their stares were like the cracking of whips.

IN THE GAME OF MIND, THERE ARE WINNERS AND THERE ARE LOSERS.

The cyborg's interference had its effects, perhaps. Or perhaps not, perhaps before the game was over, the pattern would have been the same. Craimur Delhune is dead; they gave his corpse to the swamps last evening. But the vacancy is gone from the eyes of the pudgy young dreamduster, and she is dieting and exercising even now, and when Khar Dorian leaves, he will take her back to Delhune's estates on Gulliver.

Rieseen Jay complains that she was cheated. I believe she will linger here, outside, in the city of the damned. No doubt that will cure her boredom. The g'hvern struggles to speak, and has painted elaborate symbols on its wings. The tattooed boy leapt from the castle battlements a few hours after his return, and impaled himself upon the jagged obsidian spikes far below, flapping his arms until the last instant. Wings and fierce eyes do not equate with strength.

A new mindlord has begun to reign. She has commanded them to start on a new castle, a structure shaped from living woods, its foundations rooted deep in the swamps, its exterior covered with vines and flowers and other living things. "You will get insects," I have warned her, "parasites and stinging flies, miner-worms in the wood, blight in your foundation, rot in your walls. You will have to sleep with netting over your bed. You will have to kill, constantly, day and night. Your wooden castle will swim in a miasma of little deaths, and in a few years the ghosts of a million insects will swarm your halls by night."

"Nonetheless," she says, "my home will be warm and alive, where yours was cold and brittle."

We all have our symbols, I suppose.

And our fears.

"Erase him," she has warned me. "Blank the crystal, or in time he will consume you, and you will become another ghost in the machine."

"Erase him?" I might have laughed, if the mechanism permitted laughter. I can see right through her. Her soul is scrawled upon that soft, fragile face. I can count her pores and note each flicker of doubt in the pupils of those violet eyes. "Erase me, you mean. The crystal is home to us both, child. Besides, I do not fear him. You miss the point. Kleronomas was crystal, the ghost organic meat, the outcome inevitable. My case is different. I am as crystalline as he is, and just as eternal."

"Wisdom—" she began.

"Wrong," I said.

"Cyrain, if you prefer—"

"Wrong again. Call me Kleronomas." I have been many things through my long and varied lives, but I have never been a legend. It has a certain cachet.

The little girl looked at me. "I am Kleronomas," she said in a high sweet voice, her eyes baffled.

"Yes," I said, "and no. Today we are both Kleronomas. We have lived the same lives, done the same things, stored the same memories. But from this day on, we walk different paths. I am steel and crystal, and you are childflesh. You wanted life, you said. Embrace it, it's yours, and all that goes with it. Your body is young and healthy, just beginning to blossom, your years will be long and full. Today you think you are still Kleronomas. And tomorrow?

"Tomorrow you will learn about lust again, and open your little thighs to Khar Dorian, and shudder and cry out as he rides you to orgasm. Tomorrow you will bear children in blood and pain, and watch them grow and age and bear children of their own, and die. Tomorrow you will ride through the swamps and the dispossessed will toss you gifts, and curse you, and praise you, and pray to you. Tomorrow new players will arrive, begging for bodies, for rebirth, for another chance, and tomorrow Khar's ships will land with a new load of prizes, and all your moral certainties will be tested, and tested again, and twisted to new shapes. Tomorrow Khar and Jonas or Sebastian Cayle will decide that they have waited long enough, and you'll taste the honeyed treason of their kiss, and perhaps you'll win, or perhaps you'll lose. There's no certainty to it. But there's one sure thing I can promise. On the day after tomorrow, long years from now, though they will not seem long once passed, death will begin to grow inside you. The seed is already planted. Perhaps it will be some disease blooming in one of those small sweet breasts Rannar would so dearly love to suckle, perhaps a fine thin wire pulled tight across your throat as you sleep, perhaps a sudden solar flare that will burn this planet clean. It will come, though, and sooner than you think."

"I accept it," she said. She smiled as she spoke; I think she really meant it. "All of it, every part. Life and death. I have been without it for a long time, Wis—Kleronomas."

"Already you're forgetting things," I observed. "Every day you will lose more. Today we both remember. We remember the crystal caverns of Eris, the first ship we ever served on, the lines of our father's face. We remember what Tomas Chung said when we decided not to turn back to Avalon, and the other words he said as he lay dying. We remember the last woman we ever made love to, the shape and smell of her, the taste of her breasts, the noises she made when we pleasured her.

She's been dead and gone eight hundred years, but she lives in our memories. But she's dying in yours, isn't she? Today you are Kleronomas. Yet I am him as well, and I am Cyrain of Ash, and a small part of me is still our ghost, poor sad man. But when tomorrow comes, I'll hold tight to all I am, and you, you'll be the mindlord, or perhaps just a sex-slave in some perfumed brothel on Cymeranth, or a scholar on Avalon, but in any case a different person than you are now."

She understood; she accepted. "So you'll play the game of mind forever," she said, "and I will never die."

"You will die," I pointed out. "Most certainly. Kleronomas is immortal."

"And Cyrain of Ash."

"Her too. Yes."

"What will you do?" she asked me.

I went to the window. The glass flower was there, in its simple wooden vase, its petals refracting the light. I looked up at the source of that light, the brilliant sun of Croan'dhenni burning in the clear midday sky. I could look straight into it now, could focus on the sunspots and the flaming towers of its prominences. I made a small conscious adjustment to the crystal lenses of my eyes, and the empty sky was full of stars, more stars than I had ever seen before, more stars than I could possibly have imagined.

"Do?" I said, still gazing up at those secret starfields, visible to me alone. They brought to mind my obsidian mosaic. "There are worlds I've never been to," I told my sister-twin, father, daughter, enemy, mirror-image, whatever she was. "There are things I don't yet know, stars that even now I cannot see. What will I do? Everything. To begin with, everything."

As I spoke, a fat striped insect flew through the open window on six gossamer wings that trilled the air too fast for human sight, though I could count every languid beat if I so chose. It landed briefly on my glass flower, found neither scent nor pollen, and slipped back outside. I watched it go, growing smaller and smaller, dwindling in the distance, until at last I had telescoped my vision to the maximum, and the small dying bug was lost among the swamps and stars.

The Hedge Knight

A TALE OF THE SEVEN KINGDOMS

The spring rains had softened the ground, so Dunk had no trouble digging the grave. He chose a spot on the western slope of a low hill, for the old man had always loved to watch the sunset. "Another day done," he would sigh, "and who knows what the morrow will bring us, eh, Dunk?"

Well, one morrow had brought rains that soaked them to the bones, and the one after had brought wet gusty winds, and the next a chill. By the fourth day the old man was too weak to ride. And now he was gone. Only a few days past, he had been singing as they rode, the old song about going to Gulltown to see a fair maid, but instead of Gulltown he'd sung of Ashford. *Off to Ashford to see the fair maid, heigh-ho, heigh-ho,* Dunk thought miserably as he dug.

When the hole was deep enough, he lifted the old man's body in his arms and carried him there. He had been a small man, and slim; stripped of hauberk, helm, and sword belt, he seemed to weigh no more than a bag of leaves. Dunk was hugely tall for his age, a shambling, shaggy, big-boned boy of sixteen or seventeen years (no one was quite certain which) who stood closer to seven feet than to six, and had only just begun to fill out his frame. The old man had often praised his strength. He had always been generous in his praise. It was all he had to give.

He laid him out in the bottom of the grave and stood over him for a time. The smell of rain was in the air again, and he knew he ought to fill the hole before the rain broke, but it was hard to throw dirt down on that tired old face. *There ought to be a septon here, to say some prayers over him, but he only has me.* The old man had taught Dunk all he knew of swords and shields and lances, but had never been much good at teaching him words.

"I'd leave your sword, but it would rust in the ground," he said at last, apologetic. "The gods will give you a new one, I guess. I wish you didn't die, ser." He paused, uncertain what else needed to be said. He didn't know any prayers, not all the way through; the old man had never been much for praying. "You were a true knight, and you never beat me when I didn't deserve it," he finally managed, "except that one time in Maidenpool. It was the inn boy who ate the widow woman's pie, not me, I told you. It don't matter now. The gods keep you, ser." He kicked dirt in the hole, then began to fill it methodically, never looking at the thing at the bottom. *He had a long life,* Dunk thought. *He must have been closer to sixty than to fifty, and how many men can say that?* At least he had lived to see another spring.

The sun was westering as he fed the horses. There were three; his swaybacked stot, the old man's palfrey, and Thunder, his warhorse, who was ridden only in tourney and battle. The big brown stallion was not as swift or strong as he had once been, but he still had his bright eye and fierce spirit, and he was more valuable than everything else Dunk owned. *If I sold Thunder and old Chestnut, and the saddles and bridles too, I'd come away with enough silver to...* Dunk frowned. The only life he knew was the life of a hedge knight, riding from keep to keep, taking service with this lord and that lord, fighting in their battles and eating in their halls until the war was done, then moving on. There were tourneys from time to time as well, though less often, and he knew that some hedge knights turned robber during lean winters, though the old man never had.

I could find another hedge knight in need of a squire to tend his animals and clean his mail, he thought, *or might be I could go to some city, to Lannisport or King's Landing, and join the City Watch. Or else...*

He had piled the old man's things under an oak. The cloth purse contained three silver stags, nineteen copper pennies, and a chipped garnet; as with most hedge knights, the greatest part of his worldly wealth had been tied up in his horses and weapons. Dunk now owned a chain-mail hauberk that he had scoured the rust off a thousand times.

An iron halfhelm with a broad nasal and a dent on the left temple. A sword belt of cracked brown leather, and a longsword in a wood-and-leather scabbard. A dagger, a razor, a whetstone. Greaves and gorget, an eight-foot war lance of turned ash topped by a cruel iron point, and an oaken shield with a scarred metal rim, bearing the sigil of Ser Arlan of Pennytree: a winged chalice, silver on brown.

Dunk looked at the shield, scooped up the sword belt, and looked at the shield again. The belt was made for the old man's skinny hips. It would never do for him, no more than the hauberk would. He tied the scabbard to a length of hempen rope, knotted it around his waist, and drew the longsword.

The blade was straight and heavy, good castle-forged steel, the grip soft leather wrapped over wood, the pommel a smooth polished black stone. Plain as it was, the sword felt good in his hand, and Dunk knew how sharp it was, having worked it with whetstone and oilcloth many a night before they went to sleep. *It fits my grip as well as it ever fit his,* he thought to himself, *and there is a tourney at Ashford Meadow.*

SWEETFOOT HAD AN EASIER GAIT THAN OLD CHESTNUT, BUT DUNK was still sore and tired when he spied the inn ahead, a tall daub-and-timber building beside a stream. The warm yellow light spilling from its windows looked so inviting that he could not pass it by. *I have three silvers,* he told himself, *enough for a good meal and as much ale as I care to drink.*

As he dismounted, a naked boy emerged dripping from the stream and began to dry himself on a roughspun brown cloak. "Are you the stableboy?" Dunk asked him. The lad looked to be no more than eight or nine, a pasty-faced skinny thing, his bare feet caked in mud up to the ankle. His hair was the queerest thing about him. He had none. "I'll want my palfrey rubbed down. And oats for all three. Can you tend to them?"

The boy looked at him brazenly. "I could. If I wanted."

Dunk frowned. "I'll have none of that. I am a knight, I'll have you know."

"You don't look to be a knight."

"Do all knights look the same?"

"No, but they don't look like you, either. Your sword belt's made of rope."

"So long as it holds my scabbard, it serves. Now see to my horses. You'll get a copper if you do well, and a clout in the ear if you don't." He did not wait to see how the stableboy took that, but turned away and shouldered through the door.

At this hour, he would have expected the inn to be crowded, but the common room was almost empty. A young lordling in a fine damask mantle was passed out at one table, snoring softly into a pool of spilled wine. Otherwise there was no one. Dunk looked around uncertainly until a stout, short, whey-faced woman emerged from the kitchens and said, "Sit where you like. Is it ale you want, or food?"

"Both." Dunk took a chair by the window, well away from the sleeping man.

"There's good lamb, roasted with a crust of herbs, and some ducks my son shot down. Which will you have?"

He had not eaten at an inn in half a year or more. "Both."

The woman laughed. "Well, you're big enough for it." She drew a tankard of ale and brought it to his table. "Will you be wanting a room for the night as well?"

"No." Dunk would have liked nothing better than a soft straw mattress and a roof above his head, but he needed to be careful with his coin. The ground would serve. "Some food, some ale, and it's on to Ashford for me. How much farther is it?"

"A day's ride. Bear north when the road forks at the burned mill. Is my boy seeing to your horses, or has he run off again?"

"No, he's there," said Dunk. "You seem to have no custom."

"Half the town's gone to see the tourney. My own would as well, if I allowed it. They'll have this inn when I go, but the boy would sooner swagger about with soldiers, and the girl turns to sighs and giggles every time a knight rides by. I swear I couldn't tell you why. Knights are built the same as other men, and I never knew a joust to change the price of eggs." She eyed Dunk curiously; his sword and shield told her one thing, his rope belt and roughspun tunic quite another. "You're bound for the tourney yourself?"

He took a sip of the ale before he answered. A nut-brown color it was, and thick on the tongue, the way he liked it. "Aye," he said. "I mean to be a champion."

"Do you, now?" the innkeep answered, polite enough.

Across the room, the lordling raised his head from the wine puddle. His face had a sallow, unhealthy cast to it beneath a rat's nest of sandy brown hair, and blond stubble crusted his chin. He rubbed his mouth, blinked at Dunk, and said, "I dreamed of you." His hand trembled as he pointed a finger. "You stay away from me, do you hear? You stay well away."

Dunk stared at him uncertainly. "My lord?"

The innkeep leaned close. "Never you mind that one, ser. All he does is drink and talk about his dreams. I'll see about that food." She bustled off.

"Food?" The lordling made the word an obscenity. He staggered to his feet, one hand on the table to keep himself from falling. "I'm going to be sick," he announced. The front of his tunic was crusty-red with old wine stains. "I wanted a whore, but there's none to be found here. All gone to Ashford Meadow. Gods be good, I need some wine." He lurched unsteadily from the common room, and Dunk heard him climbing steps, singing under his breath.

A sad creature, thought Dunk. *But why did he think he knew me?* He pondered that a moment over his ale.

The lamb was as good as any he had ever eaten, and the duck was even better, cooked with cherries and lemons and not near as greasy as most. The innkeep brought buttered pease as well, and oaten bread still hot from her oven. *This is what it means to be a knight,* he told himself as he sucked the last bit of meat off the bone. *Good food, and ale whenever I want it, and no one to clout me in the head.* He had a second tankard of ale with the meal, a third to wash it down, and a fourth because there was no one to tell him he couldn't, and when he was done he paid the woman with a silver stag and still got back a fistful of coppers.

It was full dark by the time Dunk emerged. His stomach was full and his purse was a little lighter, but he felt good as he walked to the stables. Ahead, he heard a horse whicker. "Easy, lad," a boy's voice said. Dunk quickened his step, frowning.

He found the stableboy mounted on Thunder and wearing the old man's armor. The hauberk was longer than he was, and he'd had to tilt the helm back on his bald head or else it would have covered his eyes. He looked utterly intent, and utterly absurd. Dunk stopped in the stable door and laughed.

The boy looked up, flushed, vaulted to the ground. "My lord, I did not mean—"

"Thief," Dunk said, trying to sound stern. "Take off that armor, and be glad that Thunder didn't kick you in that fool head. He's a warhorse, not a boy's pony."

The boy took off the helm and flung it to the straw. "I could ride him as well as you," he said, bold as you please.

"Close your mouth, I want none of your insolence. The hauberk too, take it off. What did you think you were doing?"

"How can I tell you, with my mouth closed?" The boy squirmed out of the chain mail and let it fall.

"You can open your mouth to answer," said Dunk. "Now pick up that mail, shake off the dirt, and put it back where you found it. And the halfhelm too. Did you feed the horses, as I told you? And rub down Sweetfoot?"

"Yes," the boy said, as he shook straw from the mail. "You're going to Ashford, aren't you? Take me with you, ser."

The innkeep had warned him of this. "And what might your mother say to that?"

"My mother?" The boy wrinkled up his face. "My mother's dead, she wouldn't say anything."

He was surprised. Wasn't the innkeep his mother? Perhaps he was only 'prenticed to her. Dunk's head was a little fuzzy from the ale. "Are you an orphan boy?" he asked uncertainly.

"Are you?" the boy threw back.

"I was once," Dunk admitted. *Till the old man took me in.*

"If you took me, I could squire for you."

"I have no need of a squire," he said.

"Every knight needs a squire," the boy said. "You look as though you need one more than most."

Dunk raised a hand threateningly. "And you look as though you need a clout in the ear, it seems to me. Fill me a sack of oats. I'm off for Ashford...alone."

If the boy was frightened, he hid it well. For a moment he stood there defiant, his arms crossed, but just as Dunk was about to give up on him the lad turned and went for the oats.

Dunk was relieved. *A pity I couldn't...but he has a good life here at the inn, a better one than he'd have squiring for a hedge knight. Taking him would be no kindness.*

He could still feel the lad's disappointment, though. As he mounted Sweetfoot and took up Thunder's lead, Dunk decided that a copper penny might cheer him. "Here, lad, for your help." He flipped the coin down at him with a smile, but the stableboy made no attempt to catch it. It fell in the dirt between his bare feet, and there he let it lie.

He'll scoop it up as soon as I am gone, Dunk told himself. He turned the palfrey and rode from the inn, leading the other two horses. The trees were bright with moonlight, and the sky was cloudless and speckled with stars. Yet as he headed down the road he could feel the stableboy watching his back, sullen and silent.

THE SHADOWS OF THE AFTERNOON WERE GROWING LONG WHEN Dunk reined up on the edge of broad Ashford Meadow. Three score pavilions had already risen on the grassy field. Some were small, some large; some square, some round; some of sailcloth, some of linen, some of silk; but all were brightly colored, with long banners streaming from their center poles, brighter than a field of wildflowers with rich reds and sunny yellows, countless shades of green and blue, deep blacks and grays and purples.

The old man had ridden with some of these knights; others Dunk knew from tales told in common rooms and round campfires. Though he had never learned the magic of reading or writing, the old man had been relentless when it came to teaching him heraldry, often drilling him as they rode. The nightingales belonged to Lord Caron of the Marches, as skilled with the high harp as he was with a lance. The crowned stag was for Ser Lyonel Baratheon, the Laughing Storm. Dunk picked out the Tarly huntsman, House Dondarrion's purple lightning, the red apple of the Fossoways. There roared the lion of Lannister gold on crimson, and there the dark green sea turtle of the Estermonts swam across a pale green field. The brown tent beneath red stallion could only belong to Ser Otho Bracken, who was called the Brute of Bracken since slaying Lord Quentyn Blackwood three years past during a tourney at King's Landing. Dunk heard that Ser Otho struck so hard with the blunted longaxe that he stove in the visor of

Lord Blackwood's helm and the face beneath it. He saw some Blackwood banners as well, on the west edge of the meadow, as distant from Ser Otho as they could be. Marbrand, Mallister, Cargyll, Westerling, Swann, Mullendore, Hightower, Florent, Frey, Penrose, Stokeworth, Darry, Parren, Wylde; it seemed as though every lordly house of the west and south had sent a knight or three to Ashford to see the fair maid and brave the lists in her honor.

Yet however fine their pavilions were to look upon, he knew there was no place there for him. A threadbare wool cloak would be all the shelter he had tonight. While the lords and great knights dined on capons and suckling pigs, Dunk's supper would be a hard, stringy piece of salt beef. He knew full well that if he made his camp upon that gaudy field, he would need to suffer both silent scorn and open mockery. A few perhaps would treat him kindly, yet in a way that was almost worse.

A hedge knight must hold tight to his pride. Without it, he was no more than a sellsword. *I must earn my place in that company. If I fight well, some lord may take me into his household. I will ride in noble company then, and eat fresh meat every night in a castle hall, and raise my own pavilion at tourneys. But first I must do well.* Reluctantly, he turned his back on the tourney grounds and led his horses into the trees.

On the outskirts of the great meadow a good half mile from town and castle he found a place where a bend in a brook had formed a deep pool. Reeds grew thick along its edge, and a tall leafy elm presided over all. The spring grass there was as green as any knight's banner and soft to the touch. It was a pretty spot, and no one had yet laid claim to it. *This will be my pavilion,* Dunk told himself, *a pavilion fed with leaves, greener even than the banners of the Tyrells and the Estermonts.* His horses came first. After they had been tended, he stripped and led into the pool to wash away the dust of travel. "A true knight is cleanly as well as godly," the old man always said, insisting that they wash themselves head to heels every time the moon turned, whether they smelled sour or not. Now that he was a knight, Dunk vowed he would do the same.

He sat naked under the elm while he dried, enjoying the warmth of spring air on his skin as he watched a dragonfly move lazily among the reeds. *Why would they name it a dragonfly?* he wondered. *It looks nothing like a dragon.* Not that Dunk had ever seen a dragon. The old man had, though. Dunk had heard the story half a hundred times, how Ser

Arlan had been just a little boy when his grandfather had taken him to King's Landing, and how they'd seen the last dragon there the year before it died. She'd been a green female, small and stunted, her wings withered. None of her eggs had ever hatched. "Some say King Aegon poisoned her," the old man would tell. "The third Aegon that would be, not King Daeron's father, but the one they named Dragonbane, or Aegon the Unlucky. He was afraid of dragons, for he'd seen his uncle's beast devour his own mother. The summers have been shorter since the last dragon died, and the winters longer and crueler."

The air began to cool as the sun dipped below the tops of the trees. When Dunk felt gooseflesh prickling his arms, he beat his tunic and breeches against the trunk of the elm to knock off the worst of the dirt, and donned them once again. On the morrow he could seek out the master of the games and enroll his name, but he had other matters he ought to look into tonight if he hoped to challenge.

He did not need to study his reflection in the water to know that he did not look much a knight, so he slung Ser Arlan's shield across his back to display the sigil. Hobbling the horses, Dunk left them to crop the thick green grass beneath the elm as he set out on foot for the tourney grounds.

In normal times the meadow served as a commons for the folk of Ashford town across the river, but now it was transformed. A second town had sprung up overnight, a town of silk instead of stone, larger and fairer than its elder sister. Dozens of merchants had erected their stalls along the edge of the field, selling felts and fruits, belts and boots, hides and hawks, earthenware, gemstones, pewterwork, spices, feathers, and all manner of other goods. Jugglers, puppeteers, and magicians wandered among the crowds plying their trades...as did the whores and cutpurses. Dunk kept a wary hand on his coin.

When he caught the smell of sausages sizzling over a smoky fire, his mouth began to water. He bought one with a copper from his pouch, and a horn of ale to wash it down. As he ate he watched a painted wooden knight battle a painted wooden dragon. The puppeteer who worked the dragon was good to watch too; a tall drink of water, with the olive skin and black hair of Dorne. She was slim as a lance with no breasts to speak of, but Dunk liked her face and the way her fingers made the dragon snap and slither at the end of its strings. He would have tossed the girl a copper if he'd had one to spare, but just now he needed every coin.

There were armorers among the merchants, as he had hoped. A Tyroshi with a forked blue beard was selling ornate helms, gorgeous fantastical things wrought in the shapes of birds and beasts and chased with gold and silver. Elsewhere he found a swordmaker hawking cheap steel blades, and another whose work was much finer, but it was not a sword he lacked.

The man he needed was all the way down at the end of the row, a shirt of fine chain mail and a pair of lobstered steel gauntlets displayed on the table before him. Dunk inspected them closely. "You do good work," he said.

"None better." A stumpy man, the smith was no more than five feet tall, yet wide as Dunk about the chest and arms. He had a black beard, huge hands, and no trace of humility.

"I need armor for the tourney," Dunk told him. "A suit of good mail, with gorget, greaves, and greathelm." The old man's halfhelm would fit his head, but he wanted more protection for his face than a nasal bar alone could provide.

The armorer looked him up and down. "You're a big one, but I've armored bigger." He came out from behind the table. "Kneel, I want to measure those shoulders. Aye, and that thick neck o' yours." Dunk knelt. The armorer laid a length of knotted rawhide along his shoulders, grunted, slipped it about his throat, grunted again. "Lift your arm. No, the right." He grunted a third time. "Now you can stand." The inside of a leg, the thickness of his calf, and the size of his waist elicited further grunts. "I have some pieces in me wagon that might do for you," the man said when he was done. "Nothing prettied up with gold nor silver, mind you, just good steel, strong and plain. I make helms that look like helms, not winged pigs and queer foreign fruits, but mine will serve you better if you take a lance in the face."

"That's all I want," said Dunk. "How much?"

"Eight hundred stags, for I'm feeling kindly."

"Eight hundred?" It was more than he had expected. "I . . . I could trade you some old armor, made for a smaller man . . . a halfhelm, a mail hauberk . . ."

"Steely Pate sells only his own work," the man declared, "but it might be I could make use of the metal. If it's not too rusted, I'll take it and armor you for six hundred."

Dunk could beseech Pate to give him the armor on trust, but he knew what sort of answer that request would likely get. He had traveled with the old man long enough to learn that merchants were notoriously mistrustful of hedge knights, some of whom were little better than robbers. "I'll give you two silvers now, and the armor and the rest of the coin on the morrow."

The armorer studied him a moment. "Two silvers buys you a day. After that, I sell me work to the next man."

Dunk scooped the stags out of his pouch and placed them in the armorer's calloused hand. "You'll get it all. I mean to be a champion here."

"Do you?" Pate bit one of the coins. "And these others, I suppose they all came just to cheer you on?"

THE MOON WAS WELL UP BY THE TIME HE TURNED HIS STEPS BACK toward his elm. Behind him, Ashford Meadow was ablaze with torchlight. The sounds of song and laughter drifted across the grass, but his own mood was somber. He could think of only one way to raise the coin for his armor. And if he should be defeated... "One victory is all I need," he muttered aloud. "That's not so much to hope for."

Even so, the old man would never have hoped for it. Ser Arlan had not ridden a tilt since the day he had been unhorsed by the Prince of Dragonstone in a tourney at Storm's End, many years before. "It is not every man who can boast that he broke seven lances against the finest knight in the Seven Kingdoms," he would say. "I could never hope to do better, so why should I try?"

Dunk had suspected that Ser Arlan's age had more to do with it than the Prince of Dragonstone did, but he never dared say as much. The old man had his pride, even at the last. *I am quick and strong, he always said so, what was true for him need not be true for me,* he told himself stubbornly.

He was moving through a patch of weed, chewing over his chances in his head, when he saw the flicker of firelight through the bushes. *What is this?* Dunk did not stop to think. Suddenly his sword was in his hand and he was crashing through the grass.

He burst out roaring and cursing, only to jerk to a sudden halt at the sight of the boy beside the campfire. "You!" He lowered the sword. "What are you doing here?"

"Cooking a fish," said the bald boy. "Do you want some?"

"I meant, how did you *get* here? Did you steal a horse?"

"I rode in the back of a cart, with a man who was bringing some lambs to the castle for my lord of Ashford's table."

"Well, you'd best see if he's gone yet, or find another cart. I won't have you here."

"You can't make me go," the boy said, impertinent. "I'd had enough of that inn."

"I'll have no more insolence from you," Dunk warned. "I should throw you over my horse right now and take you home."

"You'd need to ride all the way to King's Landing," said the boy. "You'd miss the tourney."

King's Landing. For a moment Dunk wondered if he was being mocked, but the boy had no way of knowing that he had been born in King's Landing as well. *Another wretch from Flea Bottom, like as not, and who can blame him for wanting out of that place?*

He felt foolish standing there with sword in hand over an eight-year-old orphan. He sheathed it, glowering so the boy would see that he would suffer no nonsense. *I ought to give him a good beating at the least,* he thought, but the child looked so pitiful he could not bring himself to hit him. He glanced around the camp. The fire was burning merrily within a neat circle of rocks. The horses had been brushed, and clothes were hanging from the elm, drying above the flames. "What are those doing there?"

"I washed them," the boy said. "And I groomed the horses, made the fire, and caught this fish. I would have raised your pavilion, but I couldn't find one."

"There's my pavilion." Dunk swept a hand above his head, at the branches of the tall elm that loomed above them.

"That's a tree," the boy said, unimpressed.

"It's all the pavilion a true knight needs. I would sooner sleep under the stars than in some smoky tent."

"What if it rains?"

"The tree will shelter me."

"Trees leak."

Dunk laughed. "So they do. Well, if truth be told, I lack the coin for a pavilion. And you'd best turn that fish, or it will be burned on the bottom and raw on the top. You'd never make a kitchen boy."

"I would if I wanted," the boy said, but he turned the fish.

"What happened to your hair?" Dunk asked of him.

"The maesters shaved it off." Suddenly self-conscious, the boy pulled up the hood of his dark brown cloak, covering his head.

Dunk had heard that they did that sometimes, to treat lice or root-worms or certain sicknesses. "Are you ill?"

"No," said the boy. "What's your name?"

"Dunk," he said.

The wretched boy laughed aloud, as if that was the funniest thing he'd ever heard. *"Dunk?"* he said. "Ser Dunk? That's no name for a knight. Is it short for Duncan?"

Was it? The old man had called him just Dunk for as long as he could recall, and he did not remember much of his life before. "Duncan, yes," he said. "Ser Duncan of..." Dunk had no other name, nor any house; Ser Arlan had found him living wild in the stews and alleys of Flea Bottom. He had never known his father or mother. What was he to say? "Ser Duncan of Flea Bottom" did not sound very knightly. He could take Pennytree, but what if they asked him where it was? Dunk had never been to Pennytree, nor had the old man talked much about it. He frowned for a moment, and then blurted out, "Ser Duncan the Tall." He *was* tall, no one could dispute that, and it sounded puissant.

Though the little sneak did not seem to think so. "I have never heard of any Ser Duncan the Tall."

"Do you know every knight in the Seven Kingdoms, then?"

The boy looked at him boldly. "The good ones."

"I'm as good as any. After the tourney, they'll all know that. Do you have a name, thief?"

The boy hesitated. "Egg," he said.

Dunk did not laugh. *His head does look like an egg. Small boys can be cruel, and grown men as well.* "Egg," he said, "I should beat you bloody and send you on your way, but the truth is, I have no pavilion and I have no squire either. If you'll swear to do as you're told, I'll let you serve me for the tourney. After that, well, we'll see. If I decide you're worth your keep, you'll have clothes on your back and food in your belly. The clothes might be roughspun and the food salt beef and salt fish, and maybe some venison from time to time where there are no foresters about, but you won't go hungry. And I promise not to beat you except when you deserve it."

Egg smiled. "Yes, my lord."

"*Ser,*" Dunk corrected. "I am only a hedge knight." He wondered if the old man was looking down on him. *I will teach him the arts of battle, the same as you taught me, ser. He seems a likely lad, might be one day he'll make a knight.*

The fish was still a little raw on the inside when they ate it, and the boy had not removed all the bones, but it still tasted a world better than hard salt beef.

Egg soon fell asleep beside the dying fire. Dunk lay on his back nearby, his big hands behind his head, gazing up at the night sky. He could hear distant music from the tourney grounds, half a mile away. The stars were everywhere, thousands and thousands of them. One fell as he was watching, a bright green streak that flashed across the black and then was gone.

A falling star brings luck to him who sees it, Dunk thought. *But the rest of them are all in their pavilions by now, staring up at silk instead of sky. So the luck is mine alone.*

———

In the morning, he woke to the sound of a cock crowing. Egg was still there, curled up beneath the old man's second-best cloak. *Well, the boy did not run off during the night, that's a start.* He prodded him awake with his foot. "Up. There's work to do." The boy rose quick enough, rubbing his eyes. "Help me saddle Sweetfoot," Dunk told him.

"What about breakfast?"

"There's salt beef. *After* we're done."

"I'd sooner eat the horse," Egg said. "Ser."

"You'll eat my fist if you don't do as you're told. Get the brushes. They're in the saddle sack. Yes, that one."

Together they brushed out the palfrey's sorrel coat, hefted Ser Arlan's best saddle over her back, and cinched it tight. Egg was a good worker once he put his mind to it, Dunk saw.

"I expect I'll be gone most of the day," he told the boy as he mounted. "You're to stay here and put the camp in order. Make sure no *other* thieves come nosing about."

"Can I have a sword to run them off with?" Egg asked. He had blue eyes, Dunk saw, very dark, almost purple. His bald head made them seem huge, somehow.

"No," said Dunk. "A knife's enough. And you had best be here when I come back, do you hear me? Rob me and run off and I'll hunt you down, I swear I will. With dogs."

"You don't have any dogs," Egg pointed out.

"I'll get some," said Dunk. "Just for you." He turned Sweetfoot's head toward the meadow and moved off at a brisk trot, hoping the threat would be enough to keep the boy honest. Save for the clothes on his back, the armor in his sack, and the horse beneath him, everything Dunk owned in the world was back at that camp. *I am a great fool to trust the boy so far, but it is no more than the old man did for me,* he reflected. *The Mother must have sent him to me so that I could pay my debt.*

As he crossed the field, he heard the ring of hammers from the riverside, where carpenters were nailing together jousting barriers and raising a lofty viewing stand. A few new pavilions were going up as well, while the knights who had come earlier slept off last night's revels or sat to break their fasts. Dunk could smell woodsmoke, and bacon as well.

To the north of the meadow flowed the river Cockleswent, a vassal stream to the mighty Mander. Beyond the shallow ford lay town and castle. Dunk had seen many a market town during his journeys with the old man. This was prettier than most; the whitewashed houses with their thatched roofs had an inviting aspect to them. When he was smaller, he used to wonder what it would be like to live in such a place; to sleep every night with a roof over your head, and wake every morning with the same walls wrapped around you. *It may be that soon I'll know. Aye, and Egg too. It could happen. Stranger things happened every day.*

Ashford Castle was a stone structure built in the shape of a triangle, with round towers rising thirty feet tall at each point and thick crenellated walls running between. Orange banners flew from its battlements, displaying the white sun-and-chevron sigil of its lord. Men-at-arms in orange-and-white livery stood outside the gates with halberds, watching people come and go, seemingly more intent on joking with a pretty milkmaid than in keeping anyone out. Dunk reined up in front of the short, bearded man he took for their captain and asked for the master of the games.

"It's Plummer you want, he's steward here. I'll show you."

Inside the yard, a stableboy took Sweetfoot for him. Dunk slung Ser Arlan's battered shield over a shoulder and followed the guards captain back of the stables to a turret built into an angle of the curtain wall. Steep stone steps led up to the wallwalk. "Come to enter your master's name for the lists?" the captain asked as they climbed.

"It's my own name I'll be putting in."

"Is it now?"

Was the man smirking? Dunk was not certain. "That door there. I'll leave you to it and get back to my post."

When Dunk pushed open the door, the steward was sitting at a trestle table, scratching on a piece of parchment with a quill. He had thinning gray hair and a narrow pinched face. "Yes?" he said, looking up. "What do you want, man?"

Dunk pulled shut the door. "Are you Plummer the steward? I came for the tourney. To enter the lists."

Plummer pursed his lips. "My lord's tourney is a contest for knights. Are you a knight?"

He nodded, wondering if his ears were red.

"A knight with a name, mayhaps?"

"Dunk." Why had he said *that*? "Ser Duncan. The Tall."

"And where might you be from, Ser Duncan the Tall?"

"Everyplace. I was squire to Ser Arlan of Pennytree since I was five or six. This is his shield." He showed it to the steward. "He was coming to the tourney, but he caught a chill and died, so I came in his stead. He knighted me before he passed, with his own sword." Dunk drew the longsword and laid it on the scarred wooden table between them.

The master of the lists gave the blade no more than a glance. "A sword it is, for a certainty. I have never heard of this Arlan of Pennytree, however. You were his squire, you say?"

"He always said he meant for me to be a knight, as he was. When he was dying he called for his longsword and bade me kneel. He touched me once on my right shoulder and once on my left, and said some words, and when I got up he said I was a knight."

"Hmpf." The man Plummer rubbed his nose. "Any knight can make a knight, it is true, though it is more customary to stand a vigil and be anointed by a septon before taking your vows. Were there any witnesses to your dubbing?"

"Only a robin, up in a thorn tree. I heard it as the old man was saying the words. He charged me to be a good knight and true, to obey the seven gods, defend the weak and innocent, serve my lord faithfully and defend the realm with all my might, and I swore that I would."

"No doubt." Plummer did not deign to call him *ser*, Dunk could not help but notice. "I shall need to consult with Lord Ashford. Will you or your late master be known to any of the good knights here assembled?"

Dunk thought a moment. "There was a pavilion flying the banner of House Dondarrion? The black, with purple lightning?"

"That would be Ser Manfred, of that House."

"Ser Arlan served his lord father in Dorne, three years past. Ser Manfred might remember me."

"I would advise you to speak to him. If he will vouch for you, bring him here with you on the morrow, at this same time."

"As you say, m'lord." He started for the door.

"Ser Duncan," the steward called after him.

Dunk turned back.

"You are aware," the man said, "that those vanquished in tourney forfeit their arms, armor, and horse to the victors, and must needs ransom them back?"

"I know."

"And do you have the coin to pay such ransom?"

Now he *knew* his ears were red. "I won't have need of coin," he said, praying it was true. *All I need is one victory. If I win my first tilt, I'll have the loser's armor and horse, or his gold, and I can stand a loss myself.*

He walked slowly down the steps, reluctant to get on with what he must do next. In the yard, he collared one of the stableboys. "I must speak with Lord Ashford's master of horse."

"I'll find him for you."

It was cool and dim in the stables. An unruly gray stallion snapped at him as he passed, but Sweetfoot only whickered softly and nuzzled his hand when he raised it to her nose. "You're a good girl, aren't you?"

he murmured. The old man always said that a knight should never love a horse, since more than a few were like to die under him, but he never heeded his own counsel either. Dunk had often seen him spend his last copper on an apple for old Chestnut or some oats for Sweetfoot and Thunder. The palfrey had been Ser Arlan's riding horse, and she had borne him tirelessly over thousands of miles, all up and down the Seven Kingdoms. Dunk felt as though he were betraying an old friend, but what choice did he have? Chestnut was too old to be worth much of anything, and Thunder must carry him in the lists.

Some time passed before the master of horse deigned to appear. As he waited, Dunk heard a blare of trumpets from the walls, and a voice in the yard. Curious, he led Sweetfoot to the stable door to see what was happening. A large party of knights and mounted archers poured through the gates, a hundred men at least, riding some of the most splendid horses that Dunk had ever seen. *Some great lord has come.* He grabbed the arm of a stableboy as he ran past. "Who are they?"

The boy looked at him queerly. "Can't you see the banners?" He wrenched free and hurried off.

The banners . . . As Dunk turned his head, a gust of wind lifted the black silk pennon atop the tall staff, and the fierce three-headed dragon of House Targaryen seemed to spread its wings, breathing scarlet fire. The banner-bearer was a tall knight in white scale armor chased with gold, a pure white cloak streaming from his shoulders. Two of the other riders were armored in white from head to heel as well. *Kingsguard knights with the royal banner.* Small wonder Lord Ashford and his sons came hurrying out the doors of the keep, and the fair maid too, a short girl with yellow hair and a round pink face. *She does not seem so fair to me,* Dunk thought. The puppet girl was prettier.

"Boy, let go of that nag and see to my horse."

A rider had dismounted in front of the stables. *He is talking to me,* Dunk realized. "I am not a stableboy, m'lord."

"Not clever enough?" The speaker wore a black cloak bordered in scarlet satin, but underneath was raiment bright as flame, all reds and yellows and golds. Slim and straight as a dirk, though only of middling height, he was near Dunk's own age. Curls of silver-gold hair framed a face sculpted and imperious; high brow and sharp cheekbones, straight nose, pale smooth skin without blemish. His eyes were a deep violet color. "If you cannot manage a horse, fetch me some wine and a pretty wench."

"I . . . m'lord, pardons, I'm no servingman either. I have the honor to be a knight."

"Knighthood has fallen on sad days," said the princeling, but then one of the stableboys came rushing up, and he turned away to hand him the reins of his palfrey, a splendid blood bay. Dunk was forgotten in an instant. Relieved, he slunk back inside the stables to wait for the master of horse. He felt ill at ease enough around the lords in their pavilions, he had no business speaking to princes.

That the beautiful stripling was a prince he had no doubt. The Targaryens were the blood of lost Valyria across the seas, and their silver-gold hair and violet eyes set them apart from common men. Dunk knew Prince Baelor was older, but the youth might well have been one of his sons: Valarr, who was often called "the Young Prince" to set him apart from his father, or Matarys, "the Even Younger Prince," as old Lord Swann's fool had named him once. There were other princelings as well, cousins to Valarr and Matarys. Good King Daeron had four grown sons, three with sons of their own. The line of the dragonkings had almost died out during his father's day, but it was commonly said that Daeron II and his sons had left it secure for all time.

"You. Man. You asked for me." Lord Ashford's master of horse had a red face made redder by his orange livery, and a brusque manner of speaking. "What is it? I have no time for—"

"I want to sell this palfrey," Dunk broke in quickly, before the man could dismiss him. "She's a good horse, sure of foot—"

"I have no time, I tell you." The man gave Sweetfoot no more than a glance. "My lord of Ashford has no need of such. Take her to the town, perhaps Henly will give you a silver or three." That quick, he was turning away.

"Thank you, m'lord," Dunk said before he could go. "M'lord, has the king come?"

The master of horse laughed at him. "No, thank the gods. This infestation of princes is trial enough. Where am I going to find the stalls for all these animals? And fodder?" He strode off shouting at his stableboys.

By the time Dunk left the stable, Lord Ashford had escorted his princely guests into the hall, but two of the Kingsguard knights in their white armor and snowy cloaks still lingered in the yard, talking with the captain of the guard. Dunk halted before them. "M'lords, I am Ser Duncan the Tall."

"Well met, Ser Duncan," answered the bigger of the white knights. "I am Ser Roland Crakehall, and this is my Sworn Brother, Ser Donnel of Duskendale."

The seven champions of the Kingsguard were the most puissant warriors in all the Seven Kingdoms, saving only perhaps the crown prince, Baelor Breakspear himself. "Have you come to enter the lists?" Dunk asked anxiously.

"It would not be fitting for us to ride against those we are sworn to protect," answered Ser Donnel, red of hair and beard.

"Prince Valarr has the honor to be one of Lady Ashford's champions," explained Ser Roland, "and two of his cousins mean to challenge. The rest of us have come only to watch."

Relieved, Dunk thanked the white knights for their kindness, and rode out through the castle gates before another prince should think to accost him. *Three princelings,* he pondered as he turned the palfrey toward the streets of Ashford town. Valarr was the eldest son of Prince Baelor, second in line to the Iron Throne, but Dunk did not know how much of his father's fabled prowess with lance and sword he might have inherited. About the other Targaryen princes he knew even less. *What will I do if I have to ride against a prince? Will I even be allowed to challenge one so highborn?* He did not know the answer. The old man had often said he was thick as a castle wall, and just now he felt it.

Henly liked the look of Sweetfoot well enough until he heard Dunk wanted to sell her. Then all the stableman could see in her were faults. He offered three hundred silvers. Dunk said he must have three thousand. After much arguing and cursing, they settled at seven hundred fifty silver stags. That was a deal closer to Henly's starting price than to Dunk's, which made him feel the loser in the tilt, but the stableman would go no higher, so in the end he had no choice but to yield. A second argument began when Dunk declared that the price did not include the saddle, and Henly insisted that it had.

Finally it was all settled. As Henly left to fetch his coin, Dunk stroked Sweetfoot's mane and told her to be brave. "If I win, I'll come back and buy you again, I promise." He had no doubt that all the palfrey's flaws would vanish in the intervening days, and she would be worth twice what she was today.

The stableman gave him three gold pieces and the rest in silver. Dunk bit one of the gold coins and smiled. He had never tasted gold before, nor handled it. "Dragons," men called the coins, since they were stamped with the three-headed dragon of House Targaryen on one side. The other bore the likeness of the king. Two of the coins Henly gave him had King Daeron's face; the third was older, well worn, and showed a different man. His name was there under his head, but Dunk could not read the letters. Gold had been shaved off its edges too, he saw. He pointed this out to Henly, and loudly. The stableman grumbled, but handed over another few silvers and a fistful of coppers to make up the weight. Dunk handed a few of the coppers right back, and nodded at Sweetfoot. "That's for her," he said. "See that she has some oats tonight. Aye, and an apple too."

With the shield on his arm and the sack of old armor slung over his shoulder, Dunk set out on foot through the sunny streets of Ashford town. The heft of all that coin in his pouch made him feel queer; almost giddy on one hand, and anxious on the other. The old man had never trusted him with more than a coin or two at a time. He could live a year on this much money. *And what will I do when it's gone, sell Thunder?* That road ended in beggary or outlawry. *This chance will never come again; I must risk all.*

By the time he splashed back across the ford to the south bank of the Cockleswent, the morning was almost done and the tourney grounds had come to life once more. The winesellers and sausage makers were doing a brisk trade, a dancing bear was shuffling along to his master's playing as a singer sang "The Bear, the Bear, and the Maiden Fair," jugglers were juggling, and the puppeteers were just finishing another fight.

Dunk stopped to watch the wooden dragon slain. When the puppet knight cut its head off and the red sawdust spilled out onto the grass, he laughed aloud and threw the girl two coppers. "One for last night," he called. She caught the coins in the air and threw him back a smile as sweet as any he had ever seen.

Is it me she smiles at, or the coins? Dunk had never been with a girl, and they made him nervous. Once, three years past, when the old man's purse was full after half a year in the service of blind Lord Florent, he'd told Dunk the time had come to take him to a brothel and make him a man. He'd been drunk, though, and when he was sober he did not remember. Dunk had been too embarrassed to remind him. He was not certain he wanted a whore anyway. If he could not have a highborn maiden like a proper knight, he wanted one who at least liked him more than his silver.

"Will you drink a horn of ale?" he asked the puppet girl as she was scooping the sawdust blood back into her dragon. "With me, I mean? Or a sausage? I had a sausage last night, and it was good. They're made with pork, I think."

"I thank you, m'lord, but we have another show." The girl rose, and ran off to the fierce fat Dornishwoman who worked the puppet knight while Dunk stood there feeling stupid. He liked the way she ran, though. *A pretty girl, and tall. I would not have to kneel to kiss that one.* He knew how to kiss. A tavern girl had showed him one night in Lannisport, a year ago, but she'd been so short she had to sit on the table to reach his lips. The memory made his ears burn. What a great fool he was. It was jousting he should be thinking about, not kissing.

Lord Ashford's carpenters were whitewashing the waist-high wooden barriers that would separate the jousters. Dunk watched them work awhile. There were five lanes, arrayed north to south so none of the competitors would ride with the sun in his eyes. A three-tiered viewing stand had been raised on the eastern side of the lists, with an orange canopy to shield the lords and ladies from rain and sun. Most would sit on benches, but four high-backed chairs had been erected in the center of the platform, for Lord Ashford, the fair maid, and the visiting princes.

On the eastern verge of the meadow, a quintain had been set up and a dozen knights were tilting at it, sending the pole arm spinning every time they struck the splintered shield suspended from one end. Dunk watched the Brute of Bracken take his turn, and then Lord Caron of the Marches. *I do not have as good a seat as any of them,* he thought uneasily.

Elsewhere, men were training afoot, going at each other with wooden swords while their squires stood shouting ribald advice. Dunk watched a stocky youth try to hold off a muscular knight who seemed lithe and quick as a mountain cat. Both had the red apple of the Fossoways painted on their shields, but the younger man's was soon hacked and chipped to pieces. "Here's an apple that's not ripe yet," the older said as he slammed the other's helm. The younger Fossoway was bruised and bloody by the time he yielded, but his foe was hardly winded. He raised his visor, looked about, saw Dunk, and said, "You there. Yes, you, the big one. Knight of the winged chalice. Is that a longsword you wear?"

"It is mine by rights," Dunk said defensively. "I am Ser Duncan the Tall."

"And I Ser Steffon Fossoway. Would you care try me, Ser Duncan the Tall? It would be good to have someone new to cross swords with. My cousin's not ripe yet, as you've seen."

"Do it, Ser Duncan," urged the beaten Fossoway as he removed his helm. "I may not be ripe, but my good cousin is rotten to the core. Knock the seeds out of him."

Dunk shook his head. Why were these lordlings involving him in their quarrel? He wanted no part of it. "I thank you, ser, but I have matters to attend." He was uncomfortable carrying so much coin. The sooner he paid Steely Pate and got his armor, the happier he would be.

Ser Steffon looked at him scornfully. "The hedge knight has matters." He glanced about and found another likely opponent loitering nearby. "Ser Grance, well met. Come try me. I know every feeble trick my cousin Raymun has mastered, and it seems that Ser Duncan needs to return to the hedges. Come, come."

Dunk stalked away red-faced. He did not have many tricks himself, feeble or otherwise, and he did not want anyone to see him fight until the tourney. The old man always said that the better you knew your foe, the easier it was to best him. Knights like Ser Steffon had sharp eyes to find a man's weakness at a glance. Dunk was strong and quick, and his weight and reach were in his favor, but he did not believe for a moment that his skills were the equal of these others. Ser Arlan had taught him as best he could, but the old man had never been the greatest of knights even when young. Great knights did not live their lives in the hedges, or die by the side of a muddy road. *That will not happen to me,* Dunk vowed. *I will show them that I can be more than a hedge knight.*

"Ser Duncan." The younger Fossoway hurried to catch him. "I

should not have urged you to try my cousin. I was angry with his arrogance, and you are so large, I thought . . . well, it was wrong of me. You wear no armor. He would have broken your hand if he could, or a knee. He likes to batter men in the training yard, so they will be bruised and vulnerable later, should he meet them in the lists."

"He did not break you."

"No, but I am his own blood, though his is the senior branch of the apple tree, as he never ceases to remind me. I am Raymun Fossoway."

"Well met. Will you and your cousin ride in the tourney?"

"He will, for a certainty. As to me, would that I could. I am only a squire as yet. My cousin has promised to knight me, but insists that I am not ripe yet." Raymun had a square face, a pug nose, and short woolly hair, but his smile was engaging. "You have the look of a challenger, it seems to me. Whose shield do you mean to strike?"

"It makes no difference," said Dunk. That was what you were supposed to say, though it made all the difference in the world. "I will not enter the lists until the third day."

"And by then some of the champions will have fallen, yes," Raymun said. "Well, may the Warrior smile on you, ser."

"And you." *If he is only a squire, what business do I have being a knight? One of us is a fool.* The silver in Dunk's pouch clinked with every step, but he could lose it all in a heartbeat, he knew. Even the rules of this tourney worked against him, making it very unlikely that he would face a green or feeble foe.

There were a dozen different forms a tourney might follow, according to the whim of the lord who hosted it. Some were mock battles between teams of knights, others wild melees where the glory went to the last fighter left standing. Where individual combats were the rule, pairings were sometimes determined by lot, and sometimes by the master of the games.

Lord Ashford was staging this tourney to celebrate his daughter's thirteenth nameday. The fair maid would sit by her father's side as the reigning Queen of Love and Beauty. Five champions wearing her favors would defend her. All others must perforce be challengers, but any man who could defeat one of the champions would take his place and stand as a champion himself, until such time as another challenger unseated him. At the end of three days of jousting, the five who remained would determine whether the fair maid would retain the crown of Love and Beauty, or whether another would wear it in her place.

Dunk stared at the grassy lists and the empty chairs on the viewing stand and pondered his chances. One victory was all he needed; then he could name himself one of the champions of Ashford Meadow, if only for an hour. The old man had lived nigh on sixty years and had never been a champion. *It is not too much to hope for, if the gods are good.* He thought back on all the songs he had heard, songs of blind Symeon Star-Eyes and noble Serwyn of the Mirror Shield, of Prince Aemon the Dragonknight, Ser Ryam Redwyne, and Florian the Fool. They had all won victories against foes far more terrible than any he would face. *But they were great heroes, brave men of noble birth, except for Florian. And what am I? Dunk of Flea Bottom? Or Ser Duncan the Tall?*

He supposed he would learn the truth of that soon enough. He hefted the sack of armor and turned his feet toward the merchants' stalls, in search of Steely Pate.

EGG HAD WORKED MANFULLY AT THE CAMPSITE. DUNK WAS pleased; he had been half afraid his squire would run off again. "Did you get a good price for your palfrey?" the boy asked.

"How did you know I'd sold her?"

"You rode off and walked back, and if robbers had stolen her you'd be more angry than you are."

"I got enough for this." Dunk took out his new armor to show the boy. "If you're ever to be a knight, you'll need to know good steel from bad. Look here, this is fine work. This mail is double-chain, each link bound to two others, see? It gives more protection than single-chain. And the helm, Pate's rounded the top, see how it curves? A sword or an axe will slide off, where they might bite through a flat-topped helm." Dunk lowered the greathelm over his head. "How does it look?"

"There's no visor," Egg pointed out.

"There's air holes. Visors are points of weakness." Steely Pate had said as much. "If you knew how many knights have taken an arrow in the eye as they lifted their visor for a suck o' cool air, you'd never want one," he'd told Dunk.

"There's no crest either," said Egg. "It's just plain."

Dunk lifted off the helm. "Plain is fine for the likes of me. See how bright the steel is? It will be your task to keep it that way. You know how to scour mail?"

"In a barrel of sand," said the boy, "but you don't have a barrel. Did you buy a pavilion too, ser?"

"I didn't get that good a price." *The boy is too bold for his own good, I ought to beat that out of him.* He knew he would not, though. He liked the boldness. He needed to be bolder himself. *My squire is braver than I am, and more clever.* "You did well here, Egg," Dunk told him. "On the morrow, you'll come with me. Have a look at the tourney grounds. We'll buy oats for the horses and fresh bread for ourselves. Maybe a bit of cheese as well; they were selling good cheese at one of the stalls."

"I won't need to go into the castle, will I?"

"Why not? One day, I mean to live in a castle. I hope to win a place above the salt before I'm done."

The boy said nothing. *Perhaps he fears to enter a lord's hall,* Dunk reflected. *That's no more than might be expected. He will grow out of it in time.* He went back to admiring his armor, and wondering how long he would wear it.

Ser Manfred was a thin man with a sour look on his face. He wore a black surcoat slashed with the purple lightning of House Dondarrion, but Dunk would have remembered him anyway by his unruly mane of red-gold hair. "Ser Arlan served your lord father when he and Lord Caron burned the Vulture King out of the Red Mountains, ser," he said from one knee. "I was only a boy then, but I squired for him. Ser Arlan of Pennytree."

Ser Manfred scowled. "No. I know him not. Nor you, boy."

Dunk showed him the old man's shield. "This was his sigil, the winged chalice."

"My lord father took eight hundred knights and near four thousand foot into the mountains. I cannot be expected to remember every one of them, nor what shields they carried. It may be that you were with us, but . . ." Ser Manfred shrugged.

Dunk was struck speechless for an instant. *The old man took a wound in your father's service, how can you have forgotten him?* "They will not allow me to challenge unless some knight or lord will vouch for me."

"And what is that to me?" said Ser Manfred. "I have given you enough of my time, ser."

If he went back to the castle without Ser Manfred, he was lost. Dunk eyed the purple lightning embroidered across the black wool of Ser Manfred's surcoat and said, "I remember your father telling the camp how your house got its sigil. One stormy night, as the first of your line bore a message across the Dornish Marches, an arrow killed his horse beneath him and spilled him on the ground. Two Dornishmen came out of the darkness in ring mail and crested helms. His sword had broken beneath him when he fell. When he saw that, he thought he was doomed. But as the Dornishmen closed to cut him down, lightning cracked from the sky. It was a bright burning purple, and it split, striking the Dornishmen in their steel and killing them both where they stood. The message gave the Storm King victory over the Dornish, and in thanks he raised the messenger to lordship. He was the first Lord Dondarrion, so he took for his arms a forked purple lightning bolt, on a black field powdered with stars."

If Dunk thought the tale would impress Ser Manfred, he could not have been more wrong. "Every pot boy and groom who has ever served my father hears that story soon or late. Knowing it does not make you a knight. Begone with you, ser."

It was with a leaden heart that Dunk returned to Ashford Castle, wondering what he might say so that Plummer would grant him the right of challenge. The steward was not in his turret chamber, however. A guard told him he might be found in the Great Hall. "Shall I wait here?" Dunk asked. "How long will he be?"

"How should I know? Do what you please."

The Great Hall was not so great, as halls went, but Ashford was a small castle. Dunk entered through a side door, and spied the steward at once. He was standing with Lord Ashford and a dozen other men at the top of the hall. He walked toward them, beneath a wall hung with wool tapestries of fruits and flowers.

"—more concerned if they were *your* sons, I'll wager," an angry man was saying as Dunk approached. His straight hair and square-cut beard were so fair they seemed white in the dimness of the hall, but as he got closer he saw that they were in truth a pale silvery color touched with gold.

"Daeron has done this before," another replied. Plummer was standing so as to block Dunk's view of the speaker. "You should never have commanded him to enter the lists. He belongs on a tourney field no more than Aerys does, or Rhaegel."

"By which you mean he'd sooner ride a whore than a horse," the first man said. Thickly built and powerful, the prince—he was surely a prince—wore a leather brigandine covered with silver studs beneath a heavy black cloak trimmed with ermine. Pox scars marked his cheeks, only partly concealed by his silvery beard. "I do not need to be reminded of my son's failings, brother. He has only eighteen years. He can change. He *will* change, gods be damned, or I swear I'll see him dead."

"Don't be an utter fool. Daeron is what he is, but he is still your blood and mine. I have no doubt Ser Roland will turn him up, and Aegon with him."

"When the tourney is over, perhaps."

"Aerion is here. He is a better lance than Daeron in any case, if it is the tourney that concerns you." Dunk could see the speaker now. He was seated in the high seat, a sheaf of parchments in one hand, Lord Ashford hovering at his shoulder. Even seated, he looked to be a head taller than the other, to judge from the long straight legs stretched out before him. His short-cropped hair was dark and peppered with gray, his strong jaw clean-shaven. His nose looked as though it had been broken more than once. Though he was dressed very plainly, in green doublet, brown mantle, and scuffed boots, there was a weight to him, a sense of power and certainty.

It came to Dunk that he had walked in on something that he ought never have heard. *I had best go and come back later, when they are done,* he decided. But it was already too late. The prince with the silvery beard suddenly took note of him. "Who are you, and what do you mean by bursting in on us?" he demanded harshly.

"He is the knight that our good steward was expecting," the seated man said, smiling at Dunk in a way that suggested he had been aware of him all the time. "You and I are the intruders here, brother. Come closer, ser."

Dunk edged forward, uncertain what was expected of him. He looked at Plummer, but got no help there. The pinch-faced steward who had been so forceful yesterday now stood silent, studying the stones of the floor. "My lords," he said, "I asked Ser Manfred Dondarrion to vouch for me so I might enter the lists, but he refuses. He says he knows me not. Ser Arlan served him, though, I swear it. I have his sword and shield, I—"

"A shield and a sword do not make a knight," declared Lord Ashford, a big bald man with a round red face. "Plummer has spoken to me of you. Even if we accept that these arms belonged to this Ser Arlan of Pennytree, it may well be that you found him dead and stole them. Unless you have some better proof of what you say, some writing or—"

"I remember Ser Arlan of Pennytree," the man in the high seat said quietly. "He never won a tourney that I know, but he never shamed himself either. At King's Landing sixteen years ago, he overthrew Lord Stokeworth and the Bastard of Harrenhal in the melee, and many years before at Lannisport he unhorsed the Grey Lion himself. The lion was not so gray then, to be sure."

"He told me about that, many a time," said Dunk.

The tall man studied him. "Then you will remember the Grey Lion's true name, I have no doubt."

For a moment there was nothing in Dunk's head at all. *A thousand times the old man had told that tale, a thousand times, the lion, the lion, his name, his name, his name. . . .* He was near despair when suddenly it came. "Ser Damon Lannister!" he shouted. "The Grey Lion! He's Lord of Casterly Rock now."

"So he is," said the tall man pleasantly, "and he enters the lists on the morrow." He rattled the sheaf of papers in his hand.

"How can you possibly remember some insignificant hedge knight who chanced to unhorse Damon Lannister sixteen years ago?" said the prince with the silver beard, frowning.

"I make it a practice to learn all I can of my foes."

"Why would you deign to joust with a hedge knight?"

"It was nine years past, at Storm's End. Lord Baratheon held a hastilude to celebrate the birth of a grandson. The lots made Ser Arlan my opponent in the first tilt. We broke four lances before I finally un-horsed him."

"Seven," insisted Dunk, "and that was against the Prince of Dragonstone!" No sooner were the words out than he wanted them back. *Dunk the lunk, thick as a castle wall,* he could hear the old man chiding.

"So it was." The prince with the broken nose smiled gently. "Tales grow in the telling, I know. Do not think ill of your old master, but it was four lances only, I fear."

Dunk was grateful that the hall was dim; he knew his ears were red. "My lord." *No, that's wrong too.* "Your Grace." He fell to his knees and lowered his head. "As you say, four, I meant no . . . I never . . . The old man, Ser Arlan, he used to say I was thick as a castle wall and slow as an aurochs."

"And strong as an aurochs, by the look of you," said Baelor Breakspear. "No harm was done, ser. Rise."

Dunk got to his feet, wondering if he should keep his head down or if he was allowed to look a prince in the face. *I am speaking with Baelor Targaryen, Prince of Dragonstone, Hand of the King, and heir apparent to the Iron Throne of Aegon the Conqueror. What could a hedge knight dare say to such a person?* "Y-you gave him back his horse and armor and took no ransom, I remember," he stammered. "The old—Ser Arlan, he told me you were the soul of chivalry, and that one day the Seven Kingdoms would be safe in your hands."

"Not for many a year still, I pray," Prince Baelor said.

"No," said Dunk, horrified. He almost said, *I didn't mean that the king should die,* but stopped himself in time. "I am sorry, m'lord. Your Grace, I mean."

Belatedly he recalled that the stocky man with the silver beard had addressed Prince Baelor as brother. *He is blood of the dragon as well, damn me for a fool.* He could only be Prince Maekar, the youngest of King Daeron's four sons. Prince Aerys was bookish and Prince Rhaegel mad, meek, and sickly. Neither was like to cross half the realm to attend a tourney, but Maekar was said to be a redoubtable warrior in his own right, though ever in the shadow of his eldest brother.

"You wish to enter the lists, is that it?" asked Prince Baelor. "That de-cision rests with the master of the games, but I see no reason to deny you."

The steward inclined his head. "As you say, my lord."

Dunk tried to stammer out thanks, but Prince Maekar cut him off. "Very well, ser, you are grateful. Now be off with you."

"You must forgive my noble brother, ser," said Prince Baelor. "Two of his sons have gone astray on their way here, and he fears for them."

"The spring rains have swollen many of the streams," said Dunk. "Perhaps the princes are only delayed."

"I did not come here to take counsel from a hedge knight," Prince Maekar declared to his brother.

"You may go, ser," Prince Baelor told Dunk, not unkindly.

"Yes, my lord." He bowed and turned.

But before he could get away, the prince called after him. "Ser. One thing more. You are not of Ser Arlan's blood?"

"Yes, m'lord. I mean, no. I'm not."

The prince nodded at the battered shield Dunk carried, and the winged chalice upon its face. "By law, only a trueborn son is entitled to inherit a knight's arms. You must needs find a new device, ser, a sigil of your own."

"I will," said Dunk. "Thank you again, Your Grace. I will fight bravely, you'll see." *As brave as Baelor Breakspear,* the old man would often say.

THE WINESELLERS AND SAUSAGE MAKERS WERE DOING A BRISK trade, and whores walked brazenly among the stalls and pavilions. Some were pretty enough, one red-haired girl in particular. He could not help staring at her breasts, the way they moved under her loose shift as she sauntered past. He thought of the silver in his pouch. *I could have her, if I liked. She'd like the clink of my coin well enough, I could take her back to my camp and have her, all night if I wanted.* He had never lain with a woman, and for all he knew he might die in his first tilt. Tourneys could be dangerous...but whores could be dangerous too, the old man had warned him of that. *She might rob me while I slept, and what would I do then?* When the red-haired girl glanced back over her shoulder at him, Dunk shook his head and walked away.

He found Egg at the puppet show, sitting cross-legged on the ground with the hood of his cloak pulled all the way forward to hide his baldness. The boy had been afraid to enter the castle, which Dunk put down to equal parts shyness and shame. *He does not think himself worthy to mingle with lords and ladies, let alone great princes.* It had been the same with him when he was little. The world beyond Flea Bottom had seemed as frightening as it was exciting. *Egg needs time, that's all.* For the present, it seemed kinder to give the lad a few coppers and let him enjoy himself among the stalls than to drag him along unwilling into the castle.

This morning the puppeteers were doing the tale of Florian and Jonquil. The fat Dornishwoman was working Florian in his armor made of motley, while the tall girl held Jonquil's strings. "You are no knight," she was saying as the puppet's mouth moved up and down. "I know you. You are Florian the Fool."

"I am, my lady," the other puppet answered, kneeling. "As great a fool as ever lived, and as great a knight as well."

"A fool *and* a knight?" said Jonquil. "I have never heard of such a thing."

"Sweet lady," said Florian, "all men are fools, and all men are knights, where women are concerned."

It was a good show, sad and sweet both, with a sprightly swordfight at the end, and a nicely painted giant. When it was over, the fat woman went among the crowd to collect coins while the girl packed away the puppets.

Dunk collected Egg and went up to her.

"M'lord?" she said, with a sideways glance and a half-smile. She was a head shorter than he was, but still taller than any other girl he had ever seen.

"That was good," Egg enthused. "I like how you make them move, Jonquil and the dragon and all. I saw a puppet show last year, but they moved all jerky. Yours are more smooth."

"Thank you," she told the boy politely.

Dunk said, "Your figures are well carved too. The dragon, especially. A fearsome beast. You make them yourself?"

She nodded. "My uncle does the carving. I paint them."

"Could you paint something for me? I have the coin to pay." He slipped the shield off his shoulder and turned it to show her. "I need to paint something over the chalice."

The girl glanced at the shield, and then at him. "What would you want painted?"

Dunk had not considered that. If not the old man's winged chalice, what? His head was empty. *Dunk the lunk, thick as a castle wall.* "I don't...I'm not certain." His ears were turning red, he realized miserably. "You must think me an utter fool."

She smiled. "All men are fools, and all men are knights."

"What color paint do you have?" he asked, hoping that might give him an idea.

"I can mix paints to make any color you want."

The old man's brown had always seemed drab to Dunk. "The field should be the color of sunset," he said suddenly. "The old man liked sunsets. And the device..."

"An elm tree," said Egg. "A big elm tree, like the one by the pool, with a brown trunk and green branches."

"Yes," Dunk said. "That would serve. An elm tree...but with a shooting star above. Could you do that?"

The girl nodded. "Give me the shield. I'll paint it this very night, and have it back to you on the morrow."

Dunk handed it over. "I am called Ser Duncan the Tall."

"I'm Tanselle," she laughed. "Tanselle Too-Tall, the boys used to call me."

"You're not too tall," Dunk blurted out. "You're just right for..." He realized what he had been about to say, and blushed furiously.

"For?" said Tanselle, cocking her head inquisitively.

"Puppets," he finished lamely.

THE FIRST DAY OF THE TOURNEY DAWNED BRIGHT AND CLEAR. Dunk bought a sackful of foodstuffs, so they were able to break their fast on goose eggs, fried bread, and bacon, but when the food was cooked he found he had no appetite. His belly felt hard as a rock, even though he knew he would not ride today. The right of first challenge would go to knights of higher birth and greater renown, to lords and their sons and champions from other tourneys.

Egg chattered all through their breakfast, talking of this man and that man and how they might fare. *He was not japing me when he said he knew every good knight in the Seven Kingdoms,* Dunk thought ruefully. He found it humbling to listen so intently to the words of a scrawny orphan boy, but Egg's knowledge might serve him should he face one of these men in a tilt.

The meadow was a churning mass of people, all trying to elbow their way closer for a better view. Dunk was as good an elbower as any, and bigger than most. He squirmed forward to a rise six yards from the fence. When Egg complained that all he could see were arses, Dunk sat the boy on his shoulders. Across the field, the viewing stand was filling up with highborn lords and ladies, a few rich townfolk, and a score of knights who had decided not to compete today. Of Prince Maekar he saw no sign, but he recognized Prince Baelor at Lord Ashford's side. Sunlight flashed golden off the shoulder clasp that held his cloak and the slim coronet about his temples, but otherwise he dressed far more simply than most of the other lords. *He does not look a Targaryen in truth, with that dark hair.* Dunk said as much to Egg.

"It's said he favors his mother," the boy reminded him. "She was a Dornish princess."

The five champions had raised their pavilions at the north end of the lists with the river behind them. The smallest two were orange, and the shields hung outside their doors displayed the white sun-and-chevron. Those would be Lord Ashford's sons Androw and Robert, brothers to the fair maid. Dunk had never heard other knights speak of their prowess, which meant they would likely be the first to fall.

Beside the orange pavilions stood one of deep-dyed green, much larger. The golden rose of Highgarden flapped above it, and the same device was emblazoned on the great green shield outside the door. "That's Leo Tyrell, Lord of Highgarden," said Egg.

"I knew that," said Dunk, irritated. "The old man and I served at Highgarden before you were ever born." He hardly remembered that year himself, but Ser Arlan had often spoken of Leo Longthorn, as he was sometimes called; a peerless jouster, for all the silver in his hair. "That must be Lord Leo beside the tent, the slender graybeard in green and gold."

"Yes," said Egg. "I saw him at King's Landing once. He's not one you'll want to challenge, ser."

"Boy, I do not require your counsel on who to challenge."

The fourth pavilion was sewn together from diamond-shaped pieces of cloth, alternating red and white. Dunk did not know the colors, but Egg said they belonged to a knight from the Vale of Arryn named Ser Humfrey Hardyng. "He won a great melee at Maidenpool last year, ser, and overthrew Ser Donnel of Duskendale and the Lords Arryn and Royce in the lists."

The last pavilion was Prince Valarr's. Of black silk it was, with a line of pointed scarlet pennons hanging from its roof like long red flames. The shield on its stand was glossy black, emblazoned with the three-headed dragon of House Targaryen. One of the Kingsguard knights stood beside it, his shining white armor stark against the black of the tentcloth. Seeing him there, Dunk wondered whether any of the challengers would dare to touch the dragon shield. Valarr was the king's grandson, after all, and son to Baelor Breakspear.

He need not have worried. When the horns blew to summon the challengers, all five of the maid's champions were called forth to defend her. Dunk could hear the murmur of excitement in the crowd as the challengers appeared one by one at the south end of the lists. Heralds boomed out the name of each knight in turn. They paused before the viewing stand to dip their lances in salute to Lord Ashford, Prince Baelor, and the fair maid, then circled to the north end of the field to select their opponents. The Grey Lion of Casterly Rock struck the shield of Lord Tyrell, while his golden-haired heir Ser Tybolt Lannister challenged Lord Ashford's eldest son. Lord Tully of Riverrun tapped the diamond-patterned shield of Ser Humfrey Hardyng, Ser Abelar Hightower knocked upon Valarr's, and the younger Ashford was called out by Ser Lyonel Baratheon, the knight they called the Laughing Storm.

The challengers trotted back to the south end of the lists to await their foes: Ser Abelar in silver and smoke colors, a stone watchtower on his shield, crowned with fire; the two Lannisters all crimson, bearing the golden lion of Casterly Rock; the Laughing Storm shining in cloth-of-gold, with a black stag on breast and shield and a rack of iron antlers on his helm; Lord Tully wearing a striped blue-and-red cloak clasped with a silver trout at each shoulder. They pointed their twelve-foot lances skyward, the gusty winds snapping and tugging at the pennons.

At the north end of the field, squires held brightly barded destriers for the champions to mount. They donned their helms and took up lance and shield, in splendor the equal of their foes: the Ashfords' billowing orange silks, Ser Humfrey's red-and-white diamonds, Lord Leo on his white charger with green satin trappings patterned with golden roses, and of course Valarr Targaryen. The Young Prince's horse was black as night, to match the color of his armor, lance, shield, and trappings. Atop his helm was a gleaming three-headed dragon, wings spread, enameled in a rich red; its twin was painted upon the glossy black surface of his shield. Each of the defenders had a wisp of orange silk knotted about an arm, a favor bestowed by the fair maid.

As the champions trotted into position, Ashford Meadow grew almost still. Then a horn sounded, and stillness turned to tumult in half a heartbeat. Ten pairs of gilded spurs drove into the flanks of ten great warhorses, a thousand voices began to scream and shout, forty iron-shod hooves pounded and tore the grass, ten lances dipped and steadied, the field seemed almost to shake, and champions and challengers came together in a rending crash of wood and steel. In an instant, the riders were beyond each other, wheeling about for another pass. Lord Tully reeled in his saddle but managed to keep his seat. When the commons realized that all ten of the lances had broken, a great roar of approval went up. It was a splendid omen for the success of the tourney, and a testament to the skill of the competitors.

Squires handed fresh lances to the jousters to replace the broken ones they cast aside, and once more the spurs dug deep. Dunk could feel the earth trembling beneath the soles of his feet. Atop his shoulders, Egg shouted happily and waved his pipestem arms. The Young Prince passed nearest to them. Dunk saw the point of his black lance kiss the watchtower on his foe's shield and slide off to slam into his chest, even as Ser Abelar's own lance burst into splinters against Valarr's breastplate. The gray stallion in the silver-and-smoke trappings reared with the force of the impact, and Ser Abelar Hightower was lifted from his stirrups and dashed violently to the ground.

Lord Tully was down as well, unhorsed by Ser Humfrey Hardyng, but he sprang up at once and drew his longsword, and Ser Humfrey cast aside his lance—unbroken—and dismounted to continue their fight afoot. Ser Abelar was not so sprightly. His squire ran out, loosened his helm, and called for help, and two servingmen lifted the dazed knight by the arms to help him back to his pavilion. Elsewhere on the field, the six knights who had remained ahorse were riding their third course. More lances shattered, and this time Lord Leo Tyrell aimed his point so expertly he ripped the Grey Lion's helm cleanly off his head. Barefaced, the Lord of Casterly Rock raised his hand in salute and dismounted, yielding the match. By then Ser Humfrey had beaten Lord Tully into surrender, showing himself as skilled with a sword as he was with a lance.

Tybolt Lannister and Androw Ashford rode against each other thrice more before Ser Androw finally lost shield, seat, and match all at once. The younger Ashford lasted even longer, breaking no less than nine lances against Ser Lyonel Baratheon, the Laughing Storm. Champion and challenger both lost their saddles on their tenth course, only to rise together to fight on, sword against mace. Finally a battered Ser Robert Ashford admitted defeat, but on the viewing stand his father looked anything but dejected. Both Lord Ashford's sons had been ushered from the ranks of the champions, it was true, but they had acquitted themselves nobly against two of the finest knights in the Seven Kingdoms.

I must do even better, though, Dunk thought as he watched victor and vanquished embrace and walk together from the field. *It is not enough for me to fight well and lose. I must win at least the first challenge, or I lose all.*

Ser Tybolt Lannister and the Laughing Storm would now take their places among the champions, replacing the men they had defeated. Already the orange pavilions were coming down. A few feet away, the Young Prince sat at his ease in a raised camp chair before his great black tent. His helm was off. He had dark hair like his father, but a bright streak ran through it. A servingman brought him a silver goblet and he took a sip. *Water, if he is wise,* Dunk thought, *wine if not.* He found himself wondering if Valarr had indeed inherited a measure of his father's prowess, or whether it had only been that he had drawn the weakest opponent.

A fanfare of trumpets announced that three new challengers had entered the lists. The heralds shouted their names. *"Ser Pearse of House Caron, Lord of the Marches."* He had a silver harp emblazoned on his shield, though his surcoat was patterned with nightingales. *"Ser Joseth of House Mallister, from Seagard."* Ser Joseth sported a winged helm; on his shield, a silver eagle flew across an indigo sky. *"Ser Gawen of House*

Swann, Lord of Stonehelm on the Cape of Wrath." A pair of swans, one black and one white, fought furiously on his arms. Lord Gawen's armor, cloak, and horse bardings were a riot of black and white as well, down to the stripes on his scabbard and lance.

Lord Caron, harper and singer and knight of renown, touched the point of his lance to Lord Tyrell's rose. Ser Joseth thumped on Ser Humfrey Hardyng's diamonds. And the black-and-white knight, Lord Gawen Swann, challenged the black prince with the white guardian. Dunk rubbed his chin. Lord Gawen was even older than the old man, and the old man was dead. "Egg, who is the least dangerous of these challengers?" he asked the boy on his shoulders, who seemed to know so much of these knights.

"Lord Gawen," the boy said at once. "Valarr's foe."

"*Prince* Valarr," he corrected. "A squire must keep a courteous tongue, boy."

The three challengers took their places as the three champions mounted up. Men were making wagers all around them and calling out encouragement to their choices, but Dunk had eyes only for the prince. On the first pass he struck Lord Gawen's shield a glancing blow, the blunted point of the lance sliding aside just as it had with Ser Abelar Hightower, only this time it was deflected the other way, into empty air. Lord Gawen's own lance broke clean against the prince's chest, and Valarr seemed about to fall for an instant before he recovered his seat.

The second time through the lists, Valarr swung his lance left, aiming for his foe's breast, but struck his shoulder instead. Even so, the blow was enough to make the older knight lose his lance. One arm flailed for balance and Lord Gawen fell. The Young Prince swung from the saddle and drew his sword, but the fallen man waved him off and raised his visor. "I yield, Your Grace," he called. "Well fought." The lords in the viewing stand echoed him, shouting, *"Well fought! Well fought!"* as Valarr knelt to help the gray-haired lord to his feet.

"It was not either," Egg complained.

"Be quiet, or you can go back to camp."

Farther away, Ser Joseth Mallister was being carried off the field unconscious, while the harp lord and the rose lord were going at each other lustily with blunted longaxes, to the delight of the roaring crowd. Dunk was so intent on Valarr Targaryen that he scarcely saw them. *He is a fair knight, but no more than that,* he found himself thinking. *I would have a chance against him. If the gods were good, I might even unhorse him, and once afoot my weight and strength would tell.*

"Get him!" Egg shouted merrily, shifting his seat on Dunk's back in his excitement. "Get him! Hit him! Yes! He's right there, he's right there!" It seemed to be Lord Caron he was cheering on. The harper was playing a different sort of music now, driving Lord Leo back and back as steel sang on steel. The crowd seemed almost equally divided between them, so cheers and curses mingled freely in the morning air. Chips of wood and paint were flying from Lord Leo's shield as Lord Pearse's axe knocked the petals off his golden rose, one by one, until the shield finally shattered and split. But as it did, the axehead hung up for an instant in the wood . . . and Lord Leo's own axe crashed down on the haft of his foe's weapon, breaking it off not a foot from his hand. He cast aside his broken shield, and suddenly he was the one on the attack. Within moments, the harper knight was on one knee, singing his surrender.

For the rest of the morning and well into the afternoon, it was more of the same, as challengers took the field in twos and threes, and sometimes five together. Trumpets blew, the heralds called out names, warhorses charged, the crowd cheered, lances snapped like twigs, and swords rang against helms and mail. It was, smallfolk and high lord alike agreed, a splendid day of jousting. Ser Humfrey Hardyng and Ser Humfrey Beesbury, a bold young knight in yellow and black stripes with three beehives on his shield, splintered no less than a dozen lances apiece in an epic struggle the smallfolk soon began calling "the Battle of Humfrey." Ser Tybolt Lannister was unhorsed by Ser Jon Penrose and broke his sword in his fall, but fought back with shield alone to win the bout and remain a champion. One-eyed Ser Robyn Rhysling, a grizzled old knight with a salt-and-pepper beard, lost his helm to Lord Leo's lance in their first course, yet refused to yield. Three times more they rode at each other, the wind whipping Ser Robyn's hair while the shards of broken lances flew round his bare face like wooden knives, which Dunk thought all the more wondrous when Egg told him that Ser Robyn had lost his eye to a splinter from a broken lance not five years earlier. Leo Tyrell was too chivalrous to aim another lance at Ser Robyn's unprotected head, but even so Rhysling's stubborn courage (or was it folly?) left Dunk astounded. Finally the Lord of Highgarden struck Ser Robyn's breastplate a solid thump right over the heart and sent him cartwheeling to the earth.

Ser Lyonel Baratheon also fought several notable matches. Against lesser foes, he would often break into booming laughter the moment they touched his shield, and laugh all the time he was mounting and charging and knocking them from their stirrups. If his challengers wore any sort of crest on their helm, Ser Lyonel would strike it off and fling it into the crowd. The crests were ornate things, made of carved wood or shaped leather, and sometimes gilded and enameled or even wrought in pure silver, so the men he beat did not appreciate this habit, though it made him a great favorite of the commons. Before long, only crestless men were choosing him. As loud and often as Ser Lyonel laughed down a challenger, though, Dunk thought the day's honors should go to Ser Humfrey Hardyng, who humbled fourteen knights, each one of them formidable.

Meanwhile the Young Prince sat outside his black pavilion, drinking from his silver goblet and rising from time to time to mount his horse and vanquish yet another undistinguished foe. He had won nine victories, but it seemed to Dunk that every one was hollow. *He is beating old men and upjumped squires, and a few lords of high birth and low skill. The truly dangerous men are riding past his shield as if they do not see it.*

Late in the day, a brazen fanfare announced the entry of a new challenger to the lists. He rode in on a great red charger whose black bardings were slashed to reveal glimpses of yellow, crimson, and orange beneath. As he approached the viewing stand to make his salute, Dunk saw the face beneath the raised visor, and recognized the prince he'd met in Lord Ashford's stables.

Egg's legs tightened around his neck. "Stop that," Dunk snapped, yanking them apart. "Do you mean to choke me?"

"Prince Aerion Brightflame," a herald called, *"of the Red Keep of King's Landing, son of Maekar Prince of Summerhall of House Targaryen, grandson to Daeron the Good, the Second of His Name, King of the Andals, the Rhoynar, and the First Men, and Lord of the Seven Kingdoms."*

Aerion bore a three-headed dragon on his shield, but it was rendered in colors much more vivid than Valarr's; one head was orange, one yellow, one red, and the flames they breathed had the sheen of gold leaf. His surcoat was a swirl of smoke and fire woven together, and his blackened helm was surmounted by a crest of red enamel flames.

After a pause to dip his lance to Prince Baelor, a pause so brief that it was almost perfunctory, he galloped to the north end of the field, past Lord Leo's pavilion and the Laughing Storm's, slowing only when he approached Prince Valarr's tent. The Young Prince rose and stood stiffly beside his shield, and for a moment Dunk was certain that Aerion meant to strike it . . . but then he laughed and trotted past, and banged his point hard against Ser Humfrey Hardyng's diamonds.

"Come out, come out, little knight," he sang in a loud clear voice, "it's time you faced the dragon."

Ser Humfrey inclined his head stiffly to his foe as his destrier was brought out, and then ignored him while he mounted, fastened his helm, and took up lance and shield. The spectators grew quiet as the two knights took their places. Dunk heard the *clang* of Prince Aerion dropping his visor. The horn blew.

Ser Humfrey broke slowly, building speed, but his foe raked the red charger hard with both spurs, coming hard. Egg's legs tightened again. *"Kill him!"* he shouted suddenly. *"Kill him, he's right there, kill him, kill him, kill him!"* Dunk was not certain which of the knights he was shouting to.

Prince Aerion's lance, gold-tipped and painted in stripes of red, orange, and yellow, swung down across the barrier. *Low, too low,* thought Dunk the moment he saw it. *He'll miss the rider and strike Ser Humfrey's horse, he needs to bring it up.* Then, with dawning horror, he began to suspect that Aerion intended no such thing. *He cannot mean to . . .*

At the last possible instant, Ser Humfrey's stallion reared away from the oncoming point, eyes rolling in terror, but too late. Aerion's lance took the animal just above the armor that protected his breastbone, and exploded out of the back of his neck in a gout of bright blood. Screaming, the horse crashed sideways, knocking the wooden barrier to pieces as he fell. Ser Humfrey tried to leap free, but a foot caught in a stirrup and they heard his shriek as his leg was crushed between the splintered fence and falling horse.

All of Ashford Meadow was shouting. Men ran onto the field to extricate Ser Humfrey, but the stallion, dying in agony, kicked at them as they approached. Aerion, having raced blithely around the carnage to the end of the lists, wheeled his horse and came galloping back. He was shouting too, though Dunk could not make out the words over the almost human screams of the dying horse. Vaulting from the saddle, Aerion drew his sword and advanced on his fallen foe. His own squires and one of Ser Humfrey's had to pull him back. Egg squirmed on Dunk's shoulders. "Let me down," the boy said. "The poor horse, *let me down*."

Dunk felt sick himself. *What would I do if such a fate befell Thunder?* A man-at-arms with a poleaxe dispatched Ser Humfrey's stallion, ending the hideous screams. Dunk turned and forced his way through the press. When he came to open ground, he lifted Egg off his shoulders. The boy's hood had fallen back and his eyes were red. "A terrible sight, aye," he told the lad, "but a squire must needs be strong. You'll see worse mishaps at other tourneys, I fear."

"It was no mishap," Egg said, mouth trembling. "Aerion meant to do it. You saw."

Dunk frowned. It had looked that way to him as well, but it was hard to accept that any knight could be so unchivalrous, least of all one who was blood of the dragon. "I saw a knight green as summer grass lose control of his lance," he said stubbornly, "and I'll hear no more of it. The jousting is done for the day, I think. Come, lad."

He was right about the end of the day's contests. By the time the chaos had been set to rights, the sun was low in the west, and Lord Ashford had called a halt. As the shadows of evening crept across the meadow, a hundred torches were lit along the merchants' row. Dunk bought a horn of ale for himself and half a horn for the boy, to cheer him. They wandered for a time, listening to a sprightly air on pipes and drums and watching a puppet show about Nymeria, the warrior queen with the ten thousand ships. The puppeteers had only two ships, but managed a rousing sea battle all the same. Dunk wanted to ask the girl Tanselle if she had finished painting his shield, but he could see that she was busy. *I'll wait until she is done for the night,* he resolved. *Perhaps she'll have a thirst then.*

"Ser Duncan," a voice called behind him. And then again, "Ser Duncan." Suddenly Dunk remembered that was him. "I saw you among the smallfolk today, with this boy on your shoulders," said Raymun Fossoway as he came up, smiling. "Indeed, the two of you were hard to miss."

"The boy is my squire. Egg, this is Raymun Fossoway." Dunk had to pull the boy forward, and even then Egg lowered his head and stared at Raymun's boots as he mumbled a greeting.

"Well met, lad," Raymun said easily. "Ser Duncan, why not watch from the viewing gallery? All knights are welcome there."

Dunk was at ease among smallfolk and servants; the idea of claiming a place among the lords, ladies, and landed knights made him uncomfortable. "I would not have wanted any closer view of that last tilt."

Raymun grimaced. "Nor I. Lord Ashford declared Ser Humfrey the victor and awarded him Prince Aerion's courser, but even so, he will not be able to continue. His leg was broken in two places. Prince Baelor sent his own maester to tend him."

"Will there be another champion in Ser Humfrey's place?"

"Lord Ashford had a mind to grant the place to Lord Caron, or perhaps the other Ser Humfrey, the one who gave Hardyng such a splendid match, but Prince Baelor told him that it would not be seemly to remove Ser Humfrey's shield and pavilion under the circumstances. I believe they will continue with four champions in place of five."

Four champions, Dunk thought. *Leo Tyrell, Lyonel Baratheon, Tybolt Lannister, and Prince Valarr.* He had seen enough this first day to know how little chance he would stand against the first three. Which left only . . .

A hedge knight cannot challenge a prince. Valarr is second in line to the Iron Throne. He is Baelor Breakspear's son, and his blood is the blood of Aegon the Conqueror and the Young Dragon and Prince Aemon the Dragonknight, and I am some boy the old man found behind a pot shop in Flea Bottom.

His head hurt just thinking about it. "Who does your cousin mean to challenge?" he asked Raymun.

"Ser Tybolt, all things being equal. They are well matched. My cousin keeps a sharp watch on every tilt, though. Should any man be wounded on the morrow, or show signs of exhaustion or weakness, Steffon will be quick to knock on his shield, you may count on it. No one has ever accused him of an excess of chivalry." He laughed, as if to take the sting from his words. "Ser Duncan, will you join me for a cup of wine?"

"I have a matter I must attend to," said Dunk, uncomfortable with the notion of accepting hospitality he could not return.

"I could wait here and bring your shield when the puppet show is over, ser," said Egg. "They're going to do Symeon Star-Eyes later, and make the dragon fight again as well."

"There, you see, your matter is attended to, and the wine awaits," said Raymun. "It's an Arbor vintage, too. How can you refuse me?"

Bereft of excuses, Dunk had no choice but to follow, leaving Egg at the puppet show. The apple of House Fossoway flew above the gold-colored pavilion where Raymun attended his cousin. Behind it, two servants were basting a goat with honey and herbs over a small cook-fire. "There's food as well, if you're hungry," Raymun said negligently as he held the flap for Dunk. A brazier of coals lit the interior and made the air pleasantly warm. Raymun filled two cups with wine. "They say Aerion is in a rage at Lord Ashford for awarding his charger to Ser Humfrey," he commented as he poured, "but I'll wager it was his uncle who counseled it." He handed Dunk a wine cup.

"Prince Baelor is an honorable man."

"As the Bright Prince is not?" Raymun laughed. "Don't look so anxious, Ser Duncan, there's none here but us. It is no secret that Aerion is a bad piece of work. Thank the gods that he is well down in the order of succession."

"You truly believe he meant to kill the horse?"

"Is there any doubt of it? If Prince Maekar had been here, it would have gone differently, I promise you. Aerion is all smiles and chivalry so long as his father is watching, if the tales be true, but when he's not..."

"I saw that Prince Maekar's chair was empty."

"He's left Ashford to search for his sons, along with Roland Crakehall of the Kingsguard. There's a wild tale of robber knights going about, but I'll wager the prince is just off drunk again."

The wine was fine and fruity, as good a cup as he had ever tasted. He rolled it in his mouth, swallowed, and said, "Which prince is this now?"

"Maekar's heir. Daeron, he's named, after the king. They call him Daeron the Drunken, though not in his father's hearing. The youngest boy was with him as well. They left Summerhall together but never reached Ashford." Raymun drained his cup and set it aside. "Poor Maekar."

"Poor?" said Dunk, startled. "The king's son?"

"The king's *fourth* son," said Raymun, "not quite as bold as Prince Baelor, nor as clever as Prince Aerys, nor as gentle as Prince Rhaegel. And now he must suffer seeing his own sons overshadowed by his brother's. Daeron is a sot, Aerion is vain and cruel, the third son was so unpromising they gave him to the Citadel to make a maester of him, and the youngest—"

"Ser! Ser Duncan!" Egg burst in panting. His hood had fallen back, and the light from the brazier shone in his big dark eyes. "You have to run, he's hurting her!"

Dunk lurched to his feet, confused. "Hurting? Who?"

"Aerion!" the boy shouted. "He's *hurting* her. The puppet girl. Hurry." Whirling, he darted back out into the night.

Dunk made to follow, but Raymun caught his arm. "Ser Duncan. Aerion, he said. A prince of the blood. Be careful."

It was good counsel, he knew. The old man would have said the same. But he could not listen. He wrenched free of Raymun's hand and shouldered his way out of the pavilion. He could hear shouting off in the direction of the merchants' row. Egg was almost out of sight. Dunk ran after him. His legs were long and the boy's short; he quickly closed the distance.

A wall of watchers had gathered around the puppeteers. Dunk shouldered through them, ignoring their curses. A man-at-arms in the royal livery stepped up to block him. Dunk put a big hand on his chest and shoved, sending the man flailing backward to sprawl on his arse in the dirt.

The puppeteer's stall had been knocked on its side. The fat Dornishwoman was on the ground weeping. One man-at-arms was dangling the puppets of Florian and Jonquil from his hands as another set them afire with a torch. Three more men were opening chests, spilling more puppets on the ground and stamping on them. The dragon puppet was scattered all about them, a broken wing here, its head there, its tail in three pieces. And in the midst of it all stood Prince Aerion, resplendent in a red velvet doublet with long dagged sleeves, twisting Tanselle's arm in both hands. She was on her knees, pleading with him. Aerion ignored her. He forced open her hand and seized one of her fingers. Dunk stood there stupidly, not quite believing what he saw. Then he heard a *crack,* and Tanselle screamed.

One of Aerion's men tried to grab him, and went flying. Three long strides, then Dunk grabbed the prince's shoulder and wrenched him around hard. His sword and dagger were forgotten, along with everything the old man had ever taught him. His fist knocked Aerion off his feet, and the toe of his boot slammed into the prince's belly. When Aerion went for his knife, Dunk stepped on his wrist and then kicked him again, right in the mouth. He might have kicked him to death right then and there, but the princeling's men swarmed over him. He had a man on each arm and another pounding him across the back. No sooner had he wrestled free of one than two more were on him.

Finally they shoved him down and pinned his arms and legs. Aerion was on his feet again. The prince's mouth was bloody. He pushed inside it with a finger. "You've loosened one of my teeth," he complained, "so we'll start by breaking all of yours." He pushed his hair from his eyes. "You look familiar."

"You took me for a stableboy."

Aerion smiled redly. "I recall. You refused to take my horse. Why did you throw your life away? For this whore?" Tanselle was curled up on the ground, cradling her maimed hand. He gave her a shove with the toe of his boot. "She's scarcely worth it. A traitor. The dragon ought never lose."

He is mad, thought Dunk, *but he is still a prince's son, and he means to kill me.* He might have prayed then, if he had known a prayer all the way through, but there was no time. There was hardly even time to be afraid.

"Nothing more to say?" said Aerion. "You bore me, ser." He poked at his bloody mouth again. "Get a hammer and break all his teeth out, Wate," he commanded, "and then let's cut him open and show him the color of his entrails."

"No!" a boy's voice said. "Don't hurt him!"

Gods be good, the boy, the brave foolish boy, Dunk thought. He fought against the arms restraining him, but it was no good. "Hold your tongue, you stupid boy. Run away. They'll hurt you!"

"No they won't." Egg moved closer. "If they do, they'll answer to my father. And my uncle as well. Let go of him, I said. Wate, Yorkel, you know me. Do as I say."

The hands holding his left arm were gone, and then the others. Dunk did not understand what was happening. The men-at-arms were backing away. One even knelt. Then the crowd parted for Raymun Fossoway. He had donned mail and helm, and his hand was on his sword. His cousin Ser Steffon, just behind him, had already bared his blade, and with them were a half-dozen men-at-arms with the red apple badge sewn on their breasts.

Prince Aerion paid them no mind. "Impudent little wretch," he said to Egg, spitting a mouthful of blood at the boy's feet. "What happened to your hair?"

"I cut it off, brother," said Egg. "I didn't want to look like you."

THE SECOND DAY OF THE TOURNEY WAS OVERCAST, WITH A GUSTY wind blowing from the west. *The crowds should be less on a day like this,* Dunk thought. *It would have been easier for them to find a spot near the fence to see the jousting up close. Egg might have sat on the rail, while I stood behind him.*

Instead Egg would have a seat in the viewing box, dressed in silks and furs, while Dunk's view would be limited to the four walls of the tower cell where Lord Ashford's men had confined him. The chamber had a window, but it faced in the wrong direction. Even so, Dunk crammed himself into the window seat as the sun came up, and stared gloomily off across town and field and forest. They had taken his hempen sword belt, and his sword and dagger with it, and they had taken his silver as well. He hoped Egg or Raymun would remember Chestnut and Thunder.

"Egg," he muttered low under his breath. His squire, a poor lad plucked from the streets of King's Landing. Had ever a knight been made such a fool? *Dunk the lunk, thick as a castle wall and slow as an aurochs.*

He had not been permitted to speak to Egg since Lord Ashford's soldiers had scooped them all up at the puppet show. Nor Raymun, nor Tanselle, nor anyone, not even Lord Ashford himself. He wondered if he would ever see any of them again. For all he knew, they meant to keep him in this small room until he died. *What did I think would happen?* he asked himself bitterly. *I knocked down a prince's son and kicked him in the face.*

Beneath these gray skies, the flowing finery of the highborn lords and great champions would not seem quite so splendid as it had the day before. The sun, walled behind the clouds, would not brush their steel helms with brilliance, nor make their gold and silver chasings glitter and flash, but even so, Dunk wished he were in the crowd to watch the jousting. It would be a good day for hedge knights, for men in plain mail on unbarded horses.

He could *hear* them, at least. The horns of the heralds carried well, and from time to time a roar from the crowd told him that someone had fallen, or risen, or done something especially bold. He heard faint hoofbeats too, and once in a great while the clash of swords or the *snap* of a lance. Dunk winced whenever he heard that last; it reminded him of the noise Tanselle's finger had made when Aerion broke it. There were other sounds too, closer at hand: footfalls in the hall outside his door, the stamp of hooves in the yard below, shouts and voices from the castle walls. Sometimes they drowned out the tourney. Dunk supposed that was just as well.

"A hedge knight is the truest kind of knight, Dunk," the old man had told him, a long long time ago. "Other knights serve the lords who keep them, or from whom they hold their lands, but we serve where we will, for men whose causes we believe in. Every knight swears to protect the weak and innocent, but we keep the vow best, I think." Queer how strong that memory seemed. Dunk had quite forgotten those words. And perhaps the old man had as well, toward the end.

The morning turned to afternoon. The distant sounds of the tourney began to dwindle and die. Dusk began to seep into the cell, but Dunk still sat in the window seat, looking out on the gathering dark and trying to ignore his empty belly.

And then he heard footsteps and a jangling of iron keys. He uncoiled and rose to his feet as the door opened. Two guards pushed in, one bearing an oil lamp. A servingman followed with a tray of food. Behind came Egg. "Leave the lamp and the food and go," the boy told them.

They did as he commanded, though Dunk noticed that they left the heavy wooden door ajar. The smell of the food made him realize how ravenous he was. There was hot bread and honey, a bowl of pease porridge, a skewer of roast onions and well-charred meat. He sat by the tray, pulled apart the bread with his hands, and stuffed some into his mouth. "There's no knife," he observed. "Did they think I'd stab you, boy?"

"They didn't tell me what they thought." Egg wore a close-fitting black wool doublet with a tucked waist and long sleeves lined with red satin. Across his chest was sewn the three-headed dragon of House Targaryen. "My uncle says I must humbly beg your forgiveness for deceiving you."

"Your uncle," said Dunk. "That would be Prince Baelor."

The boy looked miserable. "I never meant to lie."

"But you did. About everything. Starting with your name. I never heard of a Prince Egg."

"It's short for Aegon. My brother Aemon named me Egg. He's off at the Citadel now, learning to be a maester. And Daeron sometimes calls me Egg as well, and so do my sisters."

Dunk lifted the skewer and bit into a chunk of meat. Goat, flavored with some lordly spice he'd never tasted before. Grease ran down his chin. "Aegon," he repeated. "Of course it would be Aegon. Like Aegon the Dragon. How many Aegons have been king?"

"Four," the boy said. "Four Aegons."

Dunk chewed, swallowed, and tore off some more bread. "Why did you do it? Was it some jape, to make a fool of the stupid hedge knight?"

"No." The boy's eyes filled with tears, but he stood there manfully. "I was supposed to squire for Daeron. He's my oldest brother. I learned everything I had to learn to be a good squire, but Daeron isn't a very good knight. He didn't want to ride in the tourney, so after we left Summerhall he stole away from our escort, only instead of doubling back he went straight on toward Ashford, thinking they'd never look for us that way. It was him shaved my head. He knew my father would send men hunting us. Daeron has common hair, sort of a pale brown, nothing special, but mine is like Aerion's and my father's."

"The blood of the dragon," Dunk said. "Silver-gold hair and purple eyes, everyone knows that." *Thick as a castle wall, Dunk.*

"Yes. So Daeron shaved it off. He meant for us to hide until the tourney was over. Only then you took me for a stableboy, and..." He lowered his eyes. "I didn't care if Daeron fought or not, but I wanted to be somebody's squire. I'm sorry, ser. I truly am."

Dunk looked at him thoughtfully. He knew what it was like to want something so badly that you would tell a monstrous lie just to get near it. "I thought you were like me," he said. "Might be you are. Only not the way I thought."

"We're both from King's Landing still," the boy said hopefully.

Dunk had to laugh. "Yes, you from the top of Aegon's Hill and me from the bottom."

"That's not so far, ser."

Dunk took a bite from an onion. "Do I need to call you *m'lord* or *Your Grace* or something?"

"At court," the boy admitted, "but other times you can keep on calling me Egg if you like. Ser."

"What will they do with me, Egg?"

"My uncle wants to see you. After you're done eating, ser."

Dunk shoved the platter aside, and stood. "I'm done now, then. I've already kicked one prince in the mouth, I don't mean to keep another waiting."

LORD ASHFORD HAD TURNED HIS OWN CHAMBERS OVER TO PRINCE Baelor for the duration of his stay, so it was to the lord's solar that Egg— no, *Aegon,* he would have to get used to that—conducted him. Baelor sat reading by the light of a beeswax candle. Dunk knelt before him. "Rise," the prince said. "Would you care for wine?"

"As it please you, Your Grace."

"Pour Ser Duncan a cup of the sweet Dornish red, Aegon," the prince commanded. "Try not to spill it on him, you've done him sufficient ill already."

"The boy won't spill, Your Grace," said Dunk. "He's a good boy. A good squire. And he meant no harm to me, I know."

"One need not intend harm to do it. Aegon should have come to me when he saw what his brother was doing to those puppeteers. Instead he ran to you. That was no kindness. What you did, ser...well,

I might have done the same in your place, but I am a prince of the realm, not a hedge knight. It is never wise to strike a king's grandson in anger, no matter the cause."

Dunk nodded grimly. Egg offered him a silver goblet, brimming with wine. He accepted it and took a long swallow.

"I *hate* Aerion," Egg said with vehemence. "And I had to run for Ser Duncan, uncle, the castle was too far."

"Aerion is your brother," the prince said firmly, "and the septons say we must love our brothers. Aegon, leave us now, I would speak with Ser Duncan privately."

The boy put down the flagon of wine and bowed stiffly. "As you will, Your Grace." He went to the door of the solar and closed it softly behind him.

Baelor Breakspear studied Dunk's eyes for a long moment. "Ser Duncan, let me ask you this—how good a knight are you, truly? How skilled at arms?"

Dunk did not know what to say. "Ser Arlan taught me sword and shield, and how to tilt at rings and quintains."

Prince Baelor seemed troubled by that answer. "My brother Maekar returned to the castle a few hours ago. He found his heir drunk in an inn a day's ride to the south. Maekar would never admit as much, but I believe it was his secret hope that his sons might outshine mine in this tourney. Instead they have both shamed him, but what is he to do? They are blood of his blood. Maekar is angry, and must needs have a target for his wrath. He has chosen you."

"Me?" Dunk said miserably.

"Aerion has already filled his father's ear. And Daeron has not helped you either. To excuse his own cowardice, he told my brother that a huge robber knight, chance met on the road, made off with Aegon. I fear you have been cast as this robber knight, ser. In Daeron's tale, he has spent all these days pursuing you hither and yon, to win back his brother."

"But Egg will tell him the truth. Aegon, I mean."

"Egg *will* tell him, I have no doubt," said Prince Baelor, "but the boy has been known to lie too, as you have good reason to recall. Which son will my brother believe? As for the matter of these pup-peteers, by the time Aerion is done twisting the tale it will be high treason. The dragon is the sigil of the royal House. To portray one being slain, sawdust blood spilling from its neck...well, it was doubtless innocent, but it was far from wise. Aerion calls it a veiled attack on House Targaryen, an incitement to revolt. Maekar will likely agree. My brother has a prickly nature, and he has placed all his best hopes on Aerion, since Daeron has been such a grave disappointment to him." The prince took a sip of wine, then set the goblet aside. "Whatever my brother believes or fails to believe, one truth is beyond dispute. You laid hands upon the blood of the dragon. For that offense, you must be tried, and judged, and punished."

"Punished?" Dunk did not like the sound of that.

"Aerion would like your head, with or without teeth. He will not have it, I promise you, but I cannot deny him a trial. As my royal father is hundreds of leagues away, my brother and I must sit in judgment of you, along with Lord Ashford, whose domains these are, and Lord Tyrell of Highgarden, his liege lord. The last time a man was found guilty of striking one of royal blood, it was decreed that he should lose the offending hand."

"My *hand*?" said Dunk, aghast.

"And your foot. You kicked him too, did you not?"

Dunk could not speak.

"To be sure, I will urge my fellow judges to be merciful. I am the King's Hand and the heir to the throne, my word carries some weight. But so does my brother's. The risk is there."

"I," said Dunk, "I...Your Grace, I..." *They meant no treason, it was only a wooden dragon, it was never meant to be a royal prince,* he wanted to say, but his words had deserted him once and all. He had never been any good with words.

"You have another choice, though," Prince Baelor said quietly. "Whether it is a better choice or a worse one, I cannot say, but I remind you that any knight accused of a crime has the right to demand trial by combat. So I ask you once again, Ser Duncan the Tall—how good a knight are you? Truly?"

"A TRIAL OF SEVEN," SAID PRINCE AERION, SMILING. "THAT IS MY right, I do believe."

Prince Baelor drummed his fingers on the table, frowning. To his left, Lord Ashford nodded slowly.

"Why?" Prince Maekar demanded, leaning forward toward his son. "Are you afraid to face this hedge knight alone, and let the gods decide the truth of your accusations?"

"Afraid?" said Aerion. "Of such as this? Don't be absurd, Father. My thought is for my beloved brother. Daeron has been wronged by this Ser Duncan as well, and has first claim to his blood. A trial of seven allows both of us to face him."

"Do me no favors, brother," muttered Daeron Targaryen. The eldest son of Prince Maekar looked even worse than he had when Dunk had encountered him in the inn. He seemed to be sober this time, his red-and-black doublet unstained by wine, but his eyes were bloodshot, and a fine sheen of sweat covered his brow. "I am content to cheer you on as you slay the rogue."

"You are too kind, sweet brother," said Prince Aerion, all smiles, "but it would be selfish of me to deny you the right to prove the truth of your words at the hazard of your body. I must insist upon a trial of seven."

Dunk was lost. "Your Graces, my lords," he said to the dais. "I do not understand. What is this *trial of seven*?"

Prince Baelor shifted uncomfortably in his seat. "It is another form of trial by combat. Ancient, seldom invoked. It came across the narrow sea with the Andals and their seven gods. In any trial by combat, the accuser and accused are asking the gods to decide the issue between them. The Andals believed that if the seven champions fought on each side, the gods, being thus honored, would be more like to take a hand and see that a just result was achieved."

"Or mayhap they simply had a taste for swordplay," said Lord Leo Tyrell, a cynical smile touching his lips. "Regardless, Ser Aerion is within his rights. A trial of seven it must be."

"I must fight *seven men*, then?" Dunk asked hopelessly.

"Not alone, ser," Prince Maekar said impatiently. "Don't play the fool, it will not serve. It must be seven against seven. You must needs find six other knights to fight beside you."

Six knights, Dunk thought. They might as well have told him to find six thousand. He had no brothers, no cousins, no old comrades who had stood beside him in battle. Why would six strangers risk their own lives to defend a hedge knight against two royal princelings? "Your Graces, my lords," he said, "what if no one will take my part?"

Maekar Targaryen looked down on him coldly. "If a cause is just, good men will fight for it. If you can find no champions, ser, it will be because you are guilty. Could anything be more plain?"

<hr />

DUNK HAD NEVER FELT SO ALONE AS HE DID WHEN HE WALKED OUT the gates of Ashford Castle and heard the portcullis rattle down behind him. A soft rain was falling, light as dew on his skin, and yet he shivered at the touch of it. Across the river, colored rings haloed the scant few pavilions where fires still burned. The night was half gone, he guessed. Dawn would be on him in a few hours. *And with dawn comes death.*

They had given him back his sword and silver, yet as he waded across the ford, his thoughts were bleak. He wondered if they expected him to saddle a horse and flee. He could, if he wished. That would be the end of his knighthood, to be sure; he would be no more than an outlaw henceforth, until the day some lord took him and struck off his head. *Better to die a knight than live like that,* he told himself stubbornly. Wet to the knee, he trudged past the empty lists. Most of the pavilions were dark, their owners long asleep, but here and there a few candles still burned. Dunk heard soft moans and cries of pleasure coming from within one tent. It made him wonder whether he would die without ever having known a maid.

Then he heard the snort of a horse, a snort he somehow knew for Thunder's. He turned his steps and ran, and there he was, tied up with Chestnut outside a round pavilion lit from within by a vague golden glow. On its center pole the banner hung sodden, but Dunk could still make out the dark curve of the Fossoway apple. It looked like hope.

"A trial by combat," Raymun said heavily. "Gods be good, Duncan, that means lances of war, morningstars, battleaxes...the swords won't be blunted, do you understand that?"

"Raymun the Reluctant," mocked his cousin Ser Steffon. An apple made of gold and garnets fastened his cloak of yellow wool. "You need not fear, cousin, this is a knightly combat. As you are no knight, your skin is not at risk. Ser Duncan, you have one Fossoway at least. The ripe one. I saw what Aerion did to those puppeteers. I am for you."

"And I," snapped Raymun angrily. "I only meant—"

His cousin cut him off. "Who else fights with us, Ser Duncan?"

Dunk spread his hands hopelessly. "I know no one else. Well, except for Ser Manfred Dondarrion. He wouldn't even vouch that I was a knight, he'll never risk his life for me."

Ser Steffon seemed little perturbed. "Then we need five more good men. Fortunately, I have more than five friends. Leo Longthorn, the Laughing Storm, Lord Caron, the Lannisters, Ser Otho Bracken . . . aye, and the Blackwoods as well, though you will never get Blackwood and Bracken on the same side of a melee. I shall go and speak with some of them."

"They won't be happy at being woken," his cousin objected.

"Excellent," declared Ser Steffon. "If they are angry, they'll fight all the more fiercely. You may rely on me, Ser Duncan. Cousin, if I do not return before dawn, bring my armor and see that Wrath is saddled and barded for me. I shall meet you both in the challengers' paddock." He laughed. "This will be a day long remembered, I think." When he strode from the tent, he looked almost happy.

Not so Raymun. "Five knights," he said glumly after his cousin had gone. "Duncan, I am loath to dash your hopes, but . . ."

"If your cousin can bring the men he speaks of . . ."

"Leo Longthorn? The Brute of Bracken? The Laughing Storm?" Raymun stood. "He knows all of them, I have no doubt, but I would be less certain that any of them know him. Steffon sees this as a chance for glory, but it means your life. You should find your own men. I'll help. Better you have too many champions than too few." A noise outside made Raymun turn his head. "Who goes there?" he demanded, as a boy ducked through the flap, followed by a thin man in a rain-sodden black cloak.

"Egg?" Dunk got to his feet. "What are you doing here?"

"I'm your squire," the boy said. "You'll need someone to arm you, ser."

"Does your lord father know you've left the castle?"

"Gods be good, I hope not." Daeron Targaryen undid the clasp of his cloak and let it slide from his thin shoulders.

"*You?* Are you mad, coming here?" Dunk pulled his knife from his sheath. "I ought to shove this through your belly."

"Probably," Prince Daeron admitted. "Though I'd sooner you poured me a cup of wine. Look at my hands." He held one out and let them all see how it shook.

Dunk stepped toward him, glowering. "I don't care about your hands. You lied about me."

"I had to say *something* when my father demanded to know where my little brother had gotten to," the prince replied. He seated himself, ignoring Dunk and his knife. "If truth be told, I hadn't even realized Egg was gone. He wasn't at the bottom of my wine cup, and I hadn't looked anywhere else, so . . ." He sighed.

"Ser, my father is going to join the seven accusers," Egg broke in. "I begged him not to, but he won't listen. He says it is the only way to redeem Aerion's honor, and Daeron's."

"Not that I ever asked to have my honor redeemed," said Prince Daeron sourly. "Whoever has it can keep it, so far as I'm concerned. Still, here we are. For what it's worth, Ser Duncan, you have little to fear from me. The only thing I like less than horses are swords. Heavy things, and beastly sharp. I'll do my best to look gallant in the first charge, but after that . . . well, perhaps you could strike me a nice blow to the side of the helm. Make it ring, but not *too* loud, if you take my meaning. My brothers have my measure when it comes to fighting and dancing and thinking and reading books, but none of them is half my equal at lying insensible in the mud."

Dunk could only stare at him, and wonder whether the princeling was trying to play him for a fool. "Why did you come?"

"To warn you of what you face," Daeron said. "My father has commanded the Kingsguard to fight with him."

"The Kingsguard?" said Dunk, appalled.

"Well, the three who are here. Thank the gods Uncle Baelor left the other four at King's Landing with our royal grandfather."

Egg supplied the names. "Ser Roland Crakehall, Ser Donnel of Duskendale, and Ser Willem Wylde."

"They have small choice in the matter," said Daeron. "They are sworn to protect the lives of the king and royal family, and my brothers and I are blood of the dragon, gods help us."

Dunk counted on his fingers. "That makes six. Who is the seventh man?"

Prince Daeron shrugged. "Aerion will find someone. If need be, he will buy a champion. He has no lack of gold."

"Who do you have?" Egg asked.

"Raymun's cousin Ser Steffon."

Daeron winced. "Only one?"

"Ser Steffon has gone to some of his friends."

"I can bring people," said Egg. "Knights. I can."

"Egg," said Dunk, "I will be fighting your own brothers."

"You won't hurt Daeron, though," the boy said. "He told you he'd fall down. And Aerion...I remember, when I was little, he used to come into my bedchamber at night and put his knife between my legs. He had too many brothers, he'd say, maybe one night he'd make me his sister, then he could marry me. He threw my cat in the well too. He says he didn't, but he always lies."

Prince Daeron gave a weary shrug. "Egg has the truth of it. Aerion's quite the monster. He thinks he's a dragon in human form, you know. That's why he was so wroth at that puppet show. A pity he wasn't born a Fossoway, then he'd think himself an apple and we'd all be a deal safer, but there you are." Bending, he scooped up his fallen cloak and shook the rain from it. "I must steal back to the castle before my father wonders why I'm taking so long to sharpen my sword, but before I go, I would like a private word, Ser Duncan. Will you walk with me?"

Dunk looked at the princeling suspiciously a moment. "As you wish, Your Grace." He sheathed his dagger. "I need to get my shield too."

"Egg and I will look for knights," promised Raymun.

Prince Daeron knotted his cloak around his neck and pulled up the hood. Dunk followed him back out into the soft rain. They walked toward the merchants' wagons.

"I dreamed of you," said the prince.

"You said that at the inn."

"Did I? Well, it's so. My dreams are not like yours, Ser Duncan. Mine are true. They frighten me. *You* frighten me. I dreamed of you and a dead dragon, you see. A great beast, huge, with wings so large they could cover this meadow. It had fallen on top of you, but you were alive and the dragon was dead."

"Did I kill it?"

"That I could not say, but you were there, and so was the dragon. We were the masters of dragons once, we Targaryens. Now they are all gone, but we remain. I don't care to die today. The gods alone know why, but I don't. So do me a kindness if you would, and make certain it is my brother Aerion you slay."

"I don't care to die either," said Dunk.

"Well, I shan't kill you, ser. I'll withdraw my accusation as well, but it won't serve unless Aerion withdraws his." He sighed. "It may be that I've killed you with my lie. If so, I am sorry. I'm doomed to some hell, I know. Likely one without wine." He shuddered, and on that they parted, there in the cool soft rain.

The merchants had drawn up their wagons on the western verge of the meadow, beneath a stand of birch and ash. Dunk stood under the trees and looked helplessly at the empty place where the puppeteers' wagon had been. Gone. He had feared they might be. *I would flee as well, if I were not thick as a castle wall.* He wondered what he would do for a shield now. He had the silver to buy one, he supposed, if he could find one for sale...

"Ser Duncan," a voice called out of the dark. Dunk turned to find Steely Pate standing behind him, holding an iron lantern. Under a short leather cloak, the armorer was bare from the waist up, his broad chest and thick arms covered with coarse black hair. "If you are come for your shield, she left it with me." He looked Dunk up and down. "Two hands and two feet, I count. So it's to be trial by combat, is it?"

"A trial of seven. How did you know?"

"Well, they might have kissed you and made you a lord, but it didn't seem likely, and if it went t'other way, you'd be short some parts. Now follow me."

His wagon was easy to distinguish by the sword and anvil painted on its side. Dunk followed Pate inside. The armorer hung the lantern on a hook, shrugged out of his wet cloak, and pulled a roughspun tunic down over his head. A hinged board dropped down from one wall to make a table. "Sit," he said, shoving a low stool toward him.

Dunk sat. "Where did she go?"

"They make for Dorne. The girl's uncle, there's a wise man. Well gone is well forgot. Stay and be seen, and belike the dragon remembers. Besides, he did not think she ought see you die." Pate went to the far end of the wagon, rummaged about in the shadows a moment, and returned with the shield. "Your rim was old cheap steel, brittle and rusted," he said. "I've made you a new one, twice as thick, and put some bands across the back. It will be heavier now, but stronger too. The girl did the paint."

She had made a better job of it than he could ever have hoped for. Even by lantern light, the sunset colors were rich and bright, the tree tall and strong and noble. The falling star was a bright slash of paint across the oaken sky. Yet now that Dunk held it in his hands, it seemed all wrong. The star was *falling*, what sort of sigil was that? Would he fall just as fast? And sunset heralds night. "I should have stayed with the chalice," he said miserably. "It had wings, at least, to fly away, and Ser Arlan said the cup was full of faith and fellowship and good things to drink. This shield is all painted up like death."

"The elm's alive," Pate pointed out. "See how green the leaves are? Summer leaves, for certain. And I've seen shields blazoned with skulls and wolves and ravens, even hanged men and bloody heads. They served well enough, and so will this. You know the old shield rhyme? *Oak and iron, guard me well . . .*"

"*. . . or else I'm dead, and doomed to hell,*" Dunk finished. He had not thought of that rhyme in years. The old man had taught it to him, a long time ago. "How much do you want for the new rim and all?" he asked Pate.

"From you?" Pate scratched his beard. "A copper."

—————————

THE RAIN HAD ALL BUT STOPPED AS THE FIRST WAN LIGHT SUFFUSED the eastern sky, but it had done its work. Lord Ashford's men had removed the barriers, and the tourney field was one great morass of gray-brown mud and torn grass. Tendrils of fog were writhing along the ground like pale white snakes as Dunk made his way back toward the lists. Steely Pate walked with him.

The viewing stand had already begun to fill, the lords and ladies clutching their cloaks tight about them against the morning chill. Smallfolk were drifting toward the field as well, and hundreds of them already stood along the fence. *So many come to see me die,* thought Dunk bitterly, but he wronged them. A few steps farther on, a woman called out, "Good fortune to you." An old man stepped up to take his hand and said, "May the gods give you strength, ser." Then a begging brother in a tattered brown robe said a blessing on his sword, and a maid kissed his cheek. *They are for me.* "Why?" he asked Pate. "What am I to them?"

"A knight who remembered his vows," the smith said.

They found Raymun outside the challengers' paddock at the south end of the lists, waiting with his cousin's horse and Dunk's. Thunder tossed restlessly beneath the weight of chinet, chamfron, and blanket of heavy mail. Pate inspected the armor and pronounced it good work, even though someone else had forged it. Wherever the armor had come from, Dunk was grateful.

Then he saw the others: the one-eyed man with the salt-and-pepper beard, the young knight in the striped yellow-and-black sur-coat with the beehives on the shield. *Robyn Rhysling and Humfrey Beesbury,* he thought in astonishment. *And Ser Humfrey Hardyng as well.* Hardyng was mounted on Aerion's red charger, now barded in his red-and-white diamonds.

He went to them. "Sers, I am in your debt."

"The debt is Aerion's," Ser Humfrey Hardyng replied, "and we mean to collect it."

"I had heard your leg was broken."

"You heard the truth," Hardyng said. "I cannot walk. But so long as I can sit a horse, I can fight."

Raymun took Dunk aside. "I hoped Hardyng would want another chance at Aerion, and he did. As it happens, the other Humfrey is his brother by marriage. Egg is responsible for Ser Robyn, whom he knew from other tourneys. So you are five."

"Six," said Dunk in wonder, pointing. A knight was entering the paddock, his squire leading his charger behind him. "The Laughing

Storm." A head taller than Ser Raymun and almost of a height with Dunk, Ser Lyonel wore a cloth-of-gold surcoat bearing the crowned stag of House Baratheon, and carried his antlered helm under his arm. Dunk reached for his hand. "Ser Lyonel, I cannot thank you enough for coming, nor Ser Steffon for bringing you."

"Ser Steffon?" Ser Lyonel gave him a puzzled look. "It was your squire who came to me. The boy, Aegon. My own lad tried to chase him off, but he slipped between his legs and turned a flagon of wine over my head." He laughed. "There has not been a trial of seven for more than a hundred years, do you know that? I was not about to miss a chance to fight the Kingsguard knights, and tweak Prince Maekar's nose in the bargain."

"Six," Dunk said hopefully to Raymun Fossoway as Ser Lyonel joined the others. "Your cousin will bring the last, surely."

A roar went up from the crowd. At the north end of the meadow, a column of knights came trotting out of the river mist. The three Kingsguard came first, like ghosts in their gleaming white enamel armor, long white cloaks trailing behind them. Even their shields were white, blank and clean as a field of new-fallen snow. Behind rode Prince Maekar and his sons. Aerion was mounted on a dapple gray, orange and red flickering through the slashes in the horse's caparison at each stride. His brother's destrier was a smaller bay, armored in overlapping black and gold scales. A green silk plume trailed from Daeron's helm. It was their father who made the most fearsome appearance, however. Black curved dragon teeth ran across his shoulders, along the crest of his helm, and down his back, and the huge spiked mace strapped to his saddle was as deadly-looking a weapon as any Dunk had ever seen.

"Six," Raymun exclaimed suddenly. "They are only six."

It was true, Dunk saw. *Three black knights and three white. They are a man short as well.* Was it possible that Aerion had not been able to find a seventh man? What would that mean? Would they fight six against six if neither found a seventh?

Egg slipped up beside him as he was trying to puzzle it out. "Ser, it's time you donned your armor."

"Thank you, squire. If you would be so good?"

Steely Pate lent the lad a hand. Hauberk and gorget, greaves and gauntlet, coif and codpiece, they turned him into steel, checking each buckle and each clasp thrice. Ser Lyonel sat sharpening his sword on a whetstone while the Humfreys talked quietly, Ser Robyn prayed, and Raymun Fossoway paced back and forth, wondering where his cousin had got to.

Dunk was fully armored by the time Ser Steffon finally appeared. "Raymun," he called, "my mail, if you please." He had changed into a padded doublet to wear beneath his steel.

"Ser Steffon," said Dunk, "what of your friends? We need another knight to make our seven."

"You need two, I fear," Ser Steffon said. Raymun laced up the back of the hauberk.

"M'lord?" Dunk did not understand. "Two?"

Ser Steffon picked up a gauntlet of fine lobstered steel and slid his left hand into it, flexing his fingers. "I see five here," he said while Raymun fastened his sword belt. "Beesbury, Rhysling, Hardyng, Baratheon, and yourself."

"And you," said Dunk. "You're the sixth."

"I am the seventh," said Ser Steffon, smiling, "but for the other side. I fight with Prince Aerion and the accusers."

Raymun had been about to hand his cousin his helm. He stopped as if struck. "No."

"Yes." Ser Steffon shrugged. "Ser Duncan understands, I am sure. I have a duty to my prince."

"You told him to rely on you." Raymun had gone pale.

"Did I?" He took the helm from his cousin's hands. "No doubt I was sincere at the time. Bring me my horse."

"Get him yourself," said Raymun angrily. "If you think I wish any part of this, you're as thick as you are vile."

"Vile?" Ser Steffon tsked. "Guard your tongue, Raymun. We're both apples from the same tree. And you are my squire. Or have you forgotten your vows?"

"No. Have you forgotten yours? You swore to be a knight."

"I shall be more than a knight before this day is done. *Lord* Fossoway. I like the sound of that." Smiling, he pulled on his other gauntlet, turned away, and crossed the paddock to his horse. Though the other defenders stared at him with contemptuous eyes, no one made a move to stop him.

Dunk watched Ser Steffon lead his destrier back across the field. His hands coiled into fists, but his throat felt too raw for speech. *No words would move the likes of him anyway.*

"Knight me." Raymun put a hand on Dunk's shoulder and turned him. "I will take my cousin's place. Ser Duncan, knight me." He went to one knee.

Frowning, Dunk moved a hand to the hilt of his longsword, then hesitated. "Raymun, I . . . I should not."

"You must. Without me, you are only five."

"The lad has the truth of it," said Ser Lyonel Baratheon. "Do it, Ser Duncan. Any knight can make a knight."

"Do you doubt my courage?" Raymun asked.

"No," said Dunk. "Not that, but . . ." Still he hesitated.

A fanfare of trumpets cut the misty morning air. Egg came running up to them. "Ser, Lord Ashford summons you."

The Laughing Storm gave an impatient shake of the head. "Go to him, Ser Duncan. I'll give squire Raymun his knighthood." He slid his sword out of his sheath and shouldered Dunk aside. "Raymun of House Fossoway," he began solemnly, touching the blade to the squire's right shoulder, "in the name of the Warrior I charge you to be brave." The sword moved from his right shoulder to his left. "In the name of the Father I charge you to be just." Back to the right. "In the name of the Mother I charge you to defend the young and innocent." The left. "In the name of the Maid I charge you to protect all women . . ."

Dunk left them there, feeling as relieved as he was guilty. *We are still one short,* he thought as Egg held Thunder for him. *Where will I find another man?* He turned the horse and rode slowly toward the viewing stand, where Lord Ashford stood waiting. From the north end of the lists, Prince Aerion advanced to meet him. "Ser Duncan," he said cheerfully, "it would seem you have only five champions."

"Six," said Dunk. "Ser Lyonel is knighting Raymun Fossoway. We will fight you six against seven." Men had won at far worse odds, he knew.

But Lord Ashford shook his head. "That is not permitted, ser. If you cannot find another knight to take your side, you must be declared guilty of the crimes of which you stand accused."

Guilty, thought Dunk. *Guilty of loosening a tooth, and for that I must die.* "M'lord, I beg a moment."

"You have it."

Dunk rode slowly along the fence. The viewing stand was crowded with knights. *"M'lords,"* he called to them, *"do none of you remember Ser Arlan of Pennytree? I was his squire. We served many of you. Ate at your tables and slept in your halls."* He saw Manfred Dondarrion seated in the highest tier. *"Ser Arlan took a wound in your lord father's service."* The knight said something to the lady beside him, paying no heed. Dunk was forced to move on. *"Lord Lannister, Ser Arlan unhorsed you once in tourney."* The Grey Lion examined his gloved hands, studiedly refusing to raise his eyes. *"He was a good man, and he taught me how to be a knight. Not only sword and lance, but honor. A knight defends the innocent, he said. That's all I did. I need one more knight to fight beside me. One, that's all. Lord Caron? Lord Swann?"* Lord Swann laughed softly as Lord Caron whispered in his ear.

Dunk reined up before Ser Otho Bracken, lowering his voice. "Ser Otho, all know you for a great champion. Join us, I beg you. In the names of the old gods and the new. My cause is just."

"That may be," said the Brute of Bracken, who had at least the grace to reply, "but it is your cause, not mine. I know you not, boy."

Heartsick, Dunk wheeled Thunder and raced back and forth before the tiers of pale cold men. Despair made him shout. *"ARE THERE NO TRUE KNIGHTS AMONG YOU?"*

Only silence answered.

Across the field, Prince Aerion laughed. "The dragon is not mocked," he called out.

Then came a voice. "I will take Ser Duncan's side."

A black stallion emerged from out of the river mists, a black knight on his back. Dunk saw the dragon shield, and the red enamel crest upon his helm with its three roaring heads. *The Young Prince. Gods be good, it is truly him?*

Lord Ashford made the same mistake. "Prince Valarr?"

"No." The black knight lifted the visor of his helm. "I did not think to enter the lists at Ashford, my lord, so I brought no armor. My son was good enough to lend me his." Prince Baelor smiled almost sadly.

The accusers were thrown into confusion, Dunk could see. Prince Maekar spurred his mount forward. "Brother, have you taken leave of your senses?" He pointed a mailed finger at Dunk. "This man attacked my son."

"This man protected the weak, as every true knight must," replied Prince Baelor. "Let the gods determine if he was right or wrong." He gave a tug on his reins, turned Valarr's huge black destrier, and trotted to the south end of the field.

Dunk brought Thunder up beside him, and the other defenders gathered round them; Robyn Rhysling and Ser Lyonel, the Humfreys. *Good men all, but are they good enough?* "Where is Raymun?"

"*Ser* Raymun, if you please." He cantered up, a grim smile lighting his face beneath his plumed helm. "My pardons, ser. I needed to make a small change to my sigil, lest I be mistaken for my dishonorable cousin." He showed them all his shield. The polished golden field remained the same, and the Fossoway apple, but this apple was green instead of red. "I fear I am still not ripe...but better green than wormy, eh?"

Ser Lyonel laughed, and Dunk grinned despite himself. Even Prince Baelor seemed to approve.

Lord Ashford's septon had come to the front of the viewing stand and raised his crystal to call the throng to prayer.

"Attend me, all of you," Baelor said quietly. "The accusers will be armed with heavy war lances for the first charge. Lances of ash, eight feet long, banded against splitting and tipped with a steel point sharp enough to drive through plate with the weight of a warhorse behind it."

"We shall use the same," said Ser Humfrey Beesbury. Behind him, the septon was calling on the Seven to look down and judge this dispute, and grant victory to the men whose cause was just.

"No," Baelor said. "We will arm ourselves with tourney lances instead."

"Tourney lances are made to break," objected Raymun.

"They are also made twelve feet long. If our points strike home, theirs cannot touch us. Aim for helm or chest. In a tourney it is a gallant thing to break your lance against a foe's shield, but here it may well mean death. If we can unhorse them and keep our own saddles, the advantage is ours." He glanced to Dunk. "If Ser Duncan is killed, it is considered that the gods have judged him guilty, and the contest is over. If both of his accusers are slain, or withdraw their accusations, the same is true. Elsewise, all seven of one side or the other must perish or yield for the trial to end."

"Prince Daeron will not fight," Dunk said.

"Not well, anyway," laughed Ser Lyonel. "Against that, we have three of the White Swords to contend with."

Baelor took that calmly. "My brother erred when he demanded that the Kingsguard fight for his son. Their oath forbids them to harm a prince of the blood. Fortunately, I am such." He gave them a faint smile. "Keep the others off me long enough, and I shall deal with the Kingsguard."

"My prince, is that chivalrous?" asked Ser Lyonel Baratheon as the septon was finishing his invocation.

"The gods will let us know," said Baelor Breakspear.

A deep expectant silence had fallen across Ashford Meadow.

Eighty yards away, Aerion's gray stallion trumpeted with impatience and pawed the muddy ground. Thunder was very still by comparison; he was an older horse, veteran of half a hundred fights, and he knew what was expected of him. Egg handed Dunk up his shield. "May the gods be with you, ser," the boy said.

The sight of his elm tree and shooting star gave him heart. Dunk slid his left arm through the strap and tightened his fingers around the grip. *Oak and iron, guard me well, or else I'm dead and doomed to hell.* Steely Pate brought his lance to him, but Egg insisted that it must be he who put it into Dunk's hand.

To either side, his companions took up their own lances and spread out in a long line. Prince Baelor was to his right and Ser Lyonel to his left, but the narrow eye slit of the greathelm limited Dunk's vision to what was directly ahead of him. The viewing stand was gone, and likewise the smallfolk crowding the fence; there was only the muddy field, the pale blowing mist, the river, town, and castle to the north, and the princeling on his gray charger with flames on his helm and a dragon on his shield. Dunk watched Aerion's squire hand him a war lance, eight feet long and black as night. *He will put that through my heart if he can.*

A horn sounded.

For a heartbeat Dunk sat as still as a fly in amber, though all the horses were moving. A stab of panic went through him. *I have forgotten,* he thought wildly, *I have forgotten all, I will shame myself, I will lose everything.*

Thunder saved him. The big brown stallion knew what to do, even if his rider did not. He broke into a slow trot. Dunk's training took over then. He gave the warhorse a light touch of spur and couched his lance. At the same time he swung his shield until it covered most of the left side of his body. He held it at an angle, to deflect blows away from him. *Oak and iron guard me well, or else I'm dead and doomed to hell.*

The noise of the crowd was no more than the crash of distant waves. Thunder slid into a gallop. Dunk's teeth jarred together with the violence of the pace. He pressed his heels down, tightening his legs with all his strength and letting his body become part of the motion of the horse beneath. *I am Thunder and Thunder is me, we are one beast, we are joined, we are one.* The air inside his helm was already so hot he could scarce breathe.

In a tourney joust, his foe would be to his left across the tilting barrier, and he would need to swing his lance across Thunder's neck. The angle made it more likely that the wood would split on impact. But this was a deadlier game they played today. With no barriers dividing them, the destriers charged straight at one another. Prince Baelor's huge black was much faster than Thunder, and Dunk glimpsed him pounding ahead through the corner of his eye slit. He sensed more than saw the others. *They do not matter, only Aerion matters, only him.*

He watched the dragon come. Spatters of mud sprayed back from the hooves of Prince Aerion's gray, and Dunk could see the horse's nostrils flaring. The black lance still angled upward. A knight who holds his lance high and brings it on line at the last moment always risks lowering it too far, the old man had told him. He brought his own point to bear on the center of the princeling's chest. *My lance is part of my arm,* he told himself. *It's my finger, a wooden finger. All I need do is touch him with my long wooden finger.*

He tried not to see the sharp iron point at the end of Aerion's black lance, growing larger with every stride. *The dragon, look at the dragon,* he thought. The great three-headed beast covered the prince's shield, red wings and gold fire. *No, look only where you mean to strike,* he remembered suddenly, but his lance had already begun to slide offline. Dunk tried to correct, but it was too late. He saw his point strike Aerion's shield, taking the dragon between two of its heads, gouging into a gout of painted flame. At the muffled *crack,* he felt Thunder recoil under him, trembling with the force of the impact, and half a heartbeat later something smashed into his side with awful force. The horses slammed together violently, armor crashing and clanging as Thunder stumbled and Dunk's lance fell from his hand. Then he was past his foe, clutching at his saddle in a desperate effort to keep his seat. Thunder lurched sideways in the sloppy mud and Dunk felt his rear legs slip out from under. They were sliding, spinning, and then the stallion's hindquarters slapped down hard. *"Up!"* Dunk roared, lashing out with his spurs. *"Up, Thunder!"* And somehow the old warhorse found his feet again.

He could feel a sharp pain under his rib, and his left arm was being pulled down. Aerion had driven his lance through oak, wool, and steel; three feet of splintered ash and sharp iron stuck from his side. Dunk reached over with his right hand, grasped the lance just below the head, clenched his teeth, and pulled it out of him with one savage yank. Blood followed, seeping through the rings of his mail to redden his surcoat. The world swam and he almost fell. Dimly, through the pain, he could hear voices calling his name. His beautiful shield was useless now. He tossed it aside, elm tree, shooting star, broken lance, and all, and drew his sword, but he hurt so much he did not think he could swing it.

Turning Thunder in a tight circle, he tried to get a sense of what was happening elsewhere on the field. Ser Humfrey Hardyng clung to the neck of his mount, obviously wounded. The other Ser Humfrey lay motionless in a lake of bloodstained mud, a broken lance protruding from his groin. He saw Prince Baelor gallop past, lance still intact, and drive one of the Kingsguard from his saddle. Another of the white knights was already down, and Maekar had been unhorsed as well. The third of the Kingsguard was fending off Ser Robyn Rhysling.

Aerion, where is Aerion? The sound of drumming hooves behind him made Dunk turn his head sharply. Thunder bugled and reared, hooves lashing out futilely as Aerion's gray stallion barreled into him at full gallop.

This time there was no hope of recovery. His longsword went spinning from his grasp, and the ground rose up to meet him. He landed with a bruising impact that jarred him to the bone. Pain stabbed through him, so sharp he sobbed. For a moment it was all he could do to lie there. The taste of blood filled his mouth. *Dunk the lunk, thought he could be a knight.* He knew he had to find his feet again, or die. Groaning, he forced himself to hands and knees. He could not breathe, nor could he see. The eye slit of his helm was packed with mud. Lurching blindly to his feet, Dunk scraped at the mud with a mailed finger. *There, that's . . .*

Through his fingers, he glimpsed a dragon flying, and a spiked morningstar whirling on the end of a chain. Then his head seemed to burst to pieces.

When his eyes opened he was on the ground again, sprawled on his back. The mud had all been knocked from his helm, but now one eye was closed by blood. Above was nothing but dark gray sky. His face throbbed, and he could feel cold wet metal pressing in against cheek and temple. *He broke my head, and I'm dying.* What was worse was the others who would die with him, Raymun and Prince Baelor and the rest. *I've failed them. I am no champion. I'm not even a hedge knight. I am nothing.* He remembered Prince Daeron boasting that no one could lie insensible in the mud as well as he did. *He never saw Dunk the lunk, though, did he?* The shame was worse than the pain.

The dragon appeared above him.

Three heads it had, and wings bright as flame, red and yellow and orange. It was laughing. "Are you dead yet, hedge knight?" it asked. "Cry for quarter and admit your guilt, and perhaps I'll only claim a hand and a foot. Oh, and those teeth, but what are a few teeth? A man like you can live years on pease porridge." The dragon laughed again. "No? Eat *this,* then." The spiked ball whirled round and round the sky, and fell toward his head as fast as a shooting star.

Dunk rolled.

Where he found the strength he did not know, but he found it. He rolled into Aerion's legs, threw a steel-clad arm around his thigh, dragged him cursing into the mud, and rolled on top of him. *Let him swing his bloody morningstar now.* The prince tried forcing the lip of his shield up at Dunk's head, but his battered helm took the brunt of the impact. Aerion was strong, but Dunk was stronger, and larger and heavier as well. He grabbed hold of the shield with both hands and twisted until the straps broke. Then he brought it down on the top of the princeling's helm, again and again and again, smashing the enameled flames of his crest. The shield was thicker than Dunk's had been, solid oak banded with iron. A flame broke off. Then another. The prince ran out of flames long before Dunk ran out of blows.

Aerion finally let go the handle of his useless morningstar and clawed for the poniard at his hip. He got it free of its sheath, but when Dunk whanged his hand with the shield the knife sailed off into the mud.

He could vanquish Ser Duncan the Tall, but not Dunk of Flea Bottom. The old man had taught him jousting and swordplay, but this sort of fighting he had learned earlier, in shadowy wynds and crooked alleys behind the city's winesinks. Dunk flung the battered shield away and wrenched up the visor of Aerion's helm.

A visor is a weak point, he remembered Steely Pate saying. The prince had all but ceased to struggle. His eyes were purple and full of terror. Dunk had a sudden urge to grab one and pop it like a grape between two steel fingers, but that would not be knightly. *"YIELD!"* he shouted.

"I yield," the dragon whispered, pale lips barely moving. Dunk blinked down at him. For a moment he could not credit what his ears had heard. *Is it done, then?* He turned his head slowly from side to side, trying to see. His vision slit was partly closed by the blow that had smashed in the left side of his face. He glimpsed Prince Maekar, mace in hand, trying to fight his way to his son's side. Baelor Breakspear was holding him off.

Dunk lurched to his feet and pulled Prince Aerion up after him. Fumbling at the lacings of his helm, he tore it off and flung it away. At once he was drowned in sights and sounds; grunts and curses, the shouts of the crowd, one stallion screaming while another raced riderless across the field. Everywhere steel rang on steel. Raymun and his cousin were slashing at each other in front of the viewing stand, both afoot. Their shields were splintered ruins, the green apple and the red both hacked to tinder. One of the Kingsguard knights was carrying a wounded brother from the field. They both looked alike in their white armor and white cloaks. The third of the white knights was down, and the Laughing Storm had joined Prince Baelor against Prince Maekar. Mace, battleaxe, and longsword clashed and clanged, ringing against helm and shield. Maekar was taking three blows for every one he landed, and Dunk could see that it would be over soon. *I must make an end to it before more of us are killed.*

Prince Aerion made a sudden dive for his morningstar. Dunk kicked him in the back and knocked him facedown, then grabbed hold of one of his legs and dragged him across the field. By the time he reached the viewing stand where Lord Ashford sat, the Bright Prince was brown as a privy. Dunk hauled him onto his feet and rattled him, shaking some of the mud onto Lord Ashford and the fair maid. "Tell him!"

Aerion Brightflame spit out a mouthful of grass and dirt. "I withdraw my accusation."

AFTERWARD DUNK COULD NOT HAVE SAID WHETHER HE WALKED from the field under his own power or had required help. He hurt everywhere, and some places worse than others. *I am a knight now in truth?* he remembered wondering. *Am I a champion?*

Egg helped him remove his greaves and gorget, and Raymun as well, and even Steely Pate. He was too dazed to tell them apart. They were fingers and thumbs and voices. Pate was the one complaining, Dunk knew. "Look what he's done to me armor," he said. "All dinted and banged and scratched. Aye, I ask you, why do I bother? I'll have to cut that mail off him, I fear."

"Raymun," Dunk said urgently, clutching at his friend's hands. "The others. How did they fare?" He had to know. "Has anyone died?"

"Beesbury," Raymun said. "Slain by Donnel of Duskendale in the first charge. Ser Humfrey is gravely wounded as well. The rest of us are bruised and bloody, no more. Save for you."

"And them? The accusers?"

"Ser Willem Wylde of the Kingsguard was carried from the field insensate, and I think I cracked a few of my cousin's ribs. At least I hope so."

"And Prince Daeron?" Dunk blurted. "Did he survive?"

"Once Ser Robyn unhorsed him, he lay where he fell. He may have a broken foot. His own horse trod on him while running loose about the field."

Dazed and confused as he was, Dunk felt a huge sense of relief. "His dream was wrong, then. The dead dragon. Unless Aerion died. He didn't though, did he?"

"No," said Egg. "You spared him. Don't you remember?"

"I suppose." Already his memories of the fight were becoming confused and vague. "One moment I feel drunk. The next it hurts so bad I know I'm dying."

They made him lie down on his back and talked over him as he gazed up into the roiling gray sky. It seemed to Dunk that it was still morning. He wondered how long the fight had taken.

"Gods be good, the lance point drove the rings deep into his flesh," he heard Raymun saying. "It will mortify unless . . ."

"Get him drunk and pour some boiling oil into it," someone suggested. "That's how the maesters do it."

"Wine." The voice had a hollow metallic ring to it. "*Not* oil, that will kill him, boiling wine. I'll send Maester Yormwell to have a look at him when he's done tending my brother."

A tall knight stood above him, in black armor dinted and scarred by many blows. *Prince Baelor.* The scarlet dragon on his helm had lost a head, both wings, and most of its tail. "Your Grace," Dunk said, "I am your man. Please. Your man."

"My man." The black knight put a hand on Raymun's shoulder to steady himself. "I need good men, Ser Duncan. The realm . . ." His voice sounded oddly slurred. Perhaps he'd bit his tongue.

Dunk was very tired. It was hard to stay awake. "Your man," he murmured once more.

The prince moved his head slowly from side to side. "Ser Raymun . . . my helm, if you'd be so kind. Visor . . . visor's cracked, and my fingers . . . fingers feel like wood . . ."

"At once, Your Grace." Raymun took the prince's helm in both hands and grunted. "Goodman Pate, a hand."

Steely Pate dragged over a mounting stool. "It's crushed down at the back, Your Grace, toward the left side. Smashed into the gorget. Good steel, this, to stop such a blow."

"Brother's mace, most like," Baelor said thickly. "He's strong." He winced. "That...feels queer, I..."

"Here it comes." Pate lifted the battered helm away. "Gods be good. *Oh gods oh gods oh gods preserve...*"

Dunk saw something red and wet fall out of the helm. Someone was screaming, high and terrible. Against the bleak gray sky swayed a tall prince in black armor with only half a skull. He could see red blood and pale bone beneath and something else, something blue-gray and pulpy. A queer troubled look passed across Baelor Breakspear's face, like a cloud passing before a sun. He raised his hand and touched the back of his head with two fingers, oh so lightly. And then he fell.

Dunk caught him. "Up," they say he said, just as he had with Thunder in the melee, "up, up." But he never remembered that afterward, and the prince did not rise.

BAELOR OF HOUSE TARGARYEN, PRINCE OF DRAGONSTONE, HAND of the King, Protector of the Realm, and heir apparent to the Iron Throne of the Seven Kingdoms of Westeros, went to the fire in the yard of Ashford Castle on the north bank of River Cockleswent. Other great houses might choose to bury their dead in the dark earth or sink them in the cold green sea, but the Targaryens were the blood of the dragon, and their ends were writ in flame.

He had been the finest knight of his age, and some argued that he should have gone to face the dark clad in mail and plate, a sword in his hand. In the end, though, his royal father's wishes prevailed, and Daeron II had a peaceable nature. When Dunk shuffled past Baelor's bier, the prince wore a black velvet tunic with the three-headed dragon picked out in scarlet thread upon his breast. Around his throat was a heavy gold chain. His sword was sheathed by his side, but he did wear a helm, a thin golden helm with an open visor so men could see his face.

Valarr, the Young Prince, stood vigil at the foot of the bier while his father lay in state. He was a shorter, slimmer, handsomer version of his sire, without the twice-broken nose that had made Baelor seem more human than royal. Valarr's hair was brown, but a bright streak of silver-gold ran through it. The sight of it reminded Dunk of Aerion, but he knew that was not fair. Egg's hair was growing back as bright as his brother's, and Egg was a decent enough lad, for a prince.

When he stopped to offer awkward sympathies, well larded with thanks, Prince Valarr blinked cool blue eyes at him and said, "My father was only nine-and-thirty. He had it in him to be a great king, the greatest since Aegon the Dragon. Why would the gods take him, and leave *you*?" He shook his head. "Begone with you, Ser Duncan. Begone."

Wordless, Dunk limped from the castle, down to the camp by the green pool. He had no answer for Valarr. Nor for the questions he asked himself. The maesters and the boiling wine had done their work, and his wound was healing cleanly, though there would be a deep puckered scar between his left arm and his nipple. He could not see the wound without thinking of Baelor. *He saved me once with his sword, and once with a word, even though he was a dead man as he stood there.* The world made no sense when a great prince died so a hedge knight might live. Dunk sat beneath his elm and stared morosely at his foot.

———

WHEN FOUR GUARDSMEN IN THE ROYAL LIVERY APPEARED IN HIS camp late one day, he was sure they had come to kill him after all. Too weak and weary to reach for a sword, he sat with his back to the elm, waiting.

"Our prince begs the favor of a private word."

"Which prince?" asked Dunk, wary.

"This prince," a brusque voice said before the captain could answer. Maekar Targaryen walked out from behind the elm.

Dunk got slowly to his feet. *What would he have of me now?*

Maekar motioned, and the guards vanished as suddenly as they had appeared. The prince studied him a long moment, then turned and paced away from him to stand beside the pool, gazing down at his reflection in the water. "I have sent Aerion to Lys," he announced abruptly. "A few years in the Free Cities may change him for the better."

Dunk had never been to the Free Cities, so he did not know what to say to that. He was pleased that Aerion was gone from the Seven Kingdoms, and hoped he never came back, but that was not a thing you told a father of his son. He stood silent.

Prince Maekar turned to face him. "Some men will say I meant to kill my brother. The gods know it is a lie, but I will hear the whispers till the day I die. And it was my mace that dealt the fatal blow, I have no doubt. The only other foes he faced in the melee were three Kingsguard, whose vows forbade them to do any more than defend themselves. So it was me. Strange to say, I do not recall the blow that broke his skull. Is that a mercy or a curse? Some of both, I think."

From the way he looked at Dunk, it seemed the prince wanted an answer. "I could not say, Your Grace." Perhaps he should have hated Maekar, but instead he felt a queer sympathy for the man. "You swung the mace, m'lord, but it was for me Prince Baelor died. So I killed him too, as much as you."

"Yes," the prince admitted. "You'll hear them whisper as well. The king is old. When he dies, Valarr will climb the Iron Throne in place of his father. Each time a battle is lost or a crop fails, the fools will say, 'Baelor would not have let it happen, but the hedge knight killed him.' "

Dunk could see the truth in that. "If I had not fought, you would have had my hand off. And my foot. Sometimes I sit under that tree there and look at my feet and ask if I couldn't have spared one. How could my foot be worth a prince's life? And the other two as well, the Humfreys, they were good men too." Ser Humfrey Hardyng had succumbed to his wounds only last night.

"And what answer does your tree give you?"

"None that I can hear. But the old man, Ser Arlan, every day at evenfall he'd say, 'I wonder what the morrow will bring.' He never knew, no more than we do. Well, mighten it be that some morrow will come when I'll have need of that foot? When the realm will need that foot, even more than a prince's life?"

Maekar chewed on that a time, mouth clenched beneath the

silvery-pale beard that made his face seem so square. "It's not bloody likely," he said harshly. "The *realm* has as many hedge knights as hedges, and all of them have feet."

"If Your Grace has a better answer, I'd want to hear it."

Maekar frowned. "It may be that the gods have a taste for cruel japes. Or perhaps there are no gods. Perhaps none of this had any meaning. I'd ask the High Septon, but the last time I went to him he told me that no man can truly understand the workings of the gods. Perhaps he should try sleeping under a tree." He grimaced. "My youngest son seems to have grown fond of you, ser. It is time he was a squire, but he tells me he will serve no knight but you. He is an unruly boy, as you will have noticed. Will you have him?"

"Me?" Dunk's mouth opened and closed and opened again. "Egg... Aegon, I mean... he is a good lad, but, Your Grace, I know you honor me, but... I am only a hedge knight."

"That can be changed," said Maekar. "Aegon is to return to my castle at Summerhall. There is a place there for you, if you wish. A knight of my household. You'll swear your sword to me, and Aegon can squire for you. While you train him, my master-at-arms will finish your own training." The prince gave him a shrewd look. "Your Ser Arlan did all he could for you, I have no doubt, but you still have much to learn."

"I know, m'lord." Dunk looked about him. At the green grass and the reeds, the tall elm, the ripples dancing across the surface of the sun-lit pool. Another dragonfly was moving across the water, or perhaps it was the same one. *What shall it be, Dunk?* he asked himself. *Dragonflies or dragons?* A few days ago he would have answered at once. It was all he had ever dreamed, but now that the prospect was at hand it frightened him. "Just before Prince Baelor died, I swore to be his man."

"Presumptuous of you," said Maekar. "What did he say?"

"That the realm needed good men."

"That's true enough. What of it?"

"I will take your son as squire, Your Grace, but not at Summerhall. Not for a year or two. He's seen sufficient of castles, I would judge. I'll have him only if I can take him on the road with me." He pointed to old Chestnut. "He'll ride my steed, wear my old cloak, and he'll keep my sword sharp and my mail scoured. We'll sleep in inns and stables, and now and again in the halls of some landed knight or lesser lordling, and maybe under trees when we must."

Prince Maekar gave him an incredulous look. "Did the trial addle your wits, man? Aegon is a prince of the realm. The blood of the dragon. Princes are not made for sleeping in ditches and eating hard salt beef." He saw Dunk hesitate. "What is it you're afraid to tell me? Say what you will, ser."

"Daeron never slept in a ditch, I'll wager," Dunk said, very quietly, "and all the beef that Aerion ever ate was thick and rare and bloody, like as not."

Maekar Targaryen, Prince of Summerhall, regarded Dunk of Flea Bottom for a long time, his jaw working silently beneath his silvery beard. Finally he turned and walked away, never speaking a word. Dunk heard him riding off with his men. When they were gone, there was no sound but the faint thrum of the dragonfly's wings as it skimmed across the water.

The boy came the next morning, just as the sun was coming up. He wore old boots, brown breeches, a brown wool tunic, and an old traveler's cloak. "My lord father says I am to serve you."

"Serve you, *ser*," Dunk reminded him. "You can start by saddling the horses. Chestnut is yours, treat her kindly. I don't want to find you on Thunder unless I put you there."

Egg went to get the saddles. "Where are we going, ser?"

Dunk thought for a moment. "I have never been over the Red Mountains. Would you like to have a look at Dorne?"

Egg grinned. "I hear they have good puppet shows," he said.

Portraits of His Children

Richard Cantling found the package leaning up against his front door, one evening in late October when he was setting out for his walk. It annoyed him. He had told his postman repeatedly to ring the bell when delivering anything too big to fit through the mail slot, yet the man persisted in abandoning the packages on the porch, where any passerby could simply walk off with them. Although, to be fair, Cantling's house was rather isolated, sitting on the river bluffs at the end of a cul-de-sac, and the trees effectively screened it off from the street. Still, there was always the possibility of damage from rain or wind or snow.

Cantling's displeasure lasted only an instant. Wrapped in heavy brown paper and carefully sealed with tape, the package had a shape that told all. Obviously a painting. And the hand that had block-printed his address in heavy green marker was unmistakably Michelle's. Another self-portrait then. She must be feeling repentant.

He was more surprised than he cared to admit, even to himself. He had always been a stubborn man. He could hold grudges for years, even decades, and he had the greatest difficulty admitting any wrong. And Michelle, being his only child, seemed to take after him in all of that. He hadn't expected this kind of gesture from her. It was . . . well, sweet.

He set aside his walking stick to lug the package inside, where he could unwrap it out of the damp and the blustery October wind. It was about three feet tall, and unexpectedly heavy. He carried it awkwardly, shutting the door with his foot and struggling down the long foyer toward his den. The brown drapes were tightly closed; the room was dark and heavy with the smell of dust. Cantling had to set down the package to fumble for the light.

He hadn't used his den much since that night, two months ago, when Michelle had gone storming out. Her self-portrait was still sitting up above the wide slate mantel. Below, the fireplace badly wanted cleaning, and on the built-in bookshelves his novels, all bound in handsome dark leather, stood dusty and disarrayed. Cantling looked at the old painting and felt a brief wash of anger return to him, followed by depression. It had been such a nasty thing for her to do. The portrait had been quite good, really. Much more to his taste than the tortured abstractions that Michelle liked to paint for her own pleasure, or the trite paperback covers she did to make her living. She had done it when she was twenty, as a birthday gift for him. He'd always been fond of it. It captured her as no photograph had ever done, not just the lines of her face, the high angular cheekbones and blue eyes and tangled ash-blonde hair, but the personality inside. She looked so young and fresh and confident, and her smile reminded him so much of Helen and the way she had smiled on their wedding day. He'd told Michelle more than once how much he'd liked that smile.

And so, of course, it had been the smile that she'd started on. She used an antique dagger from his collection, chopped out the mouth with four jagged slashes. She'd gouged out the wide blue eyes next, as if intent on blinding the portrait, and when he came bursting in after her, she'd been slicing the canvas into ribbons with long angry crooked cuts. Cantling couldn't forget that moment. So ugly. And to do something like that to her own work, he couldn't imagine it. He had tried to picture himself mutilating one of his books, tried to comprehend what might drive one to such an act, and he had failed utterly. It was unthinkable, beyond even imagination.

The mutilated portrait still hung in its place. He'd been too stubborn to take it down, and yet he could not bear to look at it. So he had taken to avoiding his den. It wasn't hard. The old house was a huge, rambling place, with more rooms than he could possibly need or want, living alone as he did. It had been built a century ago, when Perrot had been a thriving river town, and they said that a succession of steamer captains had lived there. Certainly the steamboat gothic architecture and all the gingerbread called up visions of the glory days of the river, and he had a fine view of the Mississippi from the third-story windows and the widow's walk. After the incident, Cantling had moved his desk and his typewriter to one of the unused bedrooms and settled in there, determined to let the den remain as Michelle had left it until she came back with an apology.

He had not expected that apology quite so soon, however, nor in quite this form. A tearful phone call, yes—but not another portrait. Still, this was nicer somehow, more personal. And it was a gesture, the first step toward a reconciliation. Richard Cantling knew too well that he was incapable of taking that step himself, no matter how lonely he might become. He had left all his New York friends behind when he moved out to this Iowa river town, and had formed no local friendships to replace them. That was nothing new. He had never been an outgoing sort. He had a certain shyness that kept him apart, even from those few friends he did make. Even from his family, really. Helen had often accused him of caring more for his characters than for real people, an accusation that Michelle had picked up on by the time she was in her teens. Helen was gone too. They'd divorced ten years ago, and she'd been dead for five. Michelle, infuriating as she could be, was really all he had left. He had missed her, missed even the arguments.

He thought about Michelle as he tore open the plain brown paper. He would call her, of course. He would call her and tell her how good the new portrait was, how much he liked it. He would tell her that he'd missed her, invite her to come out for Thanksgiving. Yes, that would be the way to handle it. No mention of their argument, he didn't want to start it all up again, and neither he nor Michelle was the kind to back down gracefully. A family trait, that stubborn willful pride, as ingrained as the high cheekbones and squarish jaw. The Cantling heritage.

It was an antique frame, he saw. Wooden, elaborately carved, very heavy, just the sort of thing he liked. It would mesh with his Victorian decor much better than the thin brass frame on the old portrait. Cantling pulled the wrapping paper away, eager to see what his daughter had done. She was nearly thirty now—or was she past thirty already? He never could keep track of her age, or even her birthdays. Anyway, she was a much better painter than she'd been at twenty. The new portrait ought to be striking. He ripped away the last of the wrappings and turned it around.

His first reaction was that it was a fine, fine piece of work, maybe the best thing that Michelle Cantling had ever done.

Then, belatedly, the admiration washed away, and was replaced by anger. It wasn't her. It wasn't Michelle. Which meant it wasn't a replacement for the portrait she had so willfully vandalized. It was...something else.

Someone else.

It was a face he had never before laid eyes on. But it was a face he recognized as readily as if he had looked on it a thousand times. Oh yes.

The man in the portrait was young. Twenty, maybe even younger, though his curly brown hair was already well-streaked with gray. It was unruly hair, disarrayed as if the man had just come from sleep, falling forward into his eyes. Those eyes were a bright green, lazy eyes somehow, shining with some secret amusement. He had high Cantling cheekbones, but the jawline was all wrong for a relative. Beneath a wide, flat nose, he wore a sardonic smile; his whole posture was somehow insolent. The portrait showed him dressed in faded dungarees and a raveled YMCA Good Guy sweatshirt, with a half-eaten raw onion in one hand. The background was a brick wall covered with graffiti.

Cantling had created him.

Edward Donohue. Dunnahoo, that's what they'd called him, his friends and peers. The other characters in Richard Cantling's first novel, *Hangin' Out*. Dunnahoo had been the protagonist. A wise guy, a smart mouth, too damn bright for his own good. Looking down at the portrait, Cantling felt as if he'd known him for half his life. As indeed he had, in a way. Known him and, yes, cherished him, in the peculiar way a writer can cherish one of his characters.

Michelle had captured him true. Cantling stared at the painting and it all came back to him, all the events he had bled over so long ago, all the people he had fashioned and described with such loving care. He remembered Jocko, and the Squid, and Nancy, and Ricci's Pizzeria where so much of the book's action had taken place (he could see it vividly in his mind's eye), and the business with Arthur and the motorcycle, and the climactic pizza fight. And Dunnahoo. Dunnahoo especially. Smarting off, fooling around, hanging out, coming of age. "Fuck 'em if they can't take a joke," he said. A dozen times or so. It was the book's closing line.

For a moment, Richard Cantling felt a vast, strange affection well up inside him, as if he had just been reunited with an old, lost friend.

And then, almost as an afterthought, he remembered all the ugly words that he and Michelle had flung at each other that night, and suddenly it made sense. Cantling's face went hard. "Bitch," he said aloud. He turned away in fury, helpless without a target for his anger. "Bitch," he said again, as he slammed the door of the den behind him.

"BITCH," HE HAD CALLED HER.

She turned around with the knife in her hand. Her eyes were raw and red from crying. She had the smile in her hand. She balled it up and threw it at him. "Here, you bastard, you like the damned smile so much, here it is."

It bounced off his cheek. His face was reddening. "You're just like your mother," he said. "She was always breaking things too."

"You gave her good reason, didn't you?"

Cantling ignored that. "What the hell is wrong with you? What the hell do you think you're going to accomplish with this stupid melodramatic gesture? That's all it is, you know. Bad melodrama. Who the hell do you think you are, some character in a Tennessee Williams play? Come off it, Michelle. If I wrote a scene like this in one of my books, they'd laugh at me."

"This isn't one of your goddamned books!" she screamed. "This is real life. My life. I'm a real person, you son of a bitch, not a character in some damned book." She whirled, raised the knife, slashed and slashed again.

Cantling folded his arms against his chest as he stood watching. "I hope you're enjoying this pointless exercise."

"I'm enjoying the hell out of it," Michelle yelled back.

"Good. I'd hate to think it was for nothing. This is all very revealing, you know. That's your own face you're working on. I didn't think you had that much self-hate in you."

"If I do, we know who put it there, don't we?" She was finished. She turned back to him, and threw down the knife. She had begun to cry again, and her breath was coming hard. "I'm leaving. Bastard. I hope you're ever so fucking happy here, really I do."

"I haven't done anything to deserve this," Cantling said awkwardly.

It was not much of an apology, not much of a bridge back to understanding, but it was the best he could do. Apologies had never come easily to Richard Cantling.

"You deserve a thousand times worse," Michelle had screamed back at him. She was such a pretty girl, and she looked so ugly. All that nonsense about anger making people beautiful was a dreadful cliché, and wrong as well; Cantling was glad he'd never used it. "You're supposed to be my father," Michelle said. "You're supposed to love me. You're supposed to be my father, and you *raped me,* you bastard."

CANTLING WAS A LIGHT SLEEPER. HE WOKE IN THE MIDDLE OF THE night, and sat up in bed shivering, with the feeling that something was wrong.

The bedroom seemed dark and quiet. What was it? A noise? He was very sensitive to noise. Cantling slid out from under the covers and donned his slippers. The fire he'd enjoyed before retiring for the night had burned down to embers, and the room was chilly. He felt for his tartan robe, hanging from the foot of the big antique four-poster, slipped into it, cinched the belt, and moved quietly to the bedroom door. The door creaked a little at times, so he opened it very slowly, very cautiously. He listened.

Someone was downstairs. He could hear them moving around.

Fear coiled in the pit of his stomach. He had no gun up here, nothing like that. He didn't believe in that. Besides, he was supposed to be safe. This wasn't New York. He was supposed to be safe here in quaint old Perrot, Iowa. And now he had a prowler in his house, something he had never faced in all of his years in Manhattan. What the hell was he supposed to do?

The police, he thought. He'd lock the door and call the police. He moved back to the bedside, and reached for the phone.

It rang.

Richard Cantling stared at the telephone. He had two lines; a business number hooked up to his recording machine, and an unlisted personal number that he gave only to very close friends. Both lights were lit. It was his private number ringing. He hesitated, then scooped up the receiver. "Hello."

"The man himself," the voice said. "Don't get weird on me, Dad. You were going to call the cops, right? Stupid. It's only me. Come down and talk."

Cantling's throat felt raw and constricted. He had never heard that voice before, but he knew it, he knew it. "Who is this?" he demanded.

"Silly question," the caller replied. "You know who it is."

He did. But he said, "Who?"

"Not who. Dunnahoo." Cantling had written that line.

"You're not real."

"There were a couple of reviewers who said that too. I seem to remember how it pissed you off, back then."

"You're not *real,*" Cantling insisted.

"I'm cut to the goddamned quick," Dunnahoo said. "If I'm not real, it's your fault. So quit getting on my case about it, OK? Just get your ass in gear and hustle it downstairs so we can hang out together." He hung up.

The lights went out on the telephone. Richard Cantling sat down on the edge of his bed, stunned. What was he supposed to make of this? A dream? It was no dream. What could he do?

He went downstairs.

Dunnahoo had built a fire in the living room fireplace, and was settled into Cantling's big leather recliner, drinking Pabst Blue Ribbon from a bottle. He smiled lazily when Cantling appeared under the entry arch. "The man," he said. "Well, don't you look half-dead. Want a beer?"

"Who the hell are you?" Cantling demanded.

"Hey, we been round that block already. Don't bore me. Grab a beer and park your ass by the fire."

"An actor," Cantling said. "You're some kind of goddamned actor. Michelle put you up to this, right?"

Dunnahoo grinned. "An actor? Well, that's fuckin' unlikely, ain't it? Tell me, would you stick something that weird in one of your novels? No way, José. You'd never do it yourself and if somebody else did it, in one of them workshops or a book you were reviewing, you'd rip his fuckin' liver out."

Richard Cantling moved slowly into the room, staring at the young man sprawled in his recliner. It was no actor. It was Dunnahoo, the kid from his book, the face from the portrait. Cantling settled into a high, overstuffed armchair, still staring. "This makes no sense," he said. "This is like something out of Dickens."

Dunnahoo laughed. "This ain't no fucking *Christmas Carol,* old man, and I sure ain't no ghost of Christmas past."

Cantling frowned; whoever he was, that line was out of character. "That's wrong," he snapped. "Dunnahoo didn't read Dickens. Batman and Robin, yes, but not Dickens."

"I saw the movie, Dad," Dunnahoo said. He raised the beer bottle to his lips and had a swallow.

"Why do you keep calling me Dad?" Cantling said. "That's wrong too. Anachronistic. Dunnahoo was a street kid, not a beatnik."

"You're telling me? Like I don't know or something?" He laughed. "Shit, man, what the hell else should I call you?" He ran his fingers through his hair, pushing it back out of his eyes. "After all, I'm still your fuckin' first-born."

SHE WANTED TO NAME IT EDWARD, IF IT TURNED OUT TO BE A BOY. "Don't be ridiculous, Helen," he told her.

"I thought you liked the name Edward," she said.

He didn't know what she was doing in his office anyway. He was working, or trying to work. He'd told her never to come into his office when he was at the typewriter. When they were first married, Helen was very good about that, but there had been no dealing with her since she'd gotten pregnant. "I do like the name Edward," he told her, trying hard to keep his voice calm. He hated being interrupted. "I like the name Edward a lot. I love the goddamned name Edward. That's why I'm using it for my protagonist. Edward, that's his name. Edward Donohue. So we can't use it for the baby because I've already used it. How many times do I have to explain that?"

"But you never *call* him Edward in the book," Helen protested.

Cantling frowned. "Have you been reading the book again? Damn it, Helen, I *told* you I don't want you messing around with the manuscript until it's done."

She refused to be distracted. "You never call him Edward," she repeated.

"No," he said. "That's right. I never call him Edward. I call him

Dunnahoo, because he's a street kid, and because that's his street name, and he doesn't like to be called Edward. Only it's still his name, you see. Edward is his name. He doesn't like it, but it's his fucking *name,* and at the end he tells someone that his name is Edward, and that's real damned important. So we can't name the kid Edward, because *he's* named Edward, and I'm tired of this discussion. If it's a boy, we can name it Lawrence, after my grandfather."

"But I don't *want* to name him Lawrence," she whined. "It's so old-fashioned, and then people will call him Larry, and I hate the name Larry. Why can't you call the character in your book Lawrence?"

"Because his name is Edward."

"This is our baby I'm carrying," she said. She put a hand on her swollen stomach, as if Cantling needed a visual reminder.

He was tired of arguing. He was tired of discussing. He was tired of being interrupted. He leaned back in his chair. "How long have you been carrying the baby?"

Helen looked baffled. "You know. Seven months now. And a week."

Cantling leaned forward and slapped the stack of manuscript pages piled up beside his typewriter. "Well, I've been carrying *this* baby for three damned years now. This is the fourth fucking draft, and the last one. He was named Edward on the first draft, and on the second draft, and on the third draft, and he's damn well going to be named Edward when the goddamned novel comes out. He'd been named Edward for *years* before that night of fond memory when you decided to surprise me by throwing away your diaphragm, and thereby got yourself knocked up."

"It's not fair," she complained. "He's only a character. This is our baby."

"Fair? You want fair? OK. I'll make it fair. Our first-born son will get named Edward. How's that for fair?"

Helen's face softened. She smiled shyly.

He held up a hand before she had a chance to say anything. "Of course, I figure I'm only about a month away from finishing this damn thing, if you ever stop interrupting me. You've got a little further to go. But that's as fair as I can make it. You pop before I type THE END and you got the name. Otherwise, my baby here"—he slapped the manuscript again—"is first-born."

"You can't," she started.

Cantling resumed his typing.

"My first-born," Richard Cantling said.

"IN THE FLESH," DUNNAHOO SAID. HE RAISED HIS BEER BOTTLE IN salute, and said, "To fathers and sons, hey!" He drained it with one long swallow and flipped the bottle across the room end over end. It smashed in the fireplace.

"This is a dream," Cantling said.

Dunnahoo gave him a raspberry. "Look, old man, face it, I'm here." He jumped to his feet. "The prodigal returns," he said, bowing. "So where the fuck is the fatted calf and all that shit? Least you coulda done was order a pizza."

"I'll play the game," Cantling said. "What do you want from me?"

Dunnahoo grinned. "Want? Who, me? Who the fuck knows? I never knew what I wanted, you know that. Nobody in the whole fucking book knew what they wanted."

"That was the point," Cantling said.

"Oh, I get it," Dunnahoo said. "I'm not dumb. Old Dicky Cantling's boy is anything but dumb, right?" He wandered off toward the kitchen. "There's more beer in the fridge. Want one?"

"Why not?" Cantling asked. "It's not every day my oldest son comes to visit. Dos Equis with a slice of lime, please."

"Drinking fancy Spic beer now, huh? Shit. What ever happened to Piels? You could suck up Piels with the best of them, once upon a time." He vanished through the kitchen door. When he returned he was carrying two bottles of Dos Equis, holding them by the necks with his fingers jammed down into the open mouths. In his other hand he had a raw onion. The bottles clanked together as he carried them. He gave one to Cantling. "Here. I'll suck up a little culture myself."

"You forgot the lime," Cantling said.

"Get your own fuckin' lime," Dunnahoo said. "Whatcha gonna do, cut off my allowance?" He grinned, tossed the onion lightly into the air, caught it, and took a big bite. "Onions," he said. "I owe you for that one, Dad. Bad enough I have to eat raw onions, I mean, shit, but you fixed it so I don't even *like* the fucking things. You even said so in the damned book."

"Of course," Cantling said. "The onion had a dual function. On one level, you did it just to prove how tough you were. It was something none of the others hanging out at Ricci's could manage. It gave you a certain status. But on a deeper level, when you bit into an onion you were making a symbolic statement about your appetite for life, your hunger for it all, the bitter and the sharp parts as well as the sweet."

Dunnahoo took another bite of onion. "Horseshit," he said. "I ought to make you eat a fucking onion, see how you like it."

Cantling sipped at his beer. "I was young. It was my first book. It seemed like a nice touch at the time."

"Eat it raw," Dunnahoo said. He finished the onion.

Richard Cantling decided this cozy domestic scene had gone on long enough. "You know, Dunnahoo or whoever you are," he said in a conversational tone, "you're not what I expected."

"What did you expect, old man?"

Cantling shrugged. "I made you with my mind instead of my sperm, so you've got more of me in you than any child of my flesh could ever have. You're me."

"Hey," said Dunnahoo, "not fucking guilty. I wouldn't be you on a bet."

"You have no choice. Your story was built from my own adolescence. First novels are like that. Ricci's was really Pompeii Pizza in Newark. Your friends were my friends. And you were me."

"That so?" Dunnahoo replied, grinning.

Richard Cantling nodded.

Dunnahoo laughed. "You should be so fuckin' lucky, Dad."

"What does that mean?" Cantling snapped.

"You live in a dream world, old man, you know that? Maybe you like to pretend you were like me, but there ain't no way it's true. I was the big man at Ricci's. At Pompeii, you were the four-eyes hanging out back by the pinball machine. You had me balling my fuckin' brains out at sixteen. You never even got bare tit till you were past twenty, off in that college of yours. It took you weeks to come up with the wisecracks you had me tossing off every fuckin' time I turned around. All those wild crazy things I did in that book, some of them happened to Dutch and some of them happened to Joey and some of them never happened at all, but none of them happened to you, old man, so don't make me laugh."

Cantling flushed a little. "I was writing fiction. Yes, I was a bit of a misfit in my youth, but..."

"A nerd," Dunnahoo said. "Don't fancy it up."

"I was not a nerd," Cantling said, stung. "*Hangin' Out* told the truth. It made sense to use a protagonist who was more central to the action than I'd been in real life. Art draws on life but it has to shape it, rearrange it, give it structure, it can't simply replicate it. That's what I did."

"Nah. What *you* did was to suck off Dutch and Joey and the rest. You helped yourself to their lives, man, and took credit for it all yourself. You even got this weird fuckin' idea that I was based on you, and you been thinking that so long you believe it. You're a leech, Dad. You're a goddamned thief."

Richard Cantling was furious. "Get out of here!" he said.

Dunnahoo stood up, stretched. "I'm fuckin' wounded. Throwing your baby boy out into the cold Ioway night, old man? What's wrong? You liked me well enough when I was in your damn book, when you could control every thing I did and said, right? Don't like it so well now that I'm real, though. That's your problem. You never did like real life half as well as you liked books."

"I like life just fine, thank you," Cantling snapped.

Dunnahoo smiled. Standing there, he suddenly looked washed out, insubstantial. "Yeah?" he said. His voice seemed weaker than it had been.

"Yeah!" Cantling replied.

Now Dunnahoo was fading visibly. All the color had drained from his body, and he looked almost transparent. "Prove it," he said. "Go into your kitchen, old man, and take a great big bite out of your fuckin' raw onion of life." He tossed back his hair, and laughed, and laughed, and laughed, until he was quite gone.

Richard Cantling stood staring at the place where he had been for a long time. Finally, very tired, he climbed upstairs to bed.

HE MADE HIMSELF A BIG BREAKFAST THE NEXT MORNING: ORANGE juice and fresh-brewed coffee, English muffins with lots of butter and blackberry preserves, a cheese omelet, six strips of thick-sliced bacon. The cooking and the eating were supposed to distract him. It didn't work. He thought of Dunnahoo all the while. A dream, yes, some crazy sort of dream. He had no ready explanation for the broken glass in the fireplace or the empty beer bottles in his living room, but finally he found one. He had experienced some sort of insane drunken somnambulist episode, Cantling decided. It was the stress of the ongoing quarrel with Michelle, of course, triggered by the portrait she'd sent him. Perhaps he ought to see someone about it, a doctor or a psychologist or someone.

After breakfast, Cantling went straight to his den, determined to confront the problem directly and resolve it. Michelle's mutilated portrait still hung above the fireplace. A festering wound, he thought; it had infected him, and the time had come to get rid of it. Cantling built a fire. When it was going good, he took down the ruined painting, dismantled the metal frame—he was a thrifty man, after all—and burned the torn, disfigured canvas. The oily smoke made him feel clean again.

Next there was the portrait of Dunnahoo to deal with. Cantling turned to consider it. A good piece of work, really. She had captured the character. He could burn it, but that would be playing Michelle's own destructive game. Art should never be destroyed. He had made his mark in the world by creation, not destruction, and he was too old to change. The portrait of Dunnahoo had been intended as a cruel taunt, but Cantling decided to throw it back in his daughter's teeth, to make a splendid celebration of it. He would hang it, and hang it prominently. He knew just the place for it.

Up at the top of the stairs was a long landing; an ornate wooden banister overlooked the first-floor foyer and entry hall. The landing was fifteen feet long, and the back wall was entirely blank. It would make a splendid portrait gallery, Cantling decided. The painting would be visible to anyone entering the house, and you would pass right by it on the way to any of the second-floor rooms. He found a hammer and some nails and hung Dunnahoo in a place of honor. When Michelle came back to make peace, she would see him there, and no doubt leap to the conclusion that Cantling had totally missed the point of her gift. He'd have to remember to thank her effusively for it.

Richard Cantling was feeling much better. Last night's conversation was receding into a bad memory. He put it firmly out of his mind and spent the rest of the day writing letters to his agent and publisher. In the late afternoon, pleasantly weary, he enjoyed a cup of coffee and some butter streusel he'd hidden away in the refrigerator. Then he went out on his daily walk, and spent a good ninety minutes hiking along the river bluffs with a fresh, cold wind in his face.

When he returned, a large square package was waiting on his porch.

———

HE LEANED IT UP AGAINST AN ARMCHAIR, AND SETTLED INTO HIS recliner to study it. It made him uneasy. It had an effect, no doubt of it. He could feel an erection stirring against his leg, pressing uncomfortably against his trousers.

The portrait was . . . well, frankly erotic.

She was in bed, a big old antique four-poster, much like his own. She was naked. She was half-turned in the painting, looking back over her right shoulder; you saw the smooth line of her backbone, the curve of her right breast. It was a large, shapely, and very pretty breast; the aureole was pale pink and very large, and her nipple was erect. She was clutching a rumpled sheet up to her chin, but it did little to conceal her. Her hair was red-gold, her eyes green, her smile playful. Her smooth young skin had a flush to it, as if she had just risen from a bout of lovemaking. She had a peace symbol tattooed high on the right cheek of her ass. She was obviously very young. Richard Cantling knew just how young: she was eighteen, a child-woman, caught in that precious time between innocence and experience when sex is just a wonderfully exciting new toy. Oh yes, he knew a lot about her. He knew her well.

Cissy.

He hung her portrait next to Dunnahoo.

———

DEAD FLOWERS WAS CANTLING'S TITLE FOR THE BOOK. HIS EDITOR changed it to Black Roses; more evocative, he said, more romantic, more upbeat. Cantling fought the change on artistic grounds, and lost. Afterwards, when the novel made the bestseller lists, he managed to work up the grace to admit that he'd been wrong. He sent Brian a bottle of his favorite wine.

It was his fourth novel, and his last chance. Hangin' Out had gotten excellent reviews and had sold decently, but his next two books had been panned by the critics and ignored by the readers. He had to do something different, and he did. Black Roses turned out to be highly controversial. Some reviewers loved it, some loathed it. But it sold and sold and sold, and the paperback sale and the film option (they never made the movie) relieved him of financial worries for the first time in his life. They were finally able to afford a down payment on a house, transfer Michelle to a private school and get her those braces; the rest of the money Cantling invested as shrewdly as he was able. He was proud of *Black Roses* and pleased by its success. It made his reputation.

Helen hated the book with a passion.

On the day the novel finally fell off the last of the lists, she couldn't quite conceal her satisfaction. "I knew it wouldn't last forever," she said.

Cantling slapped down the newspaper angrily. "It lasted long enough. What the hell's wrong with you? You didn't like it before, when we were barely scraping by. The kid needs braces, the kid needs a better school, the kid shouldn't have to eat goddamn peanut butter and jelly sandwiches every day. Well, that's all behind us. And you're more pissed off than ever. Give me a little credit. Did you like being married to a failure?"

"I don't like being married to a pornographer," Helen snapped at him.

"Fuck you," Cantling said.

She gave him a nasty smile. "When? You haven't touched me in weeks. You'd rather be fucking your Cissy."

Cantling stared at her. "Are you crazy, or what? She's a character in a book I wrote. That's all."

"Oh, go to hell," Helen said furiously. "You treat me like I'm a goddamned idiot. You think I can't read? You think I don't know? I read your shitty book. I'm not stupid. The wife, Marsha, dull ignorant boring Marsha, cud-chewing mousy Marsha, that cow, that nag, that royal pain-in-the-ass, that's me. You think I can't tell? I can tell, and so can my friends. They're all very sorry for me. You love me as much as Richardson loved Marsha. Cissy's just a character, right, like hell, like bloody hell." She was crying now. "You're in love with her, damn you. She's your own little wet dream. If she walked in the door right now you'd dump me as fast as Richardson dumped good old Marsha. Deny it. Go on, deny it, I dare you!"

Cantling regarded his wife incredulously. "I don't believe you. You're jealous of a character in my book. You're jealous of someone who doesn't exist."

"She exists in your head, and that's the only place that matters with you. Of course you want to fuck her. Of course your damned book was a big seller. You think it was because of your writing? It was on account of the sex, on account of *her!*"

"Sex is an important part of life," Cantling said defensively. "It's a perfectly legitimate subject for art. You want me to pull down a curtain every time my characters go to bed, is that it? Coming to terms with sexuality, that's what *Black Roses* is all about. Of course it had to be written explicitly. If you weren't such a damned prude you'd realize that."

"I'm not a prude!" Helen screamed at him. "Don't you dare call me one, either." She picked up one of the breakfast plates and threw it at him. Cantling ducked; the plate shattered on the wall behind him. "Just because I don't like your goddamned filthy book doesn't make me a prude."

"The novel has nothing to do with it," Cantling said. He folded his arms against his chest but kept his voice calm. "You're a prude because of the things you do in bed. Or should I say the things you won't do?" He smiled.

Helen's face was red; beet red, Cantling thought, and rejected it, too old, too trite. "Oh, yes, but she'll do them, won't she?" Her voice was pure acid. "Cissy, your cute little Cissy. She'll get a sexy little tattoo on her ass if you ask her to, right? She'll do it outdoors, she'll do it in all kinds of strange places, with people all around. She'll wear kinky underwear, she thinks it's fun. She'll let you come in her mouth whenever you like. She's always ready and she doesn't have any stretch marks and she has eighteen-year-old tits, and she'll always have eighteen-year-old tits, won't she? How the hell do I compete with that, huh? How? How? *HOW?*"

Richard Cantling's own anger was a cold, controlled, sarcastic thing. He stood up in the face of her fury and smiled sweetly. "Read the book," he said. "Take notes."

He woke suddenly, in darkness, to the light touch of skin against his foot.

Cissy was perched on top of the footboard, a red satin sheet wrapped around her, a long slim leg exploring under his blankets. She was playing footsie with him, and smiling mischievously. "Hi, Daddy," she said.

Cantling had been afraid of this. It had been in his mind all evening. Sleep had not come easily. He pulled his foot away and struggled to a sitting position.

Cissy pouted. "Don't you want to play?" she asked.

"I," he said, "I don't believe this. This can't be real."

"It can still be fun," she said.

"What the hell is Michelle doing to me? How can this be happening?"

She shrugged. The sheet slipped a little; one perfect red-tipped eighteen-year-old breast peeked out.

"You still have eighteen-year-old tits," Cantling said numbly. "You'll always have eighteen-year-old tits."

Cissy laughed. "Sure. You can borrow them, if you like, Daddy. I'll bet you can think of something interesting to do with them."

"Stop calling me Daddy," Cantling said.

"Oh, but you are my daddy," Cissy said in her little-girl voice.

"Stop that!" Cantling said.

"Why? You want to, Daddy, you want to play with your little girl, don't you?" She winked. "Vice is nice but incest is best. The families that play together stay together." She looked around. "I like four-posters. You want to tie me up, Daddy? I'd like that."

"No," Cantling said. He pushed back the covers, got out of bed, found his slippers and robe. His erection throbbed against his leg. He had to get away, he had to put some distance between him and Cissy, otherwise . . . he didn't want to think about otherwise. He busied himself making a fire.

"I like that," Cissy said when he got it going. "Fires are so romantic."

Cantling turned around to face her again. "Why you?" he asked, trying to stay calm. "Richardson was the protagonist of *Black Roses,* not you. And why skip to my fourth book? Why not somebody from *Family Tree* or *Rain?*"

"Those gobblers?" Cissy said. "Nobody real there. You didn't really want Richardson, did you? I'm a lot more fun." She stood up and let go of the satin sheet. It puddled about her ankles, the flames reflected off its shiny folds. Her body was soft and sweet and young. She kicked free of the sheet and padded toward him.

"Cut it out, Cissy," Cantling barked.

"I won't bite," Cissy said. She giggled. "Unless you want me to. Maybe I should tie *you* up, huh?" She put her arms around him, gave him a hug, turned up her face for a kiss.

"Let go of me," he said, weakly. Her arms felt good. She felt good as she pressed up against him. It had been a long time since Richard Cantling had held a woman in his arms; he didn't like to think about how long. And he had never had a woman like Cissy, never, never. But he was frightened. "I can't do this," he said. "I can't. I don't want to."

Cissy reached through the folds of his robe, shoved her hand inside his briefs, squeezed him gently. "Liar," she said. "You want me. You've always wanted me. I'll bet you used to stop and jack off when you were writing the sex scenes."

"No," Cantling said. "Never."

"Never?" She pouted. Her hand moved up and down. "Well, I bet you wanted to. I bet you got hard, anyway. I bet you got hard every time you described me."

"I," he said. The denial would not come. "Cissy, please."

"Please," she murmured. Her hand was busy. "Yes, please." She tugged at his briefs and they fluttered to the floor. "Please," she said. She untied his robe and helped him out of it. "Please." Her hand moved along his side, played with his nipples; she stepped closer, and her breasts pressed lightly against his chest. "Please," she said, and she looked up at him. Her tongue moved between her lips.

Richard Cantling groaned and took her in his trembling arms.

She was like no woman he had ever had. Her touch was fire and satin, electric, and her secret places were sweet as honey.

In the morning she was gone.

Cantling woke late, too exhausted to make himself breakfast. Instead he dressed and walked into town, to a small café in a quaint hundred-year-old brick building at the foot of the bluffs. He tried to sort things out over coffee and blueberry pancakes.

None of it made any sense. It could not be happening, but it was; denial accomplished nothing. Cantling forked down a mouthful of homemade blueberry pancake, but the only taste in his mouth was fear. He was afraid for his sanity. He was afraid because he did not understand, did not want to understand. And there was another, deeper, more basic fear.

He was afraid of what would come next. Richard Cantling had published nine novels.

He thought of Michelle. He could phone her, beg her to call it off before he went mad. She was his daughter, his flesh and blood, surely she would listen to him. She loved him. Of course she did. And he loved her too, no matter what she might think. Cantling knew his faults. He had examined himself countless times, under various guises, in the pages of his books. He was impossibly stubborn, willful, opinionated. He could be rigid and unbending. He could be cold. Still, he thought of himself as a decent man. Michelle . . . she had inherited some of his perversity, she was furious at him, hate was so very close to love, but surely she did not mean to do him serious harm.

Yes, he could phone Michelle, ask her to stop. Would she? If he begged her forgiveness, perhaps. That day, that terrible day, she'd told him that she would never forgive him, never, but she couldn't have meant that. She was his only child. The only child of his flesh, at any rate.

Cantling pushed away his empty plate and sat back. His mouth was set in a hard rigid line. Beg for mercy? He did not like that. What had he done, after all? Why couldn't they understand? Helen had never understood and Michelle was as blind as her mother. A writer must live for his work. What had he done that was so terrible? What had he done that required forgiveness? Michelle ought to be the one phoning him.

The hell with it, Cantling thought. He refused to be cowed. He was right; she was wrong. Let Michelle call him if she wanted a rapprochement. She was not going to terrify him into submission. What was he so afraid of, anyway? Let her send her portraits, all the portraits she wanted to paint. He'd hang them up on his walls, display the paintings proudly (they were really an homage to his work, after all), and if the damned things came alive at night and prowled through his house, so be it. He'd enjoy their visits. Cantling smiled. He'd certainly enjoyed Cissy, no doubt of that. Part of him hoped she'd come back. And even Dunnahoo, well, he was an insolent kid, but there was no real harm in him, he just liked to mouth off.

Why, now that he stopped to consider it, Cantling found that the possibilities had a certain intoxicating charm. He was uniquely privileged. Scott Fitzgerald never attended one of Gatsby's fabulous parties, Conan

Doyle could never really sit down with Holmes and Watson, Nabokov never actually tumbled Lolita. What would they have said to the idea?

The more he considered things, the more cheerful he became. Michelle was trying to rebuke him, to frighten him, but she was really giving him a delicious experience. He could play chess with Sergei Tederenko, the cynical émigré hustler from *En Passant*. He could argue politics with Frank Corwin, the union organizer from his Depression novel, *Times Are Hard*. He might flirt with beautiful Beth McKenzie, go dancing with crazy old Miss Aggie, seduce the Danzinger twins and fulfill the one sexual fantasy that Cissy had left untouched, yes, certainly, what the hell had he been afraid of? They were his own creations, his characters, his friends and family.

Of course, there was the new book to consider. Cantling frowned. That was a disturbing thought. But Michelle was his daughter, she loved him, surely she wouldn't go that far. No, of course not. He put the idea firmly aside and picked up his check.

———

HE EXPECTED IT. HE WAS ALMOST LOOKING FORWARD TO IT. AND when he returned from his evening constitutional, his cheeks red from the wind, his heart beating just a little faster in anticipation, it was there waiting for him, the familiar rectangle wrapped in plain brown paper. Richard Cantling carried it inside carefully. He made himself a cup of coffee before he unwrapped it, deliberately prolonging the suspense to savor the moment, delighting in the thought of how deftly he'd turned Michelle's cruel little plan on its head.

He drank his coffee, poured a refill, drank that. The package stood a few feet away. Cantling played a little game with himself, trying to guess whose portrait might be within. Cissy had said something about none of the characters from *Family Tree* or *Rain* being real enough. Cantling mentally reviewed his life's work, trying to decide which characters seemed most real. It was a pleasant speculation, but he could reach no firm conclusions. Finally he shoved his coffee cup aside and moved to undo the wrappings. And there it was.

Barry Leighton.

Again, the painting itself was superb. Leighton was seated in a newspaper city room, his elbow resting on the gray metal case of an old manual typewriter. He wore a rumpled brown suit and his white shirt was open at the collar and plastered to his body by perspiration. His nose had been broken more than once, and was spread all across his wide, homely, somehow comfortable face. His eyes were sleepy. Leighton was overweight and jowly and rapidly losing his hair. He'd given up smoking but not cigarettes; an unlit Camel dangled from one corner of his mouth. "As long as you don't light the damned things, you're safe," he'd said more than once in Cantling's novel *Byeline*.

The book hadn't done very well. It was a depressing book, all about the last week of a grand old newspaper that had fallen on bad times. It was more than that, though. Cantling was interested in people, not newspapers; he had used the failing paper as a metaphor for failing lives. His editor had wanted to work in some kind of strong, sensational subplot, have Leighton and the others on the trail of some huge story that offered the promise of redemption, but Cantling had rejected that idea. He wanted to tell a story about small people being ground down inexorably by time and age, about the inevitability of loneliness and defeat. He produced a novel as gray and brittle as newsprint. He was very proud of it.

No one read it.

Cantling lifted the portrait and carried it upstairs, to hang beside those of Dunnahoo and Cissy. Tonight should be interesting, he thought. Barry Leighton was no kid, like the others; he was a man of Cantling's own years. Very intelligent, mature. There was a bitterness in Leighton, Cantling knew very well; a disappointment that life had, after all, yielded so little, that all his bylines and big stories were forgotten the day after they ran. But the reporter kept his sense of humor through all of it, kept off the demons with nothing but a mordant wit and an unlit Camel. Cantling admired him, would enjoy talking to him. Tonight, he decided, he wouldn't bother going to bed. He'd make a big pot of strong black coffee, lay in some Seagram's 7, and wait.

IT WAS PAST MIDNIGHT AND CANTLING WAS REREADING THE leather-bound copy of *Byeline* when he heard ice cubes clinking together in the kitchen. "Help yourself, Barry," he called out.

Leighton came through the swinging door, tumbler in hand. "I did," he said. He looked at Cantling through heavily lidded eyes, and gave a little snort. "You look old enough to be my father," he said. "I didn't think anybody could look that old."

Cantling closed the book and set it aside. "Sit down," he said. "As I recall, your feet hurt."

"My feet always hurt," Leighton said. He settled himself into an armchair and swallowed a mouthful of whiskey. "Ah," he said, "that's better."

Cantling tapped the novel with a fingertip. "My eighth book," he said. "Michelle skipped right over three novels. A pity. I would have liked to meet some of those people."

"Maybe she wants to get to the point," Leighton suggested.

"And what is the point?"

Leighton shrugged. "Damned if I know. I'm only a newspaperman. Five Ws and an H. You're the novelist. You tell me the point."

"My ninth novel," Cantling suggested. "The new one."

"The last one?" said Leighton.

"Of course not. Only the most recent. I'm working on something new right now."

Leighton smiled. "That's not what my sources tell me."

"Oh? What do your sources say?"

"That you're an old man waiting to die," Leighton said. "And that you're going to die alone."

"I'm fifty-two," Cantling said crisply. "Hardly old."

"When your birthday cake has got more candles than you can blow out, you're old," said Leighton drily. "Helen was younger than you, and she died five years ago. It's in the mind, Cantling. I've seen young octogenarians and old adolescents. And you, you had liver spots on your brain before you had hair on your balls."

"That's unfair," Cantling protested.

Leighton drank his Seagram's. "Fair?" he said. "You're too old to believe in fair, Cantling. Young people live life. Old people sit and watch it. You were born old. You're a watcher, not a liver." He frowned. "Not a liver, jeez, what a figure of speech. Better a liver than a gall bladder, I guess. You were never a gall bladder either. You've been full of piss for years, but you don't have any gall at all. Maybe you're a kidney."

"You're reaching, Barry," Cantling said. "I'm a writer. I've always been a writer. That's my life. Writers observe life, they report on life. It's in the job description. You ought to know."

"I do know," Leighton said. "I'm a reporter, remember? I've spent a lot of long gray years writing up other peoples' stories. I've got no story of my own. You know that, Cantling. Look what you did to me in *Byeline*. The *Courier* croaks and I decide to write my memoirs and what happens?"

Cantling remembered. "You blocked. You rewrote your old stories, twenty-year-old stories, thirty-year-old stories. You had that incredible memory. You could recall all the people you'd ever reported on, the dates, the details, the quotes. You could recite the first story you'd had bylined word for word, but you couldn't remember the name of the first girl you'd been to bed with, couldn't remember your ex-wife's phone number, you couldn't...you couldn't..." His voice failed.

"I couldn't remember my daughter's birthday," Leighton said. "Where do you get those crazy ideas, Cantling?"

Cantling was silent.

"From life, maybe?" Leighton said gently. "I was a good reporter. That was about all you could say about me. You, well, maybe you're a good novelist. That's for the critics to judge, and I'm just a sweaty newspaperman whose feet hurt. But even if you are a good novelist, even if you're one of the great ones, you were a lousy husband, and a miserable father."

"No," Cantling said. It was a weak protest.

Leighton swirled his tumbler; the ice cubes clinked and clattered. "When did Helen leave you?" he asked.

"I don't...ten years ago, something like that. I was in the middle of the final draft of *En Passant*."

"When was the divorce final?"

"Oh, a year later. We tried reconciliation, but it didn't take. Michelle was in school, I remember. I was writing *Times Are Hard*."

"You remember her third-grade play?"

"Was that the one I missed?"

"The one you missed? You sound like Nixon saying, 'Was that the time I lied?' That was the one Michelle had the lead in, Cantling."

"I couldn't help that," Cantling said. "I wanted to come. They were giving me an award. You don't skip the National Literary League dinner. You can't."

"Of course not," said Leighton. "When was it that Helen died?"

"I was writing *Byeline*," Cantling said.

"Interesting system of dating you've got there. You ought to put out a calendar." He swallowed some whiskey.

"All right," Cantling said. "I'm not going to deny that my work is important to me. Maybe too important, I don't know. Yes, the writing has been the biggest part of my life. But I'm a decent man, Leighton, and I've always done my best. It hasn't all been like you're implying. Helen and I had good years. We loved each other once. And Michelle . . . I loved Michelle. When she was a little girl, I used to write stories just for her. Funny animals, space pirates, silly poems. I'd write them up in my spare time and read them to her at bedtime. They were something I did just for Michelle, for love."

"Yeah," Leighton said cynically. "You never even thought about getting them published."

Cantling grimaced. "That . . . you're implying . . . that's a distortion. Michelle loved the stories so much, I thought maybe other kids might like them too. It was just an idea. I never did anything about it."

"Never?"

Cantling hesitated. "Look, Bert was my friend as well as my agent. He had a little girl of his own. I showed him the stories once. Once!"

"I can't be pregnant," Leighton said. "I only let him fuck me once. Once!"

"He didn't even like them," Cantling said.

"Pity," replied Leighton.

"You're laying this on me with a trowel, and I'm not guilty. No, I wasn't father of the year, but I wasn't an ogre either. I changed her diaper plenty of times. Before *Black Roses*, Helen had to work, and I took care of the baby every day, from nine to five."

"You hated it when she cried and you had to leave your typewriter."

"Yes," Cantling said. "Yes, I hated being interrupted, I've always hated being interrupted, I don't care if it was Helen or Michelle or my mother or my roommate in college, when I'm writing I don't like to be interrupted. Is that a fucking capital crime? Does that make me inhuman? When she cried, I went to her. I didn't like it, I hated it, I resented it, but I *went to her.*"

"When you heard her," said Leighton. "When you weren't in bed with Cissy, dancing with Miss Aggie, beating up scabs with Frank Corwin, when your head wasn't full of their voices, yeah, sometimes you heard, and when you heard you went. Congratulations, Cantling."

"I taught her to read," Cantling said. "I read her *Treasure Island* and *Wind in the Willows* and *The Hobbit* and *Tom Sawyer,* all kinds of things."

"All books you wanted to reread anyway," said Leighton. "Helen did the real teaching, with *Dick and Jane.*"

"I hate Dick and Jane*!"* Cantling shouted.

"So?"

"You don't know what you're talking about," Richard Cantling said. "You weren't there. Michelle was there. She loved me, she still loves me. Whenever she got hurt, scraped her knee, or got her nose bloodied, whatever it was, it was me she'd run to, never Helen. She'd come crying to me and I'd hug her and dry her tears and I'd tell her . . . I used to tell her . . ." But he couldn't go on. He was close to tears himself; he could feel them hiding in the corners of his eyes.

"I know what you used to tell her," said Barry Leighton in a sad, gentle voice.

"She remembered it," Cantling said. "She remembered it all those years. Helen got custody, they moved away, I didn't see her much, but Michelle always remembered, and when she was all grown up, after Helen was gone and Michelle was on her own, there was this time she got hurt, and I . . . I . . ."

"Yes," said Leighton. "I know."

———

THE POLICE WERE THE ONES THAT PHONED HIM. DETECTIVE JOYCE Brennan, that was her name, he would never forget that name. "Mister Cantling?" she said.

"Yes?"

"Mister Richard Cantling?"

"Yes," he said. "Richard Cantling the writer." He had gotten strange calls before. "What can I do for you?"

She identified herself. "You'll have to come down to the hospital," she said to him. "It's your daughter, Mister Cantling. I'm afraid she's been assaulted."

He hated evasion, hated euphemism. Cantling's characters never passed away, they died; they never broke wind, they farted. And Richard Cantling's daughter . . . "Assaulted?" he said. "Do you mean she's been assaulted or do you mean she's been raped?"

There was a silence on the other end of the line. "Raped," she said at last. "She's been raped, Mister Cantling."

"I'll be right down," he said.

She had in fact been raped repeatedly and brutally. Michelle had been as stubborn as Helen, as stubborn as Cantling himself. She wouldn't take his money, wouldn't take his advice, wouldn't take the help he offered her through his contacts in publishing. She was going to make it on her own. She waitressed in a coffeehouse in the Village, and lived in a large, drafty, and rundown warehouse loft down by the docks. It was a terrible neighborhood, a dangerous neighborhood, and Cantling had told her so a hundred times, but Michelle would not listen. She would not even let him pay to install good locks and a security system. It had been very bad. The man had broken in before dawn on a Friday morning. Michelle was alone. He had ripped the phone from the wall and held her prisoner there through Monday night. Finally one of the busboys from the coffeehouse had gotten worried and come by, and the rapist had left by the fire escape.

When they let him see her, her face was a huge purple bruise. She had burn marks all over her, where the man had used his cigarette, and three of her ribs were broken. She was far beyond hysteria. She screamed when they tried to touch her; doctors, nurses, it didn't matter, she screamed as soon as they got near. But she let Cantling sit on the edge of the bed, and take her in his arms, and hold her. She cried for hours, cried until there were no more tears in her. Once she called him "Daddy," in a choked sob. It was the only word she spoke; she seemed to have lost the capacity for speech. Finally they tranquilized her to get her to sleep.

Michelle was in the hospital for two weeks, in a deep state of shock. Her hysteria waned day by day, and she finally became docile, so they were able to fluff her pillows and lead her to the bathroom. But she still would not, or could not, speak. The psychologist told Cantling that she might never speak again. "I don't accept that," he said. He arranged

Michelle's discharge. Simultaneously he decided to get them both out of this filthy hellhole of a city. She had always loved big old spooky houses, he remembered, and she used to love the water, the sea, the river, the lake. Cantling consulted realtors, considered a big place on the coast of Maine, and finally settled on an old steamboat gothic mansion high on the bluffs of Perrot, Iowa. He supervised every detail of the move.

Little by little, recovery began.

She was like a small child again, curious, restless, full of sudden energy. She did not talk, but she explored everything, went everywhere. In spring she spent hours up on the widow's walk, watching the big towboats go by on the Mississippi far below. Every evening they would walk together on the bluffs, and she would hold his hand. One day she turned and kissed him suddenly, impulsively, on his cheek. "I love you, Daddy," she said, and she ran away from him, and as Cantling watched her run, he saw a lovely, wounded woman in her mid-twenties, and saw too the gangling, coltish tomboy she had been.

The dam was broken after that day. Michelle began to talk again. Short, childlike sentences at first, full of childish fears and childish naïveté. But she matured rapidly, and in no time at all she was talking politics with him, talking books, talking art. They had many a fine conversation on their evening walks. She never talked about the rape, though; never once, not so much as a word.

In six months she was cooking, writing letters to friends back in New York, helping with the household chores, doing lovely things in the garden. In eight months she had started to paint again. That was very good for her; now she seemed to blossom daily, to grow more and more radiant. Richard Cantling didn't really understand the abstractions his daughter liked to paint, he preferred representational art, and best of all he loved the self-portrait she had done for him when she was still an art major in college. But he could feel the pain in these new canvases of hers, he could sense that she was engaged in an exorcism of sorts, trying to squeeze the pus from some wound deep inside, and he approved. His writing had been a balm for his own wounds more than once. He envied her now, in a way. Richard Cantling had not written a word for more than three years. The crashing commercial failure of *Byeline,* his best novel, had left him blocked and impotent. He'd thought perhaps the change of scene might restore him as well as Michelle, but that had been a vain hope. At least one of them was busy.

Finally, late one night after Cantling had gone to bed, his door opened and Michelle came quietly into his bedroom and sat on the edge of his bed. She was barefoot, dressed in a flannel nightgown covered with tiny pink flowers. "Daddy," she said, in a slurred voice.

Cantling had woken when the door opened. He sat up and smiled for her. "Hi," he said. "You've been drinking."

Michelle nodded. "I'm going back," she said. "Needed some courage, so's I could tell you."

"Going back?" Cantling said. "You don't mean to New York? You can't be serious!"

"I got to," she said. "Don't be mad. I'm better now."

"Stay here. Stay with me. New York is uninhabitable, Michelle."

"I don't want to go back. It scares me. But I got to. My friends are there. My work is there. My life is back there, Daddy. My friend Jimmy, you remember Jimmy, he's art director for this little paperback house, he can get me some cover assignments, he says. He wrote. I won't have to wait tables anymore."

"I don't believe I'm hearing this," Richard Cantling said. "How can you go back to that damned city after what happened to you there?"

"That's why I have to go back," Michelle insisted. "That guy, what he did...what he did to me..." Her voice caught in her throat. She drew in her breath, got hold of herself. "If I don't go back, it's like he ran me out of town, took my whole life away from me, my friends, my art, everything. I can't let him get away with that, can't let him scare me off. I got to go back and take up what's mine, prove that I'm not afraid."

Richard Cantling looked at his daughter helplessly. He reached out, gently touched her long, soft hair. She had finally said something that made sense in his terms. He would do the same thing, he knew. "I understand," he said. "It's going to be lonely here without you, but I understand, I do."

"I'm scared," Michelle said. "I bought plane tickets. For tomorrow."

"So soon?"

"I want to do it quickly, before I lose my nerve," she said. "I don't think I've ever been this scared. Not even...not even when it was happening. Funny, huh?"

"No," said Cantling. "It makes sense."

"Daddy, hold me," Michelle said. She pressed herself into his arms. He hugged her and felt her body tremble.

"You're shaking," he said.

She wouldn't let go of him. "You remember, when I was real little, I used to have those nightmares, and I'd come bawling into your bedroom in the middle of the night and crawl into bed between you and Mommy."

Cantling smiled. "I remember," he said.

"I want to stay here tonight," Michelle said, hugging him even more tightly. "Tomorrow I'll be back there, alone. I don't want to be alone tonight. Can I, Daddy?"

Cantling disengaged gently, looked her in the eyes. "Are you sure?"

She nodded; a tiny, quick, shy nod. A child's nod.

He threw back the covers and she crept in next to him. "Don't go away," she said. "Don't even go to the bathroom, okay? Just stay right here with me."

"I'm here," he said. He put his arms around her, and Michelle curled up under the covers with her head on his shoulder. They lay together that way for a long time. He could feel her heart beating inside her chest. It was a soothing sound; soon Cantling began to drift back to sleep.

"Daddy?" she whispered against his chest.

He opened his eyes. "Michelle?"

"Daddy, I have to get rid of it. It's inside me and it's poison. I don't want to take it back with me. I have to get rid of it."

Cantling stroked her hair, long slow steady motions, saying nothing.

"When I was little, you remember, whenever I fell down or got in a fight, I'd come running to you, all teary, and show you my booboo. That's what I used to call it when I got hurt, remember, I'd say I had a booboo."

"I remember," Cantling said.

"And you, you'd always hug me and you'd say, 'Show me where it hurts,' and I would and you'd kiss it and make it better, you remember that? Show me where it hurts?"

Cantling nodded. "Yes," he said softly.

Michelle was crying quietly. He could feel the wetness soaking through the top of his pajamas. "I can't take it back with me, Daddy. I want to show you where it hurts. Please. Please."

He kissed the top of her head. "Go on."

She started at the beginning, in a halting whisper.

When dawn light broke through the bedroom windows, she was still talking. They never slept. She cried a lot, screamed once or twice, shivered frequently despite the weight of the blankets; Richard Cantling never let go of her, not once, not for a single moment. She showed him where it hurt.

Barry Leighton sighed. "It was a far, far better thing you did than you had ever done," he said. "Now if you'd only gone off to that far, far better rest right then and there, that very moment, everything would have been fine." He shook his head. "You never did know when to write Thirty, Cantling."

"Why?" Cantling demanded. "You're a good man, Leighton, tell me. Why is this happening? Why?"

The reporter shrugged. He was beginning to fade now. "That was the W that always gave me the most trouble," he said wearily. "Pick the story, and let me loose, and I could tell you the who and the what and the when and the where and even the how. But the why...ah, Cantling, you're the novelist, the whys are your province, not mine. The only Y that I ever really got on speaking terms with was the one goes with MCA."

Like the Cheshire cat, his smile lingered long after the rest of him was gone. Richard Cantling sat staring at the empty chair, at the abandoned tumbler, watching the whiskey-soaked ice cubes melt slowly.

He did not remember falling asleep. He spent the night in the chair, and woke stiff and achy and cold. His dreams had been dark and shapeless and full of fear. He had slept well into the afternoon; half the day was gone. He made himself a tasteless breakfast in a kind of fog. He seemed distant from his own body, and every motion was slow and clumsy. When the coffee was ready, he poured a cup, picked it up, dropped it. The mug broke into a dozen pieces. Cantling stared down at it stupidly, watching rivulets of hot brown liquid run between the tiles. He did not have the energy to clean it up. He got a fresh mug, poured more coffee, managed to get down a few swallows.

The bacon was too salty; the eggs were runny, disgusting. Cantling pushed the meal away half-eaten, and drank more of the black, bitter coffee. He felt hungover, but he knew that booze was not the problem.

Today, he thought. It will end today, one way or the other. She will not go back. *Byeline* was his eighth novel, the next to the last. Today the final portrait would arrive. A character from his ninth novel, his last novel. And then it would be over.

Or maybe just beginning.

How much did Michelle hate him? How badly had he wronged her? Cantling's hand shook; coffee slopped over the top of the mug, burning his fingers. He winced, cried out. Pain was so inarticulate. Burning. He thought of smoldering cigarettes, their tips like small red eyes. His stomach heaved. Cantling lurched to his feet, rushed to the bathroom. He got there just in time, gave his breakfast to the bowl. Afterwards he was too weak to move. He lay slumped against the cold white porcelain, his head swimming. He imagined somebody coming up behind him, taking him by the hair, forcing his face down into the water, flushing, flushing, laughing all the while, saying dirty, dirty, I'll get you clean, you're so dirty, flushing, flushing so the toilet ran and ran, holding his face down so the water and the vomit filled his mouth, his nostrils, until he could hardly breathe, until the world was almost black, until it was almost over, and then up again, laughing while he sucked in air, and then pushing him down again, flushing again, and again and again and again. But it was only his imagination. There was no one there. No one. Cantling was alone in the bathroom.

He forced himself to stand. In the mirror his face was gray and ancient, his hair filthy and unkempt. Behind him, leering over his shoulder, was another face. A man's face, pale and drawn, with black hair parted in the middle and slicked back. Behind a pair of small round glasses were eyes the color of dirty ice, eyes that moved constantly, frenetically, wild animals caught in a trap. They would chew off their own limbs to be free, those eyes. Cantling blinked and the face was gone. He turned on the cold tap, plunged his cupped hands under the stream, splashed water on his face. He could feel the stubble of his beard. He needed to shave. But there wasn't time, it wasn't important, he had to . . . he had to . . .

He had to do something. Get out of there. Get away, get to someplace safe, somewhere his children couldn't find him.

But there was nowhere safe, he knew.

He had to reach Michelle, talk to her, explain, plead. She loved him. She *would* forgive him, she had to. She would call it off, she would tell him what to do.

Frantic, Cantling rushed back to the living room, snatched up the phone. He couldn't remember Michelle's number. He searched around, found his address book, flipped through it wildly. There, there; he punched in the numbers.

The phone rang four times. Then someone picked it up.

"Michelle—" he started.

"Hi," she said. "This is Michelle Cantling, but I'm not in right now. If you'll leave your name and number when you hear the tone, I'll get back to you, unless you're selling something."

The beep sounded. "Michelle, are you there?" Cantling said. "I know you hide behind the machine sometimes, when you don't want to talk. It's me. Please pick up. Please."

Nothing.

"Call me back, then," he said. He wanted to get it all in; his words tumbled over each other in their haste to get out. "I, you, you can't do it, please, let me explain, I never meant, I never meant, please..." There was the beep again, and then a dial tone. Cantling stared at the phone, hung up slowly. She would call him back. She had to, she was his daughter, they loved each other, she had to give him the chance to explain. Of course, he had tried to explain before.

His doorbell was the old-fashioned kind, a brass key that projected out of the door. You had to turn it by hand, and when you did it produced a loud, impatient metallic rasp. Someone was turning it furiously, turning it and turning it and turning it. Cantling rushed to the door, utterly baffled. He had never made friends easily, and it was even harder now that he had become so set in his ways. He had no real friends in Perrot, a few acquaintances perhaps, but no one who would come calling so unexpectedly, and twist the bell with such energetic determination.

He undid his chain and flung the door open, wrenching the bell key out of Michelle's fingers.

She was dressed in a belted raincoat, a knitted ski cap, a matching scarf. The scarf and a few loose strands of hair were caught in the wind, moving restlessly. She was wearing high, fashionable boots and carrying a big leather shoulder bag. She looked good. It had been almost a year since Cantling had seen her, on his last Christmas visit to New York. It had been two years since she'd moved back east.

"Michelle," Cantling said. "I didn't . . . this is quite a surprise. All the way from New York and you didn't even tell me you were coming?"

"No," she snapped. There was something wrong with her voice, her eyes. "I didn't want to give you any warning, you bastard. You didn't give *me* any warning."

"You're upset," Cantling said. "Come in, let's talk."

"I'll come in all right." She pushed past him, kicked the door shut behind her with so much force that the buzzer sounded again. Out of the wind, her face got even harder. "You want to know why I came? I am going to tell you what I think of you. Then I'm going to turn around and leave, I'm going to walk right out of this house and out of your fucking life, just like Mom did. She was the smart one, not me. I was dumb enough to think you loved me, crazy enough to think you cared."

"Michelle, don't," Cantling said. "You don't understand. I do love you. You're my little girl, you—"

"Don't you *dare!*" she screamed at him. She reached into her shoulder bag. "You call this *love,* you rotten bastard!" She pulled it out and flung it at him.

Cantling was not as quick as he'd been. He tried to duck, but it caught him on the side of his neck, and it hurt. Michelle had thrown it hard, and it was a big, thick, heavy hardcover, not some flimsy paperback. The pages fluttered as it tumbled to the carpet; Cantling stared down at his own photograph on the back of the dust-wrapper. "You're just like your mother," he said, rubbing his neck where the book had hit. "She always threw things too. Only you aim better." He smiled weakly.

"I'm not interested in your jokes," Michelle said. "I'll never forgive you. Never. Never ever. All I want to know is how you can do this to me, that's all. You tell me. You tell me now."

"I," Cantling said. He held his hands out helplessly. "Look, I . . . you're upset now, why don't we have some coffee or something, and talk about it when you calm down a little. I don't want a big fight."

"I don't give a fuck what you want," Michelle screamed. "I want to talk about it right now!" She kicked the fallen book.

Richard Cantling felt his own anger building. It wasn't right for her to yell at him like that, he didn't deserve this attack, he hadn't done anything. He tried not to say anything for fear of saying the wrong thing and escalating the situation. He knelt and picked up his book. Without thinking, he brushed it off, turned it over almost tenderly. The title glared up at him; stark, twisted red letters against a black background, the distorted face of a pretty young woman, mouth open in a scream. *Show Me Where It Hurts.*

"I was afraid you'd take it the wrong way," Cantling said.

"The *wrong way!*" Michelle said. A look of incredulity passed across her face. "Did you think I'd *like* it?"

"I, I wasn't sure," said Cantling. "I hoped... I mean, I was uncertain of your reaction, and so I thought it would be better not to mention what I was working on, until, well..."

"Until the fucking thing was in the bookstore windows," Michelle finished for him.

Cantling flipped past the title page. "Look," he said, holding it out, "I dedicated it to you." He showed her:

To Michelle, who knew the pain.

Michelle swung at it, knocked it out of Cantling's hands. "You bastard," she said. "You think that makes it better? You think your stinking dedication excuses what you did? Nothing excuses it. I'll never forgive you."

Cantling edged back a step, retreating in the face of her fury. "I didn't do anything," he said stubbornly. "I wrote a book. A novel. Is that a crime?"

"You're my *father,*" she shrieked. "You knew... you knew, you bastard, you knew I couldn't bear to talk about it, to talk about what happened. Not to my lovers or my friends or even my therapist, I can't, I just can't, I can't even think about it, you knew. I told you, I told only you, because you were my daddy and I trusted you and I had to get it out, and I told you, it was private, it was just between us, you knew, but what did you do? You wrote it all up in a goddamned book and *published* it for millions of people to read! Damn you, damn you. Were you planning to do that all along, you sonofabitch? Were you? That night in bed, were you memorizing every word?"

"I," said Cantling. "No, I didn't memorize anything, I just, well, I just remembered it. You're taking it all wrong, Michelle. The book's not about what happened to you. Yes, it's inspired by that, that was the starting point, but it's fiction, I changed things, it's just a novel."

"Oh yeah, Daddy, you changed things all right. Instead of Michelle Cantling it's all about Nicole Mitchell, and she's a fashion designer instead of an artist, and she's also kind of stupid, isn't she? Was that a change or is that what you think, that I was stupid to live there, stupid to let him in like that? It's all fiction, yeah. It's just a coincidence that it's about this girl that gets held prisoner and raped and tortured and terrorized and raped some more, and that you've got a daughter who was held prisoner and raped and tortured and terrorized and raped some more, right, just a fucking coincidence!"

"You don't understand," Cantling said helplessly.

"No, *you* don't understand. You don't understand what it's like. This is your biggest book in years, right? Number-one bestseller, you've never been number one before, haven't even been on the lists since *Times Are Hard,* or was it *Black Roses*? And why not, why not number one, this isn't no boring story about a has-been newspaper, this is *rape,* hey, what could be hotter? Lots of sex and violence, torture and fucking and terror, and doncha know, *it really happened,* yeah." Her mouth twisted and trembled. "It was the worst thing that ever happened to me. It was all the nightmares that have ever been. I still wake up screaming sometimes, but I was getting better, it was behind me. And now it's there in every bookstore window, and all my friends know, everybody knows, strangers come up to me at parties and tell me how sorry they are." She choked back a sob; she was halfway between anger and tears. "And I pick up your book, your fucking no-good book, and there it is again, in black and white, all written down. You're such a fucking *good* writer, Daddy, you make it all so real. A book you can't put down. Well, I put it down but it didn't help, it's all there, now it will always be there, won't it? Every day somebody in the world will pick up your book and read it and I'll get raped again. That's what you did. You finished the job for him, Daddy. You violated me, took me without my consent, just like he did. You raped me. You're my own father and you raped me!"

"You're not being fair," Cantling said. "I never meant to hurt you. The book... Nicole is strong and smart. It's the man who's the monster. He uses all those different names because fear has a thousand names, but only one face, you see. He's not just a man, he's the darkness made flesh, the mindless violence that waits out there for all of us, the gods that play with us like flies, he's a symbol of all—"

"He's the man who raped me! He's not a symbol!"

She screamed it so loudly that Richard Cantling had to retreat in the face of her fury. "No," he said. "He's just a character. He's...Michelle, I know it hurts, but what you went through, it's something people should know about, should think about, it's a part of life. Telling about life, making sense of it, that's the job of literature, that's my job. Someone had to tell your story. I tried to make it true, tried to do my—"

His daughter's face, red and wet with tears, seemed almost feral for a moment, unrecognizable, inhuman. Then a curious calm passed across her features. "You got one thing right," she said. "Nicole didn't have a father. When I was a little kid I'd come to you crying and my daddy would say show me where it hurts, and it was a private thing, a special thing, but in the book Nicole doesn't have a father, he says it, you gave it to him, he says show me where it hurts, he says it all the time. You're so ironic. You're so clever. The way he said it, it made him so real, more real than when he was real. And when you wrote it, you were right. That's what the monster says. Show me where it hurts. That's the monster's line. Nicole doesn't have a father, he's dead, yes, that was right too. I don't have a father. No, I don't."

"Don't you talk to me like that," Richard Cantling said. It was terror inside him; it was shame. But it came out anger. "I won't have that, no matter what you've been through. I'm your father."

"No," Michelle said, grinning crazy now, backing away from him. "No, I don't have a father, and you don't have any children, no, unless it's in your books. Those are your children, your only children. Your books, your damned fucking books, those are your children, those are your children, those are your children." Then she turned and ran past him, down the foyer. She stopped at the door to his den. Cantling was afraid of what she might do. He ran after her.

When he reached the den, Michelle had already found the knife and set to work.

———

Richard Cantling sat by his silent phone and watched his grandfather clock tick off the hours toward darkness.

He tried Michelle's number at three o'clock, at four, at five. The machine, always the machine, speaking in a mockery of her voice. His messages grew more desperate. It was growing dim outside. His light was fading.

Cantling heard no steps on his porch, no knock on his door, no rasping summons from his old brass bell. It was an afternoon as silent as the grave. But by the time evening had fallen, he knew it was out there. A big square package, wrapped in brown paper, addressed in a hand he had known well. Inside a portrait.

He had not understood, not really, and so she was teaching him.

The clock ticked. The darkness grew thicker. The sense of a waiting presence beyond his door seemed to fill the house. His fear had been growing for hours. He sat in the armchair with his legs pulled up under him, his mouth hanging open, thinking, remembering. Heard cruel laughter. Saw the dim red tips of cigarettes in the shadows, moving, circling. Imagined their small hot kisses on his skin. Tasted urine, blood, tears. Knew violence, knew violation, of every sort there was. His hands, his voice, his face, his face, his face. The character with a dozen names, but fear had only a single face. The youngest of his children. His baby. His monstrous baby.

He had been blocked for so long, Cantling thought. If only he could make her understand. It was a kind of impotence, not writing. He had been a writer, but that was over. He had been a husband, but his wife was dead. He had been a father, but she got better, went back to New York. She left him alone, but that last night, wrapped in his arms, she told him the story, she showed him where it hurt, she gave him all that pain. What was he to do with it?

Afterwards he could not forget. He thought of it constantly. He began to reshape it in his head, began to grope for the words, the scenes, the symbols that would make sense of it. It was hideous, but it was life, raw strong life, the grist for Cantling's mill, the very thing he needed. She had showed him where it hurt; he could show them all. He did resist, he did try. He began a short story, an essay, finished some reviews. But it returned. It was with him every night. It would not be denied.

He wrote it.

"Guilty," Cantling said in the darkened room. And when he spoke the word, a kind of acceptance seemed to settle over him, banishing the terror. He was guilty. He had done it. He would accept the punishment, then. It was only right.

Richard Cantling stood and went to his door.

The package was there.

He lugged it inside, still wrapped, carried it up the stairs. He would hang him beside the others, beside Dunnahoo and Cissy and Barry Leighton, all in a row, yes. He went for his hammer, measured carefully, drove the nail. Only then did he unwrap the portrait, and look at the face within.

It captured her as no other artist had ever done, not just the lines of her face, the high angular cheekbones and blue eyes and tangled ash-blonde hair, but the personality inside. She looked so young and fresh and confident, and he could see the strength there, the courage, the stubbornness.

But best of all he liked her smile. It was a lovely smile, a smile that illuminated her whole face. The smile seemed to remind him of someone he had known once. He couldn't remember who.

Richard Cantling felt a strange, brief sense of relief, followed by an even greater sense of loss, a loss so terrible and final and total that he knew it was beyond the power of the words he worshipped.

Then the feeling was gone.

Cantling stepped back, folded his arms, studied the four portraits. Such excellent work; looking at the paintings, he could almost feel their presence in his house.

Dunnahoo, his first-born, the boy he wished he'd been.

Cissy, his true love.

Barry Leighton, his wise and tired alter-ego.

Nicole, the daughter he'd never had.

His people. His characters. His children.

A WEEK LATER, ANOTHER, MUCH SMALLER PACKAGE ARRIVED. Inside the carton were copies of four of his novels, a bill, and a polite note from the artist inquiring if there would be any more commissions.

Richard Cantling said no, and paid the bill by check.

George R. R. Martin:
A Retrospective Fiction Checklist

AS OF 31 DECEMBER 2006
By Leslie Kay Swigart
University Library, California State University, Long Beach

THIS CHECKLIST OF THE PROFESSIONALLY PUBLISHED FICTION OF George R. R. Martin, now in its second published version, is part of a much larger project which eventually will be as complete and thorough a bibliography of the work by, and about, George R. R. Martin as may be created by diligence, persistence, and sheer dogged research. In this future bibliography I hope to provide meticulously detailed bibliographic descriptions of all known editions, versions, adaptations, and translations of all books, scripts, short fiction, and nonfiction by Mr. Martin, as well as an annotated bibliography of all known reviews, interviews, articles, and biographical works about Mr. Martin and his work.

The focus of this more modest listing is on the first English-language professional print publications of his books, books he has edited, scripts, and his short fiction. For the books, only the first American and British English language editions are presented, with no attempt to track the reprints of these or other editions. There are several foreign-language volumes with no English-language equivalent; these volumes are not listed here. The short fiction and scripts are listed chronologically by year, then alphabetically by title, with the first publication or first air dates given, along with appearances in his collection. Pre-professional publication is noted only when the item is later reprinted professionally. For all items there is a note of those foreign languages and other formats into which they are known to have been translated.

This project began, although I was then unaware of it, one late June weekend in 1973 in Dallas, Texas. I was attending D-Con '73, a comics- and science fiction-oriented convention, as the author of *Harlan Ellison: A Bibliographical Checklist*, which was being published that weekend by the convention chairman, Joe Bob Williams, in honor of the con's guest of honor, Harlan Ellison. In attendance at the con were a group of young writers, most of whom knew each other through their SF or comics connections. Among these writers were Howard Waldrop, Steve Utley, Lisa Tuttle, and George R. R. Martin.

As far as any evidence exists, I next ran into George at the Science Fiction Writers of America's Nebula Awards weekend in spring 1974 where George took a photo of a very young and startled-looking me, a photo which I still have. By DisCon II (32nd World Science Fiction Convention, Washington, D.C., 1974), our acquaintance was off and running (quite literally!). Over the years there have been many conversations, mail and email exchanged, and meals shared as well as the occasional convention.

After a while, as George's writing career continued to prosper there were thoughts and desultory discussions about my doing a bibliography of George's work along the lines of the one I'd done on Ellison. Then, while attending a party at ConJosé (60th World SF Convention, San Jose, California) in 2002, George asked me if I'd be interested in doing a modest bibliography for the collection of his work that was being proposed for publication in time for his Guest of Honor gig at Torcon III (61st World SF Convention in Toronto) the following year. If so, he would broach the subject with his publisher, William Schafer of Subterranean Press. Then, in late September an email arrived with the subject line of "wanna do my bibliography?" Schafer was interested. Emails were exchanged. Et voilà! This second updated version was prompted by this Bantam publication of *Dreamsongs, Volume I and II* (previously published as *GRRM: A RRetrospective*).

LESLIE KAY SWIGART
Los Angeles and Long Beach, California
February 2007

The sources of this checklist are as follows:

My own collection bought in stores all over the U.S., Ontario, Germany, the Netherlands, the United Kingdom, France, and Italy, and which has been generously supplemented over the years by gifts, especially foreign editions, from George. Thanks, George!

The collection of George R. R. Martin himself, examined in April 2004 during a sabbatical leave from California State University, Long Beach. Thank you George! And thank you, CSULB!

Previous bibliographies:

Stephensen-Payne, Phil. *George R. R. Martin: The Ace from New Jersey; A Working Bibliography.* 2nd rev. edn. [Leeds, England; Albuquerque, NM]: Galactic Central [1989]. The original edition (1987) of this bibliography was the first separately published bibliography of Martin's work.

Marano, Lydia C. George R(aymond) R(ichard) Martin: Bibliography. Manuscript bibliography, dated 31 May 1994, prepared for an unrealized publication.

Miller, John J. Collecting George R. R. Martin. *Firsts: The Book Collector's Magazine,* 11 (9), November 2001: 36-45. Provides valuation ranges for first editions.

Other indexes, catalogs, and websites:

Brown, Charles N., and William G. Contento. *The Locus Index to Science Fiction (1984-1998)* [and annual supplements]. 2004-2006. [http://www.locusmag.com/index/; latest access: 2007-02-02]

Contento, William G. *Index to Science Fiction Anthologies and Collections, Combined Edition.* 2005. [http://contento.best.vwh.net/0start.htm; latest access: 2007-02-02]

George R. R. Martin Bibliography [and] George R. R. Martin Cover Art Gallery. *George R. R. Martin Official Website.* [http://www.georgerrmartin.com; latest access: 2007-01-28]

George R. R. Martin—Bibliography Summary. *The Internet Speculative Fiction Database.* [http://www.isfdb.com]; latest access: 2007-02-02]

Index Translationum, 1971–date. [print: 1971-1977; electronic: 1978-date, http://databases.unesco.org/xtrans/; latest access: 2007-02-02]

Martin, George R. R. Bibliografía general. *Términus Tríntor.* 2007. [http://www.ttrantor.org; latest access: 2007-02-10]

National Library catalogs too numerous to mention.

O autorovi: Martin, George R. R. *Daemon: Internetové knihkopectví on-line.* 2007. [http://www.daemon.cz; latest access: 2007-02-09]

Pree, Christian. *Bibliographie der deutschsprachiger Science Fiction-Stories und Bücher/Bibliography of German Science Fiction Stories and Books.* 1998-2007. [http://www.chpr.at/sfstorye.html; latest access: 2007-02-02]

Vegetti, Ernesto, Pino Cottogni, and Ermes Bertoni. *Catalogo SF, Fantasy e Horror.* 2007. [http://www.fantascienza.com/catalogo/index.htm; latest access: 2007-02-02]

WorldCat [OCLC; latest access 2007-02-03]

Order of information and the abbreviations used in this checklist:

For Books and Books Edited:

Title of Book [type of book]

 a. [Hardcover, paperback or trade paper indicator] Place of publication: publisher name, year of publication. Original price in country of publication (additional prices in other countries, if given). Note: Only first American and British editions are given, with the occasional limited edition where that edition is not the first. There are several foreign-language collections which have no English-language equivalent; these volumes are not given here.

 b. Foreign languages, adaptations, and other formats into which book is known to have been translated.

 c. Contents of collections are given based on the first American publication.

For Scripts:

a. [TV scripts] "Episode title." *Series title*, first airdate.

b. [Film scripts] ***Title***. Producing company, year of first release.

For Short Fiction:

 a. [In periodicals:] Title of story. *Periodical title*, volume # (issue number; whole issue #), date. [Abbreviations for appearances in Martin's own collections, see below.]

 b. [In books:] Title of story. *Title of collection*. Editor. Place of publication: publisher name, year of publication. [Abbreviations for appearances in Martin's own collections, see below.]

 c. Foreign languages, adaptations, and other formats into which story is known to have been translated.

Abbreviations for Martin collections in which the story also appears:

SLya = *A Song for Lya and Other Stories* [1976]
SongsS&S = *Songs of Stars and Shadows* [1977]
Wind = *Windhaven* [1981; novel based on previously published stories]
Sks = *Sandkings* [1981]
SongsDMS = *Songs the Dead Men Sing* [1983]
Nflyrs = *Nightflyers* [the collection; 1985]
TufV = *Tuf Voyaging* [1986]
Portraits = *Portraits of His Children* [1987]
Quartet = *Quartet* [2001]
GRRM = *GRRM: A RRetrospective* [2003; aka: *Dreamsongs*]

General Abbreviations:

Audio = audio recording (cassette or CD)
AudioBPH = audio recording for blind or physically handicapped
E-audio = electronic sound file/audio recording
·E-text = electronic book or other electronic-based text
Ed. = Edited, or Editor
Graphic = graphic story or comic adaptation
HC = hardcover edition
Ltd = limited edition
PB = mass market paperback edition
TPB = trade paperback edition
Video = Video recording (VHS, Videodisc, or DVD)

Books By:

A Song for Lya and Other Stories [Short Story Collection]
[PB] New York: Avon, 1976. $1.25
[PB.] Sevenoaks, UK: Coronet, 1978. 85p

Other forms: Czech; French; German; Italian; Spanish.

Contents: With Morning Comes Mistfall. The Second Kind of Loneliness. Override. Dark, Dark Were the Tunnels. The Hero. fta. Run to Starlight. The Exit to San Breta. Slide Show. A Song for Lya.

Songs of Stars and Shadows [Short Story Collection]
[PB] New York: Pocket, 1977. $1.75
[PB] London: Coronet, 1981. 95p

Other forms: Czech; French; German; Italian.

Contents: Introduction. This Tower of Ashes. Patrick Henry, Jupiter, and the Little Red Brick Spaceship. Men of Greywater Station [written with Howard Waldrop]. The Lonely Songs of Laren Dorr. Night of the Vampyres. The Runners. Night Shift. "... for a single yesterday." And Seven Times Never Kill Man.

Dying of the Light [Novel based on previously published serialized novel in *Analog* (1977) as: *After the Festival*]
[HC] New York: Simon and Schuster, 1977. $9.95
[HC] London: Victor Gollancz, 1978. £4.95

Other forms: Czech; Dutch; French; German; Italian; Polish; Russian; Spanish; AudioBPH; E-text.

Hugo Awards nominee.

Windhaven. Written with Lisa Tuttle. [Novel based on previously published stories (1975, 1980, 1981)]
[HC] New York: Timescape, 1981. $13.95
[PB] London: New English Library, 1982. £1.50

Other forms: Bulgarian; Croatian; Czech; Dutch; French; German; Italian; Japanese; Polish; Russian; Spanish; Braille (French); E-text.

Contents: Novel based on previously published stories: Storms [original title: The Storms of Windhaven]; One-Wing; The Fall (published contemporaneously in *Amazing*).

Nightflyers. [Novella expanded from the originally published story (1980)]
[PB] *Binary Star No. 5: Nightflyers* [by] George R. R. Martin, [and] *True Names* [by] Vernor Vinge. New York: Dell, 1981. $2.50

Other forms: Czech; French; Polish; Russian.

Hugo Awards nominee.

Sandkings [Short Story Collection]
[PB] New York: Pocket, 1981. $2.75
[PB] London: Futura, 1983. £2.25 ($6.95 Australia)

Other forms: Czech; German; Japanese; Polish.

Contents: The Way of Cross and Dragon. Bitterblooms. In the House of the Worm. Fast-Friend. The Stone City. Starlady. Sandkings.

Fevre Dream [Novel]
[HC] New York: Poseidon, 1982. $14.95
[HC] London: Victor Gollancz, 1983. £7.95
[HC Ltd] Burton, MI: Subterranean (forthcoming)

Other forms: French; German; Hebrew; Hungarian; Italian; Japanese; Polish; Russian; Spanish; AudioBPH; E-text.

World Fantasy Awards nominee.

Songs the Dead Men Sing [Short Story Collection]
[HC Ltd] Niles, Illinois: Dark Harvest, 1983. $35.00 [for 500 for sale copies]

[Limitation statement: "The First Edition of *Songs the Dead Men Sing* is limited to five hundred individually signed and numbered copies." Marano notes that there were also 50 presentation copies, and six proofs.]
[HC] London: Victor Gollancz, 1985. £9.95

Other forms: Czech; Spanish.

Contents: George R. R. Martin, Dark Harbinger [introduction, by A. J. Budrys]. The Monkey Treatment. ". . . for a single yesterday." In the House of the Worm. The Needle Men. Meathouse Man. Sandkings. This Tower of Ashes. Nightflyers [expanded version]. Remembering Melody.

The Armageddon Rag: A Stereophonic Long-Playing Novel [Novel]
[HC] New York: Poseidon, 1983. $15.95
[HC Ltd] Omaha [and] Kansas City: Nemo, 1983. $50.00 [for 500 for sale copies]
[Limitation statement: "This special collector's first edition is limited to 540 signed and slipcased copies, of which 500 are for sale, 14 are specially marked and numbered as review copies, and the remaining 26, marked A through Z, are reserved for the Press, having been designated as presentation copies. Six of these presentation copies are hand-bound in leather and are personalized with foil stamping."]
[PB] Sevenoaks [UK]: New English Library, 1984. £2.95

Other forms: Croatian; French; German; Polish; Swedish; Braille; E-text.

World Fantasy Awards nominee.

Nightflyers [Short Story Collection]
[TPB] New York: Bluejay, 1985. $8.95

Contents: Nightflyers [expanded version]. Override. Weekend in a War Zone. And Seven Times Never Kill Man. Nor the Many-Colored Fires of a Star Ring. A Song for Lya.

Tuf Voyaging [Short Story Collection]
[HC] New York: Baen, 1986. $15.95
[HC] London: Victor Gollancz, 1987. £10.95

Contents: Prologue. The Plague Star. Loaves and Fishes. Guardians. Second Helpings. A Beast for Norn [rewritten version]. Call Him Moses. Manna From Heaven.

Other forms: Bulgarian; Czech; Lithuanian; Polish; Romanian; Russian; Spanish.

Portraits of His Children [Short Story Collection]
[HC Ltd] Arlington Hts, Illinois: Dark Harvest, 1987. $150.00 [52 copies lettered, signed, boxed]; $39.95 [Limitation statement: "This deluxe first edition of Portraits of His Children is limited to four hundred fifty individually signed

and numbered copies.] [Note: Marano says: 75 presentation copies and 24 proofs also]

[HC] Arlington Hts., Illinois: Dark Harvest, 1987. $18.95 [2500 copies]

Other forms: Czech.

Contents: A Sketch of Their Fathers [introduction by Roger Zelazny]. With Morning Comes Mistfall. The Second Kind of Loneliness. The Last Super Bowl. The Lonely Songs of Laren Dorr. The Ice Dragon. In the Lost Lands. Unsound Variations. Closing Time. Under Siege. The Glass Flower. Portraits of His Children.

Dead Man's Hand [Novel; written with John J. Miller; *Wild Cards, 7*]
See below: Books Edited By GRRM

The Pear-Shaped Man [separate publication of short story (1987)].
[PB] Eugene, Oregon: Pulphouse, 1991. (Short Story Paperback, #37) $1.95
[HC] Eugene, Oregon: Pulphouse, 1991. (Short Story Hardback, #24) $20.00
    [Limitation statement: Short Story Hardback Issue Twenty-Four: The Pear-Shaped Man by George R. R. Martin has been published in a limited edition of 100 copies. 100 limited, signed, and numbered 1–100.]

Other forms: E-text.

A Game of Thrones [Novel; *A Song of Ice and Fire, 1*]
[The opening chapters published in a mass-market paperback format as a "preview edition."] London: HarperCollins, 1996. £0.99
[HC] New York: Bantam, 1996. $21.95 ($29.95 Canada)
[HC] London: HarperCollins, 1996. £16.99
[HC Ltd] Atlanta, GA: Meisha Merlin, 2000. [Limitation Statement: This edition of *A Game of Thrones* is limited to 500 copies, 52 lettered and 448 numbered. This is letter/number ___. A GAME OF THRONES. Book One of A Song of Ice and Fire.]

Other forms: Bulgarian; Chinese (PRC); Chinese (Taiwan); Croatian; Czech; Dutch; Finnish; French; German; Hebrew; Hungarian; Italian; Japanese; Korean; Polish; Portuguese; Russian; Serbian; Spanish; Swedish; Audio; AudioBPH; E-audio; E-text.

Nebula Awards nominee; World Fantasy Awards nominee.

A Clash of Kings [Novel; *A Song of Ice and Fire, 2*]
[HC] London: HarperCollins, 1998. £17.99
[HC] New York: Bantam, 1999. $25.95
[HC Ltd] Atlanta, CA: Meisha Merlin, 2003. [Limitation Statement: This edition of A Game of Thrones [sic!] is limited to 500 copies, 52 lettered and 448 numbered. This is letter/number ___. A CLASH OF KINGS. Book Two of A Song of Ice and Fire.]

Other forms: Bulgarian; Chinese (PRC); Chinese (Taiwan); Croatian; Czech; Dutch; Finnish; French; German; Hebrew; Hungarian; Italian; Japanese; Korean; Polish; Russian; Serbian; Spanish; Swedish; Audio; AudioBPH; E-audio; E-text.

Nebula Awards nominee.

A Storm of Swords [Novel; *A Song of Ice and Fire, 3*]
[HC] London: HarperCollins, 2000. £17.99
[HC] New York: Bantam, 2000. $26.95 ($39.95 Canada)
[HC Ltd] [Burton, MI]: Subterranean, 2006. [Limitation Statement: This special signed edition is limited to 448 numbered copies and 26 lettered copies. This is copy ___.]

Other forms: Bulgarian; Chinese (Taiwan); Czech; Dutch; Finnish; French; German; Hebrew; Hungarian; Italian; Korean; Polish; Russian; Serbian; Spanish; Audio; AudioBPH; E-audio; E-text.

Nebula Awards nominee; Hugo Awards nominee.

Quartet: Four Tales from the Crossroads [Collection; edited by Christine Carpenito]
[HC Ltd] Framingham, Massachusetts: NESFA, 2001. [Limitation statement: "*Quartet* was printed in an edition of 1200 numbered hardcover books, of which the first 200 were signed by the author and artist, bound with special endpapers and slipcased. Of these 200 copies, the first 10 are lettered A through J and the remainder are numbered 1 through 190. The trade copies are numbered 191 through 1190."]
[HC] Framingham, Massachusetts: NESFA, 2001. $25.00
[TPB] Framingham, Massachusetts: NESFA, 2001. $15.00

Contents: Introduction. Black and White and Red All Over [novel fragment]. Skin Trade. StarPort [script]. Blood of the Dragon.

GRRM: A RRetrospective [Short Story Collection]
[HC Ltd] Burton, MI: Subterranean, 2003. [Limitation Statement: This special signed edition is limited to 400 numbered copies and 52 letter copies. This is copy ___.] Note: Includes chapbook: *The Last Defender of Camelot*. Teleplay by George R. R. Martin. Story by Roger Zelazny. Burton, MI: Subterranean, 2003.
[HC] Burton, MI: Subterranean, 2003. $40.00
[HC; retitled:] *Dreamsongs: GRRM: A RRetrospective*. London: Gollancz, 2006. £20.00

Contents: George R. R. Martin [introduction by Gardner Dozois]. ONE: A Four-Color Fanboy [introduction]. Only Kids Are Afraid of the Dark. The Fortress. And Death His Legacy. TWO: The Filthy Pro [introduction]. The Hero. The Exit to San Breta. The Second Kind of Loneliness. With Morning Comes Mistfall. THREE: The Light of Distant Stars [introduction]. Song for Lya.

This Tower of Ashes. And Seven Times Never Kill Man. The Stone City.
Bitterblooms. The Way of Cross and Dragon. FOUR: The Heirs of Turtle Castle
[introduction]. The Lonely Songs of Laren Dorr. The Ice Dragon. In the Lost
Lands. FIVE: Hybrids and Horrors [introduction]. Meathouse Man.
Remembering Melody. Sandkings. Nightflyers. The Monkey Treatment. The
Pear-Shaped Man. SIX: A Taste of Tuf [introduction]. A Beast for Norn.
Guardians. SEVEN: The Siren Song of Hollywood: [introduction]. The Twilight
Zone: The Road Less Traveled. Doorways. EIGHT: Doing the Wild Card
Shuffle [introduction]. Shell Games. From the Journal of Xavier Desmond.
NINE: The Heart in Conflict [introduction]. Under Siege. The Skin Trade.
Unsound Variations. The Glass Flower. The Hedge Knight. Portraits of His
Children. George R. R. Martin: A RRetrospective Fiction Checklist, As of 31
December 2002 [bibliography, by Leslie Kay Swigart].

The Hedge Knight. George R. R. Martin, writer. Ben Avery, adaptation. Mike S.
Miller, pencils. Mike Crowell, inks. Team Kandora, colors/transparency
digital. Bill Tortolini, lettering/lithium pro design. Robert Silverberg, editor.
Elio M. Garcia [and] Linda Antonsson, thematic consultants. [Graphic
adaptation of novella (1998)]
[TPB] [np]: DB Pro [and] Devil's Due, 2003 [2004]. $14.95

Other forms: Originally released as a limited-run comic book, 2003 (August)–
2004 (April) from Image Comics, then Devil's Due. Italian; Spanish; Turkish.

Shadow Twin. Written with Gardner Dozois and Daniel Abraham. [Novella]
[HC Ltd] Burton, MI: Subterranean, 2005. $150.00 (signed lettered) $40.00
(signed limited) [Limitation Statement: This special signed edition is limited
to 500 numbered copies and 26 lettered copies.]

A Feast for Crows [Novel; *A Song of Ice and Fire, 4*]
[HC] London: HarperCollins, 2005. £18.99
[HC] New York: Bantam, 2005. $28.00 ($38.00 Canada)
[HC Ltd] Burton, MI: Subterranean (forthcoming).

Other forms: Croatian (forthcoming); Czech; Dutch; German; Hebrew;
Italian; Polish; Serbian; Audio; AudioBPH; E-audio; E-text.

Hugo Awards nominee.

The Ice Dragon. [Illustrated novella (1980)]
[HC] New York: Starscape, Tom Doherty Associates, 2006. $12.95 ($16.95
Canada)

Other forms: Audio; E-text.

Books Edited By:

New Voices in Science Fiction: Stories by Campbell Award Nominees.
[Anthology; edited by George R. R. Martin]
[HC] New York: Macmillan, 1977. $8.95

Other forms: German.

Contents: Bova, Ben. Introduction.; Tuttle, Lisa. The Family Monkey.; Thurston, Robert. Kingmakers.; Martin, George R. R. The Stone City.; Berman, Ruth. To Ceremark.; Effinger, George Alec. Mom's Differentials.; Pournelle, Jerry. Silent Leges.

New Voices II: The Campbell Award Nominees. [Anthology; edited by George R. R. Martin]
[PB] New York: Jove/HBJ, 1979. $1.75

Other forms: German.

Contents: Martin, George R. R. Preface.; Sturgeon, Theodore. Introduction.; Tuttle, Lisa. The Hollow Man.; Snyder, Guy. Lady of Ice.; Monteleone, Thomas F. The Dancer in the Darkness.; Miller, Jesse. Twilight Lives.; Robinson, Spider. Satan's Children.

New Voices III: The Campbell Award Nominees. [Anthology; edited by George R. R. Martin]
[PB] New York: Berkley, 1980. $1.95

Contents: Martin, George R. R. Preface. Asimov, Isaac. Introduction.; Varley, John. Beatnik Bayou.; Pearce, Brenda. Haute Falaise Bay.; Charnas, Suzy McKee. Scorched Supper on New Niger.; Brennert, Alan. Stage Whisper.; Brennert, Alan. Queen of the Magic Kingdom.; Gotschalk, Felix. The Wishes of Maidens.; Plauger, P. J. Virtual Image.

New Voices 4: The John W. Campbell Award Nominees. [Anthology; edited by George R. R. Martin]
[PB] New York: Berkley, 1981. $2.25

Contents: Preface, George R. R. Preface. van Vogt, A. E. Introduction; Varley, John. Blue Champagne; Foster, M. A. Entertainment.; Darnay, Arsen. The Pilgrimage of Ishten Telen Haragosh.; Vinge, Joan D. Psiren.; Reamy, Tom. M Is for the Million Things.; Budrys, Algis. Afterword: Tom Reamy.

The Science Fiction Weight-Loss Book. [Anthology; edited by Isaac Asimov, George R. R. Martin, and Martin H. Greenberg]
[HC] New York: Crown, 1983. $12.95

Other forms: Portuguese.

Contents: Asimov, Isaac. Introduction: Fat!; Aandahl, Vance. Sylvester's Revenge.; Card, Orson Scott. Fat Farm.; Merwin, Sam, Jr. The Stretch.; Lafferty,

R. A. Camels and Dromedaries, Clem.; Boyle, T. Coraghessan. The Champ.;
Wells, H. G. The Truth about Pyecraft.; Silverberg, Robert. The Iron
Chancellor.; Pohl, Frederik. The Man Who Ate the World.; West, John
Anthony. Gladys's Gregory.; Vance, Jack. Abercrombie Station.; Morrison,
William. Shipping Clerk.; Tenn, William. The Malted Milk Monster.; Reed, Kit.
The Food Farm.; Sanders, Scott. The Artist of Hunger.; King, Stephen. Quitters,
Inc.

The John W. Campbell Awards, Volume 5. [Anthology; edited by George
  R. R. Martin]
[TPB] New York: Bluejay, 1984. $7.95

  Contents: Martin, George R. R. Preface.; Anderson, Poul. Introduction.;
Chalker, Jack L. In the Dowaii Chambers.; Foster, M. A. Dreams.; Scholz, Carter.
A Catastrophe Machine.; Cherryh, C. J. The Dark King.; Cherryh, C. J.
Companions.

Night Visions 3. [Anthology; edited by George R. R. Martin]
[HC Ltd] Niles, Illinois: Dark Harvest, 1986. $49.00 [Limitation statement: "The
  deluxe first edition of Night Visions 3 is limited to four hundred individually
  signed and numbered copies." In slipcase.]
[HC] Niles, Illinois: Dark Harvest, 1986. $18.00
[HC] London: Victor Gollancz, 1987. £11.95

  Other forms: Dutch.

  Contents: Martin, George R. R. Introduction: The Horror, The Horror.;
Campbell, Ramsey. In the Trees. This Time. Missed Conection. Root Cause.
Looking Out. Bedtime Story. Beyond Words.; Tuttle, Lisa. Riding the
Nightmare. From Another Country. The Dragon's Bride.; Barker, Clive. The
Hellbound Heart.

  World Fantasy Awards nominee.

Wild Cards: A Mosaic Novel [Mosaic novel; Wild Cards, 1; edited by George
  R. R. Martin]
[HC book club edition] Toronto [and] New York: Bantam, 1986.
[PB] Toronto [and] New York : Bantam, 1987. $3.95 ($4.95 Canada)
[PB] London: Titan, 1989. £3.95

  Other forms: German; Japanese; Russian; E-text.

  Contents: [Martin, George R. R.] Prologue.; Waldrop, Howard. Thirty
Minutes Over Broadway!; Zelazny, Roger. The Sleeper.; Williams, Walter Jon.
Witness.; Degradation Rites / Melinda M. Snodgrass — [Martin, George R. R.]
Interlude One.; Martin, George R. R. Shell Games.; [Martin, George R. R.]
Interlude Two.; Shiner, Lewis. The Long, Dark Night of Fortunato.; Milán,
Victor. Transfigurations.; [Martin, George R. R.] Interlude Three.; Bryant,
Edward and Harper, Leanne C. Down Deep.; [Martin, George R. R.] Interlude

Four.; Leigh, Stephen. Strings.; [Martin, George R. R.] Interlude Five.; Miller, John J. Comes a Hunter.; Shiner, Lewis. Epilogue: Third Generation.; [Milán, Victor]. Appendix.; [2001 ibooks edition adds:] Wild Cards: A Mike Zeck Gallery; Martin, George R. R. Afterword.

The Wild Cards series was a Hugo Awards nominee in 1988.

Aces High. [Mosaic novel; *Wild Cards, 2*; edited by George R. R. Martin]
[PB] Toronto [and] New York: Bantam, 1987. $3.95 ($4.95 Canada)
[PB] London: Titan, 1989. £3.95

Other forms: German; Japanese; Russian; E-text.

Contents. Shiner, Lewis. Pennies From Heaven.; Martin, George R. R. Jube: One.; Williams, Walter Jon. Unto the Sixth Generation: Prologue.; Martin, George R. R. Jube: Two.; Zelazny, Roger. Ashes to Ashes.; Williams, Walter Jon. Unto the Sixth Generation: Part One.; Williams, Walter Jon. Unto the Sixth Generation: Part Two.; Martin, George R. R. Jube: Three.; Simons, Walton. If Looks Could Kill.; Martin, George R. R. Jube: Four.; Williams, Walter Jon. Unto the Sixth Generation: Epilog.; Martin, George R. R. Winter's Chill.; Martin, George R. R. Jube: Five.; Snodgrass, Melinda. Relative Difficulties.; Milán, Victor. With a Little Help from His Friends.; Martin, George R. R. Jube: Six.; Cadigan, Pat. By Lost Ways.; Williams, Walter Jon. Mr. Koyama's Comet.; Miller, John J. Half Past Dead.; Martin, George R. R. Jube: Seven. [2001 ibooks edition adds:] Wild Cards: The Floyd Hughes Gallery; Martin, George R. R. Afterword.

Jokers Wild: A Wild Cards Mosaic Novel. [Mosaic novel; *Wild Cards, 3*;
    edited by George R. R. Martin]
[PB] Toronto [and] New York: Bantam, 1987. $4.50 ($5.50 Canada)
[PB] London: Titan, 1989. £3.95

Other forms: German; Japanese; Russian; E-text.

Contents: This mosaic novel was collectively written by Edward Bryant, Leanne C. Harper, George R. R. Martin, John J. Miller, Lewis Shiner, Walton Simons, and Melinda M. Snodgrass, but responsibility for the individual parts is not identified. [2002 ibooks edition adds:] Wild Cards: The Tom Palmer Gallery; Martin, George R. R. Afterword.

Aces Abroad: A Wild Cards Mosaic Novel. [Mosaic novel; *Wild Cards, 4*;
    edited by George R. R. Martin; assistant editor: Melinda M. Snodgrass]
[PB] Toronto [and] New York: Bantam, 1988. $4.50 ($5.50 Canada)
[PB] London: Titan, 1990. £3.95

Other forms: German; E-text.

Contents: Leigh, Stephen. The Tint of Hatred.; Martin, George R. R. The Journal of Xavier Desmond.; Miller, John J. Beasts of Burden.; Harper, Leanne C.

Blood Rights.; Gerstner–Miller, Gail. Down By the Nile.; Simons, Walton. The Teardrop of India.; Bryant, Edward. Down in the Dreamtime.; Shiner, Lewis. Zero Hour.; Milán, Victor. Puppets.; Snodgrass, Melinda. Mirror of the Soul.; Cassutt, Michael. Legends. [2002 ibooks edition adds:] Illustrations by Tom Mandrake; Martin, George R. R. Afterword.

Down & Dirty: A Wild Cards Mosaic Novel. [Mosaic novel; *Wild Cards, 5*;
     edited by George R. R. Martin; assistant editor: Melinda M. Snodgrass]
[PB] Toronto [and] New York: Bantam, 1988. $4.50 ($5.50 Canada)
[PB] London: Titan, 1990. £3.99

Other forms: German; E-text.

Contents: Miller, John J. Only the Dead Know Jokertown.; Martin, George R. R. All the King's Horses.; Zelazny, Roger. Conterto for Siren and Serotonin.; Harper, Leanne C. Breakdown.; Cover, Arthur Byron. Jesus Was an Ace.; Snodgrass, Melinda M. Blood Ties.; Bryant, Edward. The Second Coming of Buddy Holly.; Leigh, Stephen. The Hue of a Mind.; Cadigan, Pat. Addicted to Love.; Williams, Walter Jon. Mortality.; Harper, Leanne C. "What Rough Beast . . ." [2002 ibooks edition adds:] Illustrations by Timothy Truman; Martin, George R. R. Afterword.

Ace in the Hole: A Wild Cards Mosaic Novel. [Mosaic novel; *Wild Cards, 6*;
     edited by George R. R. Martin, assisted by Melinda M. Snodgrass]
[PB] New York [and] Toronto: Bantam, 1990. $4.50 ($5.50 Canada)
[PB] London: Titan, 1990. £3.99

Other forms: German; E-text.

Contents: This mosaic novel was collectively written by Stephen Leigh, Victor Milán, Walton Simons, Melinda M. Snodgrass, and Walter Jon Williams, but responsibility for the individual parts is not identified.

Dead Man's Hand: A Wild Cards Novel. [Novel; *Wild Cards, 7*; edited by
     George R. R. Martin; assistant editor: Melinda M.Snodgrass]
[PB] New York [and] Toronto: Bantam, 1990. $4.50 ($5.50 Canada)

Contents: This novel was written by George R. R. Martin and John J. Miller.

One-Eyed Jacks: A Wild Cards Mosaic Novel. [Mosaic novel; *Wild Cards, 8*;
     edited by George R. R. Martin; assistant editor: Melinda M. Snodgrass]
[PB] New York [and] Toronto: Bantam, 1991. $4.95 ($5.95 Canada)

Contents: Simons, Walton. Nobody's Girl.; Claremont, Chris. Luck Be a Lady.; Simons, Walton. Nobody Knows Me Like My Baby.; Shiner, Lewis. Horses.; Simons, Walton. Mr. Nobody Goes to Town.; Wu, William F. Snow Dragon.; Simons, Walton. Nobody Knows the Trouble I've Seen.; Milán, Victor. Nowadays Clancy Can't Even Sing.; Simons, Walton. You're Nobody Till

Somebody Loves You.; Leigh, Stephen. Sixteen Candles.; Simons, Walton. My Name Is Nobody.; Snodgrass, Melinda M. The Devil's Triangle.; Simons, Walton. Nobody's Home.; Miller, John J. Dead Heart Beating.; Simons, Walton. Nobody Gets Out Alive.

Jokertown Shuffle: A Wild Cards Mosaic Novel. [Mosaic novel; *Wild Cards, 9*; edited by George R. R. Martin; assistant editor: Melinda M. Snodgrass] [PB] New York [and] Toronto: Bantam, 1991. $4.99 ($5.99 Canada)

Contents: Leigh, Stephen. The Temptation of Hieronymous Bloat.; Miller, John J. And Hope to Die.; Snodgrass, Melinda M. Lovers.; Milán, Victor. Madman Across the Water.; Williams, Walter Jon. While Night's Black Agents to Their Preys Do Rouse.; Shiner, Lewis. Riders.; Simons, Walton. Nobody Does It Alone.

Double Solitaire: A Wild Cards Mosaic Novel. [Mosaic novel; *Wild Cards, 10*; edited by George R. R. Martin] [PB] New York [and] Toronto: Bantam, 1992. $5.50 ($6.50 Canada)

Contents: This novel was written by Melinda M. Snodgrass.

Dealer's Choice: A Wild Cards Mosaic Novel. [Mosaic novel; *Wild Cards, 11*; edited by George R. R. Martin; assistant editor: Melinda M. Snodgrass] [PB] New York [and] Toronto: Bantam, 1992. $5.99 ($6.99 Canada)

Contents: This mosaic novel was collectively written by Edward Bryant, Stephen Leigh, John J. Miller, George R. R. Martin, and Walter Jon Williams, but responsibility for the individual parts is not identified.

Turn of the Cards: A Wild Cards Novel. [Novel; *Wild Cards, 12*; edited by George R. R. Martin] [PB] New York [and] Toronto: Bantam, 1993. $5.99 ($6.99)

Contents: This novel was written by Victor Milán.

Card Sharks: A Wild Cards Mosaic Novel. [Mosaic novel; *Wild Cards, 13; Wild Cards, A New Cycle, 1*; edited by George R. R. Martin; assistant editor: Melinda M. Snodgrass] [PB] Riverdale, NY: Baen, 1993. $5.99 ($6.99 Canada)

Contents: Leigh, Stephen. The Ashes of Memory.; Wu, William F. Till I Kissed You.; Snodgrass, Melinda M. The Crooked Man.; Cassutt, Michael. A Method of Reaching Extreme Altitudes.; Milán, Victor. A Wind from Khorasan: The Narrative of J. Robert Belew.; Zelazny, Roger. The Long Sleep.; Murphy, Kevin Andrew. Cursum Perficio.; Mixon, Laura J. The Lamia's Tale.

Marked Cards: A Wild Cards Mosaic Novel. [Mosaic novel; *Wild Cards, 14; Wild Cards, A New Cycle, 2*; edited by George R. R. Martin; assistant editor: Melinda M. Snodgrass] [PB] Riverdale, NY: Baen, 1994. $5.99 ($7.50 Canada)

Contents: Leigh, Stephen. The Color of His Skin.; Simons, Walton. Two of a Kind.; Milán, Victor. My Sweet Lord.; Harper, Leanne C. Paths of Silence and of Night.; Williams, Walter Jon. Feeding Frenzy.; Walker, Sage. A Breath of Life.; Mixon, Laura J. and Snodgrass, Melinda M. A Dose of Reality.

Black Trump: A Wild Cards Mosaic Novel. [Mosaic novel; *Wild Cards, 15; Wild Cards, A New Cycle, 3*; edited by George R. R. Martin; assistant editor: Melinda M. Snodgrass]
[PB] Riverdale, NY : Baen, 1995. $5.99

Contents: This mosaic novel was collectively written by George R. R. Martin, Stephen Leigh, Victor Milán, John J. Miller, and Sage Walker, but responsibility for the individual parts is not identified.

Deuces Down: A Mosaic Novel. [Mosaic novel; *Wild Cards, 16*; edited by George R. R. Martin; assistant editor: Melinda M. Snodgrass]
[HC] New York: ibooks, 2002. $23.00 ($35.00 Canada; £12.99 UK)

Other forms: E-text.

Contents: Simons, Walton. Introduction.; Cassutt, Michael. Storming Space.; Miller, John J. Four Days in October.; Simons, Walton. Walking the Floor Over You.; Snodgrass, Melinda M. A Face for the Cutting Room Floor.; Abraham, Daniel. Father Henry's Little Miracle.; Leigh, Stephen. Promises.; Murphy, Kevin Andrew. With a Flourish and a Flair.

Death Draws Five: An Original Novel. [Novel; *Wild Cards, 17*; edited by George R. R. Martin]
[HC] New York: ibooks, 2006. $22.95 ($30.95 Canada)

Contents: This novel was written by John J. Miller.

Scripts By:

The Last Defender of Camelot. Based on the short story by Roger Zelazny. *Twilight Zone*, 11 April 1986.

Other forms: Video; chapbook to accompany limited edition of *GRRM: A RRetrospective* (2003).

Writers Guild of America Award, for Best Teleplay/Anthology nominee.

The Once and Future King. Based on a story by Bryce Maritano, *Twilight Zone*, 27 September 1986.

Other forms: Video.

Lost and Found. Based on the short story by Phyllis Eisenstein, *Twilight Zone*, 18 October 1986.

Other forms: Video.

The Toys of Caliban. Based on a story by Terry Matz, *Twilight Zone*, 4 December 1986.

Other forms: Video; magazine.

The Road Less Traveled. *Twilight Zone*, 18 December 1986. [Original script: *GRRM*]

Other forms: Video.

Terrible Savior. *Beauty and the Beast*, 2 October 1987.

Other forms: Video.

Masques. *Beauty and the Beast*, 30 October 1987.

Other forms: Video.

Shades of Grey. Written with David Peckinpah. *Beauty and the Beast*, 8 January 1988.

Other forms: Video.

Promises of Someday. *Beauty and the Beast*, 12 February 1988.

Other forms: Video.

Ozymandias. *Beauty and the Beast*, 1 April 1988.

Other forms: Video.

Dead of Winter. *Beauty and the Beast*, 9 December 1988.

Brothers. *Beauty and the Beast*, 3 February 1989.

When the Blue Bird Sings. Written with Robert John Guttke. *Beauty and the Beast*, 31 March 1989.

A Kingdom by the Sea. *Beauty and the Beast*, 28 April 1989.

Ceremony of Innocence. Based on a story by Alex Gansa, Howard Gordon, and GRRM. *Beauty and the Beast*, 19 May 1989.

Snow. *Beauty and the Beast*, 27 December 1989.

Beggar's Comet. *Beauty and the Beast*, 3 January 1990.

Invictus. *Beauty and the Beast*, 24 January 1990.

Doorways. Columbia Pictures, 1992. [Note: Originally a pilot for a TV series.] [Original script: *GRRM*]

Other forms: Video.

Starport. [Note: Originally a two-hour pilot for a TV series (1994); not produced.] [Original script: *Quartet*]

Scripts by Others, Based on Stories by GRRM:

Remembering Melody. Scriptwriter unknown. *The Hitchhiker*. Home Box Office, 27 November 1984.

Nightflyers [feature film]. Screenplay by Robert Jaffe. Directed by Robert Collector. Vista Films, 1987.

Other forms: Video.

Sandkings. Teleplay by Melinda M. Snodgrass. *The Outer Limits*. Showtime, 26 March 1995. Two-hour TV movie.

Other forms: Video.

Stories By:

1967
Only Kids Are Afraid of the Dark. *Star-Studded Comics* [comics fanzine; ed. Larry Herndon], #10, Winter 1967. [*GRRM*]

1971
The Hero. *Galaxy*, 31 (3), February 1971. [*SLya, GRRM*]

Other forms: Czech; French; German; Spanish.

1972
The Exit to San Breta. *Fantastic*, 21 (3), February 1972. [*SLya, GRRM*]

Other forms: Czech; French: German; Japanese; Spanish.

The Second Kind of Loneliness. *Analog*, 90 (4), December 1972. [*SLya, Portraits, GRRM*]

Other forms: Czech; French; German; Italian; Spanish.

1973
Dark, Dark Were the Tunnels. *Vertex*, 1 (5), December 1973. [*SLya*]

Other forms: Czech; French; German; Spanish.

Night Shift. *Amazing*, 46 (5), January 1973. [*SongsS&S*]

Other forms: Czech; German; Italian.

Override. *Analog*, 92 (1), September 1973. [*SLya*, *Nflyrs*]

> Other forms: Czech; French; German; Spanish.

A Peripheral Affair. *The Magazine of Fantasy and Science Fiction*, 44 (1; whole no. 260), January 1973.

> Other forms: Czech; German; E-text.

Slide Show. *Omega*. Ed. by Roger Elwood. New York: Walker, 1973. [*SLya*]

> Other forms: Czech; French; German; Spanish.

With Morning Comes Mistfall. *Analog*, 93 [sic, 91] (3), May 1973. [*SLya*; *Portraits*, *GRRM*]

> Other forms: Czech; French; German; Italian; Japanese; Russian; Spanish.

> Nebula Awards nominee; Hugo Awards nominee.

1974

fta. *Analog*, 93 (3), May 1974. [*SLya*]

> Other forms: Czech; French; German; Italian; Japanese; Spanish

Run to Starlight. *Amazing*, 48 (4), December 1974. [*SLya*]

> Other forms: Czech; German; Spanish.

A Song for Lya. *Analog*, 93 (4), June 1974. [*SLya*, *Nflyrs*, *GRRM*]

> Other forms: Czech; French; German; Italian; Japanese; Russian; E-text.

> Nebula Awards nominee; Hugo Awards winner.

1975

And Seven Times Never Kill Man. *Analog*, 95 (7), July 1975. [*SongsS&S*; *Nflyrs*, *GRRM*]

> Other forms: Czech; German; Greek; Italian; Japanese.

> Hugo Awards nominee.

The Last Super Bowl Game [short version]. *Gallery*, 3 (1), February 1975; [longer version first published in:] *Run to Starlight: Sports Through Science Fiction*. Ed. by Martin Harry Greenberg, Joseph D. Olander, Patricia Warrick. New York: Delacorte, 1975. [longer version in: *Portraits*]

Night of the Vampyres. *Amazing*, 48 (6), May 1975. [*SongsS&S*]

> Other forms: Czech; German; Italian.

The Runners. *The Magazine of Fantasy and Science Fiction*, 49 (3; whole #292), September 1975. [*SongsS&S*]

Other forms: Czech; German; Italian; Japanese.

The Storms of Windhaven. Written with Lisa Tuttle. *Analog*, 95 (5), May 1975. [*Wind*]

Other forms: German; Italian.

Nebula Awards nominee.

1976

A Beast for Norn. *Andromeda 1*. Ed. by Peter Weston. London: Futura, 1976. [Revised version in: *TufV*, original version: *GRRM*]

Other forms: Czech; German; Spanish.

The Computer Cried Charge! *Amazing*, 49 (4), January 1976.

Other forms: German.

Fast-Friend. *Faster than Light*. Ed. by Jack Dann and George Zebrowski. New York: Harper & Row, 1976. [*Sks*]

Other forms: Czech; German; Japanese.

". . . for a single yesterday." *Epoch*. Ed. by Roger Elwood & Robert Silverberg. New York: Berkley, 1976. [*SongsS&S, SongsDMS*]

Other forms: Czech; German; Italian; Japanese.

In the House of the Worm. *Ides of Tomorrow*. Ed. by Terry Carr. New York: Little Brown, 1976. [*Sks, SongsDMS*]

Other forms: Czech; German; Japanese; Spanish; E-text.

The Lonely Songs of Laren Dorr. *Fantastic*, 25 (3), May 1976. [*SongsS&S, Portraits, GRRM*]

Other forms: Czech; French; German; Greek; Italian; Spanish; E-text.

Meathouse Man. *Orbit 18*. Ed. by Damon Knight. New York: Harper & Row, 1976. [*SongsDMS, GRRM*]

Other forms: Czech; German; Italian.

Men of Greywater Station. Written with Howard Waldrop. *Amazing*, 49 (5), March 1976. [*SongsS&S*]

Other forms: Czech; German; Greek; Italian.

Nobody Leaves New Pittsburg. *Amazing*, 50 (2), September 1976.

Other forms: German.

Nor the Many-Colored Fires of a Star Ring. *Faster than Light*. Ed. by Jack Dann & George Zebrowski. New York: Harper & Row, 1976. [*Nflyrs*]

Other forms: German.

Patrick Henry, Jupiter, and the Little Red Brick Spaceship. *Amazing*, 50 (3), December 1976. [*SongsS&S*]

Other forms: Czech; German; Italian.

Starlady. *Science Fiction Discoveries*. Ed. by Carol and Frederik Pohl. New York: Bantam, 1976. [*Sks*]

Other forms: Czech; German; Italian; Japanese.

This Tower of Ashes. *Analog Annual*. Ed. by Ben Bova. New York: Pyramid, 1976. [*SongsS&S, Songs DMS, GRRM*]

Other forms: Czech; German; Italian; Japanese; Spanish.

1977

After the Festival. [Serialized novel in four parts] *Analog*, 97 (4), April 1977; 97 (5), May 1977; 97 (6), June 1977; 97 (7), July 1977. [*Dying of the Light*]

Bitterblooms. *Cosmos*, 1 (4), November 1977. [*Sks, GRRM*]

Other forms: Czech; German; Japanese.

The Stone City. *New Voices in Science Fiction: Stories by Campbell Award Nominees*. Ed. by George R. R. Martin. New York: Macmillan, 1977. [*Sks, GRRM*]

Other forms: Czech; German; Japanese; Russian; Spanish; E-text.

Nebula Awards nominee.

Weekend in a War Zone. *Future Pastimes*. Ed. by Scott Edelstein. Nashville, Tennessee: Aurora Publishers, 1977. [*Nflyrs*]

Other forms: German.

1978

Call Him Moses. *Analog*, 98 (2), February 1978. [*TufV*]

Other forms: German; Japanese; Russian; Spanish.

1979

Sandkings. *Omni*, 1 (11), August 1979. [*Sks, SongsDMS, GRRM*]

Other forms: Czech; German; Italian; Japanese; Russian; Spanish; Audio; E-text; Graphic; TV adaptation.

Nebula Awards winner; Hugo Awards winner.

Warship. Written with George Florance-Guthridge. *The Magazine of Fantasy and Science Fiction*, 56; (4; whole #335), April 1979.

Other forms: Czech.

The Way of Cross and Dragon. *Omni*, 1 (9), June 1979. [*Sks, GRRM*]

Other forms: Czech; German; Italian; Japanese; Russian; Spanish.

Nebula Awards nominee; Hugo Awards winner.

1980

The Ice Dragon. *Dragons of Light*. Ed. by Orson Scott Card. New York: Ace, 1980. [*Portraits, GRRM, The Ice Dragon* (book)]

Other forms: Czech; German; Italian; Spanish; E-text.

Nightflyers. *Analog*, 100 (4), April 1980. [Expanded version in: *Nightflyers* (Dell, 1981); *Nflyrs* [collection], *SongsDMS, GRRM*]

Other forms: Czech; Dutch; French; German; Italian; Japanese; Film adaptation; Audio.

Hugo Awards nominee.

One-Wing. Written with Lisa Tuttle. [Part One of Two Parts] *Analog*, 100 (1), January 1980; [Part II] *Analog*, 100 (2), February 1980. [*Wind*]

Other forms: German; Italian.

1981

The Fall. Written with Lisa Tuttle. *Amazing*, 27 (12), May 1981. [*Wind*]

Other forms: German; Italian.

Guardians. *Analog*, 101 (11), October 12, 1981. [*TufV, GRRM*]

Other forms: Czech; French; German; Spanish.

Hugo Awards nominee.

The Needle Men. *The Magazine of Fantasy and Science Fiction*, 61 (4; whole #365), October 1981. [*SongsDMS*]

Other forms: Czech; German; Japanese; Spanish.

Remembering Melody. *The Twilight Zone Magazine*, 1 (1), April 1981. [*SongsDMS, GRRM*]

Other forms: Czech; German; Japanese; Spanish; TV adaptation.

1982

Closing Time. *Isaac Asimov's Science Fiction Magazine*, 6 (11; whole #58), November 1982. [*Portraits*]

Other forms: Czech; Italian; Russian; Spanish.

Fevre Dream [excerpt]. *Science Fiction Digest*, [1 (4), September–October 1982].

In the Lost Lands. *Amazons II*. Ed. by Jessica Amanda Salmonson. New York: DAW, 1982. [*Portraits, GRRM*]

Other forms: Czech; German; Italian.

Unsound Variations. *Amazing*, 28 (4), January 1982. [*Portraits, GRRM*]

Other forms: Czech; German; Russian.

Nebula Awards nominee; Hugo Awards nominee.

1983

The Monkey Treatment. *The Magazine of Fantasy and Science Fiction*, 65 (1; whole #386), July 1983. [*SongsDMS, GRRM*]

Other forms: Czech; German; Japanese; Spanish.

Nebula Awards nominee; Hugo Awards nominee.

1985

Loaves and Fishes. *Analog*, 105 (10), October 1985. [*TufV*]

Other forms: Czech; German; Spanish.

Manna from Heaven. *Analog*, 105 (13), Mid-December 1985. [*TufV*]

Other forms: German; Italian; Spanish.

The Plague Star. [Part One of Two] *Analog*, 105 (1), January 1985; [Conclusion] *Analog*, 105 (2), February 1985. [*TufV*]

Other forms: Czech; German; Spanish.

Portraits of His Children. *Isaac Asimov's Science Fiction Magazine*, 9 (11; whole #97), November 1985. [*Portraits, GRRM*]

Other forms: Czech; German; Italian; Russian; Spanish; Braille; E-text.

Nebula Awards winner; Hugo Awards nominee.

Second Helpings. *Analog*, 105 (11), November 1985. [*TufV*]

Other forms: Czech; German; Italian; Spanish.

Under Siege. *Omni*, 8 (1), October 1985. [*Portraits, GRRM*]

Other forms: German; Audio.

1986

The Glass Flower. *Isaac Asimov's Science Fiction*, 10 (10 [sic, 9]; whole #109 [sic, #108]), September 1986. [*Portraits, GRRM*]

Other forms: Czech; German; Russian; Spanish; E-text.

Interlude[s] One-Five. *Wild Cards*. Ed. by George R. R. Martin. Toronto [and] New York: Bantam, 1987.

Other forms: German; Japanese; Russian; E-text.

Shell Games. *Wild Cards*. Ed. by George R. R. Martin. Toronto [and] New York: Bantam, 1986. [*GRRM*]

Other forms: German; Japanese; Russian; E-text.

1987

Jube: One [through] Jube: Seven. *Aces High*. Ed. by George R. R. Martin. Toronto [and] New York: Bantam, 1987.

Other forms: German; Japanese; Russian; E-text.

The Pear-Shaped Man. *Omni*, 10 (1), October 1987. [*The Pear-Shaped Man* (book), *GRRM*]

Other forms: German; Spanish; E-text.

World Fantasy Awards nominee.

Winter's Chill. *Aces High*. Ed. by George R. R. Martin. Toronto [and] New York: Bantam, 1987.

Other forms: German; Japanese; Russian; E-text.

1988

All the King's Horses. *Down and Dirty*. Ed. by George R. R. Martin; assistant editor: Melinda M. Snodgrass. New York: Bantam, 1988.

Other forms: German; E-text.

The Journal of Xavier Desmond. *Aces Abroad*. Ed. by George R. R. Martin; assistant editor: Melinda M. Snodgrass. New York: Bantam, 1988. [*GRRM*]

Other forms: German; E-text.

The Skin Trade. *Night Visions 5*. [With Stephen King and Dan Simmons.] Ed. by Douglas E. Winter. Arlington Hts, Illinois: Dark Harvest, 1988. [*Quartet, GRRM*]

Other forms: Czech; Finnish; German; Italian; Japanese; Audio.

World Fantasy Awards winner.

1996

Blood of the Dragon [Excerpted from *A Game of Thrones*.] *Asimov's Science Fiction*, 20 (7; whole #247), July 1996. [*Quartet*]

Other forms: Italian; Spanish.

Nebula Awards nominee; World Fantasy Awards nominee; Hugo Awards winner.

1998

The Hedge Knight. [Set in the cycle of *A Song of Ice and Fire*.] *Legends: Short Novels by the Masters of Modern Fantasy*. Ed. by Robert Silverberg. New York: Tor Fantasy; A Tom Doherty Associates Book, 1998. [*GRRM*]

Other forms: Czech; Dutch; German; Hebrew; Italian; Japanese; Audio; E-audio; Graphic (English; Italian; Spanish; Turkish).

World Fantasy Awards nominee.

2000

Path of the Dragon. [Set in the cycle of *A Song of Ice and Fire*.] *Asimov's Science Fiction*, 24 (12; whole #299), December 2000.

Other forms: Spanish.

2001

Black and White and Red All Over [novel fragment]. [*Quartet*]

Starport [script]. [*Quartet*]

2003

And Death His Legacy. [Written in 1968.] [*GRRM*]

Arms of the Kraken. [Set in the cycle of *A Song of Ice and Fire*] *Dragon*, 27 (10; issue #305), March 2003.

Other forms: Spanish.

The Fortress. [Written in 1968.] [*GRRM*]

Doorways [script]. [*GRRM*]

The Last Defender of Camelot [script]. Teleplay by George R. R. Martin. Story by Roger Zelazny. [chapbook] Burton, MI: Subterranean, 2003. [Note: Issued with limited edition of *GRRM*.]

The Road Less Traveled [script]. [*GRRM*]

2004

Shadow Twin. Written with Gardner Dozois and Daniel Abraham. *SciFi.com*, 9, 16, and 23 June 2004.
[http://scifi.com/scifiction/originals/originals_archive/dozois–martin–abraham/] [*Shadow Twin* (book)]

Other forms: Spanish.

The Sworn Sword. [Set in the cycle of *A Song of Ice and Fire*.] *Legends II: Short Novels by the Masters of Modern Fantasy*. Ed by Robert Silverberg. London: HarperCollins, 2003; New York: Ballantine, 2004.

Other forms: Dutch; German; Spanish; Audio; E-text.

2005

The Toys of Caliban [script; based on a story by Terry Matz]. *Subterranean*, #1, 2005. [magazine issued in limited hardcover, and in softcover]

Story Copyrights